Fortunes Fate; a story in three acts: For Avolire, The Dragon Whisper, The Cuvar Conspiracy
Written by Adam and Adrian Chojnacki

Images courtesy of Pixabay
All characters and events depicted in this story are entirely fictitious. Any resemblance to real people is unintended and the sole result of the reader's imagination.

We bear no responsibility for the efficacy of the recipes, methods of healing, use of vegetable poisons, tricks of divination, or impact of the ballads should the reader speak them out loud. The authors condone no prejudice and none of the characters are intended to offend.

The Prophecy

When the Marked is found amongst the Maples,
And the armies of the east shall walk again,
With the Enderdetag alignment in the heavens,
Then shall be the end of good men.

When the Oracles crypt shall be opened,
And the choices we make must thrive,
The powers of evil shall be woken,
And no one alive shall survive.

From the innocent the savoir shall waken,
To the Bards he shall appear,
To reunite the Gems of Thamous,
And destroy the Lord of Fear.

1.

Methladon Heyn sat on a chunk of masonry that had fallen from the crumbling walls of the once powerful and prosperous city of Avolire. While bathed in the pale light of Mona he stared at the multitude of stars that glinted in the crystalline sky. It was the end of the first week since he had gained his freedom from the murderous mines and he felt great joy at being able once again to point his eyes at the heavens without fear of the sting of the lash.

Scanning the stars he began to reflect on how he had come to find himself in such a miserable place. Despite all the terrors endured he had much to be thankful for. He was alive and had somehow managed to hang on to his sanity by the thinnest of strings. First had come the attack on his home village of Maplehill. There his family and friends had been butchered without mercy by the Knights of Avolire. Then there was the journey through the Eastern Marsh where he had been forced to witness the murder of his fellow prisoners Mal Castor and the young child Maria Darcha who had been brutally killed by the sadist called Nictis. His thoughts moved to his arrival at the ruins of Avolire and how he had then been brought before the Lady of the Silverwynn. He had bartered for his life, the lives of his comrades, and then in the end he had destroyed the evil Nictis. Methladon fixed his gazed onto the brightest star and wondered how long he would continue to be protected by the Lady that now showed so much interest in his fate. Soon however his eyes wandered away and across to the courtyard where a gathering of wretches stood huddled around a makeshift fire. Avolire was full of unsavoury scum who had turned their backs on the authority of Phauless Gylewu and yet he felt some compassion for these unfortunates who clung on to a semblance of life in this most miserable of places. Even though his life experience in Maplehill had been dull and restricted, it had been a far better existence than that which Avolire's populace had to endure. Appearing out of the shadows he then recognised one who moved through the crowd. The beast Commander called Rhaizen pushed through the dishevelled mob and induced memories of suffering to haunt his mind.

Methladon felt the urge to scratch his birthmark that the Lady of the Silverwynn had been so interested to examine. Grateful that it no longer burned he noted how it tingled and created an irritation that he could at least tolerate. In the long days that had passed since he had been created a knight he had been subjected to several strange rituals within the highborn's mysterious chamber; the enchanted room that gave the Lady access to the powers of the Rift. With his consent she and the brown skinned Lizardman called Sslondash had manifested magic in an attempt to understand the purpose of his mark. It was obvious they wished to discover why when threatened he had had exhibited energy of a most powerful nature. After five long days of study the one thing they had been able to confirm was that the birthmark burned when either Methladon was angry or he was close to the Dagger of Kha.

During one discussion with the Lady regarding the dagger's purpose, they had touched upon the Sceptre of Urthanock and the visions that he had experienced when exposed to its light. At first Methladon had believed that the images, the visions of a great battle with him sat upon the throne of Parandor, were true insights into the future. He was not daunted by the prospect of becoming Ruler of the Realm with the Lady of the Silverwynn at his side. She had stated that she too had seen a similar story but after the five days of interrogation and subtle mental torture Methladon was no longer certain of what he had seen inside the diamond. It was as if some other was playing with his thoughts, seeking to mould him into something else, no longer the simple blacksmith's son from Maplehill but a creature far more powerful. He felt that he was losing control and that worried him greatly.

Methladon's fascination for the Lady's room of regeneration grew by the day. She seemed most reluctant to ever leave it and had not done so once during the five days of enquiry. From time to time she had visitors who interrupted her spell casting. Those who came to call included several of the Lizardmen, Commander Rhaizen, and some of his knights. At the end of each day Methladon had been allowed time to explore the multi-tiered city and to observe the comings and goings of others who visited the Silverwynn. He noted the dwarf Grovrouk enter the room on numerous occasions but never again while he was present. Whatever the reasons for the little man's visits his face always departed looking serious and agitated.

A thought squeezed its way in amongst the bubbling rivulets of Methladon's mind as he once again stared up into the star filled sky. It concerned the two men who had betrayed him in an attempt to save their own lives. In the end he had rescued them from death by pledging to join the Lady's cause. Still he could not help but wonder what had become of Dayis and Tycus and if the Lady had indeed kept to her word. It was possible that she had sent them back into the dark tunnels below the city and he vowed that should the chance arrive he would venture back into the mines and seek the evidence himself. There were so many questions that he wanted to put to Tycus; to understand more of the Prophecy of Enderdetag and the role of the saviour said to have been marked. He found it difficult to believe that he could be that chosen one yet all evidence seemed to point that way. Whatever the reason, the Lady of the Silverwynn placed much importance on his three circled birthmark.

Methladon lowered his head at the sound of an approaching footfall. When he at last looked up he saw the diminutive shape of Grovrouk the Despoiler, dressed in full armour and with concern etched on his wizen face. The little man walked towards him as fast as his stunted legs could waddle. In his arms he carried a black helmet.

"You are a hard bugger to find," growled the dwarf.

"I wanted somewhere to think, somewhere peaceful and quiet," snapped back Methladon. "I am searching for answers that no one seems willing to give."

Methladon didn't intend his response to be filled with so much anger but that was how it came over. It was true enough, no one appeared willing to give him any insight into what was happening. He was desperate to discover why the Lady of the Silverwynn was trying to unlock the secret of his new abilities and if there was anything she was concealing from him. When he had first met and shared a cage with the dwarf he could not understand any of the words that passed through the small one's mouth. For some unexplained reason, ever since his first visit to the Lady's room, he now had no difficulty in following any of the dwarf's utterances. It was as if his mind was able translate and make sense of the language from the far north despite having no knowledge of the tongue of Dirmark.

"I'm not sure why she sent me anyway!" continued Grovrouk. "I told her that you wouldn't be able to understand me but she seemed to think otherwise. Now I see that she was right."

"If you are not here to give me answers, then leave me alone. I want some quiet time."

"I'm sorry lad but I cannot be of help in that way. The Lady has sent me to find you. She has..."

"Don't tell me," snapped back Methladon. "I assume she has found another way of trying to figure out what is wrong with me. She made a promise to discover all but yet she struggles to deliver. I have sworn myself to her fucking cause so what more does she want from me?"

"I note your anger but do not spit your venom at this lowly messenger. The Lady ordered me to inform you that Commander Rhaizen will be going on a mission and she is sending you with him. If you are to be a true Knight of Avolire then you have to learn their ways. Rhaizen was reluctant as you can imagine but the Lady insisted."

"Do you know where he is going?"

"No I do not," replied the dwarf. "I was just told to fetch like a dog."

"So be it," sighed Methladon. "I guess I don't have any choice in the matter."

Methladon jumped from the fallen masonry in order to follow the dwarf who had already turned to walk away. Within seconds he had caught the little man up and thereafter reduced his pace. Walking on together Methladon could not help but notice more of the desperate refugees, asleep amongst the ruins and huddled around fires in their attempt to keep out the cold. Lost in his thoughts he began to compare them to those who he could remember from his time in the slums of Parandor. Then as the pair passed through the shadows, hypes of geckos scuttled before their feet as if watching Methladon's progress. A small patrol of armoured Lizardmen passed close by and the youth detected a twitch in the dwarf's left eye. It was as if something sinister disturbed the low walker. Once the scale patrol was out of ear shot, Methladon turned to Grovrouk.

"Does something bother you?"

"Lizardmen," replied the dwarf. "I hate the fucking bastards. In fact you'll find that the majority of the Knights of Avolire, including Rhaizen himself, detest the fork tongued scale shits."

"I thought you were all the best of mates," sneered Methladon.

"You didn't see what happened at the Grey Keep lad. That was a massacre the likes of which I would not like to see again, although with the way things are going, it may well be repeated soon."

"Is that so?" replied Methladon. "Why were you there in the first place? Why did the Lizardmen feel the need to keep you locked up in that cage we shared if you are on their side?"

"Ha! I can see that the Lady hasn't shared much with you, but as I like you I'll let you into a little secret. There was a period of time when I turned my back on those of Avolire and tried to escape the rule of the Lady. I didn't get very far and I was caught and imprisoned in the Grey Keep; but even in my brief confinement there I was not idle. In a moment of frustration I murdered my cell mate."

"So your crimes were serious enough to land you in the Grey Keep. I am impressed!"

Methladon had heard of the infamous prison although the only time he had been anywhere near it was when the Knights of Avolire had him restrained in the back of the cart. He knew only too well of the fearsome reputation of the stronghold deep within the Grey Mountains; a place which had long been in the grip of Raorick Gylewu's iron gauntlet. From the stories he had heard he had no desire to ever visit the dread provoking place of punishment.

"Do you know what the word 'Despoiler' means my young friend?" asked Grovrouk as they continued their progress through the ruined streets.

"I have a good idea," answered Methladon with a yawn.

"To despoil means to strip by force, to plunderer, and I was bloody good at my trade."

"Good enough to end up caught and incarcerated in the dungeons of Raorick Gylewu!"

"I got sloppy, that was all. Even after my banishment from the Dirmark, the need to pillage was too great for me to resist. As I could no longer count on the protection of the Knights of Avolire I needed to find a way to survive on my own. After a while I got over confident. I tried to steal a jewel discovered by those who dwell in Falahorn but I failed and was caught by the Berserkers. From there I was sentenced by the Jarls of Falahorn and in conjunction with the ancient laws of Parandor, I was cast into the dungeons of the Grey Keep alongside the man I later murdered."

"So what happened at that fortress?" asked Methladon.

"The Knights of Avolire came looking for me. Or should I say their scale cunts did. One of the slit eyed bastards had already infiltrated the defences of the Grey Keep under the guise of Raorick's bodyguard. It didn't take them long to defeat the Keep's garrison."

"Why didn't they just leave you there?" quizzed Methladon.

"The Knights of Avolire never forget their own. Even though I had tried to flee from their number and to strike out alone, they would not let me go. They never permit one who had once been party to the inner council of the Lady of the Silverwynn to be turned by the House of Gylewu, the bloodline that she had sworn to destroy. The Lizardmen were instructed to take me as Rhaizen believed that I would take my own life if I saw any of his horsemen. That is why when you first met me I was thrown into the cage; they thought I would run."

"That makes some sense."

"Does it?" replied the dwarf. "Perhaps it does."

"But why do you hold such hatred towards those from the Eastern Marsh?"

"You saw what they did to that young woman on the road, just to access the power known as the Rift. I can tell looking at the shredded skin that shows through your tattered clothes that you have been subjected to the whip of their slave masters. The swine relish inflicting pain and suffering."

"I'm surprised that they left the Eastern Marsh."

"There is no stopping them," continued Grovrouk. "Fierce fighters and more devious than you could ever imagine. They will do anything to achieve their own ends. They even have their own weird language. I guess you've heard them hissing? Well anyway, now you know all Methladon Heyn and I offer you this advice because I like you. Never trust one of their kind. Keep them at a distance. They are devious shits and no doubt they have a greater plan than they have revealed so far."

"I'll keep that in mind," replied the youth.

Methladon sensed that the dwarf talked in half-truths and that he too was hiding something of significance. The time however did not seem right to push the little man further. He was more interested in the motive behind the Lady's insistence that he accompanied Rhaizen on his new mission.

"And what about you?" asked Grovrouk. "What's your story?"

"What do you mean?"

"Come on lad, don't act the dullard," continued the dwarf. "You know what I allude to. What does the Lady see in you? What happened in the Lion Pit with that bastard Nictis? You can be honest with me Methladon for by the spirit of Egredor, I may be the one friend that you have in this stinking hole."

Methladon paused for a brief moment and stood still. Maybe the little man was right. Ever since the incident with Dayis and Tycus in the pit he felt that he was alone in the world and more than anything else he needed a friend. Despite the dwarf's offer, given all that had happened since he had left Maplehill, he was however reluctant to accept it. A suspicion from somewhere in his confused essence ordered him to remain vigilant and divulge as little as was needed to secure this new alliance.

"To be honest, I haven't a fucking clue! Ever since I arrived here and looked into that Sceptre, the Lady has taken a great interest in me. Has she ever acted like this with any of the others she has dragged out from the mines?"

"No," replied Grovrouk. "You are the first."

"Since looking into that that jewel I've not felt right. I saw images of long ago but they are visions that I don't remember and yet somehow I know them to be true. Then there was the incident in the pit. It was almost like the past was repeating itself. I keep seeing an image of a young boy tied between four horses and about to be dismembered. A boy that looks just like me."

"Maybe it was you?" said Grovrouk.

"An incident like that? I would have remembered."

"Well maybe that's what happened. You've remembered at last."

"That doesn't explain the magical fire does it? You saw it yourself."

"Aye lad," replied the dwarf. "That I did."

"And you wonder why your Lady has taken an interest in me. All I want to know is the truth. What is happening to me? Is that too much to ask?"

"Hence your pledge of allegiance to the Lady," said the dwarf.

"Indeed. Wouldn't you do the same if you had no control or understanding of what was happening inside your body in the presence of the sceptre and that fucking dagger?"

Methladon felt the burn grow on the back of his head. It was as if his anger had again triggered the strange phenomena that grew stronger as each day passed. Whatever the reason behind its presence, the Lady of the Silverwynn had failed to discover its meaning.

"I guess you had your reasons for joining her cause," replied Grovrouk. "And I suppose the Lady has her own, but let me repeat my advice to you. Do not trust any of them and in particular those forked tongued bastards… Well, it looks like we are here."

"And where is here?"

"The Armoury of Avolire" replied Grovrouk. "Rhaizen and his knights await inside."

Methladon stood and looked up to ruin of a building. At one time it would had been a magnificent architectural wonder with its pillars, grotesques, and Realmgoth arches admired by all who gazed upon it. Now it stood in a sorry state of disrepair. Just like the lower tiered church and the residence of the Lady of the Silverwynn it was another almost complete building set amongst the flattened ruins of the once mighty city. He looked at the cast iron door with its large bronze knocker, corroded by time and by the disease that rots metal. It had long ago been moulded in the image of a lion's head but its features had worn almost flat. The youth doubted that the building had always been an armoury for it looked more like the home of a guild or even a place of judgement.

Striding forward Grovrouk began to strike the metal below the lion's head. It surprised Methladon that the dwarf had to knock to gain entry while on the business of the Knights of Avolire. Perhaps they kept something important behind its doors or wanted to keep the wretches who sought refuge in the city out of one of the few remaining habitable buildings. Then he had another thought. Given what Grovrouk had told him, no doubt it was kept locked to keep out the Lizardmen. The sound of bolts being slipped was followed by the iron door creaking as it began to open. Methladon stared past the dwarf and into a gloom filled interior. The space was lit by a few candles which were either real or just another of the Lady's enchantments. He could not tell which. Then before he could move forward a tall, bald, slender man with pale skin and sunken eyes, part dressed in orichalcum, appeared at the doorway. He proceeded to search Methladon with his eyes.

"For Avolire!" saluted the man.

"For Avolire!" replied Grovrouk in an identical manner.

The strange man, turned and walked back into the shadows. He beckoned both Grovrouk and Methladon to follow him.

"Who is that?" questioned Methladon.

"That lad, is Newyn," replied Grovrouk. "A Harbinger and one of Rhaizen's trained elite. Whatever the task the Commander has in mind for us today it must be of great importance if it requires Newyn's presence. I wouldn't be surprised if we see the other three Harbingers."

"Harbingers?" queried Methladon as the door closed behind them.

"They are the chosen ones and the best of the Knights of Avolire. Rhaizen sends the Harbingers first into any difficult situation due to their excellence in the art of warfare. When they wield their weapons they are like dancers. They bring an artistry to the way that they impose death upon others. I would presume it was they who sacked your village, with Rhaizen at their head of course."

"So these are the bastards that killed my family and burned my village?" gasped Methladon as the fire erupted within his mark.

"Yes, but don't try anything foolish," continued Grovrouk. "They'd cut your balls off before you could even draw your sword. They are a fearsome elite and will avenge each other as necessary. You must curb your instincts and be careful whenever around them. There is also something else you should know. There was a fifth member of their group but you somehow found a way to take him out.

"You mean..."

"Yes, Nictis. There was a man who had never been right in the head since his brother turned against him but that is a story for another time. One thing I have learned from serving the Knights of Avolire is never keep the Harbingers waiting."

Taking Grovrouk's lead, Methladon followed the dwarf down a very short corridor. They turned the first corner and descended a small flight steps until they came before another open door that led into a well-lit room from where numerous voices emanated. Once inside Methladon found himself surrounded by weapons and pieces of armour of all shapes and sizes. Being the son of a blacksmith he recognised the majority of them although some were new to his eyes. He was drawn to some small objects that were made for hand fighting. They had the appearance of five pointed stars with small curved blades at their tips. Next he gazed upon a strange looking sword, key shaped at its end and attached to a golden hilt by a long serrated blade. He was determined to ask Grovrouk what these weapons were called as soon as the opportunity arose but then his attention was drawn to the benches at the far corner of the room. There Newyn and three others stood in silence. All were in the process of donning their armour and for a brief moment they ceased their chatter.

"I told you who it was," said Newyn.

"So this is the young warrior from Maplehill," said the largest of the four whose armour was too small for his belly size. "I thought you said a skilled warrior was to join us Mhlau, not a snot of a lad that still needs coddling."

"He is quite skilful in his own right for he is one that took out Nictis," replied Mhlau.

"Fuck me!" said the largest of the four. "I didn't realise that the Commander was sending us the little shit that killed one of our own. I say we now finish the job that Nictis started."

"Sit down Oedd," said the fourth whose face was so lacking in muscle tone that it appeared skeletal. "If the Commander wants this boy with us, then it must be with the will of the Lady. We abide by her decisions no matter how much it pains us."

"Farwolaeth, if this is the will of the Lady then we'd better have a closer look at this boy, the slayer of one of Avolire's finest."

"Have you been at the mead?" asked Farwolaeth. "Nictis was an evil bugger and we know it. I could never figure out why Rhaizen regarded him as our equal."

"We all know the reason, it was because of his brother," said Oedd as he sat down on a bench while Newyn adjusted the straps of his armour.

"Why don't you all just shut your mouths and get the boy a metal suit," snapped Grovrouk.

Methladon wondered if the Harbingers could also interpret the dwarf's strange language.

"I hear you Despoiler. We meant no harm, did we Oedd?" added the gaunt Newyn

"Nah," replied the largest of the four. "I was jesting."

"Good!" snapped back Grovrouk as he moved a step forward. "I'm pleased we have some understanding between the five of us. Now which one of you is going to find our young friend here a suit of armour worthy of his new status as a Knight of Avolire?"

Methladon watched as Newyn looked towards his three comrades and fastened the last strap of Oedd's breastplate.

"I'll find him a suit. Follow me lad," the knight replied

Newyn beckoned and Methladon moved to the centre of the room.

"Can you understand the dwarf speak?" he asked.

"Yes I can. Those who are able to converse with Grovrouk are one of two kinds. Either they have magic about them and are able to use it to understand what the hole-dweller says..."

"I can hear you Newyn," snapped back Grovrouk. "I've not lost my ears!"

"....Either that or they have learned the difficult language of the short arse race,'" continued Newyn without pause. "Have you ever been to the Dirmark lad?"

"My name is Methladon. Methladon Heyn. And no, I have never been to that place."

"Well, from what we witnessed in the pit, it seems that you understand something of the hole-dwellers. I'm guessing you have a degree of inbred magic about you, something special that has been activated. I think that's why the Silverwynn is so interested."

"I'm guessing it's something like that," replied Methladon. "But what about you, for you too can understand Grovrouk."

"Yes, I can follow the hole-dweller's words but that has nothing to do with any magic ability. I've had the unfortunate privilege of being sent into the Dirmark on numerous occasions. Once you get the idea behind it their language becomes easier to understand, that is once you learn to spit out globs of spit, use your cheeks like a floundering fish and flick your tongue about as if embedded in some whore's quim. But why anyone with any sense would want to talk to a hole-dweller is beyond my comprehension."

"Let me remind you that I am still here," growled Grovrouk.

"I am at a loss to understand why Rhaizen would allow a short arse to join the Knights of Avolire in the first place, and even more why he would to send a squad of the lizards to rescue you Grovrouk."

"Okay Newyn you've had your fun," added Mhlau as he approached his colleague.

It seemed to Methladon that Mhlau had some form of control over the man that had granted them entry into the armoury.

"Leave the dwarf be will you," added Mhalu. "He means you no harm, even though ugly."

"Do you speak the language of Dirmark too?" asked Methladon

"Aye lad," replied the knight. "But you're not here to discuss dwarf tongue unless the Commander and her Ladyship have some other perverted use for you."

"Look I'm fucking warning you four..." spat out Grovrouk.

Methladon put out his arm to restrain the little man.

"It's okay, I've got this under control," replied the youth as he looked down towards his new friend. "Why don't you take a break and step outside for a while I sort these four out."

"Like you did to poor old Nictis?" asked Oedd as he too finished donning his armour. Methladon did not respond and Grovrouk took a deep breath before he left through the armoury door. The youth from Maplehill then turned his attention back to Newyn and Mhlau.

"So are you going to suit me up, or are we going to stand here gossiping like whores desperate for a groat?"

Silence fell and the four knights looked to each other with a high degree of uncertainty. Methladon recognised their wariness with the exception of Farwolaeth whose stoic face hid his feelings. The silence was finally broken as Oedd began first to chuckle and then to laugh out loud. Soon he was joined by each of the Harbingers in turn. The laughter was infectious and a few seconds later Methladon joined in, even though he had his own concerns. Then at last the knight Oedd threw his arm around Methladon and pushed him towards the suits of armour.

"You may have killed one of our best and we will not forget that, but I think that you are going to fit in fine. Now remind us of your name."

"His name is Methladon," added Newyn. "You've been drinking too much of recent. I can always tell when you're pissed. Your memory gets fucked and you start spewing vile shite from out of that mouth of yours."

"Yes I maybe a little drunk Newyn," replied Oedd. "But you're a dim cunt and at least I can sober up! Don't you agree Meth?"

Methladon felt the thrust of a gauntlet as the large man's fist hit him in the ribs. Despite the discomfort he somehow managed a smile. On reflection he found it interesting that Oedd had chosen to call him Meth since that was the name he reserved for those who were his closest friends. Given that Llyat, Cleath, and his brothers were all dead, perhaps this was the beginning of new friendships.

"Let me take a look at your build," continued Oedd. "We must have armour somewhere here that will fit you. Harbingers, let's turn a boy into a man with balls and give him the finest suit he will ever own."

In an instant the knights began to seek out various components of armour from off the racks and to fix them to Methladon's body like four excited girls dressing their first doll. The weight of the metal upon his body was almost imperceptible and this fuelled Methladon's curiosity. His thoughts returned to the attack on Maplehill when he had witnessed the ease of the knight's slaughter. The lightness and freedom of movement of their armour had given them a significant advantage. He was sure that any knight from Parandor would give his life's savings for such equipment. Closing his eyes he savoured the sensations as the pauldrons and the cuirass were placed over the lightest chain mail that had ever graced his skin.

"Do you not have squires that do this for you?" asked Methladon without thinking.

"Do we look like the kind of people that would use fucking squires?" growled Oedd.

Methladon did not respond. Not wishing to provoke the knight further he refocused his thoughts back onto his armour. Then, as the final straps to the cuirass were pulled tight by Mhlau, Methladon noticed for the first time that etched onto the metal's surface was a coat of arms. It depicted two nighthowlers tearing a skyfawn apart while stood astride a shield of checked design.

"Whose coat of arms is this?" he asked.

"It is that of Calistorn," Newyn replied. "I'm assuming you know about the fall of that city."

"I do know some of it," said Methladon. "The Lady told me part of the story."

"Then you will know of the Knights of Avolire's pledge to assist all who have suffered under the rule of Gylewu."

"I've heard how they found a strange metal ore and went to war with Parandor..."

"Enough of this banter Newyn!" boomed a voice from the shadows.

Methladon turned to the door and there saw two and a half figures filling its space. The menacing Commander stood tall with his distinctive skull helmet gripped by his right hand. Just behind Rhaizen was the diminutive Grovrouk who was almost lost in the shadows. On the other side stood one of the brown skinned Lizardmen. Methladon remembered Grovrouk's dislike of the reptiles and somehow he sensed the dwarf's unease. Rhaizen and his companions then stepped forward into the room and the four Harbingers stood to attention and saluted their leader. Methladon mirrored their actions and joined in with their chant.

"For Avolire!"

"For Avolire," answered Rhaizen. "Stand easy."

Although he felt no fear Methladon remained guarded for this was the beast who had led the attack on Maplehill. He had previously felt the magic that had flowed from the brute's hand as it had sought to tear his body apart and he did not want to ever feel it again.

"By the will of the Lady we have a new addition to our brotherhood," began the Commander. "As you will come to understand, he has been chosen by the Lady of the Silverwynn for one purpose alone. I will tell you what that is when I feel the time is right but for now just accept that it is so. We are leaving with Ssnarkit and going out into the Dragonas to a location known only to Grovrouk."

Methladon took a deep breath and the Commander picked up on it.

"Look lad, I tolerate your presence only because of our leader. Despite my reservations and your antics in the Lion Pit, the Lady of the Silverwynn feels it appropriate that you should join our expedition into the Dragonas. She believes that your true purpose and value to Avolire will be revealed on the journey and that you may also find the answers to that which you seek."

Rhaizen moved forward and pushed his face in close. Methladon felt the tension rise

"Listen with great care lad. I hope you understand that any dissent or betrayal of my orders, or indeed that of my men will bring about a swift demise. I don't give a fuck if you are with magic or have the Lady's favour. If you so much cross me once during this journey, not even the gods will protect you from the pain that I will bring down upon you. Annoy me and you will beg me to end your miserable life. Do you understand?"

Methladon did not know what to say or how to react. He searched his mind for a smart answer, but none came.

"Do you understand me lad?" Rhaizen again demanded.

"Yes Sir," said Methladon as the irritation on his head returned.

"Good. That makes me happy."

"Sir!" said another voice.

"What is it Oedd?"

"Why are we going into that godless place?"

Rhaizen smiled and looked down at Grovrouk. "I'll let you tell them dwarf."

Methladon looked to the diminutive man and asked; "What is he talking about?"

"I am sorry Methladon," replied Grovrouk. "I have not spoken the truth thus far. I wasn't arrested and kept in the Grey Keep as I told you earlier. I was sent there to extract information. That is what I do best. My cell mate Tullage knew the location of something that we here in Avolire had been looking for. The old man had read the Lore of the Dead and he knew the location of the beast that we seek."

Grovrouk then smiled, raised his voice, and addressed the rest of those gathered.

"We search for the wyvern. We go to find Thamous."

2

Thias felt the warmth from Solaris radiate through his essence and tickle his senses as he sat upon an old wooden rocking chair on the porch of a long ago built rustic building. Looking out from under its canopy he scanned the distant horizon beyond the flatlands that led to the edge of the world. This was the Dragonas. It was the first time that the bard had crossed the Ivory Pass and viewed this wonder of the northern outreach of the Realm. He was both stunned and impressed by what he saw. All he had heard about the so called 'wasteland' was far removed from the truth of its reality. He had begun to suspect as much on first seeing the wormnose graveyard in the Ivory Pass. There he had realised that the lands beyond the pass had to have an abundance of vegetation on which the beasts could feed. Now he could see it for himself. It lay before him and by the golden light of Solaris he marvelled in its beauty.

The Dragonas was an expanse of yellow grassland that stretched as far as the eye could see and some said even beyond. Land flowed in every direction including to the distant mountains in the south. The grass covered swathes were interrupted by occasional clusters of rock laden outcrops and clumps of strange vegetation. There were many scattered hanging trees whose leaves dropped so low as to touch the ground and others where the leaves did not as they sought to caress the clouds. Yellow was the true colour of the grass and it was in stark contrast to the green vales and plains south of the Grey Mountains. Those mountains were now leagues away and as Thias reflected on their distant beauty he knew that he was lucky to be alive. The skyfawn attack on the mountain trail had been interrupted by a Berserker from Falahorn, one who had been scouting the upper reaches of Skillar. After dispatching the creature the Berserker had then helped Thias to locate Irabo who had fallen down a small but steep incline on the side of the mountain. The young warrior had hit his head with some force and rattled his head senseless. He had also chipped a small bone in his left ankle just to add to his woe. Llyat, close to death, had been taken at speed down the mountain. The Berserker had whispered that numerous Lizardmen had recently been spotted in and around the Ivory Pass. They appeared to be collecting young kulkulkath and transporting them back to Avolire. The purpose of this activity remained a mystery to those who sought to protect the land of the dragons.

Einar the Berserker was a large muscular man, bald on top but with enough facial hair on his face to make up for the lack of it on his head. He had intended to kill Thias until he realised that he was a bard. The giant had spotted Thias struggling with a sick youth and summoned other warriors to help. They had lay hidden in the fog while they sought to protect the entrance to the Dragonas. These others had taken charge of Llyat while Einar had helped Thias to find Irabo and ease him back into consciousness. Had it not been for the intervention of the Berserkers, the three travellers would have been long dead; left as easy pickings for the ever hungry skyfawn.

Thias looked away from the mountains and back towards the plains of the Dragonas. He stared at a three peaked mountain way off in the distance that somehow reminded him of the tridents carried by the bodyguard of the Lady

Flurdiana. Having examined it in some detail for several minutes the bard looked to his side where several wooden fences made up the pens of the farm that he had been brought to. The structures were strong and sturdy enough to secure the livestock, beasts that included several oxen, a couple of antelope, and a few pig like creatures with large tusks that were known as mathulath. He observed the comings and goings of several farmhands, all busy in their toil, and focused in on three other young men dressed in sleeveless fur jackets over green cloth shirts who looked out towards a distant longneck that ate from a tall tree on the horizon. Thias assumed that these few were employed to protect the farm from creatures of the wild that drooled on the prospect of sinking their teeth into the homestead's livestock. Closing his eyes he imagined them fighting off any stray kulkulkath that may have found their way down from the pass. Soon he was reminded of his foster brothers Fiat, Methladon, Grophaldo, and also Vostag, the man he had called father. Somehow he hoped that the story Llyat had told him was untrue. It was too painful to think of them all being slaughtered by the knights in black that were led by one with a skull adorned helmet.

A flock of large birds distracted Thias's attention for their flight triggered another memory. He and Irabo had promised Tonousa that once they reached Falahorn they would send a carrier bird with a message to inform her of their safe arrival. Thias had carried out that instruction some days earlier. He feared that a bird would not make it past the packs of skyfawn but the woman called Berger, on whose farm he now rested, had reassured him that the birds they used were strong and would without doubt make it through to the Capital. Those of Falahorn, she had told him, even had to evade the few remaining dragons and so had developed exceptional survival skills. What worried the bard most was not a bird getting through but the person intended to receive it. The message had been be sent to Danisun Dain of the City Watch. Tonousa had put great trust in this man and had asked her friends to do the same. Thias carried much doubt over her choice and it weighed like a boulder on his thoughts for he knew the name well. Ever since Tonousa had spoken it during their escape from the Bards Guild it had stirred old wounds. Danisun had been the acting Sergeant of the City Watch on the day that decided his family's fate for he was the one who had arrested his thieving father and dragged him to gallows to await his sentence and execution. There was little chance it could be a different man with the same name. Thias knew he had to supress his hate if he was going to conclude his investigations into the Death Tubaria murders. Right now he needed to protect the boy Llyat who was in his view without doubt 'the Marked' referred to in the Enderdetag Prophecy.

Thias sensed movement as the wooden door of the farm building opened behind him. He turned his head and focused on the rotund woman with much belly and hip fat as she walked through the door and out onto the veranda. Her long blonde hair was platted and it draped over one shoulder. The bard had spent almost five days in this woman's company and believed that she could have been younger than she looked. Years of stress had taken its toll for she lived amidst and helped to keep a great secret. She was one of the guardians committed to conceal and protect the last of the dragons. Dressed in a sleeveless fur jacket which lay over a rough hessian garment, it was to Thias's relief that it covered most of her ample figure.

Stood on the veranda besides him she stretched her arms out, and soaked up the morning warmth from Solaris. So doing she revealed that she had outgrown her clothes. The material pushed against the constrained tissue of her more than ample chest. His nose twitched at a ripe smell that reached his nostrils and his eyes flicked to a hair filled armpit. As the woman finished her stretch, Thias turned his head away from the pungent crevice and spoke.

"How are the patients this morning Berger?"

"They seem to be improving by the day," replied the woman. "Though it may be a while yet before Irabo can walk on that leg of his. It's lucky that Einar found you all when he did as I think any longer on that mountain and you would have lost both of the boys. I can remember Irabo as a youngster and how resilient he was then. Bumps, bruises, pox, you name it, he coped with them all but I doubt he has ever had a broken leg before. The five founding families of Falahorn ask me to act as nurse sometimes but as far as I know there is no fast cure for broken bones. He is just going to have to rest and allow his leg to heal."

"And Llyat?" asked Thias "The boy that the Berserkers brought in with us. How is he doing?"

"Much better. The Jarls are fantastic healers and they know how to treat the sweating sickness. That cursed disease almost wiped out our entire town some years back. You ask young Irabo for I think it was that same plague that took the rest of his family."

"How do you think he caught it?" asked Thias.

"Now that I cannot answer. It is possible that he came into contact with some bad air while making his way north from Valameer. The turmoil that you three have been through could have accelerated the onset of the disease. You're lucky all three of you didn't catch it."

"I see!" replied Thias as he pondered on the consequences of such an outcome.

He was sure that Irabo would be grateful that the Fates had not followed that particular course and it was too painful to imagine how their quest would have ended had they all caught the sweats.

"Couldn't you have healed the boy yourself?" continued Berger. "Sang him a song? Played him some of your famous magical music perhaps? You bards are supposed to be at one with the chords of the universe. Couldn't you have done something?"

"All my possessions were lost during the attack on the Guild. The clothes you disposed of on my arrival and the pendent that is sitting around my neck at this very moment were the only things of value that I managed to salvage."

"Speaking of the clothes," continued Berger. "How are you finding the new ones that you were given? If I didn't know you any better, I would swear that you could pass yourself off as one of our townsfolk."

Thias looked down at what he wore and smiled. He too was dressed in similar clothes to Berger, a sleeveless fur jacket over a hessian sackcloth which hid the bronze pendent with the inlaid amethyst. At least they fitted him better than Berger's did.

"Thanks again," he said with a smile. "Your generosity is boundless."

"Don't mention it bard. How foolish we would have been to leave you all stranded in the wilderness after all those tales you have told us? I have to say there are parts of your story that I find very hard to believe..."

"And that coming for the woman who helps to raise dragons," laughed Thias.

"That is true bard, but your story of murders in the Capital, the hunt for jewels belonging to Thamous, and then the attack upon the Bards Guild, is a stretch to believe. Forgive me but I am astounded that so much could have happened in such a short time."

"Believe me, I find it astounding too."

"Anyway my friend, you asked me to check if we had received a message back from the Capital," said Berger. "Our keeper of birds has reported that there has been no reply as yet but should anything come I have instructed him to deliver it at once."

"Thank you again, it is disappointing news yet much appreciated."

"Don't mention it. Oh how absent minded of me, I forgot to tell you. You have a visitor inside."

"A visitor!" exclaimed Thias. "For me? But no one else knows I am here."

That was indeed the truth for no one else could have known that Thias had journeyed to Falahorn. Since his arrival he had spent most of his time in the company of Berger, her husband Mium, and her two young sons Harrow and Thalik. The rest of the time he had sat alone or passed the hours in slumber. Llyat and Irabo had been taken to the largest of the nine buildings of the small town, the one that Berger said belonged to the Jarl family. That imposing building also served as an infirmary for the sick and injured. Thias had not seen either of his two companions since they been brought to Falahorn but Berger had reassured him daily that his friends were in the best of hands. Eerickk Jarl, the head of the village, was a renowned healer and from the way that Berger described him it seemed that he could have rivalled the skills of old Abrahamus Marus.

"Do not worry my young friend," she said as she winked and turned her back on the bard "Your secret is safe with me. You three are all wanted men and yet you dare to come this close to Avolire. Do not fret for your visitor is none other than your friend Irabo and I am sure you cannot wait to meet with him again, now that he is back on his feet."

Thias sighed in recognition of Berger's point on geography. Avolire had been built on the eastern aspect of the Dragonas whereas Falahorn lay on its most south-western tip. The two places were connected by one old road that passed through Avolire before it continued north towards the edge of the Realm and into the land of the dwarves. Thias smiled in the knowledge that at least one of his friends was up and moving again.

"Thank the gods he is walking so soon," he responded. "I think that we should thank Fatumai for her kindness in healing my friend so quickly."

"Yes indeed," added Berger as she stepped across her threshold. "Thanks to both Fatumai and her children. May the Moirai watch over us forever; should it pleases them to do so."

Thias followed Berger into the building and the darkness pierced only by the natural light of Solaris as it streamed in through the window. As he paced forward he thought again about the name Moirai. It was the word that Irabo had translated as the three Fates. He began to imagine their appearance and where they dwelt but once inside the room the thought evaporated as he looked around to see who else was present. There was no sign of Mium or his two children in the vast single room that acted as kitchen, living space, and bedroom. It appeared that all were out in the fields, tending to the general business of the farm. Then as his eyes grew accustomed to the gloom Thias noted a figure silhouetted against the log fire and which he recognised at once. Sat at a solid oak table was his young friend from the City Watch of Parandor.

"I am so pleased to see that you are up and about at last Irabo," said Thias as he grinned and walked towards his companion.

"It is so good to see you too Thias," said Irabo as he returned the smile. "Forgive me if I don't stand just now. Though I can walk a short distance, I still find it difficult to remain upright for any length of time, even with this crutch that Eerickk made for me."

Thias looked down to Irabo's side to where the young man's hand rested upon a wooden staff fashioned from one of the few trees that grew in the Dragonas. The warrior released his grip and the crutch fell the short distance to the floor.

"Then please, I beg you, do not stand," replied Thias "I'm just so relieved to see that you can move again."

"I am also glad. I doubt Tonousa or Commander Townsforth would allow me to remain in the Watch with only one good leg. They would no doubt try to pension me off or put me somewhere out of harm's way, perhaps as a guard at the temple of Fatumai, or worse still as a clerk in Tonousa's father's library."

"And a very good scribe you'd make," said Thias as he laughed.

Irabo also chuckled but then moved his injured leg and induced a pain that shot through it like a lightning bolt.

"Eerickk may have got me walking but I still have a long way to go," winced Irabo.

"That's why you need to keep resting and get more fluids and food inside you," added Berger, busy in the kitchen and preparing a dish of vegetables.

"Have Berger and Mium been looking after you?" asked Irabo.

"Yes," replied Thias, knowing that his host was near. "They have been most attentive."

"I see they have dressed you as one of their own."

"Indeed they have," chirped back Thias. "I thought they went a little over the top with the fur, but on the first night here I realised how much the temperature in the Dragonas drops when Mona rises. I'm amazed that the grass can survive here given the vast changes in temperature."

"It's Falahorn's secret. I think you'll find that the magic of the dragons has something to do with the fertility of the lands around here. Things shouldn't survive but they do. Take the three of us traversing the pass around Skillar. Was it by magic, luck, or divine intervention that we are still alive? If it hadn't been for the

Berserkers finding us when they did we would have lost Llyat and no doubt our own lives too. The Fates were certainly with us that day."

"For that I am grateful," replied Thias as he pondered. "I see they've dressed you in a similar manner."

Irabo wore the same style of clothes as the bard and people of Falahorn. The one difference was the addition of a metal cage around the young warrior's lower leg and which supported his broken bone. A voice floated out from the kitchen.

"I hope you are both hungry."

For the next hour Thias and Irabo dined with Berger. Half an hour into their meal they were joined by Berger's husband Mium. His blond hair and well developed muscular torso created a most impressive site but yet there was still no sign of his two children. The explanation given between mouthfuls of vegetables was that Harrow and Thalik were working down in the caverns below Falahorn, tending to a new clutch of dragons. Soon stomachs and minds returned to the food. Berger had prepared a vegetable broth and although a meagre meal without a hint of meat or bread, there was at least plenty of it; and it was hot.

As they continued to savour their morning feast both Berger and Mium described life for those who lived in Falahorn. Much of the information was new to Irabo, even though he was already familiar with this remote area of the Realm. The story was that there were nine buildings in Falahorn above ground and they were controlled by six different ancient families of surface dwellers. Thias had already had contact with Berger's family and also the Kelby's. He had heard much about the Jarls in their role as carers. In addition to these there were the Aadolfs, the Kirkwoods, the Olins, and the Selbys. Each of these last four also managed farms that stretched away from the town and across the surrounding countryside. In total there were five farms in Falahorn and they split their responsibilities such that one housed a tavern, one a communal stable, and one an infirmary. The last contained a fake mill house that concealed the entrance to the caverns below the town. The surface dwellers were assisted by those that lived underground and who helped when needed to protect the village livestock against attacks from kulkulkath, skyfawns, or nighthowlers. During the conversation Irabo repeatedly referred to the time that he and his parents and had lived in this same dwelling house that was now occupied by Mium's family. That was before the plague had taken them.

The hidden underground realm of the Berserkers was different to everything on the surface. Thias knew the stories of what lay beneath Falahorn well but it was good for once to not just to hear a story but to experience the truth first hand. He listened as both Berger and Mium offered their accounts of what lay beneath them in the tunnels created by dragon fire. Both confirmed that there were a large number of individuals that lived in the caves and passageways. There the most secretive of folk tended to the dragons in order to ensure their survival. They remained ever vigilant against those that followed the ways of Sir Belquin, the town of Griginor, or indeed anyone else who sought to hunt or harm the great beasts.

"So what do the dragons eat?" asked Thias. "You cannot expect me to believe that you produce food enough to support yourself and the dragons. I also doubt there are enough wild creatures living here in the Dragonas to sustain such a colony."

Mium guffawed between mouthfuls of broth. "It is clear you know nothing of the inner workings and eating habits of dragons."

"What do you mean?" questioned Thias. "They are living creatures are they not? They need sustenance to survive. How can you keep these large creatures from destroying your livestock?"

"It's clear he knows bugger all about dragons Irabo," said Mium with a haughty laugh.

"Dragons are not like you or I Thias," added Irabo. "Remember these beasts are born of the tears of the mother of the gods. They are creatures of pure magic and don't require the same stuff that you or I need to exist in this world. They feed off the magic of reality. Some say that there is an energy, unknown to us mortal men, that holds everything in place. These sages say that our universe is made of this dark powerful stuff and that together with the ordinary matter that we see, it forges our reality. The dragons feed off the dark stuff and the spells that hold us together. This form of invisible power flows through everything and the dragons can harness it for their needs."

"I'm surprised that the bard didn't write stories of the dragon's power source," added Berger.

"The only songs and tales that I have heard relate to when dragons have killed," said Thias.

"No doubt horrible stories of them hunting for pleasure, stories which they themselves created for dramatic effect," replied Mium.

"How interesting" replied Thias? "Is it really possible that the great lizards have developed a concept of fun? If so, how do you know this?"

Thias noted a silent exchange between his hosts as they looked at each other and thought as to whether they should answer that last question. Even Irabo looked confused but then he decided to offer his thoughts on the matter.

"The Berserkers have found a way to communicate with the dragons haven't they?"

"Yes lad, they have. However that is a story for another time," said Mium. "So, enough talk of dragons for now my friends. Please finish your food and then I can take you over to see the Jarls."

Thias had found the broth to be most filling, so much so that when Berger offered him the last ladleful he declined for his stomach could take no more.

"I forgot to tell you that your young friend Llyat has regained consciousness," said Mium as he put his spoon down to the table.

"He's awake!" said Thias, somewhat surprised. "That is indeed good to hear."

"Yes. He resurfaced a couple of hours ago. Eerickk Jarl told me that he is making good progress. Now which one of you two is going to explain the words the young lad muttered as he came back into the Realm?"

"What words did he utter?" asked Irabo.

"I am the Marked!"

Thias and Irabo looked to each other. Throughout their stay and the stories they had told their hosts they had never once talked of the Enderdetag Prophecy and Llyat's potential involvement in it. Thias felt uneasy as his mind and mouth considered what to say next.

"The words mean nothing to me," he muttered.

"Now young bard," grunted Mium. "I know a liar when I hear one, and to be honest you're a bad one. The words are a mystery to me but Eerickk Jarl has already sent word of what was spoken down into the caverns. I have to tell you that mention of the 'Marked' has spooked both the dragons and the Berserkers. Over the next few days we expect them to demand an audience with you…"

"I'm ready to see them now," replied Thias. "We seek the location of the dragon Thamous. I'm sure you have heard of him."

"I know enough of Thamous to know that the creature is not dragon but wyvern," answered Mium. "However the leader of the Berserkers, Cvyler Olin, has asked to meet with you on some matter of great importance. He will however wait until your friend Llyat is well enough to explain the meaning of words that he spoke on waking."

Thias thought long and hard. He contemplated what had spooked those below ground and the thought would not leave him. Given that Thamous was a wyvern he failed to understand what relevance other dragons were to his quest and why the people of Falahorn had been so unnerved. Another question that troubled him was how he would communicate with Thamous. He did not speak dragon tongue nor the language of the Eastern Marsh. Mium had hinted that the Berserkers had found an effective way of speaking with the great beasts but had yet to reveal what that secret was. Perhaps that could be the way forward if he could only persuade the Berserkers to share their knowledge. He prayed that in the coming days his questions would be answered. The group were then joined by two children, Harrow and Thalik, who proceeded to help their mother clear the table. Once the four Kelby family members had left the room to attend to their farm work, Thias and Irabo began to converse.

"So how are you doing" asked Thais from across the table?

"To be honest I could be a lot better," the warrior replied. "That knock on the head combined with my broken ankle have sapped much of the strength out of me, but I can at least walk."

"How long do you think it will be before you will be ready to continue on our journey?"

"I don't know. According to the Jarls it could be a couple of days or even weeks. However, from what I can gather, it isn't me that we should be worried about. You should concentrate on Llyat and on getting the boy fit to leave this place as soon as possible. Are you still convinced that he is the Marked?"

"Yes I am," replied Thias. "The more I think about the Prophecy, the more I am sure that he is the one that the words speak of. Master Ulthirn was most certain of it…"

"I am sorry. Can you remind me which member of the Guild he was?"

"Ah yes!" continued Thias. "I forgot that you had left the room by the time he had arrived and visited us down inside the sleeping chambers. Master

Ulthirn was one of the senior members of the Guild and he had long studied the skies and the heavens. He had been a follower of the astrologer Anyle Belanore and was convinced of Llyat's part in the prophecy. He had also assisted in my research into the Enderdetag mystery before your arrival at the Guild. Given that he was certain of the impending alignment of the orbs in the heavens, he was sure that the time of the 'the Marked' was imminent."

"Just as the prophecy said."

"Exactly," continued Thias. "And the attack on the Guild and the loss of the Dagger of Kha has further confirmed my suspicions. I now believe that it is up us to protect Llyat, to get him to a point when he can reunite the Gems of Thamous, reach the Oracle of Frasteria, and locate the door to the Underworld."

"Well, at least we are in agreement then," replied Irabo. "I have been thinking the same thing ever since Einar woke me from my head rattle on the pass around Skillar."

"What do you mean?" asked Thias

"I'm not a hundred percent sure but while I was unconscious I had a most strange dream,"

"And what did your dream reveal Irabo?"

"It was a strange vision about one member of the Sovereign Court, Lady Thinata Fullbane. Her voice whispered in my ears that 'a path was forming'. She was then joined by three old crones who told me that Llyat was my purpose in life, that it was my fate and destiny to protect the boy and to ensure that he fulfilled his part in what was to come."

"Well..." began Thias with a little hesitation. "You might want to keep that one to yourself. People who have dreams that predict the future or hear voices telling of their destiny are most often committed to a place of healing or are executed under the suspicion of witchery.

"I suppose you are right," continued Irabo while rubbing his chin. "Now, shall we go and see how our young charge is doing? I wouldn't mind having a chat with Eerickk Jarl as well and persuade him to give me more of his poppite juice. Right now the pain in my ankle is testing my limits."

Irabo tried to stand and as he did so he stumbled. Thias was quick to jump forward and caught his young friend before he hit the floor.

"I'm fine," snapped out Irabo in embarrassment. "It's just going to take some time."

It took the friends longer than expected to leave the Kelby's dwelling and step out onto the single dirt road that connected the wooden buildings of the village. Thias was reminded of Maplehill and in the cloudless still air Falahorn appeared at its most peaceful and serene. The air matched the beautiful vistas and all smelled pure and sweet. Without question it felt good to walk up the gentle incline towards the large house at the end of the row of buildings. The bard then became aware of someone walking towards him, a young lad of some fourteen years or so who led a creature by a rope that was tied to its ample neck. The beast was size of a horse but had the same leathery and hairless skin as the wormnose and hornnose. From the centre of its head grew a single white bony horn. The point was so strange that Thias stilled and allowed Irabo to catch up.

"What's wrong?" said the warrior. "Why have you stopped?"

"What is that?" asked the bard as he pointed towards the creature.

"Are you serious?" continued Irabo. "Have you never seen a unicorn before?"

"I thought there were just echoes from legends, just stories."

"Well..." laughed Irabo. "It's clear you need to visit the Dragonas a little more often. There are all sorts of wonderful creatures in this vast wasteland..."

"And there you go calling it a wasteland. The Dragonas is far from that."

"It's the best kept secret in the North, is it not?" replied Irabo laughing. "The people here live a simple existence, well apart from the raising dragons. Those that live in Falahorn do not want an influx of foreigners, venturing up from the south and trying to take over their lands. The desolate wasteland story is drilled into us from birth; it is part of the protection of all that surrounds us. It is also why the Berserkers patrol the Ivory Pass?"

"I guess that makes sense," replied Thias as he raised an eyebrow.

Irabo didn't respond further but started to walk on towards the largest of the dwellings. It was the one that Thias understood to be the Jarls' community infirmary. Thias followed and kept to the same slow speed as his young friend who limped on in obvious discomfort. Some minutes later they found themselves on the porch of the building. Irabo moved forward and rapped on its door. After a few seconds it opened and they were greeted by a tall slender blonde haired woman dressed in the attire of a healer.

"Good day Irabo," she said with a sweet voice and with obvious pleasure. "Back so soon?"

"Not for your healing hands this time Arnkatla," replied Irabo as he winked at the girl. "But thank you anyway. We are here to see our friend who you have cared for so well."

"Of course," replied the young woman as she turned and led the way into the building.

The corridor before them was lit from a single window. Four additional doors opened onto the passageway which was free of furniture. The only adornment was a tapestry on one wall, a pattern rather than a picture, and woven in colours of red, brown, and green. Arnkatla led Thias down the corridor to the door at the far end. She knocked and an authoritative voice from within responded with the word 'enter'. The young woman opened the door and gestured to Thias to move inside. Irabo followed. The room was of a comfortable size and in its centre stood a large solid wooden bed. Beside it and dressed in a similar white smock to Arnkatla stood a middle aged man. Thias noted the black markings on his shoulders and the black hood that covered most of his head. Sat bare chested on the bed was the youth they had come to visit.

"Nice to see you again Llyat," said Thias as he moved further forward.

"Thias, Irabo! It's great to see you both."

"Easy lad," said the man in the hood as Llyat tried to jump from the bed only to fall back with exhaustion. "Be careful. You haven't yet regained sufficient strength to move so quickly. I would not want to have to scrape you off the floor. I have put a lot of effort into getting you this far."

"I am sorry, please forgive me," replied Llyat as he turned to Thias. "It's wonderful to see you again."

"And you too Llyat," replied the bard. "How are you feeling?"

"Like I've fought fifteen ogres! My whole body aches."

"If you had fought fifteen ogres then I don't think we would ever get you walking again," said the hooded man

"I must apologise sir for I cannot remember who you are and I want to introduce you to my friends," said Llyat as his head turned fuzzy.

"Ah yes," replied the man. "I'd forgotten the extent of your mind muddling. You have been unconscious for most of the last five days and it is not surprising that your memory is a little jaded. Allow me to introduce myself. My name if Eerickk Jarl and this is my home in Falahorn..."

"So we made it!" exclaimed Llyat.

"Yes we did," said Thias. "But you are very lucky to have survived the journey."

"If it wasn't for the presence of a Berserker pack that were monitoring your movements in the fog around Skillar then you would have all been long dead," confirmed Eerickk.

"What happened on the mountain?" questioned Llyat. "I remember going to sleep..."

Thias gave an account of all that had transpired, starting with Irabo's fall, the skyfawn attack and Einar's rescue. As the story unfolded Llyat asked many questions as he sought to understand all that had happed to him. Thias managed the pace of the discussions so as not to exhaust Llyat and even found time part way through to find a stool for Irabo to rest upon as the discomfort grew in his leg. Eerickk Jarl had also become aware of Irabo's pain and asked his daughter to fetch some poppite from his apothecary elsewhere within the building.

Once Arnkatla had returned and administered potion, the story of the events on the mountain pass came to its natural conclusion. From the thoughtful expression that covered Llyat's face it was obvious to all that there was much he was trying to make sense of.

"As I said lad," continued Eerickk. "You are lucky to be alive."

"How did I catch the sweats?" asked Llyat as Arnkatla began to dress him in a clean shirt. "Where did the illness come from?"

"The cause is the most mysterious aspect of the disease. We put the blame on bad air. There are others who have come up with odd theories such as contact with fouled water sources in which the dead have lain. I know of one old man who thought it came from the fleas of the rats that are so abundant in the south of the Realm. As yet there is no still no agreement as to its cause. Have you come into contact with any such things?

"He is from the Capital," sneered Thias. "What do you expect?"

"As am I," added Irabo. "But I'm not carrying the sickness."

"It matters not what the cause is," continued Eerickk. "He is on the road to recovery."

"To which we are all most grateful and forever in your debt," replied Thias.

"Does this mean we get to see the dragons?" shouted Llyat with excitement.

"It does," replied Thias as he took the opportunity to sit on the edge of the bed. "I believe and hope that the Berserkers will be able help us find the dragon Thamous... sorry Irabo, wyvern"

"My friends," interrupted Eerickk. "It is the wish of the Berserkers that you attend an audience with them. As Mium will no doubt have explained, Llyat's words have caused them much consternation. You are lucky, for even those who live above ground in Falahorn seldom get to see the magnificent creatures close up, even though we helped raise them in the nest. Before you can go underground you must be allowed to rest and recover. As your healer I must insist that you respect my decision as to the timing of such a meeting."

Thias looked towards Llyat whose eyes sought reassurance. He nodded back.

"It's okay Llyat. We will leave you to rest and gather your strength. I am sure that you will be up and walking again in no time at all. Then we will resume our quest."

3.

For the next two days Llyat did his best to rest and aid his recovery from the oft fatal disease known to all as the sweating sickness. He had somehow managed to survive the foul distemper, an outcome reserved only for the most resilient and strong. It was usual that if Llyat succumbed to an illness that he would keep on going and fight through it but this disease was different for it had run a most severe course. Left alone Llyat would have been with the Fates and it would have been but a roll of the dice or a flip of a card as to whether he had survived. His mother had always told him that the best way to stop a fever taking hold was to fight it. That was the reason that Llyat had chosen not to inform Thias and Irabo of the severity of his symptoms on their journey through the Ivory Pass. He had developed a stubborn streak that first manifested itself during his illness. From nowhere had come the desire to master any problem, to better his problems no matter how fearful he felt at the time. Despite this new found confidence he was at present governed by the strict instructions of the healer that had saved his life. Under no circumstance was he to leave his bed or try to do anything strenuous. Llyat allowed himself to believe that the order had been given because the healer had his best interests at heart. Whether that was true or not he would have to wait and see. As the days passed in long hours of tedium he wondered what Eerickk had meant by 'strenuous' but in the end what mattered most was that he got well enough to see the dragons.

This was what Llyat wanted more than anything else. Given the events of the past few weeks, the slaughter of his family, the death of his master at the hands of the creatures from the Eastern Marsh, his second near drowning during his escape from the Bards Guild, and now the sweating sickness, he could not think of anything more curative than seeing the fire breathing lizards that he and his friends had so often discussed in the Red Mare. In a brief moment of fantasy he wondered if Cleath and Methladon would be jealous as he told them of his adventures but then the memory that they no longer walked in the realm of the living hit him hard. A darkness fell as he realised that his one moment of joy could never be shared with them. It deepened further as he then recalled those that who hunted him had accused his father of being a traitor and that Rukave Emgar may not have been his true father after all.

One further thought consumed Llyat's thinking. It was that of the woman Heliana who he had not seen since the massacre at the Bards Guild. He had a vague recollection while half asleep that Heliana had been saved from the inferno by the First Mate of the Banshees Wail. As he lay and rested in Falahorn he realised how much he loved and missed the smell, taste, and touch of the young woman with whom he had fallen in love. He prayed that Theoplous had indeed got her away to safety. Even the thought of meeting fire breathing dragons was insufficient to ease the pain of the separation from his beloved Heliana. It was as if the Fates had chosen to bring them together and then with great cruelty wrenched them apart. For whatever reason they had chosen this path, he swore that he would find her again, even if it took until the end of three summers.

On the third morning after his awakening Llyat was allowed to rise from his bed. Arnkatla had assisted Llyat to dress that morning for Eerickk wanted someone close in case Llyat should lose his balance and fall to the floor. As soon as she helped lift him from the bed Llyat's cock began to stiffen. He tried to hide the embarrassment that grew under his hessian trousers but it was to no avail. Arnkatla was so attractive that she even surpassed Heliana in beauty. He had been in bed too long and his seed begged for release, yet deep in his heart knew that Heliana would be the one to share his future. Still he knew not to mention Arnkatla to Heliana when they next met for his true love had the temper of a bear once roused.

After Arnkatla had helped Llyat to wash with a bucket of water, flannel, and even soap, the girl then proceeded to display the clothes that she had found for him. Llyat had half expected to see his old servant's attire, washed and repaired, but the new ones that hung over the chair were somewhat different.

"What happened to my old stuff?" asked Llyat as he looked at the strange garb. "Those I was wearing when I left Valameer?"

"They were filthy, ragged, and beyond repair. They most likely carried disease and so we disposed of them just in case they had some hand in causing your sweats. I have found some that are far more fitting. I do hope you like them."

Llyat looked down and was reminded of the gambeson that he had been given on his first day in Parandor but these new clothes were not of the same quality. They appeared made of a soft leather that was easy enough to bend and were similar to the armour that Irabo and Tonousa wore during their voyage on the Banshees Wail. Around the chest piece, patches of hardened metal had been attached, buckled on to the leather and crossed by a single piece of strapping that stretched down from the left shoulder to right side of the waist.

"What kind of garments are these?" asked Llyat while he held the top up high and examined it in the beam of light that crept into the room through the window.

"These are the clothes of the dragon handlers. Given the stir you have caused down below we thought it best that you wear something more appropriate for your purpose."

"My purpose? Caused a stir," replied Llyat. "I don't understand what you mean?"

"You forget my young friend that you were unconscious for several days while in my father's care. Your physical body may have been at rest but the mind is a wondrous thing and it governs us even when we not awake. Do you know that you talk in your sleep?"

This was news to Llyat. No one had ever told him this before, not even his parents. Why was it, he thought, that no one had mentioned this for his friends and family had not been the kind to shield him from embarrassment. Arnkatla helped Llyat to put the top coat over his chest and ensure that the strap sat well.

"What did I say?" said Llyat.

"You muttered two words; repeated the phrase 'the Marked', over and over again. To be honest, for I will not lie to you, I do not know what the words mean and your secrets are your own, but those two words sent old Cvyler Olin into a right state."

"Cvyler Olin?" quizzed Llyat as he buckled up his trousers.

"The leader of the Berserkers. He is the man in charge of the caverns below the town. He leaves the running of the surface to my father. Now, let's have a good look at you Llyat."

Llyat flushed once again but then realised that the young woman was referring to the clothes he was wearing. Even the boots which he managed to pull on with ease seemed well fitted to his feet. Although the clothes gave him confidence, something was missing.

"I had a sword. What happened to it?" he asked.

"Apart from the spears and shields used to keep any predators from the farms, all other weapons are stored underground in the armoury. Your own sword and the blade that belongs to master Irabo were taken there for safe keeping. Do not worry, it will not be going anywhere."

Llyat thought about the sword that had once belonged to his master and he recalled its name. Destiny's Song had saved his life in the Bards Guild when the Lizardman had attacked, the same creature that had referred to him as the traitor's bastard. A loud knock sounded at the door and a voice called out."

"May we come in Llyat?" bellowed the distinctive voice of Eerickk Jarl.

"Yes of course," he replied as he smiled at Arnkatla.

"And this is where I bid my leave of you, young master Llyat."

The door to the room opened and Eerickk Jarl stepped inside. He was dressed in identical attire to that which Llyat wore. Behind the healer of Falahorn stood Irabo, still supported by his crutch, and Thias the bard.

"Thank you Arnktala," said Eerickk with a brief nod towards his daughter.

The young woman acknowledged her father with a curtsy and then left the room. Once the four men were alone Eerickk spoke again.

"How are you feeling today Llyat?"

"I'm still confused but my body feels fine."

"Well fine will just have to do. Your progress has been monitored closely over the last few days and my daughter and your friends feel the time has come."

It was true for Llyat's friends had checked in on him several times each day. Irabo had visited the most for dragon curiosity had overtaken him. Even though he made sure that he looked in on Llyat daily Thias always said that he was busy writing a song about life in the Dragonas and couldn't stay long. Llyat wondered if this was the truth yet he did not waste time doubting his new friend. He also knew what Eerickk had meant by 'the time had come'. It was the moment he would meet the Berserkers and with luck, the dragons.

"Are we going underground?" he squealed with excitement as all concern faded.

"Yes Llyat," added Thias. "Then maybe we can make some sense of the events that have troubled us these past few weeks."

Eerickk Jarl led the way out of the building. Llyat and Thias followed but Irabo struggled to keep up and fell a little behind. As they moved outside Eerickk explained that they had left through a side entrance to the vast building and that the main door to the infirmary was in fact through a large open hall. Llyat found himself not listening for he was more interested in what surrounded the building. He looked over to the wooden farm constructions and the yellow grass that formed the expanse of the Dragonas. Then, he began to compare Falahorn with Maplehill. Although the buildings were different in their shape and structure, the layout of the ground was similar with one single road running through its length. There were however two significant differences; Falahorn was more attractive to the eye and it didn't smell so much of shit.

Llyat's attention then moved towards the distant horizon, past a heard of wormnose, a solitary longneck beast, and on towards a three peaked mountain in the far distance. As he looked at the far off summit he felt drawn towards it as if something powerful pulled on his navel. It seemed to the youth that invisible strings sought to manipulate his every move and he was reminded of the sensations he had felt when he had once dreamed of being a puppet. For a brief moment he closed his eyes and tried to imagine what the sensation meant. Then from the darkness behind his eyes he heard a low voice that hissed and spoke his name.

"Llyat Emgar."

The youth opened his eyes and looked towards the mountain. He stopped moving and stared into the distance.

"Llyat?" said Thias. "Are you feeling well?"

"I'm fine," lied Llyat for he felt confused.

He knew that if he admitted to hearing voices then the meeting with the Berserkers would be postponed and he would be sent back to his sickbed. So he took several deep breaths and sought to regain his composure. This gave ample time for Irabo to hobble over on his crutch. It was then that Llyat asked the question that most troubled him.

"Thias, that three pointed mountain in the distance. What is that place?"

"I believe it is referred to as the Gathering," replied Thias as he looked in the direction that Llyat pointed. "Berger, the woman that has cared of me, told me it is the source of the power of the dragons but she refused to explain further. She said that Cvyler Olin and the Berserkers will be able to answer any questions we have about that place. To be honest, when I spoke to her she seemed a little spooked."

"And so she should be," added Eerickk who now joined the three companions at the side of the road. "There is a strange power locked in that place and some will tell you that it has been there since the creation of these lands, long before the Realm came into existence. But like the bard and Berger said, the Berserkers will be able to tell you more about the Gathering if we ever get to meet them. Come on let's keep moving for we are wasting much time and will be late for our appointment."

Llyat sensed that Eerickk was frustrated by his break to look at the mountain and therefore picked up his pace. This time he strode alongside the healer who continued to lead them through the village. As they walked on Eerickk turned his head from time to time to ensure that both Thias and Irabo still followed. Then he began to engage Llyat in conversation.

"I understand that you have always wanted to see a dragon young Llyat."

"More than anything," he replied. "We saw one above the Ivory pass many days ago. We were just approaching the Bards Guild at the time and it was many leagues away and just a dot on the distant horizon. I have dreamt of seeing one up close ever since."

"Then today is your lucky day lad. One of the chambers we will pass through is one where the Berserkers guard the dragon's off-spring before they are released into the wild of the Dragonas. We have one in the birthing chamber at this moment. She is an ice dragon and we call her Valathaxicore. It seems to like the name."

"Valathaxicore," squealed Llyat. "What a beautiful word."

"And you have yet to see the beauty of the beast itself. Tell me Llyat, given all you have heard and the longing that you have to see one close up, what can you tell me about them. For a start, are you aware of the mistake that everyone makes? Do you know the difference between a dragon and a wyvern?"

"A dragon has four legs whereas a wyvern has two,"

"Good, very good. I see that you know the something of the basics. Tell me then, what else do you know of them?"

Llyat searched his memories and tried to think of as many facts as he could so as to impress the healer. Soon they left the centre of the village and approached the building disguised as an old mill.

"Well, I know the reasons why the dragons of old collected a horde. It was not based on greed, nor the love of gold, but for pure comfort and safety. A dragon, I was told, would much prefer to sleep on a bed that was not going to catch fire if it breathed out flame while it slept."

"A story of old," laughed Eerickk. "It sounds like you are familiar of the Ballad of Xenvagen and the Knight that Slew him?"

"It is my favourite one," said Llyat blushing, "It fuelled my love of everything Dragon."

Llyat also knew that the song told of the destruction of one of the most powerful creatures ever to fly out of the Dragonas.

"You never know your luck lad!" said Eerickk as approached the building's door. "The Berserkers are always looking for off-comers to join their mission of protection. Being dressed in the clothes of a Dragon handler's child I am sure you will fit in just fine. We are here now."

From within a pocket built into the side of his leather clothes Eerickk Jarl produced a ring of keys. They were all of different sizes and Llyat watched the healer as he searched for the one that would unlock the door. It took him a half a minute to find it by which time Thias and Irabo had caught up. At last Eerickk placed the rusty key into the lock of the old door and turned it slowly. With a sudden click the portal opened and allowed access to the building's interior.

Llyat was the first to step forward into the gloom. He half expected to see the inner workings and gears of a mill, just like the one back in Maplehill, yet that was not what he saw. There before him in the darkness stood a wooden square structure supported by numerous ropes, pulleys and wheels. Llyat noted a flickering light, sourced from a burning brazier close to the central workings. He knew from what he had already been told that this building gave access into the tunnels underneath Falahorn and as he moved forward Eerickk Jarl and Thias closed in behind. He heard the clumping of Irabo's crutch as it bounced of the dirt floor. The door then closed behind them and the room darkened in the absence of all light save for the brazier. Llyat felt something sharp suddenly dig into his back and the sensation forced him to stop moving. Fear took hold and he began to quiver at the thought of what would happen next. For a brief moment he assumed that he and his friends had walked into a trap but then a gruff voice spoke from behind.

"And who might these three be Eerickk?"

"Do not worry Geir. These are the ones that Einar rescued from the slopes of Skillar."

"The one that calls himself the 'Marked', is he with them?" asked the voice again in a less intimidating manner.

"What's going on Eerickk?" asked Irabo.

"Nothing of concern. He is just doing his job. Isn't that right Geir?"

The voice did not reply but Llyat felt the sharp object release its pressure from his back. This gave him the opportunity to turn around and face whoever had appeared from out of the shadows. Illuminated by the flickering flames was a giant of a man, much taller than anyone Llyat had ever seen before. He was dressed in similar hessian trousers and yet was shirtless. The dancing light showed off his perfect physique and well defined belly muscles. Dirt, charcoal, and scorch marks covered his body while the pelt of a nighthowler sat upon his black head of hair. A bearded face seemed to fight to constrain its own heavy growth. The nighthowler's mummified eyes looked out from on top of the man's head while the rest of its fur cascaded down over his back. Llyat knew he was looking at one of the legendary Berserkers of Falahorn. In one hand the giant carried a torch pole which he lit as if by magic. In the other he held a small knife, the point of which Llyat assumed had just pierced his leather jacket.

"This is Geir Aadolf," said Eerickk. "He is Cvyler Olin's second in command. Geir, these three are Llyat, Thias the bard, and one of our own who is now a member of the City Watch of Parandor. His name is Irabo Basequin and you may have come across him as a snot of a lad when he lived on one of the surface farms."

Llyat looked up to the giant man who in turn looked down with deep suspicion.

"You may be aware Geir," continued Eerickk. "Cvyler has sent for these three for he says he has much to ask them."

"That's as maybe," replied the giant. "Cvyler may want to meet with them but what is their purpose here in Falahorn."

"We seek the wyvern called Thamous," replied Llyat without thinking.

He knew he should not have not opened his mouth without first consulting Thias but he could not take the words back. After a further silence Geir spoke again, his fierce demeanour giving way to a soft smile.

"Then it is true what they say about you! The Marked has made it to Falahorn. No wonder the dragons are spooked."

"Why are they disturbed so?" asked Llyat. "Why do they fear my presence?"

"That is not for me to tell..."

"Then who the fuck will!" demanded Llyat. "Ever since I woke in this place I have been trying to ask questions. No one will give me any fucking answers..."

"Llyat please..." interjected Thias, but Eerickk Jarl once again stepped forward.

"The boy has a valid point Geir," said the healer. "I think it's time that we took Llyat and his friends down below where we can answer some, if not all, of their questions.

"Then follow me at once," said Geir.

The giant man moved towards the wooden cube and beckoned the others to follow.

"Here lad, take the flame from me."

Llyat followed Geir's instructions and took the torch from the Berserker's hand. The excitement of the moment was all consuming and it scrambled his thoughts. He stepped onto the wooden platform and the others followed. Llyat's attention then turned to Geir who stood by the wooden wheel attached to the main mechanism. The giant began to turn it and set the platform in motion. It required all of his strength but soon he jumped onto the platform and joined the rest of the group. After a couple of revolutions of the wheel the platform began to shake. Like a slug on a forced march it then descended into the caverns and soon the only light visible was that from the torch that Llyat carried in his hand.

For what seemed like an eternity the platform continued to descend into the rock and after some minutes had passed Llyat began to wonder if it would ever stop. He tried to imagine the distance between the village on the surface and the tunnels below and realised it must be a substantial one. He could make out the different layers in the rocks as they passed his flickering flame and he thought perhaps that some of the great beasts of the Dragonas could be buried within stone and preserved for all time. Finally the platform reached the end of its journey and came to rest with in a second wooden construction. Llyat looked up into the cavernous shaft he had descended and saw only black. His eyes then met those of Geir and the giant smiled.

"Welcome to the caverns of the Dragonas."

Llyat pushed the torch forward into the darkness and saw ahead of him several other burning flames, all attached to the walls of the tunnel and which lit up the passage that cut deep into the rock.

"The walls look like they have been burned" said Llyat when he realised that Thias was also examining them with great interest.

"No doubt with dragon fire," replied Irabo. "That is the only thing that could have melted rock so far below the surface. These tunnels must have been created by the dragons themselves."

Geir continued to lead the group forward through the shadowy passageways and soon Llyat began to hear strange noises that echoed from far away tunnels. He began to dream of what he would see once he reached the end of the unnatural passageway. His mind saw great beasts yet he had no concept of what a dragon would look like close up. Llyat closed his eyes and looked to the back of his lids. Shocked to his core he saw two red eyes that burned as if afire. They looked straight at him and tried to penetrate his soul.

"Young Emgar," said a strange voice from within. "Are you really the Marked of Maplehill?"

Llyat forced open his eye lids and stood still. Thias and Irabo collided into his back. He turned around to look at his friends, his face pale from the shock of seeing the mysterious eyes and hearing the voice in his head for a second time. With much concerned Eerickk stepped forward and asked:

"Is everything well lad?"

"Fine," lied Llyat. "I just lost my footing."

"Just be careful along here," continued the healer. "We don't want you ending up like Irabo, having to get by with a crutch."

"I hate to break into this conversation but we are losing sight of the Berserker," said Thias.

The bard was right. Geir had drifted off into the darkness and without further delay the rest raced forward in an attempt to catch up with the giant. That did not take long and several minutes later the group stopped in a new and different space. The tunnel had opened up into a large cavern, much wider and higher than the passageway through which they had come. Llyat looked at the wooden viewing platform that was fixed around the circumference of the almost spherical chamber, one again burned out of the rock by some great heat. Several other passages lead off from the edges of the platform. Llyat looked down over its edge and into the depths of the flame lit chamber. It wasn't the just the complexity of the circular platform, nor the mighty wooden supports that held it up that fascinated Llyat as he gazed into the hole. It was something far more interesting.

The scales of the creature that slept on a bed of loose rock were of the deepest blue. In its stilled state it displayed its elongated and magnificent body. At the top a slender neck sat a block shaped skull with a wide open mouth, pronounced overbite, and multiple rows of teeth. The beast's head rested upon a large black boulder as would a man upon a pillow. It had short limbs, each with four splayed digits that ended in claws. It wings ran from its shoulders to its hips and a row of snake like tendrils cascaded down its spine from the root of its neck to the tip of its tail. The creature's eyes were closed tight, much to Llyat's disappointment. While it slept it snored and let out small bursts of ice crystals from its nostrils.

"This is the dragon known as Valathaxicore," said Geir as he stood beside Llyat.

"Magnificent!" the youth replied. "An ice dragon?"

"You know your dragons well."

"She's quite beautiful," continued Llyat as he stood in awe. "May we get any closer?"

"Not while she is in her birthing cycle. We protect her more at such times than at any other. Valathaxicore has a mean temper and is best avoided when on her eggs."

"There are eggs down there?"

"I guess she is lay on them," added Irabo.

"Even though the dragons and their shells excite you, they must wait Llyat," said Eerickk, "Cvyler Olin demands your presence and so we must hurry on."

Once again Geir lead the group forward into one of the side tunnels. Eerickk was correct, the prospect of seeing more dragons this close filled Llyat with a tremendous excitement and as they continued their transit through the caves he once again started to dream. This time he was sat astride the neck of a large grey dragon, many times larger than Valathaxicore. He swooped into battle with Destiny's Song in one hand and the reins of the beast in his other. They flew together across the marshlands and destroyed all the Lizardmen that dwelt there. He felt powerful and for once in his life full of confidence.

"Llyat!" said the voice without warning.

He turned, half expecting to see the fiery red eyes but the voice belonged to Thias.

"Well young friend, it looks like we have arrived."

Llyat then looked to an ancient wooden door set back into the rock of the tunnel. Geir moved forward to open it. The giant stooped before entering the room to avoid striking his head on the frame of the door. Eerickk Jarl was the next to enter. Then Llyat moved forward and pushed his way in ahead of Thias and Irabo. The large stone room was at least five times as large as his house back in Maplehill. Its walls were different to the tunnels that had been formed by the melting of rock for these had been clearly chiselled by stone hammers in order to create the space in which they now stood. It had been dug high enough for even a Berserker to stand without stooping. Five enormous men filled its interior, each one dressed in a similar fashion to Geir with nighthowler pelts upon their heads. These new Berserkers were busy with various tasks and took no immediate notice of the newcomers. Llyat's eyes then inspected a tapestry that had been hung on one wall and appeared to depict maps of the Realm from many years past. Two Berserkers sat at a wooden table and conversed with an old man whose face was most hidden by a mass of matted grey hair that grew from the crown of his head. Even though this unique man appeared ancient, he too wore the garb of the Berserkers, except for the nighthowler pelt. The Berserkers around the table and those examining the tapestry turned to face their visitors.

Llyat felt anxious and looked to Irabo and Thias for reassurance as Geir stepped forward towards the table and beckoned the three friends to follow him. The old man stood up and stared at his visitors. After what seemed like an age he spoke. The voice surprised Llyat for it was not that of an old man but one much younger.

"Welcome my friends," said the strange one, his words creeping out through the grey hair strands that covered his face. "Welcome to the Dragonas. Forgive me if I don't stand longer and shake your hands for time has not been kind to me. Please take a seat at my table."

The old man returned to his chair and with a wave of his hand indicated to the three empty ones before him. Llyat sat down in the middle, Thias took the one on his left while Irabo flopped onto the chair to his right. The imposing presence of the healer closed in from behind.

"Thank you Eerickk," said the old man. "You are not required to stay and I am most grateful to you for looking after our guests so well."

"As you wish Cvyler."

Llyat sensed the disappointment in Eerickk Jarl's voice but they were now in the domain of the Berserkers and Cvyler Olin's orders were carried out without question. He heard the door close and when he then glanced over his shoulder he saw that Geir now guarded the entrance.

"We don't often receive visitors down here," said the old man. "New faces are a pleasant change."

Cvyler Olin moved the hair from in front of his face and Llyat recoiled at what he saw.

"Does my appearance startle you, the one who calls himself Marked?"

"Err...." stammered Llyat.

"Have some respect for our leader," boomed out a new voice.

The Berserker to Cvyler's right slammed his fist onto the table, stood up, and glared at Llyat with a ferocity that made the youth's limbs flutter.

"Calm yourself," ordered Cvyler who then raised his hand and caused the Berserker to sit. "The boy meant no disrespect. He just wasn't expecting to see such a face."

The old man's skin had both human and dragon-like features. It was as if he had fallen under some dark spell and been fused by magic with some slithering reptile. Half of Cvyler's face was covered with green scales, most evident around the left eye. His nose and jaw were elongated and formed a snout like protrusion. When he spoke Llyat was sure that he saw pointed teeth, more designed for ripping through flesh than the diet of men.

"Such is the gift of living close to magical creatures for so long," said Cvyler as Llyat shivered. "May I assume that you know of the Berserkers and their abilities?"

"I might have been told a little..." added Llyat as he looked towards Irabo for support.

"Then you should know of the effect of living in close proximity to such beasts over so many generations. Magic leeches from off their scales. It is like they have their own powerful variant of the Kundalish Aura, which I guess you may by now have heard of. The magic grants Berserkers the gift of extended life, skin strength, and hardened muscles. However we are not as invincible as the stories you may have heard suggest. We still pass away in time, once our course has run. I have lived for many a generation amongst the creatures that we have sworn to protect and..."

"How old are you?" interrupted Llyat.

"How old do you think?"

"Sixty, maybe seventy?"

"He said generations Llyat," whispered Thias.

"One hundred, maybe two," responded Llyat after a little more thought.

"A fascinating guess but still wrong. I am over six hundred years old. I was there when Sir Belquin pledged to destroy and drive the dragons from the Dragonas.

I was and still am, the first Berserker to accept the honour of protecting all such creatures."

Llyat was stunned. He did not know how to respond. The man was the ultimate hero who had achieved the impossible.

"I know that it is not the Berserkers that bring you all the way to Falahorn," continued the old man. "We have heard tell of the words that you spoke in your dreams. Young Arnkatla Jarl informed her father and Mium Kelby of what you had said and those words filtered their way down here. I need to know the stories you three have to tell for I wish to discover more about your quest and your presence here in the Dragonas. Before any of you may leave I must understand why you have come to Falahorn. But first you must tell why you believe this child to be the Marked of Maplehill, the one spoken of in the Enderdetag Prophecy."

Llyat listened as both Thias and Irabo in turn chronicled the events relating to the Death Tubaria murders in Parandor, their separate journeys north, and the attack upon the Bards Guild. They spared no detail in their telling of it. Llyat was able to pick up on the names of the other occupants of the room during the discussions that followed. The three men who stood near the tapestry were Alvida, Brant and Guldbrand and were the designated personal protectors of Cvyler Olin. The two sat on either side of the old man were Einar and Beris, the very same Einar who had saved Llyat's life on the path around Skillar. Llyat tried to place a memory inside his head should he ever have to remember the names of the Berserkers again. Then he began to think on what Cvyler had said regarding being in contact with the Kundalish Aura, the phenomenon that only became visible in the presence of Masslewort.

"Pay attention!" screamed the now familiar voice from inside his head.

Llyat sat upright and at once checked to see if anyone else had noticed his lapse in concentration. It seemed that no one had. Neither had anyone else heard the voice. As Llyat tuned back into the story, the discussion had moved on to the events at the Bards Guild and Thias was speaking a name that was unfamiliar to him.

"Who is Anal Bellmore?" asked Llyat, unaware he had mispronounced the name.

"Anyle Belanore was the great astrologer who helped found the Bards Guild," replied Thias with a chuckle and a raised eyebrow. "It was he who first decoded the Prophecy of Enderdetag through his observation of the stars."

"He was also the founder of the religion of the Cuvar," added Guldbrand. "Its followers swear on their lives that should the Marked ever appear they will do all they can to ensure the Prophecy is fulfilled."

"That is one I have never heard of," said Irabo. "I thought I knew of all the religions of the gods. I follow Fatumai, that which is followed here in Falahorn, but I have never heard of the Cuvar?"

"They are many who practice it still," continued Guldbrand. "They hide from sight and most hail from the distant Lotus Isles. There are a few in Parandor I believe. I have even heard there are some that dwell in the Dirmark who still follow the original teachings of Belanore to the letter. One place above all others that I wish I could have seen was the great Orrery at the Bards Guild and through its power the conjunction of Enderdetag itself."

"I am afraid the Orrery lies at the bottom of the ocean now" said Thias. "Destroyed by those shits from the Eastern Marsh."

"That saddens me," replied Guldbrand. "But seeing as young Llyat displayed so much Kundalish Aura in the library of Owasorin Fusepelt then we must assume he is indeed the Marked.

"If I could put it into plain speak, unlike the riddles that Guldbrand likes to talk in," said Cvyler. "The Cuvar are the people who will protect this boy from the servants of Urthanock and help him reach the Oracle with the Gems of Thamous. It does however worry me that the Lady of the Silverwynn has likely recovered two of the gems."

"I could lead a small force to Avolire and reclaim them," offered Einar.

"And reveal that the Marked is alive and amongst us?" said Thias from across the table. "Not to mention putting yourself in great danger by exposing your community to Avolire. Do not forget that the foul inhabitants of the Eastern Marsh have flocked to the aid of the Lady of the Silverwynn."

"Then what else do you expect us to do?" asked Einar in his gruff manner. "Should we just sit here on our arses and wait for the Underworld to be unlocked so that foulest of women can satiate her lust for power by bringing down Parandor and unleashing Urthanock upon us?"

"There is one other option," said Irabo.

"And what is that?" asked Beris, speaking for the first time.

"We carry on with what we always planned to do; find the remaining gems before those from Avolire get their hands on them."

"And is that is your true purpose here in the Dragonas?" asked Beris.

"Indeed it is," replied Irabo. "We have a need to find their creator and ask him where the remaining two are located. A third we believe remains hidden in Parandor and one of our friends searches for it as we speak."

"You seek that creature?" laughed Einar. "You seek the fifth tear; one of the original five?"

"And what business is it of yours if we do?" added Thias as the tension grew.

Llyat hoped a fight was not inevitable. Without Destiny's Song he would be of little use.

"Friends, please," said Cvyler as he coughed into his hand and then raised it aloft. "Of course they must meet with Thamous. Einar, you will be the one to take them there. I believe you have several unicorns readied for such a journey."

"That is correct," the Berserker replied.

"Then it is decided, the Marked shall meet with Thamous."

"Thank you so much," replied Thias while dipping his head in appreciation.

"The boy will need to communicate with Thamous when he meets him," added Cvyler. "Geir will also accompany you and provide you with a 'Dragon Whisper', the way to get into both dragon and wyvern thoughts. It will be an honour for us to take you to the lair of Thamous and we will give provisions for the arduous journey and return your weapons."

Llyat watched as Irabo rose and supported himself on his crutch.

"Are you taking us to where I think you are?" he asked. "A place no one other than a Berserker is permitted to enter?"

"That is correct friend," replied Cvyler as he too stood with difficulty. "Thamous's lair is a two day ride into the Dragonas. You will meet him at the Gathering."

Llyat smiled for his dream of meeting and talking with a great serpent was about to come true.

Thamous was waiting for he already knew that Llyat was coming.

4

Solaris rose and spread glorious light over the flat grassy wilderness. Methladon Heyn focused his eyes on the distant horizon and lost himself in his thoughts. He still wore the black armour of the Knights of Avolire and carried his metal helm beneath his left arm. The dwarf had lied to him about his true intentions and the reason behind his incarceration at the Grey Keep but the outcome had been the same. The Lizardmen had been part of the plan to break Grovrouk out of his prison once he had extracted the location of Thamous from Jonas Tullage. Being part of that contrived operation had not stopped the Lizardmen from treating the dwarf as they would any prisoner. Nor did they spare the violence that action brought with it.

On the two day journey from Avolire, Methladon had engaged the miserable dwarf in numerous conversations. The discussions had been difficult at first but in time had softened to the point where a relationship of trust had begun to form between the two who had shared time in a prison cart. Methladon had learned that even though Grovrouk the Despoiler had wanted to break away from the Knights of Avolire he could not forgo his loyalty to the Lady. It appeared that the pretence of keeping the dwarf in jail was plot hatched by the little man and his Lady; designed to cover up her true intentions and to allay the suspicions of Rhaizen, the Harbingers, and the rest of those that served under the banner of the Silverwynn. Grovrouk had told Methladon that the Harbingers found out about the deception and it fuelled their abuse and their dislike of all those who came from the Dirmark.

Methladon looked out from the ridge on which he stood and continued to ponder on all that Grovrouk had told him. The dwarf had explained that Jonas Tullage had once been a respected member of the Court of Gylewu and renowned throughout the south of the Realm. He had held the position of Grand Physician before the days of old Abrahamus Marus. Some twelve years previous, in the height of one of the hottest summers that Solaris bestowed upon the world, Tullage had come by the book known as the Lore of the Dead. Once opened and read, he became fascinated with the text and all that it revealed. No one knew where Tullage had found the tome but while being questioned by the Grey Keep's torturers he claimed to have been given it by an old woman he met while searching for medicinal herbs in the Hills of Harico. Grovrouk explained that the passages in the book then twisted and warped Tullage's mind. With the help of the secrets hidden within the Lore, Tullage then created the cult of Death Tubaria. He had recruited and collected the darkest and most evil minds from across Parandor with the intention of resurrecting Kha, the foulest of the Underworld's gods. In order to achieve this end he had planned a series of twelve murders; each of the victims to have been branded with the mark of Kha. In the end, Tullage was only caught by a swift intervention by the City Watch but the termination of the plot had not been without casualties. A swarm of Tullage's followers had swept through the Capital and left a swathe of dead in their wake.

Grovrouk had also told him it was the quick and decisive action of the Watch that had stopped the cult from murdering a particular small boy. They were about to dismember the child by using four horses pulling in different directions and the story had reminded Methladon of how Nictis had tried to kill him in front of the Lions of Avolire. The story surfaced a distant memory, one that plagued him despite it happening long ago. Methladon knew that he had lived in Parandor before his family had without apparent reason moved to Maplehill. He had very few memories of that early life but a recurring one forced him to confront the possibility that it was he, Methladon Heyn, who was the young boy described in the dwarf's story.

Not wishing to linger on the idea he began to brush such thoughts aside, save for two questions; what happened to the Lore of the Dead and how did Tullage discover the location of the creature that they now sought. According to Grovrouk, after the suppression of the uprising and the incarceration of the disgraced Lord, the Lore of the Dead had been deposited for safe keeping in the Sovereign's library. The intention was that it would remain there, only accessible for the purpose of research by a knowledgeable few and hidden from others with more evil intent. Whoever had written the book had no doubt visited Thamous and documented the location of their meeting within the Dragonas. It had been confirmed that Tullage had sought out the location of the creature and that was reason for Grovrouk's infiltration of the Grey Keep. There as planned the dwarf was placed in the same cell as Tullage and once the information had been extracted Grovrouk had silenced the physician. The place that Tullage had described lay in the middle of the Dragonas at it was known known as the Gathering. It was the spot where three mountain peaks had gathered into one and where the wyvern was most often seen.

Methladon stared out into the west to where the sky and grassland met. There were a few rocky areas between his feet and the horizon where the creature was said to be found. Rhaizen had warned them to be on their guard against ambush, either from dragons or their handlers. In the distance Methladon could just make out several small villages scattered across the land and it was to the closest that Rhaizen had sent Oedd with the order to scout it out. As he looked to the limits of his vision he saw no sign of a three pronged mountain that would fit Grovrouk's description.

The ridge had been chosen as their base camp the previous night. The four horses that belonged to Mhlau, Newyn, Farwolaeth and their Commander were tethered near to the makeshift fire which now smouldered having gone out in the early hours of the morning. Three other horses, those of Methladon, Grovrouk and the Lizardman warrior Ssnarkit, were tied nearby; the distance underlined the separation of the elite three from the other three. The tension between the Harbingers and the Lizardman had been evident right from the beginning of the journey and confirmed the intense dislike that the Knights of Avolire felt for those that were spawned in the Eastern Marsh. It was even greater than that shown by the Harbingers towards Grovrouk. According to Rhaizen, Lizardman presence was essential to enable communication with Thamous as the language of those that dwelt in the Eastern Marsh was not too dissimilar from dragonspeak. It was as if the Lizardmen were descendants of the great beasts, twisted in form as they evolved. Ssnarkit however kept himself to himself and communicated only on rare occasions. The Lizardman even ate his own rations and touched nothing else. It seemed the creature feared that poison would be used against him. The Knights of Avolire did not trust Ssnarkit and Methladon got the distinct impression that the reptile felt the same.

Despite everything that had happened to Methladon since his forced departure from Maplehill he felt proud to be now part of a military unit that strove to defeat injustice and gain supremacy over the Capital. The armour on his body seemed as it belonged there and yet the lightness of the metal never ceased to amaze him. Orichalcum was indeed the strangest material he knew.

A smell of burning wood drifted in on the air and gripped Methladon's attention as he looked down from the ridge to a small farm house near its base. The main building was on fire and cast flames and black smoke into the air. On the track that led from the burning house Methladon spotted a lone figure on horseback with something slumped over the front of the brown steed. He recognised the rider due to his large frame; it was the Harbinger Oedd returning from his scout of the countryside. As he got a little nearer Methladon began to make out the nature of the object draped over the saddle. Oedd had taken a prisoner.

"He returns!" shouted Methladon over his shoulder for he had been given the role of lookout by Commander Rhaizen in order to prove useful in some way or other.

The other Harbingers had been readying their horses to move out when Methladon uttered his cry. Rhaizen, who sat upon a gnarled tree stump sharpening his sword with a small knife, looked up and then nodded his understanding of the message. It did not take long for Oedd to re-join the group gathered on the edge of the ridge. As the mount reared and then came to a halt at Oedd's command, the knight cast his prisoner down from the front of his horse and dropped him before Methladon's feet. It wasn't long before all had gathered around the prisoner.

An old man writhed in the dirt. He was dressed in peasant's rags and had been beaten around his eyes and nose. Oedd had not spared the man's features.

"Who is he?" asked Rhaizen looking down.

"A farmer of no importance," replied the Harbinger as he slipped off his horse.

"That's right," replied the old man as he quivered with fear. "I'm no one. Do not harm me."

"Then why bring him here?" asked Rhaizen.

"He threatened to call out the Berserkers. Alert them to our presence."

"You should have let him," added Farwolaeth. "I'm itching for a fight."

"As am I," said Newyn. "Any engagement with Berserkers is a challenge worthy of the Knights of Avolire."

"Please," pleaded the old man, oblivious to the conversation being conducted over his head. "My wife and my children, I must go back and save them. Your friend left them tied in the barn and now it is on fire."

Methladon heard the cries of the old man and knew that he was telling the truth. He had witnessed the burning of the farm down amid the grasslands. His thoughts were with the peasant and his dying family. Part of him wished he could go up against the knights, free the poor wretch and save his wife and children, but he knew that he was outnumbered and outmatched. There was nothing he could do except pray that the gods brought a speedy end to the farmer's torment. Then he was reminded of the attack on Maplehill and how the Knights of Avolire had shown no mercy to his family. He felt helpless yet angry for there was just nothing he could do.

Rhaizen approached the old man and dropped down onto one knee. Without raising his voice he spoke again.

"Do you know who I am?"

"No I do not. My wife, my daughters. I beg you, let me save them."

Rhaizen clicked his fingers and the old man fell silent. Some mysterious form of control had befallen the man whose skin then turned white as he began to sweat in torrents. Methladon assumed it to be another example of Rhaizen's magical powers.

"I'm going to ask you a question," said the Commander without change in tone. "I am about to release my grip and you are going to answer with the truth. My men are hungry for a fresh kill, something that has been denied them for several days, and it would not be in your best interests to lie. I will order your execution should you try to speak untruths. Do you understand me?"

The old farmer nodded his acknowledgement as Rhaizen returned to his feet. The Commander then snapped his fingers and released the man from the spell.

"Thank you. Thank you kind sir!" wept the farmer as he crawled over to kiss Rhaizen's feet.

The Commander kicked out and caught the farmer in the face. The peasant collapsed back into the dirt and as he did so the Harbingers and Ssnarkit laughed. Only two watched on in silence, Methladon and Grovrouk the Despoiler.

"The question is a simple one," said Rhaizen. "The Gathering, where is it?"

Methladon prayed that the man would answer.

"I'll ask you one again," shouted Rhaizen. "The Gathering, where is it?"

"Please, please, my wife, my daughters."

Rhaizen unsheathed his blade and pointed its tip under the farmer's neck. A pungent smell hit the air and Methladon realised that the farmer's control had failed him.

"Say 'please' once again or mention your wife and daughters and I will drag them out of the barn myself, ravage their cunts and slit their throats!" bellowed Rhaizen.

"I would answer the Commander if I were you," shouted Mhlau.

"Answer, please answer," whispered Methladon to himself.

"The Ga...Ga...Gathering," stuttered the old farmer as he pointed towards a group of trees and rocks on the distant horizon. "Aim for those. Two days ride to the west. There you will find the three peaked mountain."

"At last! Thank you," replied Rhaizen as pulled back his blade and then turned his back on the peasant. "Oedd, kill him."

Methladon wanted to shout out in horror at the Commander's order but he knew that if he did then he too would be dead. He dared not cross the beast with the skull helmet.

"P...P...Please," stuttered the farmer as dark yellow stains forced their way through the stitching of his cheap trousers. "My wife. My daughters. You said you would let me go."

Rhaizen turned to face the old man.

"I said nothing of the kind. Oedd shut this fucker up; give my ears a rest."

Methladon looked on as the Harbinger unsheathed his sword and moved towards the old man. As the farmer quivered in his own filth on top of the desolate ridge, the knight raised his sword high into the air. He was about to bring it down and split the peasant into two when Rhaizen raised his hand once again.

"Stand down Oedd," he ordered and the knight obeyed without question.

Methladon was confused. Something was not right. He saw the look in the farmer's eyes and noted that they relayed the same bewilderment.

"Methladon," said Rhaizen.

"Sir,"

"You do it. Prove your commitment to our cause."

Methladon was taken aback and for a moment wondered if indeed the order had been directed at him. He looked towards Grovrouk who signalled with a simple shrug of the shoulders that he had no real choice in the matter. Methladon felt sick and yet he could feel the mark on his neck encouraging him to proceed. As the rest of the Harbingers and Ssnarkit watched on Methladon placed his hand upon the hilt of his sword and pulled it from its sheath. He saw and felt the farmer look at him. An old soul pleaded with bloodcurdling eyes.

"Kind sir, please. My wife. My daughters."

"Kill him now!" shouted Rhaizen.

Methladon hesitated. He was torn between the order he had been given and his feelings for the plight of the innocent farmer.

"Kill him now Methladon!" shouted Rhaizen, "Or I swear you will suffer in his stead."

Methladon screamed. He felt the growing pain in the back of his neck. Choosing the expedient option he closed his eyes and raised his sword high while screaming aloud;

"For Avolire!"

With his eyes still shut he brought the blade down in one swift movement. He felt it strike and cut through something. Then as he opened his eyes instead of seeing his sword lodged in the farmer's skull he saw that it had missed the head and cleaved down through the man's shoulder and on into the centre of his chest. The man coughed and spat out a great bolus of blood which hit Methladon's boots with a splat. The victim of such needless violence began to convulse and while so occupied Methladon pushed the body free of his sword with his right reddened and sticky boot. He looked towards the others in turn before at last staring at his Commander. Without knowing what else to do he raised his blade to the air and cried out with all the strength he could muster.

"For Avolire!"

"For Avolire!" replied the others.

A feeling of invincibility took root inside Methladon's core. All of a sudden there was nothing that he could not do. He kept his sword aloft and breathed in a great pocket of pungent air. The burning sensation on the back on his neck had gone and had been replaced by a warm glow the likes of which he had never felt before. He was filled with a great sense of achievement and not the intense guilt that he had so expected. As he began to lower his sword he noted Rhaizen watch his every move.

"Good boy. Very good indeed. That was a nice clean kill," said the Commander.

Rhaizen did not linger before he turned to address the rest of the group.

"We move out at once," he ordered while setting off towards the horses. Then he, gestured towards Grovrouk. "Newyn, tell the hole-dweller to look after the boy. Somehow the lad understands the tongue of the Dirmark. Get the stump to watch over the lad and make sure he remains sane."

The group dispersed and readied themselves for departure. Methladon found himself sanding motionless over the body of the dead farmer while he stared down at the blood that seeped out of the wound that ran between the man's shoulder and stomach. He felt warm and excited. His breathing became ever more rapid, and he was filled with confused emotions. In this heightened state he did not hear Newyn ask Grovrouk to look after him but the dwarf soon came up, gripped him by the arm, shook it, and forced his voice into Methladon's ears.

"Are you okay?" asked the Dwarf.

"Yeah, fine," replied Methladon while his breathing rate slowed a fraction.

"If I hadn't been at the Lion's pit when you killed Nictis, then I would have said this was your first proper kill."

"I don't want to talk about it right now."

The youth looked once again to the fallen farmer as his state of confusion waxed and waned. The dwarf was almost right for apart from Nictis there had been but one other, a member of the Knights of Avolire that he had killed during the attack on Maplehill. Yet that kill had seemed far easier compared to the murder of an innocent.

"Suit yourself," replied Grovrouk. "Sometimes it's better to talk about these things."

"I don't want to talk."

"Then do me a favour," continued the Dwarf. "Put your fucking sword away. You don't need it now. Sheath it and get your horse ready. Rhaizen says we are moving out and given his current mood we should not keep him waiting."

Methladon looked to his blade which dripped deep red globules of the farmer's life flow. The blood did not bother him in the slightest and it held a fascination of its own. At last he sheathed the sword and then with his eyes closed he sighed, placed his black helm over his head and covered his face. It blocked out all signs of his confusion. Two reddened eyes peered out through the slit like hole but no tears flowed.

"Come on then Grovrouk," he said without a hint of emotion. "Let's go."

It didn't take them long to mount their steeds although the dwarf required assistance to lift him into place. Then amid the midmorning light of Solaris, Rhaizen led the group out in single file, down from the ridge and onto a trail that traversed the grassy wilderness of the Dragonas. The smell of charred flesh floated in on the wind for the farmer's family were well cooked and would never see Solaris rise again.

Several hours later, having passed numerous villages and farms, there was still no sign of the three peaked mountain known as the Gathering. Rhaizen brought his horse to a halt at the edge of a huge canyon that stretched deep into the earth and blocked the way forward. It had no doubt been carved out of the ground by some ancient river that had long since changed its course. The great gash in the land had not been visible to Methladon nor indeed any of the others as they had journeyed from the ridge. The deep ravine stretched out for as far as the eye could see, league upon league both to the north and the south. Below him Methladon scanned for any signs of the long forgotten river but there were none visible. In ages past such a flow of water must have supplied vast areas of the Dragonas. Why, he wondered had it fled, leaving the once lush land so much drier. It was a question that had little relevance and so he let it dissipate on the wind. All that mattered now was how to cross the canyon that stretched as far as eyes could see.

"We could go south to the Grey Mountains," said Newyn as he looked into the vast gully.

"Or north for that matter," added Oedd.

"Either way it would add several days travel onto this already long journey," replied Rhaizen. "I don't want to spend any unnecessary time in this place. There are things in this wilderness other than dragons to be concerned about and I don't desire to face them. Mhlau, Farwolaeth, one of you head north the other take the south. See if you can find an easier way down. Ride until Solaris is at its fullest then return. The rest of us will wait for you here."

"Yes Sir!" they replied in unison.

In no time at all Mhlau and Farwolaeth had set off at a gallop in opposite directions and left the rest of the party encamped at the edge of the canyon. Methladon climbed off his horse and beat an iron spike into the ground to which he could tether his horse. He then looked out across the great cut in the land and scanned it for any sign of life. As the Harbingers and Grovrouk set up camp Methladon felt strange and uncomfortable. It was as if someone or something was pulling him forward across the canyon. He stood still but the compulsion to move forward and throw himself over the edge began to build. Then as he fought the strange feeling, he squinted and focused on the distant horizon. He was sure that he could make out the three peaks of the distant mountain which they sought.

"Sir!" shouted Methladon. "I've found the Gathering. I can see it; it's ahead of us."

Both Rhaizen and Ssnarkit soon joined Methladon on the edge of the canyon. The Commander removed his skull helmet and held it under his left arm as his right hand moved to shade his eyes.

"Where lad?" he asked, looking out in the direction that Methladon pointed.

"In the distance, there, straight ahead of us. Can't you see it?"

"Yes lad," replied Rhaizen. "I can just about see it now. Your eyes are keen and sharp. That is a talent the Knights of Avolire will value."

Methladon looked again towards the three peeks as the strange sensation continued to pull him on and manipulate his senses. He felt a great need to travel at speed towards the mountain in the distance but then in a moment of rest his eyes dropped to the canyon floor and he saw something move. There were five of them, grey skinned horse like creatures that moved through the rocks in search of food or fresh water.

"Are they unicorns?" asked Methladon as he pointed them out to the others.

"Yes, turd brain," replied Ssnarkit with a hiss. "They are found in just two locations."

"I am guessing you mean here and the Eastern Marsh," sneered Rhaizen.

"I do!" hissed Ssnarkit. "But within the Dragonas there are many more diverse creatures than could survive in the Eastern Marsh. Likewise many of those that dwell in my home would wither in this dry and miserable place."

"Fascinating! I am sure we have all benefited from your insight," sneered Rhaizen.

"You asked," hissed Ssnarkit.

"It was I that asked what the creatures were," added Methladon. "All I wanted to know was if they were unicorns."

Methladon waited for a response from both the Lizardman and his new Commander for he knew that either would take his life in an instant should the mood take them. He then sensed a shadow pass over as if the densest of clouds had extinguished all light.

"Yes, Methladon," said Rhaizen. "The five beasts are indeed unicorns."

"Four." hissed Ssnarkit.

"Fuck off!" barked Rhaizen. "It is clear there are five..."

The Commander stopped his sentence in mid flow as he followed Methladon's gaze to the floor of the Canyon where the unicorns had scattered in all directions. The shadow passed over again as the travellers looked on with interest. Methladon counted four and wondered what had happened to the fifth.

"There were five, I swear....."

"Fire Drake!" screamed Grovrouk as a roar from above drowned out all other sounds. The ground shook with great violence while the three warriors looked up in awe at the sky.

"In name of all the gods, she is magnificent," shouted Methladon.

"This is not the time for wonderment," yelled Rhaizen as he turned back.

"Arm yourself men. We have a fucking dragon to slay."

The beast screeched again. Methladon unsheathed his sword as it flew overhead, close enough to see all its stunning detail. Its large size and impressive wing span was enough on its own to strike terror into the hearts of most men. The body was a deep metallic red, serpentine in shape, and it terminated in a great long and slender tail. All four of its muscular legs were tucked up into its body while it glided over the cliff tops with only the occasional flap of its two mighty fan-like wings. The dragon then soared high into the sky on an updraft of air and turned in circles. Methladon tried to get a good look at the creature's head when without warning it dived into the canyon once again. It was a misshapen head with a crown of exposed bone at its forehead. In the midst of its dive the creature screeched. It was a deafening sound that filled the land as if the beast was trying to split the air. Through its open mouth Methladon saw two rows of razor sharp teeth and a long forked tongue that stretched out from the back of its throat.

"Methladon, quit dreaming and grab your shield," ordered Rhaizen. "Trust me, you don't want to be flash fried. Ready yourself with some protection."

The youth snapped out of his trance and looked up to the beast that had returned to the sparse high cloud. How he wished that Llyat and Cleath could have seen the creature but then his attention switched to his own survival. He raced at speed the short distance from the canyon edge to where his horse stood and quaked in fear while still tethered to the ground. Once there he unfastened the black orichalcum shield that was attached to side of the saddle. The four other members of his company were busy doing the same while the dragon continued to circle high above. It howled and it shrieked with an intense ferocity that tightened Methladon's sphincters. He somehow sensed all was not how it should be. There was something that was not quite right.

"It didn't kill the unicorn," he shouted to Rhaizen as the others formed a circle with their shields pointed outwards.

"Shut the fuck up Meth," snapped Oedd as he prepared for an impending attack.

"Keep your thought's to yourself boy and get ready," cried Rhaizen. "We won't protect your worthless hide if you don't pull your weight."

"There's something wrong. There is something amiss."

"Keep silent you festering turd," screamed Oedd.

"I'm telling you, the beast up there did not kill the unicorn. There is another...."

The dragon swooped down lower than before and swept over the fearful group, its wings taught and outstretched as it glided past. Methladon could almost feel the scales of the dragon comb through his hair as the beast dived over his head. In a state of panic he swung his sword at the creature and he was not alone in so. Each one of his party attempted to strike it and yet all missed. Grovrouk, wielding his axe, tried to jump up in order to implant his weapon into the creature's side. All failed miserably due to the great speed with which the beast travelled. As it dipped down into the canyon they all threw themselves to the floor such that if the dragon returned it would take their horses instead.

"That was close," gasped Newyn.

"Too fucking close," replied Rhaizen before shooting a glare towards Methladon. "What did you think you were doing, shouting and making so much noise?"

Before Methladon could answer back a second cry filled the air of the Dragonas. It was deeper and fiercer and it echoed out from the base of the canyon.

"Shit there is another one down there," gasped Rhaizen.

"That is what I was trying to tell you," said Methladon. "Something down there took one of the unicorns while we stood here talking. If we hadn't been so focused on what was happening above we would have spotted the other one much sooner."

"Go and find out what is happening," ordered Rhaizen.

Methladon sighed and closed his eyes. He inhaled deeply and savoured the air for as far as he knew it may have been his last breath. If this was what he needed to do to prove to Rhaizen that he was worthy of Knights of Avolire then he was up for the challenge. He crawled forward on his belly towards the edge of the canyon, surprised how easy it was in armour that did not restrict movement. Once at the edge he looked down into the depths of the canyon. There were no signs of the unicorns but something else gripped his attention. The fire dragon now occupied the same spot where the unicorns had been sighted. Its wings were retracted back into the side of its body and four extended legs pushed its body free of the ground. As its long tail swished through in the air Methladon watched it throw its head from side to side amongst the dirt. It was attempting to take something between its mighty jaws.

"What is it doing?" he said out loud.

Then he saw something thrash within the beasts mouth. It seemed to be the tail of some other creature that was part concealed beneath the clouds of topsoil thrown up from the canyon floor. Without warning a burst of energy expelled dirt and rocks into the air around the fire dragon. Methladon guessed what must have happened although within the chaos he could not be certain. The dragon that had swooped from above had spotted the presence of second, camouflaged and hidden in the dirt. It now held that other's tail in its mouth.

The brown earth dragon, identical in size and shape except in the colour of its scales, hollered as it tried to break free from the fire dragon that held it in its jaws. Then it turned on its captor and with one swipe of its right front claw, slashed down across the face of its adversary. The earth dragon's tail was released from the fire dragon's jaws. Methladon was mesmerised as the two beasts fought on. They clawed, bit, scratched and snarled as both tried to get the upper hand. It was a most ferocious battle between two gigantic beasts. Methladon guessed that the earth dragon must have been waiting for the unicorns and taken one while the remaining four had scattered. The fire dragon had not seen Methladon and the rest of those gathered on the edge of the canyon for it had been focused on finding the other reptile camouflaged in the dirt and whose presence challenged ownership of the surrounding lands. Somehow Methladon sensed that the fire dragon was a juvenile and he suspected it had made a fatal mistake in challenging the far superior creature that it had found hidden in the canyon floor.

"Magnificent aren't they?" hissed a voice.

Methladon glanced to his right and saw that Ssnarkit had moved forward to join him. Then he turned again to watch the battle rage on below.

"This is fascinating," said Methladon. "Is it true that you understand their language?"

"Who told you that?" hissed the Lizardman.

"Commander Rhaizen. He told me that the language of the Eastern Marsh is similar to that spoken by the dragons."

"He did not lie," continued Ssnarkit.

"Are you related somehow?"

"Do we fucking look like we're related? We may have had some link many, many, many, many generations ago, but the connection has been lost if indeed there ever was one. Do you care to have a wager?"

"Sorry?" replied Methladon, distracted as the fire dragon spewed out a great bolus of flame that covered the earth dragon without any apparent effect.

"Who do you think is going to win?"

Methladon was not one for gambling but from the lack of damage so far inflicted on the earth dragon, he knew which one he would put his money on.

"I side with the brown one. It's older and wiser and probably knows a trick or too."

"And slower,"

"What do you mean?" asked Methladon.

"Just wait and see. I can understand every grunt, howl, and screech that each of those bastards make. Even up here I can follow everything they scream at each other."

Methladon watched the fire dragon stop exhaling flame, pause to catch its breath, and then make ready to attack again. That was when the earth dragon launched its own assault. It pounced forward with what strength it had left and knocked the red dragon from its feet. With surprise on its side it began to claw, rip, and bite at the exposed belly flesh of its opponent. Never before had Methladon seen such power as the brown one ripped into the red, tore through its scales, and caused its black blood to gush from the deep slash wounds it had inflicted. The beast's body fluid seemed to have a life of its own as it tried to escape its containment and hide amongst the rocks and boulders of the canyon floor.

"Care to put your money where your mouth is Ssnarkit?" said Methladon.

"Keep watching," hissed the Lizardman.

They didn't have to watch for more than a few seconds before the fatal blow was delivered. It did not come from the earth dragon as Methladon had expected but from its opponent. One mighty swing of a powerful claw struck the earth's face and removed its right half. As the magnificent creature stumbled forward Methladon watched its life extinguished. The fire beast howled and launched itself into the sky. There it screeched as blood poured out from its belly and down onto the canyon floor. The creature then turned and flew off into the distance.

"Won't it bleed to death?" asked Methladon as the dragon became just a dot on the horizon.

"Dragons are made of stern stuff," replied Ssnarkit. "Its wounds will heal in time. But now perhaps you will understand why these creatures are almost extinct. They hate each other, just as we Lizardmen hate you of the man kind."

"How did you know the fire dragon would win?" asked Methladon. "What were they telling each other?"

"It was a fight for dominance. The alpha was the earth, and the fire challenged for supremacy over this area of the Dragonas. The earth was old and was about ready to give up but it was too proud go down without a fight. The fire drake had sensed this."

"You mean it wanted to actually die?"

"Correct," hissed Ssnarkit. "Let's return to the others for all is safe again."

Methladon rose to his feet, turned his back to the canyon and walked the short distance back to the horses where Rhaizen and the Harbingers stood waiting with shields still raised and weapons drawn. The first to catch his gaze was Oedd.

"Well?" asked the knight.

"It was as I first thought," replied Methladon. "The creature wasn't after us. There was a second one down in the canyon and that was its target."

"Where is that other fucker now?" asked Rhaizen as he lifted the visor of his skull helmet and exposed his face. "We saw the first fly off."

"That was the fire drake. The other was an earth dragon and it is dead," added Ssnarkit.

Methladon thought perhaps he had found a new ally in the Lizardman that the others despised.

"Thank fuck for that," said Oedd as he spat on the ground.

"One dragon we could have coped with," said Newyn. "Two may have been difficult. Now what do we do?"

"Nothing has changed," answered Rhaizen. "We wait for Mhlau and Farwolaeth to return. If they haven't fallen foul of something out there in the Dragonas we will then decide on the best route to take us to the Gathering. If we can find an easy way across this gash and keep up our current pace then we will have but a day and a half ride ahead of us. And before I forget Methladon..."

"Yes sir?"

"Good work lad. You showed courage to scout the edge of the ridge alone."

Methladon smiled. It seemed the Commander was now beginning to accept him into the ranks of his Harbingers. While they waited for their colleagues to return all conversations dried up just as had the mighty river that had once forged the gorge. Methladon stared out to the east and on towards the three peaked mountain. He felt the pull of the Gathering grow ever stronger. Whoever or whatever was drawing him there would no doubt reveal themselves very soon.

5.

By noon on the second day out from Falahorn six grey leather hides and their riders arrived at the foot of the rock strewn mountain. The vast natural structure rose so high as to almost touch the sky and perhaps even the heavens beyond. Wispy clouds of moisture circled its three separate peaks and hid much of them from view. Ever since the start of their ride to the north and the east, the lands had overflowed with the yellow grass that covered most of the Dragonas and gave life to an unending variety of fauna. Yet for the last hour of the arduous trek the ground around the foot of the Gathering had turned from soft soil into the hardest of rock. Llyat knew from his time on Chirth Hadra's farm that nothing could grow in this new desolate area of the Dragonas.

On leaving Falahorn, Destiny's Song had been given back to Llyat by the Berserker called Beris Kirkwood. Irabo had been reunited with his weapon and Llyat felt reassured when Thias, even though he preferred to use his limited magic skills, had also been presented with a blade. Einar, who led the expedition, had insisted that the bard carried a weapon for he stated he did not trust in the ways of sorcery. As they had prepared their mounts in Falahorn, Llyat had watched mesmerised as the three Berserkers armed themselves. Einar, Guldbrand, and Geir had all chosen the same weapons of war; a pair of battle axes that they had strapped to their naked backs underneath the nighthowler pelts that hung from their heads. He had watched the three pack their 'special' supplies onto the backs of the unicorns, several small jars of the fighting juice that which would cloud their thoughts, turn their eyes red, and transform them into the most ferocious of fighters. They had enough of the liquid to last several days of fighting but Einar had insisted that Llyat never sample the strange amber potion for those who had not been initiated and who were untrained in its effects went insane once it reached their brains. When Llyat had asked Einar where the liquid had come from and who made it the Berserker had fallen silent. This happened a lot whenever Llyat asked Einar questions. It was as if the giant had much to hide.

The unicorns had covered the ground from Falahorn at speed but for the last half hour their gallop had dropped to a slow trot as they negotiated the boulder field at the base of the high peaks. Llyat sniffed; he could feel it in the air. There was something palpable in the vapours, something about the place that it reminded him of death. Whatever he sensed made Llyat shiver although he knew not what it could be.

"I don't like this place," he said at last as he pulled on the reins of his unicorn and brought it alongside the beast that carried Guldbrand. "It feels too eerie to be a good place."

"Apart from the canyon, the course of the old river that ran out of the Grey mountains, this is the one place in the Dragonas where nothing grows." replied Guldbrand.

"Don't worry Llyat, I find it strange and creepy too, and I'm from Falahorn," added Irabo who passed him on his right hand side.

After circling around the base of the Gathering, Einar led the group towards an opening in the side of the rock face, the entrance to a vast cave that led down into the bowels of lands seldom visited. Llyat noted an old wooden pole that rose from the ground by the cave's entrance. It had been left there by previous visitors in order to secure their beasts while they explored the mountain's inner secrets. On either side of the entrance two braziers burned. They were kept alight by some form of magic for they were devoid of fuel. Their flames flickered against the darkness of the cave and a small amount of light crept into its interior as if determined to conquer the all-pervading black. On the jagged wall adjacent to each brazier had been left a wooden torch, ready to be ignited by those prepared to risk a journey into the unknown.

As he dismounted from his unicorn, Llyat was spellbound by the sight of the colossal cavity. He turned to Irabo to tell to him of his amazement but the warrior was already engaged in conversation with Thias.

"What do you think" asked Irabo as he tethered his unicorn to the wooden post.

"I don't know," replied the Bard, peering into the vast opening.

"It's very unlike you not to have an opinion Thias."

"That is very true, but there is something at the back of my mind that I cannot work out. I have a deep concern over the events spiralling around us. We did not receive a carrier bird back from Tonousa and I am worried she may be dead and that our secret died with her. There is also the possibility that she has been caught by the enemy and that they are aware that we move against them. I hope we are not walking into a trap."

"That is just your paranoia," said Geir as he joined them to tether his steed. "The Gathering has that effect on everyone, well those who ever get this far."

"What do you mean?" asked Llyat.

The voice inside his head that he had first heard in Falahorn had continued to visit Llyat and he sensed much foreboding. He had begun to question the possibility that hearing the voice was the first stage of madness. Einar secured his unicorn as Geir spoke.

"There are many things that dwell out here in the Dragonas; kulkulkath, unicorns, and wormnoses to name but a few. Then of course there are the dragons themselves and those who defend the land against the followers of Sir Belquin. All are barriers before the Gathering and few travellers ever make it this far. You three are the first in a very long time."

"What Geir is trying to say is that we kill anyone who dares trespasses in this part of the Dragonas and feed their carcasses to the wild beasts that roam here about," added Einar, "At least their recycled bodies then provide some benefit to our soil."

Llyat laughed through his nervousness. Maybe it was the place or maybe it was Einar's attitude that fuelled his fear of venturing inside the mountain. He shivered then tuned into Thias as the bard addressed the Berserker.

"I know someone you should meet Einar, Phauless Gylewu's Fool. I'm sure that with some hard work he could teach you to smile."

Llyat paused for a moment. His thoughts returned to the jester that he had met in the Citadel of Parandor; the idiot named Lolly. He began to imagine what the fool was doing at that very moment, no doubt entertaining the Court and even Phauless Gylewu himself. He reckoned that it must take a great deal of bravery and confidence to act the Fool and that was something Llyat longed for in himself. He was desperate to understand how he too could become less self-conscious and find his true self. If he ever made it back to Parandor he would join a Fool School, if such an establishment existed. Once Llyat had secured his unicorn and checked his possessions he moved away from the grey leather beasts and with the others headed towards the opening of the cavern. Just as he took his first steps into the Gathering he felt Thias's hand upon his shoulder.

"Are you feeling okay Llyat?" whispered the bard.

"Nervous, that's all."

"And so he should be," grumbled Einar.

"Einar, cut it out," mumbled Guldbrand.

"Maybe I will!" muttered the giant under his breath

Llyat turned and felt the tug around his navel as once again it sought to pull him deep underground. This time he did not hear the voice yet he felt a great compulsion to move into the dark. Despite his fear he edged forward. Some latent power of the gods seemed determined to pull on his life strings and drag him towards his destiny. Llyat resisted the temptation, stood still, and then refocused on the conversation around him.

"So what we do now, fearless leader," asked Thias.

"I take the boy to see Thamous," replied Einar in his gruff manner.

"Good. At least we will get some answers today," said Thias.

Einar thrust out an arm and prevented the bard's further progress.

"Just the lad,"

"But…." stuttered Thias.

"Do not worry Thias. I can handle this," said Llyat.

"But I don't trust them," replied Thias as he stared into Einar's eyes, bestial globes that poked out from under the nighthowler pelt. "Even if they did save all our lives on Skillar."

"The boy goes alone, or not at all."

"But…."

"Let him go Thias," added Irabo as the young warrior limped over on his crutch. "What's the worst that can happen to him? Eaten by a wyvern! Anyway I don't fancy the descent with this useless leg of mine."

"May I have one minute alone with my friend," said Thias, his gaze still fixed on Einar.

No answer came as usual and the tension rose. Llyat saw Thias's hand fall upon the hilt of the weapon and he wondered if the bard had it in him to start a fight. He had never seen a Berserker in action and was not sure if the bard's magic would be powerful enough to take one on.

"Fine," said Einar at last as he lowered his arm to allow Thias to pass.

The bard moved Llyat to one side of the cavern and out of earshot of the rest of the company. Llyat felt awkward about the developing the situation but realised that Thias had a point for he too was unsure if they could trust the Berserkers. He had told them everything and yet they had blocked his requests for information saying 'all would be revealed in time'. In reality Llyat's small group knew little more now than they had on leaving Valameer. For a brief moment Llyat thought about Heliana and how he wished to be back in her arms and between her thighs. An image of the beautiful Arnkatla Jarl broke through his thoughts and she asked him to join her in her bed. Llyat shook his head. He had to get that girl out of his mind. Thias spoke again.

"Llyat, I hope..."

"Thias, I am going to be fine," Llyat replied with an arrogance that masked his insecurity. "If I am the Marked then I am not going to get killed in there am I? Don't forget I am supposed to be everyone's fucking saviour! "

"Don't be so bloody cocky lad," replied Thias. "I like confident, but not the arrogance of a rustic snot. It is not a fitting characteristic for anyone, least of all a grubby peasant."

Llyat sensed there was something wrong. An unknown malady troubled the bard.

"Thias are you feeling well?"

"I just worry for you lad."

"Why the concern for me? I appreciate your desire to protect me but you do not really know me. Why start worrying after me now?"

"There is another story you need to hear, but it is for a different time. After the events at the Guild it is now my duty to protect you. I will explain once you return and we are on our way again."

Llyat noted the change in Thias's voice and in it the seriousness of their current situation.

"Now remember Llyat, question everything. It is imperative that you find out the locations of the remaining gems. It is critical that we find them before the Lady of the Silverwynn. Do you understand? "

Llyat nodded in silence as he heard the voice of Einar call.

"Times fucking up!"

"Do you understand what you need to do Llyat?" asked Thias.

"I do."

Llyat glanced over Thias's shoulder and saw the bulk of Einar approaching with a burning torch in hand. The Berserker clutched something hidden in his other hand but Llyat could not make out what it was.

"Come on lad, let's not keep Thamous waiting," ordered Einar as he passed deeper into the cavern. There he turned his head towards the others and called across to them. "Guldbrand, Geir, look after the bard and the one with the crutch. Answer any reasonable questions they may have."

"Of course," replied the giants together.

"And don't let them follow us."

Einar turned and made his way into the dark. Llyat looked back at Thias who signalled his approval and without further thought he chased after the Berserker's flickering flame. He tried to take in what little he could of his surroundings.

The cavern was vast and it sloped down into the belly of the earth. Its walls had a natural appearance unlike the tunnels made by the dragons below Falahorn. He became fascinated by the magnificent formations of stalactites that hung down from the roof like icicles on houses in the deepest of winters. Large stalagmites formed transient obstacles around and through which the path ran. The pair walked on at pace and soon the light source behind them disappeared to leave only the amber glow of the torch that Einar carried. The flames cast dancing shadows across the stony formations and added a sinister eeriness. Llyat realised that even the largest of the dragons would feel dwarfed within this mountain. The ice dragon Valathaxicore could extended her wings here to swoop through the darkness like a giant bat. In time the silence got to Llyat and he just had to speak.

"Why could my friends not follow and see the wyvern for themselves?" he asked although not expecting an answer.

"Cvyler Olin gave a clear instruction that you and you alone should have an audience with Thamous. That is because you are the Marked. Here take this."

Llyat looked at what Einar had passed him. It was a small white oval stone set upon a piece of crafted metal and to which a sturdy metal chain was attached.

"What is it?" asked Llyat.

"This is what we call a 'Dragon Whisper'," replied Einar "Cvyler Olin instructed me to give it to you. Wearing this stone around your neck will enable you to understand what the Great Thamous says.

"Is this is how you learned to communicate with the Dragons?"

Llyat waited for an answer but nothing came back.

"How does it work?" he asked and once again Einar failed to respond.

The youth placed the metal chain around his neck and allowed the stone to dangle over his scrawny leather clad chest. It swung in a gentle sideways rhythm as he moved ever deeper underground. At last they reached the end of the large natural cavern and came across a smaller opening in the rock wall, illuminated by two additional torches, one either side of the entrance. Even though smaller than the main cavern it was still large enough to accommodate an erect Berserker. Einar stopped and spoke again, the first time since Llyat had asked about the Dragonstone.

"Carry on down the tunnel until you reach the next cavern," ordered Einar as he thrust his torch into Llyat's right hand. "Thamous awaits you."

Llyat gulped with trepidation. "Are you not coming in with me?"

"Thamous insists that I wait here."

"Well I never heard anything," continued Llyat. "Just the crackling of the torch."

"That's because he wasn't talking to you. Now go, for he awaits."

Llyat's tremulous legs propelled him into the gloom of the tunnel and before long he sensed he was completely alone. After some fifteen paces he turned around to see if the Berserker had followed and saw nothing but the black outline of the passageway. Holding the burning torch out ahead he clutched the Dragon Whisper with his free hand. All the while he prayed that he would not meet any beast coming in the opposite direction. He had just enough courage to meet with the wyvern but not a nighthowler, skyfawn, or stray kulkulkath that may have wandered underground.

"Llyat!"

The voice hissed out his name as if giving a command and the youth sought to ignore it. He refused to submit to madness. Denius Castor had heard voices and there was no way he was going to end up like that pitiful wretch. The floor of the tunnel then widened. As Llyat swung his torch ahead of him the flickering flame revealed yet another vast cavern which blended into the distant dark. In its centre he noted a strange curved mound, no higher than a house, which twisted and turned in the darkness before it tapered off into a point. It seemed to his befuddled thoughts that a mass of black larva lay between him and the distant cavern wall. Then as Llyat moved from the passage down onto the cavern floor he noted that unlike the tunnel and the previous cavern, this space was devoid of stalagmites. He could see a few short stalactites that hung down from the roof high when he lifted the torch high but the ground was empty of stone needles.

"Llyat!" hissed the voice in his head.

"Fuck off and leave me alone! You will not drive me insane." he shouted back to the black.

Llyat sensed no answer and was troubled by the increased frequency that the voice was breaking through. It was the very last thing he needed given everything else that was happening to him. The youth knew he had a duty to fulfil the prophecy; he had to stave off the madness until he could complete his mission and all that was expected of the Marked. He looked again towards the mound and thrust his torch forwards. If Thamous was hiding somewhere in the cavern then he would have a better chance of finding the beast if sought a higher vantage point. Llyat summoned up the little confidence available and moved further into the gloom. Without a second thought he made his way over to the tip of the small hill and one hand after another began to climb upon its surface.

On reaching its summit Llyat looked around and in the restricted light could see nothing that would pass as a wyvern. He held the torch higher and clutched the Dragon Whisper around his neck. Then he began to walk the length his new vantage point while hoping he would find some clue as to the whereabouts of the beast. Not knowing what to do next he sat down and started to think about the songs and tales of the dragons of old, in particular the story of Mighty Xenvagen and the Knight that slew him.

That ballad concerned the town of Griginor during the time of Pietos Qrakus, it's then Lord Mayor. One day each month a dragon by the name of Xenvagen would beat a path of destruction across the countryside where it killed peasants, destroyed homes, and devoured livestock. According to stories Llyat had heard in the Red Mare, the dragon had taste for eating young maidens, just for the fun of the kill. It could only be appeased if a virgin was left in front of the entrance to its cave at each month end. Pietos Qrakus tried valiantly to put a stop to Xenvagen's lust fest but even his bravest and mightiest knights fell to the beast's fiery breath. And so each month a young virgin was chosen by lottery and yet Pietos Qrakus would never enter his own daughter Vanda into the ballot lest she was picked. Great warriors from near and far fought for the prize that Qrakus had promised to the one that slew the beast. A thousand gold coins was the reward on offer but no brave soul ever returned to claim it. One day Vanda felt so ashamed that she rigged the ballot such that her name would be chosen. She was a headstrong young girl and after a disagreement with her father she had decided to show the Realm that not even the Mayor's daughter was untouchable. She would sacrifice herself and go without fear to meet her gods. In desperation Qrakus promised his daughter in marriage to anyone who could defeat the dragon and save his only child from its fiery breath. A knight from the Parandor who went by the name of Sir Belquin just happened to have been visiting Griginor and accepted the challenge without hesitation. As he was also a learned man who had spent as much time with his head in books as in training to do battle, he came up with a cunning plan. Having recalled the effects of chemicals in an old alchemy book he had once read, Sir Belquin stuffed a lamb with sulphur and left it outside the dragon's lair. Even if the dragon did not need to eat meat, it had developed a taste for it along with good wine. The beast soon ate the offering and suffered an intense thirst as the sulphur burned its way into the walls of its stomach. Xenvagen turned to the river that some once called the Wistulla and which ran northwards towards the Dirmark. For relief it drank and it drank but no amount of water could quench its blistering belly. Having consumed half of the river the beast exploded. All that was left was the head although some variations of the tale ended with Sir Belquin fighting Xenvagen with his sword and decapitating it. However, in every version of the story that Llyat had heard, Sir Belquin dragged the head of the creature behind his horse all the way back into Griginor. The enormous skull was proof of his success and he used it to support his claim for the right to deflower the Lord Mayor's daughter. It was said that the girl howled long into the night.

"An interesting story, that of Sir Belquin the bastard," said the now familiar gruff voice and it caused Llyat to jump back to his feet.

"Who are you?" shouted Llyat as he swung his torch in circles, trying to locate the origin of the voice. "Get out of my fucking head?"

"I am the one that you seek. I am Thamous."

"Show yourself, and stop messing with me!" screamed Llyat into the dark.

"Just open your eyes," laughed the voice.

"What do you mean?"

"Your mind and eyes betray you," said the voice. "Yet your feet are doing wonders for my aching scales."

The shifting ground beneath his feet caused Llyat to lose his footing and fall down onto the slope of the mound. The once rough rocks felt surprising smooth but even as he tumbled he kept hold of his torch. A second later Llyat collided with the true ground. He stood up ready to climb once again when he saw an enormous eye staring back from out of the dark.

"You're... you're......" garbled Llyat, his words refusing to leave his mouth.

"And you are Llyat Emgar," replied the voice. "Allow me to illuminate my abode. My eyesight isn't as it used to be. Promethelumous."

A great ball of flame erupted over the youth's head. The cavern lit up as if in the presence of Solaris while the light hovered in the roof space against the will of gravity. Llyat watched as the wyvern uncoiled and then rose onto two large feet. Thamous stood in full glory and pushed out long semi-transparent wings before returning them to its side. The creature's skin was earth brown and appeared hard like granite. Llyat was not ashamed he had mistaken the beast for a mound of earth for most would have done the same in the dark. The wyvern's serpentine head coiled down and in fear Llyat thrust his burning torch forward and placed his other hand on the hilt of Destiny's Song.

The head moved closer and looked Llyat up and down. It seemed somewhat amused as its green lidless eyes tried to penetrate Llyat's essence. Then the wyvern opened its mouth, flicked out its tongue, and tasted the air. Llyat gazed upon rows of razor sharp teeth and then back to its magnificent eyes. The voice came again.

"You're smaller than I was expecting and much ganglier. Aren't you are a bit puny for a hero!"

"And you're the most magnificent and terrifying thing I have ever seen," replied Llyat.

He realised that Thamous was somehow able to communicate with him. Even though answering the beast, Llyat's mouth had not moved. Then he remembered the Dragon Whisper. Moving his hand from his sword he then clutched the stone that hung from his neck.

"That's interesting coming from a lad that has sent the dragons all a flutter. Tell me Llyat Emgar, are you really impressed by what you see?"

"You are magnificent."

"That's what they all say before I roast and eat them."

Llyat gulped but was determined that his fear would not get the better of him. He had to make sure that this time he did not faint from terror. He continued to stare at the creature's face and for a brief moment suspected the wyvern had smiled. Then the voice laughed.

"No need to worry my young friend. I have no intention of eating you, well not at least just yet. But first take that trinket from around your neck."

"But I need to wear this to understand what you are saying?" replied Llyat.

"You could hear me when you first woke in Falahorn. You heard me in the tunnels below that town and as you journeyed across the Dragonas. You do not need one of their whisper stones. No Llyat Emgar, you are something different."

"So it was you I heard? What have you done to me?"

"You have the ability to understand me without tricks or magic," hissed Thamous as with some reluctance Llyat removed the chain from around his neck and placed the stone into one of his pockets. "I have only sensed three others with whom I could mind-talk without the use of a whisper stone. You have met one of them, Cvyler Olin, and Sir Raulyn is long dead. But there is another I have sensed and I do not know his name. He too however makes his way here and seeks an audience with me.

"So how is it I can hear your thoughts," asked Llyat as the wyvern coiled again?

"What do you know of dragons Llyat?"

"Just what little I picked up from tavern stories and bard songs, and a bit more from the folk of Falahorn."

"Then you must know that we are creatures of dark magic. We are not governed by the laws of reality; we bend it to our will. There are those who have studied such laws and learned the secrets of harnessing the energy centres of their bodies. Then there are those that have tried to manipulate the pockets of darkness that bind our realities together and to use its power for their own ends like the scum of the Eastern Marsh. They have discovered how to use the power of the Mighty Rift and it allows them to travel over many leagues. What do you know of the Rift Llyat? To understand its true nature is part of the destiny of the Marked."

"And by that you mean me?" answered Llyat with half a hope that Thamous would say no.

"Of course you are the Marked. You are the one that the Prophecy speaks of."

Llyat closed his eyes. His fear morphed to anger and it heightened all his senses. It brought out a confidence that he never thought he had. Then in that moment Llyat forgot where he was and he began to rant.

"Speak sense Thamous and quit messing with me. What makes you so sure that I am the Marked and what the fuck is the true purpose of the Enderdetag Prophecy? Why was my father a traitor? Go on, answer that one you great lump of snake scale! Where are your gems? Where is the door to Underworld? Why did my family have to die? Why are you messing with my head? What the fuck do you want from me?"

"Ha! So many questions for such a puny runt!"

"I'm seventeen."

"And yet still a child in the ways of the world. But with regard to the questions that you seek answers for, let me first tell you about Sir Raulyn and his defeat of Urthanock."

"Whatever…if it helps. Just get on with it."

The wyvern dropped its head and Llyat looked into its great lidless eyes. The playful look had gone and in its place was the stare of a seasoned killer.

"There is no need to be sarcastic or indeed fearful. We creatures, born out of tears of the mother god Chalis, only hunt humans for fun or to silence an insolent child."

Llyat jumped backwards as the wyvern's jaws snapped forward. The movement produced a loud crunch but the beast stopped short of its kill. It was close enough however for Llyat to smell the putrid odour of the creature's breath

"I'm sorry," mumbled Llyat as he fought the urge to faint.

"Apology accepted. After all you have gone through since leaving Maplehill you do deserve an explanation of events although I cannot answer all of your questions. I do not know why others accused your father of being a traitor or why you have been chosen as the Marked. I will however attempt to answer the other questions you posed. Let's start with Sir Raulyn and Urthanock. When Raulyn defeated that evil swine and his armies of the mire, he came to me asking for help. The Oracle of Frasteria had spoken and he needed my help to understand all that was said to him. He had been ordered to create a powerful spell, one so strong as to keep the door to the Underworld sealed, a portal behind which the dormant spirit of Urthanock would be forever contained. Sir Raulyn gave me five gems, each of them of a different nature. I cracked them open with dragon fire and poured the darkest magic inside. Then I burned them into one. Together they formed the means by which to lock the door to the Underworld. Once Urthanock was bound inside his realm, the portal was to be sealed for eternity. When this had been done I spilt the 'One' back into the five and advised Sir Raulyn to scatter the Gems in remote and hidden places; just in case anyone in the future would be fool enough seek to unleash Urthanock and set him amongst us. Of recent I have detected an increase in the activity in this projection of the Great Reality. I sense an ongoing attempt to break through the spell that the Gems cast upon the door. But the portal cannot be fully opened or sealed without those Gems. You may be surprised to know that even I do not know of the doors location, but imagine for a moment some invisible power pushing on a sheet of glass. Once the pressure is high enough, cracks will start to emerge and before long it will shatter."

"And is this what is happening now?" asked Llyat while struggling to understand it all.

"The Prophecy of Enderdetag speaks of the Marked vanquishing the Lord of Fear forever," continued Thamous. "I believe Urthanock is gathering strength and that the dark energy behind the doors of the Underworld is trying to break him out. Think about the glass again and the cracks that I spoke of; fractures have been evident in our reality for some time now. This is what those of the Eastern Marsh refer to as the Mighty Rift. This is what they have been harnessing and using as a source of their power."

"Is the Lady of the Silverwynn intent on releasing Urthanock just to harness his power for herself?" asked Llyat.

"From what I read in your thoughts and in the minds of the others who now approach, I think she is indeed naive enough to break the seal of the door in her lust for domination. She intends to use that power to rain doom upon her enemies, Phauless Gylewu and the highborn of Parandor. I sense the bitch is stupid enough to release the dark one. I also suspect that Urthanock himself has chosen the Lady as a vessel which he can manipulate in order to allow him to once again to walk in this world."

"What do you mean by that?"

"The Lady has spent too much time in the vicinity of the rift. Urthanock has been dead for many centuries and his essence is no longer able to sustain its own form. I assume that he is looking for another vessel to inhabit. As to why he would choose to possess her above all others I can but speculate. It is the Marked's duty to ensure the Lady does not succeed, that the locking gems are located, the door to Underworld opened. Only then can the spirit of Urthanock be destroyed in that darkest of places before he can once again take physical form. The door must then be resealed."

"And what of the Prophecy of Enderdetag? If the Underworld is sealed already, why do I have to open it? Can't Urthanock just stay in the Underworld where he is?" asked the bemused youth, overcome by the enormity of his task.

"As the pressure of dark energy builds in the Underworld it will become too great for the door to hold back. Remember what I told you about the glass. In the end it will shatter. The same goes for the Mighty Rift and the cracks between the realities. Once shattered all the horrors of the Underworld will be released into the Realm, including that of Urthanock. You must destroy his essence Llyat but you will not be alone. You will have help in this task."

Llyat fell silent and tried to gather his thoughts.

"It's a lot to take in," he shouted. "I am still not clear on this matter. Why can't I use the gems to close the door and seal Urthanock behind it? If I open the door and let his essence out he will destroy us all."

"You have not understood me yet Llyat. The power of Urthanock will continue to grow if unchecked and the ultimate fracturing of the two dimensions between our Middle Realm and the Underworld will bring the end of days as we know them. Someone, you Llyat, needs to first open the door, enter into the evil beyond and destroy Urthanock in his dimension for he cannot be destroyed in ours. That is your task but I do not yet know how you can do it. Yet do it you must or the race of man will cease to exist. Do you understand me now?"

"This is complicated and scary shit!"

"Within the wider world the important things are always complicated," replied Thamous. "I like you Llyat Emgar. I sense the strength of the Kundalish Aura in you and yet you say that you have had no contact with magic until a few weeks ago."

"Can you explain that?" replied Llyat.

"I cannot, but the phenomenon excites me."

Llyat looked to the creature that towered above him. Even the mighty Thamous could not explain his spectral show within the library tower of the Bards Guild. He tried to piece together all the information that the wyvern had shared but there was still the question of the location of the Five.

"Where are the Gems hidden?" he began, but the wyvern interrupted.

"I was wondering when you were going to raise the one question that the bard Thias Calavan sent you to ask. I have also been inside his mind and examined his life. His story humours me. From what I have picked up from his brain chatter it appears you had one in your possession but lost it to those from the Eastern Marsh."

"Yes, it was an emerald encased in a golden dagger," muttered Llyat with shame.

"No matter," continued the wyvern as it rose upon two towering legs and began to pace the cavern in search of memories from a distant past. "The other four will need to be found. The first, the Seer's stone is a diamond placed in the Sceptre of Urthanock. It has the power to induce false prophecy. From what my gecko spies tell me, the Lady has found the Sceptre and is already trying to use its power on all that oppose her will. Of the remaining three, one is a sapphire that Sir Raulyn embedded into his axe that he named Fortune's Edge. Then there is the ruby which if I remember is heart shaped, and the last is an amethyst."

"So where are these others located?" demanded Llyat as he chased behind the head of the great beast only to collide with it as it turned to face him once again.

"I see that you are devoid of the virtue called patience Llyat but I will try and give you the answer which you seek. I have a strong connection to the Gems but even my far sight is no longer as accurate as it once was. I sense the sapphire rests within the great pyramid of Barad Elestor, far to the north and east in the midst of Thengar Forest. The amethyst I see lost within the Eastern Marsh. It is hidden from the eyes of the scum that dwell in the swamps even though resting under their snouts."

"And the ruby?"

"I am having difficulty seeing that one," mumbled Thamous. "Some kind of odd substance is blocking my sight line. It is possible that those who use the powers of the Rift have located it already. All I can tell you is that it still lies somewhere in Parandor and is well hidden..."

The wyvern looked beyond Llyat's diminutive frame towards the cavern exit. Llyat then sensed that the creature was troubled; some danger beckoned.

"What's wrong?" asked Llyat.

"I'm afraid that we must end our conversation now Llyat and get you to safety."

"What is it? What's happening?"

"That other that I spoke of. He arrives much sooner than I expected and he is not alone."

"Who is he and who are they?" asked Llyat. "Can you sense their names like you did with me?"

"No, something is clouding my vision. Whoever approaches is imbued with strong magic."

"The Lady of the Silverwynn?"

"No, that bitch would never step within these halls. It's someone else."

Llyat drew Destiny's Song from its scabbard and gipped with all his strength.

"We will fight them together!" he shouted as he stood under the chest of Thamous.

"No that is not your purpose nor my plan. You must escape while there is still time. Find the remaining Gems and somehow retrieve those already taken by our enemy. Go at once and find Einar. He will lead you to safety."

The great burning mass in the cavern roof disappeared and the vast empty space turned back to dark save from the torch that Llyat still clutched in his hand. He scanned what little area he could and looked for the tunnel through which he had entered. Thamous spoke again.

"Remember lad, the Lady of the Silverwynn must never be allowed to get her hands on you. She cannot be allowed to control the Marked... that you must prevent at all costs, even at the expense of your life."

Llyat knew his audience with the mighty beast had ended and so he ran towards the tunnel entrance. Whispers echoed through his skull, one final cryptic message from the wyvern that etched itself into his memory.

6

"And don't let them follow us."

Einar's parting words on entering the gullet of the Gathering did not sit easy with Thias. The young bard sat upon the rock strewn base of the three peaked mountain and felt most aggrieved. How dare the Berserker treat him in such a way for he had every right to hear what Thamous had to say? There was something about Einar of Falahorn that did not bode well with Thias and he loathed to trust the giant, one whose mighty muscles carried a head of little intellect and great dullness of character. Ever since Llyat and Einar had passed deeper into the cavern, Thias had rested his weary legs by the side of its entrance. There he had passed time in deep thought over Llyat's role in the Enderdetag Prophecy and the great challenge that now fell upon the peasant boy's shoulders. It was not long before his anger at being left behind began to infuriate him. He struggled to understand why he had been forbidden to speak with the wyvern for he was after all the Sovereign Ruler's secret envoy. He was also the last surviving representative of the once mighty Bards Guild of Valameer.

"And don't let them fucking follow us!" he muttered to himself as he mulled things over. "Who the fuck does he think he is telling me where I can and cannot go?"

Thias was interrupted when Irabo limped over and placed his ample backside upon an adjacent rock.

"Whatever is irking you let it go Thias," said the young warrior of the Watch. "Let the pain abate, it's not worth it."

"But he's is just a lad," exclaimed Thias. "He may not remember all that he was told to ask."

"The burden given to him in Valameer is his alone," replied Irabo. "He is the one who will fulfil the prophecy..."

"But he is..."

"Thias, calm down. Geir and Guldbrand are watching."

Thias looked towards the two burly Berserkers who a short distance away guarded the six unicorns still tethered to the old post.

"If we pose a threat they will kill us out without hesitation," added Irabo. "That is the Berserker way; threaten one, threaten all."

Thias did not care for the ways of the Berserkers and how Einar had dodged every question that he or Llyat had put to him on their journey to the Gathering. He then felt Irabo's iron grip surround his wrists. As he attempted to pull them from the young warrior's grasp Thias felt a sudden warm sensation flood through his body. His essence was then flushed clean with a wave of reassurance.

"Don't struggle," ordered Irabo as the pressure increased.

The bard soon felt relaxed and serene as if all his worries had somehow left him. He looked up from where Irabo's fingers pressed between the bones of his forearms and smiled.

"An interesting trick,"

"Taught to me by healers in the Temple of Fatumai. It has its uses."

"I wasn't aware you were schooled in the ways of magic?" replied Thias.

"Not magic as such. Just a distraction trick. See you feel better already."

Irabo removed his hands from around Thias's wrists and allowed the bard to stretch out his fingers. The young warrior was right, Thais did feel better. The shadows of two nighthowler pelts fell suddenly upon them.

"Is there a problem?" asked Geir.

"Nothing I can't handle," replied Irabo.

"Don't worry about the lad," added Guldbrand "Einar will take care of him."

"That is what I am afraid of," replied Thias.

Geir then pushed his head forward and squared up to Thias. The bard saw that something had snapped inside the Berserker's head. His words had triggered an unexpected change in the giant's persona.

"What's your problem bard?" snarled Geir.

"I don't trust any of you, that's all"

"Thias!" gasped Irabo, shocked at the bard's blunt words.

"No, let the arse licker speak," answered Geir. "Let's hear what he really thinks of our kind."

"Geir stop provoking him" ordered Guldbrand.

"I want to hear the truth that festers in his pus filled brain," continued Geir as he ramped up the tension.

Thias closed his eyes and leapt to his feet. He felt his anger rise and then lost all control.

"I'll tell you what I think," he shouted amidst a fountain of spittle which flew into the face of the Berserker. "And then I'll wipe the fucking floor with you."

"Go on then string plucker, just try it if you dare," snapped back Geir.

"Thias, you don't have to do this; it will not help our cause. Please stand down," pleaded Irabo as he rose and tried to manoeuvre between Geir and his friend.

"Well string plucker, what do you want to get off your chest?" growled Geir.

Thias clenched his fists. It would just take one word and a flaming mass of magic would eliminate the Berserker. He was at tipping point and longed to sever Geir's head from off his shoulders. Irabo's voice demanded to be heard.

"Thias, for the love of Fatumai, what are you doing?"

"I'll tell you what I'm about. Ever since the attack on the Guild by those shape shifting cunts of the Eastern Marsh, I have struggled to trust what others say or do, except of course for yourself and Llyat. That bastard Dayis taught me a powerful lesson. Berger and her family were very hospitable, and even Cvyler was understanding to some degree, but these bastards keep their secrets wrapped in treacle. Their unwillingness to share information is just..."

"You thankless turd," shouted Geir. "We have put our lives at risk to bring you to the Gathering. You've eaten our food, you've ridden our unicorns, and you dare to speak to us with such ingratitude."

"Then what are you hiding."

"That's it!" screamed Geir reaching for the axe strapped to his back. "I've had enough of the bile that spews from your stinking mouth."

Thias clenched his firsts and he began to shout "Promethelu…"

The magic incantation was interrupted by a most unexpected turn of events. From out of nowhere a fist connected with Geir's face. It caught the Berserker under the jaw, and lifted him clean off the ground. The giant was thrown backwards where he then slumped down onto the barren earth.

"Geir, stop this nonsense at once," shouted Guldbrand as he brought his fist down, shook out its tension, and turned to Thias. "You might want to go and stand over there. Geir needs to be taught a lesson and you should not be party to what I plan for him. Irabo take the bard away."

"No need," replied Thias as he turned and strutted off towards the entrance to the cave.

Thias did not look back but he heard the sounds of cursing and the fist fight that then began. Taking several deep breaths he continued to walk on. He heard the tapping of Irabo's crutch as the warrior sought to follow and catch up with his friend.

"You see Thias, what did I tell you? Please don't provoke them so. Why did you have to confront Geir like that; now of all times?"

"I'm sorry, I'm just so worried about Llyat," began Thias. "The boy has lost his family, his friends, and a lot more shit has happened. Someone has got to look after him and I just wish we were by his side down there with Einar and the dragon."

"Wyvern," corrected Irabo.

"Fuck off!"

Thias turned and walked away leaving Irabo at the cavern's entrance. He was not in the right frame of mind to deal with Irabo's pedantic comments concerning the classification of reptiles. Picking up his pace he then strode out into the wilds of the Dragonas. With his face away from the Gathering he headed out east toward Solaris while the minutes of his life raced on. As he wandered without aim he tried to come to terms with his emotions and his fears for young Llyat Emgar. At last he came to the conclusion that both Llyat and Irabo were now as family to him, ever since they had survived the attack on the Guild and the trek over the mountains. He saw himself as an older brother to both young men and in particular Llyat. It was just like the three Heyns had been in his youth following his father's execution.

Looking out into the distance Thias focused beyond the desolation that surrounded the Gathering. His eyes roamed over the distant horizon and the start of the yellow grasslands. He took more deep breaths to calm his nerves and soon he began to remember a story that Vostag Heyn had once told him about the mastery of anger and how to deal with difficult emotions. The story concerned a young boy who had lived in the slums outside the walls of Parandor. This boy had been cursed by the gods with the foulest temper that anyone in the Realm had ever witnessed. He was spiteful, resentful, and antagonistic towards every aspect of his life. One day after he had lashed out and struck his mother in a fit of rage, a blow that had led her to miscarry, the boy's father decided to teach him a lesson. It wasn't a harsh beating as before but an attempt to change the boy's way of thinking. The father gave his son a bag of nails and told him that every time he lost his temper he was to hammer two nails into the fence that surrounded their home. It was a task that required considerable effort for the posts were made of solid oak. At the end of the first day of this new practice the father found that the boy had driven forty nails into the wooden fence. Over the weeks that followed, the number of nails hammered each day dwindled as the boy sought to control his temper. It soon became evident that it was easier to hold his temper than to drive the heavy nails into the fence. Several months later, the day came when the boy didn't lose his temper at all. When he told his father about this the response was unexpected. He was ordered to pull out one nail for each day that he was able to hold his temper. By the end of the second year he returned to tell that all the nails were gone. The man then took his son by the hand and led him to the fence.

"You have done well," he said. "Now look at the deep scars that you have left."

"But that is what you asked me to do," cried the boy as tears cascaded from his eyes.

"Yes but the fence will never be the same again. It is just like when you used to be so angry. Every time you took your venom out on others it also left scars in the memories and emotions of those that you abused."

Thias remembered that as a child he had been confused by Vostag's story and that Methladon and Grophaldo had also struggled with its meaning. Fiat being the eldest of the four had understood what their father had been getting at and was the one who in the end explained it to the rest of the children.

"It's a simple idea unless you're dim-witted. No matter how many times you say you are sorry when you do things in anger, the wound remains, not just in the memories of others but also inside your own heart. As those wounds grow in number you learn to like yourself less and less and others seek to avoid you. Then you just get angrier. But it is not the Fates that can change any of this; you must do that yourself from within."

Thias, being a curious boy at the time, had the courage to ask Vostag the name of the young boy in the story. His adopted father confessed that the child was none other than Vostag himself. It was this experience that had driven the blacksmith to train his own boys in combat and swordsmanship; to give them an outlet for any anger that they would develop later in life. As Thais thought about the story and his failure to remain calm in the presence of the Berserkers, a tear formed in his eye. Stood in silence he wiped it away with the sleeve of his shirt. Taking a deep breath he decided to begin his return to the cavern entrance when something moved on the horizon and caught his eye. He squinted and tried to make out what it was that approached at speed.

Thias raced back to the Gathering. There he found that Geir and Guldbrand had stopped fighting and were sat tending to their wounds. Geir nursed his bloodied nose and Guldbrand a bruised left eye socket. Irabo still sat by the cavern entrance in anticipation of Llyat's return. The bard ran over to his friend and pointed in the direction of the objects he had seen on the horizon, black specks which moved towards the Gathering.

"Irabo, you are from Falahorn and have great eyes. What is it that comes from the east?"

Irabo stood tall, supported himself on his crutch, and stared out towards the direction that Thias indicated.

"I don't know. I can't make them out."

Thias called towards the two Berserkers.

"Geir, Guldbrand, what are those things that approach?" he demanded.

"Fuck off!" replied Geir before Guldbrand turned on his friend once again.

"Geir, we agreed no more of this."

"Sorry! Where? What are you talking about?"

"To the east," shouted Thias. "Below the disc of Solaris. Something moves on the horizon."

Within seconds the Berserkers climbed onto the rocks that rose up from the base of the Gathering. Both held their hands above their eyes as they scanned the far distant land.

"Geir, your eyes are better than mine," shouted Guldbrand. "What do you make out?"

"Riders. Eight of them on horseback."

Thias pondered on who could be out riding towards them at such speed. A bad feeling festered in his already troubled mind and he shouted back to two giant men.

"Is it a Berserker patrol?"

"It is not," replied Geir. "That is not our formation. We ride single file, not side by side."

"Then who could they be?" shouted Irabo from alongside Thias.

"I'm not certain," answered Geir. "But they are dressed in black armour and ride from the direction of Avolire."

Thias then felt sick as he understood the enormity of the situation that they now faced. He looked to Irabo and saw the same recognition etched on the young warrior's face. It was a frown that spelled out danger and both knew they would have to act at once.

"The Knights of Avolire! We must leave now," ordered Thias.

"What about Llyat," said Irabo?

"I'll go and fetch him," replied Thias without thinking. "You ready the unicorns."

"Why are the Knights of Avolire all the way out here," asked Guldbrand who had descended from his rocky vantage point."

"The same reason as we I guess. They must also looking for Thamous. We cannot be here when they arrive."

"No Knight of Avolire scares me," bellowed Geir who moved towards the unicorns.

"Geir, no!" shouted Guldbrand but it was to no avail. The unicorn was already on the move and it headed out towards the eight small specks on the horizon.

"Shouldn't you go after him?" shouted Thias.

"Too late for that now. If I know Geir he will gain us enough time to find your friend and get out of here."

"Thias, find Llyat now," yelled Irabo as he limped towards the unicorns "Guldbrand and I will ready the remaining beasts, cover their tracks, and clear their shit to hide that we have been here."

"Whatever happens don't let them into the cavern until I return," replied Thias, echoing Einar's earlier instructions.

"I'll do my best. My crutch is at the ready!"

Thias watched his friend limp off alongside Guldbrand and then raced into the cavern. Given the torches from the entrance had been already taken he closed his fists and focused the energy that flowed through his body.

"Promethelumous!"

Thias's fists ignited. He ran as fast as his legs would carry him across the cavern floor. In between the stalagmites he snaked, avoiding them with ease as his heightened reflexes led him on in his search for Llyat. As he scuttled and dodged the memory of the formation that the Knights of Avolire took when they chased down and executed the defenceless farmer in the lands outside of Maplehill filled his thoughts. He could fight, yes, and he had survived the attack on the Bards Guild, but to take on the Knights of Avolire in the open would be suicidal. After some minutes he came upon Einar who rested against a gigantic stalagmite. The Berserker was engrossed in sharpening an axe with a small rock. Upon seeing Thias, Einar jumped to his feet and readied his weapon in both hands.

"You!" shouted the Berserker. "I thought I told you never to enter this place."

"You must hear me out Einar and listen well," demanded the bard. "Where is Llyat? We are all in danger."

"I'm here," came a voice from out of the darkness.

Seconds later Llyat appeared, torch in one hand and sword in the other.

"We are in real trouble," continued Thias.

"What kind of trouble," asked Llyat?

"Knights of Avolire approach at speed."

"Then we fight," snarled Einar.

Thias could tell from the look in the Berserker's eyes he too had understood the gravity of the situation. Even though outnumbered and without armour the Berserkers would be formidable opponents. Their thick skin could deflect most blows from sword, axe, or arrow, but Llyat, Irabo and Thias had no protection of note.

"That is out of the question," yelled Thias. "We are outnumbered and Llyat's safety is paramount."

"We Berserkers do not run."

"But in this case we have to," continued Thias. "You must help us live to fight another day."

"Any threat to Thamous must be eliminated. It is not in our blood to flee."

"Yet if we stay your blood will soak into the very ground we stand upon. We have to go now."

In desperation Thias punched outwards with his left arm and sent a ball of flame from his fist which slammed into the ground. As the fireball struck the rock the cavern shook and caused the three to stagger. Thias was surprised by the result for it was the first time the spell had ever caused a structure to shake. The cavern rumbled and small amounts of dirt and pebbles fell from its rocky ceiling. Thias prayed that he hadn't set off a chain reaction that would bring the roof down. Einar's eyes betrayed the giant's fear for the flaming mass that the bard just created.

"I understand," grumbled the Berserker. "Let's get out of here now."

"Could you see who was leading them?" asked Llyat.

Thias noted that the youth had already drawn Destiny's Song. He wondered if Llyat had been warned of the imminent threat or had even found Thamous and questioned him. Then he remembered Llyat's story of the fall of Maplehill, the death of his family and friends, and in that moment he knew exactly what Llyat was thinking.

"I could not make out sufficient detail," replied Thias.

"Did one have a skull shaped helmet?" demanded Llyat.

"I didn't…" began Thias's but his response was too slow for Llyat had already started his run towards the exit.

"Llyat come back here! Wait for us you impetuous bugger," shouted Thias. "Are you with me Einar?"

"Of course."

"Then come on, we have no time to lose."

Both men started back towards the surface, Einar with his battle-axe readied and Thias with his fiery hands lighting the way. It didn't take long for the long striding Einar to pass Thias and race on ahead. The bard struggled to keep up but as he snaked his way back through the rocks and stalagmites he marvelled in Einar's athleticism. The Berserkers had already demonstrated their keen eyesight, and now Thias could appreciate their fleetness of foot. If this was what they were like before they took their amber juice then he could not wait see them at full charge. After a few minutes Thias caught up to Einar who had stopped to restrain Llyat at the cavern entrance. A swift pull on the back of Llyat's hair had caused him to drop both his sword and torch. The flames had been extinguished and the smouldering wood sent small puffs of smoke high into the air.

"Thank the gods you caught him," said Thias before extinguishing the flames around his wrists with a single shake of his hands. "Don't be so stupid Llyat, you cannot take them on alone."

"I'm know," replied Llyat while picking up his sword. "I just saw red. The mention of the Knights of Avolire just filled me with such…"

"I understand but we must all control our anger for the dangers are great and we must remain clear in thought. We have to leave this place at once."

"Where is Geir?" asked Einar as looked out from the entrance to the cave.

"He's gone to delay them. His anger also got the better of him," replied Guldbrand who had come over to see what was happening. "He went to buy us some time."

"Whatever else we do, we have to leave right now," stressed Thias as he pointed to the unicorns which Irabo now led towards them and despite the hindrance of his crutch.

"Where shall we go?" shouted Irabo. "We cannot head back to Falahorn and let the Knights follow us there. The village will not survive long once the Knights become aware of its exact location."

"Irabo is right," said Guldbrand. "We dare not risk leading them to Falahorn."

"Then where?" asked Thias with mounting anxiety.

"Thengar Forest," added Llyat.

"North East?" added the Berserker? "Why the fuck would you want to go there of all places."

"I can't explain now... just trust me!"

"Then don't explain. Let's just leave," snapped Thias. "You can tell us why later."

"Won't we be spotted," asked Irabo?

Thias tried to process Irabo's comment for it was indeed true that if they were to head out towards the north and east there was a strong possibility they would be spotted by the approaching riders. Despite that logic there seemed no other choice and Thias felt he had to trust in Llyat's suggestion. He turned to Guldbrand who was busy scanning the eastern horizon.

"Let's prey that Geir keeps them occupied for long enough," added Thias.

"I've lost him from my sight line, but the riders are on the move again," replied Guldbrand.

"Then let's go," snarled Einar.

Thias helped Irabo to mount his steed and then proceeded to climb upon his own. As he sat into the saddle he realised that Guldbrand had decided to go no further and stood with axe in hand to await the impending arrival of the Knights of Avolire.

"Guldbrand, come on," Einar exclaimed.

"We can't leave Thamous unprotected," he replied.

"Neither may we leave the Marked," added Thias.

"I've made my decision," said Guldbrand.

"Is your hatred of the followers of Sir Belquin worth dying for?" shouted Einar.

"I will forfeit my life to stop these bastards. The tear of Chalis shall not be wasted."

Thias looked towards Einar: "We can't leave him to die here alone."

"He has made his choice. He will not change it."

"Go at once, they are almost upon us," shouted Guldbrand.

Thias looked towards the east and could see the eight horsemen clearly as they approached.

"Let's head north around the base of the Gathering before we then strike out to Thengar Forest. That way they may not see us," suggested Thias.

"Goodbye dear friend," said Einar as he placed his hand upon Guldbrand's shoulder.

"And good luck," added Thias.

"And may the Fates be with you all," replied the Berserker.

Guldbrand smiled and then winked at Thias. The bard knew this was to be the Berserker's last stand. Here the Fates would roll the final dice that governed the Berserker's life, alone in the depths of the Dragonas. Then as the unicorns and their riders gathered together the lone warrior readied his battle-axe and spoke his last farewell.

"The Moirai will guide you on your quest. Fortune to you all."

Thias kicked the sides of his unicorn with both feet and gripped the reins with his fists. He then set off with the others away from the approaching horsemen and soon Guldbrand disappeared as they galloped on. The bard still had no idea if Llyat had met with Thamous or why he was leading them into the fearsome depths of the Thengar Forest.

7

The nighthowler pelt hung over the head of the giant such that it hid most of his bruised face. It did not however cover the sweat that dripped from his muscular torso and which glistened like pearls in the bright glare of Solaris. Geir the Berserker sat astride the spine of his leather skinned unicorn as together man and beast barred the way to the three peaked mountain.

Methladon Heyn rode at speed alongside the dwarf at the rear of the patrol that had set out from Avolire. Without warning he was forced to pull hard on the reins of his horse to avoid ramming the back of the Newyn who rode a short distance ahead. All the Knights of Avolire forced their steeds to stop at the sight of the strange rider, who from out of nowhere had borne down on them with malice aforethought. Amid a cloud of dust thrown up from the unicorn's hooves the strange giant pulled up a short distance from Rhaizen's troop.

"Whoa," shouted Methladon as he tugged even harder on his reigns.

The youth was determined not to let a simple animal embarrass him for he still had to prove himself worthy to his fellow Knights. He collected his horse together and at last it stopped and snorted.

"Who the fuck is that?" he heard Oedd shout as the others fought for control of their beasts.

"Just another obstacle," shouted Commander Rhaizen through the visor of his helm.

Methladon looked through the gaps between his comrades and on towards the giant man and unicorn ahead. He could see that the stranger was intent on making trouble and given his physique he reckoned he would not be easy to subjugate. Yet he felt no fear for he had seen the Knights of Avolire in action and was aware of their devastating fighting capabilities. It was they who should be most feared although they seemed to have no impact on the stranger. The giant then spoke with a firm and authoritative voice.

"What brings the Knights of Avolire deep into Berserker territory?"

"None of your fucking business," shouted Mhlau from the middle of the group.

Methladon half expected for Rhaizen to turn and silence the Harbinger but he did not.

"Best turn around then. There is nothing for you in the Dragonas," continued the giant.

Methladon was unsure as to what the stranger implied. Whoever the odd looking man was he held the full attention of his fellow knights who waited in heightened anticipation for someone to make the first move. He turned to his right to where Grovrouk still sought to retain control of his horse.

"What does he mean? Who is this man?"

"A Berserker," replied Grovrouk without taking his eyes off the giant. "A sworn protector of the Dragonas and all that inhabit its lands."

"I don't understand!"

"Don't you know the history? Avolire supported Sir Belquin, the first to vow to kill all dragons."

"So he would know where…" began Methladon but he did not have time to finish his question.

"Get out of our way, dragon fucker!" shouted Rhaizen.

"This is your last warning," bellowed the giant.

The Berserker reached behind his back and pulled out a battle axe. He gripped it in two hands and held it aloft for all to see. Methladon was surprised by the move for he had not noticed the weapon having been preoccupied by the man's size and the fur pelt which covered the head and rear of the Berserker's muscular frame.

"Turn around and be on your way," ordered Geir as globules of spit flew from his mouth.

Methladon looked on as the strange man clambered off the back of the unicorn and stood his ground before the Knights of Avolire. He appeared ready to fight all eight of them and Methladon couldn't believe that anyone could be so stupid. Even a giant would struggle against eight.

"We haven't got time for this shit!" muttered Rhaizen before shouting his out his next command. "Farwolaeth, deal with this wazzock."

"My pleasure," replied the black clad Harbinger whose raised sword flashed amid the fierce light of the day.

Farwolaeth dismounted and then moved towards the Berserker. Above the noise of the nervy horses, the guttural throat grunts of the unicorn, and the clunking of armour as it moved across Farwolaeth's body, Methladon heard the Berserker shout out once again.

"Is that all you send to confront me? This lanky piece of shite."

"Stand aside," replied the knight as he gripped his curved blade.

"It will be better for you if you were to just turn around and piss off," snarled Geir.

"So be it. Don't say you didn't ask for this," replied Farwolaeth.

The Knight circled his sword around in an effortless manner. What happened next surprised all of those who watched. As he span forward in an attempt to land the blade of his sword upon the Berserker it connected with his opponents axe and the knight's blade shattered. It threw Farwolaeth off balance and caused him to stumble forward towards his opponent. The giant unleashed a second axe with his free hand and brought in crashing down into the gap between the Knight's helm and breastplate. It sliced deep into the neck and forced Farwolaeth to drop to his knees. Crimson liquid sprayed out as would a fruit fountain at a feast. The knight then fell to the floor amid a clamour which spooked both the free horse and the unicorn, both of which then galloped off in different directions. Farwolaeth was no more and he lay in an ever expanding pool of blood. It had all ended in an instant.

No one moved or said anything in the first seconds that followed but Methladon placed his hand upon the hilt of his weapon. He sensed what was coming next but glancing towards Grovrouk he witnessed a negative shake of the head which caused him to think otherwise. It was not his turn to die for some other would take care of the Berserker.

"Do any more of you black shiny turds want to have a go?" shouted the Berserker as he moved forward over the corpse of Farwolaeth, his feet making ripples in the red lake. "Or are you going to do as I suggested earlier and fuck off?"

Methladon stared in awe at the Berserker and feared his next move. Then his line of sight was obscured as Rhaizen moved forwards towards the giant. He half expected his Commander to draw his own weapon but instead he raised his hand and snapped his fingers.

"We haven't got time for this," Rhaizen shouted through his skull adorned helm.

The Berserker rose from the ground. In the next instant the giant's arms and legs stretched out like a cross and his two mighty battle axes fell to the ground. Geir's face changed to a grimace and his face flushed wine red. Beads of sweat then dripped from his forehead and rolled down onto his cheeks. It was obvious that the giant was in great pain.

"Now are you going to let us pass, or do I have to finish you myself," snarled Rhaizen.

"Go lick my arse!" spat back the Berserker through his yellowing teeth.

Rhaizen snapped his fingers once again Geir screamed out as his limbs and head were ripped from his torso by some unseen force. Body parts pulted in different directions and left arches of crimson droplets suspended as a mist before they too fell to the ground some distance away. The remaining horses snorted their displeasure and all except Methladon laughed.

"Shite of the gods!" exclaimed the youth.

"Is something wrong boy?" shouted the Commander.

"No, nothing Sir!" he replied as a great wave of fear rippled through his body.

If he hadn't been astride a horse with his rump pressed against the saddle Methladon was sure that he would have soiled himself. He had been subjected to the same powers in Avolire and had seen first-hand the effects of Rhaizen's abilities when he had silenced the old farmer on the top of the ridge. The Lady of the Silverwynn had confirmed that the Commander was a direct descendant of an old order of the Knights, men more powerful than the bards but yet not as strong as the wizards in the ways of magic. He struggled to comprehend a greater power for if Rhaizen's was so strong, what would the wizards' be like; he prayed he would never have to find out.

"Now what?" shouted Newyn? "What next Commander?"

"We continue on without further delay and remove any more such obstacles that dare to impede our progress," replied Rhaizen as he turned to the west and the three peaked mountain.

The horse that carried Ssnarkit moved forward along the line of Knights, passed Rhaizen, and stepped over the fallen Farwolaeth and the limbless torso of the Berserker. The hooves of the reptile's steed splashed in the red gloop as the Lizardman's hand pointed towards the north.

"There on the horizon... can you see them?" hissed a forked tongue.

Methladon looked as directed, as did others. He squinted into the distance but there was nothing that his eyes could make out. Then he heard Oedd respond.

"What is it? What do your slit-eyes see?"

"Four riders leaving the base of the three peaks and heading north," hissed Ssnarkit.

Methladon looked again. If he squinted hard enough he could just make out four tiny dots that moved across the ground. He could not tell if they were riders and neither could Grovrouk as he too scanned the horizon. Rhaizen turned his horse.

"It is of no consequence. Berserkers no doubt and I assume they have spotted us."

"And if they have?" asked Mhlau.

"Then they will suffer the same fate as their friend. Let them go for we have a more important mission to complete. Now, let us ride on."

With a swift dig of his heals into the sides of his horse Rhaizen set off and the rest followed. It did not take long to reach the foot of the Gathering where Methladon soon spotted the single unicorn tethered to a post outside the mouth of what appeared to be an enormous cave. He looked at the strange creature and realised that the giant that had tried to bar their progress had not been alone. There was another nearby and for a brief moment he wondered if the four riders that Ssnarkit had seen upon the horizon had left to fetch help. Perhaps they would return with the army of the Dragonas.

"I don't like it," whispered Newyn as he climbed off his horse and looked towards the unicorn. "We may be walking into a trap."

"Are you sure this is the right place hole-dweller?" asked Oedd as he dismounted.

"Yes," replied the dwarf. "Tullage confirmed that the beast lay below the three peaks."

"For your sake he'd better not have been lying," replied Newyn.

"Fuck you," spat back Grovrouk.

Methladon looked to his new friend and for a brief moment it seemed the pair were ready to fight but Rhaizen put a stop to any such nonsense.

"That's enough Newyn. We've already lost Farwolaeth. We can't turn on our own, not now, not ever. Cease sniping or you will both feel the effects of my wrath."

Newyn and Grovrouk shot each other a look that would have withered the dead but neither responded. Methladon was once again thankful that he didn't have to intervene on behalf of the dwarf but somehow he sensed that one day soon he would be forced to do so. Until then Grovrouk would be on his own. A small amount of dirt fell from above the entrance to the Gathering. Something or someone had disturbed its roof. Methladon looked up but could not see anything amiss, yet from the expressions of his companions he knew that they too had also seen the disturbance. The hands of the knights moved to the hilts of their swords and they made ready to defend themselves.

"Show yourself," demanded Rhaizen.

A second giant jumped to the ground. In an instant the Berserker straightened himself and stood menacingly before Rhaizen and the Knights of Avolire.

"What do you buggers want in these lands?" demanded the giant.

Methladon noticed the bruising around this second Berserker's eye and the two mighty battle axes strapped to his back. He wondered why both carried significant facial injuries. It seemed strange and perhaps they we all like that. Maybe it was custom in the Dragonas to sport a facial blemish as a symbol of prowess.

"So appears another lanky bastard!" exclaimed Oedd.

"Do you know why we are here dragon fucker," added Newyn?

"No I do not," sneered the Berserker moving closer. "What do you buggers want?"

Methladon reached for the hilt of his sword for he felt sure he would soon have to defend himself. He hoped he would be up to the task. Then as the giant moved closer Newyn unsheathed the curved blade that hung at his side.

"Stand down Newyn. That is an order," shouted Rhaizen

"Yeah Newyn," laughed Oedd. "Stand down you dumb shit."

Mhlau was quick to join in the laughter and even Methladon felt a smile creep across his face. Rhaizen then barked out his next command.

"Silence," he bellowed before turning to address the Berserker. "Stop pissing me off. I believe you know where the beast dwells; I ask you to direct me to its lair."

"And which beast is that?" snarled the Berserker.

"The Mighty Thamous," added Rhaizen without raising his voice. "We seek an audience with the creature that dwells under this barren three peaked hole."

Methladon watched as the Berserker looked over his shoulder into the cavern and then back.

"Fuck off!"

Rhaizen took a step towards the giant man.

"I won't ask again."

"I said fuck off and I won't bother to repeat myself either," growled the Berserker while he pulled his two battle axes from the straps on his back. The gap between the two combatants shank and the tension grew.

"Look you festering mound of pox pus, we don't need your permission," snarled Rhaizen. "Your friend said similar things and now he's gone to meet whatever gods you assholes worship. Isn't that right Meth?"

The startled youth looked towards his Commander and even though Rhaizen was looking away he felt the need to display his affirmation.

"That's right, your friend is dead!" he stuttered.

"I'm not going to ask again..." continued Rhaizen but the Berserker was quick to interrupt.

"Did you not understand the first time, you shall not enter!"

Rhaizen turned and signalled towards the remaining Harbingers.

"Oedd, Newyn, Mhlau. Take him out."

"My pleasure," replied Oedd.

Methladon heard the unsheathing of the swords and then saw the glints as three were held aloft. He felt the urge to use his own blade to aid his companions in their fight but he had not been mentioned in the order. Then something most unexpected happened. The Berserker dropped both axes and adopted a submissive posture with his hands pushed forward for protection.

"Wait, wait, wait," shouted the giant without any hint of anxiety.

"At last some sense," said Rhaizen. "It seems this one is too like an old hen to fight."

"Oh, but I do want to fight you," responded the Berserker as he lowered his arms and walked towards the still tethered unicorn at the cavern entrance. "I just think you ought to know what you are dealing with before I rip your arms off and force you to eat their ends."

"What the fuck are you babbling on about?" shouted Oedd.

The Harbinger, it seemed, had lost all patience with the Berserker. Then Methladon noted that Grovrouk and Ssnarkit had also drawn weapons. The giant opened the saddle bag that hung from the unicorns back while he continued to speak with his back to the Knights of Avolire.

"Do you know why we are called Berserkers?" he asked while searching through the bag.

"No we don't but if it is so important then spit it out before we spill your guts," growled Oedd

"Be patient, I am about to show you," laughed the Berserker as he turned with a small jar of amber liquid clutched within his hands.

"Why doesn't the Commander use his magic like he did on the other?" Methladon whispered to Grovrouk.

"Don't you know the laws of magic yet Meth? Right now he is drained of all of his power. He has to recharge."

Methladon was unsure as to what Grovrouk meant but events moved on at pace.

"Come on dragon fucker, we are waiting for your explanation," laughed Oedd. "Do not keep us in suspense any longer."

"As you insist, then so be it," replied the Berserker.

With that the giant man pulled the bung out of the glass container and consumed the liquid in a single gulp and without spilling a drop. The giant closed his eyes and drew in several deep breaths. Methladon wondered what the strange liquid was and what effect it would have on the man who stood before them.

"Well?" shouted Newyn. "We are waiting."

The Berserker reopened his eyes but what Methladon saw was not human. It was something more primal and two maddened globes stared back from within deep pitted sockets. The giant then changed his stance and never again lost eye contact with the Knights of Avolire. His back hunched in a grotesque manner while all watched on transfixed. The attack came without warning. The giant man pounced towards the three Harbingers knocking all to the ground with a single swipe of his large hands. Oedd, Mhlau and Newyn did not know what had hit them. The Berserker pummelled Oedd on the chest as he sought to rupture his armour. The horses scattered in every direction and almost ran Methladon down. Having to jump out of the way he too watched dumbfounded as the Berserker let out a guttural howl. Rhaizen was upon the Berserker in a flash. He mustered whatever strength he had left to pull the creature off the knight. As the giant regained his feet he turned and snarled at his foe. Mhlau charged forward with his blade drawn but the Berserker pounced himself and in an instant brought the Knight to the ground and snapped his neck. Then the red eyes made contact with Methladon's and the giant howled again.

"Sweet mercy mother of mountains," Methladon exclaimed in terror.

In the next instant both Grovrouk and Ssnarkit jumped in front of Methladon, their weapons readied as the rampant creature moved towards them.

"Methladon, into the cavern," shouted the dwarf while he pointed backwards. "Take cover. Get out of here now."

Guldbrand sprang forward but this time he ran on all fours towards the blacksmith's son. The youth froze with terror and as he did so he felt the mark on the back of his head start to burn again. He did not have time to think more about it for something seemed to snap inside. Rhaizen moved next and bore down upon the Berserker. In one swift swing of his blade he sliced off the giant's left arm. The Berserker let out another guttural howl and immediately turned on the Commander. Each swipe and punch that the Berserker made with his remaining hand was countered by Rhaizen's blade, yet nothing would stop the incensed giant. Through the sounds of metal on flesh and the screeches of the Berserker, Methladon heard the Commander scream.

"Die, dragon fucker!"

Oedd and Newyn regained their feet and charged back into the fight. The Berserker turned to confront them for Rhaizen, part stunned, had broken off from the skirmish and fled towards the cavern entrance. Methladon felt it prudent to follow his Commander and seek the safety of the underworld. Then in the blink of an eye the Berserker was upon Rhaizen. He had moved with stunning speed and knocked the Commander to the floor. Methladon kept on running as the urge to flee took precedence over all other thoughts. Then he heard footsteps close behind and knew he was not alone

"This is it, I'm done for," gasped Methladon as his lungs sought to burst.

An intense scream rang in his ears. It was the voice of his Commander. Methladon stopped, looked back, and as he did so he saw the Berserker throw Rhaizen high into the air and onto the rock wall above the mouth of the cavern. The Commander bounced off the stones, dropped to the floor below, and did not move again. Methladon then looked towards the Berserker and held his breath. He could no longer see Newyn or Mhlau but Grovrouk and Ssnarkit were still by his side. An unearthly groan then rose from the roof stone and Methladon immediately looked up to its origin. As dust and small cobbles started to fall, Grovrouk screamed and charged at the Berserker. The giant man charged back. The dwarf leapt upon several boulders to his left and then launched himself into the air as he swung his axe down towards his intended target. The blade travelled with great momentum and with a snap embedded itself deep into the skull of the Berserker. Two tree trunk legs tottered before the giant fell to the floor, twitched, and then lay still. Before Methladon could make sense of all that was happening an even louder tremor shook the cavern walls. He looked up again as more debris rained down on his head. Then he glanced over to Grovrouk who sought to drag Rhaizen out of harm's way. As their eyes met the dwarf shouted out.

"Methladon, flee inside, the cavern is collapsing."

Grovrouk was right. Before Methladon could answer the roof began to fall around him. The impact of Rhaizen body striking the wall above the cave's entrance had been the catalyst that brought the ancient entrance down. Methladon turned and ran into the depths of the cave. He did not stop to look at the devastation behind him as the air was then filled with voluminous quantities of dust and powdered debris. The deeper recesses of the cavern were plunged into darkness, broken only by the odd ray of light that seeped in through cracks in the pile of rubble. On the youth ran until he was sure that he was safe. Eventually exhaustion overtook Methladon and he fell upon the hard stony ground. From his low position he turned his head and realised in that instant that there could be no going back. The cavern entrance was blocked with an immovable quantity of boulder and stone. He would have to find another way out.

"Methladon?" hissed a familiar voice through the dust as it settled.

"Ssnarkit? Is that you?"

"Yes."

"Please tell me if your eyes can see in the dark?"

"Yes they can. There is another tunnel ahead. It leads further down into the mountain. We might be able to get out that way."

Methladon jumped as he felt the reptilian hand of Ssnarkit grab hold of the pauldron on his right shoulder. He was then propelled forward in to the dark. As the Lizardman dragged him along he prayed that this place would not be his tomb. As much as he disliked the idea, he knew he would have to trust in Ssnarkit if he was to ever get out alive. Then he thought about the others who had fought the Berserker and wondered if any had survived. On he stumbled amid the black and all the while he speculated as to whether Grovrouk had managed to pull Rhaizen to safety before the cavern roof had collapsed. If the others had survived and failed to find a way into the mountain perhaps they would then abandon their mission and return to Avolire. He would be given up for lost and consigned to the slowest of deaths. After several more minutes had passed Methladon noticed a small light that flickered ahead. It danced in the dark and it seemed to entice him forward.

"Ssnarkit." he asked. "That light! What is it?"

"It looks like a burning torch fixed to the wall. I believe it marks the way forward. Perhaps we may yet find what we came here for."

"But what about a way out. Do you think the tunnel you saw could lead to the surface?"

"I'm not sure. It looks to me like it goes further into the mountain," hissed Ssnarkit.

It did not take the pair long to traverse the cavern floor to the point where the torch illuminated a secondary passage that led even deeper into the wall of stone. Methladon was relieved when he found that the torch could be removed from the iron bracket that held it fixed to the wall. At least there now seemed some hope in his moment of despair. He felt scared and yet a strange sensation gripped his body. Some entity drew him forward as if pulling a hook through his navel. He entered the rocky tunnel and with his new light Methladon allowed himself to be dragged belly first along the narrow passage. After a short distance the tunnel opened up into a much larger cavern and both man and reptile came to a halt before entering its dark confines. There they stood motionless and looked into the black.

"Impressive," mumbled Ssnarkit. "You could house an entire army in here and there would still be room for another. This cavern is enormous."

Methladon did not answer. He felt his birthmark tingle but this time it was the most strange of sensations. As if with a life of its own it started to crawl up the back of his head and into his mind. Whatever the phenomenon was, it was caused Methladon to twitch as if his body was trying to expel some giant roach that was eating away at his soul. The movements did not go unnoticed by Ssnarkit.

"Are you okay lad?"

"I don't know," replied Methladon. "It feels like someone's inside my head?"

"So you are the one that I could sense?" spoke a voice.

"Who said that?" shouted Methladon as he reached for his sword only to find he had lost it somewhere during the rock fall.

"So I was right?" said the voice.

"Who are you? Show yourself!" the youth cried out while swinging the torch back and forth in order to illuminate the cavern.

"Haven't you already guessed?"

"Methladon be careful," shouted the Lizardman as the burning stave almost hit his head. "We may yet need that flame that you carry."

Methladon was not listening. The feelings inside his skull continued to amplify the voice that spoke to him. At that moment Ssnarkit seemed insignificant.

"Who are you?" he cried.

"Who are you talking to?" demanded Ssnarkit with much concern. "There is no one but us two. I cannot detect any other presence and my hearing is most acute."

"I am the Mighty Thamous?" said the voice. "You hear my thoughts and I yours."

"How did you get inside in my head?" shouted Methladon into the darkness.

"There is no one here," bellowed Ssnarkit and his voice echoed around the cavern.

"You are with magic," said the voice "I sense a strong Kundalish Aura."

"If you're so fucking mighty, then show yourself!" shouted Methladon amid the grip of fear.

"I have long waited to do so," laughed the voice.

"Who are you talking to Methladon?" demanded Ssnarkit "There is no one out there. Has a rock fallen on your head?"

Without warning an upturned enormous serpentine head appeared at the junction of the tunnel and cavern. It was attached to a long neck that disappeared into the darkness above. Methladon and Ssnarkit jumped backwards as two great jaws opened and then snapped shut. Thamous had tried to reach them in the tunnel and had missed by a matter of a fingertip.

"Fuck" shouted Ssnarkit as he pushed his blade forward.

"Are you not impressed?" asked voice.

The beast's nostrils flared and snorted as it in took voluminous quantities of air.

"You're nought but an overgrown lizard," shouted Methladon as he brandished the torch as if a weapon. "A slimy winged serpent spawned from the bile of the gods."

"A wyvern please, I must insist," said the voice as it laughed and continued to block the way forward. "But as a fellow user of magic I will let you get away with the insult, just this once."

"Behold the Mighty Thamous, Methladon Heyn," added Ssnarkit before moving a step forward to look deep into the pair of giant nostrils that filled the entrance to the tunnel. "We have found the prize we seek."

"I don't think much of the company that you keep lad," added the voice.

"Magnificent isn't he..." said Ssnarkit.

Methladon's thoughts were elsewhere. He feared that he was going mad, cracking under the strain of his plight, and the last thing he needed was to end up crazy like Denius Castor. For whatever reason the voice was real to him and it had a name. It called itself Thamous.

"Do not worry Methladon Heyn. The creature from the Eastern Marsh who stands beside you cannot hear the words that I project inside your mind. You are safe from its prying ears and that is most important given the conversation we are about to have."

"What do you mean?" asked Methladon. "We are here because we seek the Gems."

Ssnarkit hissed and the wyvern's head moved again as if trying to get closer to the two who still sheltered within the tunnel's opening. Methladon held up the flame and watched as the wyvern opened its jaws to reveal multiple rows of razor sharp teeth and a long forked tongue. Without warning the beast emitted a half hiss, half screech, and the mark on the back of Methladon's neck flared again. He was astounded for he could understand everything that the wyvern had said.

"And why do you seek the keys to the underworld" demanded Thamous, this time speaking such that Ssnarkit could hear the words.

"It is not necessary that you know the purpose," replied the Lizardman as it moved a fraction forward. "I demand to know their location. I order you to tell me..."

"Arrogant swamp scum, just as ever," sneered the beast.

Before Methladon could react, Thamous snapped his jaws forward causing the youth to stumble and fall back heavily upon the ground. When he looked up from where he lay, still with the torch gripped in his right hand, he could no longer see any sign of Ssnarkit save for the creature's sword that lay upon the rocky floor of the tunnel; but there was no mistaking the cries and screams as the wyvern munched and crunched upon the Lizardman's scaly carcass. Then with one almighty gulp the beast silenced Ssnarkit's cries forever. Methladon looked up towards the pair of huge eyes and then at the wyvern's teeth with evidence of its kill stuck between them.

"I never expected one of the lizard kind to taste like that!" said the voice. "It reminded me of chicken but with the texture of rancid skyfawn."

Methladon continued to stare into the face of the wyvern. From its expression he wondered if the creature was laughing or was it just some trick of his mind.

"Don't worry lad. I know you can hear what I say. You will do well to remember that I am in your thoughts and that I can sense your fear of death.

"I understood what you said to him," replied Methladon as his legs shook. "I've heard the cries of other dragons but could not understand them. Ssnarkit could, because he said you shared an ancient common language. How is it that I can understand you?"

"Because I choose to let you lad."

"My name is Methladon, Methladon Heyn."

"Still a child either way, but names matter not," continued Thamous. "Please remove yourself from the floor. It is not fitting for a magic user to prostrate himself in the dirt."

Methladon rose from the ground and once again held his torch in front of the wyvern. Its flickering flames reflected off brown scales while the words 'magic user' reverberated through his thoughts. If the beast could read his mind then perhaps it could explain the strange effects that he had experienced before the Lions of Avolire.

"Magic user?" Methladon asked, seeking to bait the creature. "I've never used magic before. I wouldn't know how to start."

"An interesting lie and yet you freed yourself with ease when confined in the Silverwynn's pit. I never believed the once proud people of Avolire could be so cruel."

"You know what happened?" gasped Methladon as he recalled the green flames and flash of light that had erupted from his limbs and saved him from dismemberment. "Can you read all my thoughts?"

"Yes, yet your mind amuses me, just like the other youth before you."

"Youth?" asked Methladon. "What youth?"

"It matters not lad. Your mind is far from simple yet despite the complex thoughts that course through your being I sense that you are filled with doubt and mystery. You also carry the great gift..."

"What gift?" questioned Methladon for he had no idea what the riddle meant?

"Did you ever wonder from where your magic ability originated?" continued Thamous. "Did the bitch Lady not tell you? Did she not spell it out?"

"I have no magic."

"You are a poor liar," snapped back the beast as it moved its head forward and caused Methladon to jump once again. "I know that you question yourself. You ask why you have been granted these powers. I hear the doubt inside your head."

"Then explain it all to me. Give me the answers that I seek. Why am I so plagued? "

"First look upon my full form and see the wonder that is Thamous, created so long ago from a tear of Chalis. Behold what you must deal with for I am more powerful than you could ever imagine and I hold the truth that you seek."

Methladon hesitated for he was concerned that the creature was trying to trick him, to get him to move forwards so he too could be eaten like Ssnarkit; yet he had no other option but to trust the wyvern if he was ever to discover the truth of what was happening to him. He stepped out of the tunnel and moved past the creature's head and neck. Once inside the vast cavern he stopped and looked around. Staring up to the roof through the flame of his torch he followed the snake like neck of Thamous up into the darkness and there saw the rest of its body coiled in the cavern's ceiling. Two legs gripped onto a massive stalactite and a snake tail wrapped around another. There was no doubt that the beast was magnificent, far more impressive than the fire and earth dragons that he had seen out in the Dragonas.

After some minutes Methladon returned to the passageway where the head and neck of the Thamous now lay besides its opening. Once again the voice mindspoke.

"Well! What do you think?"

"Most impressive!" replied Methladon. "I take back all that I said about you being just a dragon. You are really something else, something far grander. Now tell me what you see in my thoughts and explain to me what is going on inside my body."

The voice laughed again and the creature's expression gave way to a sly smile.

"Tell me now!" demanded Methladon as the pain of his mark burned like a poker in the coals.

"A lad pulled taut between four horses," began the voice. "Stretched out with the purpose of dismemberment and death. A brand of magic placed on the back of a head on discovery of a mystical dagger. The creation of one who should have died and yet still walks amongst us. A magical brand that should have brought about his death but didn't."

"You mean...I'm not...You can't...?" stuttered Methladon as images of his time in the pit came flooding back.

"Yes of course I mean you. You may search for the gems but your mind has chosen to forget that you came into contact with one of the five in your youth. Do you not remember the emerald embedded in the hilt of a dagger? It was that which caused the mark to form on the back of your head. It was the dagger that your fool of a father failed to destroy."

"But this cannot be so! That was but a dream. A distant fantasy."

"And yet your subconscious tells you otherwise. You have been marked young man, marked for a very long time."

Methladon paused once again. If this was true then his whole life had been a lie. He could not remember that far back to his childhood and yet things were now starting to make sense. What he thought was a simple birthmark had in the past burned only when he was angry. Of late it had done so in the presence of that which the Lady of the Silverwynn called the Dagger of Kha. It was now clear that the weapon was of greater significance than he had ever realised. The dagger which the Lady claimed held one of the five Gems of Thamous stirred memories and questions that both Tycus and Lancet had put to him down in the mines. They concerned the Prophecy of Enderdetag and an individual known as the Marked; someone destined to save the Realm. He began at last to understand the wyvern's cryptic message. He, Methladon Heyn, had to be the very same Marked that Tycus and Lancet had spoken about. He was the one spoken of in the mystical prophecy.

"So this is why I am cursed, because of a fucking dagger containing one of your gems?"

"You should have died at the hands of Death Tubaria but the Fates deemed that you should live on," continued the voice. "Whatever their reason or purpose was it has caused an imbalance in the laws of nature. You are an anomaly, someone who should not exist. The powerful magic that grows inside you is all that is keeping you grounded in this reality. You are leaching power out of the cracks between the dimensions. Take that ability away and you will fall back into the Underworld, the place where you truly belong."

"But what does all this mean?" cried out Methladon as his mark burned like white hot steel.

"It matters not," laughed Thamous.

"It fucking matters to me!"

"But that is not why you are here. I know what she has sent you to find," said Thamous.

"So you know that she hunts for the means with which to destroy Parandor."

"I know very well what that bitch wants and how she intends to use the power of the Rift for her own ends. She will seek to use you and your mark if you let her. Have you not already tasted what the Rift bestows on her?" added Thamous

"I don't...."

Once again the voice of Thamous had talked in riddles. Methladon knew that he would have to persevere if he wanted to discover the truth of his role in the events that had taken over his life.

"A room of four walls that sits above one of the cracks in reality," continued Thamous. "Walls that harness the energy of the Underworld and focus its power through fissures onto the room's occupants. I can see in your thoughts that the coin of clarity has fallen into place. It is these cracks, these fissures between worlds, which your anger feeds upon. This is the same reason that you can understand both myself and the language of your friend from the Dirmark, Grovrouk the Despoiler. The crack between the realities, the Mighty Rift, is awakening your full potential. Your mind has been unlocked and your powers are growing stronger with each day that passes."

"What else can you tell me?" asked Methladon.

He so hoped that Thamous would continue his explanation. The quest for the gems could end now for all he cared. He had at last found answers as to why he was the Marked of Maplehill.

"What else do you see?" he demanded and once again the amused wyvern looked back.

"Now that would be telling. Your mind is unlocked and I can see both your past and some of your future. I sense the fears and uncertainty that fester deep within; fears that feed the mark. You blossom in your anger. Something most special has taken hold of you. It is a power that cannot be dispelled and one that shields you from my magic. Yet while you stand before me under this place known as the Gathering I am able to keep it in check."

"A power? What power? Tell me more," demanded Methladon.

"It matters not!"

"Stop fucking saying that," shouted Methladon. "Tell me what I want to know."

Methladon waited but the answer never came, just the sounds of laughter.

The youth was infuriated and he felt his ire rage through his body. He screamed out and his spittle sprayed into the face of Thamous.

"If you're not going to answer me you stupid bastard of a bog beast then I will be on my way. Tell me where the three remaining gems are located and I will be gone. Where will I find the stones to unlock the Underworld? If you can read my thoughts then you will have known of my intentions from the moment I was chased into this shit hole. Quit stalling and playing for time. Answer the question that my reptile friend posed before you ate him."

"And why would I tell you such secrets, servant of the Lady that demeans her title?"

"Tell me you vile serpent," bellowed Methladon.

"That bitch will never sit on the throne of Parandor. The powers of the Underworld will never be hers to control. Already those who oppose her search out and seek to protect the Gems of Thamous from the armies of Avolire. Now piss off back where you came from. I bid you goodbye and I never want to cast my eyes on you again."

The wyvern's head and neck retracted back into the depths of the cavern. Methladon raced forward and held his torch high in order to fight the darkness and seek out the great beast. He caught a brief glimpse of a shadow, nothing more, as mighty wings expanded to enable flight. Methladon then screamed as loud as he could. The words echoed around the cavern.

"You serpent swine. You fucking beast! Come back here now. Who opposes her? Was it those horsemen? Who were those four?"

The wyvern turned around mid-flight and glided back towards the ground. It landed upon the cavern floor with its two enormous legs and brought its head down to face the blacksmith's son.

"Fucking beast!" said the voice "You should have stopped at 'serpent'."

"Tell Me!" screamed Methladon as his anger burst forth from his mind.

Then, in a most bizarre turn of events, Methladon no longer saw though his own eyes but those of another and he witnessed something most extraordinary. He found himself looking at a great warrior, fitted out in the orichalcum armour of the Knights of Avolire. He sensed that he was looking through the eyes of Thamous himself? Then as he closed his eyes he saw the image of a dense frost covered forest, no, more of a jungle, with the spires and pyramids of an ancient civilisation reaching up out of the trees. It was followed by visions of a tomb and a skeletal knight upon a stone plinth. In the body's hands rested a mighty battle axe with a sapphire embedded in its head. As these images flashed through his mind the voice muttered a few final words.

"Barad Elestor………Sapphire………Tomb."

Methladon shook his head and opened his eyes. He looked again at the creature which now appeared to be writhing in pain. He noticed that he had dropped the torch that he had carried and that his hand was glowing as he pointed his finger towards the creature. Yet when Methladon next spoke the voice that came out of his mouth was not his own. It was deeper and inhuman. It was bestial.

"A forest to the north you say?"

"Get out of my head foul Lord," howled Thamous but Methladon was past caring for he realised that somehow he now had the creature within his control. He could read the wyvern's thoughts and he sought to enforce his will upon the beast.

"Tell me what I need to know," ordered Methladon although the voice was still not his.

"I am warning you lad."

"I can cause you even more pain," said Methladon as he thrust his glowing hand forward. "I can give you pain like you have never felt before."

"This is your last chance…" screeched Thamous.

"Tell me now where the remaining Gems are hidden."

"The Vessel must die!" bellowed the beast.

Those were that last words that Methladon heard. As he looked towards the head of the wyvern his eyes made contact with those of the creature. Thamous's cavernous mouth opened and a great bolus of air, smoke, fire, and heat basted out from the wyvern's throat. It hit Methladon full on and the youth was engulfed in flame.

8

The dismal cell, deep within the rectum of the Citadel of Parandor, was identical to the one in which her father had suffered his last days in the Realm. It had the same cold walls and a similar ante-chamber but with perhaps a greater quantity of mould that grew out from in between the cracks in the mortar that held the stones together. Iron rods and a gate prevented Tonousa Amberstone from moving into that antechamber and barred her way to the stone stairs that climbed up onto a higher level. A small window, set at the end of a long air tunnel in one wall, looked up and out into the courtyard beyond. It too was grated to prevent any possible means of escape. The room itself was one of the better prison cells that Tonousa had ever visited. There were others that were void of any fixtures at all and that when the cell door was closed would be plunged into total darkness. In such a hole as those it would be impossible to distinguish between night and day. Tonousa knew them well from her work for the City Watch and had deposited many a wretch there to suffer a lingering death.

She was also aware of the few forget-me-not cells, oubliettes as the highborn called them; places where people were put to be erased from memory. She thanked the gods that she had at least been spared the experience of such an evil hole. Most in the Watch had heard accounts of the unfortunates that had been deposited there and a left to rot. Most times they were reserved for the vilest scum of the city, people so evil that they would sell their own children to the sex merchants of the savage lands beyond the Howling Hills. They were the kind that everyone was pleased see disappear; people that if you ever met them you would wish that you had not, for their memory would haunt you for the rest of your days. But this was not to be Tonousa's fate. She still had a purpose to fulfil and would strive to ensure that she would never be forgotten.

From her place of rest upon the sparse straw covered floor, Tonousa looked up to the small window through which the light of Solaris streamed and bathed her with a comforting warmth. She had tried to keep track of the duration of her incarceration and her way of doing so had been by counting the number of sleeps that had passed. Even then she was not sure how long she had been there for sometimes she slept during the day and stayed awake through Mona's passage. Since the events on Stukeley Knoll and her subsequent arrest at foot of the Richemanus Folly, Tonousa had calculated that she had been incarcerated for about seven days. They were long days that lingered in the pain of their passing and amid the vivid memories of her father's brutal execution.

Her jailer, Tharik Mastisan, under the instructions of Sir Byddin, had been ordered to make sure that she was made as comfortable as possible given the limitations of her predicament. She knew that pressure must have also been applied by Lord Commander Townsforth and she guessed that it was the Watch who had ensured that she had been provided with bowls of warm water and a bucket in which to drop her solids. The metal container was even emptied each day, something unheard of in the routine of Parandor's prison. But even the City Watch had limited influence and beyond these few simple comforts they could not interfere with the day to day existence of the prisoners beneath the Citadel, let alone have one released. Freedom was only possible with the expressed permission of Phauless Gylewu himself, the Head of the Sovereign Guard Sir Byddin, or from the man she wished she could beat to mush, Xix Blackfayer, the swine who had betrayed her father.

Through that small window she watched feet pass in the courtyard and thought on what she would do if she ever came face to face again with that slithering snake man. She knew it would be difficult to ever again restrain herself in his presence. All she could deduce from the facts and clues that she had accumulated so far was that somehow her father and Xix Blackfayer were key players in the events that linked the murderous cult with the Knights of Avolire and those that dwelt in the Eastern Marsh. She tried to imagine Xix and her father as they attempted to protect the Lore of the Dead and prevent it from falling into the hands of the devotees of Death Tubaria. She wondered what would have happened to Blackfayer had he been found in possession of the book rather than her father and whether he too would have been sentenced to death at the hands of Sir Richemanus. The warrior was not convinced that would have been the case. Then her father's last words came back to haunt her and once again she tried to work out what it was that he had been trying to tell her.

Tonousa heard the bolt at the top of the stone steps unlock. After a few seconds the door creaked open and the sounds of heavy footsteps followed. She didn't have to look up to know to whom the feet belonged to for the jingle of keys gave his identity away.

"You have a visitor," snorted Tharik the keeper of the keys.

"Who" replied Tonousa without removing her gaze from window above?

"One of your City Watch friends."

"Which one? I have so many," replied Tonousa, knowing that to be a lie.

There were but two individuals that would bother to come to her aid. One of them was responsible for her incarceration and had been her arresting officer. The other was travelling the far ends of the Realm with a bard and the boy that all recent events seemed centred on, the youth called Llyat Emgar.

"Well Tharik, who has come to pity me?" she asked at last. "I'm waiting to hear."

"Hello Tonousa, how are you?" said the visitor from the stairs.

Tonousa recognised the voice at once and even though she thought of him as a trusted friend, he was the one who had led to her confinement.

"What the fuck do you want?" she demanded.

"That is no way too receive your greatest friend and admirer," said Danisun Dain.

"I am not talking to you, so just fuck off."

"Tharik, please leave us. I have things to discuss with the prisoner in private," ordered Danisun.

Still staring at the window Tonousa heard the jailer begin to ascend the stairs and pass his keys over to Danisun. It was this degree of awareness and deductive capacity that had made Tonousa so good at her job. Within seconds Danisun stood at the bars that separated him from his prisoner.

"Tonousa, we need to talk" he ordered.

"And how many times do I have to tell you, I have nothing to say to you."

"And yet I twice saved your life. It was shear madness to attempt to assault Xix Blackfayer, then steal a fellow officer's weapon at Stukeley Knoll ..."

Tonousa glared at the ginger bearded face on the other side of the bars. She stood up on the hard floor, thankful that Tharik had let her keep her shoes and clothes. Yet even the protection they provided could not warm the feelings she had towards Danisun Dain at that moment.

"I thought you understood what was going on," she snapped back. "Did you not sense the severity of the situation? I was mistaken in the hope that I could trust you."

"You can trust me Tonousa. I had to act on impulse. You were not going to accomplish anything if you were under suspicion yourself. Xix would have seen to it that you shared the same fate as your father given the history between you and what your father had been accused of. I had to remove you from the situation, at least for a while, and allow you to gather your senses. How was I to know you would turn up at the Richemanus Folly...?"

"My father was about to be executed," shouted Tonousa. "Of course I would go there. Talk sense or just fuck off and leave me to my fate."

Danisun did not respond. Instead he looked over his shoulder towards a three legged stool that had been pushed to one corner of the anteroom. It was the same stool that Tonousa watched Tharik take his afternoon naps on when he shut himself off from the world. Danisun reached for it, placed it in front of the iron bars, and then he sat down to face Tonousa. He removed the leather helm from around his head, placed it on his lap, and allowed his dirty red hair to cascade out and down. His lips formed into a weak smile before he spoke again.

"I need the full story right now, without lies or embellishment. Commander Townsforth must make his report to the Sovereign Council this afternoon. Llys Emeny has called the Court together on the order of our Sovereign Lord and she wants all interested parties to be present. The Commander will personally represent the Watch on this matter. He requires that I report to him with your honest story. For the record I need to hear it once again. I need to hear the full truth..."

"But you know the truth..." she screamed back.

Had the metal bars not separated her from her colleague would have grabbed Danisun by the throat and throttled him so hard that his ears would have burst.

"Please Tonousa. I need to hear it again," he repeated. "This isn't some fireside chat about the colour of Lady Lorst's dress, or who sank the ship bound for the Lotus Isles. No, this is much more serious shit. People have been murdered and there are many gaps that I need to fill in order to solve the puzzle. I need more proof if I am to believe that the Eastern Marsh, the Knights of Avolire, and the resurgence of the cult of Death Tubaria are all connected."

Tonousa sighed and then after a few moments of deliberation she began her story. She started from the beginning with how she had been approached by Commander Townsforth to accompany him to the Citadel where they had been instructed to investigate the murders of the past months. Following the trail that the perpetrator had left it became apparent that the crimes were similar to those committed by a previous cult. She spoke of a clue discovered by Grand Physician Abrahamus Marus who was assisting her and her appointed partner Irabo Basequin with the investigation. Following this they had sought the help of the bards, given that magic had been evoked in the crimes and because of the suggestion of a link to an old order of magic users, the Knights of Avolire. Tonousa continued her story by describing the events at the Bards Guild and the attack led by the Lizardmen of the Eastern Marsh which had split her group. Then at last she told how those who had survived the Guild's inferno had gone their different ways in order to pursue the various clues they had unearthed.

"Thank you Tonousa," said Danisun after a brief pause. "Now once again, and just so I can report back to Commander Townsforth, what happened to Irabo Basequin?

"Look Danisun, haven't you been listening to a word I said? I told you on numerous occasions that he travels in secret on his way to Falahorn with a bard and that boy we fished out of the river.

Danisun did not answer but a smile crept across his face and Tonousa spotted it at once.

"What is so funny?"

"Well at least I can confirm that part of your story to the Lord Commander," he added.

"What do you mean by that?"

"We received a carrier bird this morning," replied Danisun as Tonousa stared back in shock. "Young master Bluehill found the bird and the message. He brought it straight to me as I was acting duty officer. You'll have to thank the gods that the boy Bluehill cannot read."

Tonousa sat with her mouth wide open and stared. She thought perhaps this meeting's purpose had been some form of test and she wondered what Danisun was really up to. Perhaps he too was caught up in the crimes for he was well placed to be the killer. She could not be certain but the sign that she had waited for, one to say that her friend Irabo was safe in Falahorn, brought sweetness to her ears.

"Thanks be to Solaris that they arrived in one piece?" said Tonousa while composing herself.

"I wouldn't say in one piece. It appears that Irabo broke his leg defending himself from a skyfawn attack and the young boy that was in his charge came down with the sweating sickness. Sounds like a healer in Falahorn is taking care of them."

"Did they say anything else? Was there more in the message?"

"Not much that I could tell. The bard called Thias Calavan, the sullen bugger that used to skulk in the shadows of the Court and the one you told me was Phauless Gylewu's private investigator; he appears to have accepted responsibility for your friends and has reported that he is going to stick with them until they complete their quest."

Tonousa smiled to herself. At least her friends were safe and that fact warmed her heart.

"May I see the letter," she asked while she searched Danisun's eyes for further clues.

"I destroyed it for I felt that was the safest course of action. If what you told me is true and that some spy has infiltrated the Court, then I thought it was for the best. I wouldn't want such information getting into the wrong hands and compromising my investigation."

"That at least is some good news," replied Tonousa

She began to wonder how the investigation could move forward and then it dawned on her that the responsibility for solving the murders had passed to Danisun. Perhaps his checking of the validity of the message was the true reason for his visit but maybe he also had other questions to ask her. There were several that she had for him.

"If you've finished asking your questions, have you any further insight as to what happened to my father at his execution?"

"To be honest with you, that is why I am here."

"What do you mean?" asked Tonousa as a cloud of confusion cast its shadow across her mind. "I thought you were here to just kiss ass and pad out Townsforth's report?"

"Like I just said, after the events of the Richemanus Folly, your investigation was passed to me by order of our Lord Commander. He said that he needed someone you would trust and openly confide in. Therefore I am leading the investigation in your temporary absence. I was tasked with unearthing the truth and you know I can be deceptive in my own way.

"You mean..." added Tonousa as the truth of the situation became apparent.

"Yes. I'm here to release you."

While Danisun spoke he removed the jailer's keys from underneath the leather helm on his lap and waved them in front of Tonousa. There they jangled amid the silence of the stone cell.

"Well then, in the sight of the god's, get me out of this shit hole."

Danisun stood up from the milking stool and made his way over toward the gate. He fumbled with the keys as he tried to find which of the iron objects would set his comrade free. Tonousa made her way over towards him and timed her arrival with the opening of the metal bars. With haste she walked through them and into freedom. Tonousa then smiled at Danisun and he reciprocated. Then she clenched her fist and punched him on the jaw with all the strength she could muster.

"That is for knocking me senseless," she cried.

Danisun reeled backwards and staggered from the shock of the unexpected assault. As Tonousa recoiled with the impact pain from her fist she watched the man who claimed to be her friend spit blood and a piece of tooth out onto the floor. Then he wiped his face with his leather sleeve.

"I guess I asked for that," he muttered before laughing. "I am pleased to see you are back to your normal self!"

"Thank you for getting me out of here but I do have to ask you how you managed to get Blackfayer to agree to my release. How did you convince him after all that has happened?"

"Blackfayer will no longer be a thorn in your side."

"Oh is that so!" replied Tonousa. "Did that weasel finally grow a pair of balls?"

"There is much that I need to tell you. A lot has changed since the events of the Richemanus Folly and your father's execution. I will fill you in on the details on the way."

"On the way?" asked Tonousa "Where are we going?"

"All I will say is that I am taking you to someone I think you will be quite pleased to see."

Tonousa saw no point in questioning Danisun further for she knew he would keep his secret until he himself was ready to divulge it. Events were moving faster than her thoughts could follow and it didn't take them long to leave the cell. Danisun passed the keys back to Tharik who for once had not been listening at the door. He then led Tonousa out of the labyrinth of tunnels, into the courtyard, and then on through the same exit from the Citadel that Tonousa and Irabo had used one month before when they had carried one of the Death Tubaria victims through it on the orders of the Grand Physician. That day seemed such a distant memory as she traversed the yard where the Lords and Ladies of the Court moved about on their private business. Many eyes stared and sought to penetrate the leather armour that she wore and she sensed the highborn were casting their preconceived assumptions of her guilt. What, she wondered, would it take to prove her innocence. Whatever had to be done she would do it. She would bide her time until the truth about the events on the Richemanus Folly were uncovered.

Danisun led the way through the outer wall of the Citadel. Minutes later the pair exited through the Barbican and into the warren of streets beyond. Solaris was already warming the town and given what Tonousa had endured during the past week she felt a flush of well-being ripple through her essence. They walked on and passed the few citizens out and about and dodged the foul waste piles that lay where they had been dropped from above. As the weary souls of the city passed her, Tonousa could sense in them a great urgency and she then realised that the streets were much quieter than usual for the time of day. Something had happened that Danisun had not yet told her about.

"So what have I missed?" she began. "Why is this place so deserted?"

"Where to begin?" pondered Danisun. "Ever since the curse mark showed itself at the Richemanus Folly, the whole city has been in disarray."

"What do you mean? Say more."

"Our Sovereign Lord and the rest of the Council thought they could contain the secret of the resurrection of Death Tubaria but after what happened on Stukeley Knoll they soon realised their error. You know the sort of gossip that spreads through the taverns and markets. The news that your father bore a curse mark after his unexpected swift beheading spread like the fires of the great dragons themselves. The city threw itself into turmoil. There was panic in the streets, looting in the market place, and most of the population then went into hiding. They locked themselves into their homes and now venture out only when necessary. No one trusts his neighbours and there is great unrest. Commander Townsforth is trying hard to regain control. He has imposed a night curfew and enlisted more men into the City Watch with the support of the Sovereign Council. Yet those who have so far joined are far from combat ready. They are mostly farmers and boys and none of them have held a sword before. Sir Rayner Byddin loaned us some of his men but even so we do not have enough to stop the vigilante attacks that have started across the city."

"That's all we need, people taking the law into their own hands. As if we haven't got enough to deal with," added Tonousa as she shook her head with disbelief.

"Nedes Karoly is the worst of the bastards," continued Danisun. "Townsforth suspects him of the horse rustling that been going on but we haven't enough evidence to pin it on him as yet. More worrying than missing horses however is the rumour that Karoly and his friends have sworn to root out any magic users and lynch them on the spot. You can imagine how much concern this is causing the Wizard's Guild. Archmage Iqotrix and his ilk, recluses at the best of times, have sealed themselves inside the walls of their Guild. Until the activities of the vigilantes has been brought under control we will remain in a state of anarchy. "

"What about the threat from the Eastern Marsh and that of the Knights of Avolire? What about the group of riders that Townsforth sent out and that you were part of? What more did you discover?"

"We found the massacre at the Grey Keep, just like your bard friend said had occurred. It was the basis of my report when you gate crashed the Council meeting on your return to Parandor. The Eastern Marsh does appear to be in the ascendancy. Sir Byddin has called in the reserves and the armies of Parandor are preparing for war. More troops from the Fifteen Keeps have been arriving every day and have made camp on the outskirts of the city. At least we can call on some of them if we do not soon return order within the Capital. Sir Byddin has even sent an envoy north to Valameer to meet with the Lady Flurdiana, to inform her of the murder of her betrothed and to ask her for her support against those that oppose us. We may yet need the assistance of her Trident Guard."

"Good luck with that," answered Tonousa as she remembered the morning of the attack on the Bards Guild. "The last time I saw her she was more concerned with breaking her fast than assisting those who had fled the reptiles' slaughter."

"That may be the case but the Trident Warriors of Valameer are a formidable force and from a rumour that Lolye Throissler of the South Gate tells me, Sir Byddin has also sent a carrier bird to Falahorn to ask for the help of the legendary Berserkers."

"If war is imminent then we are going to need all the help we can get."

"It's those that dwell in the slums outside the city gates that I feel sorry for," continued Danisun. "The arrival of fifteen battalions has pushed them out of their homes and the destitute have flocked into the city."

"I thought Blackfayer would have prevented such an act given his dislike of the slum scum."

"The Sovereign Council had no choice in the matter. Phauless Gylewu gave the order himself for the gates to be opened, much to the disdain of Lady Emeny and Lord Ystafell. Both I believe fell on bended knee to beg our Sovereign

Lord to change his mind but Phauless ignored them and gave the charge of the poor to the Royal Priest that sits on the Sovereign Council… what's his name again?"

"Heward Teulu"

"Yes that's him. Well, Teulu has brought all of the temples of the different faiths together and they are now in the process of giving sanctuary to those that previously lived in the slums."

Tonousa smiled. There were not enough people in the Realm with such a selfless heart as Heward Teulu. The kindness of the priest reminded her of the inhabitants of Valameer and how they had assisted those who had survived the destruction of the Bards Guild. She was also reminded of Irabo and his devotion to the following of Fatumai, the way that he offered charity to those who needed it most, and how he was always the first to put his own life at risk in the service of others. Yet she had not ruled the priest out as being the possible infiltrator. It would be perfect cover for a Lizardman changeling.

"Hang on a minute Danisun," said Tonousa. "This isn't the way to the barracks."

Danisun stopped and turned to face his colleague.

"We are not going to the barracks Tonousa. The people who want to meet with you did not wish a venue where they could be discovered by the infiltrator. They insisted on much more inconspicuous place."

"Who is it that wants to meet with me?"

"All that I was told was that once I had released you, I was to bring you to straight to them and that is where we are going. Given current events and what they had to say transpired in Valameer, I thought it was for the best. They asked that I didn't name them out in the open for reasons of secrecy and their personal security. They say we cannot trust anyone."

"And I thought that it was just the bards that talked in riddles," said Tonousa although she had suspicions as to who Danisun referred.

"Quite so. I must insist that we carry on walking as I fear a sky fall from that window that has just opened."

The pair moved off just as the stinking solids fell. Tonousa demanded to know more.

"So is there anything else that I have missed? Things of significance that I should know of? Has Blackfayer pardoned my father yet given the events on the Richemanus Folly? And where has that rat faced weasel of a snake been during all the time that I was locked up."

"Well…"

"Spit it out man," ordered Tonousa.

"Xix Blackfayer is dead!"

"You've got to be fucking kidding me!" exclaimed Tonousa as the shock of the words hit home. "How did he die?"

"He took a sleeping draft and never woke up. The suicide note said he couldn't live with what he had done and that everything was his fault. He mentioned nothing of your father,

"What had he done? What was his fault? I am so shocked that I cannot take all this in."

"The letter was ambiguous," Danisun continued. "But from the words as written it has been assumed that he has been guilty of high treason. Sir Byddin and Phauless Gylewu have thrown the resurfacing of the cult of the Death Tubaria at his feet now, hence the reason I have been able to release you. You are no longer a suspect."

"I smell a rat. This sounds like a set up and that Blackfayer has been made a scapegoat. I feel our murderer is becoming even more sophisticated and devious."

"My feelings also," added Danisun as he turned and marched off.

"And there was no sign of the mark of Death Tubaria?" called out Tonousa as she followed.

"No, none at all. Given all that you had told me and from what I was already aware of, I made sure it was the first thing that the Watch checked for. My theory is that Blackfayer took his own life because he couldn't cope with the guilt of having your father executed. "

"But why Danisun? Why would he do such a thing?"

"That is the question I would like answering myself. It's just one of many such loose ends that we have yet to come to understand."

"Who's taken his place?" asked Tonousa as the thought of no longer having to deal with Blackfayer sank in. "Who has stepped into the void of power that he has left behind?"

"Llys Emeny. It was a unanimous vote by the rest of the Sovereign Council. As she had been the Royal Judge she will bring a very different approach to the role of Sovereign Advisor. From what I have heard from Sir Lightmain and Sir Cragtalon, she is putting her mark on the Realm already..."

Tonousa did not register the last words that spilled out of Danisun's mouth for once again she was lost in her own thoughts. She tried to piece together the bricks of evidence that were building around her and tried to understand what Xix and her father had been up to. She still could not work out how they could they have allowed the theft of such a vital piece of evidence, the process that would allow the Knights of Avolire and the Lizardmen of the Eastern Marsh to resurrect the cult of Death Tubaria. It was so strange that following the taking of the Lore of the Dead the two did not confess to it being stolen and that they ended blaming each other instead of seeking to prevent the troubles that had since been brought within Parandor's walls. For a brief second Tonousa felt saddened over Xix's demise but then she shrugged the thought from her mind. It was a moment of weakness that she put down to her elation at being freed from captivity.

Her thoughts were interrupted once again when Danisun stopped in the street outside a familiar building. Tonousa recognised the strong oak door and sign in the shape of a wolf that hung above it; one which swung back and forth upon its rusted chains. There was however none of the usual clamour from within The Murdered Wolf, a fact which Tonousa at once picked up on and thought most odd. Given that the drinking hole was known throughout the Realm to attract the worst of the dross, it was strange to find it so quiet.

"Well here we are?" said Danisun as he pushed open the door and stepped inside the tavern's gloomy interior. "Come on, follow me."

Tonousa did as instructed and marched inside. She was surprised to find that apart from the lone figure of Isambard Hotch, busy in his task of cleaning tankards with his spittle, the place was empty. There was a distinct absence of serving girls, whores waiting to sell themselves, and of course customers. No fire burned in the hearth. Parandor's problems must indeed be severe to empty The Murdered Wolf. If this was happening to all the small business of the once bustling Capital, then Parandor itself was at risk of dying.

On seeing the two enter Isambard growled but the warriors ignored the sound.

"See what you've gone and done bitch. You've scared off all my custom with your Death Tubaria stunt at the Stukeley Knoll. What has Parandor become if its own City Watch isn't able to catch a murderer? All my business has gone down the sewers. Thank the gods for men like Nedes Karoly..."

Tonousa continued to ignore the barkeep for she wasn't in the mood for trouble. Instead she sneered back at him and followed Danisun into the small corridor that led off from the main room. She passed by the door where she had once interrupted Highroar pleasuring a whore and at last came to the largest of the doors. Danisun rapped upon the solid oak with his hand several times in a unique and specific rhythm. Tonousa recognised it as one of the first secrets that he had taught her during her training. However before she could comment the door opened from within and revealed those gathered in the room.

"Tonousa!" screeched the young girl who had opened the door. "He got you out then. How wonderful"

"Hi Heliana," Tonousa replied as she stepped into the room.

Tonousa was not altogether surprised to see the young woman she had last seen in Valameer. Also present was the dark skinned sailor whose face had been cratered by the pox. Theoplous Danmar sat on the mattress of an unmade bed in the corner of the room.

"Theo, I'm so glad to see you? How long had have you been back in the city?"

"They arrived three days ago, just turned up at the barracks as if out of nowhere," added Danisun as he enter the room in Tonousa's wake. "Said they were looking for you and that they had been told that they could trust me. I explained to them the events of the Richemanus Folly and they filled in some of the gaps in my knowledge. I managed to persuade old Isambard to find them accommodation and with a little threat or two even managed to persuade him to procure them some of new clothes. This was the best place I could think of to hide them. It has to be the safest and furthest from the eyes of the spy that stalks the Citadel.

"You call The Murdered Wolf safe, that's the best joke I have heard in ages," replied Tonousa.

"Well as I said, it's one of the most secure places I know of. You've seen the scum that..."

"Yes, yes, yes," rambled Tonousa as she dismissed his words. "Heliana, how are you? Well?"

Tonousa hugged both in turn despite being aware of the filthy state of her attire and the stink left over her from her incarceration. How she longed for a scrub and a bath.

"We're fine, thanks to Danisun here," said Heliana as she tried not to notice the reek.

"Well, I must say Heliana that dress sits better on you than on one of Isambard's whores?"

"Well thank you Tonousa," laughed the young girl as she twirled on the spot. "I've always wanted a dress like this and now I have one. Blue and black is just my colour."

Tonousa looked at the dress that Heliana wore. It had seen better days but the girl was right. Despite the grime stains and the frayed fabric, the dress did indeed look as if belonged on Heliana. It showed off her cleavage, her trim waist, and her rounded hips.

"Do you know what Heliana," added Tonousa. "To be honest with you, when the light of Solaris shines on it, it almost looks white and gold. But it matters not, even when you step back into the gloom it still becomes you. But to more serious matters, after our parting in Valameer I carried much guilt for what had happened to us all."

"Don't be so bloody silly," the girl responded. "If it wasn't for you and Theo then I would have died at the hands of those slime scaled bastards from the swamps."

"Yes, and once again, I'm sorry that I hit you so hard," added Theoplous.

"How is the head?" asked Tonousa.

"It's been better but the lump has at least started to go down."

Without warning the door behind her closed and caused Tonousa to turn. Her eyes shot past Danisun and on to another occupant of the room, one who had remained hidden behind the door ever since her arrival.

"It's good to see you again," said the man in his soft voice.

"Darchus!" exclaimed Tonousa. "What in the name of the gods are you doing here?"

Tonousa smiled as the man from Valameer stepped towards her. Out of all the people in the Realm, Darchus Arillius of Valameer was the last person she had expected to see.

"I have Captain Highroar and Theoplous to thank for bringing me to Parandor," replied the cordwainer. "The Captain would, if you asked him, say that he sought me out, but the truth is that I have too many questions that I need you to answer Tonousa Amberstone."

"Darchus approached us the day we were due to set sail," added Theoplous. "He said that he had unfinished business with a woman from the City Watch of Parandor. He offers you his services in gratitude for your actions in Valameer."

"That's all very well, but haven't you got a wife and child? Where are they? Don't tell me you left them to follow me here on the hope of finding the answers to a few questions."

"No I did not leave them, they came with me. I couldn't abandon them with the Lady Flurdiana unwilling to defend her own city. Highroar is out finding them some accommodation at this very moment. He said he could pull some strings with his sailor friends and secure them somewhere to stay near the Southern Gate."

"I wouldn't leave them alone for too long with that one…" began Tonousa before Theoplous cut her off.

"He's under instructions,"

"I'm so glad to hear it," replied Tonousa.

"I don't think he likes taking orders from his First Mate but I think he understands the new pecking order and the need to keep his mind away from his cock just now."

Tonousa smiled. The thought of Highroar being put in his place lightened her mood. It drove away many negative thoughts and began to lift her veil of confusion; but then she was brought crashing back down as Heliana spoke.

"Are you going to explain what is going on? I think you owe the three of us some answers. What do you know that we don't?"

Tonousa sighed. She didn't relish repeating the story yet another time but given the critical nature of their situation she felt that those present deserved a detailed explanation of the complex events that were unfolding in their midst. As the four occupants of the room gathered around her, Tonousa sat down upon the bed and began to relate the confused and convoluted story once again. It took a while for she did not miss out any of the details.

After a long time answering questions about every critical point of her story Tonousa at last finished and paused for breath.

"So Llyat is still alive," asked Heliana?

"Yes and I am so sorry for the deception but Thias Calavan, that sullen bard we met in Valameer, swore me to secrecy," added Tonousa. "Thias needed to get Llyat as far from Valameer as possible before his mission was discovered. I feel safe to tell you this now, given the time that has passed since they headed off into the wilderness, but you must not repeat this secret to anyone else."

"Wait until I get hold of him!" exclaimed Heliana as her face flushed an angry purple. "I'll rip his fucking balls off, leaving me like that without so much as a message and me thinking that he was dead. Why, I swear to you all here and now, I will have his guts made into tie-ups for the fat Lady's stockings."

Tonousa tried not to laugh but the sight of Heliana's ire amused her greatly.

"Well it all makes sense at last," added the cordwainer.

"Does it!" exclaimed Heliana. "How does any of it make sense? We don't know which one of the Sovereign Council is a shape changer. It could be anyone of those highborn paps."

"And even then how may we be sure that it is one of the Council?" asked Theoplous. "Remember Tonousa what you told us back in Valameer. The Lizardman infiltrator could be anyone of us. You even seemed to suspect those involved in Highroar's card game on the night before we set out on the Banshees Wail."

Silence descended until Danisun cut it with words.

"Tonousa, you have our full attention now so how do you want to proceed? It's your call. How will we begin flush out the shape changer? I mean it's not like there is a give-a-way sign like they are devoid of emotion or something."

"Danisun, may I suggest that we begin to investigate this like any other crime," she replied "We have do this the old fashioned way, by careful questioning, probing, and using our combined powers of deduction. We must pray to our collective gods to guide us on this quest and unmask the traitor within our midst. We can do it and we will do it. This is our time Danisun and we will make the City Watch proud of our deeds."

"And the rest of us?" asked Theoplous.

"I can't ask you get involved in these most dangerous investigations. You've already done far too much for me. For your own safety you must distance yourself from the Watch."

"I'm involved now whether you like it or not," snapped back the sailor.

"As am I," added Heliana.

"And me," added Darchus.

"Oh shit!" sighed Tonousa.

The reactions of the three pleased Tonousa and ideas began to form in her mind.

"It looks like I'm not going to be able to deter any of you from this quest. So given that I am stuck with you this is how I propose we proceed. All must be done with the utmost of caution. First of all, Danisun, you need take Darchus here and induct him into the City Watch. He will then have the authority to help us with our formal investigation. A fresh unbiased mind may be essential in the coming days if we are to flush out someone who is already familiar to Danisun and myself. However, we must keep the real reason behind his assimilation a complete secret. Not even our Commander must know for Townsforth still remains a potential suspect.

"I will try Tonousa, but you know our Commander, he will ask many pointed questions."

"I trust your judgement and skill to handle this Danisun," added Tonousa.

"And what about Heliana and myself?" asked Theoplous.

"If you think I'm joining the City Watch then think again," sneered Heliana.

"No girl, I will not ask that of you," said Tonousa as she smiled. "Even though a feisty nature would be of great value within the ranks. Remember that despite your master the Grand Physician being no longer with us, you still remain in service to the Court. It is a position that will be terminated only on your death. You may say it's a job for life and yet you are in a perfect position to search the Citadel. No doubt you have contacts with most of the other servants who may also be able to help us, in particular the ones that pander to the whims of the Sovereign Council. Should one of the Gems of Thamous be hidden within the Citadel, we will need to call on all the eyes and ears that we can recruit to discover its whereabouts and keep it from our infiltrator. Use your knowledge well and see what you can find out."

"I'm on it," replied Heliana.

Tonousa turned to Theoplous.

"Theo, I need you find out all you can from Highroar about that bloody card game and who played it with him. Also question old Isambard downstairs. Be very careful but find out what he knows about the Oracle of Frasteria. He maybe pissed off at the City Watch for driving all his customers away but you might be able to get some information out of him. Try dangling some coins in front of his trough. The barkeeps of Parandor are an infinite source gossip and rumour. He may know something that could assist us."

"Of course," affirmed the sailor. "I have many years of practice in seeking information from within such bug huts."

"We will reconvene back here tomorrow at the same time," continued Tonousa. "When we do Theo there will be some answers that I need from you. I want to know how you fit into all of this. Your story is far from complete and there is much more that we need to discuss."

"Why not ask me now and I will answer all that you need to know."

"It can wait and I trust you Theo."

"And you Tonousa?" asked Danisun. "What next for you? Why are you so keen to end this meeting now?"

"I stink and I need to dump in haste. I need a bath above everything else and some fresh armour. I cannot stand my own stench any longer. There is somewhere I have to go; it's the one place that I know where to start from."

Thoughts of her father's execution once again flooded Tonousa's mind.

9

Yellow and red flames flickered in the fireplace and as they jumped and crackled Llyat felt their warmth against his skin. His time in the Dragonas had taught him that days were warm but nights were much colder than he could ever have imagined. He was most grateful for the fire that Einar and Thias had managed to cobble together at short notice and out of almost nothing. Dusk had fallen an hour past and it was almost half a day since he and his companions had fled north from the Gathering on their unicorns. They had left the three peaked mountain with barely time to escape from the Knights of Avolire who had been spotted riding there at speed. Llyat had mixed emotions regarding the heroic sacrifice of the Berserkers Geir and Guldbrand who had stayed behind to confront the enemy and buy sufficient time for him to escape. He knew he would have been useless in fighting those who had massacred his family and friends and yet part of him still wished that he had stayed to confront the beast with the skull adorned helmet. Alone in his thoughts Llyat looked deep into the fire and attempted to find comfort on the wooden floor of the abandoned farm house which was now their place of refuge. The Berserker who had joined in the exodus from the Gathering had recommended this particular farmstead for it was well hidden in the north eastern quadrant of the Dragonas. Einar reckoned it was the safest place he knew although he never explained why.

The farmhouse, like the rest of the cluster of buildings that surrounded it, had long been abandoned and was in a state of advanced decay. Einar however had convinced the others that it would suit their purpose for the upcoming night. They had entered the ramshackled building after securing the unicorns inside an old derelict stable that had a trough built into one wall and which had of recent filled with rain water. It was a perfect place for their steeds to quench their thirst from the long ride that they had endured. Once inside the farmhouse Llyat had looked around with great curiosity. He had half expected to find more Berserkers hiding out in the remains of the old building but there was no sign of their presence. Apart from the small family of field mice that had been disturbed and forced out through a gap in the woodwork there was nothing of any significance that had captured Llyat's interest. After searching the farmhouse and adapting it as a shelter as best as they could both Einar and Thias had been quick to gather some old firewood from outside its door and which they had used it to make the fire that would provide warmth through the long cold night. Thias had used the Promethelumous spell to ignite the kindling while the Berserker saw to the placing of the wood. Llyat had then assisted Irabo in creating a straw mattress in the one room to still have a roof. After consuming a small vial of poppite the Warrior of the watch had fallen asleep. The drug, plus the fatigue of the ride had induced a deep and peaceful sleep.

But that was then and now Llyat gazed into the flames and wondered how long he had been at the hearth. Time passed slower than a slug crossing a leaf and Llyat drifted in and out of his thoughts. He could hear Thias moving about in the farmhouse having checked in on Irabo. The youth felt safe in the presence of the bard and was certain that some deeper connection had begun to link the two of them. Whatever the attraction was, Llyat was oblivious to its meaning. He looked over his shoulder to where the bard moved through the shadows and then back into the flames. The last words that Thamous had whispered to him as he had left the cavern under the Gathering continued to demand attention. The wyvern's message circled around his mind and yet as he thought about each word he struggled to understand their collective meaning. Pulling the Dragon Whisper from his pocket he stared at the stone but it just added to his confusion. He was certain that sooner or later Thamous's words would manifest their meaning but until that time their significance would remain a mystery.

Llyat's musings were interrupted by a creaking sound. It came from the door of the farmhouse. Turning his head he witnessed Einar step in from the cold. The giant walked over towards an old bench that stood close to where Llyat lay and he too looked at the fire. Llyat changed his position and sat crossed legged such that he could talk with greater ease.

"Is everything quiet out there?" he asked.

"The lands are still," replied the Berserker. "Not a creature stirs."

"That's good to hear," added Llyat as he placed the Dragon Whisper back into the pocket of his pants. "How are we doing for rations?"

"We're running low," replied Einar. "I thought we'd find something hidden here but I was wrong. It appears that the last Berserker stash was emptied a long time ago. All we have left is enough water to last us a day at the most and a bit of meat. Nothing more to sustain us after that! Whatever we decide to do now we must factor in supplies. We need fresh provisions if we are going maintain our energy levels and outrun those swine from Avolire."

Llyat and his stomach agreed. What use would any of them be if they ran out of food?

"How is your friend doing?" asked the Berserker.

"He is out for the count," added Llyat. "I think he has also used the last of that poppite stuff so I guess his pains will just get worse over the coming days."

"He's going to be fine," added Thias as he walked into the room and joined Einar on the bench that faced the fire. "Another couple of days and he should be able to take full weight on his leg."

"That is good to hear," replied Einar.

Llyat wanted to laugh. The Berserker's honest assessments were something that made him smile and he felt reassured to have Einar watch out for him.

"And what do you make of our current predicament?" asked Thias. "Are there any signs of the Knights of Avolire out there? Are we being followed?"

"It appears not. Like I was telling the lad just now, there is not a creature in sight. No dragons, no wormnose, no kulkulkath, and no fucking knights. It looks like Geir and Guldbrand bought us enough time."

"I'm sorry about what happened back there," added Thias.

"Don't be. They knew what they were doing when they stayed behind," responded Einar with pride in his voice. "I must assume that Geir and Guldbrand are long dead but I will meet them again in the Halls of the Fallen, on the day of my judgement and before the Moirai themselves. Then we will we be reunited beneath the beams of ever-flowing honour."

Llyat looked towards the Berserker for the words had intrigued him. He struggled to understand what the giant man had meant by the Halls of the Fallen and the day of his judgement. He scanned his memory of the many stories that he had heard from the bards and Denius Castor. He tried to recollect some image that would give meaning to the words. A vision soon appeared behind his eyes and in it he saw a white marble hall filled with Berserkers of old. There at long tables the dead ate the finest of foods and drank the sweetest mead. At the head of the table sat the Moirai, the children of Fatumai, with wrinkles as deep as a furrowed field. It seemed so real despite being nought but a simple day dream.

"So Llyat," said Einar. "Are you going to explain to us why we are heading north east and ever closer towards the one place we should wish to avoid above all others? What truths did Thamous reveal during your meeting?"

Llyat glanced towards Thias and waited for a nod of approval.

"Yes Llyat, do tell," said the bard while smiling. "I cannot go off faith alone. No matter what Irabo and Einar say about fate and destiny, I need facts to function."

Llyat understood his companions needed more information. Once again it felt like he was not in control of his life and that something or someone was attempting to manipulate his strings. If he was to avoid madness he had to hold onto the belief that he could control his own destiny. Each time Irabo said everything was pre-determined he felt anxious and helpless.

"Did he tell you where the remaining gems are to be found?" asked Thias.

Llyat took a deep breath and began his tale. Even though the events of the Gathering were so recent they seemed to have occurred an age ago. He found it easy to remember the detail of the words that the wyvern had implanted in his mind and that worried him a little for he was not usually so good at recalling facts. Thamous had first confirmed that he, Llyat Emgar from Maplehill, was indeed the one referred to in the Prophecy. Llyat described how the wyvern had revealed the location of two of the gems. The third he had confirmed was still in Parandor but that some substance continued to block the beast's ability to locate it. Throughout the telling of the tale, other than the sound of field mice that scuttled about in the rafters, a deep silence pervaded the farmhouse.

"So Barad Elestor and the tomb of Sir Raulyn and then somewhere in the centre of the Eastern Marsh. It's not much to go on, but at least it's a start," said Thias at the end. "Did Thamous tell you anything else?"

Once again the wyvern's words flicked back and forth around Llyat's mind. They teased him with their hidden meaning and confused him even more. The youth had promised not to divulge them.

"No," replied Llyat. "He left it at that."

"Are you sure?" asked the Berserker as he sensed the obvious lie. "Are you certain he did not tell you anything else?"

Llyat hesitated and found it impossible to reply as the Berserker watched him with searching eyes. He felt his heart pump faster and his rate of breathing increased. He sensed the sweat appear on his forehead and wondered if he was sat too close to the fire. Llyat had never been a good liar and there was always something in his mannerisms that gave him away whenever he told an untruth. He so wanted to disclose the wyvern's last message but he had made a solemn vow to keep it secret until the appropriate time.

"No, he didn't," he finally forced himself to utter.

Llyat paused as Einar and Thias raked him with their eyes. All he could think of doing in that moment was to turn his back upon his friends and once again look into the flames of the fire.

"Are you okay Llyat?" asked Thias. "Is there something bothering you?"

"Why didn't you let me stay and fight the bastards?" replied Llyat in an attempt to deflect the conversation away from his meeting with Thamous.

"I'm sorry, what do you mean?"

"The Knights of Avolire?" continued Llyat. "The men that killed my father and mother. The cunts that destroyed my home and murdered my friends. Why did you not let me stay and face them?"

Llyat focused on the burning embers and the smoke that drifted up through the chimney.

"I couldn't let you go to your death for that is what would have happened?" said Thias.

Llyat turned and jumped to his feet with the intention of confronting the bard. He was consumed by a sudden anger, fuelled by the thought of the man who had butchered his father, and he needed to vent that anger before he exploded in a violent rage.

"But there were six of us," he shouted. "Three Berserkers, Irabo, you, and me."

Llyat noticed a second glance of concern that passed between Thias and Einar. His nostrils flared and his fists clenched. Yet his anger was not uncontrolled.

"And then what Llyat?" answered Thias. "From what you told us of events at your village, the Commander with the skull helmet has a magic far greater than my own or anyone else in our company. I can manipulate heat and fire, but that bugger can do a great deal more. Even if I could perform more wondrous feats, Irabo can only just walk and would be a hindrance in any fight."

"I can speak for myself, thank you!" shouted a voice from the adjacent room.

"Sorry," replied Thias. "I didn't realise that you were awake."

"I will forgive you bard," replied Irabo as he laughed out loud. "The poppite is taking its time to work. I must be getting used to it. I somehow don't feel at all drowsy."

"As I was saying Llyat," continued Thias. "Irabo has confirmed that he taught you basic sword skill but you are not yet ready to fight the Knights of Avolire. I doubt that even Guldbrand, Geir, or Einar could take on eight of their riders."

"You have never seen a Berserker in action," said Einar as he almost fell off the wooden bench.

"No, I haven't and I have no desire to do so."

"I guess you're right," added Llyat as his anger abated. "I would have been useless. In fact I am no fucking use to anyone anymore."

"Now enough of that Llyat."

Thias moved to where Llyat stood, gripped him by the shoulders, and looked into his eyes.

"There is something that I have noticed about you lad. You have to start believing in yourself more and let go of all the black shit. You can accomplish anything if you put your mind to it. Even the great warriors of the past needed to find a hidden strength to accomplish feats against impossible odds. Look at Sir Raulyn who cast Urthanock down. If you believe the stories we bards sing about, he started out as a mere shepherd boy. Even the most timid can leave a substantial mark on this world if they can find but a morsel of courage."

"Perhaps if there was some weakness we could exploit," replied Llyat while he tried to hold back the tears that began to form his eyes. "If there was then we may stand a chance if they catch up with us.

"There is," added Einar in his matter of fact manner. "The join between the helmet and the breast plate. Something we Berserkers know of and pass down through our ranks. One sharp blow there will penetrate their armour shield."

Llyat felt the bard release the grip on his shoulders.

"That doesn't really help," growled Thias.

"I'm just telling how it is," added Einar.

"Well don't, not just now."

Llyat felt overwhelmed again. It was as if the burden he carried was about to submerge him in a pool of irretrievable despair. He felt trapped and isolated within his own mind for the bard and the Berserker didn't know how he felt. It wasn't their burden to bear; it was his alone. Llyat started to gasp for air as panic wrapped around his heart. His pulse began to race, he felt that had to flee, to escape the torment of the conversation. Without warning he raced towards the farmhouse door and opened it with such force that it's rusted hinges rattled in the stone door frame.

"Where are you going now?" he heard Thias shout.

"I need some fresh air."

Llyat knew how stupid his comment must have sounded for most of the roof of the old farmhouse had long since disappeared. He walked across the road that ran through the old farm buildings and on towards a small wooden fence that separated the dirt track from the yellow grassland of the Dragonas. There he took many deep breaths in order to steady himself. When he then closed his eyes and tried to shut out the world he became aware of approaching footsteps. If only he had picked up Destiny's Song from against the wall besides Einar's battle axes. He took another deep breath and turned to face whoever it was who approached. Much to his relief it was Thias and he wiped the tears from his eyes.

"Llyat, look, I know there is something bothering you, so just tell me what's wrong. I can't help you if you continue to bottle things up and get so consumed by anger."

"I'm just so overwhelmed given my role in this quest" sniffed Llyat. "Why me? Why have I been chosen? Why do have to be the fucking Marked?"

"I wish I knew Llyat, I just wish I knew."

"And why do you care so much about me anyway? Why have you taken to me so? What is it that you want from me?"

Llyat expected the bard to argue back in some way but he didn't. Instead Thias placed his hand upon Llyat's shoulder and smiled.

"Walk with me a while," he said in his softest of voices.

There was something about the smile that relaxed Llyat and together the pair started down the dirt track between the buildings and on beyond the stables where the unicorns were tethered. On and on they walked and while they tramped Llyat felt his anger drift away on the light night breeze.

"It's strange that I feel so protective about you my young friend," said Thias at last. "It is something I have thought about long and hard, ever since we first met. I don't claim to understand the true nature of my interest Llyat and so I tell you what I know to be true. Ever since that first night when I saw you in the Red Mare in Maplehill, sat with three brothers Methladon, Fiat and Grophaldo Heyn…"

"How do you know their names?" asked Llyat, taken aback and believing the bard had also infiltrated his thoughts. "I don't remember them introducing themselves that night and I don't think I have ever discussed my dead friends with you before."

"There is much about my link to those three that you do not know and understand."

"What do you mean? Are you telling me that you already knew them?"

"I think you may understand better Llyat if I start from the beginning," began Thias. "Do you remember what I said back in Valameer? I told you where I found the Dagger of Kha. It was given to me by its owner."

"I know you found it in Maplehill but apart from someone hiding it all of these year how is this relevant to your knowledge of the Heyn brothers?"

"I'm sure the name Vostag rings bells inside your skull?"

"He was their father."

"Come on Llyat do I have to spell it out," sniggered Thias in a manner which irritated Llyat. "I was given the dagger by their father."

"You mean Vostag had one of the Gems the entire time I was living in Maplehill?"

"That is correct. Like I said, I took possession of it during my meeting with Vostag. I had heard a rumour that he had moved from the Capital with his wife and boys and I confirmed that to be true when I saw the four of you that night in the tavern. I had been appointed by Phauless Gylewu to investigate the Death Tubaria murders. The Heyn family had a strong connection with the previous rise of the cult that had been led by Lord Tullage. I knew that Vostag had the dagger way back then and that it had curse-marked his youngest son, your best friend Methladon…"

"Whoa, slow down a minute," yelled Llyat as the bard's words hit him like a rock fall. "Are you telling me that Methladon was cursed by the dagger? He was a…"

"Yes, that is exactly what I am saying," replied Thias as the two continued their walk. "Methladon Heyn was the final victim of Death Tubaria all those years ago. I say victim in a different sense for although the cult had targeted him for death by dismemberment he was saved by the City Watch. They rescued him somehow and prevented his murder but the curse mark could not be reversed."

Llyat felt amazed on hearing Thias's words. He had known Methladon Heyn for almost ten years and in all that time his closest friend had never once discussed the events that the bard had described. He found it hard to believe that given their close friendship that he knew nothing of the attempt on Methladon's life. It was the kind of story that best friends would share in order to strengthen their bond.

"So how do you know all of this?" asked Llyat after a moment's thought. "Were you a family friend?"

"Much more than a friend Llyat. When my father was executed for theft, the Heyns took me in and treated me as one of their own. They became my foster parents and their children my brothers. I lived with them for two years until I decided to choose the way of the bards and leave for Valameer. It broke Ruta's heart when I left and she never forgave me for it. It was during the two years that I was with the family that the cult of Death Tubaria surfaced. Methladon found the dagger one day and was cursed by its magic. Don't tell me you've forgotten about the curse marks of Death Tubaria, the three circles..."

"Meth, Methladon I mean, yes...he had a birthmark like that!" exclaimed Llyat. "Well, he said was a birthmark."

"And there you have it Llyat, the curse mark of the Death Tubaria."

"But if Methladon's father had the dagger all this time, who has been carrying out the murders in the Capital? There was no way it could have been Vostag. The Grand Physician said that all the bodies were found with the same three circle mark. If the dagger with the emerald did not cause their marks then who or what did?"

"In all truth, I don't know Llyat. It has been something that has been troubling me ever since the Gathering. It was there staring me in the face and I didn't noticed it. The marks had appeared in the absence of the dagger. Someone has somehow replicated the evil magical process and I pray that our friends in the City Watch realise the significance of what we now know. They are using foul trickery unconnected to the methods supposedly written down in the Lore of the Dead. I wish I had figured it out sooner just so that I could have warned Tonousa. I would have sent her a message by carrier bird."

Llyat thought hard. Questions bubbled up and troubled him. It couldn't be as simple as Thias alluded. It seems they had all been distracted from the truth about the murders in the Capital and become blind to their real nature. Llyat was not sure what to think but he still believed that everything that had occurred since he was pulled from the river Tiaryer was somehow connected in a strange and mysterious way. Once again he felt like a puppet in some other greater game. Then there were his friends who had been slaughtered in Maplehill. The notion that his best friend and his father were involved in the sequence of events began to trouble him. He became consumed with thoughts about the Dagger of Kha and whether he would have still ended up in the Dragonas if it had never been brought to Maplehill. He remembered that the knight in the skull helmet had been looking for a family and one youth in particular. They had called him the 'Marked' and he realised that it could have been Methladon that they sought, not himself. Then there were the words spoken by the Lizardman who had killed the Grand Physician of Parandor.

'The traitor's bastard' it had said and the words were pointed at him although he still had no idea why. Finally he realised that he did not have a clue as to what was going on.

Llyat opened his mouth to speak but stopped when Thias pulled out a pendent

"What is that?" asked Llyat.

"It's just a memory that's all, one from the Bards Guild and another family now destroyed."

"I'm sorry..." added Llyat, but the bard cut him off.

"In response to the question you posed when you asked why I care so much about you; there was something that I was going to tell you before you went underground to meet with Thamous. If you remember, I told you that it could wait. You see Llyat, when I saw you in Valameer and you revealed yourself as the Marked of Maplehill, a title until then I believed was reserved for Methladon Heyn, I knew that fate was taunting me as she dangled your connection and friendship with the family that took me in and called me their own. I was like a brother to those boys and in our time together Llyat I sense a similar feeling. Even if you do not also feel it I will still protect you as any brother would. Llyat, you are like this pendent for you remind me of those who I held most dear. You are both precious and I shall protect you until my last breath drifts away from my mouth."

Llyat did not know what to say. From the emotion in his voice it was clear that Thias spoke with sincerity but it was all too much to take on board. The thought of the bard being the foster brother of his dead friends filled him with sadness and tears once again welled in his eyes. Indirectly the bard was a piece of Maplehill, part of his extended family and the place that was once his home.

Llyat reached and touched the pendant briefly before Thias put it away.

"We ought to head back," said the bard. "Einar and Irabo will be wondering where we are."

Llyat looked to the cloudless sky with just the stars and Mona to illuminate the darkness. He was surprised to see how far they had walked from the ruined farmhouse and their friends. Despite Mona's pale light the building had hidden itself in the darkness.

"You're right" replied Llyat "It's getting spooky out here."

Llyat and Thias turned and trekked back in silence along the dirt road. Soon they came within site of the farm house where Einar stood waiting by the door. For the briefest of moments Llyat was reminded of his mother back in Maplehill. She had stayed up and waited so many times after his long evenings in the Red Mare with the three Heyn brothers. It had always played out in the same manner. His mother would greet him with a stern look and ask 'Where have you been 'til now?' But that was not the question that the Berserker asked.

"What the fuck have you two been up to?"

"Nothing," replied Llyat.

"Despite the tension between us at the Gathering I must thank you Einar for all that you have done so far," added Thias. "I don't think many would have helped us as you have done."

"That was not an issue. I was under instructions from Cvyler Olin to escort you to and from the Gathering but given the events at the three peaks you are going to need all the help you can get to find the remaining gems. You will need my skills if you are to have any chance of stopping the forces of Avolire."

"Does that mean you will join our quest?" asked a voice from within the doorway.

Llyat glanced past Einar and saw Irabo propped up by his crutch.

"If it means helping destroy those swine from the pens of Avolire, then of course I am," replied Einar. "Given the nature of the quest and the fact that I saved your lives when you took the pass around Skillar, I cannot abandon you all now."

"For that we are most grateful," responded Thias as he offered his hand to the Berserker.

"So what now," asked Llyat?

"I would prefer if it we were indoors before I answer that question," replied Thias. "The night air may be still but sounds travels far. Even though all is quiet it doesn't mean there isn't anyone or anything listening. Who knows what foul creatures the Lady of the Silverwynn has placed as her spies out here in the Dragonas."

"If there were such creatures a Berserker would know," added Einar.

"Either way, I would rather be safe than sorry," added Thias. "We can talk inside."

The four men made their way back to their places around the fireside. Llyat once again took to sitting cross legged on the floor before the wooden bench where Thias and Irabo sat. Einar stood by the fire with his elbow resting on its stone mantle.

"So now what," repeated Llyat?

Thias took a deep breath and then tabled his proposition.

"This is how I see it. Following on from Thamous's information regarding the location of two of the Gems, as I remember from maps of the Realm, the nearest of the two would be the Temple of Barad Elestor and the tomb of Sir Raulyn, deep inside the wilds of Thengar. The vast forest is about a day's ride north east from here, over the canyon that once housed a great river and then on towards the snow covered mountains that mark the boarders of Dirmark. As I recall there is a village called Fallguard on the outskirts of the forest. It sits on the road that once served as the main trade route between Avolire and the lands of the dwarves. Who knows what we will find there but the main thing is we will be able to get some supplies. I'm sure that one of the unicorns will fetch a fair price."

"That at least sounds like a plan," added Irabo.

Llyat did not disagree but he still had major concerns about those who may still be following.

"The Knights of Avolire may pick up our trail and track us across the Dragonas."

"I must be honest with you Llyat," replied Thias sighing. "I believe that their presence at the Gathering was to gain the same information that we ourselves were after. They were not I think looking for us. This tells me a couple of things. They would have to confront Thamous to gain knowledge of the location of the remaining Gems and I don't see the wyvern divulging that information, do you? Had Tullage disclosed the location of the gems to Grovrouk, the Knights would not have bothered to cross the Dragonas. There is another thing that troubles me. As the Dagger of Kha was not linked to the recent murders in the Capital, this Death Tubaria business back in Parandor must just be a cunning diversion. I suspect the Lady of the Silverwynn is using the memories of the old cult to instil fear and misinformation. With the use of her devious agents of evil she must be attempting to create sufficient distraction to allow her to build-up of her forces in Avolire before unleashing them on Parandor. If she ever were to gain possession of the remaining Gems then she would unleash a power greater than any of us could imagine."

In the silence that followed Thias's speculations, the crackling of the wood on the fire became ever more noticeable. Then Einar spoke up.

"I'll tell you something thing bard and no doubt Irabo will back me up being himself a follower of Fatumai. It all doesn't seem right. The Moirai are acting in a strange manner and this is no ordinary quest that we find ourselves on. There is a great game being played out by the three crones. We are being manipulated and pulled in strange directions. I fear we will be sacrificed as and when the three choose. Our fates have already been decided."

Llyat smiled to himself for he did not share the giant's concerns. Then as Einar signalled that he would take the first watch, Llyat allowed his thoughts to drift back to Thamous's parting whisper. Perhaps this was the time that everything was going to change?

10

Her father's old chamber in the Citadel was basic in its extreme. Its meagre contents included a single cupboard, a bedside set of drawers, and a straw filled mattress covered in faded linen. Tonousa was surprised to find it in such an austere state for the room was most unlike that befitting the man she thought she once knew. When she had first been inducted into the City Watch and her father promoted to Head Librarian his chambers had been filled with items of luxury and drapes made of the finest of materials. The vision that now greeted her as she walked into the room was different from all that she remembered from her youth. Something strange had taken place and her father had changed from the man she knew of old. If the Royal Chamberlin, Gilebin Ystafell, was to be believed then the only thing that had been removed from the room after her father's arrest was the Lore of the Dead. Nothing else had been disturbed or taken; this was how he had lived.

While standing in the doorway of the stone walled room Tonousa's thoughts ruminated on her father's last words; *'should any person seek to remember me and enquire as to the cause that I die for then I require them only to follow and seek the truth within the walls of the Citadel'*. She could not get rid of the notion that her father had spoken out to someone in the crowd, to declare his innocence and direct them to seek out the evil that was undermining Parandor? Whatever the meaning behind his words, it still alluded her.

Tonousa stepped with care about the room and searched in minute detail. She concentrated hard as she looked for clues but there was nothing that seemed out of place or unusual. The air was still and quiet save for the caw from a solitary crow which sat upon an outside windowsill and called to the morning. She was surprised and yet relieved to have been allowed access to her father's chambers given the events of the Richemanus Folly and her subsequent incarceration in the Underkeep. At first she believed that Danisun Dain had tugged on the strings of the new Sovereign Advisor, or that Commander Townsforth had used his rank to gain Tonousa access to her father's belongings; then as she had collected the key from the Lord Chamberlin she found out the truth of the matter. It had been Gilebin Ystafell himself that allowed her access and for no other reason that she was Lord Amberstone's one living relative and someone had to sort out his personal possessions. Ystafell had ordered that anything that remained after her visit would be disposed of as Mona rose that same evening.

Attracted by its dark plumage Tonousa moved towards the solitary widow and caused the ever watchful bird to take flight. Once it had disappeared out over the roof tops of Parandor she looked down towards the courtyard where various members of the Royal Guard were sparring with each other. She watched for some minutes as they slashed away with their swords in preparation for the inevitable war with Avolire. Tonousa sighed and wondered in that brief moment what would have happened if Commander Townsforth had not pulled her into the Death Tubaria investigation. She would no doubt also have been down there with them, homing her skills for battle. Soon she began to think about her colleague Irabo and how he would fare in the north without her. There were so many dark possibilities that they made her shiver but there was one particular thought that returned to haunt her. If she had listened to her father when he had come to inform her of the theft of the Lore of the Dead then maybe she could have prevented his arrest and caught the killer before travelling to meet with the bards.

Tonousa turned and walked back into the centre of the room. She heard the peel of temple bells which signified the start of the many and varied religious practices permitted within the edifices of Parandor. She was not a believer in fantasy and preferred not to be ruled by fate or holy fiction. Her mind had always sought evidence rather than the divine whims of invented gods but right at that moment she felt that a little faith in some religion or another would not go amiss. Even if her prayers came to nothing it was surely worth a chance. She sighed and sat down upon the bed, faced the stone wall, closed her eyes, and clasped her hands together. There she began to utter her words of prayer.

"Solaris, thank you for the warmth you bestow upon us," she muttered against the muffled sound of the bells. "Mona, thank you for your light that gives clarity to the night and for showing me the way through my darkest hours. And as for the rest of you buggers, whichever one of you that may be listening right now, please send me a sign or way to..."

Tonousa stopped midsentence, surprised at what was she doing. There were no gods. It was all just a trick to help guide the gullible through the misery of their pitiful existence. There was no one listening and there would be no help nor sign that would appear as if by magic. She would have to do this herself and her instincts would have to show her the way. The dream in which she had seen the Lady Fullbane had been but a false hope for a significant path had failed to form in her mind and she was still no closer to solving the mystery. She sighed amid her troubled thoughts, opened her eyes wide and then focused on the stone wall before her. There was something about the central blocks that did not look right; there was no mortar around their joints. Several appeared much newer, less weathered, and had not been faded by the light of Solaris that bathed them each day from the window. She looked to the floor below the bricks and saw a small pile of dust and sought to figure out where or what had been disturbed. *'Seek the truth within the walls of the Citadel.'* Then in a flash Tonousa jumped from the bed and began to pull the loose stone blocks away from the wall. As she dropped them to the ground she was at once filled with hope. Then at last she revealed the hidden compartment that her father had constructed.

"Thank you, whichever god was still awake" she mumbled as her eyes looked up to the ceiling.

It seemed her prayers had indeed been answered and that a miracle had occurred. Peering into the space, one no larger than her own head, several small objects lay and awaited her inspection. The first was a strange device made of a substance which Tonousa presumed was the famed ivory of the legendary wormnoses. It was formed of two flat discs, one a little larger than the other, and joined together by a single central pin which allowed the two parts to turn around and over each other. Tonousa had never seen such an object before and as she held it to the light of Solaris she saw that around their edges each of the two discs were engraved with the twenty six letters of the common language of the Realm.

Whatever the device was it was a most peculiar instrument. Tonousa placed it into the leather satchel that hung from her side.

Once again she looked deep into the hidden compartment. This time she pulled out four small pieces of parchment, each one oblong in shape, stained white, and the size of a hand. She inspected each in turn and concentrated on the pictures and the words written beneath them that had been painted on one side. Tonousa had never thought of her father as a player of cards, dice, or chance. The first carried the image of a set of scales and the word 'Judgement'. The second was of a single sword with the word 'Justice' below. The third card bore a picture of a fisted gauntlet with the word 'Strength' and upon the fourth card the word 'Temperance' had been written beneath the image of a winged person pouring some liquid between two vessels. The cards meant nothing to Tonousa and their significance was a complete mystery. They seemed like something that Captain Highroar would have owned and better placed in some tavern or on the Banshees Wail rather than in her father's chambers. Either way Tonousa secreted them alongside the alphabet device in her satchel and reached back into the depth of the compartment. She then removed the final object that her father had hidden there. Once in her hand she gave it her full attention.

It was a rolled up parchment, stained, ink grimed, and with letters scrawled on one side. Tonousa looked long and hard at their combinations but they seemed to make no meaning. She wondered if it was the language of the Dirmark and that she would need to find a dwarf to translate it. Then she remembered that she had once been told that Dirmark words were all more than five letters in length so it couldn't be that tongue. Their meaning remained an enigma and Tonousa sensed that her investigation had stalled once again.

"Why do you taunt me so," she said as once again she looked up to the ceiling.

No answer came and with a long deep sigh she placed the parchment alongside the cards and lettering device inside her satchel. Wasting no time Tonousa replaced the stone blocks and swept up the dust that had fallen to the floor lest anyone else follow in her footsteps. Then she took one last look around her father's chamber. This was her one chance and it was important that she missed nothing of importance. Apart from a few clothes still inside the cupboard she found nothing else of value. With a second long sigh Tonousa made her way out of her father's chamber and locked the door behind her. The rest of the contents would be left to Lord Ystafell to dispose of as he pleased. The strange objects within her satchel were now her main hope of unlocking the mystery but she had no idea of how she would begin to understand their meaning.

It did not take Tonousa long to reach The Murdered Wolf. Isambard was hard at work behind the counter as usual. He made eye contact as she entered but neither of them spoke. Tonousa then made her way across the tavern floor, passed the few customers that had dared to venture out, and entered the corridor that led to the rooms at the back of the building. She opened the first door on her right and entered into the space beyond. The room, like that of her father's, had few contents. There was a small round wooden table with several chairs. Danisun had hired it on behalf of the Watch as a place from which to conduct their investigation. Given that Isambard now had few customers he had been grateful for the income that it provided. In fact the barkeep had been most helpful and as agreed in the contract he had provided spare blank parchment, a quill, a jar of ink, and a flagon of water with six tankards. If beer was needed it would be extra. All had been left in place for the City Watch on the table in the centre of the room. Tonousa was pleased if not somewhat surprised that Isambard had been so cooperative given the fact that he blamed the Watch for his lack of business. She made herself comfortable on one of the chairs at the far end of the table and poured some of the murky water from the flagon into one of the pewter tankards. After the first sip its stench caused her to vow only to drink beer should her thirst get the better of her senses. She removed the objects she had found inside her father's wall and paced them upon the table. First she looked at the piece of parchment and its strange grouping of letters before then focusing on the first line.

IDIWT RJGKG TIWPI IPZTH BNEDH XIXDC DCRTX PBVDC

Tonousa became transfixed by the sixth group for there she saw the letters XIX. She knew her reading skills were not the best but she did know her letters and the three that stood out spelled a name that she recognised. This puzzled her and she wondered what her father could have stumbled on and how it could concern Xix Blackfayer?

A knock at the door gained Tonousa's attention.

"It opens," she shouted.

There followed a brief moment of silence before the door moved and Theoplous strode into the room. A new sword hung at his side and as he entered he greeted Tonousa with a smile.

"Ah Theo, good morning," said Tonousa with a cheerful air.

"And good morning to you," replied the sailor.

"Any luck with Isambard last night? Did he have anything of use to tell?"

"I asked him about the Oracle of Frasteria and if he knew anything about it, just as you had asked," continued Theoplous as he too took a chair and sat down. "He is mightily pissed off about his lack custom and still blames the Watch for not maintaining order."

"Let him vent his frustrations how best he chooses. The Watch can but do their best in such dire times," added Tonousa. "We cannot stop all the rumour and speculation."

"All I could get out of him, and which he prattled on about at great length, was that there was an old hermit who could be found around the Barrow of Harico and who it is said knows something about the Oracle. That was the one thing of note he could remember from conversations overheard in his bug hut. I could push him further if you wish, perhaps break a few bones..."

"That won't be necessary. Hotch may have a grudge against the Watch but he is a harmless dolt. He won't be a threat to us and I'm sure if he remembers anything useful he will pass it on. The lardy lump is too stupid to concoct lies and his head contains more bone than filling."

Tonousa then saw that Theoplous was looking with great interest at the strange disc-like object she had taken from her father's study. It lay on the surface of the table and induced the sailor to comment on its presence.

"Well I'm glad we have that conversation out of the way before the others arrive but I see from the presence of the Lotus Isle code wheel that you have many more interesting questions for me."

Tonousa was both stunned and surprised. A hope sprang into her heart as she sensed that the sailor knew what the object was. Then she also felt alarmed for the First Mate's connection with her investigation now appeared to run deeper than she had ever thought likely.

"Code wheel?" snapped out Tonousa. "Is that what it is? I found it in my father's chambers. How do you know of such things?"

"I'm sorry, I thought it was the code wheel you wished to discuss, and my connection to the Cuvar."

"Cuvar?" quizzed Tonousa. "I have not heard that word before."

"The followers of Anyle Belanore, the ones who understand the Enderdetag Prophecy..."

"What in the name of Solaris are you talking about?" exclaimed Tonousa. "You're not making the slightest bit of sense."

"So this wasn't what you wanted to talk to me about?" asked the bemused sailor.

"Not at all. I wanted to know your story, your part in all of this. I just came across this object, this code wheel as you call it, this morning in my father's rooms."

Silence fell and seconds passed in awkward stillness.

"In a way Tonousa my story is connected to the code wheel for both are linked to the Cuvar."

"You have my full attention so tell me your story. Back in Valameer you said that you were searching for the boy and that you had overheard conversations to suggest that Llyat was the one known as the Marked," said Tonousa.

"That is correct. It stems from my studies back on the Lotus Isles and in particular the teachings of Anyle Belanore. Furthermore, it is because I am Cuvar that I am committed to protecting the Marked. We don't follow any of your gods but we worship the heavens and the stars themselves. Not long after the fall of the Dark Lord Urthanock, Anyle Belanore was studying the orbs of the heavens and he came to understand the meaning of what we now know of as the Enderdetag Prophecy. As you are aware the verse describes the rise of the Lord of Fear and the one known as the Marked of Maplehill."

"And do you still believe this Marked to be Llyat?"

"Ever since I met you all on board the Banshees Wail I sensed something about that boy that was special and my attention was further drawn to him during to your conversations with Highroar. Suspicions about his destiny were confirmed in Valameer's Guild when he displayed intense Kundalish Aura and revealed himself to the bards, just as the Prophecy had predicted. In case you are unaware Tonousa, we are entering into the alignment of Enderdetag at this very moment in time. The great orbs of the sky are in conjunction and Urthanock wakes once more. He is waiting..."

"Yes, yes, yes," interrupted Tonousa, concerned that the conversation was about to descend into areas she would not understand nor be able to control. "Enough of all this prophecy stuff. Let us deal in facts alone."

"Yet even after all you have heard and witnessed since Valameer?"

"Yes, even after Valameer. I have to keep an objective mind if I am to root out the infiltrator. I cannot let all of this nonsense cloud my thoughts."

"You will believe one day," replied Theoplous with a knowing smile. "I have much faith in you."

"Please return to your story," said Tonousa as she gripped the ivory object and passed it across the table to the sailor. "So you are a Cuvar? What has that got to do with my father and this code wheel?"

"Am I right in thinking the wheel wasn't on its own when you found it?" asked Theoplous as he took hold of the device.

"Yes. There were four strange picture cards with the words Temperance, Justice, Strength and Judgement on the bottom and this parchment filled with what I thought at first was nonsense apart from three letters that make up the word Xix. If you are sure that this object is a code wheel then perhaps with it you could decipher the text on the parchment."

Theoplous looked down at the four picture cards and studied each in turn before he at last brought his attention to the parchment and its strange text. Tonousa could only wait and hope that Theoplous would be able to make sense of what her father had been trying to communicate.

"The cards are of little meaning to me," he said at last. "I'm sure Highroar will be able to shed some light on their purpose and significance. Being addicted to games of chance I'm sure that he will know of them. However the words on this parchment interest me more and as the text was found in the presence of the code wheel, it can mean one of two things. Either your father knew someone who was Cuvar, or like me your father himself had followed the teachings of Anyle Belanore. Is there anything he ever said or did that would confirm this?"

"He never once mentioned the Cuvar to me," replied Tonousa.

The thought of her father being somehow tied into the Enderdetag Prophecy was hard for Tonousa to come to terms with.

"He kept himself to himself."

"That sounds about right," affirmed Theoplous. "The Cuvar hide in plain sight and we promise never to reveal ourselves until the appropriate time. We are scattered and hold many varied positions throughout the Realm. We are the protectors of the Marked and will sacrifice ourselves in order to ensure the Enderdetag Prophecy is fulfilled."

"I find it hard to believe that my father was protecting Llyat for he had never met the boy."

"There could be a different explanation for all of this," continued Theoplous "It may be that your father found the items and was keeping them safe for somebody else. There is also the possibility that he was himself investigating some other in the Citadel. You have said before that he been trying to work out who had stolen the Lore of the Dead. He even told you of its theft. Is there anyone you think he suspected?"

Tonousa closed her eyes and once again lost herself in her thoughts. She heard the voice of Thinata Fullbane speaking to her through her dreams and telling of the opening of a path. Her mind raced as she tried to remember if there was anyone that her father had suspected of stealing the Lore but only Blackfayer came and stayed in her thoughts. Coupled with the recognition of the three letters in the coded parchment he had to be the one behind the murders. He must have known he was about to have been uncovered and that was the reason behind his suicide. That had to be it. Her father had got close to unmasking the traitor.

"So please explain the code wheel to me?" said Tonousa. "How does it work?"

"The Cuvar use these wheels as a way of keeping their messages secret from prying eyes," answered Theoplous after which he proceeded to demonstrate the mechanism of the device. "As you can see on each of two bone discs there are the twenty six letters of our common language. The single pin in the centre of the two wheels allows them to rotate and align each letter with another, top to bottom, do you see? Just like this. The top letter being the one you wish to code, whereas the letter on the wheel below it is the new letter for the disguised word. The wheel contains twenty six different code possibilities. The coded letters are then arranged into groups of five letters to disguise them even more and to confuse anyone attempting to decipher the message."

"So can you translate it? The code I mean?"

"I should be able to in time," affirmed Theoplous. "All I need is a bit of parchment, a quill, and some ink which it appears you have already procured for me. I'll have a go now and see if I can find out what your father was hiding. I just need to discover the right initial setting for the first wheel."

"May I ask what that is?" said a familiar voice that came from the open doorway.

Tonousa glanced up and saw Danisun Dain as he looked on with great interest. Darchus stood behind him, dressed in the leather armour of the City Watch.

"Good morning Danisun, and also to you Darchus," she answered.

"Good to see again Tonousa," answered the man from Valameer.

"How long have you been standing there" she asked?

"Long enough to hear about a possible code that may throw some light on your father's activities," replied Danisun as he and Darchus entered the room.

"So now you're one of us," said Tonousa, pointing to Darchus's uniform. "A member of the City Watch of Parandor!"

"And proud to be able to assist," added Darchus with gusto and as he sat at the table.

"That's enough of the sweet chatter" grumbled Danisun. "Are you going to explain what you have found or do we revert to guessing games?"

"I'm sorry Danisun, I didn't mean to give offence with my curt greeting," said Tonousa "I have just found out what this object is myself, thanks to Theo."

"Explain what you have found then?" demanded Danisun.

"Very well, I've....." began Tonousa, but before she could continue she was interrupted a second time.

The bright voice of Heliana breezed through the air and took command of the room.

"Sorry I'm late," she said as she rushed in and sank into the empty seat at the table next to Darchus. "I've just been released by my Lady but only for an hour. She said that Ourri would take care of her personal needs this morning and that I was free to return to more menial tasks. I must not though be late to serve her lunch."

"No need to apologise," added Tonousa as she noted the servant's attire. "It seems you have settled back into your role with ease. Which Lady did the Lord Chamberlin allocate you to this time?"

"The Lady Fullbane of all people. Lord Ystafell said Fullbane was still not herself, ever since the murder of poor Golda Flintwind and...."

"Yes, yes, and I suppose this is all very exciting," grumbled Danisun as he grew ever more impatient. "We are here for a specific task so let us begin to focus on the issues at hand. Tonousa, explain what you were discussing with the sailor when I entered the room."

"Sure," replied Tonousa who then set about her explanation.

She covered all the events of that morning, what she had found inside her father's chamber, and the true purpose behind Theoplous's involvement in their investigation.

"So your purpose in this dog's dinner of a plot is to protect Llyat!" said Heliana once Tonousa had finished her story.

"That is correct," replied Theoplous.

"Then why under the shadow of Mona's breasts are you here and not protecting him in Falahorn?"

"Well, I..."

"Bollocks!" interrupted Heliana as she turned to make eye contact with Tonousa. "I've met his kind before! All talk and nothing between the ears. So what does the message say then?"

"Theo and I were just about to attempt to translate it when Danisun and Darchus arrived."

"If Theoplous is as he has declared then he should crack the code in no time," added Danisun with suspicion evident in his tone.

"I'll try my best," said the sailor as he took hold of the quill and pulled several sheets of the parchment towards him along with the ivory object.

"And what about the rest of us," added Heliana. "Are we all just going to sit around here like peeled turnips while he tries to work the meaning of the words?"

"I think we all need to clear our heads and start again from the beginning," replied Tonousa as she sensed the tension that Heliana brought to the table. "We need to establish the hard facts from all the surrounding tripe."

"I agree Tonousa," added Danisun. "Though please remember, this is still officially my investigation. So take us through it with care, step by simple step."

Tonousa looked to the four members of her audience and wondered where to begin. She searched her memories of all the events surrounding the Death Tubaria crimes. There was just one way she felt she could start and while Theoplous focused on the code wheel she began to address the others.

"First of all, as far as we know, there have been seven deaths that bore the curse mark of the cult. Let me remind you of them. There was Lord Fabius Colt, Lord Tobius Faros, Sir Britta Rainmark, Golda Flintwind, Webb Underscroft, Mikus Danbury, and my father. Each one was linked in some way or other to the Citadel but there must be a deeper connection between these seven. There has to be some common knot in the thread that we are missing and which we must unravel. Then we ought to consider the theft of the Lore of the Dead from my father's library. It would simplify things if we assume our spy and the thief to be the same person. That's the way that it looks to me."

"Yet the book was found in your father's chambers!" added Danisun

"Yes, and I was coming to that. The Lore of the Dead was indeed found in my father's rooms but should we in all honesty believe that he had become so careless. Would he have left the book out on purpose, long after its disappearance and allow it to be so discovered? I don't think so. I never got on with my father but I don't believe that he would be that stupid if he had been the one who had stolen the Lore of the Dead in the first place. Everything I have discovered this morning leads me to believe my father was already getting close to identifying the perpetrator of the crimes. As I have already pointed out, there are three letters in the code that spell out the name of the last Sovereign Advisor. It is also possible that my father told Xix Blackfayer the truth of what he knew and that Xix didn't believe him. Call it an intuitive guess but I think my father came close to unmasking our villain and was then framed by that same person. There remains yet another possibility, that after the events at the Richemanus Folly, Xix realised that my father had been telling the truth and the guilt of not believing him caused the slimy snake to take his own life."

"Xix Blackfayer! Feelings of guilt!" sneered Dansiun. "We not talking of the same man?"

Tonousa glared at her colleague from across the table and her eyes silenced him.

"I'm sorry, please carry on," he muttered under his breath.

"I believe Blackfayer was innocent of these murders and our suspicions have been false trails," continued Tonousa. "I am convinced that the one who framed my father is the same assassin who tried to kill Phauless Gylewu. I further believe that this bastard is also supplying the potions that Golda Flintwind and Webb Underscroft were peddling. Even Webb's dead collector father thought there might be such a connection when I spoke with him."

"Unless there is another, you must mean Cassius who lives down by the docks," said Danisun.

"The very same," continued Tonousa, "Now the horses Danisun. Tell me more about the horse rustling that's going on in the city. From what you have already told me I gather this is more than just an isolated incident?"

Tonousa looked across the table at Theoplous who continued to write down letters on the parchment as he examined the wheel.

"There is not much to tell. Just that horses have been disappearing right across the city. The Watch seem to think it is the work of Nedes Karoly and his cronies but each of them has a good alibi for the times the crimes were committed. Townsforth has sent men to question the Thieves Guild but they are finding their leaders impossible to find. Cassius Underscroft reports they have gone underground."

"I think we can dismiss Nedes Karoly and the Thieves Guild from this one," said Tonousa. "I thought about what you told me yesterday and I do recall that Treveyn the Stable Master had reported his horses missing the day we found Mikus Danbury. It is possible that Mikus was murdered the way he was..."

"He had a fucking big rock dropped on him," exclaimed Heliana.

"Who told you that?" demanded Danisun as he shot a glance across the room. "I thought no one outside of the Watch and Blackfayer's people knew the details of how Danbury met his end?"

"I guess it was just servant's gossip," added Tonousa as she jumped to Heliana's defence.

"It wasn't gossip," replied Heliana. "Okay it was."

"Then who told you?" demanded Danisun.

"It was the Fool Lolly who told me all about it!" she continued. "He said that Xix Blackfayer and his bodyguards were in a right state that morning after my master, the late Grand Physician, may his soul rest with Solaris, took the boy's body back to the Underkeep. Xix was his usual pompous self, well at least according to Lolly. Yet the two members of his guard, Sir Digory Berthellemy and Sir Horace Mandleworth who had been with him were as grey as sheets."

"The idiots slipped in the boy's blood and dropped the body," added Tonousa. "But it's of no consequence. I'm sure that if we speak to the Lord Chamberlin he will soon silence Lolly. That is if Gilebin Ystafell isn't our infiltrator of course. I know for a fact that he will come down hard on any servant of the Citadel who speaks loose words, no matter what their status."

Tonousa paused for a moment. It wasn't the first time that Lolly had been caught out. His too willing tongue and fondness for gossip may have placed her investigation in jeopardy. She then remembered a similar conversation she had with Irabo when the body of Mikus had first been discovered but it mattered not. She would deal with the Fool in her own way but for now there were more pressing matters at stake.

"As I was saying," she continued. "It is possible that Danbury was murdered because he had disturbed our infiltrator in the act of stealing the horses from the stables. Now we have to try and deduce how those bastards from the Eastern Marsh knew of our journey to Valameer and when best to strike? Somehow they got wind we would be there because they were looking for Llyat. I keep asking myself, did someone tell the infiltrator of our intentions on purpose or did he find out by accident? Either way, there were but a select few who knew of our intentions to journey to Valameer and all of them apart from Highroar are either in this room, travelling in the north somewhere, or dead. I have been wondering if the card game hosted by Hotch holds the key to this mystery. By his own admission Highroar confirmed to me that he had told several people of our journey that night. Isn't that right Theo?"

Tonousa looked across the table again as the sounds of quill upon parchment had ceased. Theoplous focused on the writing before him, oblivious to all else that was going on.

"Theo!" repeated Tonousa.

She wondered if there was something wrong with the sailor as all at the table fell silent. Each waited for a response from the First Mate and after what seemed like an eternity Theoplous raised his head and looked towards Tonousa.

"That's it!" he exclaimed with a hint of excitement in his voice. "That was the correct setting. I know now what the message says."

Tonousa moved around to Theoplous's side, looked over his shoulder, and stared down at the parchment on the table. The rest of the group watched on in hope and anticipation as Tonousa tried to make out the detail of the sailor's scrawled handwriting and the message that he had decoded.

"Well man, don't keep us hanging in a fog of our own farts!" exclaimed Danisun. "What does it say?"

"I've got the first few words down and it confirms my suspicions. It has nothing to do with Xix as you had thought. The message starts thus..."

'TO THE CUVAR THAT TAKES MY POSITION ONCE I AM GONE.'

Tonousa felt her stomach flutter as she tried to keep control of her emotions. Whatever her father had hidden was now about to be revealed.

"So what does the rest of it say?" she asked.

"Give me a couple of minutes and I'll be able to translate the entire thing."

Tonousa looked on as the First Mate wrote down more letters while comparing them to those on the code wheel. Then with a sigh he placed the quill down.

"Finished."

"Well!" added Danisun, "What does the message reveal?"

Theoplous picked up the translated parchment and began to read.

"To the Cuvar that takes my position once I am gone. I must be brief and warn you of the plot to bring down the Sovereign Household. The Eastern Marsh has infiltrated the Citadel with one of their shape changing shamans whose sole purpose is to strike fear throughout the heart of the Capital and prevent the enactment of the Prophecy of Enderdetag. It is the same individual that stole the Lore of the Dead and now uses the old cult of Death Tubaria to create panic and discord throughout the city. Through the evidence I have uncovered I am certain that the shaman has taken the form of one of the Sovereign household and I conclude that it can only be one of four individuals. The cards you will find with this letter represent those four. Sir Richemanus, Justice. Lady Llys Emeny, Judgement. Sir Rayner Byddin, Strength. Heward Teulu, Temperance. You must finish this task for all now depends on you. These are my last words."

"Fuck me," mumbled Danisun under his breath.

"It looks like your father was more involved than you ever thought," continued Theoplous as he handed the parchment over to Tonousa in order to read the message once again. "From what he says and as I suspected, I can confirm he was indeed Cuvar, a follower of my religion, and a protector of the Marked."

As Tonousa reread the words the she became nauseous and she felt the blood rush from out of her head. Despite a desire to faint, for the sake of the investigation and her father's honour, she was determined to hold herself together. She owed it to all in the Realm to discover who was behind the evil plot. Somehow she would avenge her father's death and yet right now all she wanted was to race out into the street and throw up.

"Are you feeling okay?" asked Darchus as Tonousa's colour changed.

"I've never felt better!" she lied, determined not to reveal her vulnerability.

"So now what" asked Heliana?

"At least we seem to have narrowed the list of suspects down a bit. There are just four if Tonousa's father is to be believed," replied Danisun as he picked up the cards and examined them.

"And do we have any reason not to believe him?" asked Theoplous.

"Apart from Sir Richemanus, the other three, Lady Emeny, Sir Byddin and Heward Teulu are trusted members of the Sovereign Council," continued Danisun as he examined each of the four images in detail. "It couldn't be them..."

"Why not Danisun?" said Tonousa "Remember, the swine is a shape shifter. The individual he imitates will be long dead."

The group plunged head first into awkward silence while Tonousa hoped Danisun understood the magnitude of her words. She wished Irabo was with her to support her views but he was lost somewhere in the north lands. If Danisun did not believe her then she would be on her own again and her fight to find the infiltrator would get ever more difficult.

"He mentioned evidence," said Darchus as he half smiled at Tonousa. "Was there anything else in the message?"

"No," replied Theo. "I have told you all there is."

"So we are back to square one." added Danisun.

"I'm not so certain," said Tonousa as her confidence returned. "I'm sure of this much Danisun; I trust in my father and I call on Solaris to strike me down now if I am wrong. Despite my previous lack of faith I sense that Fatumai herself may have led us to this point. We must forget for now those who were at the card game in The Murdered Wolf and of course our Commander. We must focus on the four that my father has identified. I'm sure that one of them will slip up if we question them with skill. A shape changer is bound to do or say something out of character."

"Hold on a minute, we can't go rushing in and pointing fingers at such important people without good evidence," replied Danisun as he grew a little flustered. "Given the fear that gips the Capital, if we choose the wrong one there will be a lynching or even worse if Nedes Karoly has anything to do with it."

Danisun had made a good point and Tonousa knew it. He was correct that as members of the City Watch, one of the oldest and respected groups of Parandor, they could not go flinging wild accusations at members of the Sovereign Council, no matter the severity of the crime under investigation.

"Your point is well made Danisun and I understand your concern," added Tonousa as she took her place again at the table. "We must let the Council know of our intentions and the reasons why..."

"But wouldn't that put Irabo, Llyat, and that bard in danger." exclaimed Heliana.

"I am afraid we must," replied Tonousa. "We have bought them some time in their quest but that time is now up. We must be honest with those who we question in an attempt to get to the truth. We should still focus on the four, Strength, Justice, Judgement and Temperance. We must conduct ourselves with the utmost of sensitivity and must not move or make any arrests until we are sure of the infiltrator's identity."

"But..." added Danisun.

"No Danisun! I appreciate that you got me out of jail to aid in this investigation that you have been charged with completing. I also understand that I am not in a position to argue with you but do not forget that I was the one first ordered to investigate the Death Tubaria murders by Phauless Gylewu. I must complete the task that our Sovereign gave to me. If you have a better plan I would love to hear it."

"Point taken," replied Danisun.

"From what we know already, I suggest that we start with cards Strength and Judgement, Sir Byddin and Lady Emeny. If you recall Danisun, both had approached my father with questions about the Lore of the Dead. They sound like the ones to call on first."

"Yes, I remember that," muttered Danisun as his authority began to diminish.

"Good," continued Tonousa. "This is what we are going to do. Danisun, do you think you will be able to get Commander Townsforth to arrange a meeting between myself and Sir Byddin?"

The Man-at-Arms paused for a moment as he thought on the request.

"I'll try," he began. "From what I know they are caught up with the arrival of the armies of the Fifteen Keeps outside the city walls. Commander Townsforth is sending our own amongst them to ensure they respect all our laws and don't cause trouble. However I'll see what I can arrange."

"Good, and I thank you for that. Heliana, please remember you have a most important task yourself. See if you can find out any information about the ruby, but I also want you to keep a close eye on Lady Emeny. Make a note of her movements and report back to me as soon as possible."

"Of course," replied Heliana, happy at being treated as an equal.

Tonousa looked again to her friends around the table and felt that she could rely on each and all of them. She then stared down at the four cards, the ivory code wheels, and the message from her father. Then she spoke.

"At last we are now one step ahead of the bastard."

11

The smell of burnt flesh filled the nostrils of the bard as he stood and looked down at the charred corpses that lay on the floor before him. It had been several hours since they had crossed the large gorge that had threatened to halt their progress. Einar had directed them through one of the paths that the Berserkers knew well and by which his people had traversed the vast canyon for many centuries. After several hours had passed on the land beyond the great split, the four travellers and their weary grey leather skinned beasts had come across the remains of a burnt-out farmhouse at the bottom of a high ridge. The building was very much like the one they had spent the previous night in although this one had been blackened and reduced to ash.

Llyat had been the first to spot the two charred human remains, huddled in what appeared to be the remnants of a barn as he searched the outbuildings of the homestead. He had been on the hunt for anything that may have been of value to the group of travellers. Irabo pointed out that the fire was recent for there were still a hint of hot embers amongst the blackened and soot stained timbers. While the four companions stood and looked at the blackened corpses Llyat spoke and broke the tension.

"What or who could have done this?"

"I don't know," replied the bard as he too felt a deep foreboding as to how the two souls had met their end.

"Maybe it was a dragon!" suggested Llyat.

"I also had that thought," answered Thias. "But we have seen no sign of the great winged creatures during our time crossing the Dragonas."

"This is not the work of a dragon," added Einar. "They may kill beasts for sport, but they never attack the farmers of the Dragonas."

Einar moved amongst the remains of the building and it seemed to Thias that he looked for something very specific. Then after a few minutes the Berserker called over to his companions and brought their attention to what he had found.

"Something else did this; look at the burn pattern," he said as he pointed to the floor where the scorch marks appeared most concentrated. "Dragon fire would have created a deep single singe in the centre of the ground but from what I see there are several points where the fire started from. This place was deliberately torched."

Thias looked at the marks. He had little experience with fire except for the Promethelumous spell that he used to ignite his fists and yet it was obvious even to him that the farm had been set alight on purpose and its occupants incinerated.

"The poor bastards," said Irabo but no one replied.

Thias clambered through the wreckage of the building and back to the two skeletons. There he knelt down in the dirt to investigate further. After a few minutes he found evidence that confirmed the cause of the fire.

"It Looks like they were bound and tied as the fire burnt around them," he added.

"You mean...?" he heard Llyat ask.

"Yes Llyat," replied Thias. "They were cooked alive for some reason."

Thias heard a small sniff and the sound of material as it rubbed against skin. He knew that Llyat had shed a tear for the two unfortunates that had been reduced to almost ash. It then dawned on the bard that this foul crime had brought back memories of how Llyat's parent's lives had been taken by the Knights of Avolire. Then with a brief sigh of his own Thias stood up from where he knelt and pulled Llyat in close. He embraced him with his arms and gave the youth all the comfort he could generate. As he attempted to console Llyat he reflected on the fact that both of their respective father's had been killed in front of them. The empathy he felt drew him closer and strengthened the bond between the two young men. Llyat was a brother to him now and he reaffirmed his vow to do all that he could to protect him from the darkness that was to come.

The sound of movement by his side caused Thias to pull away. The young farmhand dried his eyes and tried to compose himself.

"Do you still want to head towards Fallguard?" asked Einar with a hint of concern. "Given that it's in such close proximity to Avolire and the evil that you say is gathering there. I could take much us further north and then veer across to Thengar Forest..."

"I see your point," replied Thias. "If we had supplies of food and water then I would agree with your proposal. I thought we might have found something of use amongst all this debris but there is nothing. Whoever burnt down this place, wiped all its contents from existence. I'm afraid we must venture on to Fallguard even if it does lead us even closer to the Lady because we don't have sufficient supplies to make any other option viable."

The group gathered themselves, mounted their unicorns, and once again set off on their trek. Led by Einar they navigated the terrain up to the top of the ridge and over onto the grasslands beyond. For the next few of hours they continued on towards the east. No one spoke for all were deep in thought, pondering on the chain of events that had swept them along on their perilous journey. Thias wondered where the road would take them and what they would find there. He prayed to the memory of the bards for help in thwarting the Lady of the Silverwynn's attempt to release the dark powers of the Underworld. Then he thought about the murders in the Capital and it seemed so long since Phauless Gylewu had given him the task which now took him towards Thengar Forest. He sensed he would soon discover what the Fates had in store for him. Sometime later the yellow grass lands of Dragonas transitioned into the familiar green landscapes that Thias had long travelled throughout in the south of the Realm. The clouds turned grey and began to block out the blessed rays of Solaris. While the unicorns carried them on Thias began to think about what they would discover in Fallguard and if they would find a welcome there. If it was true that Avolire's forces grew more numerous in anticipation of a march on Parandor, then the sooner they moved away from the influence of that ruined city the better. Three hours out from the burned farm they came across a road that dissected their path. Here Einar raised his hand and signalled for all to stop.

"The Old North Road," he said, pointing to the dirt track before them. "To the south, Avolire. To the north, Dirmark, Fallguard, and Thengar Forest."

Thias scanned the road in both directions as it snaked through the grasslands. There was nothing visible to the south but miles of grass but he realised that despite their current isolation Avolire was still too close for comfort. He then focused to the north and on the distant horizon he saw the faint peaks of the cold hard mountains that signified the boarders of Dirmark.

"I know which direction we're heading in," said Llyat and he turned left and onto the north road.

Einar and Irabo followed without question as Thias reflected on Llyat's new found confidence. The young man no longer seemed the same snivelling runt that had presented himself at the Bards Guild to Grand Musician Owasorin Fusepelt. Ever since their escape from the Gathering, Thias had noticed subtle changes in Llyat's behaviour. He also sensed that the youth was hiding something for he had been avoiding all questions regarding his conversation with Thamous. Given time, Thias hoped that Llyat would tell all.

The four companions trekked north, league upon league and always sticking to the dirt track made by the passage of feet, hooves, and wheels throughout the memory of man. Thias noted that the temperature of the air dropped with each hour along the road and after the day's light began to fail he watched the condensation on his breath as he exhaled. It formed wisps of vapour like that from the mouth of the ice dragons. The cooler air caressed his skin and he was thankful for the fur jacket that Berger had given him back in Falahorn. It would surely provide protection against the frosty winds that kicked up from the north. Then as it continued to get ever colder Thias began to realise that if they didn't reach the warm fires of Fallguard by the end of the day then all except the Berserker would freeze to death. As his eyes looked to the ground at either side of the road he saw a peppering of snowflakes begin to settle on the grass. When he then looked up he saw heavy clouds ready to dump their frozen load and he sensed a blizzard was imminent. The warmth was draining from Llyat and Irabo, a fact confirmed as their bodies shook from raging shivers and chattering teeth. Each exhaled plumes of frost filled vapour into the air. The bard looked towards the giant Berserker sat astride his beast, dressed in nothing but thin trousers and with two mighty battle axes still strapped to his back. The giant did not appear in any away affected by the cold and Thias remembered conversations regarding the Berserkers' thickened skin; a consequence of living close to dragons.

"It's fucking freezing'" shouted Llyat from the head of the group. "How much further is it?"

"Not much more than an hour at the most," added Einar.

"If we don't reach cover soon then we will all be lost," moaned Thias.

It was in fact just half that time before they saw the tree line that signified the start of the dense expanse of Thengar Forest and the many buildings that made up the town of Fallguard. They moved forward with much greater energy over the snow covered ground as the town came ever closer. The buildings of Fallguard were mixed stone and timber constructions, similar in design to those that Thias had seen in villages such as Maplehill and some in Parandor. Snow covered their rooves and icicles hung from eaves and windowsills. The latter created perfect daggers of ice that reached almost to the ground. In contrast to the warm weather of the Dragonas, Fallguard felt as if it had never known heat throughout all of its existence. Thias was surprised how life managed to survive this far north in such cold conditions. Given its proximity to Avolire he had expected more people to be present on its streets and amid an uneasy atmosphere the group traversed its frozen road. The few well wrapped people that they passed watched the four companions and their beasts with great suspicion. Thias felt nervous and untrusting. He was determined not to risk their identity being discovered for then messages could be passed to the Lady of the Silverwynn and result in their slaughter as they slept. First things first, they had to find supplies, they had to find shelter, and they had to find warmth.

"I don't like this one bit," moaned Irabo though chattering teeth while passing a street walker.

"Thieves, bandits, and dragon slaying scum," replied Einar "I wouldn't trust any of them."

"Remember what the sailor said back at the Guild," added Thias. "He had heard there were all sorts of low life travelling north to join the Lady of the Silverwynn in preparation for her strike against Parandor. Whatever happens while we are in this place, we must be on our guard at all times. We cannot risk Avolire knowing that we move against them."

"And what shall we do if we're asked our purpose here in Fallguard?" replied Einar.

"Leave that to me. First of all let's get out of the bloody cold."

A short time later Thias recognised a sign of salvation, a building that stood out from all the others due to its size and form. Even though snow and ice covered every aspect of the two story building he knew that it was an inn. It would be a place of fortitude against the harshness of the cold. Then the bard spotted the wooden sign above the door, carved in the shape of a bed, and which indicated the name of the establishment; 'The Three Sisters.' The travellers dismounted their unicorns which somehow seemed unaffected by the cold.

"This looks like the sort of place we need," chirped up Irabo as he rested on his crutch.

"It's perfect," agreed Thias as a plan formed in his mind "Let me do the talking. Einar will you please stay outside and watch over our animals? Given the scum that no doubt infest this place, I'm not happy to leave them unattended."

"Of course, you three go inside and get warm. The cold doesn't bother me the same way."

Thias led Llyat and Irabo up the single step of the building and then pushed open the large wooden door. It wasn't much warmer in the small room that opened before them but it was better than standing outside for at least it was free from the wind. As he walked forward and surveyed this new space Thias noted the counter upon which had been placed a single ink pot and quill. Behind it was a wooden stairwell which he assumed lead to any rooms that may be still vacant. A single door to his right led into the main part of the building and from behind it he could hear the sound of voices.

Thias approached the counter and noted that it was full of small holes where woodworm had once settled but since moved on. A lone man rose up from behind the counter, placed a large ledger onto its surface and made ready to greet the new visitors to his establishment. He was of mid age, rotund, and with shaggy hair that sprouted from his face and head. He wore furs, no doubt to save money on heating his abode. Thias was struck by the blackened skin around the man's nose which appeared both charred and decayed. He could only assume that this was the result of frost bite.

"Good afternoon to you sir," said Thias with authority. "Long may Solaris warm your heart and favour you."

"And the same to you young sir," replied the man. "What brings three strangers here?"

"My name is Vostag. I am a bard from the lands around Falahorn," lied Thias. "These are two are called Fiat and Grophaldo and also hail from that distant town. We seek supplies and a place to sleep for the night before continuing our journey into Thengar Forest tomorrow. My friends have long wished to see the ancient ruins of Barad Elestor..."

"And more fool them," answered the man as he cut Thias off mid-sentence. "I wouldn't venture into that place for all the wealth of Dirmark. What business do you have in that old dump?"

"Our business is our own."

An awkward silence followed and in that moment Thias wondered if he had already said too much. However before he could think further or embellish his lies the man spoke again.

"I meant no offence young bard. With all these strange folk travelling to and from old Avolire, I've got to be cautious. I don't want any trouble here."

"As is your duty sir," replied Thias.

"So how may I help you out," grumbled the man? "Or should we just stand and continue in idle chatter?"

"As I said, we seek supplies," continued Thias. "Food and drink for our journey northwards and a bed for the night."

"Then you've come to the right place."

"The thing is, we are a little short on coin," added Thias.

The innkeeper looked at the Bard for a brief moment and then laughed.

"Then why are you wasting my time. Fuck off and be gone, all of you."

The man turned his back and began to move towards the single door behind which the sounds of voices could still be heard.

"Wait on good sir, we are willing to offer you another form of payment. Something much more valuable than money," added Thias. "Outside this building, we have four of the finest unicorns ever bred in the Dragonas. We are willing to trade you two of the noble beasts for a room and the supplies that we need."

"Now you are talking," said the man as a greedy smile formed on his face. "Unicorn meat is very hard to come by and I can make a fortune with its horn in the right market."

Thias contemplated what the man meant by the 'right market' or to what possible perverted uses that the inhabitants of Fallguard would have for the horn. Then he realised that he was being just as suspicious as the folk he had passed in the street. Fallguard seemed to create mistrust out of the very air that permeated its streets. The man then stepped from behind the counter and headed for the door.

"Let's take a look at them shall we," he mumbled as he moved past the three travellers.

Thias followed the man out through the door and left Irabo and Llyat inside the building. Night had arrived and visibility was poor and as Mona rose she fought to illuminate the land. The bard stood in the doorway as the man made his way over towards Einar and the four unicorns. There he began to examine each one in detail. As the he poked and prodded each beast, Thias made his way over towards Einar who watched the man with great suspicion. After some minutes the innkeeper turned around.

"I'll take three to meet your needs. Yes, three will pay for everything you have requested."

"Two and that's my final offer," replied Thias, his direct tone suggesting that he would not be easily be made a fool of.

"Three or no deal," uttered the man, moving back into the Three Sisters.

"Wait, I'm sure we can strike some kind of deal," shouted Thias in desperation.

The bard then gave chase and followed the innkeeper back into his establishment. As he ran the force of his movement caused the bronze pendent he wore around his neck to bounce upwards and out of the confines of his shirt. Within seconds he had passed by Llyat and Irabo who just stood and watched on with confused interest. The innkeeper then turned and laughed.

"It sounds like you are desperate," sneered the man. "You should never let on how keen you are to make a contract for you just reveal your weakness. I like the look of you and your friends, Bard of Falahorn, even though you keep company with a Berserker. So I'll tell you what, I will make you another offer."

"And what would that be?" asked Thias.

"Two unicorns and that pendent around your neck. What is it made from?"

"Bronze."

"Bronze and amethyst, very nice indeed. The metal alone will fetch a hefty sum from those who dwell in holes."

"Thias, no, you cannot do it!" Llyat exclaimed. "You cannot sell your last memory."

Thias hesitated for Llyat was right; it was all he had to remind him of his time at the Bards Guild. Their needs were however great and their cause was just. Thias knew he had no option but to sacrifice his precious trinket for the sake of the quest.

"It's a deal," replied Thias, thrusting out a hand to confirm the agreement.

The innkeeper's smile increased as he shook hands and sealed the deal. Then he insisted that the three men sign the ledger on the counter. After Irabo and Llyat had signed the book with their false names Thias also made his mark upon the parchment. Their host then proceeded to show them upstairs to their room which was sparse and basic with only a single bed in one corner and a dresser in the other.

It was decided that Irabo would take the bed due to the injury to his leg while Thias and Llyat would make do with the floor. When the three at last returned downstairs they were joined once again by the innkeeper but also Einar who informed them that the four beasts had been moved into to the stables at the back of the building. Two had already been claimed and separated from the others. Thias then took Einar to one side and explained the details of his agreement. He then removed his pendent and passed it over to the innkeeper who dropped it into one of his deep pockets.

"It has been a pleasure doing business with you," smirked man while Thias prayed he could be trusted.

"I'll tell you what," continued innkeeper. "I'll get one of my boys to collect the supplies you require for your journey to Barad Elestor, along with some furs, and then have them sent up to your room. I'm guessing the Berserker won't need any additional covering. Those buggers are immune to the cold but given this dreadful weather you others are going to need all the protection you can get if you intend to visit that most desolate of places."

"Once again I thank you," replied Thias. "Your hospitality is much appreciated."

"Seeing as I'm such a generous man and how much I like the look of you, head into the room next door and speak to my wife Kaylee who runs the bar. Tell her that Garret promised you a meal on the house. Give her this and she will understand your intentions."

With that the black nosed Garret reached into his pocket and pulled out an iron disk which he then pressed into the bard's hand.

"Thank you again," said Thias. "Long may Solaris warm your bed and keep it active."

"And yours!" came the response.

With that Garret spat on the floor and then retreated behind the counter. Thias looked to his companions who stood and waited.

"A free meal?" asked Llyat.

"That's what he said," replied Thias as he examined the iron disk.

"I sense something amiss," added Einar. "This all feels too convenient and it doesn't sit right with me. I have had the strangest feeling that we have been watched ever since we entered this place. I won't be able to rest until I've had a close look around this town."

"As you please. See what you can find out but be careful my friend."

"I always am."

Einar turned and made his way out through the entrance door. The cold wind and frost swept past him as he stooped so as not to hit his head on the door frame. Once the wood had closed, Thias stepped through the second portal and into the room of never ending chatter.

The atmosphere was just as one would expect inside a ramshackled tavern situated deep in the arse end nowhere. It oozed gloom and suspicion. Built into the room was a short single counter in front of several barrels that no doubt contained the local brew. There were also several tables that were squeezed onto the tavern floor, some of which were occupied and some not. The space was illuminated by a solitary candle on each table and in the centre of one wall there was a large stone hearth that was devoid of fire. This space too was also almost as cold as the street outside. The silence that fell as the three companions walked through the door was palpable and the few customers seated at the tables sealed their lips, turned their heads, and stared at those who had just entered. Around one table sat three hooded old women who looked up for a brief moment before resuming their private conversation. At another sat two rough looking men, dressed in dark colours with some leather armour strapped to their bodies beneath cloaks of fur. Thias noticed that they carried swords by their sides and he assumed from their attire they were mercenaries, wanderers who offered their swords for hire. Even these two returned to their own conversation after a quick evaluation and paid no further attention to the newcomers.

"Great crowd." whispered Thias. "Be on your guard at all times."

"Understood!" replied Irabo as his hand fell to the hilt of his blade.

The noise in the room rose to its previous level and a voice from behind the counter shouted out towards the three companions. Thias looked to its origin and there saw a squat manlike woman with greasy hair and large red pustules on her face. She stood behind the counter, an imposing figure and most terrifying sight. Thias guessed this must be the Kaylee.

"Now you buggers, we'll have no disturbance here," the woman shouted.

"I can assure you that you will have no trouble from me, my good woman." replied Thias in his best reassuring voice.

"Then take a seat and I'll be over in a second."

Thias made his way towards one of the empty tables beyond the centre of the room. Irabo and Llyat followed like cows to the milking shed. He looked towards the two sellswords that sat nearby and they stared back through their suspicious eyes. The three chose a table close to the stone fireplace and next to that occupied by the mercenaries. Thias continued to feel uncomfortable, for just like Einar, he too had the distinct feeling that their presence was being monitored. Kaylee's voice then hammered in his ear as she stood ready to take their order.

"So what you want then?" she asked before spitting on the floor.

"Garret sent us," replied Thias handing over the iron disc. "He said I was to give you this."

"I'll sort you out something to eat then," she mumbled as her demeanour became a fraction friendlier. "But in the meantime what may I get you handsome fellows to drink?"

"Got any mead?" asked Llyat.

"Where do you think you are, fucking Parandor?" snorted Kaylee.

"My friend meant no disrespect lady," answered Thias, attempting to diffuse her ire. "The youngling is used to finer beverages than the rest of us but he will make do with whatever you have on offer. Tell us what may we quench our thirst with?"

"We have ale," replied Kaylee. "And also we have ale."

"Well if that be the choice, we will have three ales," replied Thias with a smile.

Kaylee towered over her guests before turning her back and retreating behind her counter.

"Wonderful hospitality," mumbled Thias once Kaylee was out of earshot.

"Did you ever frequent The Murdered Wolf during your days in Parandor?" asked Irabo.

"No, I can't say that I did."

"Well I must tell you this place is luxury in comparison."

Thias then felt Llyat's elbow in his side. He turned to face the young lad who then nodded towards the corner of the room.

"Over there," whispered the youth. "Sneak a peep as soon as you can."

Thias soon glanced over his left shoulder to where Llyat had indicated and was surprised that he hadn't noticed them sooner. There sat at a table, part hidden in the dark shadows and deep in conversation, sat two unmistakable figures. They were dressed in the cheap metal and leather armour of the Eastern Marsh and Thias suspected that this was the probable source of his paranoia.

"Lizardmen!" he whispered. "Let's not do anything that will bring attention to ourselves. Einar was right. We are being watched."

"Here you go then lads," shouted Kaylee as three tankards were slammed down onto the table forcing some of their contents to slosh over the brims of the earthenware vessels. "Three Blessed Beasts. Food is on its way."

Thias watched Kaylee walk away, convinced she had to be a man for he had never seen a woman look more like one. His attention was then captured by the mercenaries' conversation. Their words were of great interest and hinted at the movements of the Knights of Avolire.

"Those fucking Harbingers have been seen on the road heading east" said the first, one who had a distinctive scar across the left hand side of his face.

"It seems like war with Parandor is inevitable," replied the second and the younger of the two.

"Her armies are growing and the Knights become ever stronger while their number increase daily. It has taken the Lady years to rebuild since her defeat at the hands of Britta Rainmark. Now every sick fuck in the Realm is flocking to Avolire. I also saw the Harbingers moving a month ago as they headed down the Avolire road, towards Griginor, the Grey Mountains, and the old pass that once allowed access to the Southern Kingdom."

Thias knew that the pass that they mentioned lay several days north of the road that led from the Capital to the Grey Keep. It had once been the main route between the northern and southern halves of the Realm but it had not been maintained and had long ago fallen into disrepair. Mountain tree roots had undermined its foundations and fallen firs blocked its lower passage in several places. It had also become home to the most dangerous types of wild creatures.

"Well, if anyone can make it through that old road then it's the Knights of Avolire," added the younger man. "Even the kulkulkath would think twice before attacking them."

"From what I got out of old Garret, I hear that they have some secret intent," continued the man with the scar. "It has something to do with striking fear into the southern highborn and is somehow linked to that missing Historian, long since forgotten in these parts, but essential to the Lady's plans."

'Historian' pondered Thias. This was new information regarding the Lady of the Silverwynn. He picked up his tankard and took a sip of ale so as not to make it obvious that he was listening to those behind. Then he moved his chair backwards a fraction so that he could hear with greater clarity and catch any further insights that the two may share.

"Historian?" queried the younger of the two mercenaries. "What kind of a title is that?"

"From what Garret told me, I believe the man was someone close to the Lady many years ago. He was essential to the Lady's plan to bring down the House of Gylewu and put her on the throne. They say the Historian disappeared one day and blocked the Silverwynn's schemes. It was his desertion that undermined her thinking and led to her defeat at the hands of Rainmark."

Thias struggled to think who this Historian could be for he had never heard mention of one before. How he wondered could such a book reader fit into the plans of Avolire and what information he could have discovered that could help overthrow the forces of Parandor. Thias was unprepared for what he next heard.

"Garret also told me that the Harbingers were sent south because the Historian had been traced to one of three villages, Maplehill, Oakwood or Ashview on the banks of the Tiaryer."

Thias spluttered on his ale, loud enough for the two mercenaries to hear and the three old crones on the table beyond to notice. As soon as he could Thias engaged Llyat and Irabo in conversation, although as he did so his thoughts continued to churn the new information and try and assimilate it into what he already knew of the threat to Parandor. Then as he talked over the surface of his ale the two mercenaries returned to their chatter. A thought began to seep into Thias's mind. He began to speculate that the Historian could have been Llyat's father for the Lizardman that attacked the youth in the Bards Guild had referred to 'the traitor's son'. This could perhaps be the reason why the Knights of Avolire were looking for Llyat, something to do with him being the 'Marked'. Thias continued to eavesdrop but he also knew he could not speak to Llyat on the matter until he was certain of its implications. He leaned back again and tuned in to the conversation behind him.

"You know that one of Fallguard's own, the one known as Nictis, was amongst those Knights who went south to find the Historian."

"Now there was a man worthy to fight for the Lady of the Silverwynn," stated the younger.

"I am sure you remember the rumours about Nictis and his brother?" said the scarred one.

"Sort of. My mind is a little fuzzy on the detail. Please remind me."

Thias leaned back even more, hungry for further insights to help counter the intentions of Knights of Avolire. He was already aware of one weakness, the gap in their armour that Einar had spoken of, but information about any other vulnerabilities was not common knowledge. Thias slurped on his ale and tilted his chair as the voices of the two dropped to a whisper.

"There was a pregnant woman who turned up in Fallguard many years ago," began the scarred one. "Said she had fled the south for her husband used to abuse and beat her. In the few months she was in Fallguard before her premature demise, she was taken in by the keeper of this very place and who at that time treated her well. He ensured she was looked after and even arranged for her to be married. However the union was short lived as the woman, whose name I recall was Rebekha, died during the birth of twin boys. The brats survived and were later named Nictis and Filian. It was said by the midwives that attended the birth that Nictis was born grasping the heel of his brother in an attempt to pull him back into the womb in order to be born first."

"Bull shit!" laughed the younger of the two.

"I kid you not my young friend. That's how the story was told to me. Both sons of Rebekha grew to be opposites in every way. Nictis strong, brash and violent, whereas Filian turned out soft spoken but quick of wit. The old innkeeper adopted the pair as his own for he had sired no children himself. He vowed that his mother's limited wealth and the property would be split in equal parts between the two boys when they came of age. Just as the brothers had turned fifteen, Filian came home one day from the fields. He was very hungry and pleased to find his brother had returned from a hunt with fresh game. At first Nictis refused to share the spoils of his catch but then agreed to give Filian a half share under the condition that he would give up his inheritance in exchange for the food. So hungry was the youngest twin that he agreed and therefore in the eyes of the gods themselves, he forfeited all his rights."

"So if Nictis was in line to inherit this place, how did he end up joining the Knights of Avolire?"

"About three years ago when the Lady was gathering her forces, her commander, that guy with the skull adorned helmet... what's his name? ...Ah yes, Rhaizen. Well, Rhaizen and his platoon of Harbingers showed up and gathered us all together. He then selected one of us to act as the spokesperson for Fallguard. That was Nictis. He was then given the instruction to choose another of the village to surrender to the knights for the purpose of enslavement. This unfortunate one would held as hostage in order to secure the loyalty of Fallguard to..."

Thias overestimated the degree that he had been leaning back on the chair. As he strained further to listen it collapsed backwards and the bard landed at the feet of the two mercenaries. Their conversation came to an abrupt halt and the two jumped to their feet and drew their swords. The room fell silent and even the two Lizardmen ceased their chatter and looked down to the floor.

"Do you have a problem?" shouted the man with the scar.

Llyat rushed to help Thias from the ground.

"I told you, no trouble," shouted man-woman from behind the counter.

"I've got this under control Kaylee," shouted the mercenary as he pointed his blade at the bard's neck.

"I do apologise my friend," said Thias in his most humble of voices.

He pushed Llyat back on to his chair next to the bemused Irabo. Then holding up his hands to bare his palms Thias pushed the blade away from his neck and smiled.

"I meant no offence sirs and I apologise for listening into your conversation. I admit I shouldn't have done so but I couldn't help but over hear what you were saying to your friend about this guy called Nictis. As the bard of Falahorn I travel the villages and towns of the Realm listening and looking for stories to tell and songs to write. Where I come from the story of Nictis and his brother would be much appreciated and I could make a lot of money from singing about it. There is nothing more sinister behind my actions I assure you; it was a great story and it caught my interest."

"Birds from the south have told another story. Do you know that the Bards Guild went up in flames?" sneered the young mercenary as he re-sheathed his weapon.

"Birds say a lot of things," added Thias, "but never stories of any interest so don't believe all that you hear on the wind."

"Aye, that may be so," added the scarred man who remained ready to strike Thias down. "But it matters not. You and your friends, though made welcome to drink here by Garret and Kaylee, need to be more careful. I like the look of you bard and so I'll give you a piece of advice. Keep your nose out of other people's affairs and you might survive the night."

"I thank you for that advice," squirmed Thias.

The bard waited for a response. The tension between the two rose. It would take was just one wrong word for Thias to ignite his hands and initiate a lethal conflict yet he was a man of his word and he had promised Kaylee there would be no trouble. He focused on calming himself and then looked around the room for inspiration as to how he could talk his way out of his predicament. All eyes present honed in on him including those of the three woman that sat in silence at their table. The two Lizardmen in the corner strained to hear each word and they monitored the situation that now hung on a knife edge.

"So what is your name bard?" asked the man with the scar.

"Vostag," lied Thias with conviction. "These are my companions Fiat and Grophaldo Heyn."

"Pleasure to meet you," added Llyat as he continued Thias's lie and stepped forward to offer a hand of friendship only to be pushed back by Thias's hand.

"Likewise," snapped back the younger of the two mercenaries.

"I am called Ventes and this young runt here is Dint L'Fare," added scar face. "So Vostag of Falahorn, what business do you have in Fallguard?"

With Ventes's sword still readied to strike at his throat Thias continued his chain of untruths. He so hoped that Llyat and Irabo would continue to play along with his deception.

It took Thias some ten minutes to spin out his tale, how the three friends had ventured forth from Falahorn with the purpose of seeing the majestic temples and tombs that legend said were to be found within the frozen depths of Thengar Forest. The two mercenaries appeared to believe all that was said and not once did Thias hint at the true purpose of their journey to Barad Elestor.

"Well, I can't understand your desire to see such a dark place, a collection of old stone ruins, but your business is your own," said Ventes after which he sheathed his weapon and offered his hand to Thias. "If you are as you say a bard, why don't you sing and entertain us all?"

"I don't think..."

"You don't have a choice, not if you want to keep your fucking tongue," growled Ventes.

The mercenary tapped the hilt of blade before turning towards the counter.

"Kaylee, are you up for a song?" he shouted.

"Just as long as there is no further trouble and you all stop acting like twats."

Thias scanned the room where all waited on his response. He looked down at Irabo who shrugged his shoulders and laughed. With no other option available Thias turned to face the mercenaries and smiled.

"Very well. I'll try my best to entertain you all for never have I had such an esteemed audience! Most often this song would be accompanied by an instrument of some sort but I lost mine on my journey here. I will try and to make do without it! Ladies, gentlemen, and creatures from the Eastern Marsh, I give you the tale of The Maiden and The Tower."

With that said Thias began to sing.

It began on a cold bitter evening,
I the most honest Bard around,
She was the fairest of maidens,
With golden hair down to the ground.

She was my lover,
My fair lover,
My maiden,
My maiden fair.

They say we complemented each other,
Back then in times long ago.
We wanted our love eternal,
But our futures were destined for woe.

She was my lover,
My fair lover,
My maiden,
My maiden fair.

Then one frost bitten evening,
The Fates decided to flower.
Her family moved her, and locked her away,
In the darkest moss covered tower.

She was my lover,
My fair lover,
My maiden,
My maiden fair...

Thias continued on for several minutes. At the end of his rendition he half expected applause, but none came. The Lizardmen returned to their deep conversation and he noted that the three old woman had left the inn sometime during his song. He looked once more to Ventes and wondered where events would go next but then the man laughed.

"Absolute shite, although it made a change from Kaylee's squawking."

"Fuck you Ventes," shouted Kaylee from behind the counter.

"Later my lover, later," replied the mercenary as he too laughed and turned to his young companion. "Come Dint, let's leave these fools to their ale. Avolire beckons."

Thias waited until the two mercenaries had left the tavern before he sat once again at the table. For the next half hour, none of the three companions spoke except to thank the Kaylee for the food which after a long wait she had brought for them to eat. Following the meagre meal the three companions retired to the room they had procured earlier that evening. Einar was still absent and presumed scouting the town. Soon Irabo fell asleep on the bed leaving Llyat and Thias to talk as they sat by its edge and tried not to disturb the weary warrior.

"I thought that you sang well," said Llyat. "Like you said, it is better when there is music to accompany it but you carried off the tune."

"Thank you dear Llyat, your critical acclaim is most appreciated," replied Thias.

"Here I want you to have this?" said Llyat.

The youth reached into his pocket and pulled out a white oval stone set upon a piece of crafted metal and to which a small chain was attached. Llyat then held it aloft for Thias to see and then hold.

"What is it?" asked Thias.

"Remember when I was in the tunnels under that three peaked mountain conversing with Thamous. This is a 'Dragon Whisper' that Einar gave to me. It is the way to communicate with dragons and wyverns. You gave away your pendent in order to us buy food and supplies. You sacrificed your precious memory and I no longer have use for this magic stone. I want you to have it."

Thias looked at the object as he held it aloft in his hand. The dim light from the one candle in the room reflected off the stones surface and caused it to sparkle.

"Thank you so much."

"Don't dwell on it," replied Llyat.

Since re-emerging from the cavern below the Gathering he had always intended to pass the stone onto Thias.

"Please don't tell Einar that I have given it to you though. Best keep it a secret between us."

"Of course. I'll keep it hidden. I'll keep it safe," answered the bard.

12

"Thank you for agreeing to meet with me Sir Byddin," said Tonousa to the stern man.

The imposing knight half smiled in acknowledgement of her presence while Tonousa's eyes were drawn to the patch that covered his left eye. Sir Byddin was dressed in steel and bronze armour which glinted in the light from Solaris. Being the most polished its shine distinguished him from the rest of Royal Guard.

"You're most welcome Tonousa, daughter of the late Lord Amberstone," he replied while shaking Tonousa's hand. "I am pleased to meet you even though at such short notice. I have had to leave Sir Redgrave in charge of the massing troops from the Fifteen Keeps so please make this brief. As you will no doubt of heard, Redgrave is not the most reliable of people and I dare not leave him long without him creating mayhem. War is at last coming but you need have no fear for whatever happens in the coming weeks and months ahead, be rest assured that you and this city will be well protected."

Tonousa looked through the crenulations of the outer city wall that surrounded Parandor. It was midday and Solaris sat high in a cloudless sky. It had been three days since Danisun Dain had released her from the Underkeep and already events had spiralled out from the starting point of her investigation. They twisted and turned in her mind as she sought to make progress in her endeavours. Behind her back the fortress and towers of one particular building provided an imposing yet ethereal backdrop; it was known by all as the home of the reclusive Wizards. Stood in the shadow of the Guild's highest tower, Tonousa's energy was focused on the task of unmasking the shapeshifter that had taken the guise of one of the members of the Sovereign Council. She was not alone with Sir Byddin for beside her on the battlements stood Darchus of Valameer, now a member of the Watch and Tonousa's co-investigator. She would have paired herself with Irabo had he not been away in the north of the Realm for he was a good a foil to her thinking and would have thrown in new insights as the interrogation progressed. Darchus had yet to prove his value in this respect but Tonousa was still thankful for his company. Her decision to meet with Rayner Byddin overlooking the northern slums of the city was based on her desire to question him away from the shadows. It would be safer that way.

"I can handle myself in any conflict that may come to these walls," Tonousa responded. "I am sure you are aware of my position in the Watch."

"Yes indeed and I understand you are a most formidable opponent. At least that is what my new recruits have heard while training under the instruction of Danisun Dain and Townsforth. I will be proud to have a warrior such as yourself watching my back once we begin the defence of the inner city. The Knights of Avolire will have great difficulty penetrating those defences, if they manage to break through the outer walls. As you can see below, we prepare the engines of war for our defence with the upmost urgency. Those bastards from Avolire will not get through, not even with the help of those forked tonged shits from the marshes. I am still hopeful that we may yet receive assistance from Valameer and Falahorn despite the fact we have had no response as yet from our request for help. Even so, without their aid we will still triumph."

Tonousa noted the knight's arrogance and bravado but it was true that the defences he was preparing were formidable. She looked at Darchus and for a brief moment wondered if he felt the same given his experience in organising the citizens of a Valameer.

The two officers of the Watch looked down from the great wall towards the slums and observed Sir Byddin's troops as they busied themselves in their preparations. The gathered throng from the Fifteen Keeps, strongholds interspersed across the lands before the Grey Mountains, moved in organised chaos across the ground as they sought to complete their defence of the ground before Parandor's gates. The armour worn by those from the provinces was distinctively different to that of the Royal Guard of Parandor. The design of each of their pauldrons varied and depicted the many coats of arms that were unique to their Lords and Ladies. Men were hard at work constructing large wooden structures behind a deep ditch and palisade of oak spikes that now circumnavigated the Capital. These engines of war were being built at regular intervals along the base of the city wall. Tonousa knew from knowledge passed onto her as a child by her father that the mechanical beasts were called pults. She had no concept of the science behind the workings of these contraptions but she knew that they could launch a heavy stone or bolus of burning material in to the path of an oncoming enemy, or in the case of a siege, into or over a defensive wall. Sir Byddin was right, the Capital would be well defended but she could not help but wonder if the effort would be sufficient.

Tonousa then turned her attention back to Sir Byddin while Darchus's eyes followed her every move. Then as her demeanour became more seriousness, she spoke again.

"Did Danisun Dain tell you why I asked to meet you here?"

"He did," replied Sir Byddin, somewhat irritated. "Although I am both surprised and disappointed to think that you would include me as a suspect in the Death Tubaria murders. Yet I do feel that I owe it to the memory of your father to answer any questions that you and your friend may wish to put to me. Following those most disturbing events at the Richemanus Folly I am now certain that he was but an innocent counter in some other's devious game.

"Your co-operation is noted and appreciated," continued Tonousa. "Allow me to introduce Darchus Arillius, a new member of Parandor's Watch. Although new to us he is well experienced in the workings of the world. He hails all the way from Valameer and has served the Lady Flurdiana."

"I am most pleased to meet you sir," responded Sir Byddin as he tipped his head in a sign of acknowledgment.

"Likewise," replied Darchus as he mirrored the knight's actions.

In the brief awkward silence that followed Tonousa noted the chirp of a bird on the air. It reminded her not to waste the knight's valuable time.

"Sir Byddin, please tell us all you know about the series of murders that I am tasked to investigate. Please began with the death of Sir Tobius Faros, one from your own Royal Guard."

Tonousa watched and listened as Byddin began to recount his knowledge of the circumstances of the deaths of each of the victims. It took him many minutes to cover the key points as he saw them. Sir Faros had hung himself. Sir Rainmark had drowned. The two servants had both been poisoned, or so it had seemed, just like the Royal Treasurer, Lord Colt. While he spoke Tonousa recalled that the three poisonings had likely been a consequence of Nightshade, a conclusion drawn by the late Grand Physician, Abrahamus Marus. Tonousa then noted Sir Byddin's interesting observation that each of the five victims had been found in the early hours of the morning, a detail she had not until then realised linked the crimes. Then she remembered that the exception to this pattern was the death of Golda Flintwind, the servant to Lady Thinata Fullbane, who was found one evening down in the servant's quarters of the Underkeep.

"Thank you for your detailed account Sir Byddin," said Tonousa once he had finished. "Let us return to the first five murders, the ones that occurred before our Sovereign Lord asked for the assistance of the City Watch. Can you tell us of any relationship you may have had with any or all of the deceased."

"What is there to say? Sir Faros and Sir Rainmark were both members of my elite Royal Guard. They were both loyal and brave men. I was most surprised when I heard that both of them had died. Well, more so Sir Rainmark than for Sir Faros, who despite being a good knight and an exceptional fighter, let darkness take hold of his thinking after the death of his wife and daughter. Therefore his demise did not at first raise suspicions of more sinister events. As for Sir Rainmark, his mind was in a good place, one where his merriment was at the forefront of his being; so when they found him face down in the Tiaryer I never for the slightest moment believed he could have taken his own life. In all of my years in the service of Lord Gylewu he was the last person I would have expected to have ended his life in such a manner. The revelations that the cult of Death Tubaria had a hand in his death begged the question as to why the cult would pick him out for that purpose. Did you know that he led the forces of Parandor against the Knights of Avolire some six years ago? I guess that was the reason."

"Yes indeed, I am sure that everyone in the Realm is aware of the heroism of Sir Rainmark." added Tonousa. "I was one of those ordered to stay back and safeguard the Capital with the rest of the City Watch. If it wasn't for his victory then we wouldn't be standing here now. It is truly dreadful that the Knights of Avolire would resurface in such a way and use the cult of Death Tubaria to instil fear amongst our populace."

"My thoughts are the same," replied the knight.

Tonousa recalled that without the swift actions of Sir Rainmark, the forces of Avolire could never have been defeated. Was this the connection she wondered, that Britta Rainmark was targeted because he had played such a key role in the previous defeat of the enemy. Yet that did not explain the reasons for the murder of the two servants.

"So what about the others, Lady Fullbane's servant Golda and the kitchen boy Webb?"

"I never knew them. Didn't have a reason too."

Tonousa sensed his answer to be truthful. Why after all would the head of the Royal Guard and the Army of Parandor be acquainted with Lady Fullbane's personal servant and her kitchen boy lover?

"That brings me to Lord Fabius Colt?" she added. "How well did you know the Treasurer?"

"That fat balding bastard? Everyone in Court knew Lord Colt. He controlled the funds that greased the workings of the Capital's cogs. There was no deal done nor monies exchanged that didn't first pass through Lord Colt's jam stuck fingers. From where your questions are leading, I assume you're going to ask me if I know the names of those in debt to him, but I can tell you now, I know nothing about what happens with other people's money. I cannot keep track of the few coins that find their way into my own pocket."

Tonousa could not help but smile. At least Sir Byddin was being open about his finances. She could not tell for certain whether he was being honest with her but was sure that if she gave him enough rope he would hang himself on a length of spoken untruths.

"So there was no one, not a single member of your own guard or indeed others that confided in you on issues of money lending?" asked Darchus.

"Well there was one," replied Byddin after a moment's hesitation. "But I believe that he had cleared his debt some months ago."

Tonousa was hooked by the statement.

"Who" she asked with great urgency and the Knight closed his one eye? "Sir Byddin, please give me the name of the one who was in debt to Lord Colt?"

Tonousa noted small beads of perspiration form on the knight's forehead. He was it seemed becoming uncomfortable as Tonousa probed on this issue which she sensed to be of great importance. Byddin turned, placed his hands upon the crenulations of the wall and looked out to the distant horizon. When he spoke again Tonousa sensed that his words brought relief. It was as if a great weight had been lifted from his shoulders.

"Sir Richemanus of the Nightfall. He likes a drink you see…"

"A fitting pastime for an executioner," she replied, making mental notes.

Sir Byddin turned to face Tonousa while he rested his back against the stone wall.

"I think he was in great debt to the Crown. You know what it costs to live in Parandor. Nothing comes cheap if when like Richemanus you have many vices, whores and ale being greatest amongst them. He was addicted to both and those in the know say he owed money to a great number of people. I even fear he owed money to the Wizards Guild and maybe even that of the Thieves."

"Why do you think no one has tried as yet to reclaim his debts?" asked Darchus.

"Would you dare challenge Phauless Gylewu's executioner, a man so skilled with a blade and who wields his huge axe with such great aplomb? Not even the Court Fool would dare cross Sir Richemanus."

"Yes, that makes sense," replied Tonousa. "Richemanus is not a person to anger."

"Correct!" replied Byddin and he lifted his right hand up to the patch over his left eye and gently tapped on it. "Did you do know that it was Richemanus who took my eye?"

"No, I have not heard that story."

Tonousa hoped she was about to hear something relevant to her investigation and to make progress she knew she would have to humour the old man.

"May I assume that during your training you were made aware of the practice of Hog?"

"Yes, you can," replied Tonousa. "However I have always struggled in passing on its concepts to new recruits."

"I am sorry to interrupt but what is this Hog?" asked Darchus.

"It stands for 'Hands of the Gods'," replied Tonousa. "It is a self-defence technique to be used when attacked by someone wielding a dagger or another similar small weapon. In its simplest form it is a collection of moves to disarm an opponent and deliver a lethal strike, just using your hands alone."

"That's quite a good description Tonousa," continued Sir Byddin. "Well, there I was up on the Folly in the days of my youth, sparing with Richemanus and practicing Hog. He is a formidable opponent at the best of times but on that particular day he wasn't going easy on me. I remember being distracted by a dog and I moved the wrong way. Instead of avoiding his knife I pushed my own eye ball onto the pointed end of his blade. At least I think it was an accident. "

Tonousa yawned. It wasn't that she was bored with Sir Byddin's story but she struggled to link its purpose to that of her investigation. She had to get back on track and stop Sir Byddin from rambling.

"You have your own scars too don't you Tonousa?"

"Yes I do," she replied as she thought back to her beating for insulting Xix Blackfayer and then Karoly's assault on her in the barracks. "I carry the reminder of my mistakes with me for all time. Those who scarred me have been punished. May we please get back to the reason for meeting me here today? I want to ask you about Mikus Danbury, the stable boy? What was your link to that young lad?"

"My very loose connection with Danbury was that he looked after my horse sometimes."

Tonousa raised an eyebrow and wondered what Sir Byddin meant but the Knight continued without a pause.

"He tended to Jakovs before he was stolen," he added with a mischievous smile which Tonousa failed to register for she was too busy trying to decide on her next question.

"So having explored your links with those murdered, the question I now would like you to answer is..."

"Where was I at the times these deaths took place? That's what you want to know isn't it? You want to know if I have an alibi don't you. Ever since Danisun Dain sent me the request for me to meet you here on the battlements I knew that question was going to be asked and it has caused me significant consternation. You must understand me when I say that I wish I had a water tight excuse for all of the events, some evidence that would put me in the arms of whore or the like. Alas I have no such facts to put before you and your colleague. You see I confine myself to my chambers during the evenings to read old maps and stories of the great battles long in the past. During the day I'm always escorted by my own men who will swear that I have never left their sight. However, as the majority of the murders happened at night, in the first hours of the morning, I have to admit that I was always alone at those times. I have no witnesses to call on who would confirm my activities on the nights in question."

Tonousa sighed. She had hoped that Byddin would have been able to give an alibi for at least one of the deaths and that she could eliminate him from her investigations. She was still no closer to the truth.

"May I ask why I happen to be one of your suspects?" he then asked. "Why not the dwarf, Grovrouk the Despoiler once locked in the Grey Keep, or one of the devoted followers of Jonas Tullage, long since forgotten by most in this Realm?"

"Please remember Sir Byddin that the City Watch sent out riders into the lands that lay before the Grey Mountains," answered Tonousa. "And didn't Danisun Dain himself report back to you that all in the Grey Keep had been massacred and that the Dwarf was gone?"

"There, you see my point Tonousa. The dwarf could be the one behind all of this, so why do you question me?"

Tonousa glanced towards Darchus who nodded back his affirmation of her intent, an action that was noticed by Sir Byddin.

"Well, are you going to tell me or not?"

Tonousa sighed. It was clear to her that she would need to manage Sir Byddin's frustrations if she was to have any chance of maintaining control over the interview.

"I have nothing to hide," she said. "Of course I will tell you."

"I thank you for that. It will help me offer you any further support that I can."

Tonousa then explained the events that led to her discovery of the parchment, the code wheel, and the strange picture cards that had been concealed in the secret compartment within her father's private chambers. Sir Byddin listened with great interest to all that she had to say, in particular the breaking of the code by the sailor known as Theoplous. She went on to explain how this seasoned mariner had previous knowledge of such devices and how they had deduced that each one of the cards were representations of her father's prime suspects and that the four were all prominent members of the Court. Once her story came to its natural conclusion Sir Byddin's curiosity got the better of him.

"Do you mind if I take a quick look at those cards?" he asked.

Tonousa reached into the leather pouch that hung at her side and retrieved the four cards. She passed them over to the knight who scanned each in detail and sought to decipher their hidden meaning. A minute passed.

"So the strength card represents myself, I get that as a possibility, but what of the others?"

"Judgement is Lady Emeny, Justice is Sir Richemanus, and Temperance is the Royal Priest."

"Heward Teulu," added Sir Byddin, correcting Tonousa in her failure to name the holy man.

"Yes Sir Byddin. That's the name that was in my father message."

Byddin handed the cards back and Tonousa replaced them inside her pouch. She could tell from the knight's demeanour that he was growing impatient and she feared she may extract little more from him. Indeed, she had told him far more useful information than he had given in return.

"So is that all of your questions?" said Byddin, confirming her fears. "Am I free to leave?"

"I'm sorry Sir, just bear with me for a moment longer," added Tonousa while she sifted through her thoughts in the hope that she could find another line of questioning that would bring her closer to solving the mystery.

"There's another question that I need to ask you," she added at last.

"Then spit it out Tonousa Amberstone, for I have nothing to hide."

"Once again I thank you for your cooperation in this matter. My question concerns the two servants Golda Flintwind and Webb Underscroft. From conversations that I have had with both Lady Fullbane and the dead collector, Webb's father Cassius Underscroft, it has become apparent that both servants were connected to someone peddling illicit compounds within the Citadel's walls. Is this something that as Head of Royal Guard you were aware of, or did this activity pass you by while engaged with all your other responsibilities?"

The statement seemed to shock the Knight. His face turned ashen and his one remaining eye opened wide as if at any moment it would pop out of its socket.

"Well, I..." stuttered Sir Byddin as he tried to get his words to flow.

Tonousa then realised that even if Byddin was not the Lizardman infiltrator he knew something of great significance and from the look on Darchus's face it was clear that he felt the same. She could not let him go now; she had to push for answers.

"Sir, whatever you know, you must tell us now. It may be of great help."

"Yes, I am aware of what you speak of," he replied with a stutter. "Though you would have to seek out others if you want to identify who is responsible for the sale of such stuff. Even then I doubt they would tell you the real name of the culprit who seems to hide in the shadows and protect his identity with ease."

"Any information you have, however small it may be, could be critical to my success. What is it that are people buying? Is it the Nightshade perhaps, because that is what was said to have caused the deaths of Golda Flintwind, Webb Underscroft and Lord Colt? Can you tell me why your Royal Guard did not stop the potion's distribution at source?"

"Well for a start it's not Nightshade, no, far from it. As far as I understand things, the word passed amongst my men ..."

"Your men!" exclaimed Tonousa, unable to believe that Sir Byddin was implicating those under his command. "Don't tell me that the Royal Guard themselves are taking potions that alter their perception."

"Not all of them but to be honest with you there are several. They are good men at heart and I would trust each and every one of them with my life.

Therefore I tend to look the other way on the condition that it never interferes with their duties to protect Phauless Gylewu, and that they are never caught taking it on duty. I am ashamed to tell you that was my way of handling the issue until of course the attempt on our Sovereign Ruler's life."

Tonousa could not believe that the knight she had once so respected had confessed to being complicit in the use and distribution of mind altering substances. It confirmed all that she had suspected ever since the beginning of her investigation. Byddin's honest answers had highlighted two major failings of Sovereign's Guard. First there was the theft of the Lore of the Dead and then the attempted assassination of Phauless Gylewu himself. It was now clear that the Guard were both incompetent and unfit for purpose.

"However in answer to your question Tonousa," continued Sir Byddin. "Any alchemist or physician that you consult will tell you that the white powder most sought after in the Citadel is a refined concentrate of the Lillywort flower."

"Lillywort?" queried Tonousa for it was the name of a plant she had never heard of.

"It is a white flower that grows in the Eastern Marsh. Anyone who has ever been near that stinking shit hole would tell you that it flourishes amongst the marsh grass."

"Do you think there is any possibility that one of the others my father implicated could be taking or even dealing in this substance; given what you have already implied about the stuff being openly peddled inside the Citadel?" she asked.

"An interesting question! I do know that Lady Emeny, although stern in her demeanour when at Court, is a bucket of nervous tremblings most of the time. I would wager that she takes something to help her calm her shakes, but whether she does partake of the Lillywort I could not say."

Tonousa thought for a moment. Things were starting to make a little more sense and as Lady Fullbane had foretold in her dream, a path could perhaps be forming. If the Lillywort was only to be found in and around the edges of the Eastern Marsh, whoever supplied it to members of the Sovereign Household must have access to a supply from that place. It seemed that part of the infiltrators plan was to create and spread addiction and to undermine the ability of the Royal Guard to protect all within the Citadel. Sir Byddin had been most helpful, if not perhaps a little too helpful. There was part of her that wondered if there was truth in anything that the knight had divulged. He could after all have lied and set false trails. She still could not rule him out from being the shapeshifter that she sought?

"There is one more question I need to ask you before you are free to go about your duties."

"Then ask away."

"What was your interest in the Lore of the Dead?" asked Tonousa as she watched for any change in the knight's demeanour.

"I'm sorry!" replied Sir Byddin as a look of concern formed on his face.

Tonousa threw a glance to Darchus and wondered if he too had also picked it up.

"I will repeat the question if you wish. What was your interest in the Lore of the Dead? I am referring to the book that Tullage found?"

"Yes, yes, yes. I know what the Lore of the Dead is."

"Then answer the question please Sir. What was your interest in that book before it was taken from my father's library?"

"Do you dare to accuse me of that crime too Tonousa? It was found in your father's room remember. The implications are quite obvious, even if they do not fit with your theories, code wheels, and cards. As much as it may pain you, look to your father not to me. Be careful. Be very careful Tonousa Amberstone and do not single me out for that particular crime. Should you persist you will carry yet another scar to keep your others company. Do not incur my wrath further."

Tonousa once again looked towards Darchus for support. She wondered if her friend realised that Byddin was simply using aggression to avoid answering her question.

"I am not accusing you but do you have something to hide?" she asked.

"I assumed from your question you already know what that bloody book contains," grumbled Sir Byddin. "In addition to the incantations that would release the dead from the Underworld and so forth, there is information that points to the location of a great weapon buried somewhere within the ruins of Barad Elestor."

Sir Byddin then paused and looked at Tonousa through his single searching globe.

"Before we continue, what makes you certain that I had or have any interest in that book?"

"I read your name in the library ledger," lied Tonousa as she sensed the possibility of Byddin's hand in the murders.

"I had asked for that information to be destroyed," he snarled with a sudden upsurge of anger. "But it seems the damage has been done. Then let me explain a little more. Within the passages of the Lore of the Dead there are descriptions of a weapon that could turn the tide of any war."

"Weapon?" snapped back Darchus. "What kind of weapon?"

"It takes the form of a battle axe in which a rather special sapphire was set. All This happened way back in the distant past. Together they wield a power that exceeds anything that the Wizards can throw at an enemy. Imagine what such a weapon could do in the right hands. It could determine the outcome of our impending war if used against the forces of Avolire. We could at last put an end to the bastards that have sought to destroy our lands across the years. With such a powerful weapon to hand, all would serve whoever owned it. They would rule unchallenged..."

"Is that what you want Sir Byddin?" interrupted Tonousa. "Is that what you desire for yourself, to sit on the throne of Parandor?"

"Fuck that and fuck you!" roared back the knight as he clenched his fists, his face turning plum red. "Now you're putting words into my mouth and making more accusations. Phauless Gylewu is ruler of this Realm, no one else. I am true and loyal to our Sovereign and I will flay anyone who commits treason against him. You are accusing me again and I do not like it madam. Sir Richemanus is always looking for new dancers on his stage so be very careful indeed young Tonousa..."

"I apologise again Sir. I continue to mean no offence but I have a job to do and these matters are most serious."

"Just be very precise in what you say next," the knight replied.

"This weapon you just mentioned. What more can you tell me about it?"

Sir Byddin looked out over the crenulations of the battlements towards the slums of the city and the armies stationed beyond.

"Once I became aware of the legend of the weapon I sent many good knights to explore Thengar Forest and seek out the Temple of Barad Elestor that resides somewhere within its dark recesses. None however returned and I have given up on finding that weapon. I have tried to forget that it ever existed. That was until now when you come along asking all your damned questions."

Tonousa's attention was then broken by the sound of running steps. She turned at once to investigate the source of the commotion and saw the young servant Arfon who once had served Xix Blackfayer. The youth ran along the battlements and weaved in and out of the sentries who stood and watched over the land before the Grey Mountains.

"Sir Byddin, Sir Byddin!" shouted Arfon as he ran towards them.

"What is it?" shouted back the knight.

"Sir Redglade is urgently looking for you. He said it couldn't wait; said it was something to do with the inner workings of the Narrow Gate."

The Narrow Gate was one of two set into the western wall and was the only one of all the Capital's gates that had both a portcullis and a pair of iron doors that opened inwards towards the city. Tonousa knew at once what the boy referred to by the inner workings of the gate. She was already aware that the portcullis mechanism was in need of urgent repair. The solid metal grate that when closed prevented access into the city was prone to jam. Its movements were unreliable and no longer could it be relied on to work when asked. Sir Byddin's demeanour changed as he resumed his authoritative posturing. Freed from his conversation and induced anger he spoke again.

"I guess that is my cue to leave you Tonousa Amberstone."

"One last question please Sir Byddin, if you don't mind."

"Well make it quick."

"If it is true that one of the Sovereign Council is a serial murderer, who would you suspect?"

"Let me have quick look at those cards again."

Tonousa retrieved the four stiff pieces of parchment from her leather pouch and handed them over to Sir Byddin. He scanned the four and then handed them back, but left one that stuck out to highlight it above the others. Tonousa looked at the card and noted it was the one that depicted Judgement.

"If the Royal Guard were investigating this matter instead of having to prepare the Capital's defences then I would point to Lady Emeny. Given her new position as Sovereign Advisor, she is close enough to Phauless Gylewu to do significant damage. I wouldn't be surprised if she poisoned Blackfayer in order to gain her new status. Perhaps Xix did not commit suicide after all."

Sir Byddin paused as Tonousa and Darchus looked back through quizzical eyes. Even Arfon raised an eyebrow at the accusation that Byddin had just thrown out.

"I would appreciate it if you didn't repeat what I have just said," added the knight. "She may be a heifer but she has one hell of a temper."

"You have our word on that," replied Tonousa as she placed the cards back into her pouch.

"I would also advise you seek to find out how the Lillywort is coming into the city. My hunch is that it is the same person who is responsible for both the murders and the corruption of the Citadel. They must be one and the same."

"Sir Byddin, please," interjected Arfon in attempt to gain the knights attention.

"Yes Arfon, I'm coming. Interrupt me again and you'll spend the next week in a cell."

Arfon fell silent and he dropped his head. Then Byddin spoke again.

"I'll talk with Lady Emeny and see if I can arrange for you to meet with her. Given her hectic duties it may be a couple of days before I can get you an audience but I will do my best."

"Thank you once again Sir," answered Tonousa.

With that said she shook hands with the knight who then turned and followed Arfon off along the line of battlements. As the two walked away Tonousa heard Byddin order the young servant keep his mouth shut on all matters that didn't concern him. Once out of ear shot Tonousa turned to her colleague. She felt she had accomplished much during her discussion with the Head of the Royal Guard and wanted to Darchus's opinion on all that had transpired.

"So what you made of all that?"

"He is hiding something," replied the man from Valameer. "He went very quiet when you mentioned the two servant's use of potions, the possible implications for the Royal Guard, and the rest of the Council. He also was very quick to defend himself when you hinted that he may want to gain the fabled weapon from Barad Elestor and use it for his own ends."

"Yes I noticed that too," affirmed Tonousa. "Anything else?"

"He pointed the finger of suspicion onto two of our other suspects, the Royal Executioner and the new Sovereign Advisor. I feel he has also failed to lift any doubts that we may have of him. He was rather quick and willing to answer any question you raised."

"I thought so too," replied Tonousa. "It was almost too easy."

"Back in Valameer it was common knowledge that the Trident Guard would always suspect those most willing to assist in any investigation," continued Darchus. "Nine times out of ten they were correct in their assumptions. We should first look closest to home."

Tonousa thought for a second. Darchus's idea interested her for even though she had picked up some points of interest from her direct questions, there was nothing that could eliminate Sir Byddin from her list of suspects.

"Was there anything else that you noticed?" continued Tonousa.

"There was just one other thing," added Darchus.

"And what was that?"

"The book, the Lore of The Dead. From all I have heard and from what you have told me since my arrival in Parandor, it strikes me that even though it was stolen many years ago and was then found in your father's chambers, no one has asked the obvious questions. Where is the book now and who controls it? This is something we must find out if we are to prevent further murders by the cult."

"That is a most interesting observation," replied Tonousa. "I was so caught up with the message from my father's room that I allowed that fact to slip from my mind. That is why I asked you to accompany me here Darchus. It's for times like this I need a fresh pair of eyes, to see things from another point of view, and to pick up on what I may have missed."

"I'm just pleased to have been of service."

It didn't take the pair long to return to The Murdered Wolf. As they walked on together Tonousa again noticed the absence of fearful residents who hid in their homes and now ventured outside only when forced to. The events on the Richemanus Folly had played to the infiltrators plan. He had the Capital where he wanted it, in a heightened state of fear.

On reaching the tavern they made their way through to the back of the building. There was no sign of Isambard Hotch and Tonousa was surprised that the lardy barkeep had left the tavern unattended despite having no customers. They made their way into the same room in which her father's message had been deciphered and were pleased to find that Theoplous already present. There was however no sign of Heliana or Danisun Dain, nor was there any indication they had been there that day. Tonousa looked towards another who sat at the table beside Theoplous and whose rotund figure was unmistakable. No other in the Realm matched such belly with a cascade of greasy hair and deep pox scars scattered across his face. Captain Highroar rose to his feet as soon as Tonousa and Darchus entered the room.

"Tonousa Amberstone!" he exclaimed. "You've more lives than my ship's cat!"

"And nice to see you again Captain," she answered before addressing Theoplous. "Did he come without a fight?"

"Of course. Just threaten his cock with the point of a knife and he'll do anything."

"I've just had it up to here with your sick quips, you dark bastard..." growled Highroar, but Darchus cut him short.

"We suffer no racist talk here Captain. Here we are all equal. Now tell me, how are my wife and daughter?"

"They are doing fine," snapped back Highroar as he took his place back at the table. "Captain Whitebeard of the Master's Catch was true to his word. He has agree to let them stay with him in his hovel just inside of the southern wall. I told you I would make them safe but they are always asking when they will get to see you again."

"Then please pass back how much I love and miss them and tell them that I will visit them soon," replied Darchus with sadness evident in his voice.

Tonousa did not know love in the sense that Darchus felt for his wife and child and could not imagine the magnitude of the pain he felt being separated from them. She was however pleased that Highroar had kept his promise and not abused them in the way that she had most feared. As Tonousa and Darchus took a seat at the table Highroar placed both of his hands upon its surface and began to demand answers.

"So what is it you wanted to see me about? Another voyage perhaps? Where do you want to go to this time, the sun drenched shores of the Lotus Isles?"

"No Captain, that is not why we asked to meet with you here today," replied Tonousa. "I wish to ask you about these."

She reached into her pouch and pulled out the four parchment cards which she then threw face up onto the table before the Captain. Highroar picked them up and started to analyse each of them in turn. Then after he had looked at the fourth he spoke.

"Theoplous did say that you wished to show me some cards but from what I have seen these are not the type I am accustomed to playing with. They are not used in games of chance although I have seen them before and I do know of their purpose. Yes, there is no doubt in my mind, these are Fortunes Fate cards."

"Fortunes Fate!" muttered Tonousa as she looked across the table to Theoplous who just shrugged his shoulders.

She had hoped that the Cuvar follower would have had some better understanding of the cards but then she remembered that Theoplous had also been bemused when first shown them.

"Are sure that you have not heard of them?" asked the Captain.

"I have not seen them before," replied Tonousa.

"From what a whore who once sold me her snatch upon the steps of a temple told me, they are a set of cards used by a certain religion in the foretelling of the future. There are forty seven cards that the priests use as they try to second guess the will of the goddess Fatumai and her three daughters. Yes my friends, as strange as it may sound, they are used to try and predict what may yet come to pass."

"But is there anything special about them?" asked Tonousa for she hoped that somewhere hidden deep within the Captain's perverse thoughts would be the key that would unlock their secret. "Is there anything unusual about them that we should know of?"

Captain Highroar looked again and then shook his head.

"No, they just look like normal cards to me. I cannot see any hidden clue."

Tonousa sighed. This was yet another dead end.

"Captain, can you tell us any more about how these cards are used? Do you have any insight as to the method of predicting the future?" asked Darchus.

"Now such things I do not know. You will have to ask a priest on that one. I can however tell you what the cards are made from and where you could acquire a full set but I don't claim to know how they work or how the priests use them. All I do know is that it is supposed to be the best way to explore your possible destiny. I guess it is a life game of sorts...a game of Fates, you might say."

"Are you certain that is all you know on this matter?" asked Tonousa.

"I'm afraid so. I cannot help you further."

Tonousa closed her eyes and thought for a brief moment.

"Thank you captain. Could you procure a complete deck for me? I would be most grateful and forever in your debt."

"I'll see what I can do," replied the Captain as he leered, no doubt fantasising about what his reward would be.

Tonousa turned in disgust and looked at the cards that lay upon the table. Thanks to Sir Byddin and Captain Highroar a way forward had begun to form within the fog of her thinking. She attempted to piece together all of the information she had accumulated. The memory of the voice of Lady Fullbane probed her mind and repeated again and again, 'a path is forming'. Tonousa sensed that wherever the path led it would contain many more twists and turns before the mystery was solved.

13

Young eyes flickered open but they saw nothing but darkness. Spasms of agonising pain surged through the youth's body even though he remained motionless and made no attempt to move. The pain was the one thing he could hold onto. It was the reality of that intense agony that proved to him that he was neither dreaming nor dead. Had it been an imagining, the great distress would have woken him from his nightmare and then it would have gone away. If he was dead then he had been sent to Plains of Eternal Terror for other than Kha no deity would allow such dreadful torment in the afterlife. He had lived a good life and so could not believe he had been condemned to that most awful of places. No, he had to be alive and that was all that mattered. He did not know how long he had lain on the hard rock floor but he then remembered his journey into the depths of the mountain and what he had found there. He recalled with horror the heat of the fire as it had belched forth from out of the Wyvern's throat.

Lay on his back he stared into the pitch black that swallowed him whole. He sought out the slightest speck of light that would give him some indication as to the way out of his isolation; but there was nothing. There seemed no hope left for him and that the darkness was destined to last for ever. The youth then noticed of the coolness of the armour that he wore and it soothed the flesh that underneath the metal had been burned and charred in a most hideous way. He felt the damp wetness of a multitude of ruptured blisters as they oozed salt laden fluid which trickled over adjacent areas of sensitive flesh. Whenever he tried to move the burns rubbed against the rough edges of his armour and caused him to tremble amid intense discomfort. It was as if someone had stabbed him with a million daggers. To move was to be in pain and to be in pain was to want to move.

The youth sighed down to the soles of his boots and then cried out.

"Somebody help me. Please, somebody help me,"

He continued to shout into the darkness, over and over again until his voice grew hoarse. Once exhausted he sensed that he had to wait to regain his energy for he did not know if help would ever come. He was all alone in the impenetrable black of the cavern but he had to keep fighting to survive. Amid his trembling terror he prayed that someone, anyone, would come and find him. Once again he tried to move his left arm only to feel an excruciating pain shoot through his limb. It was no good, he was lost, and he felt devoid of hope. There was no way that he could escape from the confines of the cavern without assistance and realised that he was trapped and would die in this god forsaken place. His bones would remain there forever, at least until they crumbled to ash.

Methladon Heyn closed his eyes and wondered how long it would be before he would pass into the next world where the gods would repair his body so that he could exist alongside them. He knew that he could go for a week without food for he had often done so during his time in Maplehill when sustenance was often scarce. However, without water he knew he could not last more than a few days and not even that long given the severity of the burns that he had suffered. If he didn't get treatment for them soon the black flesh rot would set in and then the pain would then increase tenfold. Methladon realised in that moment that he was fucked.

He closed his eyes, at least he thought he had closed them as the pain the action produced shot through his entire head. His eyelids had perhaps been burned away or at least reduced to their roots. Methladon then realised that it had been the orichalcum that encased his body which had provided protection against the fiery breath that had emanated from the bowels of Thamous. From the first time that he had seen it, he had realised that the mysterious armour of the Knights of Avolire had great properties and was able to resist the most severe physical insults. This rarest of all metals had saved his life.

Unsure of how time passed or how much he had left of life, the youth tried to recall what had so angered the wyvern so much that it had unleashed its fiery inferno. He remembered pushing Thamous for answers as he had become angered in his belief that it was withholding information from him. He remembered the sensation growing on the back of his head and then a feeling that someone had begun to control him. Yes, that was it, somehow he had projected his mind inside that of the wyvern in order to see the creature's thoughts and to cause it pain. It was that coming together of minds that had startled the creature and caused it to seek to kill him.

He then remembered screaming after the initial blast had hit him, followed by a second and a third. The creature had not intended him to survive. Amid the heat and the burning agony that engulfed him, he had seen the flailing of his own limbs as he had sought to extinguish the flames and push them back. The creature had then retreated into the darkness of the cavern. The fire that had pierced gaps in his armour had then started to cook him alive as if he was enclosed within one of the twin Lions of Avolire. Once his arms had beaten back the flames a he had fallen into unconsciousness and his world had turned black.

"Wake up dolt!" demanded a voice.

The words caused Methladon to jump. He screamed out in agony as the cooling metal of his armour rubbed once again on the open sores of his skin. It was an inhuman and guttural utterance that had surfaced somewhere inside his skull. He thought for a brief moment that the wyvern had returned to torment him and finish the job it had started, but then he realised that the voice was different.

"Who's there?" shouted Methladon as he tried to use what was left of his facial muscles.

No answer came. No help came either and his fear and sense of isolation grew. He attempted to close his eyes and breathe through the pains that shot through his body. He focused on the one thing that that made him fight to remain alive, the memory of his family, his father, his mother, and his two brothers. Even in the darkness that crushed him, Methladon was able to picture the faces of his loved ones. He saw visions of happy times when he had defended Maplehill from skyfawn and nighthowler attacks with his two brothers and father. He pictured the tasty meals that his mother had conjured up from the little food they had to survive on. He remembered the fireplace at the Red Mare and the times he had spent with his friends Llyat and Cleath, listening to stories of the old times that flowed out of the garrulous mouth of the dimwit Denius Castor. In his delirium he could taste, smell, and hear all the details of each event. He felt he was slipping into another reality.

Then the image of a young boy stretched between four horses in a darkened street in a fortified city started to break through the happier visions that had begun ease his suffering. Methladon knew that image well. It had been the very one that had haunted his dreams for years, an event that he had once believed was just a fantasy, a mere illusion caused by his subconscious memory. Yet, if Thamous was to be believed, then this frightening vision was not fiction but an actual event. It was a distant memory of something that had happed to him way back in his past and which he had sought to bury deep inside his soul. He searched his mind and tried to recall his distant youth but each time he tried, the furthest back he could remember was the memory of waking up in Maplehill at the beginning of his teen years. No matter how hard he pushed something in his head continued to block more distant memories. It was as if that someone or something did not want him to know of his roots and would use any means, even the darkest of magic, to prevent him from knowing his past.

"So are you just going to lie there?" said the voice. "You know damn well that death isn't going to come for you here. You are an anomaly. One with power over fear and death itself. You cannot and will not die."

Methladon lay confused and listened to the words as they echoed through his head. He realised once again this was not the voice of the great beast for this new one was much more human. For a brief second he wondered if his dehydration was sending him insane but yet he knew that all was real.

"How do I know that you are there?" he asked.

A sudden crushing weight seemed to push the armour of his chest down on to the burnt skin beneath it. Methladon cried out in agony. One question teased him; had the pressure had been induced by falling debris or the presence of another. Surely there had to be someone else there with him in the blackness of the cavern.

"Okay," Methladon screamed. "You win. You are real. But who the fuck are you and why won't you let me die in peace."

"Like I keep telling you," continued the voice. "Remember what Thamous said, you are an anomaly. You should have died when that mark was etched on the back of your neck; yet you survived somehow and now the deepest of magic percolates through your energy centres. You are immortal. You cannot ever die."

Methladon started to weep and as he did so the salty tears seeped down his blistered cheeks and added to the agony. The thought of lying awake for an eternity in this darkest of tombs filled him with an intense dread. The attempt on his life by a fanatical cult had robbed him of the one thing that would end his suffering, the ability to die. He felt very afraid.

"Quit that pathetic howling," shouted the voice. "Do you think that crying like a young girl is going save you? Only you can do that Methladon Heyn, only you. You know what you saw in that sceptre, witnessed what your future demands of you. It is the choices you make right now that will determine your fortune and your fate. This is your moment to grasp your destiny and make it so."

Methladon hesitated for he could not work out how the voice knew what he had witnessed inside the diamond. It was true that he had seen a future where he sat on the throne of Parandor with the Lady of the Silverwynn by his side. He had also seen a great battle around a walled city where a gold and a black knight fought on the corpses of the dead. Then he remembered the image of flying and his flesh melting and falling to the ground. He sensed that this was what the sceptre had showed him, his cremation by the will of the wyvern Thamous? Despite his moribund state Methladon felt his anger increase. He was troubled by the fact that whoever the other person with him was, they knew far too much about his life.

"Who are you?" he demanded. "Can you see me?"

"Of course I can see you lad and I see the predicament you now face."

"Then who are you?" screamed Methladon "Stop avoiding the question."

"My name!" sneered the voice with a sinister undertone. "My name is not yet for your ears. It is a prize that you must earn."

"What must I do to have you speak it?"

"You have to get yourself out of this mountain. Only then will my name be revealed."

Methladon was dumfounded. He could not comprehend what the voice had suggested. He could not move let alone find his way through the darkness of the Gathering.

"Are you mad?" he shouted through half absent lips.

"Only as mad as you choose to believe, but if I can walk then so can you."

"What about my injuries..." began Methladon, but the voice was ready for him.

"From what I can tell, your armour took the full force of the fire. Any mortal man, even wearing plate from of the orechalcic seams of Calistorn, should have perished and be now nothing but ash. But you cannot die Heyn. You are at one with the gods. You are immortal. Pain and fear are just different states of mind for you to overcome. You can accomplish anything, if you set your mind to it."

Methladon sighed. He would seek to put the stranger's theory to the test and inch by inch he began to raise his left arm from the ground upon which he still lay. Intense pain shot through it and caused him to drop it back onto the rock. Methladon hollered hard.

"Heed what I say. I'm going to go now but I will be back in a short time. When I return, I want to see you on your feet or I'm going to leave you down here forever. Do you understand me lad?"

"But..." began Methladon yet once again the voice cut him off.

"I will accept no excuses. If you are not on your feet by the time I return then I'll leave you here to rot."

"I thought I couldn't die," replied Methladon.

No reply came and he did not hear the footfall of the stranger as he left. It was as if he had just floated away.

"Help me, I have so much to live for, so much good I can still bring to this world."

Methladon then closed what remained of his eyelids and began to think hard. Whoever the stranger was his threat to abandon him if he could not stand was all too clear. Furthermore, this other seemed to have insight as to what was happening to him, including the mark on the back of his head. Methladon then began to wonder if the three circles had been destroyed by the flames. If the stranger knew such details then maybe he could explain why he could not remember his childhood and why as Thamous had put it, he had started to leach energy from out of the Rift. He needed answers to those questions and to do that he would need to get onto his feet by the time the stranger returned. Taking a deep breath and then using the armour that encased him to support his battered body he rolled onto his side. He uttered a high pitched scream which rose to fill the cavern. It was then that he realised that the pain he had just experienced did not have the same disabling impact as previous ones had done. It was now somehow different, less intense, and that realisation confused him.

"Here goes," he muttered as he mustered all of his courage to push himself up on to his knees.

It was a feat that should have been impossible given his circumstances but somehow Methladon managed to move with a little more ease within the confines of his armour. The pain that once was unbearable began to give him a great strength with which to overcome the impossible. He used his hand to manipulate his weight and pulled himself to his feet. Dizziness then struck. He staggered forward, put his hands out to stop himself from falling, and then collided with the wall. Even this no longer caused the agony that he had previously endured. He took another deep breath and then put his full weight on to the balls of his feet. He was upright again. The lightness of head passed and he began his wait for the stranger to return.

A thought then came to Methladon. What if the mysterious person had been telling lies and intended to leave him in the darkness. Fear started to grow but then he managed to catch his breath and slow his pounding heart. He would not give into fear. If he could force himself to stand and conquer the pain, then as the stranger had implied, he could do anything.

"So you did it then?" said the voice from his side. "Do you now believe me? Everything is possible for one who has courage."

"Where are you?" asked Methladon and he reached out in an attempt to grab the stranger.

Yet all his hands touched were the walls and no matter how hard he tried he could not put his hands upon the person he prayed was destined to be his saviour.

"I'm right ahead of you."

"Then let me touch you," demanded Methladon but the voice did not answer.

Methladon wondered why the man taunted him so and then it dawned on him that perhaps the reason the owner of the voice could see in the dark was due to it being either of lizard or dragon kind. And yet the voice sounded human and somewhat familiar.

"So are you coming?"

"Which way?" he replied. "I can't see anything."

"Reach out and put your hand on the wall. Feel for the rock. Keep them there and continue to follow its course. You will find salvation soon enough my friend."

"Wouldn't it be easier if I..."

"No it wouldn't, for if you were to touch my body you would lose all hope of getting out of here alive. You would lose your strength and your courage. I can but guide you out of here with my words, the rest is up to you."

"But..." interrupted Methladon as once again the voice fell silent.

Methladon placed his hand out towards his side and in a blind swinging motion he tried once again to locate the wall. Some minutes later he touched the rock wall and placed both hands up its hard surface. The pain in his hands had long since gone, overcome by the power and focus of his will. An insight of significance then struck home. He did not know which way to go. Should he move to the left or to the right? His spatial awareness had been lost within the unending darkness. The one thing he knew for certain was that the rock wall was in front of him.

"Which way?" Methladon demanded of the darkness but again no answer came.

He closed what remained of his eye lids even though it made no difference to the black that engulfed him and then directed his thoughts towards prayer. He grovelled with all the belief and faith that he could muster that some god would look down upon him and show him the way forward.

"Right it is then," he said with a sigh and then began his shuffle along the wall.

Methladon continued to inch sideways. He placed hand over hand, foot over foot, and edged like a somnolent slug like along the cavern wall. His fingers felt every rocky crevice and outcrop that appeared before his raw minced digits. On occasions he staggered forwards and almost fell but somehow he managed to stop himself from going over for that would have disorientated him even further. He heard no further sound from his would be saviour as he crept forward, nor from the monstrous creature that had caused his desperate predicament. Soon he began to feel the ground slope downwards and knew that he had begun to descend further into the wyvern's roost. Perhaps an hour later the floor levelled out and still Methladon clung onto the wall. On the rare occasions that he let go of it he panicked and at once replaced his hand upon the stone. He could not afford to get lost inside the bowels of the Gathering.

"So you've got the hang of it," whispered the voice. "Do you see what I mean? You are doing very well indeed."

"How far do I have to go? Tell me the truth; is there another way out of this hell hole or am I trapped in here forever. Are you going to say anything useful?"

"You are doing just fine. You are getting the hang of it at last."

Methladon sighed in deep frustration and continued his stumble through the dark. There was no way of telling how long he had been negotiating the twists and turns of the cavern's walls but it seemed that it must have been hours. He wished for just the smallest glint of light, a morsel that would be enough to give him hope; but again none came. A bitterness started to creep into his thoughts, born from being abandoned in the depths of the Gathering. A hatred fermented and he directed it towards those that he thought were his friends and yet had left him for dead. If he ever got out of his tomb he would make them pay. He would make them all suffer. Then as if his bitterness had been heard by the gods, Methladon noticed the smallest pin prick of light that seemed to hang in the darkness above. At first he thought he was dreaming and that the small speck was some ethereal spirit that had come to release him from his torment, yet the longer he stared the more his hope grew. It had to be the way out that the voice had teased him with, his means of escape.

"Is that my way to freedom?" he shouted into the darkness.

"Why don't you check it out and see for yourself?"

"But how far is it? How high do I have to climb?"

The voice did not answer and Methladon felt the bitterness towards his tormentor grow. He felt around the rocks with his hands and realised that he was stood within a small recess, cut into the rock wall, and below the pin prick of light.

"You want me to climb, is that it?" Methladon asked of the dark.

"Now perhaps you understand what you have to do to get out of here."

"For once give me a straight answer," he snapped back as his curse mark burned.

"Good boy," said the voice. "Give yourself up to the darkness within your soul. Embrace your fear and agony. Let these be your salvation and climb Methladon Heyn. Let us ascend the wall together like no one else would ever dare to do."

The words of the voice did not register as Methladon looked up to the speck of light. Then with all of his strength he gripped hold of the rock and attempted to pull himself up. His progress did not last for the weight of his armour, as light at it was, pulled him back down to where he had started.

"I can't do it," sighed Methladon as the hopelessness of his situation gripped his heart.

"There is no such word as can't," said the voice. "You can and will succeed. Stop feeling so sorry for yourself. You know what you need to do to get out of here. So just do it."

"Then fucking tell me!" screamed Methladon. "What do I need to do?"

"Discard your armour. Discard everything and lighten your load."

Methladon hesitated. The strange voice that tutored him seemed to speak some sense. If he discarded the metal suit then he might stand a chance of climbing up to the light above. Doing so would also give him greater freedom of movement and he would need that because one false step would bring him crashing back down to the cavern floor where his bones would shatter in to a thousand shards. He removed his helmet and for a brief of moment felt the intense pain return as his burnt flesh stuck to the metal of the helm. He screamed once again and this time an answer came back from within the darkness. The sound was bestial, something very reptilian. He was sure it was the sound of a dragon or even worse, a wyvern.

"What was that?" shouted Methladon as he dropped his helm.

Ignoring the resurgence of pain he succumbed to his fears. It was as if his body was on fire with excitement. Sensations urged him to choose between fighting the beast that hid in the dark or fleeing up the rock and on to freedom.

"What do you think it was?" asked the voice. "You know that sound?"

"That was the wyvern," he replied.

"Why are you just standing there? Get a fucking move on."

Methladon did not have to be told twice. Several minutes later he had pulled off all the remaining parts of his armour and cast them away into the black. He cried out as each piece that had welded to his flesh ripped open further wounds. Then after removing his metal boots he stood naked, vulnerable, and alone. Once again he sought out the recess in the cavern wall. It didn't take him long to find where he needed to be and soon he relocated the light source above his head. Reaching up with both of his hands he started to pull himself up the rock. He took each boulder in turn and continued the slow climb, always seeking a good foot hold and a secure place in which he could grip with his charred and blistered fingers. He was not sure if his guide followed him and so cried out to the darkness.

"Are you there? Are you coming with me?"

"Don't worry about me. Focus on getting yourself out of here."

"But you can't face that creature alone," replied Methladon as he remembered what Thamous had done to the Lizardman with whom he had entered the Gathering.

"Your problem is that you care too much about others. Think only of yourself or you will not survive. Only you can make it happen; no one else."

Methladon continued on his climb up the rock. He groped, gripped and dragged himself ever higher. As he moved up he could feel the roughness of the stone against his skin and it scraped away at his already pulverised flesh. On he went minute by minute, hour after hour. He heard no further sounds to indicate the presence of the wyvern but neither did he hear his saviour climbing beneath him. The youth's arms and legs began to weaken as the fatigue of his climb took its toll on his depleted energy reserves. His muscles ached more than they had ever done and they combined with spasms of lightening pain to try and destroy his will. The bright light above grew ever larger with each handhold that he secured and he began to feel in control at last. Now he understood how right the voice had been; *'If you put his mind to it, you can accomplish anything.'* For what seemed like an infinite stretch of time Methladon approached the light source that hung above his head. He climbed into its beginning, now grown large, and it bathed him in the reflected light from Solaris. He listened in the quiet stillness but still could not hear anyone below. It did not seem to matter for he was close to the sweet fresh air of the outside world and it would make a welcome change from the stench of cooked flesh that he had endured for so many hours. His heart quickened as he approached his salvation.

Many of the rocks under his right hand moved and fell away. Several of those dislodged from the rock face were the size of a fist and they plummeted down into the dark pit below. With his left hand only attached, Methladon hung on for his life while seeking further cracks to grip with his right hand and feet. With great effort he managed to stabilise himself and the immediate terror passed. The dangers he faced became magnified for he was tiring, becoming complacent, and struggling to maintain attention. His drive to escape had been great and it had clouded his judgement. There was a strong possibility that the debris he had dislodged could have fallen upon the one who followed and he feared that they may have sent his saviour crashing to his doom. Inhaling deeply he shouted to where he thought the voice would come from.

"Please tell me you are still there."

"Just focus on the task. It's not over yet. There is still a significant distance to cover."

Methladon returned his attention to the rock and continued his ascent up through the now gaping hole in the mountain. After what seemed another life time he at last climbed out into the cool mountain air and allowed the direct light of Solaris to fall upon his seared flesh. There he paused and gazed upon the vastness of the opening he had just passed through. He was reminded of the wing span of the wyvern Thamous, the beast who had left him to die in such a pitiful state.

"This must be the creature's gateway into the mountain," he mumbled weakly as he clung on to life in his nakedness.

The light of Solaris soothed his raw skin rather than adding to the pain from his burns. He sensed he had emerged from the darkness like a fledgling from the nest, new born and intent on savouring a new world. With all of his strength he pulled himself up and over the final lip of the entrance and allowed himself to roll down a steep slope of dirt and gravel before coming to a halt some distance away. Lay on his back he stared up the sky. The grime that clung to his many wounds no longer caused discomfort for he had conquered both pain and fear. They were but subjective experiences that he would no longer permit to hinder his thoughts. Lying helpless he began to laugh with sinister undertones. Methladon Heyn then screeched to the burning disc of Solaris.

"I am still fucking alive!"

The strange laughter built to a crescendo and it echoed around the sides of the mountain.

The sound of approaching men as they moved over the gravel brought Methladon out of a transient delirium. The noise of feet was soon joined by the sound of shouts and they came from voices that he recognised. They belonged to three who he had journeyed with from Avolire.

"I told you. See, I told you," shouted the grumpy voice of Oedd.

"What is it?" replied Commander Rhaizen.

"There by the cavern entrance," shouted the Harbinger. "I knew that I had heard someone."

After a distinct pause a third voice joined in with the others the pace of the men's footfall hastened.

"Meth? Methladon Heyn?" shouted Grovrouk the Despoiler.

The youth focused on the footsteps of his companions as they raced towards him and seconds later he found himself staring into the eyes of the dwarf.

"Meth, is that you? What the fuck has happened to you? We thought you were lost."

"Water!" gasped Methladon as for the first time he realised the extent of his dehydration.

"Oedd, give the boy something to drink," ordered Rhaizen as he too then came into view.

The large form of Oedd produced a bladder of water and pushed it forward with an outstretched hand. Methladon felt the dwarf and the Commander reach down and lift him so as to aid him to drink the cool life giving liquid. As the water passed his lips he half expected the burnt flesh of his face to sting but there was no pain, just the soothing cold of the liquid.

"What happened?" demanded Rhaizen. "Did you find the creature? What happened to Ssnarkit? Where is your armour and why are you naked? What happened to your fucking skin?"

Methladon did not answer the Commander's barrage of questions. Instead he allowed his thoughts to his focus on the stranger who had guided him throughout his escape. He needed to know if he too had made it out of the mountain.

"Answer me lad, what happened down..." said Rhaizen but Methladon cut him off.

"There is another you must aid, someone who helped me escape? Where is he?"

"Oedd, check around and see what you can find," shouted Rhaizen.

"Is there anything you can do for him?" Methladon heard Grovrouk ask Rhaizen.

"For fucks sake speak with man tongue and not that drivel you call a language," replied Rhaizen and in that moment Methladon remembered that it was his magic, the power that had sustained his life and made him immortal, which allowed him to understand the words of the Dirmark.

"Is there anything at all that you can do for him?" Methladon heard Grovrouk ask again, this time in a language that others could understand.

"We need to get him back to Avolire as soon as possible," said Rhaizen. "My magic is not strong enough to save his life and heal these hideous wounds. Only the Lady and the power she taps from the Rift could do that."

"Then let's get him away from here as soon as possible," added Oedd on his return.

"Was there any sign of anyone else?" asked Rhaizen as he helped Grovrouk to lift Methladon from off the hard ground.

"There is no other, my nose would have told me otherwise"

"But there was someone," moaned Methladon. "He helped me escape."

"You've been down there for two days without food or water," continued Rhaizen. "You are delirious."

"But I am telling you..."

It was then that Methladon realised the truth behind his escape. He recalled the way that the voice would not allow any contact nor answer his questions. It knew certain secrets that no one else could ever have known. There was the nature of the voice itself which he had at last recognised. It was his own. He had been talking to himself. He alone had been responsible for his escape and in that moment of enlightenment he felt truly reborn.

14

Einar returned at the midpoint of Mona's watch and explained the reasons for missing the meal in the Three Sisters. Llyat and Thias, happened to be both still awake and talking. The Berserker then told how he had spent his time scouting the land in and around the small town of Fallguard that lay in the shadow of the great pines of Thengar Forest. The cold had descended sooner than anyone had expected and even though he was immune to it Einar knew there was something unnatural about the weather that blew down from the lands of the Dirmark. He reported he had seen nothing sinister about which they should be fearful. The bard enquired of the two mercenaries that had confronted him in the tavern and asked if Einar had seen them leave the village. The giant confirmed that he had seen two men that fitted Thias's description leave the town and that they had headed south along with two Lizardmen. However as it was very dark the time he could not be certain that they were the two that Thias had described.

Despite little sleep Llyat was the first to rise the next morning. Even though grey snow laden clouds hung over the town and blocked Solaris's rays, there was enough light to illuminate the room and cause him to stir from his slumber. He recalled the dream that had played out in his head just before he woke, one where he had found himself in back in Parandor, making love to Heliana on the bed of Grand Physician Abrahamus Marus, nuzzled between her breasts, warm, comfortable and safe.

Once his companions had risen and dressed, the group made their way to the ground floor of the Three Sisters where the innkeeper Garret had been true to his word. Assembled for them were the supplies that the travellers needed for their onward passage into the wilds of the forest. Llyat had half expected Garret to have gone back on his word and stolen the remaining unicorns, maybe even have attempted to murder them in their sleep; but he had not and instead had provided enough provisions to last for at least ten days. In his generosity the innkeeper had also left for them a crude map that showed the main routes through Thengar Forest and in particular the one that led to the ruins of Barad Elestor. For this Thias was most thankful. The bard shook the innkeepers hand in gratitude and no doubt hoped it was not false information designed to do lead them astray and to their eventual doom.

After persuading Kaylee to allow Einar to eat breakfast with them, a meagre meal that consisted of something that resembled milky oatmeal, the four companions left the Three Sisters and began their journey over the snow covered ground towards the forest. Llyat watched the eyes of those that saw them leave and wondered if any would dare follow or indeed attack them in the streets or along the road beyond the town. He was relieved that there was no sign of Ventes, Dint L'Fare, Lizardmen, or indeed the strange sisters with whom they had shared space and time the previous evening.

Wrapped in the new furs that the Garret had provided and which Einar confirmed as nighthowler pelts, the group laboured on through the deep snow. All were on foot and Thias led the way with Llyat by his side. Irabo followed without his crutch which he had at last decided to abandon. The two unicorns, even though saddled for riding, were weighed down with the supplies and were led through the snow by the still bare chested Einar. Each moved at their own pace as they crunched through the crisp white blanket of snow. Llyat did not speak as they moved into the darkness of the dense forest for his mind was preoccupied with random thoughts. The first was that he was glad that the snow had ceased falling along with the better cold wind that had blown against them. The second was his gratitude for the furs for even though he wore the leather armour of the dragon handlers of Falahorn he was mindful of the extra warmth that the pelts generated. However, the most important thought that consumed him was the Dragon Whisper for he could not help but wonder what Thamous had meant by his parting message,

> 'When things begin to change, give the Whisper to the bard. With a beacon of hope his suffering will end.'

He thought back to the bronze pendent which Thias had given up for supplies and wondered if that was what the wyvern had meant by the Bard's suffering. If it was, then Llyat realised that the Dragon's Whisper he had carried out of the Dragonas could be key to ending any pain that Thias felt by giving up his one connection to the place that he had once called home.

After trekking the first mile from Fallguard and deep within the forest the four companions stopped to check their bearings. They looked up amid the great gnarled oak trees interspersed with ancient pines with their snow covered needles that overhung the path, ready to fall and bring their white burden down upon the travellers. None however moaned as they looked out with awe and apprehension. As he stood in silence Llyat began to wonder what new dangers lurked ahead in the darkness of the dense forest that had occupied this land since the world first formed. He wondered briefly if any of his companions felt the same, that they should turn back and leave the mysterious place unexplored. He knew they would not agree and so shook the thought out of his head and searched for his new found confidence. Once grasped, he took his first step forward into his uncertain future.

Sometime later while crossing a most uneven section of forest floor, where the roots of great oaks surfaced only to disappear once again beneath the snow and dirt, Llyat came across the first sign of danger from within the midst of the ancient creaking timbers. On the ground, with his back against one of the larger trees, and covered with a layer of snow that had found its way down through the dense foliage, sat a knight in fine armour. His visor was down and he was as stiff as iron from the cold. It was immediately clear that the warrior was long lost from the world. As the group gathered round the figure they found no obvious sign of injury. Thias moved forward to try and discover the identity of the deep frozen warrior.

"Who was he?" asked Llyat.

"From the sigil on his pauldron he was a member of the Royal Guard of Parandor," replied Thias as he knelt in the snow and examined the corpse with its covering of ice crystals.

Llyat also moved forward and in an instant recognised the colours and the same pattern that he seen hanging from the ceiling of the Great Hall back in the

Citadel. The depiction of a golden cross dividing a background in four equal parts of copper-red, bronze, silver, and grey was unmistakeable. He was pondering on who the man could be when he heard some movement behind. It was Irabo limping towards him.

"What in Mona's tears are members of the Royal Guard doing all the way up here?"

"I'm not sure I can answer that," replied Thias as he examined the Knight with great care. "It is most strange. During my time at of the Court of Phauless Gylewu, I was never made aware of an expedition sent this far north from the Capital. Whoever he is... sorry was, he has long since departed on his journey to the afterlife."

"No shit!" snorted Irabo.

Llyat heard further movement as Einar then circled and sniffed the air for danger. The unicorns he had led remained alone a short distance away.

"I don't like it," whispered the Berserker as he made his fears known.

"I don't think there is anything to like about it," replied Thias as he lifted the knight's visor to reveal the lilywhite frozen flesh of the man's face.

"What do you think killed him?" asked Llyat, his nerves trembling as he assumed that whatever it was could still be lurking in the shadows.

"I cannot say," continued Thias as he looked over the warrior. "There are no visible wounds or signs that he was attacked. If I was to take a guess then it could be that the poor bugger simply froze to death and that his companions, if he had any, just left him here. I don't think we should linger in this place. Let us pray to Solaris that it wasn't Kaylee's food, tainted by the pus from one of her numerous carbuncles."

Without further comment the four companions set off again and trudged ever deeper into the gloom filled expanse of Thengar Forest. Their progress was snail slow as they manoeuvred through the dense foliage and trees, hindered by Irabo's struggles as he sought to get used to walking on two legs again. On the four went, mile after long mile. They stopped from time to time to recover their strength and in the little light available check their position against the directions on Garret's map. At nightfall when the temperature plummeted even further the travellers stopped and huddled around the best fire that they could make given the dampness the wood collected during the day. They took it in turns to be on watch in case any danger should approach in the night. To Llyat the cold felt like nothing he had ever experienced before and the further north they travelled, the greater was its effect on his morale. Late into the hours of the first night Llyat was most thankful for the warm nighthowler fur. Einar's presence ignited curious thoughts in Llyat's mind as the Berserker kept guard over the two unicorns and the group's precious supplies. The stoic nature of the giant and the ability to remain bare chested in the deep frost caused a look of gormless wonderment to settle on Llyat's face as he sought to invent stories to tell in the Red Mare if he ever got back home.

In the morning of the second day they broke through the darkness of the forest and entered a small glade which would have been a most beautiful sight in the frost covered forest had it not been for the two iron cages in its centre that contained the frozen remains of two naked men. Scattered around were the pieces of armour that had once belonged to knights and it was clear that these two had been captured and forced to remove their metal protection before being and confined within their icy tombs. As the four travellers looked in silence at the carnage in the glade, Thias spoke the words that Llyat was too frightened to utter.

"More members of the Royal Guard."

"It's horrible," whimpered Llyat as he joined Thias at the first cage.

Llyat looked to the head of the frozen corpse. Its exposed skull had oozed brain for the hungry carrion to eat before it had frozen solid. It seemed as if someone had struck the knight from behind, perhaps with a rock, shattered his skull, and then left him to rot.

"Looks like ogres to me," said Einar who looked into the second cage and found similar signs. The Berserker then sniffed the air as he sensed something nearby.

"What would ogres be doing this far north of the Grey Mountains?" asked Irabo.

"I'm not sure," answered the bard. "I'm reminded of what Theoplous said; that the Lady was recruiting all manner of evil to her cause. It looks like she may have gained the trust of the ogres."

"May we go please?" asked Llyat as he pulled on the Bard's sleeve like a child demanding tit. The sight of the carnage had unsettled Llyat and the horrific visions fuelled his fear.

"Sure," replied Thias as he threw out a comforting arm. "We won't linger here any longer."

"How far do you think it is to Barad Elestor?" asked Irabo.

"Could be a couple of days more," replied Thias. "Although from studying the almost illegible scrawl on old Garret's map I'm not that sure."

"May we go right now please?" moaned Llyat with added urgency.

Thias looked back, nodded and smiled. Llyat sensed the bard, even though curious about the two caged men, was equally as apprehensive about what lurked in the darkness of the forest. The youth did not have to ask again and soon all four companions resumed their long trek. Snow began to fall and it peppered their progress. Just a fraction fell to the ground and Llyat knew that much more accumulated in the branches of the tall trees and threatened to engulf the travellers. Llyat then noticed the complete absence of life save for that of his companions and the trees. There were no birds, no nighthowlers, skyfawn or indeed any other creature that would threaten their journey. The forest seemed to be dead. Then out of the corner of his right eye, set amongst the whiteness of the snow that part covered it, he spotted a single red rose. It was a most beautiful object amid the oppressive gloom of Thengar Forest and Llyat wondered if it was a trick of his imagination. He stopped to admire the ruby rich redness of the solitary flower and as he looked at it in detail he smiled. He realised in that simplest of moments that anything was possible. The flower was a symbol of hope. Just as the rose had found a way to survive in the ice hell forest then so would he. With a warm glow in his heart Llyat raced after his companions who had moved some distance ahead. It had been but a fleeting moment in his life and yet one of great significant. No one asked him why he had stopped and for that Llyat was grateful. It was a private memory from the journey that he would cherish for as long he walked in this world.

The light of Solaris failed to break through the snow clouds at the midpoint of the third day. Amongst the trees, the four companions came across yet another clearing in the middle of the forest. They stepped out into its vast openness and were surprised to find several large hessian tents erected in the centre of the clearing. Each one flew from its central pole the flag of the Royal Guard of Parandor. The travellers moved forward with much trepidation and soon came across many fallen knights that were scattered across the ground. All were dressed in identical armour, some decapitated, some dismembered, and others with their helms smashed into the bones of their skulls. Each had spilled their crimson onto the white snow which had long frozen but now was part hidden under the most recent fall. It was impossible to say how long ago the massacre had occurred for the ice and cold had preserved the remains of the dead. While the group stepped amongst the carnage Llyat noticed that Thias had stopped and bent forward to examine one of the fallen warriors. After a few moments the others gathered around to deliberate on their next move.

"I'm beginning to sense a pattern here," began Thias once they had all assembled. "I think Einar is correct; there are ogres in these woods."

"That's just great." added Irabo.

"If there are ogres near here then we're not likely to come across any other Realm folk who could impede our quest," responded Thias. "No one in their right mind would linger here when those foul beasts are close."

Llyat focused on Thias's less than comforting comment. The bard had confirmed Llyat's fear as to why they had encountered no others on their journey through the forest. He had heard stories about the ogres of the Grey Mountains from Denius Castor. From what he understood they were large, mottled, grey skinned creatures, with pig-like heads too big for their bodies. He also knew that these creatures were strong and not as dumb as commonly believed. After hearing one of Castors stories Llyat knew that the ogres had high intelligence, an ability to think, and make plans. This made them one of the most dangerous types of creatures in the entire Realm. Even worse, Denius Castor had told him that there were some ogres who had mastered the magic arts and this further strengthened the view in the tavern that the creatures had exceptional intelligence.

Then Thias spoke. "Let's see if there is anything that we can find that could be useful. We might as well rest for the time being. Llyat, can you pass me Garret's map, it's in the satchel on the side of the first unicorn. I want to check our bearings."

The youth made his way over to the unicorns which Einar had tied to a tree. There he began to search through the satchel for the map that was hidden within it dark recesses. As he looked his hand touched upon on a small glass bottle which he then he pulled out to examine. It was one of the flasks of amber liquid with which the Berserkers of Falahorn transformed into their fearsome bestial state. As he held it up to the little light that came through the clouds Llyat heard a crunch in the snow. He turned to find Einar watching with concern.

"Careful with that lad," said the Berserker and as he snatched the vial from Llyat's hands. "If there are ogres in these woods then we're going to need all of the help we can get. One sip of this and you would feel the full power of the Dragonas. Remember what I told you though, it's not for the uninitiated. One gulp would drive a lad like you insane. I only have two bottles, so we can't afford to spill any."

"I'm sorry, I understand, I won't touch it again," answered Llyat.

It didn't take Llyat long to find the map amid the other contents of the pouch and he took it straight to the waiting bard. As Einar and Irabo began their search of the tents and the fallen warriors, Thias began to study the map while Llyat looked over his shoulder.

"From what I can make of Garret's scrawl, it looks like we have a half a day's journey from this clearing. See here, there is a trail that heads north east that will lead us to Barad Elestor. Once there it is just a matter of finding the missing gem. Did Thamous say where in the city we should look for it?"

"No. He just said it was in the tomb of Sir Raulyn, somewhere in the ruins of Barad Elestor."

Before he could comment further Llyat heard a disturbance from within the largest of the tents. A second later Irabo's voice boomed out.

"In here, now!"

Thias rushed to the tent and Llyat followed. Whatever Irabo had found it seemed of great importance. The pair entered within seconds of each other. The interior contained a single hammock and a desk upon which there were a vast number of maps and papers scattered in a haphazard heap. Sat at the desk on a small three legged stool was another frozen corpse. It was slumped over the table with a sword that penetrated its back and pinned it to the desk. Llyat tried to make out what lay before the dead man and guessed that it was a small leather bound book, a journal of some sort.

"What is it? What have you found?" demanded Thias.

"It looks like this was the Commander's tent," replied Irabo. "This must have been their base camp."

Thias moved over towards the corpse and looked over its shoulder. The knight had no helmet to cover his ghost-like head and his face carried the terror that was captured by the ice until a thaw came and the flesh rotted. Thias examined the warrior first and then the blade that passed through his back.

"I think this was Sir Elot Searl," said Thias at last. "He was second in command to Sir Byddin before he went missing some months ago. He was then replaced by Sir Britta Rainmark."

Llyat did not care who the dead man was. He was more interested to hear what had caused Irabo cry out.

"What else have you discovered?" he asked.

"I suspect these knights were looking for the same thing as were are."

"Are you sure?" asked Thias. "How can you tell?"

"From the name in this journal," replied Irabo and he indicated the leather bound book that he had searched for clues.

"Look at the words," continued Irabo. "They spell out 'Sir Raulyn'. There are entries that suggest that these men were sent north by Sir Byddin. There are many comments about their journey from Parandor and their search for a weapon in the central pyramid of Barad Elestor."

"A weapon?" replied Llyat aghast. "It could be Sir Raulyn's Battle Axe?"

"It would appear so," added Thias as Irabo passed him the journal and allowed him to flick through its pages. "Just remember that Sir Byddin is on the Sovereign's Council and he is therefore one of suspects that Tonousa is determined to uncover. Given that the Lady who controls the infiltrator is looking for the Gems of Thamous, then this small book is evidence to suggest that Sir Byddin is the one behind the murders in the Citadel. But then there is another possibility...."

"And what is that?" asked Llyat.

"That it's all one big coincidence," replied Thias.

"Or even fate," added Irabo.

"Which ever it is, I hope Tonousa is having more luck than we are," continued Thias. "It still troubles me that we didn't receive a carrier bird from her before we left Falahorn and I still wonder every day if our journey remains hidden from the eyes of the Lady of the Silverwynn. I am not sure if it is fate or coincidence that the Knights of Avolire showed up at the Gathering at the same time that we did. Perhaps we will never know the answer. Despite all this we must keep pushing on to complete our quest. We must honour of those who have died so far and ensure their great sacrifice has some reward."

Llyat agreed with all that Thias had said. It seemed there had been too many coincidences on their travels from Valameer. He thought about Irabo's comment on fate and wondered if Fatumai or her three daughters were with them on their journey. He was about to throw out his own thoughts when Thias added;

"Well at least we have a starting point for our quest, the central pyramid of Barad Elestor."

Einar had drifted off to search the fallen outside the tents. Once located, the four companions set off once again along the ice path indicated by their map. They made good progress throughout the rest of the day for the trail became more open with less of the great mesh of roots to hinder their foot placements. More light from Solaris fought its way through the clouds and helped illuminate the way through the shadow filled land. Thias had interpreted the almost illegible map well. Half a day's trek to the north and east the group once again came to a sudden halt. To a man they stood in awe as they looked upon the great stone ruins that broke out from the forest's canopy. While the ice worms wriggled beneath his feet Llyat's eyes locked in on the large pyramid that reached high into the sky. His jaw dropped low as happens when peasants of the Realm are forced to marvel at remarkable constructions of which they cannot conceive how they were built. Llyat turned with a smile of excitement as he heard the words he so much wanted to hear.

"Welcome my friends to the ancient city of Barad Elestor," said Thias.

The group of weary travellers, energised by what they had seen, began to move through the stone ruins which wind and ice had eroded and undermined. Llyat became lost in the magnificence of the fallen edifices that threated to engulf the four men and their unicorns. The wonder of the structures flooded through Llyat's consciousness but not a single bird call signalled their arrival. Each building was a marvel of architectural design, adorned from top to bottom with carved pictographs of the long forgotten civilization that had first worshiped Solaris. Barad Elestor was the most impressive place that Llyat had ever seen. To him it ranked higher than Parandor's Keep or the once mighty Bards Guild of Valameer. Whatever this place used to be, Llyat wished that he had lived in the time when he could have been a part of it. A feeling of foreboding then began to penetrate the sparkle of his thoughts as he passed through what appeared to be a square stone arena with terraces for seating on all sides.

"What kind of a place is this? I never believed something so beautiful could be so spooky? Who lived here and why would Sir Raulyn have been laid to rest in such a place?"

"That Llyat is even beyond my knowledge," began Thias. "All I can tell you is that this city was once home to those known as the 'Ancients'. Have you heard of them in any of the stories you have listened to?"

"Not in any of the tales I have heard. The Grand Physician did once speak of them, back in Parandor when he asked me to assist him with his examination of one of the murder victims. There were runes cut into the young man's body and my master said it was the language of the Ancients. He then sent me to collect a book of arcane knowledge from the library in order to decipher their meaning."

"Yes Llyat," said Thias with a smile. "The old man was right. Runes were the way that the Ancients recorded their language and there are still some who know the mystery and meaning behind them."

"Who," asked Llyat without thinking?

"Those that dwell in the Eastern Marsh."

"Oh shit," responded Llyat, wishing he had never asked the question. "So who were the Ancients and why did they die out? What happened to them?"

"Like I said Llyat, my knowledge is very limited about this city and its former inhabitants. Do you remember Master Ulthirn of the Bards Guild? Well perhaps you do not as you spent most of your time in his presence unconscious. From the historical studies that Ulthirn undertook at the Bards Guild, it seems that the Ancients were the first race of men to ever settle here in the Realm and they came from an unknown and distant shore. Over centuries they built their civilization in these forests with the help of the dwarfs of Dirmark. Their city prospered and was the established site of power for all the Realm. This continued for many centuries, long before the foundations of Parandor, Calistorn, Griginor, and Avolire were ever laid. The Ancients worshiped Solaris alone and anyone who disagreed with their practice were either executed or banished from their great city and the lands that surrounded it. Those that were exiled and managed to survive the journey south, set up villages beyond the Grey Mountains. Some of those hamlets over time, became towns and one grew into the city you know today as Parandor."

"But Parandor looks nothing like this place," said Llyat. "This city is beautiful. Erie but beautiful. Parandor is a..."

"Shithole?" added Einar who had moved closer and tuned into the conversation.

Thias continued. "There are still several structures in the older parts of Parandor and indeed other parts of the Realm which mimic the architecture found here in Barad Elestor."

"I'm guessing you could say that the Temple of Fatumai as one of them," chipped in Irabo as he too appeared at Llyat's side.

"That is correct," continued Thias. "Whoever designed that temple had access to the knowledge of the architects of the Ancients. If my memory serves me well, several towers and the walls of the Wizard's Guild share similar styles of ornamentation."

"But if Parandor still stands, what happened to this place? How can something once magnificent fall into such a state of ruin," asked Llyat?

"I don't know. Like I said, my knowledge of this place is somewhat limited, but from what I learned at the Bards Guild, the civilisation based in Barad Elestor disappeared in a single night following one of the many great battles it had endured against the forces of Urthanock. There are those who say that Lord of Fear's armies wiped them out, while others say the Ancients just gave up and decided to return to where they had come from, somewhere across the sea where they were never heard of again. No one knows the true reason. Perhaps we may find some answers to your questions here today."

Sir Raulyn's tomb got ever closer as the travellers continued to weave their way through the fallen masonry. The pyramid, just as described in Sir Searl's book, loomed so large that it threatened to block out all light. As Llyat approached he looked up at the almost sheer sides of the four sided structure. Each face had had built into its centre a flight of steps that led up to the square temple on its pinnacle. That was the structure that all assumed would house the tomb.

"So why would they choose to put the dead knight all the way up there?" asked Llyat pointing.

"Again Llyat, my knowledge is incomplete," replied Thias.

"You don't know much do you bard," chipped in Einar

Llyat expected Thias to respond but instead he continued unruffled.

"On the subject of the Ancients. I agree with my friend from Falahorn. As much as Ulthirn's history lessons were important, they were also pretty boring. I wish now that I had listened more during my training. I can tell you all one bit of interesting information though for it was one of the key points of every lecture given by the Masters of the Guild."

"And what is that?" asked Llyat.

"All modern day magic has its roots here in Barad Elestor. The ancient scholars of this place were the ones who first discovered how to harness power from the energy centres of the body. I am not talking about the magic practiced in the Eastern Marsh but the stuff that the bards, wizards, and others have mastered. It is the magic that can be learned."

A short time later the four companions found themselves at the base of the ice covered steps of the south facing wall of the pyramid of Barad Elestor. Thias moved forward and tested the surface of the imposing stone steps and as he did so it dawned on Llyat that even the ruins were death silent. The absence of bird song added to his growing apprehension. Whatever the cause of the quiet, one thought played over and over again in his mind. There were ogres somewhere in the darkness recesses of Thengar Forest and their presence filled him with dread. He thought back to the red rose in order to clear his fears. It worked and helped him regain his focus.

"We might want to take this next part with great care," said Thias. "The steps are covered in thick ice. One slip and it will be more than just a leg or arm you'll end up breaking."

"Then let's pray to the gods that we don't have to leave in a hurry," replied Irabo.

Given his previous accident on the pass round Skillar, Llyat understood why the young warrior feared such an icy climb. If truth be known so did he.

"We ought to find a place to tie these two up," added Einar as he pointed to the unicorns that were still in his care. "If they were to bolt now with our supplies, I wouldn't fancy the walk back to the Three Sisters on an empty stomach."

"You and me both," agreed Irabo.

After finding a strong tree on the land adjacent to southern aspect of the pyramid, Einar secured the unicorns with a Berserker knot designed to resist the pull of a startled beast. After much deliberation it was decided that one of the ropes included in Garret's supplies would be tied around each of the companion's waists such that they were strung together in one long line. Einar would lead the climb up the side of the Pyramid as he was the strongest and would use the sharp points of his battle axes to create secure leverage points as they ascended the hundreds of treacherous steps. Irabo made the point that if Einar lost his hold and fell back then his sheer size and weight would be enough to rip all of them from the face of the pyramid. Given that no one could not think of a better plan they decided to stick with their original idea.

Minutes later the four had tied themselves in a line. The climb was slow and calculated as each of the companions distanced themselves as much as their rope line would permit. Despite the slow speed, progress was good, and it wasn't long before they had climbed halfway up the side of the pyramid. Llyat tried hard to maintain his confidence and not be overwhelmed by fear. Visions flashed past his eyes as he imagined being disconnected from his companions. He looked down towards Irabo and back up to Thias and Einar as they slipped and skated about on the icy stones. Llyat's stomach began to turn and he knew the feeling well. His innards craved expulsion as his fear knotted his stomach. He paused for a brief second, gathered his thoughts and breathed through his anxiety. He was determined to make it to the summit and prove himself worthy of his quest.

The youth felt a small fragment of ice fall from above, hit him on the right shoulder, and brake his focus of concentration. Looking up he saw that Thias had lost his footing and was trying to secure himself back onto the side of the pyramid. He prayed that his own sudden pause had not caused the bard to slip. Thias dangled by the rope from Einar's waist but as Llyat managed to control his fear he reached up with one hand and pushed it against Thias's boot. He then forced the bard back against the side of the pyramid.

"Next time give me some fucking warning before you fall," shouted Einar from above. "It'll give me chance to cut you free "

"Are you alright Thias?" shouted Llyat.

"Yes, no problem. I just slipped that's all."

The climb resumed and Llyat once again fixed his concentration upon the icy steps. He now knew for certain that one slip would be fatal. So it was that he decided to whisper another small prayer and pleaded with any gods awake to deliver him to the summit. Then he thought about how they would get down again once they had searched the tomb and his limbs trembled. Forcing the idea from his mind he spoke to himself; 'One step at a time. Focus on the here and now."

Whichever of the gods had heard his plea ensured that the remainder of the climb was uneventful. The four companions stood at last on the platform in front of the opening of the tomb. They disconnected from the rope and Llyat waited with impatience as Einar coiled it up once again and slung over his shoulder. Llyat's legs and arms quivered from both the effort of the climb and the intense cold that threatened to freeze his marrow. He turned slowly and looked out to lands that swept in their majesty before his goggle-eyed gaze. In the distance, over the tree tops of Thengar Forest, he made out the line of mountains that stretched from east to west appearing as jagged skyfawn teeth sticking out of the jaws of the land. He knew that he was looking at the Grey Mountains and as he squinted he began to make out what appeared to be the remains of city in the distant south. It had to be Avolire and he was surprised how close it was to the southern edge of the forest.

Thias was the first of the four to enter into the dark confines of the ancient temple. Llyat watched as his friend raised his right hand.

"Promethelumous," Thias cried and his hand burst into flame while a welcome light cut through the gloom.

Llyat allowed his eyes to grow accustomed to the contrast between the light and shadows. Soon he was able make out details of the tomb's interior. As his eyes strained to make out fine details he noted that the room had been constructed from large stones. Its flat base covered all of the squared top of the pyramid. In each of the walls he noted many large holes that penetrated the dark and let no light inside. He moved forward into inspect one and realised that each of the dusty cobweb filled recesses were in fact the resting places of long deceased people, void of any flesh or internal organs. Bone and rusting armour were all that was left to give clues as to who had been laid to rest there.

The youth then moved further into the tomb's interior where his eyes further adjusted to the limited light. He began to focus on a square raised section that rose to a height some three times that of the Berserker. It stood in the middle of the chamber and its summit could be accessed only by a narrow flight of stone steps. This central plinth was so high that Llyat could not see what rested on its upper surface. The eeriness of the room stirred his fears and he sought to hold on to his courage. Inside this strange tomb, lost in the middle of a vast ogre infested forest, he sensed there was yet worse to come. He thought of the rose and sought to channel his strength of will for he was determined to master his inadequacies. He had to be strong and he had to have confidence in himself. His hand drifted forward until it rested on the hilt of Destiny's Song.

Llyat looked to Thias and wondered if the bard had any knowledge of those who had been interred in in this place, now long erased from the memory of most men. He looked on as Irabo took an old torch from the floor and ignited it using the flame that burned from Thias's hand. The result was an instantaneous doubling of the light.

"So which one of these buggers is the one we seek?" said Einar as his eyes searched the room.

"Well young Llyat," said Thias. "It's up to you now. Which one is it?"

Llyat felt the pressure of Thias's statement. He was the one who had conversed with the wyvern and he was sure that he had told his companions every word of that fateful conversation. But still he wondered if he had remembered everything. Then, as if the Fates were manipulating his thoughts, a word thrust itself to the fore front of his thinking. That word was 'axe'.

"The gem that we seek is a sapphire," began Llyat. "It is embedded in Fortune's Edge, the battle axe of Sir Raulyn. I guess that's what we should look for, a pile of bones with a big battle axe."

Llyat beamed with pride having made such a positive contribution and as the broad grin stretched across his face his confidence soared.

"Then let's all look for one with the axe," ordered Thias. "I'd rather not stay in this place longer than we have to. There is something foul about its air. Something I don't like."

"I agree with you," added Einar "Let's search with a purpose and urgency."

The four companions began their examination of the niches and alcoves of the various tombs. Einar searched one half of the room with Irabo while Llyat explored the other with Thias. The progress of the two pairs was obscured from each other's line of sight by the central plinth of stone. Despite all their endeavours amongst the grime infested alcoves and the haunting skeletal remains there was no sign of anything that indicated the presence of Sir Raulyn or the battle axe with its sapphire.

It then occurred to Llyat that even though they were inside a tomb there was no sign of any casket or coffin. The dead had been left in the open to rot away with the passage of time. In his village the dead were buried in wooden coffins, three cubits under the loose dirt on the edge of Maplehill. This alternative disposal of the dead stirred up a great curiosity that got the better of his mouth.

"What was the purpose of this place?" asked Llyat as he and Thias searched their fifth set of remains. "Why were they not buried underground and left so exposed?"

"To be honest Llyat, I don't know that either. I must assume that it is some form of tradition, some weird rite that was specific to the Ancients. Master Ulthirn's teachings never covered their death rituals, just the study of their magic. If I was to hazard a guess, I would suppose that whoever these individuals were in their life they wished to be laid to rest as close as possible to the gods that ruled above them. I presume that this way they were ready for a quick exit out of this world. Remember what I told you about the Ancients worshiping Solaris? Well, it's just my opinion but this pyramid is the highest point of Barad Elestor and when the dead were put here it was because this was the ideal spot from which to leap."

"I guess that makes some sort of sense," agreed Llyat as he rubbed the stubble on his chin.

"Leaving them in these open niches and alcoves would, I presume, allow their spirits to travel unhindered. There would be no need to fight through the caskets or the dirt under which we bury our own dead."

"And Sir Raulyn, where could he be and why would he have been lain to rest here?"

"Let me think for a moment. Yes, that must be it. If Sir Raulyn is amongst these Ancients, then there is only one other possibility, something that the songs and stories of his defeat of Urthanock did not cover."

"And what is that?" asked Llyat.

"That Sir Raulyn was one of the Ancients."

Before Llyat could respond a noise from behind caused him to turn and his hand tightened around his weapon. He then walked around the plinth to where Irabo and Einar stood with deep despondency etched onto their faces.

"Found anything?" asked Thias as they all reunited.

"Not a thing," replied Irabo as he shook his head. "Nothing but lots of old bones and no sniff of an axe. There are no clues to indicate which one could be Sir Raulyn."

Just as Llyat had begun to feel that they would never find the sapphire, a sudden thought came to him. If Sir Raulyn was indeed the greatest figure in the history of the Ancients then perhaps he would have been treated differently to the rest. In that instant he knew where they needed to look.

"Did you go up on the top of there?" asked Llyat as he pointed to the plinth. "If Sir Raulyn was top knight then he would be lain to rest in the highest of places."

Thias smiled and ruffled Llyat's hair in a friendly but patronising way.

"Good thinking Llyat, let's take a look shall we?"

The four companions climbed the stone stairs that led up to the summit of the plinth. Llyat smiled for his assumption had been correct. There before them was a large stone slab, waist high, the sides of which were covered in pictographs and runes. Upon its grey stone surface lay another skeleton clad in old, ornate bronze armour that had been part eaten by the ghosts of time. In the skeletons bony hands and resting upon its chest age was a mighty battle axe.

"I think we've found him" whispered Thias as the four stood and gawped at the remains of the legendary warrior.

"Sir Raulyn the Grand, Slayer of Urthanock the Lord of Fear" declared Irabo. "Along with his battle axe, Fortunes Edge, the very weapon that ended Urthanock's evil reign."

15

High upon the plinth Llyat was the first to break the group's sensation of awe.

"Let's snatch that Sapphire quick and fuck off out of here."

Thias grabbed hold of Llyat's furs and prevented the youth from moving towards the remains of Sir Raulyn.

"Wait!" he ordered. "This is far too easy. If, as Sir Byddin and others believe, his axe is a weapon of great strength and power then why has it been is it left unguarded?"

Thias then pointed towards the far corner of the edifice on which they stood and brought everyone's attention to yet more human remains. He had noticed them the moment that Llyat had begun to take his first step forward. There underneath outer furs and preserved in ice was a skeleton in the unmistakable armour of the Royal Guard of Parandor.

"See everyone, another of Searl's men... over there," continued Thias. "He must have been the only one to have made it this far and yet he got no further."

"So, do you think we've walked into a trap?" asked Irabo as he moved alongside the bard.

"I can't be certain," replied Thias. "Given all that we have seen during our journey through Thengar Forest it does look like he was the last of the group. How he alone managed to make it this close to the jewel, I guess we will never know."

"So what do you propose we do now?" demanded Einar.

"Let me think a moment."

The bard moved forward, step by tentative step. He held his hand aloft as the flames he had summoned lit the darkness. There with care he examined every crack on the floor and on the walls that surrounded him. With much suspicion he sought out the unusual for he feared that one inappropriate foot placement would trigger some ancient mechanism devised to protect the contents of the sacred space. He had heard stories of such death traps, those that that could collapse walls and bring ceilings down. As far as he knew they were just tales but Thias was not of the mind to take any chances. With each step he felt his heart beat ever faster. Nothing however happened. The floor remained solid and unmoved. Everything appeared in order as his companions watched in silence and relief.

Once he had reached the central stone Thias looked down at Sir Raulyn's remains and the battle axe that the corpse still clutched in its hands. He began to examine it in detail when in a flash he saw amid the years of dust and accumulated cobwebs the bluest stone that he had ever seen. It was stunning to behold and it glinted in the artificial light that emanated from his fist. Its colour and sparkle outshone the eyes of even the fairest of maidens. There, sat in all its glory was the stone they had come to find, one of the legendary Gems of Thamous.

Thias reached forward to take the axe from out of the bony hands but he suddenly stopped mid action. He turned his head back towards his friends and then once again towards Sir Raulyn's weapon. A compelling sense that something was wrong overtook him as he leaned in closer to look at what was left of the long since deceased Knight. He then noted that the head of the battle-axe rested on what appeared to be several well balanced stones, large pebbles that would no doubt shift if the weapon were to be moved. Perhaps their displacement could trigger some diabolical chain of events. For no obvious reason he then felt compelled to look down to his feet. There in the floor, leading into unknown darkness, were many holes that circled the Knights resting place and which were part hidden by centuries of icy aggregates. Thais began to put two and two together. The mechanism that Sir Raulyn's axe lay on had to be connected to the holes drilled into the stone floor.

Once again he turned to face his companions as they stood waiting in anticipation.

"Please, no one move; not even a midge twitch," he ordered as he began to retrace his steps.

"What is it!" exclaimed Llyat. "What have you found?"

"I'm not sure," added Thias. "It looks like there is some form of trap rigged to activate once the battle axe is moved. Irabo, would you pass me your blade."

"My pleasure," replied the warrior as he drew his sword from under his furs, "but I can't understand what you are seeking to accomplish....."

"You'll see. Just trust me," added Thias as he took hold of the sword with his non burning fist.

The bard turned and made his way back to the remains of Sir Raulyn, noting where the holes were positioned on the floor. He leaned forward towards the central stone while holding Irabo's sword in front of him and then stretched out towards the axe. Placing the tip of the blade under the handle of the weapon he then attempted to lift it off what he believed to be a trigger mechanism.

Thias saw the stones slip and heard a mechanism snap into place somewhere below his feet. As the battle axe fell from the skeleton, metal spears shot from out of the holes on the ground to the height of a grown man. Their firing had been accompanied by a loud clunk and then a distant clatter. They remained upright as a fence of steel around the corpse that lay at their centre. One had passed through the bones of the Royal Guard and Thias realised that is was not the first time that it had been deployed.

"Fuck me!" exclaimed Llyat as he took a step backwards.

"So now you see the reason for my caution," added Thias. "In your haste to hold the gem you would have been impaled. Let that be a lesson to you lad. We must remain vigilant at all times."

Irabo moved forward past Thias towards the remains of Sir Raulyn and set about examining the mechanism that protruded through the corpse and under the displaced stones.

"It looks like a basic counter weight system," he said at last "When you dislodged the axe handle, the pressure imbalance triggered the firing of the spears. I guess that's what happened to that unfortunate knight."

"But if the spears killed the poor sod after he had sought to take the axe, then who reset the mechanism?" asked Llyat as he moved forward to join the others.

"Good point. Be alert for there is more to this than just a simple tomb," added Thias as he handed the sword back to Irabo. "Our Parandor friend never stood a chance. By the Fates Llyat, be mighty pleased that I managed to stop you in time."

As Thias spoke his thoughts drifted back to the meeting in the Bards Guild when he had sent Llyat to retrieve the Dagger of Kha from the secret compartment and witnessed his subsequent display of Kundalish Aura. Thias had been unable to stop that chain of events but at least now he had prevented something far worse, death by spear. He looked towards Llyat and noted that all colour had drained from the youth's face. A most dreadful disaster had been averted and he began to believe that the Fates had indeed intervened.

"Now, let's take the Sapphire and get out of here," he ordered as he squeezed through the spears.

As Thias sought to grasp the axe it slid off the crumbling ribs, went over the edge of the central plinth and dropped down into the darkness of the main hall of the tomb. Thias hesitated and remained motionless.

"Is everything okay?" he heard Irabo ask over the clatter below.

"Perhaps!" replied Thias. "It's just that I knocked the axe over the edge."

"I'll get it," shouted Llyat and in an instant he set off running down the stone steps. As he did so Thias held his burning right hand aloft in an attempt to illuminate the way for the youth. Within a matter of seconds Llyat had picked had up the axe from where it had fallen.

"Here it is," he shouted as he stared back through the Bard's ethereal light.

"Is the stone still in there?" exclaimed Thias.

"Yes. It's the bluest thing I have ever seen."

"Can you detach it?" Thias shouted. "Can it be removed?"

"I think so."

Thias stared back down into the gloom as Llyat rested the handle of the battle axe on the floor and sought to detach the grime covered sapphire from its rough and rusted clasp. What happen next shocked everyone. As Llyat grasped the sapphire he let out an ear piercing scream that echoed throughout the confines of the tomb enclosure. As the sound left his lips Llyat ignited into a ball of Kundalish Aura so intense that its glow lit up the lower depths of the tomb, the alcoves, and all the niches that surrounded him. He appeared to be in great pain as he sought to detach the sapphire which had somehow fused to his hand. Llyat continued to scream as Thias, Einar, and Irabo stared down with concern. Then he fell quiet and dropped like a sack of turnips thrown from a waggon. Thias watched on with even greater concern as Llyat released his grip on the stone and the gem rolled off into the dark. The bard soon reached the bottom of the stone steps and stood over the still glowing youth. He checked to see if Llyat was still breathing and some minutes later the boy began to stir again.

"The Kundalish Aura again! What just happened?" asked Thias.

"I know where to find the next jewel," stuttered Llyat.

"You've already told us that," exclaimed Thias. "The Eastern Marsh somewhere."

"No, more than that," added Llyat as he stood and gathered his senses while the Aura continued to flare. "What I mean is, I know where the amethyst is hidden. The sapphire gave me the foresight to see its hiding place."

"What do you mean?" asked Thias. "What did the jewel show you?"

"The Eastern Marsh," continued Llyat. "Within the mud, slime, mist, and water, I saw a city; one populated by Lizardmen on the eastern edge of the marshlands and within a vast hidden lake near where the swamps meet the sea."

"They have their own city!" exclaimed Irabo who joined them "How can this be?"

"Are you sure?" added Thias. "I always thought that those that dwell in the marsh were scattered in many small villages. I have never heard anyone say that they had constructed a city. To be honest I didn't think they were capable of such a feat."

"I'm positive," continued Llyat as his strange glow began to fade. "It is a vast city of wood, grass, and mud that floats upon a raft of reeds amid a sulphurous shite filled lake. The amethyst is amongst many other captured treasures piled high on an enormous altar, a shrine built for one of their greatest heroes. In front of that shrine there is a massive statue of a great warrior but I could not make out any of its details. Thamous was right, the gem has been under their noses all time and they just didn't realise it."

Thias, even though unnerved by what had just happened, felt excited by what he had heard. The power locked within the sapphire had revealed a most valuable secret. Yet the thought of their being an unknown city deep within the Eastern Marsh filled Thias with much dread. The quest that had started out as a simple murder investigation linked to the cult of Death Tubaria continued to suck him into ever deeper discoveries. His perception of the Realm expanded exponentially.

"I still can't believe the scale shits have their own city," exclaimed the bard. "Parandor has been blind and duped. They must have been growing in strength for a great many years. By the gods, given their alliance with the Lady of the Silverwynn and her Knights of Avolire they may yet succeed in bringing Parandor to its knees. Did you see anything else in your visions Llyat?"

"I saw many warriors. I guess you could call it an army. All primed and ready for war."

"Then we have to warn the Capital," exclaimed Irabo with great urgency."

"And in time we will," replied Thias, "but we must not abandon our quest just yet. Even if the alliance between the Lady of the Silverwynn and the Eastern Marsh grows stronger by the day, I don't think they would dare to attack the Capital without the powers of the Underworld behind them. They may have the numbers but Parandor is a phenomenal fortress and it has never yet fallen to a siege. The armies of the house of Gylewu have always prevailed."

"I agree with your assessment," responded Irabo. "However, we now know there is an army of Lizardmen who are at this moment preparing for war. I feel a loyalty to our brothers back in Parandor and somehow we need to warn them at the same time as continuing with our quest."

Thias pondered the good point that Irabo had made. If Parandor was not made aware then there was a distinct possibility it would fall to a surprise attack. He sensed Tonousa Amberstone would have already warned the Sovereign of the growing threat from Avolire and that by now she might also have discovered the identity of the spy who lay hidden amongst the Court. Yet Tonousa was unaware of the scale of the evil that grew within in the marshlands. As if stuck by a thunderbolt, a thought directed him to one specific line of the Enderdetag Prophecy.

'And the armies of the East shall walk again,'

Thias had always assumed that the 'armies of the east' referred to the Knights of Avolire. Now, given what Llyat had said about a hidden city in the swamps he was convinced that the reptiles were the real enemy. If only he knew their true intentions. He shook his glowing hand with vigour until its light was extinguished and then relied on Irabo's torch to keep them from the darkness.

"Well at least you've stopped glowing Llyat," he added as he threw a comforting arm around the youth's shoulder. "I've never seen the aura flare without Masslewort. Llyat Emgar, you are unique in this world. I'm just wondering why you didn't glow like this when you touched......."

Thias's memory was again transported back to the events within the Grand Musician's library. There he had revealed the dagger to those who had arrived seeking assistance from the bards. It seemed like months ago but in truth only three weeks had past. He recalled showing the dagger to all those present and then how Llyat had emitted the Kundalish Aura on contact with the herbal mixture. It was as if ten thousand candles had ignited together in his mind for it all became much clearer to him. Something else had happened to ensure that Llyat had revealed himself as the Marked.

"You didn't touch it did you," said Thias.

"Touch what?" added Llyat, somewhat bemused.

"The Dagger of Kha," continued Thias. "The Emerald in its hilt."

"I'm sorry, I don't follow you."

"Try and remember back to your time in the Guild. I sent you to retrieve the dagger but you contrived to cover yourself in Masslewort before you managed to retrieve it. As I recall, I don't think you ever touched the dagger...It doesn't matter now... What's done is done!"

Thias found himself reciting the words of the Prophecy and once again he was drawn to one particular line.

'To the Bards he shall appear,'

If there had been any lingering doubts in his mind that Llyat was the one the prophecy spoke of, the events that had transpired in the Great Pyramid of Barad Elestor erased them. The boy just had to be the Marked of Maplehill.

"So what now" asked Llyat?

"We will take a lead from your visions lad. We will locate this floating city and take possession of the amethyst. We have enough supplies to reach the other side of Thengar Forest and I'm sure we will find a farmhouse or a small village between there and the Eastern Marsh from where we can replenish our needs. We can also hunt game in these woods."

"If we can find any," replied Llyat. "Didn't you notice the lack of bird song in the trees? We haven't seen a living thing on our journey through this most desolate of places?"

"You are right Llyat," continued Thias. "I think we have already spent far too long in this forest. At least we have avoided the ogres that seem to have passed this way but we cannot go unnoticed for ever."

"In that case might I suggest we move on," added Irabo. "Even though I can walk unaided, it is going to be some time before I can fight as I would like. If we do come across ogres I am going to more of a liability than a help, just like a sword without a blade."

"Then it's settled then," said Thias. "We will leave. Now where did that Sapphire go?"

"Over there," said Llyat as he pointed into the black. "It rolled into that alcove."

"Well, given what happened the last time you touched it, I think I should retrieve it!"

Thias made his way over and into the darkness of the nearest alcove. With a small piece of fur that he ripped from his jacket he picked up the dirt covered sapphire from amongst the bones in which it had come to rest. He placed it in a pocket in his tunic beside the Dragon Whisper pendant that Llyat had earlier given him. He did not notice the mild tremor that occurred as the two stones touched. Then as he turned he noticed that Einar was missing and had yet to join them on the lower level of the tomb.

"Einar, is all well up there?" shouted Thias.

"Where is he? Has something happened to him? " asked Llyat.

"I left him at the top," confirmed Irabo. "I split the torch so he could some have light just before I came down here to see if Llyat was okay."

"Einar!" shouted Thias again and this time the Berserker replied.

"You three might want to come back up here and see this."

In no time at all Thias, Irabo, and Llyat climbed the steps to the top of the plinth. When they reached its summit they were surprised to see Einar on his knees before the spears. He was looking at the side of the slab on which the remains of Sir Raulyn rested. There in his solitude he studied the pictographs, hieroglyphs, and the runes that were carved into the stone, some more prominent than others, though all had faded over time.

"What is it? What have you found?" asked Thias as he made his way over to the giant.

"I may be wrong but your suspicions were infectious," replied the Berserker. "This particular pictograph here depicts a figure surrounded by a glow and five coloured stones. The colour of the stones has waned but the figure reminds me of Llyat."

"What!" said Llyat as he moved forward? "How can it be me?"

"Let me have a look." ordered Thias.

Einar moved aside to allow the bard full access to the markings and soon Thias confirmed the giant's observations. The pictograph did indeed resemble Llyat. As curiosity got the better of him Thias then searched the four sides of the stone slab and scanned the rest of the markings that were etched into the stone. Some of the words were clear but some made no sense.

"Hieroglyphs and runes," mumbled Thias as he walked round. "At first glance this looks like the history of Sir Raulyn and the slaying of Urthanock but do I see what you mean; that particular image does look very much like Llyat. I assume that bit there is the Kundalish Aura and here the Gems of Thamous that are depicted around the figure."

"Can you translate what it says?" asked Irabo.

"The Hieroglyphs, yes, and some of the runes," replied Thias "A lot have been distorted over time and there are some symbols I cannot claim to understand, but I can give it my best shot."

Thias looked at the markings before him and knelt down to decipher them as best he could. Then after wiping a layer of dust from the stone he uncovered more of those masked by time and grime. So he began to translate the meaning behind the marks.

"These runes depict a story from over nine hundred years ago. They describe the time when these lands were in anarchy, an everlasting war between the armies of the Ancients and those that dwelt within the Eastern Marsh. Things are then a bit hazy and these few words I do not understand. However there is something about one specific inhabitant of the Eastern Marsh who rose out of the waters, a creature that displayed unique powers and was stronger than anything the Ancients had ever encountered before. There is more stuff I cannot decipher but they do go on to name that creature."

Thias hesitated for the next word had taken him by surprise.

"Don't just stop there!" exclaimed Einar. "What was this Lizardman's name?"

Thias looked to each of his companions in turn. What he had just read changed everything he that had been brought up to believe.

"Thias!" shouted Llyat. "What was his name for fucks sake?"

"You're not going to believe this but the most powerful of the Lizardmen was Urthanock."

Thias saw the look of surprise fall across the faces of his three companions. It was as if the battle axe itself had descended upon their heads.

"Urthanock was a Lizardman!" gasped Llyat. "That's not what the stories I've heard said."

"Well, that's what it says here," replied Thias.

"I don't believe it," said Llyat in utter disbelief. "I always assumed that he was human. A powerful man who had perfected mastery over fear and brought darkness across the land."

"As did I," added Einar with equal astonishment.

"And me," confirmed Irabo.

"I can't believe it myself," said Thias before Llyat jumped back in.

"Heliana told me that the stories from long ago often got things wrong. She said that Urthanock was not killed by a shepherd boy as I had been led to believe by Denius Castor, but by Sir Raulyn. I never realised how much the stories had drifted away from the truth."

"That's the same with all famous legends Llyat," said Thias. "An element that was once true gets distorted and changed over the many years that pass since its first telling. In the nine hundred since Urthanock fell there has been more than enough time for the story tellers and bards to change every detail. In the end very little of the truth remains.

"So before we get lost in what may be either truth or fantasy," added Irabo. "What else does the inscription say?"

Thias moved around the central slab and began to wipe away more of the dust.

"There is something here about a promise made by Urthanock to Kha, to provide him with fresh innocent souls in defiance of the wishes of Egredor, Chalis, and their children. With each life he took, Urthanock's power grew ever more powerful and after fifty years of fighting the Ancients of Barad Elestor he had grown invincible. Wow, if Master Ulthirn could have read this, he would be have been ecstatic."

"Keep to the point bard," grumbled Einar. "You're wandering off track. Is there anything else of use apart from the fact that the bastard was into human sacrifice?"

"There is a bit more here concerning Sir Raulyn," continued Thias as he scanned more of the runes. "The story confirms my suspicions that he was one of the Ancients who was bound to a mighty quest; to find a way to vanquish Urthanock once and for all. It gets a little vague from here on but it seems that he made a deal with the Oracle of Frasteria in order to gain their help. Next there is a word whose meaning I did not understand until you explained it to me on the slopes of Skillar."

"And what word would that be," asked Irabo?

"The name for the Fates... Moirai."

"So the Moirai are involved!" exclaimed Irabo. "I knew the three would have a hand in this. Let's just pray they are on our side."

"Perhaps," continued Thias as he pointed to some other markings. "This pictogram here seems to suggest that it was the Moirai with whom Sir Raulyn struck a deal and that they are one and the same as the Oracle of Frasteria."

Once again Thias's thoughts returned to the Prophecy of Enderdetag and another specific line.

'When the Oracles crypt shall be opened'

Thias paused as his reading of the signs started to make sense at last. Once again he thought back to events of the Bards Guild and a conversation between himself, Master Ulthirn, and Parandor's Grand Physician. Ulthirn had believed that the burial place of the famous Oracle of Frasteria lay somewhere near an ancient barrow located in the Harico Hills. It was now so obvious. The Moirai, the legendary daughters of Fatumai, had a key role in the realisation of the Enderdetag

Prophecy. Thias felt a strange certainty infuse his thinking. Could it be that he and his companions had been led to Barad Elestor by the three Fates and not by their own volition?

"What did the Moirai want with Sir Raulyn?" asked Irabo. "What did they ask of him?"

"Like I said, it's all a little hazy," continued Thias as he returned to the text on the tomb. "Shit! It seems that Sir Raulyn gave them a child in return for their help."

"Sir Raulyn sacrificed a child!" exclaimed Llyat in astonishment.

"That's what the inscriptions suggest," continued Thias. "And from what it says here, he did it for some greater good."

"Greater good?" sneered Llyat. "What the fuck is that supposed to mean?"

"I'm not sure," said Thias.

"Well is there anything else you can decipher?" asked Irabo with concern. "Is there any more to the story?"

Thias looked again at slab.

"No that's it. My guess is that the Moirai, in exchange for the child, told Sir Raulyn that Thamous could help him seal the doors of the Underworld."

"There is so much more to this than I ever believed possible," added Irabo. "This inscription changes much and throws what we already know into confusion. From Llyat's visions of the city in the Eastern Marsh, we must assume that the great warrior statue that he saw is a shrine to Urthanock. It all points to those slimy buggers from the swamps worshipping that evil being as a god!"

The bard glanced at his friends and saw a mixture of confusion and bewilderment. Even Thias found it hard to believe that the Lord of Fear, the evil that the Lady of the Silverwynn had threatened to unleash in her lust for power, was in truth a Lizardman that had risen to power many centuries ago. Thias then remembered the meeting with the leader of the Berserkers. Cvyler Olin had talked of people who sought to protect the 'Marked' to ensure that the Enderdetag Prophecy was fulfilled. They went by the name of the Cuvar and Thias was determined to find out more about them. Perhaps they had information that would help lift the mists of confusion that covered the events of the past.

"What should do we do now?" asked Llyat.

"We carry on as planned," replied Thias. "We make for the Eastern Marsh and take possession of the amethyst."

The journey to the bottom of the pyramid passed without significant mishap despite the treacherous icy steps and the almost vertical descent. They used the same method as for their earlier climb and attached themselves to each other by means of the rope. This time Einar came down last as it was felt that should others slip his strength and axes would act as anchors and break their fall. Most of the way they descended on their backsides and took each step in turn down the almost sheer drop of the ice that covered pyramid's stones. Once at the bottom they disconnected from each other and made their way across to the tree line where they had tied the two unicorns that carried their supplies. To their astonishment and horror both unicorns had disappeared. There was no sign of them save for hoof prints in the snow that led off into the depths of the ruins of Barad Elestor. But they were not the only footprints.

"Where are the unicorns?" exclaimed Llyat.

"I thought you had tied them up," said Thias as he looked to Einar.

"I did. They would have never broken free from one of my knots."

"They didn't," said Irabo as he held up the pieces of rope that were once tied around the nearest tree. "These ropes were cut. Our animals were set free on purpose."

Einar snatched the rope from Irabo's hands and held the cut ends to his nose.

"Ogres," he snarled. "I'd know their stench anywhere."

"We've got to find those supplies," moaned Thias. "We are as good as dead without them."

"Have you got some form of death wish bard?" uttered Einar. "In all seriousness do you think that the four of us would stand any chance against an ogre, or even worse, several of the buggers?"

"It is not my wish to take on a pack of ogres let alone one, but without supplies we will never make it out of this place alive."

"I have to agree with Thias," added Irabo. "I have no wish to fight an ogre either but I do not wish to starve to death in this cold and miserable place."

"It's settled then," said Thias as he once again took charge of the situation. "We find the unicorns first and then we get the out of here as fast as we can."

"And how do we find then?" asked Llyat.

Thias pointed to the tracks in the snow and amongst them he could see other prints, bigger than those made by man or Berserker.

"I think fate is once again on our side for there appears to be only one of them," continued Thias. "It seems that our thief has left us a trail to follow. Look, the tracks lead off into those ruins."

"Then let's get after that thieving swine," shouted Irabo.

"Remember to use stealth and guile. Do not give it warning of our approach," added Thias.

The bard led the way as he tracked the ogre at speed through the snow. The others followed close behind and with each passing step Thias grew ever more alert as his eyes searched the derelict buildings for danger. It was not long before they heard a noise that caused them to stop, the recognisable guttural snore of a beast. There was no mistaking the nature of the sound, amplified tenfold as it echoed off the walls of ancient stones.

"What the fuck is that?" added Llyat. ,

"That is the sound of our good fortune," replied Thias. "Our thief has decided to take a nap."

"You mean...?"

"That's right Llyat. It's the noise of a snoring ogre."

Thias gave Llyat a moment to reflect before he set off once again. Back they raced into the large rectangular stone arena that they had passed earlier.

Entering through a small opening in the collapsed fourth wall Thias paused beneath a small stone circular stone that protruded out of the wall at the height of a man's head. In a different time and space these type of structures would have fascinated Thias but this was no time for an exploration of ancient archaeology. The footprints had led them to that which they searched.

One of the unicorns, still loaded with the supplies bartered for in Fallguard, wandered free in the centre of the arena. The bloody remains of the second lay close to one of the outer walls, its guts and innards splattered across the ground as they created crimson patterns in the white snow. What supplies had once been carried on the beast's back were scattered amongst the blood and gore. Sat close to the scene of slaughter was the sum of all Thias's fears, for leaning against the stone edifice was a large grey creature with inhuman features forged upon an oversized head. It had a mass of hair upon its grizzled face and was dressed in ornate armour. A mighty steel cleaver rested by its side.

"This is our chance," whispered Thias. "Irabo, Llyat, you two secure the unicorn. Einar and I will try and save what else we can. Whatever you do, do not wake it. Be as quiet as you can."

Llyat and Irabo tiptoed towards the unicorn as it roamed about in the snow. Thias turned and with stealth moved towards the remains of the fallen creature. As Einar followed, Thias kicked through the destroyed remains of their supplies and noted that there was nothing worthy of salvage. Thias then saw that Einar was walking towards the ogre with one of his battle axes drawn and poised for attack.

"Einar what are you doing?" whispered Thias with great concern.

"I have no intention of letting this thing follow us," began the giant. "It's already killed and consumed one of the unicorns and from the mess on the ground, half of our supplies. I do not wish to be woken late in the night in the middle of the forest if the beast decides to give chase."

"Don't be stupid," whispered Thias as his concern mounted.

Without warning the snoring stopped and Thias looked to Einar who in turn looked down towards the motionless ogre. The creature's eyes flickered and then opened. The beast then swung out with an arm. It hit Einar square in the chest and sent him flying into the air, across the arena, and into the wall on its opposite side. Thias closed his eyes. The worst thing possible had happened for the creature had woken.

The bard then watched in awe as the ogre rose to its full height and rubbed its eyes. He glanced towards the last unicorn and noted that Llyat had restrained it by the end of what remained of its reigns. Irabo raced through the snow to where Einar had fallen and Llyat followed.

"And what the fuck do you want little man?" boomed the voice above Thias.

"We are just passing through these ruins," replied the bard, fists clenched and readied.

"Then move right along," replied the creature. "Can't you see I'm taking a nap?"

"I apologise for my friend over there," lied Thias. "It's just that he had never seen a real ogre before and curiosity got the better of him."

"So it would appear," replied the ogre. "He ought to be...."

Thias watched as the creature glanced to where Llyat and Irabo tended to the unconscious Einar. Its gaze then fell upon the unicorn and it snorted.

"Oi, that's my fucking dinner," it bellowed and in one swift motion it reached down and grasped the steel cleaver which it then swung it out in Thias's direction.

Thias ducked and then rolled out of the way as the weapon dropped for a second time. It connected with the space that Thias had just occupied. Quick to his feet the bard dodged the third and fourth swings. He closed his eyes and hoped that he had enough magic left to survive.

"Promethelumous," he shouted but his hands did not ignite.

Thias's power reserves had been depleted on top of the pyramid and a feeling of emptiness screeched from out the depths of his belly. The ogre charged again and brought its cleaver down in a quick succession of swipes. Each one came at Thias from a different angle and yet the bard managed somehow to dodge them all. Then as the steel weapon came at him for the twelfth time, Thias tripped and fell backwards into the snow. As he tumbled he felt his life flash before him but the giant's blow did not connect. The sound of steel against steel rang out. Irabo had deflected the blow.

"You might want to move now," suggested Irabo as he parried several more blows.

Thias did not wait to be told a second time. He rolled away at once and clambered to his feet. Then as he looked back he watched the young warrior lead the ogre a merry jig. Irabo ducked, dodged, and scampered around the centre of the arena as if a dance master teaching class back in Parandor. Thias knew that Irabo could not defend so well for much longer. He looked to Llyat and then ran towards him.

"Your sword," he shouted. "Give me your sword."

Taking Destiny's Song from its scabbard Llyat threw it forward.

"Get yourself to safety lad, do not worry about us..." shouted Thias while catching the blade.

"But..."

"Don't argue. Just do as your fucking told."

Thias turned and raced back to the dance of death. Once there he joined in the fray without hesitation. The ogre now had no choice but to split its attacks between the two skilled fighters. And so it continued as the ogre swung its cleaver with one hand and punched out with its other. Thias made several hits on the beast with Llyat's blade but despite scratching the surface of the metal armour he inflicted no injury of significance.

"Irabo," shouted Thias as he deflected a further blow that had been aimed at his head. "Go to Llyat. Get him to safety."

"And what about you?" he heard the young warrior shout back.

"I can handle this lump of shite myself. You must to protect Llyat and finish this quest."

"No, you cannot kill this beast alone."

Thias ducked once again as the ogre swung at him. This time the impact skimmed off his blade and it hit Irabo as he moved in close. As the weapon smashed into the young warrior it knocked him down to the ground where he then too lay motionless.

"Get away from my friends you ugly bastard!" bellowed a gruff voice that cut through the air.

The fighting ceased in an instant and Thias turned to look at where the fearsome voice had originated. He noticed that the ogre had stopped as it too stared out towards the origin of the unexpected noise. There in the open, clutching an oversized battle-axe in one hand and a small jar of amber liquid in the other, stood Llyat. He was ready to do battle.

"And what do you think you are going to do about it?" said the ogre.

"You see this," shouted Llyat as he held the jar high." Do you know what it is?"

"Dwarf piss no doubt," shouted the ogre. "No one steels my lunch and gets away with it."

"Llyat, no!" shouted Thias but it was already too late.

Llyat removed the stopper from the neck of the vial and consumed the contents with one single gulp before throwing the empty container down onto the snow covered earth. He then screamed. It was not of human kind but something much more bestial. The youth stood as would a wounded animal and he clutched his head as if in torment. Thias knew what Llyat had drunk, the potion that Einar had warned them never to try, the juice that enhanced the fighting ability of the Berserkers but which to the uninitiated resulted in madness.

"Oh fuck," exclaimed Thias. "What have you gone and done lad?"

Llyat stopped screaming and glared at Thias and the ogre. Then he hollered into the air like some great wolf god, squeezed the battle axe in both hands and charged towards the ogre. Llyat covered the distance from the centre of the arena in seconds and launched himself upon the ugliest of beasts. He brought down Einar's axe with tremendous speed and smashed it into the ogre's sword arm. The blow removed the creature's limb and sprayed crimson globules high into the air where they then rained down upon the snowy ground.

The ogre screamed as it clutched the bloody stump where its arm used to be. Then with all of its strength it lashed out with the intent of connecting with Llyat. Thias looked on in disbelief as Llyat swung his battle axe down once again and removed the creatures remaining hand. Once again the creature recoiled in pain. Thias then moved in as the ogre kicked out. He thrust his own leg onto the one that that the ogre balanced on and the contact dropped the beast to the ground. It writhed on the floor and then hollered and screamed. Thias took Destiny's Song and drove it down through the front of the ogre's right eye socket and into the great cavity that contained its inhuman brain. Silence.

Llyat stood motionless, still clutching the battle axe in two hands while his breathing grew heavier and his teeth began to grind. He then let go of his axe, hollered out in pain, and fell to the ground amid the red speckled snow. There he continued to clutch his head as he writhed, just like the ogre had done just a few seconds earlier. Leaving the blade in the ogre's head, Thias raced over towards Llyat. Once there he dropped to the ground in complete exhaustion and took the youth in his arms.

"Your name is Llyat Emgar," shouted Thias as he tried to cancel out Llyat's screams.

"You are from Maplehill. Your master was Grand Physician Abrahamus Marus. You were saved by your friends Irabo and Tonousa. You are in love with Heliana."

"Hell-ee-arr-nar," growled Llyat through his gritted teeth.

"That's right Llyat, Heliana," continued Thias as he held his ward close and felt the boy's rapid heartbeat begin to slow a little. "The beautiful blonde girl from the Capital."

"Hell-ee-arr-nar," repeated the maddened youth.

"That's right Llyat. The one who willing gave herself to you. Hold on to that thought. Come back to us."

"Hel-i-ana!" shouted Llyat as his voice became more human.

"That's it Llyat. Beautiful Heliana."

Thias repeated the girls name over and over again as the seconds turned into long minutes. At last Llyat slowly returned to normal.

"What the hell just happened?" he asked as he tried to work out why he was lying on the floor in the arms of the bard.

Thias did not have time to respond before he heard the approach of armour. He jumped to his feet and gazed towards the entrance to the arena.

"Oh fuck!" he said as he looked at seven more of the giant beasts.

The fight with the first ogre had been won, but the noise had summoned its friends. The largest of the new arrivals moved forward and looked down towards its fallen comrade. Thias sighed for now there was no possible means of escape.

16

"I must be honest with you Heliana, I never expected Lady Emeny to send you of all people with her summons," said Tonousa as the two women and Darchus walked along the upper corridors of the Citadel and onto the next phase of their investigation. "I thought you were in the service of Lady Fullbane just now. If I had known you were serving the Sovereign Advisor then I would not have waited for Sir Byddin to have set up this meeting."

Tonousa had been surprised to have been asked to meet with Lady Llys Emeny at such short notice. It had been several days since her meeting with Sir Byddin on the battlements adjacent to the Wizard's Guild and she had passed each day in hope that he would facilitate a meeting with Xix Blackfayer's replacement. After a few days of silent disappointment Tonousa had begun to doubt if Sir Byddin would be true to his word and had started to think of other ways to progress her investigation. During those painful hours of waiting Tonousa had tried to re-establish herself back into the routine of the Watch. She had assisted with the training of the new recruits that each day poured through the gates of the Barbican. With the influx of displaced citizens arriving inside the city walls, evicted from the slums by the ever growing armies of the Fifteen Keeps, the Watch had its work cut out to maintain any semblance of control. It required all the expertise of its senior officers to keep order amongst the restless populace. At a curt meeting with Commander Townsforth it was evident that the events of Richemanus Folly continued to trouble the leader of the City Watch. Despite Danisun's support for her valued expertise and undoubted skills she had only been allocated training tasks and had not been permitted to conduct patrols inside the Capital. Danisun had further stressed Tonousa's great insight in the investigation and for which Townsforth had been most grateful; yet her superior felt it necessary to say that if she brought any further trouble before him she would be returned to the Underkeep and the key to her cell thrown into the fast flowing Tiaryer.

Heliana's surprise arrival at the barracks had interrupted one such training session. Having left Danisun with the new recruits it was with both excitement and apprehension that Tonousa realised the next stage of her work was about to kick off. So with Darchus to accompany her as her witness she had followed Heliana back into the Citadel and on to her longed for meeting with the new Sovereign Adviser.

"The Lady was meeting with my mistress when she ordered me to find you," said Heliana as they moved along the flame lit corridors. "She was about to ask her own errand boy to take the summons but I let it slip that I knew where you would be and somehow found myself volunteering for the task."

"Has Lady Emeny agreed to assist us with our investigation?" asked Tonousa.

"Sort of," continued Heliana. "She has invited you to take afternoon refreshments in her chambers. My mistress, the Lady Fullbane, will also be in attendance."

Tonousa sighed. It wasn't the perfect environment in which to conduct her interrogation but she realised that she may not get another chance. Thus the invitation for an afternoon of food and drink would have to do. With Lady Fullbane present it did at least mean there would be less likelihood of a hostile reaction from the Sovereign Advisor and yet Tonousa realised that she would still need to remain on her guard. If Lady Emeny was the one that she sought to unmask, she reckoned that the creature would not reveal its true nature in front of the Lady Fullbane. Tonousa recalled that there was no love lost between Fullbane and Emeny and she began to wonder why the Sovereign Adviser had invited the big one to join in the discussion. She hoped it was not some devious trick.

"At least we will be able to ask her some questions. It's been a couple of days now since we gained anything useful and it's just a matter of time before our murderer strikes again," continued Tonousa. "I had begun to think that Sir Byddin had forgot my request."

"The talk amongst the servants is that the Lady has had a lot to do, taking over the role of Sovereign Advisor and all that," continued Heliana. "She has spent most of her time in meetings with Phauless Gylewu and Sir Byddin in order to ensure sufficient protection for the city. They have been directing the armies to prepare for an attack from the north or from the east. It seems that all the necessary weapons of war have been constructed and put in place."

Tonousa recalled her time with the knight on the battlements where she had witnessed the construction of the large wooden pults outside the city walls. The excuse for Lady Emeny's lack of availability was understandable given that preparation for war was not an easy matter. She was just grateful that Sir Byddin had been true to his word.

"The rest of the time Lady Emeny has confined herself alone in her chambers," continued Heliana. "Tecwyn Hennion, that strange young lad that acts as her cupbearer, though I would call him more of a slave, told me that her nerves have been all over the place since the incident at Stukeley Knoll. He said she had sent him to every apothecary in the city to find something strong enough to steady her nerves."

Tonousa raised an eyebrow. The words seemed to confirm Sir Byddin's comments.

"And has she found something that helps?" asked Darchus.

"Tecwyn said his mistress had managed to get things under control and that she had found something that helped a lot. It's not legal stuff though, so she had best be careful!"

"Did the boy say what she was taking?" probed Tonousa.

"No, that much escaped his knowledge. He did swear me to secrecy and told me that no one was to know where she got it from."

"Don't worry Heliana, I'll not mention your name."

"Thank you for that. You had better not for a gossiping servant is not tolerated even though we all do it and permanent privy duty does not sound that appealing."

"Your secret is safe with me," added Tonousa with a smile. "But did Tecwyn say where she got this substance from?"

"No, he didn't. Lady Emeny and Sir Byddin walked in and interrupted our conversation. I felt it best not to push for an answer."

Tonousa could not help but feel disappointed. It was as if she was still being fed crumbs of information for them then to be pecked away as if by some dark and mysterious beak. The voice of Lady Fullbane returned to her thoughts, *'A path will form'*, but for Tonousa it not forming fast enough. Then she remembered that her investigation was but a part of a much deeper mystery. There was the issue of the gem, hidden somewhere in the Citadel and lost amongst its vast wealth.

"And what about you?" asked Tonousa. "Have you had any luck in finding the fabled ruby?"

Heliana half-smiled and Tonousa wondered why.

"What's so funny?" she asked.

"Well, given all that has happened, the murders, the events of the Bards Guild, your father's death, and the possibility of a spy from the Eastern Marsh walking amongst us, you still doubt the possible existence of the Gems of Thamous?"

"She makes an honest point," added Darchus as he smirked.

Tonousa sighed for Heliana was right. How she could still doubt what had to be done, even if she could not believe that a greater force was at work. All she could hope for was to focus her actions and somehow solve the awful crimes that had been carried out within the confines of the Capital.

"Well, in response to your question," continued Heliana as they approached a large set of wooden doors at the end of the corridor. "I spoke to the servants that work for Lady Calendrial Lorst, Lady Antviane Rirert, and even Gilebin Ystafell. It appears there are many rubies within the walls of the Citadel. Several of them are of a significant size and quite a few heart shaped. Most were gifts from the rulers of the Dirmark and are locked away in the Citadel's vaults. To be honest it's going to be like sniffing out a fart in a forest."

"Well thank you for at least trying," sighed Tonousa as yet another glimmer of hope disappeared. "We just have to keep looking. I'm sure there must be some clue somewhere that we have missed, one that could lead us its hiding place. It could be right under our noses so we will need to be vigilant."

"And the Oracle?" asked Heliana. "Has Theo found out anything of use?"

"Not yet. Highroar has had Theo working on the Banshees Wail and I think he is making preparations to flee when war breaks out. It will be a sad loss if Theoplous goes with him for we would lose his expertise on all matters relating to the Cuvar and..."

Tonousa did not have time to finish her sentence before the noise of something breaking sounded against the other side of the door. It was followed at once by the raised voice of Llys Emeny.

"How dare you," she shouted. "Get out of my sight."

"I'm so sorry my Lady," replied a second voice

It was just as loud as the first, and Tonousa recognised it as the Fool's.

"Piss off and don't come back," shouted Lady Emeny, her words followed by a second crash.

Tonousa reached for the handle and pulled open the door. As she did so a pewter goblet soared past her face and just missed her nose. She was then taken aback as Lolly raced past her into the corridor and then onwards until he disappeared down a side passage. Lady Emeny's shouts followed him.

"You'd better run faster than that, you devil's dick. If I so much as clap eyes on you again today then so help me I'll get the Royal Guard to find the foulest stinking hole in the Underkeep for you to live out your useless fucking life. Do you hear me you arsehole?"

Tonousa stepped into the room. Heliana and Darchus followed as the warrior moved towards the red faced Lady. The new Sovereign Advisor was dressed in a full length green velvet gown that covered her slender figure and contrasted painfully with her red cheeks. Anger was etched deep into her highborn face. Tonousa made ready to duck again as the Lady clutched a book and made as if to throw it towards the door. On spotting Tonousa and Darchus she lowered her arm and sought to regain her composure.

"Ah late as usual," she grumbled. "What is the City Watch coming to when they cannot turn up on time, even to escort a simpleton out of my presence?"

"I apologise my Lady," began Tonousa as she noted the other presence within the room.

Flopped on and around a large chair to the side of the chamber rested the enormous form of Lady Thinata Fullbane. Heliana moved forward and addressed the red headed Lady.

"What just happened? What has that stupid Fool done now?"

"That knobnut was reciting a tale of the Richemanus Folly, about all those who bore the title of 'the Nightfall' before our own current executioner took the role. Then the cheeky bastard began to remind us that our gracious Lady Emeny had fainted on the viewing platform. He said that she had lain there 'like an underfed crow.'"

"The fucking cheek of it," grumbled Lady Emeny as her face began to flush once again. "He has insulted me for the last time..."

The Lady stopped midsentence and looked towards Tonousa and Darchus who still stood waiting to be announced. Then with a forced smile she spoke again.

"Please, my friends. Do come in and make yourself comfortable."

Tonousa looked to Darchus who shrugged his shoulders and then took a step forward over the broken pottery that lay by the foot of the door. While she passed between two brass lions that lay on either side of the portal Tonousa made her way to a similar velvet cushioned chair to that which Lady Fullbane occupied. Darchus followed Tonousa's lead and Lady Emeny took her place on the seat beneath the only window in the room.

The room was darker than Tonousa had expected. She was thankful for the solitary wall window from which light shone down on an empty wooden table before the gathered group. This illumination also highlighted the many shelves that covered most of the wall space and which were crammed with books, manuscripts and scrolls. Tonousa assumed they were necessary references with which, as Court Judge, Emeny presided over the laws and decrees of Phauless Gylewu. She then noticed numerous strange objects scattered on what little space was left on the shelves. She had never seen their like before and did not have the slightest idea of their purpose. Her mind was drawn for a moment to the withered hand in the secret compartment back at the Bards Guild, the very one Thias the Bard had stopped the lad Llyat from touching. Tonousa shuddered for there was something most odd about the collection.

"I do apologise Tonousa for my outburst," said Lady Emeny at last. "My nerves have not been good these last two weeks; ever since your father's execution. I understand that the Sovereign Council have yet to apologise to you for the grave injustice that took place that day."

"I told you," interrupted Lady Fullbane. "Mathias Amberstone could never have been a traitor. He was as loyal to Phauless as any of us. If my Enguerrand had been alive today..."

"Yes, yes, yes, Thinata, I think Tonousa gets the message," said Lady Emeny before the fat woman could finish. Having silenced her friend with a wave of her authoritative hand she turned to Heliana who stood against the wall. "Girl, some refreshments for our honoured guests."

"At once my Lady," replied Heliana who then curtsied and made eye contact with Tonousa.

"A good girl that one," said Lady Emeny to Lady Fullbane once Heliana had closed the door. "I feel some sympathy for the poor lass, what with the murder of the Grand Physician and such. That reminds me, we still need to fill that position Thinata, but Heliana is a great find for you. I think you would struggle to find a more honest and loyal girl than that one."

"Yes, in a way I'm glad the old coot..." began Lady Fullbane before she was silenced once again.

"I don't believe that I've had the pleasure," said Lady Emeny as she turned to address Darchus.

"Darchus Arillius, my Lady."

"I am sure the pleasure is all mine," she continued as she offered her hand for the young man to shake. "From the accent, I am guessing that you hail from Valameer?"

"You are indeed correct Lady."

"Well I think he's a bit tasty if you ask me," added Lady Fullbane with a lick of her lips.

"Nobody asked you Thinata," snapped back Emeny.

Once again the Sovereign Advisor's character darkened and that precipitated an awkward silence. Tonousa glanced across the table towards Fullbane and wondered if the obese woman would respond but she did not. Instead Tonousa allowed her eyes to wander across to the strange objects and implements that cluttered the spaces of the shelves and she contemplated whether any could contain the ruby that she sought. She was snapped out from her thoughts as Lady Emeny took a deep breath and began speak.

"Sir Byddin requested that I meet with you. He said that you wished to ask me some questions about the events that have gripped Parandor in a fist of fear, the murders of the Death Tubaria. He said that you had found some cards that you thought were someway connected to the crimes."

"That is correct my Lady," affirmed Tonousa.

"May I take a look at them while we wait for Heliana to come back with our refreshments? Sir Byddin said you carried them with you at all times."

Tonousa did not hesitate. She reached into her leather satchel and removed the four pieces of parchment which she then passed over. The Sovereign Advisor then began to study each one of them in turn. Tonousa noticed that Lady Fullbane also watched on with intense interest and much suspicion.

"They're called Fortunes Fate cards," added Tonousa as the Lady studied them. "I believe some priests of the local faiths use them to tell the fortunes of their followers and anyone else who may wish to pay good money to know what their future holds."

"Well, I'm not a priest and have little time for holy claptrap. Therefore I cannot help you much. You might want to ask Heward Teulu when he returns from his mission to Valameer."

"So he's gone to Valameer has he," said Tonousa as she raised an eyebrow in surprise. "What would be his purpose in going there?"

"I maybe Sovereign Advisor to Phauless Gylewu and sit on his Council, but I seldom care about the whereabouts of the other members, least of all Heward Teulu. However, if I recall our last meeting he did say something about going to help the injured following the attack on the Bards Guild. He left several days ago along with the some of his priests. The rest have stayed behind to tend to the sick and the needy that have flocked in from the city slums and taken refuge around his temple."

"Did he say when he would be back?" asked Tonousa.

"No he did not. His business is his own. Nothing to do with me!" continued Lady Emeny before lifting the cards in her hands. "So what have these got to do with the murders?"

Once again Tonousa found herself explaining what she had found within the walls of her father's chamber and how the note which accompanied the cards had suggested that one of four was responsible for the crimes committed in the name of Death Tubaria. Tonousa did not mention Heliana's role in searching through the rooms of the Ladies of the Citadel, nor that it was Theoplous the sailor who had deciphered the message and its meaning. She not mention the link to the Cuvar, those destined to protect the Marked and fulfil the Enderdetag Prophecy for the Lady did not need to know such detail. While Tonousa recounted her tale Darchus filled in gaps at various points. Both Emeny and Fullbane were hooked into the story but when Lady Emeny's name was mentioned as a suspect, a look of deep shock settled on her face. Lady Emeny turned red with rage.

"You dare to suggest that I am implicated in these murders?" she snarled.

"Would you like me to leave Llys?" added Lady Fullbane as she persuaded her shocked lips into action. "I'm sure you don't want your secrets paraded out in front of me of all people."

"No Thinata, you can stay. In fact I insist for I need a witness to this slander," replied Emeny without removing her eyes from her accuser. "Whatever Tonousa Amberstone has to say, she can say in front of us both. Remember this is not the first time she has accused a Sovereign Advisor of misdoings. Do you recall how they say she burst into Xix's chambers and threatened his life with some foreign blade? Is that what you are expecting Tonousa, to push me over the edge so that I take my life like Blackfayer? Are you trying to punish us all on the Council for what happened to your father? How dare...."

Emeny's face deepened to plum purple and Tonousa feared the Lady's head would burst. She expected the nearest object to fly her way but then Lady Fullbane intervened to calm her friend.

"Llys. Take a deep breath. Count to ten."

Tonousa watched with concern as Lady Emeny rose from her chair, dropped the parchment cards to the floor and paced the room for several minutes. While so engaged she took in several deep breaths before exhaling to allow the fires in her head to dampen. Then without prompting she made her way across the room to one of the shelves and from amongst the strange objects she pulled out a small wooden box no bigger than the palm of her hand. She opened it at once and took out something which she then thrust into her mouth. Whatever the object or substance was it soon calmed the Lady and allowed her to resume her place back upon her chair. With dignity restored she spoke.

"I'm sorry. My nerves have been all over the place of recent. The strain of being second in command of this Realm weighs heavy on me. It is a great responsibility you know."

"And yet it was a position you always craved Llys," added Lady Fullbane. "Something you once said you would kill for, given the chance."

Lady Emeny did not respond to Fullbane's words but both Tonousa and Darchus understood their significance.

"I apologise Lady Emeny for these accusations," continued Tonousa. "I am also sorry that you have been out of sorts. However, I hope that you will understand that I have to follow up all lines of enquiry. The City Watch have been charged with solving the murders while the Royal Guard prepare for war."

"I understand that Tonousa Amberstone, and if you tread with care I may accept your apology. What is it that you would you like to know from me? How may I assist you?"

"Let's us start with the victims," began Tonousa. "How well did you know Lord Tobius Faros, Sir Britta Rainmark, Lord Fabius Colt, the servants, Webb Underscroft, Golda Flintwind, and the stable boy Mikus Danbury?"

After a brief pause for thought Lady Emeny began her answer.

"Sir Rainmark was one of Sir Byddin's men, so I never had anything to do with him. Lord Colt was the treasurer and the late Xix Blackfayer dealt with him most of the time so I didn't know him very well either. Lord Faros was just a miserable old tosser."

"Ooo... Lys, how unbecoming and vulgar," added Lady Fullbane in a mixture of contrived shock and laughter which both Tonousa and Lady Emeny chose to ignore.

"I'm sorry, what you were saying," added Darchus as he picked the cards up from the floor and tried to move the conversation along.

"Lord Faros had a lot of emotional issues," continued Lady Emeny as she turned her gaze away from the fat lady. "The sweating sickness that once plagued the northern villages took his wife and daughter. Because he couldn't live without them I still believe that he took his own life by hanging himself from the tallest tower of the Citadel. As for the two servants, I knew them by name and saw the girl in the occasional presence of Thinata. I knew little of them and didn't have reason to do so. As for stable boy Danbury, the same would be for him. Apart from tending to my horse, which I believe has still yet to be recovered, there is nothing I can add to what you may already know about him."

"So in that case Lady Emeny, are you able to vouch..?" began Tonousa.

"I was alone in my room each night that a murder was committed. I was sound asleep. You can ask young Tecwyn, the boy that serves me. He can vouch for my whereabouts each evening and that I take a sleeping draught every night. You see it helps me sleep but also steadies my nerves. I've not been well of late."

"And so you keep reminding us," chortled Lady Fullbane after which she sniffed in air through her nostrils and rattled the phlegm at the back of her nose. Tonousa leaned in closer to probe further.

"Forgive me for asking but the substance you take must be rather potent if it allows you to sleep with ease. I'm having similar difficulty myself at the moment, ever since my father's death, and I wouldn't mind giving anything a try to help me rest my weary body. What have you been taking? I have a mind to try some myself."

"Just a little something off a local market vendor" replied the Lady. "Nothing special!"

Tonousa knew that she was lying.

"It wouldn't be Lillywort would it?" asked Darchus in contrived innocence. "That white flower found on the edges of the Eastern Marsh."

"Ooo Lys, you haven't been indulging in that stuff again have you?" sneered Lady Fullbane.

Lady Emeny's skin turned ghost corpse white. Even though surprised at Darchus's sudden mention of Lillywort, Tonousa was pleased that the issue had been broached. The reaction confirmed what Tonousa had already suspected. The substance Lady Emeny had taken from the small box was the same one that Sir Byddin had implied was being distributed by a mysterious 'other'.

"Has Tecwyn been talking?" asked Lady Emeny.

"No, not Tecwyn," replied Tonousa. "He is an innocent in all of this I assure you. You have confirmed what we already knew to be true, that Lillywort is being brought within the walls of the Citadel."

"I don't see what this has got to do with anything," said Lady Emeny. "I thought I invited you here on Sir Byddin's request to discuss the Death Tubaria murders. This Lillywort business is a subject I wish to remain untouched. It must remain confidential and the knowledge you have just gained must never leave this room."

As her last statement left her lips she glared at Lady Fullbane who simply sat and grinned.

"I understand," continued Tonousa. "However, I have to ask who provided you with the..."

"I never saw his face," insisted the new Sovereign Advisor. "Kept his hood over his head the whole time. It was dark and wherever he took me it smelt like something had long since died there.

"Did you recognise his voice?" asked Tonousa as she sensed a path forming.

"No, I did not. There was a lot of hissing and sloshing of the mouth as if the man had a deformity of his tongue or something."

Tonousa raised an eyebrow. The idea that the Lady had met with a creature from the Eastern Marsh confirmed everything she already suspected. Llys Emeny had succumbed to the temptations of Lillywort and the connection to the Marsh was too good to be dismissed. Tonousa continued with her new line enquiry.

"And where did you meet first him, Lady Emeny? This man who peddles the potion?"

"That I will not divulge. I do not want you to go out of here and arrest the one person who allows me to sleep at night. You can take me in if you feel that you must, but as you know from your dealings with Xix Blackfayer, my position is one of great power and I assure you that I can and will make your life very difficult Tonousa should you try to cross me."

"Is that a threat Lady Emeny?" asked Darchus.

Emeny shot a fearsome look at Darchus and the venom that flowed from her eyes took Tonousa by surprise. Even Fullbane sat in silence and dared not speak. Tonousa felt the need to respond but it was Darchus who acted. He stood up from his seat and placed both of his palms outwards as if to divert the aggression that had between generated by the two women.

"Both of you, please!" he began. "We must keep calm and not allow this meeting to descend into something that we will all regret."

Tonousa looked up to Darchus who then took a deep breath and returned to his seat. She was most impressed by her new recruit for his intervention had instantly calmed the proceedings. His next words came as a surprise to all.

"Lady Emeny that is an interesting pair of Lions you have by the door?"

Fullbane raised an eyebrow as if to speak but then felt the better of it.

"Yes, they are a replica of the fabled Lions of Avolire," said Lady Emeny with pride. "Most of the artefacts you see dotted around this room are from a time long forgotten."

Tonousa looked at the two brass lions that stood in the doorway and then on towards the cluttered shelves that surrounded the room. She now began to understand why her father believed Emeny to be a prime suspect. The Lady was a collector of all things from Avolire.

"I never realised you were such a fanatic for the foul artefacts from that evil place," said Lady Fullbane with obvious disdain.

"I'm not a fanatic Thinata, I assure you," added Emeny as her anger began to abate. "Just a collector of the strange, the interesting, and the unusual. I have been amassing such items ever since Sir Rainmark led our troops to his first victory over the Knights of Avolire all those years ago. You should understand this desire Thinata as your Enguerrand was also collector of the unusual. I can still recall him spending time with his wandering friend that claimed to be a Historian from way north of Avolire. What was his name again dear, I seem to have forgotten?"

"I'm sorry Lady Emeny," interjected Tonousa before Fullbane could answer. "Please may we return to my investigation of the Death Tubaria murders."

"Now, I guess it is my turn to apologise," added Lady Emeny.

"And it is accepted," replied Tonousa. "You just mentioned that you have an interest in the unknown and the unusual. I've seen from the library records you sought access to the Lore of the Dead. Can you confirm why you would have done that?"

A knock at the door drew attention away from Tonousa's question. As it opened three people entered the room. The first was Heliana who carried a silver tray laden with strange and exotic delicacies such as grapes, plums and Lotus Isle fire berries. Behind her trotted the olive skinned boy called Ourri. He carried a large flagon and four pewter goblets. The third to enter was Emeny's short statured serving boy, Tecwyn, with a bowl of water and linen cloths for the guests to wash and dry their hands before eating. Lady Emeny signalled to the servants and pointed to the empty table.

"Put the food down here will you Heliana, there's a good lass."

Once Tecwyn had placed the bowl and cloth before his mistress Lady Emeny began to wash her hands. As she did so Tecwyn moved away to join Heliana and Ourri by the door. Tonousa waited for Emeny to respond but it soon became apparent that the Lady had forgotten the question having become preoccupied with the ritualistic cleansing of hands.

"Lady Emeny, the Lore of the Dead?" Tonousa asked again.

"Ah yes!" came the replied as she passed the bowel to Lady Fullbane. "Your father always kept good records. I did indeed enquire over the Lore of the Dead, the history of the book, and its connection to the dark times of Urthanock. Your father permitted me to see it just the once. Most of its text made little sense to me. It was written in some strange old language that I could not understand. All those incantations were enough to put anyone off wanting to read it. I can't believe that Jonas Tullage managed to decipher what was on those cursed pages. That is why I insisted that Xix Blackfayer, before he killed himself, sent the Lore to the towers of the Wizards Guild in order for it to be translated and kept under the protection of their strongest magic."

"I'm sure that Archmage Iqotrix will keep it secure," replied Tonousa despite having little faith that the wizards would be helpful.

"It will at least be away from the clutches of Sir Byddin there," continued Lady Emeny as she signalled Tecwyn to pour wine from the flagon. "I know that old one eye searches for a weapon to end the threat from Avolire, but the dabbling in the black arts must be treated with great care."

"I don't know about that Llys," added Lady Fullbane as she bit into a plum and allowed its ripened juice to run down her chin and on into her more than ample cleavage. "I could use such magic to help me lose all of this weight. I'm sure there must be something wrong with my glands."

"No magic would not be strong enough to do that Thinata," replied Lady Emeny. "Maybe if Sir Richemanus cut off both your hands then you could perhaps lose a little."

The room fell silent once again. Lady Fullbane carried on chewing after which she plunged her fat fingers into the mound grapes before her and pulled out a large sprig which she then consumed at great pace. The meeting fell into disorder as the two Court highborn began to surface their inherent dislike for each other.

"Speaking of Sir Richemanus," continued Tonousa. "Were you aware of his mounting debt to Lord Colt and the treasury?"

"I think that is something that the whole of the Citadel was aware of. Bad drinking debts and whoring, but I suppose each of the buggers on the Council has at least one vice, isn't that right Thinata?"

Lady Fullbane did not answer but instead let out a horrendous belch.

"I know that Fabius Colt called in his debt as Sir Richemanus did not frighten him one jot. He even got Jasper Redglade and Horace Mandleworth to pay him a visit in order to retrieve some of what he was owed. But after Lord Colt's murder, well, I don't think anyone in their right mind would go up against Richemanus again, not even Sir Byddin. I do remember a comment from Mandleworth saying that he wondered if Richemanus had been responsible for Colt's death, but that was before they found that curse mark on his bald head."

Tonousa looked to Darchus and then back to Lady Emeny. There were others who suspected Richemanus of at least one of the crimes.

"Did you know that it was Sir Richemanus who was responsible for the loss of Sir Byddin's eye?" asked the Sovereign Adviser.

Lady Fullbane slurped and munched as she devoured a fist full of fire berries.

"Yes, I did know that," replied Tonousa. "Byddin mentioned it when I met with him."

"It put him out of the field for it restricted his usefulness on the battlefield. They say that's the reason for his promotion to Commander of the Royal Guard."

"And a better place the Citadel has been since his appointment," added Lady Fullbane after which she belched again and then took another gulp of wine."

A thought then occurred to Tonousa. How would the Sovereign Advisor react if she knew that some of the Royal Guard where abusing Lillywort and thus had compromised the safety of the Citadel. She considered mentioning it but did not for she did not wish her investigation to be further deflected.

"Anything else?" asked Lady Emeny, now bored with the conversation.

"Just a couple of more questions please," said Tonousa.

"Then speak them at once. Let's get them out of the way so that we can all move on."

"You mentioned earlier that Heward Teulu was on his way to Valameer to assist those wounded after the fall of the Bards Guild. I am guessing his stated reason was his duty to his gods and yet it does seem rather convenient that he has waited until now to start his travels."

"The priest's business is his own, but yes, I did wonder why he hadn't set off earlier. Many of us raised an eyebrow when he dallied after the Flurdiana's carrier birds brought news of the slaughter," added Lady Emeny.

Fullbane threw a grape up into the air and caught it in her mouth.

"So you too think his absence is suspicious?" asked Tonousa. "Has he anything to hide?"

Tonousa watched as Lady Emeny pondered the question. She half expected that Lady Fullbane would comment, but she didn't. The fat lady continued to fill her face with all that her hands could snatch from the table. Several seconds later Lady Emeny laughed.

"Heward Teulu, something to hide. Now that's a good one."

"What you mean by that," asked Darchus.

"I'm sure you must have heard about the death of his wife? The reason that he turned his head to the gods?"

"That story has been kept far from the ears of the City Watch," replied Tonousa.

"She was a young woman. Came from a village out towards the north and east. I think it was called Ashview... Yes that was the place. Well, as the story goes, Teulu came home one evening to find his wife sliced open, quim to throat, her organs removed and thrown over her shoulder. Her entrails had been left for the rats to feast upon."

Tonousa looked across the table as Lady Fullbane attempted to stuff a whole plum into her mouth. Once again the juices sprayed froth, swept down her chin, and cascaded onto her clothes.

"Heward Teulu, as the first to discover his wife's body, was the prime suspect for her murder. Commander Townsforth of your City Watch was the investigator at the time. This was before he rose to the rank of Commander. It does surprise me that you haven't heard this story before, Tonousa."

"There are many things that my Lord Commander keeps to himself."

"Well, maybe this was before you joined his merry band of men? Who knows? Anyway the story goes that Heward Teulu had no alibi for the time of his wife's murder and the people of Ashview made ready to hang him from a crude structure they had erected in the market place. They intended to burn his corpse as it danced on the end of the rope. In his final moments before the crowd he bellowed aloud to the goddess Fatumai and demanded she send a sign to those present that would prove his innocence."

"And what happened?" asked Darchus with great interest.

"The gallows were struck by a bolt of lightning cast down from the heavens by Hamthor, and they were destroyed," continued the Lady as she sipped more wine. "Rain then dropped in torrents and damped the wood so much it could not be burned again for a month. With Heward Teulu's public prayer answered the people set him free. From that day on he found his vocation within his church and after the years slipped by he became the Heward Teulu that we know today."

"Perhaps Fate had intervened," suggested Tonousa.

Tonousa's mind flashed back to past conversations with Irabo. Her focus then became fixed on Lady Fullbane who clutched at her throat as she turned redder in the face. Something was amiss with the enormous woman and it had been a significant length of time since she had passed comment.

"Well whatever divine power stepped in, it saved him from joining the wretches who dwell in the Underworld. But I can tell you one thing more, I sense this is the answer to your questions as we bring this interview to a close. You want to know who out of your four suspects I believe the murderer is. Of course I rule myself and of the other three I would look to Richemanus and our Royal Priest. If it's not..."

Lady Emeny stopped speaking as she too became aware of Lady Fullbane's difficulties. The whale's enormous face had turned regal purple and it darkened further with each passing second.

"Thinata, you've gone red, have I said something to embarrass you?" asked Lady Emeny, but Tonousa had guessed what was happening.

"Shit, she's choking!" she exclaimed as she jumped to her feet.

"Somebody help us!" shrieked Lady Emeny.

Tonousa jumped over the table towards the shocked lump whose colour had now turned blue. Two eyes bulged in their sockets and threatened to pop out and join the grapes on the fruit platter. In no time at all Tonousa was by Fullbane's side while the woman's great dimpled arms flapped around with no semblance of control. Ignoring the cries for help from the Sovereign Advisor, Tonousa forced the Lady forward and began to pound on her back with her clenched fist.

"Heliana, Tecwyn, somebody help us, send for a physician," screamed Lady Emeny.

The two servants moved forward to help support Lady Fullbane as she began to lose consciousness. All the while Tonousa continued to pound on her back.

"It's no good," shouted Tonousa. "Whatever she has swallowed is lodged in her windpipe."

Amid the chaos that descended Tonousa had a darker thought. Perhaps something was not lodged in Lady Fullbane's throat and a sinister power was at work. It could be they were about to witness another murder linked to the cult of Death Tubaria. Even so, Tonousa was determined to do everything she could to prevent the mountainous woman from dying.

"Heliana, and you boy," shouted Darchus as he pointed to Tecwyn. "Help me stand her up and support her."

"We'll never pick that up," shouted back Tecwyn.

"Just do as you're bloody told," screamed Lady Emeny.

"Darchus, what are you doing?" demanded Tonousa as she, Heliana, and Tecwyn fought to support the enormous dead weight between them.

"Trust me on this one," replied Darchus

In one swift move he punched upwards with all his strength into the woman's voluminous stomach. As his fist disappeared within the folds of fat, the plum stone that had been lodged in Fullbane's throat flew out from her mouth amid a shower of spittle and juice. It flew across the room like a bolt from a pult and hit Lady Emeny square in the centre of her forehead. The Sovereign Advisor's eyes rolled back into her skull and she fell to the floor in a faint.

"She's not breathing," shouted Heliana as she examined Lady Fullbane's mouth and chest.

"Quick, lie her down," ordered Darchus after which he turned to the dumbfounded Ourri and shouted aloud. "Quick lad see to Lady Emeny."

Darchus dropped to his knees by the side of Fullbane's shoulders. He ripped open the top of her dress to expose the rolls of fat around her upper chest and breasts. Then he joined and placed his hands one upon the other in the centre of the Lady's breast bone. A second later he began to push up and down in a rhythmical motion.

"Darchus, what are you..."

The man from Valameer did not answer. The others stood and watched as Darchus continue with his strange magic. He stopped every so often, put his mouth against the spittle covered lips of the woman whose life he attempted to save and exhaled into her chest. Tonousa had never seen such actions before but whatever Darchus was doing she prayed that it would save the Lady's life.

Then without warning Lady Fullbane lurched forwards and began to cough and splutter in a most violent manner. She projected more spit and fruit residue over Darchus who did not once flinch at the insult. At last her eyes opened and began to take in her surroundings. Thinata Fullbane then began to smile. A mischievous grin spread across her face as her tongue licked across her lips and savoured a new taste.

"After so many years a young man has once again dared to press his sweet lips upon my own."

Tonousa smiled and let out a deep sigh. The whale had been saved.

17

Methladon woke with a start and sat bolt upright. His breath heaved while he encouraged his eyes to make sense of his surroundings. The nightmare that had tortured him ever since he had been roasted by the wyvern amid the darkness of the mountain had continuously played out as he slept. Once he was awake his fears dissipated amid the cocoon of the soft sheets that lay wrapped against his skin. There on the bed he felt relieved to at least be still alive. He allowed his eyes to accustom to the darkness that enveloped him in a room illuminated by a solitary candle that stood upon a stone mantelshelf. He tried to understand where he could be for the last thing he remembered was his climb out of the blackness beneath the three peaks and his rescue by the Knights of Avolire. The room seemed somewhat familiar and when his eyes at last adjusted to his new surroundings Methladon knew where he was. He had seen the room before and he remembered its significance. The four walls and roof inside which he rested sat upon the crack known as the Mighty Rift. It was this very fissure that fed the Lady of the Silverwynn the power with which to rule over Avolire. Now the chamber was being used for a different purpose and his intuition told him what that was. The Lady had begun to heal his hideous burns using the magic that the room bestowed.

From atop the Lady's bed Methladon looked towards the twin oak doors which alone permitted entry into the room. He reached up, looked at his right hand, and saw that the weeping blisters that had once covered most of his body had almost disappeared. The room had done its job well although Methladon had no idea of how long he had lain within its confines. He scanned his arm in more detail and there saw areas of disfiguring white scar tissue. It was as if reptilian scales now covered the once open sores. He then looked under the sheets and noted that the rest of his body was also scarred. Much to his relief his private parts looked intact. He felt his head and then his lower limbs and found that he was without hair from crown to toe and that the scars were everywhere except on one side of his face. He concluded that he must have turned his head away at the precise moment that the wyvern had belched out its fiery breath. In an instant of insight he felt reborn. Despite the damage to his skin he realised he had retained all the wyvern's information and that his brain had somehow survived intact.

Methladon sat and listened to the faint crackle from the candle. He watched its flame flicker in a draft that blew from behind his bed towards the oak doors. The faint hint of air movement wafted over his exposed skin and caused him to reach up and touch the altered side of his face. The roughness of the disfigurement caused him to want to gaze upon it. He was sure there would be a mirror somewhere within the Lady's bedchamber and in that moment he sought to find it. Once he had jumped out from beneath the sheets that covered him and allowed his feet to connect with the cold hard stone of the floor, he wrapped his naked form in the covering which he ripped from off the bed. He made his way over to the flickering candle gripped its holder and held the light high. There was no sign of a mirror anywhere that he could use to examine his face but he soon found a polished bronze vase that was filled with dried flowers. Picking it up he sought to try and catch his reflection in the little light that was available to him. There in the ghoulish reflection he managed make out the hideous scars that covered the right-hand side of his face and above which grew the few sparse hairs he still had left on his head. The memory of the Lion Pit returned and he felt a great empathy for the brother of Nictis whom he been forced to see cooked alive.

He then felt a crawling sensation on the back of his neck and it started to build as if with a mind and will of its own. It sought to add to his anguish. Anger at his disfigurement had begun to fester but for some unexplained reason this time the sensation was different. He focused on it, fought it, and then it disappeared. Once he had replaced the vase a loud knock from the door echoed through the hollow room. He pushed his candle forwards to light the entrance as best he could.

"Who is it?" he demanded to know. "Who's there?"

"It's me," replied a familiar voice, muffled by its passage through the wood.

"What do you want?" shouted Methladon.

The oak doors opened inwards and allowed light to fall upon the spot where Methladon stood. As it bathed his form the young man squinted while he sought to determine who approached. All he could see was a diminutive blur.

"I've come to see how you are," said the dwarf as he stepped inside the room.

The sudden arrival of Grovrouk troubled Methladon. He dropped the candle to the floor, launched himself onto the bed, and tried in his desperation to cover his scarred and deformed face.

"Get away from me," he shouted as he forced his head into the feather pillow.

"Is that how you great a friend?"

"Friend?" muttered Methladon as if he could not comprehend the word.

"Of course I'm your friend,"

"Stay away from me."

"What happened to you down in that cavern Meth?" asked Grovrouk as he moved forward and ignored his friend's command. "Whatever went on down there has changed you greatly, and I don't just mean your looks."

Methladon lay motionless while Grovrouk's voice penetrated deep into his thoughts. He closed his eyes and visualised Rhaizen, Oedd, and the dwarf finding him on the side of the Gathering. Others would have given up on him, left him to his fate, but they came to his aid and gave him water. Yet he failed to understand how they knew to search outside the entrance of a cave that was half way up the mountain.

"By what powers did you locate me?" he asked.

"We saw the beast fly off from the mountain, high up from the side of the middle peak of the Gathering. We assumed there had to be a second entrance somewhere. It took us a couple of days to find it for Rhaizen had injured his arm during the fight with the Berserkers and he struggled to keep up on the climb. Oedd was the first to hear you shout and he led us to your smouldering body. What did happen down there? Fuck, but you were lucky to have survived it."

"How long have we been back in Avolire?" asked Methladon for he was at still a loss as to the length time he had been unconscious. "How long have I been here in this bed?"

"Three days now," replied Grovrouk who then clambered onto the bed and sat with his legs hung over its side. "The Lady of the Silverwynn has been tending to your wounds ever since you returned. She was most insistent that you did not die. It seems you are too special and important to her plans to be lost to her cause."

Methladon strained his eyes and tried to make out what Grovrouk was wearing. The little man no longer wore the armour of the Knights of Avolire and was draped in the most simple of linen cloth, the colour of which he could not make out in the gloom.

"Meth, come on, tell me what happened to you in the cavern? What became of Ssnarkit?"

Methladon closed his eyes. He began to wonder if the dwarf was showing genuine concern or just trying to trick him once again in order to gain information. He recalled how Grovrouk had earlier told him of his skill at deception and how he had infiltrated the Grey Keep in order to glean knowledge of the wyvern's location. Yet despite his concerns he felt the need to talk of all that had happened.

"I should have died when I was young," began Methladon. "I should have perished at the hands of the cult of Death Tubaria but somehow I survived when I was supposed to have been ripped apart. Thamous could sense it and he told me things that I wish had remained unheard. He said that I have caused an imbalance in the laws of nature, an anomaly he called it, and it means that I cannot die."

"So that's what you meant!" exclaimed the dwarf as his demeanour changed. "Now I understand what you meant by 'anomaly'."

"What are you getting at?" asked Methladon.

"You spoke in your sleep Meth. You've been lost to this world ever since we found you at the Gathering. Don't ever ask how we managed to get you down the mountain and back to Avolire for it was with the greatest of struggles that we did so."

"So what are you trying to tell me?"

"You speak in your sleep. I've been visiting you these past three days to see if you would survive your ordeal. Despite our Lady caring for you and the power of this room I was still unsure if you would survive."

"Where is she?" he asked.

Grovrouk jumped down from the bed. Methladon followed him and dropped naked to his knees beside his diminutive companion.

"Where is the Lady now? Why isn't she here? Why has she left me alone like this?"

Methladon pointed to his body not knowing if Grovrouk could make out the scars upon his face or understand the source of his distress. His anger intensified and yet once again he was somehow able to control it. He closed his eyes to allow the emotion to settle and then turned his attention back to the dwarf.

"Why isn't she here with me Grovrouk?"

"She had other pressing matters with an envoy from the Eastern Marsh. One of their high priests has turned up with information of great importance to her cause."

"Why would such a person come to her? What does the forked tongued bastard want?"

"I haven't a clue. To be honest I wasn't present at their meeting in the old chapel. Rhaizen alone was allowed to go with her to meet Ssonsh."

The name Ssonsh sounded familiar to Methladon but he had more urgent concerns than that of a Lizardman's name. He needed to understand the Lady of Silverwynn's intentions for him and her next move in the war against Parandor.

"Have you got anything useful to tell me Grovrouk; like why you are here?"

"Stop being so arsey Meth, I don't like this new attitude of yours. You'll find out soon enough but you need to understand that the Lady has changed since your last meeting with her. She is still the same person that you first met but she has aged somewhat."

Methladon recalled his first visit to the Lady's bedchamber, how he had attempted to assault her with a metal bowl and how she had repelled him with unseen energy. It had been channelled through the room by the forces of the Mighty Rift and manipulated by the Lady herself. He remembered being pulted across the chamber and then seeing a haggard old crone where a young and beautiful woman had once stood. He tried to work out why her power would fade and if he had been the cause of it. The wyvern had also told him that being the anomaly he leached power from the Rift. Perhaps he was he was stealing that which she had once claimed hers alone.

"What do you want Grovrouk?" he asked with cutting sharpness.

"To see how you are. We found you barely alive on that mountain side and I swear you ought to be dead, no matter what you say about being an anomaly. I'm concerned for your health..."

"Well don't be," snapped back Methladon as he threw himself down onto the bed and covered his naked form once again with the bed sheet. "Your concern is false and I will never trust a short arsed hole-dweller again. I can look after myself. I got myself out of that bloody pit didn't I?"

"Meth..." stuttered Grovrouk, shocked at the venom and force of insult.

"Just fuck off and leave me alone."

It was a second voice that had spoken over his own. It was of deeper tone and the very same one that had confronted the wyvern. Grovrouk was shaken and after a brief pause he turned his back on Methladon and made his way out through the oak doors without bothering to shut them. A minute later the doors closed of their own volition.

The voice that had spoken over his own did not concern Methladon. Even though it was new, something that would have disturbed others, he liked the sound that it had made. It had given him authority and was not one to be challenged. Ever since the fiery breath of the wyvern had scorched his body he had discovered the ability to conquer both his anger and his pain. He was now determined to control this other voice for it had a power that he also sought to manipulate. A minute later he climbed off the bed, made his way to where he had dropped the candle, and picked it up. In the darkness of the room he sought a way to reignite it and explore his surroundings in greater detail. Then to his surprise the candle fired up and cast its eerie light across the room. All the other candles present, dozens which Methladon had until then failed to notice, also burst into flame and created a multitude of dancing shadows across the strange and magical space. It was clear that his link to the Rift was being amplified through his presence in that strangest of rooms.

His eyes then focused on a dresser with an accompanying stool at the far side of the room. Unseen forces pulled him towards it. As he approached he noticed two familiar objects upon its shelves. The first was the jewel encrusted dagger with an emerald in its hilt, the Dagger of Kha. It was the object that had once caused him extreme pain but for some reason it no longer had that same effect on him. The second was the one that had been used to look into his mind and through which he had experienced visions of his skin burning and then sitting on the throne of Parandor with the Lady of the Silverwynn by his side.

"Look into the stone again," said Methladon's inner voice. "Witness the ripples of change."

He wondered what the voice meant but he trusted it for it had helped deliver him from the darkness of the cavern. He had trusted it then and he would trust it now. Thus Methladon Heyn placed the illuminated candle onto the dresser before him and took a seat on the stool. There he took a deep breath and then exhaled as slow as he was able. Gripping the sceptre in his right hand he looked into the diamond and the light that shone from within its core. Just like the first time he felt his consciousness lurch from out of his body and enter into the fog like limbo that was the soup of his thoughts. Within seconds the mist had cleared away and Methladon found himself looking at a grand marble hall which he assumed to be the throne room of Parandor. It was filled with golden banners and the sounds of a trumpet fanfare that rose above the clamour of the many that gathered in the Court. He knew this vision well but this time as he looked into the stone he saw something different. The mass of people parted to reveal a white marble throne on which he himself sat. His burned and deformed head, with a single gold band upon its summit, stared down at the crowd below. The Lady of the Silverwynn was no longer by his side but instead at his feet lay the haggard corpse of a wizened old crone, face down with her head turned away so as to obscure its features.

"All hail Methladon the First," sounded the fanfare which was followed by a chorus from those gathered in the hall: "Hail to our Sovereign Ruler of Parandor, Keeper of the Peace, Savoir of Avolire, and Guardian of the Underworld."

"All this power is yours to take. You just have to want it," whispered the voice.

"All hail Methladon!"

Then a new voice entered onto his consciousness, a female one that he recognised.

"Do not look too deep into the darkness Methladon. You do not know what you will find."

Methladon lurched back into reality, dazed and confused. He found himself staring back at the Seer's Stone a few inches away from his eyes. He felt beads of sweat upon his brow but he no longer held any fear for what the Stone would show him. A second later he span around and turned his attention to the now open doors and where three figures stood and observed his actions. The first he recognised was Rhaizen, who like Grovrouk before him was dressed in linen of green and brown, one arm in a make shift sling attached around his neck. The second was the Lady of the Silverwynn, who just as Grovrouk had described, looked much older than the last time he had looked upon her face. No longer did she have the youthful features he had seen on his first encounter yet neither was she the haggard and ancient form he had witnessed after the abuse of his private parts. The third of those present he also recognised at once. It had been sometime since he had seen the rotund Lizardman who with great brutality had sacrificed Mal Castor in order to open the Mighty Rift to facilitate the passage of Rhaizen's Knights from the Eastern Mash. He then understood who Grovrouk meant when he talked of an envoy from the Marsh. The creature's name came back to him but he could not shake the vision of Mal Castor's murder from his thoughts.

"What is that foul fucker doing here?" he demanded of the Lady.

"Less of the lip talk lad; show some respect and remember who you are talking too," ordered Rhaizen after which the Lady spoke with a voice still strong and confident.

"This Methladon, this is the priest of the Eastern Marsh, Ssonsh. I never..."

"Yes, we've met," interrupted Methladon as he rose to face his three visitors. "That slimy bastard killed Mal Castor."

"Who" asked the Lady with no clue as to whom Methladon referred?

"She was taken from Maplehill with me. That thing sacrificed her on it's alter."

"It matters not Methladon Heyn," continued the Lady "In the greater plans that are unfolding she was an insignificant..."

"Insignificant! She was a dear and close friend until his piece of scale shit murdered her."

"And yet you are still alive," added the Lady.

"Despite all that you've put me through. Yes, I'm lucky to be alive. You sent me to my death out there in the Dragonas just to further your own ends. It was no thanks to you that I escaped from the beast that dwells beneath the Gathering."

"And yet you were successful in your mission. You found out what you were sent to discover, although we are unsure as to whether it was you or Ssnarkit who conversed with the creature, given that you do not speak its language. You found out the location of one of the missing gems that we search for although you won't remember telling me; it is just that you talk in your sleep. A forest temple, covered in snow! The tomb of a fallen knight that went by the name of Sir Raulyn. That image can mean but one place, the temple in Barad Elestor. As if by fate, I had already placed one of my servants there pending the inevitable war that is to spread across the Realm. If the Gem of Thamous does rest in that temple then General Brosizrug and his ogres will....."

"Fuck you!" screamed Methladon as he allowed his anger to flow. "Fuck you and fuck your desire for revenge."

Rhaizen moved forward and stood between Methladon and the Lady as the creature from the Marsh took one step back and continued to watch events unfold. Even with his broken arm Rhaizen was still able to project authority into the chamber.

"Stand down!" he ordered.

"And you," spat out Methladon as he switched his attention. "You call yourself a Commander. Your ancestors would turn in the earth pits had they witnessed your failure in the Dragonas. You couldn't even protect yourself from a couple of pissed off Berserkers."

"I'm telling you to stand down," ordered Rhaizen as he took another step forward.

"Fuck you!" spat back the youth.

Rhaizen held up his good hand and Methladon knew at once what Rhaizen intended. This time he would not allow the Commander to control him. He held out his own hand and focused his anger towards the tips of his fingers. Then as he felt the Commander's attempt to take control of his body Methladon screamed out and a wave of unseen power flew from the tips of his fingers. It hit Rhaizen in the chest and threw him backwards onto the far wall.

Methladon moved several paces towards the Lady and her envoy. The Lizardman priest looked on with concern but the Lady did not seem at all surprised by the youth's new found abilities. The former blacksmith's son then looked towards his fallen Commander, watched his chest rise and fall and realised that he had not yet killed him. He lowered his hand and addressed the Lady that he served.

"I have learned to control my power," he added with considerable calm. "I figured it out myself without any help from you. My climb out of the darkness taught me a lot of things and my anger no longer holds dominion over me. The power given to me by the curse mark of Kha has made me stronger than you could ever imagine. I am all powerful."

"Good, very good!" said the voice inside Methladon's head. "You have their attention now."

"So now that you have decided to grace me with your presence I demand to know the truth," he replied.

"And what truth would that be?" said the voice

"What the fuck is going on?" shouted the deeper voice.

The Lady of the Silverwynn looked towards Ssonsh and then back towards Methladon before beginning to chuckle.

"Methladon Heyn, I'm afraid the darkness in your heart seems to have taken control of you."

"Tell me now!"

The Lady looked towards the Lizardman who seemed to affirm his approval. Rhaizen had already started to climb back to his feet and offered no immediate challenge. The Lady then began.

"To understand the true depth of my vendetta against Parandor, there is someone I think you should meet. He is a major player in this..."

"Stop your delaying tactics bitch and tell me now!" demanded Methladon.

"Please keep your anger under control, just as you said you could," continued the Lady without flinching. "You will just scar yourself further. The answers you seek will soon be revealed."

Once again Methladon felt his anger bubbling in the cauldron beneath the surface of his disfigured skin. It was as if the Lady of the Silverwynn toyed with him, teased him with clues, and yet held back the one vital piece of information that held everything together. Given all that had happened since his capture in Maplehill, his enforced slavery, his attempted dismemberment at the hands of Nictis, and the inferno generated by the wyvern, he felt that the Lady owed him the truth. He was determined not to let her leave without disclosing the full extent of her plans.

"Don't listen to what she says," said the voice. "She cannot inflict further pain and you will be victorious. Her days are about to pass."

Methladon believed in both the voice and its message. The vision he had seen in the Seer's Stone had shown that he alone would sit upon the throne of Parandor. The Lady of the Silverwynn, ravaged by time, would lie at his feet in submission to his power; if he permitted her to live. He was now the all-powerful one. Just as she had used him it was now his turn to dominate her and all that she had once controlled. He stared at the Lady who had begun to converse with the Lizardman priest.

"Ssonsh, the room is yours," she began. "Find out why it no longer bestows the power of the Mighty Rift upon me and why I now wither. I will take Methladon to meet with Ssleptaz, though we need to find him some clothes first. It looks like he's forgotten already what gifts this room bestows."

For the briefest of moments Methladon wondered what the Lady meant and then he remembered his nakedness beneath the sheet that he still clutched to his body. As he focused his thoughts onto clothes he felt the sheet fall away to be replaced by a covering of black leather that stretched from neck to toes. It hid all his scars, save for the deformities on the right side of his face. After checking this new attire which was perfect for his needs, Methladon once again gave his full attention to the Lady of the Silverwynn. Without further ado she beckoned him to follow her out of the room.

"Come Heyn, we have important things to do and to discuss."

Methladon moved forward but Rhaizen stepped before him to prevent further progress.

"Do you think this is wise Lady," he asked. "Given his power and the purpose you have for him, does he need to know all the details of your plans?"

Methladon glared at Rhaizen. He felt sure that he could destroy the Commander in an instant but before he could act the Lady spoke again.

"I'm sure I can handle the boy."

"Then I must insist in accompanying you," he answered, glaring.

"There is no need Commander. I may be older and weaker but I can still control him."

Methladon returned Rhaizen's stare.

"My duty to protect you is paramount," continued Rhaizen. "Considering what we now know about him and his ability to use of the power of the Rift against me, I insist that you have me by your side at all times while in his presence."

Methladon readied himself for another confrontation.

"Very well if you insist," she replied.

Rhaizen smirked as the Lady of the Silverwynn left the room. Then he turned and followed her and left Methladon alone with Ssonsh. The frog priest signalled with its fat head for Methladon to follow the others out of the room and that is what he did. He raced forward without further thought and soon caught up with the Lady and her troubled Commander.

For several minutes Methladon passed through the ruins that surrounded the Lady's bedchamber. Soon he stepped out into the light of Solaris and then followed the others through the crumbled remains of several buildings and courtyards where the followers of Avolire still huddled around their braziers. All watched the three pass in weary acceptance of their Lady's presence. As they progressed through the encampment Methladon's heightened senses tuned into the whispers and side conversations that passed between those that sought to survive in the old city. He picked up ancient stories of Avolire, theories as to why their Lady had begun to age, and how the Harbingers had been defeated on their quest inside the Dragonas. Even the scuttling geckos that swarmed over the ruined walls of the city seemed to watch Methladon with great interest as he moved among them.

Some ten minutes later the Lady led them to yet another wooden door. She knocked upon it and a few moments later Methladon heard the sound of the lock turn. Then as the door opened the Lady stepped into the candlelit room. The others followed.

"Who is this youth that you dare to bring before me?" hissed a voice.

Methladon looked towards the centre of the old space. A large Lizardman sat at a solitary table upon a rotting chair. It was more muscular than those he had encountered before and its scale skin bulged out from the under linen clothes rather than the poor armour that the rest of the creatures wore.

"My name is Methladon Heyn."

The scarred youth stared at the reptile and given that no response came back he switched his gaze to the Lady of the Silverwynn and her Commander.

"Allow me to introduce the wonderful Ssleptaz," she began. "One of my chief conspirators."

"Why haven't I seen him before?" asked Methladon.

"Who is this boy?" hissed the creature, irritated by Methladon's presence. "Is he the one you have talked about since my return, the one with the mark?"

"I'm waiting for an explanation," demanded Methladon as he held back the second voice that demanded to speak.

His eyes danced between Lady of the Silverwynn, Commander Rhaizen, and then back towards the creature who remained at the table. He wondered who would be first to respond. Then through ancient lips the Lady spoke.

"I told you that you would soon have answers to your questions young Heyn. You have no doubt heard that in our quest to overthrow the House of Gylewu and bring Parandor to its knees, we have infiltrated the Citadel of Parandor and placed a spy within its walls. My special one continues to cause much trouble and instil fear amid their Sovereign Council."

"And why are you telling me this? What are you alluding to," asked Methladon.

He had been told the spy story by the dwarf during their journey to the Gathering however he could not understand why the Lady had brought him before yet another foul Lizardman.

"Methladon Heyn," began the creature as it stood up and moved from behind the table. "The point that our Lady is making is that I am the one causing mayhem."

"You," sneered Methladon.

"Yes me!" hissed Ssleptaz as he looked towards the Lady for permission to continue with his great secret. "I am a shapeshifter and with that ability I have managed to undermine the defences of Parandor. With the help of much Lillywort I have control of so many that the Royal Guard will do my bidding when I demand it of them. Once I cut off their supplies they will be brushed aside like dust from the table. I have them stuck to the web of my hand and have even managed to get the Council to believe in the resurrection of the cult of Death Tubaria. It has caused much panic amongst the sots."

"Ssleptaz, this lad has first-hand experience of the Cult of Death Tubaria," added the Lady.

Methladon tried to understand how the Lady knew so much about his past. He thought perhaps she had deduced the truth behind his curse mark which until recent days even he believed had been present from his birth. Perhaps she had been lying to him unless of course he had revealed the information in his sleep. There was no other way for the Lady to have known of his childhood link to the cult of Death Tubaria.

"You look confused Methladon," she said. "I sense from the look on your face that you are still wondering what all this has to do with you and why I have brought you to meet with Ssleptaz."

"Not at all," lied Methladon.

"From your knowledge of Death Tubaria, I assume you will have heard of Lord Jonas Tullage."

"The name is somewhat familiar," replied Methladon. "Grovrouk told me of him once. The Lord who found a book called the Lore of the Dead, the source of Death Tubaria's power."

"The hole-dweller speaks too much," added Rhaizen who was then silenced by the rising of the Lady's hand.

"Please continue Ssleptaz so that Methladon can understand the true extent of what I intend."

"The Lore of the Dead, that dusty relic of the Ancients, will be the downfall of Parandor." hissed the reptile. "All I had to do was mimic the action of the cult and cause the Court to believe it had resurfaced. This I achieved by killing a few and by invoking magic to brand them with a copy of the cult's curse mark. The Capital has since fallen into a gauntlet's grip of fear. Not even the agent of the Cuvar who watched over the Citadel was able to stop me, though on many occasions he had come close to..."

"Look I am failing to see the point of all this. What has any of this got to do with me?"

As the three conspirators looked at him, Methladon noticed the Lady smile.

"As Ssleptaz causes his mischief, the forces of Parandor are distracted and fail to understand the depth of my plan," she continued. "As the sole survivor of Calistorn, the once proud city destroyed for a seam of orichalcum, I have aligned myself with the Knights of Avolire. These once proud descendants of the Ancients, and those that dwell in the Eastern Marsh, will ensure my victory. The people of the swamps have promised me access to the Underworld and to a power so strong it will wipe Parandor off the face of this Realm."

"You've told me all this before and it's all getting rather boring," replied Methladon before turning his attention back to the Lizardman. "If you're supposed to be in the Citadel causing havoc then what are you doing here?"

"The City Watch of Parandor have been asking too many awkward questions. I murdered seven, each branded with the imitation mark of Kha. I even managed to frame the Cuvar who had been investigating my role in the attempted murder of Phauless Gylewu. He became my seventh victim at the hands of the executioners axe. Yet somehow the City Watch is following on from where Lord Amberstone left off. I am here to decide the next steps with our Lady from Calistorn."

"So where do I fit into your plans? I sense there is something you are not telling me?"

Methladon watched as the Lizardman glanced towards the Lady of the Silverwynn.

"He doesn't know does he?" hissed the creature.

"Doesn't know? What don't I know?"

"Our Lady told me that you have conversed with Thamous and that the mark of Kha also saved you from dismemberment in the Lion Pit."

"Then you knew what it was all this time," snapped Methladon. "You lied to me bitch. All that you talked of helping me understand what was happing was nought but falsehood."

"I will admit to a little deceit..." began the Lady.

"I trusted you and you fucking lied to me!" he screamed.

"I promise I won't lie to you again, and that's the best I can do in the way of reassurance. I suggest you calm yourself and take a seat for I am sure you will want to listen to what I have to say."

Methladon swallowed air, sat at the table, and looked to the three.

"Start talking then!" he grumbled as the Lady took a step towards the table.

"After what we witnessed in the Lion Pit and from your visions the first time that you looked into the Seer's Stone, it was obvious that some greater power resides inside of your essence. It was something that I could not ignore. I would have had you executed after what happened in the Pit were it not for the fact that you carry the true mark of Kha on the back of your head; the one person in the Realm to have ever done so and lived. Just as you confirmed in your sleep, you are an anomaly, you are something that cannot and should not exist. That is why I sent you with Rhaizen and his Harbingers to find Thamous? I knew that the beast would recognise a power as great as his own, one over life and death itself."

"So if you knew I was that special why didn't you didn't tell me!" exclaimed Methladon. "You sent me to my death."

"And yet you found the truth about yourself in those caverns. Thamous did indeed intend to kill you and yet with the mark of Kha on your skin he could not do so. It proves just one thing; that you truly cannot die. I wanted to confirm the extent of your abilities and so at last the truth has come out."

"So your interest in me is clear," replied Methladon. "It was nothing to do with the pact that we struck, which if you remember included freeing my friends. Tell me then if you can speak in truths, did you keep to your part of our bargain and release them?"

"Your slave friends were sent south as promised although as you will be aware the road to Parandor is fraught with many dangers. The pass through the mountains which the old road takes is filled with many terrors, including the deadly kulkulkath."

"Then so be it," continued Methladon as he dismissed all thoughts of Dayis and Tycus from his mind. "Lady, you have my attention. I have a great power but why should I use it to help you? What threat can you pose to me if I cannot die? I could just walk out that door and you could not stop me. I have no desire to support you or your cause, not after all you have done. You can all just piss off back where you came from."

"Good, very good," whispered the voice. "Here it comes. You have their attention now."

"Because of who you are; that is why you should help me," continued the Lady. "And because of the Enderdetag Prophecy which talks about opening the door to the Underworld where the greatest of powers resides. There lies the means to destroy the House of Gylewu. When the door is opened, the one who opens it cannot survive the energy it that will be released through them. That is except for one who cannot die. That is you Methladon Heyn. You have a purpose now. Leave the life you once knew and become the one to lead us to victory. Help me control a power even greater than yours."

"I am sorry, I still don't get it. What's in it for me, why should bother to help you?"

"For what you saw in the Seer's Stone. The prize above all prizes. You can rule Parandor by my side for the diamond has revealed your inner desires. You crave great fame Methladon Heyn even if you do not want to admit it."

"She knows us too well," whispered the voice.

Methladon looked in turn to the Lady, the changeling, and Rhaizen. He sensed something was missing. She was however correct. He did desire to sit upon of the throne of Parandor and yet she had not revealed the full details of what she expected of him.

"But why have me rule alongside you?" he asked. "Where do I fit into your plans?"

"Nineteen years ago there was a Historian who once served Avolire as one of our chief advisors. He was a most loyal subject until the day when the first of the Gems of Thamous were found in some ruins on the boarders of Dirmark. I had sent him there to dig for he hailed from beyond the home of the dwarves. The gem, a ruby, had been placed in a niche in the rock where an ancient inscription was carved upon an adjacent stone. There besides the jewel were the words of the Enderdetag Prophecy which the Cuvar hold in such reverence. The Historian one day realised the truth about the power source that I wished to harness. Still, I did not expect him to do what did next."

"What happened to him? Where is the ruby now?"

"The Historian fled Avolire. He headed south to the Grey Mountains where he disappeared. He took the ruby with him along with his adopted son. The boy was descended from one of the oldest families of Avolire and that boy is essential to our plans. You see, that child is the one that the Enderdetag Prophecy speaks of. That boy is the 'Marked'."

"What!" exclaimed Methladon? "The child of the Historian is the Marked, not me?"

"Correct!" continued the Lady. "The boy was sired from the seed of the highest of families, a direct descendent of Sir Raulyn the Grand. Now you see Methladon there is another who can fulfil the Prophecy. The child that was marked by the seed of Sir Raulyn is the only other person who can open and close the doors to the Underworld and survive. You Methladon Heyn are my insurance for it appears the other is lost. You must be the one to open the door and bequeath to me the power of Kha."

"And this Historian, who was he and what happened to the jewel that he found? Don't you need all of the Gems of Thamous to open the door?"

"The traitor went by the name of Rukave Emgar," added Ssleptaz.

Methladon was stunned by the mention of his best friend's father's name. Even though he felt sure that Llyat was dead he could not now help but wonder if he was alive somewhere and in hiding. Before he could comment Ssleptaz hissed again.

"The Historian was tracked as far as Parandor and then we lost all trace of him some years ago. It was as if he had disappeared from the Realm but then we got lucky. The traitor was discovered by a loyal supporter of Avolire, a farmer who moved to one of the villages along the Tiaryer. It was he who recognised the name Emgar and tipped us off. He was silenced by the Harbingers once the information was confirmed, just in case he tried to double-cross us. When the traitor's general location had been revealed to us, Rhaizen set out with his Harbingers to bring the Marked and the ruby back to Avolire. He was also ordered to dispose of the Historian."

"So if you haven't worked it out by now, that's who we were looking for when we destroyed your village and slaughtered the scum that lived there," growled Rhaizen. "We found our traitor, but not the boy or the Ruby. Emgar even swore to his last that he did not have a son."

"But little did we know that the Fates would lead us to you Methladon on that very same night, the one who will enable Avolire's victory over the House of Gylewu," said the Lady as she crossed her right arm across her chest and shouted "For Avolire!"

"For Avolire!" replied Rhaizen and Ssleptaz as they mirrored her actions.

"So the truth is out at last," whispered Methladon's inner voice, but the youth ignored it for he too jumped to his feet and joined in with the salute.

"For Avolire."

A loud knock shook the door to the room which then swung open. Oedd the Harbinger entered in haste. He was dressed in his orichalcum armour and carried a sheathed blade. As he approached the Lady he stopped and saluted before speaking.

"Word from Barad Elestor," he exclaimed mid salute.

"What is it Oedd?" demanded Rhaizen.

"A bird message sent by General Brosizrug," continued the Harbinger. "He has apprehended four travellers in the ancient ruins and has taken them prisoner. They had the Sapphire that we seek in their possession. Brosizrug is making his way to the ogre's encampment near Calistorn."

Methladon watched as a look of excitement fell across the Lady's wrinkled visage. She then turned to face her Commander.

"Do you think you can ride with that arm?" she asked as she pointed to the sling.

"Yes my lady."

"I need you to get into your armour and ride at once to Calistorn. I want that sapphire in Avolire as soon as you can get it here. If the message is to be believed then once we hold the sapphire, it will point us to the other two Gems."

"I understand my Lady."

The words that passed between Rhaizen and the Lady of the Silverwynn dropped to a whisper as she then ushered both Rhaizen and Oedd out of the room and left Methladon alone with Ssleptaz. As the door to the room closed Methladon turned towards the Lizardman for he still had one more burning question to ask.

"So who in the Citadel have you replaced?"

"See for yourself," replied Ssleptaz.

Then in the flickering candle light he watched the creature change shape and take on a different form. Methladon would never forget who then appeared before his eyes.

18

"Run that by me again," mumbled Danisun Dain from across the table.

"The stone hit Emeny on the forehead and she passed out," replied Tonousa.

It had been but two hours since Darchus had saved the life of Lady Fullbane in the presence of the new Sovereign Advisor and Tonousa was in the process of relating the tale to her colleague from the City Watch. Both realised that Fullbane's choking, albeit funny in retrospect, could have turned into a woeful tragedy. Had it not been for Darchus's quick thinking and display of strange and unusual skills, they would have had another corpse to explain to their Commander.

"And Lady Fullbane?" asked Danisun with concern as he leaned over the table to make himself heard over the background noise of the tavern.

Tonousa was not sure why Danisun had chosen to hold their meeting in the main room of The Murdered Wolf given that Hotch's business was once again on the up. The occupants of the tavern seemed to have forgotten that the city was preparing for war. It was as if the scum were in complete denial of the dangers that they faced. The armies of the Fifteen Keeps on the land beyond the outer walls could not after all be missed. The readying for war had forced the inhabitants of the slums to take refuge inside the City and that had at last boosted business for The Murdered Wolf. The fact that there were still no signs of the enemy's approach was a great relief for everyone including Tonousa and her colleagues. Drinking away the thoughts of what may yet come was now the most popular way of diffusing anxiety.

"Recovering I guess," Tonousa continued. "Had it not been for Darchus she would have joined her husband in the afterlife. Then how to dispose of a mountain of lard?"

"I just did what anyone less would have done," mumbled Darchus who sat between Tonousa and Danisun Dain. "It was just knowing what to do that was important. The technique was taught to me by my father and it was passed down from his father before him. I know it may seem a strange skill for a cordwainer to have mastered but given the circumstances it was most useful."

"I'm glad you were there," said Tonousa. "I do not know what I would have done if alone?"

"I'm sure you would have acted in a most appropriate manner," replied Darchus. "I saw how you relieved the suffering of the old bard in Valameer. You would have done all that you could even if you did not know the best way to revive the large Lady. She probably would have died but at least you would have tried to save her."

Tonousa began to reflect and despite the drunken uproar that filled the tavern she recalled the one called Ulthirn whose life she had taken. She remembered how the act had affected her. It seemed like a dream and she still could not believe she had done it. Darchus thought her unselfish but she was not so sure of her own motives.

"So let me get this straight," began Danisun as he tried to gain Tonousa's attention. "If what you discovered from Lady Emeny is true, then the majority of the

Royal Guard and many others who dwell within the Citadel are hooked on Lillyweed?"

"Lillywort," corrected Tonousa. "And yes, that would seem to be the case. Both Sir Byddin and Lady Emeny both confirmed that fact."

"It would at least explain the behaviour of certain members of the Royal Guard," added Danisun. "I am thinking in particular of those two that used to follow Xix Blackfayer where ever he slithered, Berthellemy and Mandleworth. It would also explain Lady Emeny's erratic behaviour."

Danisun paused for a moment and as he did so Tonousa tried to guess what he was thinking. She could read her friend like a book but of recent times his body language had become more difficult to interpret. It was as if a stakewall had been erected between them.

"Given what you have heard, do you think that Sir Byddin or Lady Emeny is the spy we are looking for?" he asked.

"Sir Byddin, yes, I think he could be the one," replied Tonousa. "Remember, he has a fascination for the Lore of the Dead and the weapon from Barad Elestor that he so desires to obtain. I sense he knows much more about that book than he has so far admitted. He is in prime position to provide his men with Lillywort and has strong connections with all of those who have so far died at the hands of Death Tubaria. I keep thinking of Lady's Emeny's description of where and how she got her supply. It could have been Sir Byddin in a hooded cloak, who under the cover of darkness, provided her with the potion to help her sleep. If he is our infiltrator then he is also in a position to leak the detailed operations of our army and how Parandor will seek to defend itself."

"And what about Lady Emeny?" asked Danisun

"I think we should eliminate her from our investigation; her strings are too tight. Her behaviour earlier today showed that that she doesn't have the control and temperament needed to mastermind such a devious plan and manipulate the buffoons that walk the Court. I think we should forget Fullbane's comment that Lady Emeny has always wanted more power and control."

"Unless it was a double bluff of course and her behaviour was an elaborate act to put us off her trail," interjected Darchus.

The shoemaker's words caused Tonousa to revaluate her statement.

"That's a good point," she added after a moment's thought. "I'm glad to have you..."

A shadow then fell across the table where the three colleagues sat. Darchus and Danisun looked beyond Tonousa and noted its source. Tonousa heard a familiar voice rise above the background din. It was one she did not care to engage with for it belonged to Nedes Karoly.

"I'm surprised you dare show your face in here again but your quim would be welcome, if it still can open."

Tonousa sensed that Karoly stood right behind her but she was determined not to acknowledge him. However her words came out nonetheless.

"Fuck off Nedes."

"It's all down to you, the mess that this City is in right now," goaded Karoly. "You and your traitorous father have brought the Death Tubaria on us once again. I'm surprised old Isambard hasn't throw you out on your scrawny arse after what you did to his business but I guess he's a wimp when it comes to…"

"I'm warning you Nedes…." growled Tonousa as her hand moved to her weapon.

"It's just another City Watch fuck up," he continued. "Just one after another ever since you joined them and now here you are trying to solve the unsolvable. We all saw it; at the Richemanus Folly when your father's head released its curse mark upon this City. Even a brainless …"

"That's enough Nedes," ordered Danisun before Tonousa could respond but the man behind her took no notice and continued his tirade.

"As I was saying, even a brainless cunt like you should know that magic is behind all this shit. So why don't you do what the citizens of Parandor should have done years ago, root out the wizards who have sealed themselves in their towers and lynch the bastards."

"Is that a confession to a crime you are about to commit, Nedes?" asked Tonousa, believing a fight to be inevitable.

"None your fucking business bitch."

Tonousa was about to stand but Danisun was first to his feet. He stood tall and leaned across the table with authority. With his hand gripped upon the hilt of his blade he glared with menace.

"I sense there is an issue to be investigated Nedes?" said Danisun with anger in his voice. "I'm sure that Commander Townsforth and the Royal Guard would like to talk with you about the horses that have gone missing in and around the Capital. You wouldn't know anything about that would you?"

Tonousa looked across the table towards Danisun and then glanced to Darchus who still sat to her left. She was sure that Karoly was riled and spoiling for a fight. His heavy breath and close presence increased her anxiety but she had no intention of submitting to his intimidation.

"Fuck you!" Nedes exclaimed. "And fuck the lot of you."

Tonousa heard the lout move away. She glanced back over her right shoulder to witness the former member of the Watch disappear amid the crowd of low life. Sighing deeply she then addressed the Man-at-Arms.

"Danisun…" she began.

"Don't mention it," he replied as he returned to his seat.

"I can handle Nedes Karoly you know."

"Yes and that's what I am afraid of. At your father's execution you stole a fellow officer's weapon; you cannot be seen to be the cause of further trouble. You have only to put one foot in the wrong place and Townsforth will throw you off this investigation."

"I understand what you are saying and your point is well made," she replied.

Danisun was right as usual. Tonousa's continued contribution to the unmasking of the spy relied on her controlling her temper. It would help no one if she were to act like an imbecile. There was no doubt that her father had been framed but she would not avenge that injustice if locked inside the Underkeep and left to rot with only the rats and lice for company.

"As we were saying before that idiot tried to pick a fight," began Danisun. "We are still left with Sir Richemanus and the priest, Heward Teulu."

"I did learn from Emeny and Fullbane that holy Heward is not in the Capital. He has gone up to Valameer in order to comfort the surviving bards. They also said that Richemanus is up to his neck in debt with many of the Sovereign Household. From what Emeny said, Lord Colt tried to call in the debt owed to him but his sudden death put a stop to that. Convenient don't you think?"

"Well you could always ask him face to face and get him to confirm what you already know," added Danisun.

"I intend to," replied Tonousa. "There is a lot I wish to ask that man."

"I know you do," continued Danisun while he nodded his head in the direction of the door. "He's just walked in... over there."

Once again Tonousa looked over her shoulder and into the crowd that filled the tavern's tables. She scanned the faces and backs of those between the door and the counter where Isambard Hotch was trying his best to serve the swarm that had descended upon his nectar. Eventually she spotted the imposing figure of the executioner, dressed in dirty leather and without a single hair on his head. Even without his official uniform there was no mistaking the distinctive presence of the monstrous Sir Richemanus of the Nightfall. The crowd parted as if by some unseen communication and allowed the executioner free passage to the counter.

"It's not that often that you see him down in this neck of the slums," muttered Danisun as Tonousa watched the enormous man part the crowd. "He tends to stick to the taverns around Stukeley Knoll..."

As Danisun continued to speak Tonousa's attention was pulled away and it focused on Sir Richemanus as he sat down at a wooden tables in the darkest of the alcoves. She then noticed that another also sat at that same table. Dressed in the loose fitting brown and white woven robes of the Badland nomads was an individual that Tonousa had come across in the past.

"I wonder what Richemanus wants with Falaz Al Hizdor?" asked Danisun.

"I don't know," replied Tonousa. "But now is a good opportunity to find out!"

Before Danisun had time to answer Tonousa was on her feet. She began to push through the crowd towards where the two had engaged in a deep discussion. As she edged forward she saw Falaz slip out a small leather purse from under his robes and place it down on the table. A second later he pushed it towards Richemanus.

The pair fell silent as Tonousa approached their table, her eyes fixed upon the purse.

"What's in the bag Falaz?"

"None of your business," he replied.

"This is no concern of the City Watch," growled Sir Richemanus. "The contents will not interest you. It would make me very happy if you went about your business and moved along..."

"I have just made this my business," responded Tonousa. "I have had a very interesting conversation with Lady Lorst, who I believe under Lady Emeny's instructions, and with a recommendation from Phauless Gylewu himself, has been appointed Keeper of the Treasury. It seems that the City Watch has bought out the debt you owed to Lord Fabius Colt."

Tonousa bit her lip. She hoped that the lie she had just told would be enough to rattle Richemanus and persuade him to speak with her in private, away from the prying ears of the southerner that sat opposite. An exchange of looks passed between Richemanus and Falaz and she tried to second-guess what it was that they had to hide.

"Are you threatening me Tonousa Amberstone?" the executioner barked out.

"Not at all Sir, but I am pleased that you recognise me. I need to ask you some questions."

After further furtive glances Richemanus nodded his head and waved to dismiss his friend.

"We shall discuss terms later Sir," grumbled Falaz as he rose from his chair, snatched the leather purse and hid it under his robes. "When we are alone and in more congenial company."

Falaz Al Hizdor turned and flounced off into the midst of the crowded Tavern, no doubt to spread mischief and mayhem elsewhere within the Capital. However, the southerner was of little immediate concern to Tonousa for she had a bigger fish to hook and in Parandor none came any larger than the monstrous executioner. Having once again made eye contact with the knight, she took the seat vacated by Falaz. She stared at the man before her, noted his nostrils flare and the anger that rippled across the skin of his face. Her interruption had enraged him.

"This had better be fucking good," he barked.

"There is no need to be so aggressive. You may be Parandor's executioner and have the title of the Nightfall, but you will find that intimidation does not scare the City Watch nor detract them from their work. I am here on official business and so would appreciate your cooperation."

The two egos glared at each other. In the silence that followed Richemanus leaned back in his chair and inhaled deep to his bladder.

"Let's get this over and done with then," he said.

"As you are aware, even before my father's execution..." began Tonousa.

"Which I carried out on the orders of our Sovereign Lord..."

"And as you are aware, even before my father's execution," repeated Tonousa. "The City Watch, under the command of Brynn Townsforth, were appointed to investigate matters relating to the recent murders. Those that have been linked to the resurgence of the cult of Death Tubaria."

Tonousa tried to remain focused. She could not allow her personal feelings to cloud her judgement and yet she was determined to prove her father's innocence. There was a job to finish and an infiltrator to unearth.

"So what have the murders got to do with me?" said the executioner as he folded his arms across his chest."

"Evidence in my possession implies that you are involved with the Death Tubaria murders and likely responsible for the deaths linked to that cult."

"Evidence?" roared Sir Richemanus as he stood and rose to his full height. "What evidence do you have, you spawn of a traitor's dick?"

Tonousa glanced backwards and saw that Darchus and Danisun were watching and monitoring her progress. She felt vulnerable as the man towered over her and yet she knew she had to continue.

"Sir, please sit down and let us talk in a more reflective manner. In case you hadn't noticed I am here with two others from the Watch. They observe us at this very moment and please believe me, I will have no hesitation in seeking their assistance to take you away for questioning should this tavern not suit. Now if you would please take your seat again so that we can discuss this properly and without further incident. There are questions that need answering. They may cast light upon new evidence brought before us."

Tonousa gestured with her hand and after a few seconds the executioner sat down.

"Like I said Sir," continued Tonousa. "The City Watch has come into possession of certain evidence that links you to the Death Tubaria murders and appears to indicate you as the sole perpetrator of the crimes."

"So what evidence do you have?" grumbled Sir Richemanus. "What do I stand accused of?"

"I will come to that in a minute but first of all I need to ask you about your axe."

"My axe!"

"Yes your axe Sir, the black metal blade that that you wield at executions. When you put on your show at the Folly your axe is usually so blunt that it takes several attempts to cleave through a victim's neck. It causes the condemned to nod as if in acknowledgement of their guilt. Only this time..."

"So this is all about your father..." he interrupted.

Tonousa leaned across the table. "You're damn right that I am talking about my father. If your weapon should have been as blunt as all the stories tell then why did it cleave through my father's neck with such ease? Given that his head was then found to bare the curse mark of Death Tubaria, I have to know how your axe had been sharpened. Did you do that yourself and if not who did it? Had it been enchanted in some way? Where is it kept when not in use? Who else had access to it?"

Tonousa's sudden outburst drew attention from the drunken crowd.

"Enchanted! My axe? No more than my arse is you stupid bitch. Now there's a good tale to tell. I think everyone in Parandor would love a story such as that. Remind me to tell you the one about the one legged whore, the goat, and the obsidian..."

"Sir Richemanus!" snapped Tonousa, frustrated as the interview flew from her control.

"I put the speed at which I cut through your father's neck down to sheer strength and the heighted excitement of having such an important victim to dispatch. He was a traitor to the Realm. He deserved everything he got and so I may have swung a bit harder than normal."

Tonousa felt sick in her stomach. Richemanus was enjoying tormenting her.

"But in response to your question," he continued. "All of my instruments of torture and execution are kept within the Citadel's Armoury when not in use. The only time the axe sees the light of Solaris is when I perform upon the Folly. Anyone who had a key to the armoury would have had access to it without my knowledge. Mandleworth, Berthellemy, and even Cragtalon. In fact all the Royal Guard have access and it is even possible that Sir Byddin tampered with it. Did you know that he has magic skills and can influence metal?"

"That fact has so far escaped me. Please say more," replied Tonousa.

"How do you think he lost his bloody eye?"

"He told me it happened while you were sparing with him," responded Tonousa. "He said he got distracted for a moment in the middle of Hog."

"Oh, did he? That's interesting. The stupid sod was trying to show off. Said he could manipulate our weapons such that the metal was stronger than the very stone that supports the Citadel. Said it was a very simple process to turn the properties of one object into another. Well to cut a long story short, the spell he used backfired and as we sparred together his enchanted blade shattered and sent a slither deep into his own eye. The Grand Physician couldn't save it and had to cut the whole thing out to prevent infection spreading. So you see, Byddin knows some magic and as I said before, he would have had access to my axe."

"That would further explain his interest in the Lore of the Dead," muttered Tonousa under her breath, low enough such that Richemanus did not hear her words.

If this new information was true and from what she already knew of the changeling, then someone with the power to alter metal would be a prime suspect. Byddin had told her about losing his eye to Richemanus but he had left out any reference to magic.

"So," began Richemanus after a long pause. "Now that I have answered your questions about my axe and Sir Byddin, you can answer mine."

"Sir Richemanus I'm..." began Tonousa, but the executioner was too quick for her.

"What evidence do you have that implicates me? What have you discovered?"

Tonousa hesitated and felt uneasy that Sir Richemanus was taking control of the conversation but if she was to obtain anything meaningful from the man she knew she would have offer something to keep him compliant. Sighing, she reached into the leather satchel and removed the four cards which she then handed over to the executioner.

"So what have we got here?" began the executioner as he scanned the pieces of parchment in his hands. "Of all the things you could have shown me these are the last thing I would have expected. What links these cards and the murders to me?"

Once again Tonousa explained what she had found within the walls of her father's chamber. She then told how she had discovered a coded note that a sailor had deciphered for her. It had pointed to four suspects and he, Richemanus, was one of them. As she did so Tonousa watched for any change that would give a clue as to the executioner's guilt. There was nothing that she picked up on and the only movement he made was to summon a serving wench. The girl came over to the table and Richemanus ordered another tankard of Blessed Beast. Once the girl had left Tonousa continued to explain the meaning and purpose of the four cards. She pointed to the one marked Justice.

"That is rather strange evidence if you ask me," sneered the knight as he handed them back. "I am sure that within the laws, your evidence is nought but bull's pizzle and would not be admissible in any court. You might want to speak to Lady Emeny about its usefulness, she being a judge and all that."

"Do not worry Sir," replied Tonousa. "I have already done so. She was most interested."

Tonousa smiled. Lady Emeny had indeed taken great interest in her story and the pieces of parchment. Together it had all been enough to fuel the new Sovereign Advisor's suspicion. For a brief moment her thoughts left Sir Richemanus and returned to the words that Darchus had muttered some minutes earlier, 'Unless it was a double bluff of course and her behaviour was an elaborate act to put us off her trail'.

"So who else have you spoken too?" asked Richemanus. "Who else do your cards accuse?"

"So far Sir Byddin and Lady Emeny, although both of them pointed their fingers at others."

"You don't say, fancy that!" sneered Richemanus.

"To be honest, they both pointed to you."

"Now there's a fucking surprise."

"Both had reasons to suggest your involvement in the crimes."

"I bet they did!"

"Why would they want to implicate you Sir?"

"You tell me," he replied.

"Both Sir Byddin and Lady Emeny confirmed that you have a drink problem."

"And what the fuck has that got to do with them?" he spat out as he leaned back into his chair. "What's wrong with liking a drink? That doesn't give me reason to murder anyone."

"I do not believe it to be the drink that fuels your intentions although I wouldn't put it past most of the scum in here, those like Falaz Al Hizdor for example. It's easy to imagine a killing spree when the tank is full of Blessed Beast."

Tonousa's annoyance grew as her interrogation once again lost focus but hers was not the only anger on the rise.

"Get to the fucking point," spat out Richemanus as the wench returned with the ale.

"It's not the drink Sir that concerns me," continued Tonousa as the serving girl left the table, "but rather your spiralling debts and your lack of means to pay them. It is how you may have treated those you owe money that gives you a clear motive. Do you deny that Fabius Colt tried to call in your debt just before he was murdered?"

Tonousa stared across the table. The tankard had not yet touched the executioner's lips and he placed it back down. Something had spooked the grotesque man who just moments before had been red with anger. He had turned frost white and he trembled.

"Are you feeling well Sir?" asked Tonousa, knowing that she had regained control. "Is there something amiss?"

The executioner leaned forward and dropped his voice to a whisper. His eyes shot glances to all corners of the room as he began to whisper.

"Shush, not so loud. Let me be honest with you Tonousa Amberstone. There are others in here who would find this conversation very interesting; those who belong to the Thieves Guild for example like that bastard Nedes Karoly. I owe money to many and all are unaware of my debts with others. If the truth were to be made public I would be in serious trouble, in particular if it became common knowledge that Colt had tried to call in his. Given the fear that now stalks this Capital I wouldn't put it past the likes of Karoly to demand immediate repayment. For most, the only thing that keeps them from tearing down my door is my position and title. The 'Nightfall' still strikes fear into most of the scum."

"I understand," she whispered back. "Is there anyone I should be made aware of that could help with my investigation? Let me be clear, to who else did you owe money that also suffered at the hands of Death Tubaria?"

Once again Richemanus fell silent. Tonousa sensed a reluctance to divulge more.

"Sir, I need to know. Did any other of your money lenders fall victim to Death Tubaria?"

"Britta Rainmark," replied Richemanus, so low that Tonousa could just about hear. "I guess you would find out soon enough. I borrowed a significant amount of money from that bastard and then the turd set about blackmailing me. He pushed his extortion to the limit and demanded a repayment far greater than I could ever have agreed too; an amount way beyond collection."

"Blackmail!" exclaimed Tonousa as she tried not to raise her voice. "What knowledge did Britta Rainmark have to be able to blackmail a man with such fearsome reputation?"

"Look this is rather difficult. But for the record, let's just say that Rainmark knew about my many problems."

"And what problems would they be? I must ask you to be more specific, no matter how much it pains you to be honest with your answer," replied Tonousa.

"Like I said, it is rather a sensitive issue."

"Sir Richemanus!" snapped back Tonousa as her voice rose to display authority. "I will not be brushed aside. You must answer in truth if you want to clear your name. Whatever you say to me will be kept in the strictest of confidence."

"Very well then. If it is the only way that I can convince you of my innocence then I will share my secret with you; but you alone. I will have to take that on trust. As I have already told you, I like a drink in an evening. Well, to be truthful, it's more than just one Blessed Beast and sometimes it can seven or eight per night. I also have a fondness for quim. I like a woman in my bed each night and it doesn't matter who, for they are all the same between the legs. I'm sure if you asked Isambard he could point you in the direction of every woman I have ever fucked in his rooms back there. I can lose myself down here in The Murdered Wolf though more often the taverns around the Stukeley Knoll. Most of those to who I owe money wouldn't be seen dead in the shit holes I frequent and those that do are too pissed to care or notice."

"Don't tell me that you owe money to Isambard Hotch as well," added Tonousa as she glanced across the crowded room towards the rolling barkeep.

"Yes, I am sad to say that I do. Excuse me for I have digressed."

Tonousa was pleased that the knight had begun to open up at last. The threat of calling in his debt had rattled him and she sensed she had already discovered more than she had thought possible at the start of her interrogation. Her mind tried to process the relevance of Sir Byddin and his knowledge of magic, the dishonourable behaviour of Sir Rainmark and Nedes Karoly's link to the Thieves Guild, a fact she was surprised that she hadn't already known.

"Continue and do not hold anything back," added Tonousa as she pushed on.

"Back to my problem with the drink," said Richemanus as he lifted his tankard. "Some people say that it is a family curse, for all my ancestors have been troubled by it. Even though I have often tried to cut back, it always ends up the same. I will do anything to satisfy my cravings for ale and wine. It is the drink which fuels my passion for quim, why I eat too much, and why I am in so much debt. There is however another problem that plagues me and which you will be keen to understand..."

Richemanus hesitated as he looked around the tavern with suspicion.

"In your own time Sir."

"I assume being a woman that you have little understanding of the curse that afflicts a man who consumes too much ale and who wishes to shag thereafter."

"You are correct Sir," smirked Tonousa. "I am not partial to men's best kept secrets."

In fact Tonousa knew exactly what Richemanus meant but continued to act in ignorance.

"Some call it the 'bane of the beast' while others just the 'curse', but most call it 'dick droop'. Whatever name is chosen, it still means the same. All the years of heavy drinking have turned my cock into a shrivelled worm that even the slags in this whorehouse struggle to raise and ride, even for all the coin I manage to scrounge. Well, that's where I need help."

Richemanus fell quiet and for the briefest moment Tonousa felt sorry for the hated man, up to his eyes in debt, the city's most famous inebriate, and one who had lost the power to perform where it mattered most. All that he had left was his name that still struck fear into the citizens of Parandor. She realised in that moment that underneath his monstrous facade he was just like everyone else, full of self-doubt with his own bucketful of insecurities.

"You asked what was in the bag earlier," he continued "It was powdered horn from the north of the Grey Mountains. Ask Falaz Al Hizdor if you don't believe me; that is if you can ever find him again. He has access to a supplier whose special powder has the ability to turn my shrivelled worm into a fearsome spitting snake."

"I think we are digressing somewhat," said Tonousa for she had begun to feel uncomfortable as images of Richemanus's affliction flitted through her imagination. "Let us keep to the issue at hand. Apart from Lord Colt and Sir Britta Rainmark, what links did you have with the others who fell victim to Death Tubaria? Lord Tobius Faros, the two servants of the citadel, the stable boy Mikus Danbury and even my father? Did you owe money to any of them?"

"Your father, no way! Why would I owe money to a fucking Librarian?"

Tonousa smiled and pointed towards the tankard in his hands.

"I see, well... point taken," he replied.

"And the others?" continued Tonousa. "Do you have any connection to them?"

"Well, I suppose..."

"Sir, I insist that you tell me everything."

It was clear there was even more that he sought to hold back. With each passing moment any fear that Tonousa once held for the executioner melted away. She sensed his growing discomfort with her questions and knew that if she continued to press him further she would reduce him to a floundering wreck which would not serve her best interests. If she pushed him over the edge he would clam up and his usefulness would end.

"I'm guessing you're aware of Tobius Faros's personal history," added Richemanus.

"I was told that he lost his wife and daughter to the sweating sickness," replied Tonousa. "Soon after that he was found swinging by the neck from the highest tower of the Citadel."

"It is true. Lord Faros had numerous issues. Old Abrahamus Marus, the one you failed to protect on your boat trip to Valameer, called it the 'black dog of despair'. It was an ever present companion to Lord Faros, always lurking in the shadows yet just out of sight; growling, menacing, and capable of overwhelming him at any moment. Before they found that fucking mark on his head, everyone believed that it was the black dog that drove him to take his own life."

"What are you alluding to Sir? What is the connection between yourself and Death Tubaria?"

"Lord Faros's dog stopped him from finding rest at night. He came to me one day in search of something to help him find peace. Mandleworth sent him to me as he knew that I could help the poor bugger sleep. It was another of the products that I purchased from Falaz Al Hizdor."

"More unicorn parts I suppose, Let me guess, its balls!"

"No Tonousa, something more potent that any part of a unicorn and even more lethal in the right dose than kulkulkath venom. Falaz was always giving me such things to sell in the Citadel so that I could fund my vices. All I had to do was ask..."

"So what else did Falaz give you?"

"Have you heard of a flower called Lillywort?" whispered Sir Richemanus.

"Perhaps," replied Tonousa as another path opened.

"You may then be aware that it alters reality for those who take it. In much smaller amounts Lillywort has a calming effect. That's what Lord Faros bought from me and what I got from the nomad. You need to be aware of something else. Falaz claims there were others who distribute Lillywort inside the Citadel."

"The two servants, Webb Underscroft and Golda Flintwind?"

"You got it first time," added the knight. "The connection you seek is the flower."

"And the Lillywort, do you know how Falaz Al Hizdor obtains it? Who is his supplier?"

"I haven't the slightest idea. Flowers are not something I know much about. If you want to extract a confession from a prisoner, be them guilty or innocent, then and I'm your man; but if you want to know of things that grow in the wild you had best consult a woman, an apothecary, or a priest. Those that spout the holy drivel often know a great deal about poisons."

"What do you mean by that?" she asked.

"Do you know where the dead are taken by Cassius Underscroft and his like?"

"Remind me," replied Tonousa.

"It is usual for the dead collectors take the bodies of the deceased beyond the walls of the city and dispose of them in one of several large pits which they then cover with lime and soil. The exceptions to this practice are the dead of noble birth and high status who are entombed within the catacombs beneath Parandor's temples. If you've ever seen the bodies in the niches of the crypts then you will know how well preserved there are despite the years that pass. Have you ever wondered what secret ingredient is added to the embalming fluid in order to preserve the flesh of the dead?

"It has never crossed my mind," answered Tonousa.

It was true, such matters had never once entered her thoughts. The processes of the temple priests were unknown to her.

"From what I was told they use all sorts of flowers in their embalming process but Lillywort is the most important of them," added Richemanus."

The confirmation of the presence of Lillywort by three of her suspects pointed to it being the most significant factor that linked the murders. Perhaps her father had also know of this connection. She tried to imagine him investigating the white flower of the Eastern Marsh without informing others of his suspicions. Despite her confusion she felt she was at last making progress. It was easy to conclude that whoever was responsible for the resurrection of the cult of Death Tubaria was the one peddling the Lillywort. Tonousa then realised that she needed to speak to Heward Teulu with some urgency and hear what he had to say about the powerful marsh plant. She also needed to find and question Falaz Al Hizdor and explore his connection to the murders and the name of his supplier.

"Thank you for the information regarding Lord Faros and the Lillywort you obtained from Falaz. Your disclosure will save me considerable time. Is there any other connection you have missed or forgotten to tell me?"

Sir Richemanus paused and took another gulp of his beer. Tonousa sensed there was more to come. She still had to work out why her father named him as one of his four key suspects.

"I may regret saying this as it could incriminate me further, but in addition to knowledge of my drinking, whoring, and spiralling debts, Fabius Colt also discovered the identity of the person running the Lillywort racket. Colt confronted me, threatened to expose Falaz as my supplier and he began to demand half of the profit that I gained from my peddling. I was well fucked."

Tonousa heard the tremor in the executioner's voice. The once large and much feared man had become a shell of his former self as his miserable existence began to unravel around him. If Sir Richemanus was the shape changer of the Eastern Marsh then all of what she had heard would have been a most impressive act.

"So let me get this straight Sir. You were being blackmailed by Sir Rainmark and Lord Colt? Is there anyone else I should be aware of?"

To Tonousa's annoyance Richemanus once again fell silent. For a brief moment she longed for the physical presence of Theoplous, Irabo, Darchus, or Danisun. With just a little physical intimidation she sensed she could break the gruesome knight. She had one chance and she had to go for it.

"Sir, will you please answer!" she ordered.

"There was indeed one other. The stable boy, Mikus Danbury," Richemanus whimpered. "The one who died before the events at the Folly."

"And what did the boy have over you?"

"The horse rustling. The animals of the rich are being sold as meat to the scum. The boy found out that it was me that let the horses out of their stalls and turned them over to Nedes Karoly for a hefty sum. Karoly was acting as an agent for the Thieves Guild and between them they screwed me over the price. The stable boy was in the wrong place at the wrong time and he saw me free the horses. He threatened to tell old Treveyn but we came to an agreement on the price of his silence. It was one I could only afford by passing over all the money I had prised out of the Thieves Guild. I thought no one would find out about my involvement after the boy was crushed under that fucking rock."

"I think you'd better stop there Sir, or I am afraid I am going...."

"I did it just the once out of desperation," the knight howled aloud and his noise threatened to incite the tavern's crowd. "I didn't kill the boy though. I swear that is the truth for even I could never have lifted that enormous rock. I'm not saying any more. I have already said far too much."

"Sir Richemanus you've..." Tonousa's words were interrupted as a couple who were fucking on their feet in the next alcove lost their balance and fell across the table. The contents of the knight's tankard spilled onto the table, ran to its edge, and pooled within Tonousa's lap. In reflex action she jumped up out of her chair.

"Watch what you're doing!" she shouted.

"Piss off," replied the drunk who lay sprawled beneath the whore.

"Get out of here, you disgusting piece of shit," ordered Tonousa.

Without warning the whore grabbed the man's hand, pulled him off the table. She dragged him into the crowd and disappeared from sight. Tonousa looked to the now empty seat where Sir Richemanus had sat only moments earlier.

"Damn!" she exclaimed.

"What's up?" said a familiar voice.

Tonousa turned and saw Danisun close by her side.

"Just when you think you're making progressing, Fate intervenes."

"I thought you didn't…" added Danisun, but he did not get to finish his sentence.

"Fuck off. Let's not go there again."

Tonousa scanned the crowd for signs of Richemanus and then turned to her colleague.

"Danisun, you might want to have a chat with Nedes Karoly about the horse rustling. Richemanus as good as confirmed that Karoly is behind it. There is another I need to speak to as soon as possible and I will need the assistance of the whole Watch to seek him out."

"Who would that be then?" asked Danisun as Tonousa smiled to herself.

19

As the swirling amber fog broke behind his poison red lids, Llyat tried to open his leadened eyes. He squinted as the midday glare from Solaris beat down on him and warmed his body. He felt as dreadful as a boy could be and yet still be alive. It was as if all of his energy had been removed and dumped him within a vacuum of woe. An orchestra of pain hammered away inside his head and every bone burned as if tossed upon a fire. Whatever minor movements he tried to make, they felt like trying to shift the whole world. He reached up to feel his dry throat and winced at the intensity of its burning. A severe thirst threatened to choke him and his hand trembled having broken free from his control. He could feel the motion of the metal through the straw bedding that lay between him and the hard moving ground beneath. Enclosed inside the mobile cage, each bump and jerk of its wheels brought feelings of intense nausea and a churning sensation to his stomach. Llyat tried to recall what had happened inside the ruins of Barad Elestor but struggled to concentrate as the waves of sickness coursed through his body. He then attempted to sit upright using his hands and arms to steady himself. Each sound that he made was amplified and every movement a struggle. He was weakened to the point of eternal collapse. Moving his upper body up with great difficulty Llyat managed at last to support himself with his arms which transmitted his pounding heart beat into each of his bulbous fingertips. Once again he squinted through his lashes and in the midst of the searing light he tried to make out where he was.

"Welcome back to the realm of the woken," said a shadowy figure, silhouetted against the glare from Solaris.

"Thias! Is that you?" groaned Llyat as he recognised his friend's voice. "Where are we?"

"Somewhere in the southern part of Thengar Forest," replied the Bard, his voice ringing in Llyat's ears like hammers against a great anvil.

"My head hurts so much," moaned Llyat, clutching his temples while the floor of the cage bounced beneath him. "What amidst the mercy of the gods happened to me?"

"You drank one of my potions, you daft bugger," growled Einar. "The one I warned you against ever touching."

Llyat tried to recall the amber liquid as images raced through his mind. He sought to relive his attempt to rescue Thias and Irabo from the ogre that they had encountered within the ruins of the Ancients, but no matter how hard he tried he could not remember what had happened. His concentration failed him and his head continued to pound. He turned to see where the voice of the Berserker had come from and he opened his eyes wider. After several minutes he began to make out the blurred form of the Berserker who sat with his back against the metal cage and whose voice boomed out once again.

"I'm surprised you survived. The uninitiated most often go mad or even worse still..."

"Yes, yes, Einar," interrupted Thias.

This comment gripped Llyat's attention. He turned his head towards the bard while the world span.

"I think Llyat gets the point. He shouldn't have touched your brew but without him we would all be dead. Why did you have to go and wake the ogre? You are one dense bastard Einar."

"Do you dare threaten me bard?" snapped back the Berserker, his voice beating away against Llyat's consciousness.

"Considering the mess you got us into, I wouldn't...."

Thias did not have time to finish before Llyat called for quiet.

"Please stop it. My brain is fucking killing me as it is without you two shouting. Can you not whisper? Tell me what happened in the softest of voice. Why are we in a cage?"

Llyat's vision returned sufficient for him to realise that the three of them were in the centre of a metal box that sat upon a bed of filthy festering straw. The closer he shuffled towards Thias and Einar the better he could focus on their faces. But he saw no sign of Irabo. If he too was in the cage he could not see him. Neither could he make out what lay beyond the metal bars.

"You passed out when the first effects of the Berserker's brew wore off," continued Thias. "I managed to talk you down before the madness took hold but I doubt you will remember that it was your cries that attracted the rest of the ogres; the friends of the one you killed in that arena. There happened to be seven of them nearby and they were not pleased with what you had done to their brother. I surrendered us all in order to save our lives."

Llyat tried to recall his fight with the ogre but even though his vision was improving as each minute passed and the intensity of the light no longer blinded him, he still struggled to remember anything after the point at which he had rushed to the aid of Thias and Irabo. Then he recalled the reason for being in Barad Elestor, the jewel in Sir Raulyn's axe.

"The sapphire!" cried Llyat with complete disregard for the noise that echoed through his ears. "Where is the sapphire? Do you still have it?"

Llyat watched as Thias hung his head low and shook it from side to side.

Once his confusion had cleared a little Llyat became aware of the cold crisp air that hung around them and was again grateful for the protection the animal pelts that he still wore.

"I am sad to report that the ogres have it now," replied Thias a minute later. "Along with the rest of our belongings and the pendent you gave me."

"What pendent," asked Einar?

"He means the Dragon Whisper," said Llyat as he at last managed to focus on the Berserker. "I do not need it anymore as Thamous can speak to me without it. Thias had given up his own precious jewel to buy us food and lodgings in Fallguard so I felt it was only right to give it to him as a replacement for his loss."

"It wasn't yours to give boy," muttered Einar.

"Are you going to make a problem out of this?" growled Thias.

A soft yet stern voice spoke from further along the side of cage. Llyat squinted once again and his eyes focused on Irabo who lay on his back while staring at the grey metal roof.

"We are in enough trouble without fighting amongst ourselves," said the young warrior. "Bickering will serve no useful purpose. We must not show our captors any sign of weaknesses and we must keep strong if we are going to survive."

It then dawned on Llyat that ever since he had woken he had not seen any evidence of these so called captors. With great effort he managed to stand to his feet although he stood hunched and bent forward due to the low roof height. He then steadied his core by taking hold of one of the metal bars and squinted forwards. The metal box in which he was confined was harnessed to four enormous black horses. They were far larger than any that Llyat had ever seen before and they trudged on and dragged the cage over the icy ground. The beasts meandered through the trees and dense woodland of the forest as if bred to do so. The ogres, beyond the horses, walked in a straight line and Llyat noticed that all three wore ornate steel armour and sported a mass of bedraggled hair upon their heads. Ahead of these three and sat upon another gigantic horse was a fourth ogre. This one wore a steal helmet with its visor pulled down over its face and it appeared to be the leader of the group. Llyat turned back and looked through the bars at the rear of the cage. Three more ogres walked in single file. One of them carried a wooden cage on its back inside which several large birds perched. These birds did not hold Llyat's attention for long for his gaze soon fixed upon the largest of the three ogres. The creature was devoid of hair and had a metal chain that hung from its nose to its right ear lobe. Llyat made eye contact with it for a brief second but then ripped his eyes away.

"Any idea what they want with us?" asked Llyat.

"Well, for the last couple of days...." began Thias.

"I've been out for that long!"

"You're bloody lucky you didn't die," grumbled Einar from the corner.

"Let it be," snapped Thias. "As I was saying, you've been out of this world for two days and we've been locked in this cage the whole time. They've not let us out once and have forced us to wallow in our own filth with just stale bread and foul water to pass through our lips. From what I overheard when they once stopped, they are taking us towards Calistorn and then on to Avolire."

Llyat then became aware of the stink that hung heavy in the air. At first he had thought it was just the straw in the cage that was damp but the aroma of excrement that filled his nostrils soon reminded him of Maplehill. He had grown up with such an odour but within the confines of the cage it felt far from pleasant.

"Thias, what do they want with us?" asked Llyat.

"I had to tell them a few lies to save our lives although I imbedded a few grains of truth to make the story believable. I told them that we were explorers, searching Barad Elestor for treasures of the ancients and that we had come across a jewel in the tomb of Sir Raulyn. Their leader, the one at the front with a steal helmet over its stunted forehead, goes by the name of Brosizrug. He said we would make excellent slaves and would be set to work in the mines under Avolire, once the Lady had finished with us..."

A deep voice boomed from outside the cage.

"I see the shit that murdered my brother is awake."

Llyat turned to see the ogre with the face chain beside the cage.

"And hello and good morning to you too Ikeg," replied Thias with as much sarcasm as his weary mind could generate.

"I'm glad that my name has stuck inside that chicken skull of yours," spat back the ogre. "If it wasn't for the General I would have killed all four of you bastards in the arena."

Llyat quaked and was thankful for the protection that the metal bars provided.

"Well, Knuckles, I am glad you didn't for we would not have this quality time together."

"Thias," hissed Irabo. "In the name of Fatumai, stop goading him."

Llyat looked on as the Ikeg stared contemptuously at the Bard before increasing the pace of his march forward. The ogre then stumbled on the roots of a gnarled tree and swore in words that no one understood. Llyat experienced a flash back of the events in the ruins; how he had rushed to save Thias and Irabo and consumed Einar's potion. A moment later his thoughts cleared completely and he remembered all that had happened up to the point of his collapse.

"You're time will soon come string plucker, as will it will for the youth that you protect," shouted the ogre. "If the marked one wasn't wanted by Avolire then I would gut you both and leave your entrails for what little wildlife remains in this fucking forest."

Ikeg spat onto the ground and raced forward to join the ogres at the front of the procession.

Llyat turned to Thias while his thoughts darkened and his skin flushed with anger.

"I don't believe it! You told them I was the Marked!" exclaimed Llyat. "What did you have to go and do that for?"

"No Llyat. You have got it all wrong. I was about to tell you before Knuckles interrupted us. They were going to kill us in the arena, but then the largest of them, that one up front with a dented breastplate said something most significant. He mentioned the Knights of Avolire and that chance remark gave me an idea as to how I could save our lives."

"But you've delivered us straight into the hands of Lady of the Silverwynn..." moaned Llyat.

"If you will let me finish please Llyat. I told them that we are four travellers who had been searching the ruins of Barad Elestor for one of the Gems of Thamous. I said that we had it in our possession and that I was the person known as the 'Marked of Maplehill' that the Lady of the Silverwynn was looking for. It seemed to work and settle the anger inside their thick skulls. Despite Ikeg's fury after you killed his brother Dokur, I managed to persuade their leader that the Lady of the Silverwynn would want us all delivered alive. To be taken to Avolire in a cage seemed a better option than being dismembered within the ruins of Barad Elestor. I have bought us some time."

"But why would you want to give away so much information?" asked Llyat. "It was all that came to me in the moment. This was my idea. If we can gain entry to Avolire we will be near to the other gems that the Lady already has in her possession. It would give us a chance to take them all."

"But why would you want to risk doing that?" questioned Llyat.

"I will be honest," added Einar. "It's not been one of your better suggestions bard."

"So say's the idiot that got us put in this cage in the first place," snapped back Thias.

"Look you two, pack it in," said Irabo. "I have to agree with Einar and Llyat on this one, it was not a great idea. You didn't think this through Thias."

Llyat looked across the cage at the bard and watched the tension grow.

"Alright, I admit it," grumbled Thias. "I improvised. My original idea was to persuade the ogres that I was the Marked in the hope that I could persuade them to let you three go free. I didn't take into account the wrath of the brother of the one that Llyat slew."

Llyat sighed for no matter which way he looked at their situation he saw problems. The sapphire had fallen into the hands of those loyal to the Lady and it meant that she now had three of the five lost gems. They had helped her to take a step closer to her goal of destroying the House of Gylewu.

Llyat no longer felt quite as dizzy and the booming sounds inside his head had abated. The murderous hangover had left him hungry. Shaking his head free from its residual fuzziness he turned to face the bars of the cage and with each of his hands he took hold of one of the metal rods. Using all his strength he tried to pull the rods apart but was left frustrated as they would not budge an inch. Llyat turned towards the bard as an idea formed in his head.

"Thias, your 'fire fists' spell!" he exclaimed. "Can you not at least melt these bars so they will bend and let us through?"

Thias shook his head dismissively.

"It doesn't work like that I am afraid. I can use the spell to ignite my fists but the heat and energy would be insufficient to change the metal. Also, the use of magic in front of the ogres would just draw further attention to us and that is the last thing we need to do right now. Even though ogres are said to be gifted in the use of magic themselves, they seldom use it unless forced too."

"Have you any other ideas to get us out of here?" pleaded Llyat as he imagined being gutted.

"Not at this time."

"Then you're not much use to us bard," snarled Einar.

"Knock it off you two!" exclaimed Irabo as he jumped to his feet without thought to his injured leg. "As I have already said, we must work together if we are going to get out of this trap."

Thias and Einar turned away from each other. Llyat also knew that further bickering and infighting would threaten the bonds of friendship that the four had forged on their long and arduous journey.

The ogres' procession meandered through the snow covered trees of Thengar Forest for a further two days. Even though the beasts stopped to make camp and feast on the remains of the last unicorn, the four companions were never let out from their cage. However, the creatures did not let their captives starve and three times a day they were given more mouldy bread and a metal cup of brackish water. On several occasions Ikeg had suggested that the captives should be left to starve but Brosizrug would have none of it. He insisted they obeyed the Lady of the Silverwynn orders and kept the prisoners alive. During the times that the ogres made camp Llyat noticed that Thias watched and listened to their every word as he sought to concoct an escape plan. In the early morning of the third day since waking from his intoxication Llyat watched with some amazement as the dense woodland dissolved away into a hard rock covered land. Its porous pumice like stones crunched under the wheels of the cage as it trundled along. Llyat recalled the tunnels which he had passed through under Falahorn. Those rocks that had been burnt by dragon fire and had been smooth to the touch. This new type of crunching stone seemed also to have been created from heat and fire but whatever the cause, it wasn't the result of dragons. A strong stench of rotten eggs oozed from out of the stone and became so strong that it masked the stink from the foul straw on which the captives were still forced to sit.

Chilled suddenly by the frost filled air Llyat began to notice falling flakes of snow. Each failed to settle on this new ground and instead evaporated inches above its surface. The rocks were clearly much hotter than he had at first thought. He looked towards Thias who knelt and deliberated on the strange phenomenon.

"I don't think this strange cold weather is the result of magic," said Thias.

"What are you going on about now?" asked Llyat.

"It's just something that has been bothering me ever since we left Fallguard and entered Thengar Forest. I thought that some great magic had taken a hold over these northern lands but now we have left the forest I am convinced it is just a bout of unseasonal weather. Fatumai would not torment us with such cold on purpose."

"Then you don't know Fatumai," mumbled Irabo, lying against the side of the cage. "She will test us in whatever way amuses her!"

"Which reminds me of another thing," continued Thias. "Something else troubles me."

"Just one thing?" asked Einar.

"On Sir Raulyn's tomb, if you recall... There was mention of the Oracle of Frasteria and the word which you said meant the daughters of Fatumai; the Fates. I am sure the word was 'Moirai'."

"And what of the Moirai?" asked Irabo.

"I am not a follower of religion Irabo, in fact far from it. I have never visited the Oracle and any knowledge that I have comes from legends of old and the songs of the Bards Guild. They talk about a power that can grant the gift of foresight to those who seek it. Can you clarify who these daughters of Fatumai are supposed to be?"

"Now where should I begin..." said Irabo before Einar interrupted again.

"Please don't rush, we have all the fucking time in the world!"

Llyat looked across the cage to Thias, then back to Irabo, and then Einar who also lay on the floor. The young man of the City Watch rolled his eyes in frustration.

"I must first state that the connection to the Oracle of Frasteria was also a surprise to me when you translated the inscription on the side of Sir Raulyn's tomb. Let me give you some understanding about the Moirai. You are at least asking the right person..."

"Get to the point," snapped Einar.

"In legend the Moirai were the daughters of Fatumai and in most of the old stories there are always three of them. Their real names have been lost over the years but tales told around Falahorn describe the three as 'the Spinner', 'the Allotter' and 'the Cutter'. Do correct me if I am wrong Einar."

"You're right so far," mumbled the Berserker.

"The Moirai are assigned tasks by their mother to ensure that the fate of all men follows a predetermined course. These daughters are not equal to the gods but do have divine powers with which they can manipulate the way our world progresses. Each of us as we walk the Realm are governed by threads of life. It is the job of Spinner to create and spin the threads from her distaff and place them onto her spindle. Then her sister, Allotter, defines the length of the threads with her measuring rod. It is then the job of Cutter to decide the manner and time of everyone's demise. Our death occurs at a time and place of her choosing. When ready, she cuts and life ends."

While Irabo spoke, Llyat closed his eyes and tried to imagine the gruesome three. The vision of ancient woman dressed in grey cloaks, huddled over a fire, cackling as they decided the fate of each person in the Realm formed in his imagination. He pictured the threads of his father and mother being spun and woven before then being measured and cut. He saw his father murdered at the hands of the man with the skull helmet and his mother cooked as their house collapsed around her in a mass of burning timber. All the time he struggled to come to terms with the concept that three crones could have dictated how his family had died?

"Are you following me Llyat?"

Llyat opened his eyes and saw that Thias and Irabo were looking at him. Even Einar sought to make sense of Llyat's sudden stupor.

"I think so," said the youth as he felt the flush of embarrassment. "Please continue."

"Let me tell you what those who follow my religion say," continued Irabo. "In the series of texts called 'Fatumai and the Fates', the ability to see and decide how long we live on this world and by what cause we die, was given by Fatumai to her blessed daughters. It was a gift of foresight that enables them to foretell and then determine the future using a technique called the 'Grey Eye', the 'All Seeing One'. After many years of study by generations of priests, the current interpretation of the original texts suggest that this 'Grey Eye' is an actual game played between the three sisters. It is a game of cards and dice which is translated into our common language as 'Fortunes Fate'."

"If I understand what you are saying, the Fates, these Moirai, the Oracle of Frasteria or whatever they wish to be called, are playing a game to determine how long we all live!" offered Thias. "As I have said many times before, I'm not a religious man so a simple confirmation of this point will suffice."

"That is correct."

Llyat found his thoughts returning to the top of the pyramid of Barad Elestor, the tomb of Sir Raulyn, the runes and the hieroglyphs that Thias had translated. A thought then gestated inside his head. It was something that had not been addressed when they had stood in the gloom of the tomb and it began to eat away until he could restrain himself no longer.

"Why would Sir Raulyn give the daughters of Fatumai a child?"

"I'm sorry?" asked Irabo, surprised by the youth's sudden comment.

"Back at Raulyn's tomb, the inscription that Thias translated said that Sir Raulyn gave the Moirai a child in order to learn the secret of how to defeat Urthanock. Why would he do that? What would the gruesome three want with a child?"

"That I am afraid I do not know," said Irabo. "Though I wish I did for now that you mention it does seem rather odd?"

"I'm sure we can ask the crones that question when we get to meet them," added Thias before jumping to his feet and facing the front of the cage.

"Thias, what is it? What's wrong?" asked Irabo as he moved across to where Thias stood. Llyat stepped forward and the three stared through the bars.

"It looks like we're stopping," whispered Thias.

"What do you think the buggers have seen?" asked Irabo

The cage and the horses lurched to a stop. Llyat looked over to where the ogres had congregated around their General. Brosizrug looked up into the distant sky and one by one so did the other members of his troop. Then Llyat spotted the reason for the sudden halt. A small black bird flew at speed in their direction. In no time at all it had swooped down and perched itself on the arm of the ogre that carried the birdcage.

"Is it one of yours Lizvig?" asked Brosizrug.

"It looks like it," replied the bird carrier.

Llyat watched as the ogre pulled a small piece of parchment from the metal ring around the bird's foot, and proceeded to examine it.

"What does it say?" demanded the General.

"It's a message from Avolire," said Lizvig say as he passed the parchment to the General who then began to share the contents aloud.

"The Lady writes that the prisoners are to be taken to the encampment outside of Calistorn. They are to be treated with care and we must make it our priority to get them there in one piece. She is sending the Commander of the Knights of Avolire to take possession of the sapphire and the prisoners.

"Doesn't she trust us?" snarled Ikeg.

"I guess not," continued the General, "but if she is sending the one who wears the skull helmet then the scum we captured must be who they say they are."

Llyat gulped when he heard the ogre's words. It was possible he would cross paths once again with the man who had murdered his parents. He would now be able exact his revenge. So many thoughts began to collide in his already overloaded mind that he was caught unawares when Ikeg stuck his brutish face before the bars of the cage and shouted.

"It looks like you four get to live and suffer a little longer."

Llyat did not care what the creature had to say. He was consumed by thoughts of vengeance, so much so that he missed the order from General Brosizrug for the company to continue their march and barley noticed when the cage began to move. He focused on the one thought that preoccupied him.

"The skull helmeted Commander..." said Llyat as he sought confirmation of what he had heard.

"Yes Llyat," replied Thias as the others looked on "I heard that too and there is no doubt that the Commander who now rides out to meet us is the same one that murdered your father. He has been hunting you ever since that day."

"We cannot just sit inside this cage and wait until he arrives," said Einar.

"I agree," continued Thias while deep in thought. "My story may have saved us so far but if the Commander recognises Llyat then all will be lost. They will take him back to Avolire and kill the rest of us."

"Then we need to get him away from here as soon as possible," chipped in Irabo. "The boy needs to escape and continue in his quest to find the other Gems."

"I'm with Irabo on that one," added Einar. "The boy cannot stay here."

Llyat looked to each of his companions in turn and thought of many questions. Were they serious about attempting to escape and how would they ever get out of the cage? Even if they did manage to break free of its confines they would still have to deal with the brute called Ikeg. One ogre had been bad enough but now there were seven. Llyat became overwhelmed.

"But how are we going to get out of here?" he sobbed. "You said yourself that you can't use magic to free us. What else can we do?"

"I have got us this far," said Thias. "There may have been a few minor problems along the way but I haven't let you down yet. I have been watching our captors and each one of those brutes has a set of the keys attached to their belts; one of which will be certain to unlock this cage. All we have to do is relieve one of them of a set and free ourselves at a time of our choosing."

"If the Commander of the Knights is on his way from Avolire, it doesn't give us much time," added Irabo.

"The General said that we were to be taken to a camp just outside of Calistorn," continued Thias. "If I am correct, it will take us at least another two days to reach that ruined city. It will also take the Commander at least two days to make it there from Avolire. We do have a little time left."

"We must somehow get the lad out of here by then," added Einar.

Thias continued and as he spoke Llyat felt drawn to a deeper meaning of his words.

"The three of us have a clear duty to protect Llyat. He must fulfil whatever plans the Fates have decided for him. As we were told back in Falahorn, the Cuvar have always dedicated themselves to the protection of the Marked mentioned in the Prophecy. I pledge here and now to protect Llyat until my last breath. I take up the mantle of the Cuvar."

"As do I," added Irabo.

"Me too," mumbled Einar.

"And what about the rest of us. What plan do have in place for us?" asked Irabo.

"We will let the game of Fates play out. I suggest you pray to Fatumai and ask her to keep Cutter away for a while. An opportunity to escape will arise. I am certain of it and in fact I have half a plan already!"

20

The Narrow Gate, as most of the citizens of Parandor knew only too well, was named from the fact that it was the oldest and smallest of those that breached the city walls of Parandor. It was located in the western quarter towards its most southern extremity and was a popular passage of transit for both traders and smugglers alike. Tonousa did not know or understand why she had chosen this place to meet with the sailor Theoplous. It had just popped into in her subconscious as she tried to think of an ideal spot to meet in private with the First Mate of the Banshees Wail.

Stood in the shadows of the iron portcullis, set into the grey stone wall and hidden from the warming glow of Solaris as it rose in the east, Tonousa searched beyond the ancient metal gate that obscured her line of vision into the slums. She then switched her attention to a patrol of guards and then to a group of the warriors from the ever growing army that continued to gather outside of the wall. Soon her eyes moved back to the portcullis and she began to examine its iron mechanism, set in a part covered chamber above the gate. In that seldom visited space was housed the workings that governed the rise and fall of that most solid defensive structure. When opened the gate was so narrow that it just permitted the passage of three people abreast, two if travelling in the opposite direction. If Sir Byddin's men had been efficient then the gate's faulty mechanism would by now have been restored but Tonousa saw no evidence of any remedial work. The war with Avolire seemed inevitable and Tonousa and the City Watch would be responsible for the protection of all who dwelled inside the city, while the manning of the gates, walls, and the ground before them was the responsibility of the Royal Guard. Outside the thick solid walls, the armies of the Fifteen Keeps were controlled and marshalled by Sir Byddin. For the flow and deployment of troops during any attack it was important that all of the entrances, in and out of the city, were maintained in full working order, and that included the Narrow Gate. It was also vital that they could to be closed at once should the army be forced to retreat inside, or opened in an instant should the order be given to abandon the city. Sir Byddin however would only resort to a siege defence if he had no other option. Abandoning the city was unthinkable and Tonousa prayed that the repair work would soon be started.

As she stood in the shadows, she turned and leaned against the wall to the left of the gate. There she became aware of two people who passed, busy on their business of the day. Even though not doing anything inappropriate, Tonousa was drawn to them for the clothes that they wore made them stand out and attract suspicion. They were draped in the garb of those from the distant south of the Realm, from the Badlands beyond the Harico Hills. It was the same style of dress as the man she sought, Falaz Al Hizdor.

Following her conversation with Sir Richemanus in The Murdered Wolf it had become obvious that Falaz was connected to the murders she had been tasked to investigate. All fingers pointed to him as the supplier of the mind altering substance derived from the Lillywort plant. Richemanus had proved helpful once Tonousa had reduced the monstrous man to tears and broken through his tough exterior. Against the wall in the shadows she reflected on how she had been too quick to dismiss the southerner from the table. That had been a great mistake and ever since she had regretted acting on impulse. The possibility that Falaz knew which of her four suspects was the perpetrator gnawed away at her mind. She recalled that according to the executioner, Falaz was the key link to the swine who supplied the Sovereign Household and the Royal Guard with Lillywort. Tonousa sighed, closed her eyes and lost herself in her thoughts. Ever since her meeting with Richemanus she had made it a priority to find Falaz and discover all that he knew. Yet the elusive southerner seemed to have vanished without trace. Those who stood guard on the gates to the city had denied seeing him pass through. They would have recognised him from past encounters but there hadn't even been a sniff of hump sweat in the air. Even after Danisun Dain had persuaded Commander Townsforth to dedicate a team of men to the search for him, there was still no sign of Al Hizdor. He had disappeared as if by magic carpet.

A thought then occurred to Tonousa as she opened her eyes wider and watched the two innocent southerner's pass on into the cramped streets surrounding the gate. She reflected on her conversation with Ligart Highroar following the attack upon the Bards Guild and the card game he had been involved in, the one where he had let slip the purpose of the journey to Valameer. She closed her eyes as she tried to remember the details and soon smiled to herself as she began to make connections once again. According to Highroar, Falaz Al Hizdor had been one of the participants in that card game and therefore could have passed on that information to the infiltrator. The more she thought about it, the more she convinced herself of its truth.

"So has there been any news of our friends in the north?" said a familiar voice.

The words forced Tonousa to open her eyes. Her pupils constricted and she focused on the rough and well-worn face of Theoplous the sailor.

"None whatsoever," she replied without showing signs of her frustration. "Not even a single bird, not one hint of a message to say where they are or even if they are still alive. I'll not forget or forgive them for their lack of consideration. "

"I am sure that the bard is looking after the boy and your friend," added Theoplous as he too leaned against the stone of the outer city wall.

"Since they sent their message from Falahorn, they seem to have dropped right off the edge of the world. I am so angry as well as concerned," continued Tonousa. "Part of me believes that they must be still alive, whereas the other part of me..."

"The other part?"

"I don't know what to believe," replied Tonousa as she sighed. "So much has happened these past few months. Everything I ever believed in or held dear has been thrown out of the window like a bucket of waste."

The First Mate tried to assimilate her words then spoke again.

"From what you say, I presume you mean the defence of the city? The integrity of the City Watch and the Royal Guard in particular!"

"They all seem to be somehow connected to the evil plant from the Eastern Marsh which is being used to twist and corrupt the minds of those that inhabit the Citadel. Even the highest of the highborn seem to be linked to Lillywort," continued Tonousa.

"I am guessing from that comment that you mean the four assigned to the cards?"

"Yes I do," added Tonousa.

"So I can assume you've now spoken to all four of the suspects?"

Tonousa sighed once again and shook her head.

"All but one of them. It's getting a bit complicated."

She paused for a moment as she wondered if Theoplous would judge her for not having moved with greater haste.

"Sir Byddin pointed his finger at Lady Emeny and Sir Richemanus, whereas the new Sovereign Advisor pointed hers towards the priest Heward Teulu. Sir Richemanus was quick to point his back at Sir Byddin, but also seemed to implicate Heward Teulu as being responsible for the Lillywort coming into the city. He claimed it was part of the embalming process of the highborn corpses that lay in the tombs underneath the Temple of Fatumai."

Tonousa looked to Theoplous and noted how engaged he was with her words.

"And Heward Teulu, what did he have to say about all of this?"

"Like I said, I have not yet talked to all four. He's the one I have still to interrogate," replied Tonousa as she hung her head low. "I didn't get chance to question him before he fucked off to Valameer, just after my father's execution. I must wait until he returns to find out what he knows."

"What about his priests, all those others who are ordained into his order. Wouldn't they be able to help you? Couldn't you question them about Teulu in his absence?"

Tonousa sighed, "To be honest Theo that is something that crossed my mind ever since my meeting with Richemanus. I did put that suggestion to Danisun but he then reminded me that the priests of Fatumai would never betray one of their order, not least someone as high up in their ranks as Heward Teulu. If I was to seek to talk to them, they would need the permission of the highest member of their order…"

"And of course that would be Heward Teulu himself."

"Precisely."

Again Tonousa felt feelings of frustration creep unannounced into her voice. No matter how hard she tried to keep her emotions in check, the failure of not having resolved her investigation hung over her like a storm cloud and dragged down like the great anchors on the sides of Lotus Isle Caravels. A solitary tear formed in her eye and she felt her nose begin to run. She sniffed quickly hoping that Theoplous would not see her at her most vulnerable.

"Now tell me what is bothering you?" he said, not being fooled.

"I'm sorry, what do you mean?"

"I may have known you but a couple of weeks Tonousa Amberstone but I feel I have got to understand you quite well. Your hard exterior is not as thick as you would like others to believe. It has cracked and I can sense the emotions that you seek to hide. I am skilled at such observation but it doesn't take a Cuvar to know that something of great significance bothers you."

"I'm fine," lied Tonousa.

She sniffed again, uncertain as to where the conversation was heading.

"Look Tonousa, it's obvious that something troubles you. We have been through a lot together already. You can trust me. I am not going to abandon you or this cause."

Once again Tonousa hesitated. As she looked into the brown eyes of the man who stood before her and felt the honesty that he brought to his presence. Deep down she sensed that she could trust him but still something held her back. Her emotions, many that she had never felt before, churned like a curdled stew in her cauldron of her skull. Taking a deep breath she realised that if her day was to move with any hope of success she would have to confide in her new friend; she would have to overcome her feelings of embarrassment and find some way to fill the cracks that had begun to appear in her defences. Taking yet another deep breath, Tonousa's feelings flowed through the gaps in her teeth.

"I thought it would be simple to root out the infiltrator but whatever I manage to discover, the clues always seems to lead down more rabbit holes, to more and more questions, and they fill my head with great doubt and uncertainty. I feel unsure about everyone and everything. Whoever this shape changing bastard is, he is a master of his craft. The one he has replaced seems beyond suspicion and has established themselves so deep into the workings of the Citadel that he or she moves about unnoticed, unquestioned, and unchallenged. By the gods bollocks he is bloody good at what he does."

"But what of the four," said Theoplous? "From what you know so far of your father's suspects, who does your gut say it is?"

"It could be anyone of them. They all have motives of one kind or another. I just thought we would be closer to finding out who our spy is by now. There is so much information to consider that it is hard to keep track of it all."

"Then break it down to its most simple form," advised Theoplous as he dropped his hands from Tonousa's shoulders. "What key questions are still outstanding? What do you need to know?"

"I need to know who the fucking infiltrator is!" snapped Tonousa in a flurry of angst. "Haven't you been paying attention? Then there is the missing ruby, that bastard Gem of Thamous or whatever it is fucking called. It supposed to be somewhere in the city but it could be anywhere. Heliana is still searching all the Royal apartments and sooner or later she is going to attract unwanted attention, or worse still, lead the enemy straight to us."

Tonousa took another deep breath and resisted the urge to scream. She was then taken aback when Theoplous pulled her in towards his chest and wrapped her in his arms. For a brief moment she was intimidated by this sudden encroachment into her personal space but then her emotions melted and she found pleasure in the sailor's embrace. Tonousa somehow understood his benign intentions.

"Don't worry so much," he whispered. "Things have a way of working out. A path will form."

Tonousa pulled away and looked at Theoplous in disbelief. The words he had spoken reverberated inside her head and merged with the memory of those uttered by the voice of Lady Fullbane in her dream.

"I beg your pardon! What did you just say?"

Theoplous looked back at her with great curiosity.

"I said a path will form. Something will in time appear and lead you to the knowledge that you seek. It will happen when you least expect it but you must be ready for it. Once it appears you must not hesitate to take it. The path will form."

"Yes, I know what you said," replied Tonousa. "But why did you chose those words in particular?"

"Which words?" he asked, still quite unclear as to what Tonousa alluded?

"A path will form, you said. They are the words from one of my dreams; 'A path will form. Make sure you take it.'"

"You've lost me now. What words? What dream?"

From Theoplous's obvious perplexed expression Tonousa realised the sailor had no idea about what she was talking about. Before he could ask any further questions she relayed the details of the visions she had experienced after Danisun Dain had rendered her unconscious; the moment he had sought to save her from the wrath of Xix Blackfayer. She kept her story short and to the point but missed out none of the key details of her strange dream. Throughout its retelling Theoplous concentrated, sought to process the information, and consider what it had all meant.

"Please tell me that I'm not losing my mind," said Tonousa at the end of her discourse.

"Not at all," replied the First Mate. "It is obvious that the dream has much greater meaning than it first appears. My words and that of the Lady Fullbane may just be a coincidence although I suspect there is much more to it than that."

"I'm glad you at least now understand the reasons for my reaction," added Tonousa. "Given my lack of progress with the investigation and failure to prevent my father's execution, I never gave the dream its due consideration. Only now, since all other leads have dried up, have the images from that unconscious dream begun to creep back into my mind. The words you chose brought Lady Fullbane back to the pinnacle of my attention."

Tonousa looked into Theoplous's eyes in the hope that he would be able to offer her an interpretation of her dream, just as he had explained the encrypted message found hidden in her father's wall. In the end the silence between the two was too great for Tonousa to endure.

"Well! Have you nothing more to offer?"

"Let me just say this. Unlike you, I never ignore anything that could be classed as a coincidence," he began. "May I assume you know the story of Wilihas Kundter of the Lotus Isles?"

"I have never heard of him. I don't know much at all about that remote region of this world."

"I think you would like my islands," replied Theoplous. "The buildings there are not as grand as some of those in Parandor, nor as magnificent as the old ruins around the Barrow at Harico, but they do have a unique charm of their own.

The beaches, well, they are something else. With the whitest and purest of sands while the grass that grows beyond them is thick and heavy. The air has a sweetness you will find nowhere else. It carries the slightest hint of cinnamon and..."

"Theo, your story," urged Tonousa. "What were you about to tell me about coincidences?"

"Walk with me," he said as he offered Tonousa his arm.

Tonousa linked arms with her friend after which they then began a slow walk amid the constricting streets of Parandor and away from the Narrow Gate. Then amongst the filth lined streets of the Capital, devoid the slightest hint of cinnamon, Theoplous began his tale.

"When two unconnected events appear together at an important moment in time they must never be ignored. It is all part of the game that the Fates play. They use our pitiful souls as players in the game that we call life. So let me tell of what happened to Wilihas Kundter, a student of the great Anyle Belanore. Kundter was one of the first adopters of the order that I belong to, that which we call Cuvar. Being a devotee he dedicated his life to the search for 'the Marked'. As the years passed he became ever wiser and one day old Wilihas decided to make a journey across the sea to Parandor."

"Sorry I'm failing to see..."

"I'm getting there; be patient woman. The night before his voyage old Wilihas had a dream. In it he saw Hamthor strike down his boat and all on board drowned as it sank beneath the froth of the foaming waves. Wilihas was shaken for until then he had not been a superstitious man. The next morning, down by the harbour, an old hag shouted out that she sensed an almighty storm was approaching from the west. The crone went on to tell him that it was one so great that it could sink a thousand ships. Anyone venturing out on the water that day would put themselves in great peril. Despite the glorious morning's weather Wilihas was spooked and taking note of coincidence he decided against boarding his ship which later sailed without him. Despite the derision and insults of other seafarers, he sat by the side of the harbour and waited for signs of the storm. The tempest came late that afternoon and sometime after the full force of its fury had abated old Wilihas was informed that the vessel that he should have sailed on had been lost at sea. Just some timber from its mast had been recovered. As you can guess the experience troubled him greatly."

"So he had a gift of foresight," said Tonousa. "Could he see into the future?"

"No, not at all. Old Wilihas had no such gift nor any magical ability that could have explained how he had avoided death that day. As he told anyone who would listen thereafter, it was just a coincidence of the ship's demise in a dream and the crone's warning. The dream may well have been the result of some mouldy cheese, or a bit of undigested pork, but either way, it had surfaced from out of his subconscious. He linked the two events and called them 'the great coincidence' that had saved his life. From that moment on he would never ignore any coincidence and being both a scholar and teacher, he added this story to all of his lessons. It was even written on his tomb stone when he passed away, 'Never ignore a coincidence'."

Tonousa reflected on the tale and wondered if there was any truth at all in Theoplous's story. Perhaps her own dream ought to be linked to other events. While she walked by the sailors side she tried to make connections between her dream, recent events, and the information that she had unearthed over the past few weeks. Paths had begun to find their way into her consciousness and one of them was directing her search for Falaz Al Hizdor. Perhaps Lady Fullbane's words were part of some greater coincidence. Tonousa could not yet tell.

"You might also recall how I joined your party back in Valameer," Theoplous continued as the pair of souls emerged from a narrow street and into one of the wider thoroughfares of Parandor. "As I have already told you, the Cuvar have been searching for the boy mentioned in the Prophecy of Enderdetag for a very long time. Was it coincidence or fate that allowed me to hear your Grand Physician talking about the lad that young Irabo fished out of the river? A youth that came from Maplehill..."

Tonousa stopped walking and raised her hand to stop his flow of words. She felt the conversation was spiralling out of her control.

"You're beginning to sound like Irabo," she said.

In the seconds that followed it crossed her mind that Irabo had deceived her and that he too was Cuvar, just like Theoplous and also it seemed her father. Then another thought struck home. Perhaps the rescue of young Llyat from the waters of the Tiaryer was more than just a random event. It could have been a defining moment in some greater coincidence. She began to think on other significant events that occurred at that time and the word 'coincidence' seemed then to dominate her every thought. If the gods were playing some twisted game then it all seemed far too fanciful to be true.

"I may indeed sound like Irabo for we share a similar faith in our guiding power..."

"I like to believe I am in charge of my own destiny," replied Tonousa.

"Let me just say this. Think about all that has happened to you since Irabo pulled Llyat from the river and reflect on the teachings of Wilihas Kundter. How can all those events be connected? Never ignore a coincidence no matter how insignificant they may at first appear."

The pair moved on at pace and Tonousa focused on her friend's words. She wanted to believe there could be truth in what Theoplous had said but somehow couldn't bring herself to do so. Even the many conversations with Irabo had failed to sway her from her long held beliefs but as Theoplous had put it, a lot had happened to her that she could not ignore.

"There is one thing I've been meaning to ask you," she said. "It's something that has been bugging me since Danisun released me from the Underkeep."

"What is it you want to know?"

"It is about Llyat. Ever since the messenger bird from Falahorn confirmed their arrival, you have not expressed any desire or intention to go out and search for the lad. This is despite your professed duty to protect the Marked. I don't think that I am the only one of our group who have noticed that fact. Therefore tell me now, why are you still here in Parandor?"

Tonousa looked deep into the sailor's eyes. He simply smiled and then began to laugh. His response added to Tonousa's confusion.

"What's so funny?" she asked.

"There are more ways to help the boy fulfil the Prophecy of Enderdetag than being by his side. Allotter and Spinner have chosen my mission. They have steered me to this city and this is where I must stay until the Fates decide to direct me elsewhere."

"Once again you have lost me," added Tonousa. "Who are those two? I have never hear of them."

"Their names matter not. The point that I am making is that my purpose here in the Capital will be revealed by some chance happening or a specific coincidence. I have chosen to aid you in your search for the infiltrator as this will assist Llyat by helping him locate and retrieve the Gems of Thamous. We have established that one of the Gems is somewhere within this city's walls and it is our job to identify the spy and thus prevent the enemy from getting its hands on that ruby. We must find it and give Llyat a chance to seal the Underworld. Until our spy is unmasked and the Gem of Thamous found, I must stay by your side and aid you in your work. Even if Highroar says otherwise, I will not leave this city until the Fates instruct me otherwise. I hope that makes some sense to you."

"I think so...." added Tonousa after a brief hesitation.

"Are you ever going to tell me the reason why you wanted to meet me in the shadow of the Narrow Gate?"

"I need your help with something very important," replied Tonousa, "and I know that I can trust you. I need to find...."

Tonousa's sentence was cut short by the cries of another who shouted her name. She stopped walking and looked back into the congested street that she and Theoplous had just left. Her eyes then focused on another member of the City Watch who raced towards her while waving his arms in most agitated manner. She recognised Karkis Snouth at once.

"Tonousa! Tonousa!" cried the youth. "Thank the gods that I've found you."

"Karkis, what is wrong!" she exclaimed.

"It's Danisun, and that man from Valameer..."

"What about them," she demanded. "What of Danisun and Darchus?"

"They've found him," he gasped. "I don't know how, but they have."

"Who are you talking about," asked Theoplous?

"Where is he?" exclaimed Tonousa.

"Who!" exclaimed Theoplous?

"For fuck's sake let me catch my breath," bellowed Karkis.

Tonousa grabbed the young warrior by the shoulders and shook him.

"Where is he?"

"Who," demanded Theoplous?

"The Southerner, Falaz Al Hizdor, is that who you mean?" spat out Tonousa.

"And what do you know about Falaz?" demanded Theoplous with shock and concern.

"They have located him," uttered Karkis between his gasps for air. "Danisun and the man from Valameer have found him hiding in the old abandoned abattoir on Shaylotte Street, the one around the back of Stukeley Knoll. They have him trapped in there."

"Think again, that swine would never allow himself to be cornered," sneered Theoplous.

"What do you mean?" asked Tonousa.

"Falaz Al Hizdor would never be caught like a rat in a pipe."

"So you will help me find and apprehend him?" asked Tonousa.

"Of course I will, come let's hurry to Shaylotte Street."

The moment Karkis had mentioned the slaughterhouse, Tonousa knew exactly where Danisun and Darchus had located Falaz. Shaylotte Street was known throughout Parandor as the shortest street in the city. It measured fifty one paces in length and just several in width. She also knew that there were but two buildings there that opened up onto the narrow cobbled street. The first was an old apothecary that had long since lost its trade and was now an empty shell at risk of collapse. The second was the abattoir inside which it seemed her friends had trapped the southerner.

It took the two members of the City Watch and the sailor a ten minute run to reach Shaylotte Street. On assessing the situation they saw no obvious signs of human presence within the dark confines of the street. Tonousa looked through the shadows for any sign of Danisun or Darchus. Then in the distant gloom she spotted a mud caked vagrant slumped against the edge of a wall; but there was still no sign of her friends.

Tonousa turned to Karkis.

"Well!" she began. "Where are they?"

Before Karkis could respond the vagabond's groans captured Tonousa's attention. She recognised the cry of the man at once and realised how stupid she had been. There lay the Man-at-Arms of the City Watch and he projected a most pitiful image.

"Danisun!" she exclaimed as she ran to her friend. "What's happened?"

"I don't know," he mumbled.

The eyes of the warrior flickered and then opened. Tonousa saw that he tried to make sense of his predicament and ascertain where he was and why he was slumped in a pile of filth.

"I think some bastard must have hit me from behind."

Tonousa dropped to her knees and noted streaks of blood around his head, mixed in with the dirt from where he had fallen. She assessed the rest of his body but found no other obvious wounds. While the relief in finding her friend still alive was palpable, she realised that the situation was worse than she had first realised. She looked back in the direction of the abattoir's open door and then back to her injured comrade.

"Danisun," she demanded while shaking her colleague. "Where is Darchus?"

The Man-at-Arms did not have time to answer before a crash came from within the Abattoir.

"No need to answer that," she said as she stood up and placed her right hand on the hilt of her blade.

Tonousa turned towards the open door while leaving Karkis to support Danisun. Then as she took her first step forward she felt a hand upon her shoulder. In an instant she turned to see who held her back.

"Tell me what's going on," ordered Theoplous. "Why have you decided to entangle yourself in the affairs of Falaz Al Hizdor?"

"He has information," replied Tonousa and she brushed the sailor's hand from her shoulder. "I suspect he is part of a murderous web of intrigue and I need understand all that he knows."

"The man is very dangerous," shouted the sailor but Tonousa could think of nothing but the perils that Darchus faced inside the slaughterhouse.

"I know that," she said as she reached the door. "The Watch has had previous contact with Falaz. It's not like we don't know his style. Besides, he is not skilled in the use of magic. He's just scum."

"I don't care what you think or say, I'm going in there with you."

Tonousa sighed and sensed there would be no reasoning with the sailor.

"No!" she ordered. "You and Karkis need to stay here and protect Danisun. As you are not enrolled in the Watch you cannot act on their behalf. I can handle Falaz alone."

"Don't be such a stubborn bitch," moaned Danisun who now sat propped up against the wall. "Your pig-headedness will get you killed one of these days..."

Tonousa heard Danisun's words but he was not in a position to give orders.

"Look you dolts, I need you both to stay here," demanded Tonousa. "I'll assess the situation first and will call if I need assistance. I promise."

With that said she stepped forward, pushed through the opening to the Abattoir, and disappeared into the gloom beyond. The fetid stench of rotten flesh smacked against her nostrils as she entered. She held her free hand to her nose in an attempt to block the nauseating odour of fresh maggots that threatened to turn her stomach inside out. Then she began to move through the darkness and the small shafts of light that penetrated the dark by way of holes in the ceiling and broken shutters embedded in the walls. She passed the various stone slabs and butchers blocks upon which rancid flesh crawled with maggots. Flies filled the air and their collective hum broke the otherwise eerie silence. Tonousa almost slipped on the slimy innards of some once proud beast that were being picked at by several rats, none of which showed fear of her presence. She kicked the nearest one as it licked at the discarded entrails and it grunted as the air was expelled from its puny chest. The rest scuttled away but returned once she had passed. Tonousa continued to inch forward and fought hard to repel the urge to vomit. With her senses overwhelmed she hoped that she had not misjudged her prey and that Falaz was not as dangerous as Theoplous had described. Her sole focus was to find and rescue Darchus. A metal object crashed to the floor in the dark. Tonousa jumped and drew her weapon from its sheath. She pointed forward towards a crack of light which indicated the presence of yet another room.

"Falaz show yourself, I know you are here," she shouted. "We have the place surrounded."

"And yet you come inside alone" replied a voice that did not belong to Al Hizdor.

The sound of movement as someone walked towards her from out of the dark shadows caused Tonousa's heart to race. It then became obvious that there were two on the move, one that walked with purpose and one that struggled. Both became visible as they crossed a beam of light.

"Nedes, let him go!" shouted Tonousa.

She pointed her sword towards the blacksmith who held Falaz by one arm while his other pushed a blade into the southerner's back.

"I knew you would come," laughed Karoly. "Do you remember Fieggis?"

Tonousa had not the faintest idea of whom he referred too. Her prime concern was the man that Nedes held with his hands. Falaz was bound and tied with a bloody rag, his headdress unravelled and crooked upon his head.

"I don't know who the shit..." she replied just before the sharp tip of a blade pressed into her own back from one who had entered in silence from behind.

"Drop your sword bitch," demanded the unseen other.

Tonousa did not attempt to answer yet responded to his request. Her sword fell and clanged against the stone. She raised her hands above her head to show they were empty. A moment later she sensed the other had started to move around her while still ensuring that she still felt the pressure from his blade. It was not long before Tonousa looked down to where her assailant's right hand should have been only to see the blade fixed into a wooden stump and secured to its owner's wrist by leather straps.

"You didn't say it would be this bitch that would show," said the other.

"I didn't think it would be," replied Karoly as he maintained his grip on Falaz's arm and his knife across the southerner's throat. "I guess the Fates have blessed us twice."

"Let me kill her now," demanded the man that Tonousa assumed was Fieggis.

"You'll have your chance soon enough," replied Karoly.

"That bitch took my fucking hand! It is my right to dispose of her in any way I see fit."

Tonousa now knew who Fieggis was. He was the one whose hand she had cleaved off in The Murdered Wolf when Karoly and his henchmen had threatened her. Even though it had been just a few weeks past, it seemed like an eternity. She was in a most perilous position but it would not stop her seeking to regain control and take Al Hizdor in for questioning. As her thoughts raced she realised that there was still no sign of Darchus in the foul dark interior of the abattoir. She prayed Karoly and his friend had not already murdered and disposed of the most honourable man who had followed her south with his family from Valameer. For a split second she wondered how she would break the news to his wife and children.

"Where is my colleague?" she demanded to know.

"He's over there," Karoly replied.

With a nod of his head he indicated a section of the floor by a slab on which lay a large putrefying pig with its attendant swarm of flies. Tonousa followed his eyes and behind the slab she recognised the distinctive boots of the City Watch of Parandor.

"Is he..?" asked Tonousa.

"Not yet. He'll have one hell of a headache though when he wakes up, if he ever does."

Relieved that at least Darchus was still alive Tonousa needed to assert her authority.

"You can let Falaz go now for I need to take him in for interrogation. He is wanted as part of my investigations and it will not help any of us if you harm him."

"Not until I have exacted revenge on this southern bastard," snarled Karoly while he pressed his knife edge against Falaz's throat and threatened to draw blood. "I bring retribution on behalf of all who have died at the hands of Death Tubaria. I will do what the City Watch should have done already if they weren't so fucking incompetent."

"Falaz is not responsible for the Death Tubaria murders Nedes and you know it!" shouted Tonousa, grasping at the hope that the blacksmith would succumb to reason."

"Listen to the woman," whimpered Falaz as he struggled to get his words out and as the knife dug deeper into his throat. "She is right. I am innocent."

"One more word and it will be your last," replied Karoly.

"Nedes, let him go," ordered Tonousa. "It's not too late for us to walk away from this."

"I knew all this time you had been looking for a magic user," said Karoly. "I saw what happened at the Richemanus Folly. Someone invoked the old spells of Death Tubaria and a little bird whispered that you were looking for Falaz..."

"Who told you that?" asked Tonousa.

"No one, well not to my face," sneered Karoly. "But in future you might want to keep your voice down when you're in The Murdered Wolf with the likes of Richemanus."

"So which slime bag eavesdropped on my private discourse?"

"It was me, bitch," added Fieggis with smile of satisfaction.

"It matters not how we got to him," continued Karoly. "The main thing is we found him before you did Tonousa Amberstone. Now the poor folk of this city will be able to exact their revenge."

"Please, I beg you all," moaned Falaz. "Let me go and I will tell you everything I..."

Karoly dug the knife even deeper into Falaz's neck and this time it did draw blood.

"Shut your festering mouth!" he demanded. "Or I'll seal it for good."

Tonousa had had enough and her blood raged.

"Stop it now you stupid bastards!" she screamed as she glared at the two men before her. "Vigilante justice is not the answer. Falaz Al Hizdor, despite his past history of ill intent, is innocent of the murders. I swear this to you. He just holds some valuable information that I need to hear."

"Listen to her..." begged Falaz.

"One more word from that arse shaped of a mouth of yours and you will meet your gods sooner than planned," spat out Karoly.

"Please, may we talk about this," said Tonousa. "Falaz's information may be key to identifying the perpetrator of the Death Tubaria murders. Help me Nedes, please. Yet I swear this to you, get in my way and I will see you hang for it."

"Kill him and be done with it and then we can turn our attention to her," sneered Fieggis.

As Tonousa refocused she noted that Karoly had loosened his grip on Falaz while pushing him down onto his knees. She could not be certain but she hoped that the blacksmith was at last relenting. Even though he had disgraced himself before the Watch, deep down she hoped he still carried some semblance of morality.

"Nedes?" she pleaded once again.

Karoly stared back and then looked down towards the nomad. Then with a nod of affirmation he lowered his knife.

"Ask him your questions now," he said after which he kicked Falaz in the back such that the southerner prostrated himself on the floor. "Go on, ask him, he's not going anywhere."

"Please leave me be," moaned Falaz.

Tonousa knelt down by the side of the terrified man in order that he could hear her questions. A plan had formed and she hoped she would have the southerner's full cooperation.

"Falaz, I will let them kill you now if you don't answer my questions. Do you understand me?"

"I do,"

"Sir Richemanus of the Nightfall told me that you procured a specific compound for him. It was a mind altering substance that you suggested he could sell on to Lord Faros at a profit and thereby settle your debts. Faros was one of those murdered. The flower from which the compound is made is the Lillywort. From where did you obtain your supplies of that poison?"

Despite the bruises and blood on the southerner's face Tonousa could tell that he had turned phantom pale. It was as if his as if his body had expelled every last drop of the crimson fluid that sustained his life. It showed that Al Hizdor knew something of great significance.

"Falaz," said Tonousa. "You must tell me all that you know."

"I'd be a dead man if I ever spoke his name," whimpered Falaz. "He would kill me for sure."

"And Nedes and Fieggis here will kill you the moment I give them word and that won't be long from now if you do not tell me the truth. I don't care how scared you are..." replied Tonousa.

"There is an ancient passage that leads from the Underkeep to the Temple of Fatumai. He said no one knows of it except him. He has great plans for the use of the Lillywort ...."

"Who," interrupted Tonousa?

"I cannot tell you. He will kill me should I reveal his identity."

"Who the fuck is he?" bellowed Tonousa, unprepared for what happened next.

"I've had enough of this shit," shouted Fieggis.

The one-handed man grabbed Falaz by the scruff of his neck and pulled his head backwards to expose the bare flesh of his throat. In one swift motion he sliced forward with the blade that was fixed to the stump of his wrist and then dragged it through Falaz's throat. Blood spewed forth as Fieggis released his grip. The southerner fell to the floor, rolled onto his back, and shook in brief spasms before his life force gurgled out through his severed wind pipe. All Tonousa could do was scream.

"No!" she cried.

Tonousa attempted to place her hand over the slit like wound on the nomad's neck. In vain she tried to prevent the coming of his death but only succeeded in forcing the blood to pool in the hollow between the top of his chest and the remnants of his damaged voice box. She glared at Fieggis who stood over her with his blade pointing at her head. In that moment she realised how foolish she had been to enter the slaughterhouse alone.

"What did you go and do that for?" she bellowed at Fieggis.

"I was pissed off with his bullshit," the scab replied before turning to Nedes Karoly. "The bitch is ours now. Let's finish her good and proper."

"You arse," shouted Tonousa at the top of her voice. "I haven't got time for any of this..."

Tonousa ducked low and rolled to the right to where she had previously dropped her weapon. As the blade attached to Fieggis's wrist swung down to try and end her life, Tonousa grabbed hold of her sword and parried the blow. She deflected several more attempts to strike her down as Fieggis lost control of reason amid his frustration and anger. The final sweep of Tonousa's sword severed the blade from the stump that had once held his right hand. She then lashed out with her right leg and struck Fieggis with her foot in the centre of his right knee. The agonising blow dropped him in an instant and gave Tonousa time to jump up to her feet and ready herself. The next attack came from Nedes Karoly who thrust out with his knife but Tonousa deflected his blade and sent it spinning from his hand. It fell some distance away.

"I haven't got time for this shit!" snarled Tonousa.

The next assault came from behind as Fieggis launched himself into the air and wrapped his arms around Tonousa's neck. Given Tonousa's good height and Fieggis's short stature, his legs were left swinging off the ground as he hung onto her with his one complete arm.

"Do it Nedes," cried Fieggis as Tonousa attempted to shake him off. "Slice her proper; slit her from quim to tit."

Tonousa manoeuvred out of the way as Karoly lunged forward having retrieved his knife from where it had fallen. Tonousa fought to maintain a grip on her sword and keep the two men at bay. Then with all the force she could muster, she managed to push her torso back against one of the blood soaked slabs, crushing Fieggis against it in the process. She pressed back with all her weight and sought to release his grip from around her neck while at the same time continuing to deflect the stabs and slashes of Karoly's knife. Fieggis screamed out in pain as Tonousa managed to swing her left elbow back into his balls. He cried out to his gods as the pain shot through his groin, released his grip on her neck and fell to the floor in distress. In the blink of an eye Tonousa turned and thrust her blade deep into Fieggis's throat and sliced it from right to left. It opened up just as the nomad's had done a few minutes earlier. Yet again copious quantities of crimson flowed onto the already reddened stone floor of the slaughterhouse. Fieggis slumped forward, air gurgled out of his neck, and seconds later his essence departed the Realm. Tonousa turned to face Karoly who stood with his back to the now open door which led further into the depths of the building

"Enough is enough," screamed Tonousa as she prepared for Karoly's next attack. "Let's talk about this. It's clear that you're pissed off but by letting your grudge against me fester..."

"So bitch, do you admit defeat at last,"

Tonousa snarled in anger as the blacksmith continued to try to compromise her investigation. Deep down, she knew that she was the better fighter and she had lost all hope that a fight to the death could be avoided. After yet another deep breath she threw her sword down to the floor and beckoned Karoly forwards with her hands.

"Come on then you bastard," she cried at the top of her voice. "If you want to kill me come and do it now."

"There's no need to rush," he replied Karoly. "I want to savour the moment."

"Come on you bastard, just try it!" she shouted while tracking the movement of a shadow.

"I've been looking forward to this moment for such a long time," said Karoly as he edged forwards. "Amberstone bitch, you are going to get what you deserve. There is no one who can save you now and I will fuck your corpse when you're dead."

Tonousa glanced towards the dark recess of the doorway in which her saviour stood. She knew that it was the time for him to act and she shouted to the shadow in the portal.

"Just do it now."

"My pleasure," said Karoly unaware of the figure behind him.

The blacksmith thrust forwards and managed to flick his blade against the skin over Tonousa's neck where it drew a trickle of blood. Theoplous swung out with his fists and dropped Karoly to the floor. Then with a quick kick of his foot he sent Karoly's knife towards the base of one of the filth strewn slabs.

"Are you okay Tonousa?" asked the sailor after which he kicked Karoly in the groin in order to check if he was conscious.

"I've been better," she replied as she wiped the blood from her throat.

"I told you to watch out for yourself, Falaz was never anything but trouble."

"Thank you anyway," she responded. "I'm kind of glad you came in when you did."

"Like I said before Tonousa, I wasn't going to let you face this alone. I have been in the shadows for a while, awaiting an opportunity to intervene."

"The bitch will never win," muttered Karoly from the ground as he drifted back into consciousness.

Karoly suddenly attempted to sit up. Tonousa punched out hard with her fist and connected with her assailants jaw. From the impact pain within her hand and the cracking sound that followed she was certain that she must have broken a bone in it. Karoly collapsed and lay still. Tonousa then glanced at the carnage around her and let out a sigh of relief. Whatever path had led her to this place, it seemed to terminate in death. The one person with vital information, Falaz Al Hizdor, now lay still upon the floor of the slaughterhouse in the shortest of the streets of Parandor.

The door then burst open whereupon Karkis Snouth and a still shaken Danisun Dain entered. They had already drawn their weapons but relaxed once they realised that Tonousa and Theoplous appeared to have everything under control.

"What were you thinking, coming in here alone?" asked Danisun.

"I wasn't going to abandon Darchus to die," she replied.

"Then where is he?" asked Danisun as he scanned dark recesses.

"He's over there," said Tonousa

She pointed to the pair of boots that stuck out from the edge of one of the stone slabs. Behind a swarm of flies lay the carcass of a once handsome pig. Tonousa looked on as Danisun moved across the room and knelt adjacent to where Darchus lay. Danisun checked for signs of life and Tonousa feared that they had lost Darchus as well as Falaz.

"Is he dead?" she shouted.

"I've been better," replied the young man from Valameer as Danisun helped him to sit

"He's alive and that's the main thing," shouted Danisun.

"What should we do with Karoly?" asked Karkis who stood over the body of blacksmith.

"Take the bastard to the Underkeep," replied Tonousa. "We've got him on more than one charge now. Horse rustling, his lead role with the vigilantes, and now murder. There's no way he can worm his way out of this last crime.

"And Falaz?" asked Theoplous. "Was it worth it? Did you find out what you needed to know?"

"No I did not," she replied. "Karoly saw to that."

Tonousa moved to where Falaz lay motionless. As she then looked down she became transfixed by the wound in the southerner's throat and the blood that had pooled in the niche where the neck met the rib cage. Something powerful drew her towards the crimson pool but she did not know what it was. She became aware of a muffled conversation between Danisun and Darchus but her eyes had been drawn beyond them to the carcass of the enormous pig.

"What happened?" muttered Darchus.

"Take it easy," added Danisun "You've had a nasty blow to your head."

"I followed him in here, then all I remember is being stuck from behind."

"Well, it looks like it was your turn to be saved?" said Danisun.

"I don't follow you," muttered Darchus

"The Lady Fullbane, remember her? Tonousa told me how you saved her life a few days ago."

Tonousa felt relieved. It was good to hear Darchus speak and watch him move. Then the name Fullbane seemed somehow to grow in significance as her eyes moved backwards and forwards from the rotting pig to the pool of crimson blood at root of Falaz's neck. The red clot sat there like an enormous heart shaped jewel and it glinted in a ray of light that broke through one of the cracks in the ceiling. It triggered a memory that was too much of a coincidence to ignore. Theoplous's words bounced around in her mind and she guessed this was an example of what he said should never be dismissed. She jumped to her feet with a rush of excitement and she shouted for all to hear.

"You're never going to believe this but I know where we can find the ruby."

A coincidence had focused Tonousa's thoughts.

21.

"Promethelumous."

Thias listened to the words that Llyat had uttered in the Ancients' language. He then looked on as the young man clenched his fists, tightened his eyes, and attempted to conjure up the magic spell once again. A small flame flickered on top of the boy's fists before it then shot through the air and onto a pile of dry unsoiled straw which then ignited. The small fire would perhaps not have mattered much, just a small glitch in Llyat's attempts to master the ancient ways, had not the flames landed in the same spot on the cage floor that the giant Einar had chosen to sit with his legs spread wide apart. The fire spread through the dry straw and the heat grew in intensity as it began to encroach upon the Berserker's groin. Thias knew that Einar would not feel the pain of the fire and as such was at risk of serious injury. But the flickering flame caught Einar's eye and he jumped up from his place of rest in an instant. His arms flailed and he cursed like a bellowing wormnose.

"Fuck... bastards... shit!"

"I'm so sorry Einar," cried out Llyat.

The giant then tried to extinguish the flame that had taken hold on the cloth of his trousers by slapping his privates with considerable force.

"If you're going to continue to practice that fucking spell please do it somewhere else or point your scrawny hands in another direction," screeched the Berserker.

Irabo, who had been observing Thias's lesson in magic, stamped out the remaining flames amongst the straw strewn base of the cage. The bard then covered the area with some discarded animal pelts that had been piled in one corner. Even though there was still a trace of frost in the air, the rocky ground that crunched under foot gave off sufficient heat for those within the cage to suspend their needs for the furs of Fallguard.

Once he was convinced that he had extinguished the fire that had threatened his cock, Einar looked towards Thias with a stare so fierce that it would have petrified even the fiercest of the Badland's beasts. The Berserker was far from happy which was unfortunate for the others had found the event hilarious. Thias wanted to laugh so much that he almost wet himself but with great restraint he held his emotions back for he knew that to show them would just incur more of the giant's wrath.

"I too am sorry Einar," giggled Thias. "It won't happen again, I promise you."

The Berserker did not reply. He just grunted, snatched a singed fur from off the floor and lay down amongst the odorous straw. He then turned his back on Thias and covered his head with the fleece as if to block out the world until he regained his composure. If he couldn't see the others then they couldn't see him.

Despite all that had occurred within the cage, Thias was surprised that none of the ogres that marched either ahead and to either side of them had taken any notice of the magic lesson or of its fiery outcome. The ugly monsters kept their heads down and trudged on, one long stride after another. It was almost as if their brains and their feet had been mesmerised by their march. Their sole focus on the long walk to Calistorn was the avoidance of the hot pools of a tar like substance that bubbled up through the ground. Since the beginning of the journey, the only time that the ogres had interacted with their prisoners was to give them the bread and water on which they were expected to survive. For the rest of the time they tended to keep away from the cart. There was of course one exception to this rule of general indifference, the ogre with the chain between nose and ear. The one called Ikeg took it upon itself to repeatedly throw insults at Llyat for having killed his brother.

Thias glanced to where Llyat still knelt amongst the straw and looked towards his finger tips that had moments earlier erupted in flame. Then he looked upon Llyat's face and noted how disappointed the youth looked.

"I'll never get the hang of it," mumbled Llyat in a trough of despair.

"Of course you will, it will come with time, just keep at it," Thias replied.

"No, I'm sure I'll never master it," continued Llyat as he looked in disgust at his fingers before returning them to his side. "I might as well just give in now. I feel like giving up on everything and abandoning our quest. I'm just a worthless turd dropped out from the arse of the Realm."

"Llyat, please look at me," ordered Thias. "I'll have no such nonsense, not here, not ever. Just look at all you have accomplished in the past few weeks. You've survived drowning and a conflagration. You then overcame the sweating sickness and you've talked to a wyvern. You even found one of the Gems of Thamous that our quest depends upon."

Llyat looked back towards Thias who saw that there were tears in the boy's eyes.

"But I can't even manage one simple spell."

"You talk such nonsense. I managed to learn how to do it and I have to tell you it took me a couple of years to do so. You've just been practicing for a day."

"But it's hopeless. I just feel so pathetic. I just want to give up."

Thias sighed and looked to Irabo and Einar and who were both following the conversation. He wondered if they too had noted the loss of what little confidence Llyat had left and he realised he would need to act at once if he was to salvage the youth from out of his pit of despair.

"Never give up Llyat," said Thias. "Have faith in yourself. You are not as worthless as you think."

"But..." quivered Llyat.

Thias looked around for inspiration when as if by some strange coincidence he saw a small spider making its web between two of the metal bars of the mobile cage and which bounced upon the strand that it sought to anchor as the cell bumped along the uneven ground.

"Just look at this common creature," continued the bard while pointing to the tiny beast. "Time and time again it tries to build a trap to catch its food. Climbing up the slippery walls of the bars of our cage. Each time it falls it climbs back up, ready to begin again until... "

Thias hesitated long enough to see if Llyat was engaged with his story.

"Until what?"

"Until it at last manages to fix a strand onto some place where it can continue to weave its web. It will not accept failure. This mindless beast and it's never give up attitude has inspired many a great man and ballads have been written about it throughout the ages. The spider will always complete that which it sets out to accomplish and that is what we must also do. We have to bring closure on what we have started. None of us can abandon this quest for we are in it to the end."

As Thias looked deep into Llyat's eyes he could tell that the youth had begun to understand the point he was making, even if it had taken more than a moment of thought.

"He's not a fucking spider," spat out Einar from under his fleece.

Thias looked to where the Berserker lay and saw the giant's face as it peeped out from under the makeshift cover. He glared and left Einar in no doubt that he should keep his mouth shut and not interfere. Just when it looked as if he was about to speak again Irabo kicked out with his foot and sent his boot into Einar's side. The giants hand shot forward and crushed the spider.

"No, he's more than that," added Irabo as he made sure that Thias's work was not undone by the Berserker.

"Quite so Irabo," replied Thias. "He is the 'Marked'."

Einar moved his ample arse back through the remains of the burnt straw and sat upright once again. There the Berserker began to speak his mind and Thias knew at once from the tone of voice that something significant bothered him. The giant had begun to lose patience.

"That was fucking fascinating," he ranted. "Spiders and fucking shite. Haven't you forgotten one critical fact from your stupid childish story? We are still locked inside this stinking shit infested cage. I thought you had a plan bard. If you delay any longer the swine with the skull helmet will have arrived and then whatever plan you had will be as worthless as one of your pointless stories."

Thias smiled back at Einar and realised that the Berserker had made a good point. He had indeed promised to get them out somehow but he was running out of both time and ideas. The only viable way forward was to somehow get hold of one of the sets of keys that each of their captors carried but to do that he would have to be on the other side of the bars.

"So, what's your plan string plucker? How we are going to get away before skull face turns up?" sneered Einar.

"I'm working on it, just give me time."

After several minutes of silence Thias saw that Llyat was busy looking out of the cage into the land that passed them so slowly and illuminated by the last throws of Solaris.

"Where are we?" asked Llyat. "What is that place over there?"

Thias looked out over the rocky ground towards the old ruins of a once magnificent city. Time had not been kind and the bard felt a great sadness for the once great metropolis that had long fallen into decay. The place of legend was a most sorry sight.

"That Llyat, is Calistorn," replied Thias.

"Calistorn! Please remind me, which place is that? My peasant's brain has been addled by all the shite we have been through these past weeks. I seem to have a hole in my head regarding that name."

"You must recall the word Calistorn Llyat," replied Thias

"Tell me again."

"That city has lain in ruins ever since the ancestors of our Sovereign Lord crushed the infamous rebellion led by the Silverwynns. Calistorn was the ancestral home of the Lady herself."

"But what happened to it?" asked Llyat while he continued to stare out at the ruins.

"That I'm afraid I don't know. We never got round to discussing that back in Valameer. Our thoughts became distracted and focused on that sailor fellow you brought with you."

"Well that I can answer," added Einar. "I guess you know what these lands are famous for?"

"I once heard that a precious metal was mined here," replied Irabo.

"And what you heard was correct," continued Einar. "These lands were the source of the legendary orichalcum. It was the presence of that precious ore that led to the downfall of the city?"

"Is that true?" asked Thias. "Are you saying that the reason for the war between Calistorn and Parandor was all down to orichalcum? They killed each other in the thousands just for the sake of some black metal?"

"Not just any old metal but orichalcum," grinned Einar, proud to hold such knowledge.

"I'm sorry, but what is orichalcum?" asked Llyat.

Thias, having forgotten Llyat's sheltered childhood, replied in a condescending manner.

"Do you mean you have never heard of it? A metal said to be the strongest of materials that man can work with. It is the most robust and yet, so the legends say, weighs almost...."

Thias paused midsentence. A memory had forced it way into his thoughts and when he looked up he saw his puzzled companions waiting for an explanation.

"Are you okay?" Llyat asked.

"Sure," the Bard replied. "Something just clicked inside my skull and it made sense of many muddled thoughts I believed were long forgotten."

"Stop talking in riddles," demanded Einar.

"There was a farmer," began Thias. "I ran into an unfortunate who was being hunted by the Knights of Avolire. The armour they wore was unique and it permitted them to move far faster than steel could ever have allowed. What they wore looked solid enough but yet it appeared so light that it took no effort at all for those who wore it to move their limbs. I'm convinced now that what the knights wore was fashioned out of the black orichalcum you just described."

"I would go along with that conclusion," added Irabo.

A moment later the four occupants of the cage lurched forward as the metal container that had been their home for many a day lurched to a standstill. Thias, being the only one who was stood up at that time, stumbled forward but soon regained his balance after colliding with the bars. From the front of the cage he tried to ascertain the reason behind the sudden halt. Then as he glanced through the bars and past the stationary beasts that had pulled them along, beyond the ogres and General Brosizrug who still sat upon his mighty steed, he saw what lay before them. Having been so preoccupied with looking out towards Calistorn and the talk of orichalcum, Thias and the others had failed to notice their arrival at the ogre's encampment.

Thias scanned the area and noted that they had stopped in front of several large tents. They were not made of the hessian sheets that the armies of Parandor used, the type they had seen deep in the frozen depths of Thengar forest. These were larger in size, each big enough to house at least four of the hideous ogres and they were made of something else. It was a dark grey material that looked as if it came from something that once was alive. Thias then recognised the nature of the covering for it looked identical to that of the makeshift shelter that they had found on their journey through the Ivory Pass. It was without any doubt wormnose hide. He then looked through the openings of various tents and saw several more ogres milling around the encampment as they carried out their allotted tasks. He studied every single one of them for he sought to identify any weakness that he could exploit in order to break free from his cell. He saw nothing that could help, not even a hint of anything useful. Time was running out to enact a means of escape.

"Where are we?" asked Llyat with more than a hint of apprehension.

"This looks like their forward encampment, north of the Grey Mountains," replied Thias while he continued to watch the movement of the ogres. "I guess it's no surprise that they brought us here although I'm surprised how few of them there are."

Thias pushed up against the bars of the cage and attempted to listen to the orders that Brosizrug shouted to all that had gathered around him.

"Lizug get a fire going."

"With what," responded the ogre?

Thias looked about and the beast was right. Unless they had a hidden store of wood somewhere the order would be difficult to implement. The ground was parched and there was very little vegetation to be seen amongst the rocky landscape.

"Use what bit of sense you have left between your thick skulls," added another. "First collect whatever scraps of plant will burn. You know as well as I do that we walk on top of a rocks that flame. Smash your way through the surface and the ground will sustain the fire. That's what we have done while you have been away in the forest."

Thias watched as the two ogres walked off into the centre of the camp. Once they had disappeared from view Brosizrug turned his attention to Livzig, the ogre that carried the cage of birds.

"Has there been any further word from the Lady?" he asked.

"No, nothing."

"Then we must assume that her Commander has already been dispatched. He must be must be well on his way from Avolire by now. I reckon that we still have time to rest before he arrives and takes custody of the prisoners and blue gemstone."

With that Brosizrug tapped the leather satchel that hung from his side at the level of his belt and in that instant Thias knew where the sapphire was being kept. No doubt it was not alone but alongside the pendent that Llyat had given him, the Dragon Whisper.

"What is there to eat?" barked Ikeg.

"Nothing but stinking maggoty bread, and flat ale," replied another of the ogres.

"We could eat one of them," said Ikeg while pointing backwards towards the cage. "And I know which one I will choose."

Thias heard Llyat gulp. It seemed that the ogre still intended to take its revenge out on the youth and he sensed Llyat's fear of what the beast would do if he got his hands on him. Thias too shuddered as mental images of the creature's strength flashed before his eyes. He tried all he could to shift them but they were most reluctant to leave.

"You know full well what our orders are Ikeg. So back off and stop talking shite," ordered the General as he squared up to the one with the chain. "They go to the Lady unspoilt and alive."

"But..." stuttered Ikeg.

Brosizrug lurched forward, grabbed Ikeg by the neck, and lifted his subordinate off the ground in a display of incredible strength. The rest of the ogres soon gathered around to witness the outcome of the confrontation. Thias watched on like a hawk to a vole and he soon sensed the possibility of escape.

"Ikeg, do not spew another word out of that stinking mouth of yours. If you as much as utter one word of dissent I will choke you with the chain that joins you snout to lug. Then I'll slit your gizzards and serve your balls up in a stew, you heap of dragon turds. Now listen with care. You are now in charge of finding us meat. There must be a stray animal lurking out somewhere in this wilderness even if it be skyfawn."

"But..." uttered Ikeg.

The bald ogre grasped and clawed at the hands that were locked around its throat. It tried to free itself but Brosizrug was too strong and soon threw the underling to the ground. The General then placed his heavy metal boot upon Ikeg's neck. One further challenge would no doubt be Ikeg's last. Even to Thias who watched through the bars it was clear that the General had been pushed to the limit of his tolerance. Ikeg understood that too.

"I obey," sputtered the ogre as the pressure increased.

At last Brosizrug removed his foot from his Ikeg's neck and allowed the creature to stand and move away. The wounded beast glared at Llyat as it passed the cell while it ran its right index finger across its neck to indicate Llyat's fate should he ever get hands upon him. Once Ikeg had moved out of sight Thias looked back towards the General who had regained his composure and soon shouted out his next orders.

"What the fuck are you all looking at? Get back to work. I want no more nonsense. Get this camp in order and ready to receive the Lady's servant."

With that the rest of the ogres dispersed and Thias knew that none would challenge their General again. Brosizrug then turned towards the cage and made eye contact with Thias.

"I guess you found that rather amusing," he said as he moved to the side of the cage.

"It was hard not to laugh," replied Thias.

"You do not have to worry. The others will respect my orders. It's just Ikeg that's an issue, but he is denser. They say his mother had no brain at all, born without one, but with a great pair of pendulous paps and an arse that any ogre would die for... The Lady of the Silverwynn has ordered that you be taken to Avolire alive and that is what will happen. Despite the grudge that Ikeg has with your friend, the four of you will not come to any harm on my watch. I hope you understand that."

Thias was most surprised by the General's words. It was almost as if he was trying to befriend him in some way but the bard was determined to keep up his guard. If it was just a ploy to gain his trust, he would not fall for it.

"That's as clear as a fogless fortnight," replied Thias as his eyes focused on two objects on the Ogre's belt, the leather satchel containing the sapphire and the ring of rusting keys.

"I have a use for you this evening," continued Brosizrug with a wry smile. "Given that you also profess to be a bard."

"Oh, is that so! Please tell me how I can be of service to you."

"You'll find out soon enough," grunted the ogre as it walked away from the cage.

Thias could but wonder what the General had in mind but whatever it was it had to be better than being locked in the filthy stinking cage that had been his home for days. He then became aware that Llyat, Irabo, and Einar were all watching and waiting for him to say something. Llyat spoke first.

"Thais what's troubling you now?"

"Don't worry Llyat. I think I know what the General plans for me. If I am right it may give me the opportunity to free us all. Trust me, everything is going to be fine. Like I have said already, we will let the Fates play out their game and seek to bring it to its conclusion. I have half a plan to get us out of here and I just hope that it works."

Sometime later Mona reached the summit of her journey across the night sky and illuminated the barren rocky landscape through intermittent breaks in the grey cloud. This was the moment when Brosizrug and another of the other ogres came to collect the bard that they had been led to believe was also the Marked. Thias was in the process of debating the deeper purpose of their mission with his companions and with much help from Irabo was getting close making sense of everything that had happen so far. Once again the discussion had centred on whether or not the Fates directed events. However he did not have time to finish before the cage door was opened and he was pulled out and thrown to the ground.

"Right then bard," said the General as Thias picked himself up. "It's time to perform for us."

Brosizrug made to grab Thias by the arm but the bard moved away and left the General clutching at air.

"I can walk well by myself," he snapped back.

"So be it," replied the General. "Just don't try any funny tricks."

Thias glanced back towards the cage. He knew that Llyat would be concerned for his safety however the youth still had Einar and Irabo to look after him. He, however, was alone and would have to put his trust in the Fates, an act of faith he still found difficult to come to terms with.

Brosizrug pushed the bard forward into the centre of the encampment where he soon became aware of a red glow that came from the ground. At once he realised that the ogres had been successful in breaking through the rock to find the source of heat that raged below the soil's crust. As he moved closer to it a roar of laughter rose from the ogres who sat around the fire. They all appeared content as they ate, drank, and share in their merriment. Whatever they had been drinking had made them more affable, if you could ever say that of an ogre. Thias longed for a sample of whatever the creatures quaffed for after his recent incarceration he was desperate for strong drink.

Over the fire pit in the centre of the circle the creatures had erected a makeshift base on which rested a spit. It straddled the hole from where an intense heat bubbled upwards. A metal rod pierced the carcass of some animal. Thias tried to work out what beast Ikeg could have provided for this party and soon concluded it had to be nighthowler. He then turned to face the General who made ready to address his comrades. With each moment that passed he became more certain of what was about to transpire.

"Here for your entertainment, you scum of the mountain scree, is the bard, the so called marked one, spawned from the loins of she-devils. He is your treat for the evening, brought to you here outside the great city of Calistorn at great personal expense. He will, I am sure, take your minds off the foul taste of the beast that Ikeg the snout-picker has brought to our fireside."

Thias looked at all of the faces of the ogres and soon spotted Ikeg sat amongst his companions. The troublesome ogre glared back at yet another personal insult. The glow from the burning ground served to heighten the red ire in Ikeg's eyes. As yet another roar of laughter erupted and Thias smiled. The plan he had fermented earlier was at last playing out, just the way he intended. 'Fuck the Fates, I'll do this my way' he thought as he then turned to face the General at the edge of the ring.

"So you want me to sing for bastards formed from the snot of Kha's bollocks?"

"Is that going to be a problem for you Bard?" demanded the General. "Perhaps a fight to the death with Ikeg would suit you better?"

"No, not at all, I am most happy to sing for such an esteemed audience."

Even though his plan was coming together well, he still had to be careful not to provoke his captors beyond the limits of their tolerance. He faced his inebriate audience while they jeered and laughed at him. In their drunken stupor they waited on his every word.

"Well then you great lumps of lard and bone, it's going to have to be an unaccompanied song for my instrument...."

Thias did not finish his sentence before the drunken uproar grew ever louder. Even the General sniggered.

"The sad fucker longs to pull on his instrument," shouted one who had stood up and rubbed away at its groin while laughing at its own joke.

Despite the merriment Thias missed the lyre he once carried round his neck, now lost forever following the assault on the Bards Guild of Valameer. He sighed and then spoke, his voice growing ever louder as it demanded the attention of his audience.

"I was going to say that my instrument has long since gone but I see now that it would be wasted on such swine as you."

Thias rattled through his mind and wondered how best he could proceed to the next stage of his plan. They wanted him to sing but he needed to choose the right song; one that ogres would understand and join in with.

"I guess you know the story of The Cat of Ballos Anerirah."

The ring of Ogres fell silent and Thias felt the ire of each and every one of them as they growled back at him. It was as if he had uttered the foulest of all profanities. He turned to face the bemused General, determined to continue.

"I'm sorry, I didn't think you would mind that tale, given one of its characters is an ogre."

"I like you Bard," said Brosizrug as he then laughed. "Just spew out whatever tripe wants to come from your mouth. Of course we don't mind that story. What Ogre doesn't? It's just not many people have the balls to speak of it in our presence."

"The story is..." began Thias, before being interrupted.

"Enough of the prattle bard, just get on with it," snarled the General. "I want to hear what humans have to say about the Cat of Ballos Anerirah, but don't start at the beginning with all the shit about where the cat came from, where it was born, and all that fucking nonsense."

"As you so desire," replied Thias. "And as you asked in so polite a manner, I will now begin."

With that said the bard broke into song.

There was a cat,
That often sat
Beneath an old oak tree.
And there it meditated all its days,
And came to understand the ways,
Of how it could be free.

An Ogre with tremendous power,
Kept cat like a precious flower,
In its Fortress dank and black.
But then cat devised a way,

To make a break for freedom day,
And get its life on track.

The Ogre had a wondrous skill,
To change its form just at its will,
From lion to even mouse.
The cat then planned the way ahead,
To wake the Ogre from its bed,
And transform it to a louse.

When next afore the Ogre's throne,
The cat a story did bemoan,
Like a tragedy from some ancient lore.
It told the Ogre of its desire,
To set the world of man afire,
And to make their skin right sore.

Such pain did Puss wish to create,
That man would choose death as his fate,
As he scratched forever throughout his house.
But what Puss needed now you see,
To carry the pestilence was a flea,
"Oh, Yes!" cried Ogre "I shall be that louse."

The Ogre shank with a magic spell,
So small, that few could see or tell,
Whether he still mattered.
But Puss had eyes good as the best,
And when his paw slammed on the pest,
Its vital parts were splattered.

And so the cat usurped the throne,
And not one citizen did bemoan,
The passing of the creature.
For since that day there was no ague,
Nor hint of pestilence or plague,
Just a sodding cat like preacher.

Once Thias had finished the circle of ogres burst into a spontaneous round of applause. He had been unsure of the reception that his tune would invoke and was astounded at how well it went down. The General walked towards him and began to clap his hands in a slow and deliberate manner.

"Not bad. Not bad at all Bard," laughed Brosizrug. "But there was one thing you lacked."

"And pray tell what was that?" asked Thias.

"Rhythm. Don't you agree boys?"

"Yes, we can give him rhythm, right up his hairy arse!" shouted one above the drunken uproar.

"More! More! We want more," chanted the ogres.

"You heard them?" continued the General. "They demand an encore. Sing it again."

"Oh very well, if you insist," replied Thias as he shrugged his shoulders. "How could I refuse such fawning arse bandits?"

Thias took a deep breath and once more broke into song. He repeated the lyrics for a second time and if anything was a little more out of tune. This time however he was accompanied by the clapping of hands and the clanging of whatever metallic objects the ogres found close to hand. Thias noticed that even Ikeg joined in the tympanic cacophony that the enormous drunken creatures created. With much trepidation and anxiety Thias adjusted the rhythm of his song to that of the ogre's beat. As he belted out the words he was reminded of the Court Fool of Parandor and how he would skip, jump, and dance whenever he entertained Phauless Gylewu and the Sovereign Court. So as Thias repeated the song a third time he too danced along. He pranced around the fire and even enjoyed entertaining this most unusual audience. His shame had long since gone for this was a dance for survival.

As the circle of ogres jeered and attempted to sing along, Thias grew more energetic and each expressive movement of his improvised dance became ever more exaggerated. He was their fool and they lapped it up. But when Thias reached the line in the song which exclaimed, *"Oh, Yes!" cried Ogre "I shall be that louse.",* Thias tripped on purpose over the large metal boot of the ogre called Lizug and fell head first into the lap of the next beast along which just happened to be Ikeg.

Ikeg rose to his feet and pushed Thias to the floor. His mood changed in a flash and it was obvious that the ogre's blood had fermented. The circle of others fell quiet as their eyes fell upon Thias. All clapping and laughter ceased as tension built between the bard and the ugliest of the beasts.

"What the fuck do you think you are playing at?" shouted Ikeg. "Get your stinking, festering flesh off me."

"I do apologise," shouted Thias as he dragged himself up from the ground.

"You'll do more than that when I'm finished with you, you bastard."

Ikeg then took several paces toward Thias. The ogre's hand rose as if the strike and Thias screwed his eyes, waiting for a blow to land.

"That's enough Ikeg," boomed the authoritative voice of General Brosizrug.

A second passed before Thias felt it safe to open his eyes. Ikeg sat back down with the rest of the ogres and began to whisper to those nearest to him. Thias felt uneasy and imagined the creature plotting to kill him in his sleep, long before they reached Avolire. Then Brosizrug appeared by his side.

"I'd best get you back in the cage bard. I don't want any further trouble."

"And I'll do my best not to cause any," replied Thias.

The General led the way back to the place of confinement on the outskirts of the camp where one solitary ogre sat and guarded the cage. Brosizrug unlocked it with his bunch of keys and Thias clambered inside. His friends soon gathered around, anxious to check that no harm had come to their bard. It was obvious from the look on their faces that they had seen all that had happened around the camp fire, including Thias's altercation with Ikeg.

"What was all that about?" asked Irabo once the two Ogres had moved away re-join the party.

"What did you do to provoke them?"

"Me?" said Thias with a grin on his face. "Oh nothing, nothing at all."

"Then why are you smiling like a dog that's just licked a twat?" demanded Einar.

"Believe it or not," continued Thias, "I have just secured our means of escape."

Thias opened his right palm which he had kept tight shut since his fall into Ikeg's lap. There lay a single brass key and its purpose was not lost on any of the Thias's companions. All smiled.

"How did..." exclaimed Llyat.

"Shush!" said Thias as he put a finger to his lips. "Not so loud."

"Sorry," replied Llyat. "But how did you manage to get hold of that?"

"It's a skill I'm not proud of," replied Thias. "It's a technique that my father taught me many years ago. It's best you do to know how such things are done. All I can tell you is that ugly bastard Ikeg is going to be in an awful lot of trouble when the General finds out that we are gone and whose key is missing."

"You are one crazy turd of a bard," snorted the Berserker.

"You said yourself Einar that we needed to get out of here and I have kept my promise. We just need to wait for that drunken lot to fall sleep and then we can make our move."

It took longer than Thias had expected for the Ogres to end their drinking session and even longer for them to collapse inside their tents of wormnose hide. Once Thias was sure that each and every one of the creatures had drifted out of consciousness he took the key and placed it into the lock of the cage. He found it odd that no ogre had been left to guard them and he put it down to the General's naivety. Brosizrug must have been certain that there was no escape possible, but he was so wrong. Once the key had turned in the lock and Thias heard the click of success, he pushed against the bars of the cage door and opened it. He half expected a rusty screech to come from the hinges as he loosened the door but no sound came to alert the ogres of the prisoner's flight. Thias climbed out first and dropped to the rocky ground. He was followed a once by Llyat, and then by Irabo, who winced when his injured leg took his full weight. It didn't help that they had been locked in the cage for several days and that he had been thrown to the ground by the ogre back in Barad Elestor. The last out was the Berserker who declined any assistance. On hitting the ground he began to stretch his body in every way possible, groaning as he did so. Due his great size the giant was the happiest to be outside the confines of the metal container. Einar then reached back into the cage and retrieved his nighthowler pelt from its floor. Even though stained with stale urine he returned it at once to its rightful place upon his head.

"Well played bard," whispered the giant. "I owe you an apology."

"Save it for when we've put enough distance between Brosizrug and ourselves. We are not out of danger yet, not by a long way. Now let's get out of here."

"Agreed," echoed Irabo.

There was no further talk as the four companions made their way from the edge of the ogre's encampment into the darkness of the nightscape. Thias's intuition told him where the best place for them to hide would be, in the shadows of the ruins of Calistorn. Moving through the darkness he led the others on towards that goal. It was as dark as night could be for thick clouds had rolled in and blocked out all light that Mona had to offer. As long as he could hear the sounds of his companion's footfall he felt reassured. After they had walked for fifteen minutes or so across the hot crunching ground, Thias glanced backwards to where they had begun their flight to freedom. Even though they had only been travelling a short time they had covered a good distance from the camp which showed as an illuminated speck in the distant dark.

Thias stopped and Irabo bumped into his back.

"Are you okay?" asked the warrior as the others gathered around him.

"We have a problem?" replied Thias.

"What is wrong with you now Bard?" whispered Einar. "We have to keep moving."

"We have forgotten something important," continued Thias.

"What," grumbled Einar?

"The sapphire. Brosizrug still has it. There is but one option left to us," he whispered while pointing back to the camp.

"You've got to be fucking joking," replied Einar.

"I wish I was. There is no other option."

"What is he on about?" asked Llyat failing to grasp the enormity of the suggestion.

"We cannot leave the Gem of Thamous in their possession," continued Thias. "The sapphire must not reach Avolire; the Lady of the Silverwynn must never be allowed to get her talons on it. She already has two of the Gems and we dare not let her get hold a third. Do not worry, I will go back alone and retrieve it."

"But you can't," exclaimed Llyat. "You'll wake them. You'll get killed. You'll...."

Thias turned to Llyat and placed his hands upon the youth's shoulders.

"I have no choice Llyat," he added. "It has to be done."

Thias then dropped his hands and turned to face the others.

"Einar, Irabo, get Llyat away from here and make for the ruins of Calistorn. I'll join you as soon as I can. If I haven't caught up with you by the time Solaris hits his peak tomorrow then do not wait for me. Finish the quest by yourselves. Go and seek the gem that lies hidden in the Eastern Marsh and then head back to Parandor. There you can regroup and decide what to do next. Do not worry about me for I can look after myself. I will find a way to survive."

"There must be …" said Irabo, but Thias stopped him mid-sentence.

"Do as I say Irabo. This is not a request it's an order."

Before either of his friends could argue further Thias broke into a run and raced off back towards the ogre's camp.

In no time at all Thias had covered the short distance to the tented village. With great care he crept along its outer edge while always keeping to the shadows. He used all of the techniques he had learned from his father and the Thieves Guild of Parandor. He was determined not to let history repeat itself and get caught. As he passed one of the innermost tents he formulated his plan to gain access to the satchel that contained the sapphire and which he assumed was located inside the General's shelter. Crouching down at its corner he took hold of the leathery skin that covered the tent, closed his eyes, and whispered.

"Promethelumous."

Thias jumped backwards as the tent ignited. He hadn't expected it to immediately burst into flames and he rolled back into the darkness. The speed that the fire took hold had to be the result of oils used to coat the leathery canvass in order to give it additional protection from the elements that Hamthor threw against it. Thias watched the flaming structure from the shadows and soon heard sounds of coughing and shouts of terror which erupted from within the interior of the burning tent. In an instant two of the large brutes, including the ogre who had carried the cage of birds, lumbered out hollering.

"Fire!" shouted Lizvig, naked apart from a pair of soiled shorts.

"Help!" shouted the second ogre as it coughed and spat out smoke and spittle.

The noise spread around the camp. More shouting filled the night air the as occupants of the other tents were shocked out their drunken slumber. The screams of their terrified and tethered steeds added to the tumult. Amid the drifting smoke the land was illuminated for some considerable distance around the encampment. Thias had wanted to cause confusion although his means of doing so was beyond what he had planned. The fire had done its trick for the ogres were awake, confused, and drunk. The bard's gaze was then drawn to the entrance of another tent and as the ogres poured out in various stages of undress. General Brosizrug strode out into the camp's middle and made his presence known. Wearing just a loin cloth that didn't quite cover everything he held the centre of the camp and scanned the chaos that unfolded around him. He was as angry as an ogre could be and they can get very angry indeed.

"What the fuck is going on?" bellowed the General.

"Fire!" cried one of the ogres.

"I can see that you thick tosser. Then don't just stand there, put the bloody thing out."

The General continued to assess the chaos while several of the near naked creatures attempted to extinguish the fire. Then Brosizrug's gaze reached the cage which now stood empty.

"Who was supposed to be watching the prisoners?" he shouted as he strode towards it.

"I'm buggered if I know," replied one.

Thias did not wait to find out how that conversation played out. He knew which tent belonged to the General. As Brosizrug directed his men to leave the fire and find the prisoners, Thias made his way through the shadows towards the General's tent and slipped into its dark interior. A solitary candle offered insufficient light to cut through the gloom.

"Promethelumous."

His eyes roamed at speed around the tent's interior as he sought out the satchel that contained the Sapphire. Soon he located it on top of a small chest which lay next to a canvass hammock where the ogre slept. Ignoring everything else, Thias made his way past the General's armour to the wooden box, turned off the flame from his hands, and retrieved the bag and its contents.

"Thank you Solaris for bringing me luck at last," he mumbled to himself as he opened the satchel and checked that the Sapphire was still there. When he looked inside he was startled by a second glow that filled the inside of the pouch.

"What in in the name of..." he muttered.

The bard picked up the source of light; it was the stone that Llyat had given him. He held onto its golden chain and looked into the milky light that strange object emitted. Then Thias was thrown into sudden confusion as a voice entered his head and called him by name."

"Thias, Thias Calavan," whispered the voice.

"Who's there? Who are you?"

"We need to talk," said the voice.

"And what the fuck do you think you are doing bard?" exclaimed a second voice, one not inside his head but close behind. The shock caused Thias to drop the pendent back inside the satchel. When he turned around he looked straight into the eyes of the General. Thias made to run but the ogre blocked his exit.

"Not so fast you swine of the maples," snarled the General. "I may have been able to protect you from my men before this attack on our camp, but not now. You have awakened their wrath and this time I will allow Ikeg to do whatever he pleases, once I have finished with you myself."

Thias made a sudden dash for the entrance but a swing of the General's arm sent him hurtling down to the floor where he dropped the satchel and its contents. He then steadied himself and began the process of reigniting his fists. However before he could repeat his spell he was overpowered by the huge ogre who grabbed him by the throat to stifle his words and then dragged him out of the tent and along the hard stony ground beyond its entrance. There the ogre threw him down and as Thias again tried to induce the flame in his hands it became obvious that his energy store was depleted. He felt the intense pain as the stones of the ground dug into his flesh and he sensed its surface crumbling under his weight. Thias knew he was lucky not to have broken his back and spasms of pain shot through his torso while his face contorted in throes of agony. Somehow he still managed to keep his focus and observe the chaos that he had caused. The tent he had set afire still burned with great ferocity and lit up several of the ogres who beat away at the flames.

"Get this slimy bastard back into his cage," bellowed the General, "and find the others."

"We've got one of them already," yelled the closest ogre as it moved towards the General. "We found him crouching down behind that hump of earth over there."

Thias looked towards the cage and felt sick. He was thrown into even greater confusion and disappointment as he tried to comprehend what Irabo was doing there? Before he could react further the sound of approaching horses gripped everyone's attention. Out of the darkness sped two large steeds and upon each sat an armoured knight, one of whom had a helmet fashioned like a skull and one arm in a make shift sling. The Knights of Avolire had arrived and as they pulled up in front of the General they at once sought to assert their authority.

"It appears we have arrived just in the nick of time," shouted the knight with the skull adorned helmet. "What's going on here? Can't the Lady trust you with anything Brosizrug?"

"That's General to you Commander," replied the ogre.

Thias sensed the tension between the knights and the ogre rise and as he looked on he saw the Commander draw his curved blade from its sheath. It was a sword that Thias had seen before, the very one used to kill the farmer in the land outside of Maplehill.

"Explain yourself General," barked Rhaizen.

"The buggers have escaped," replied Brosizrug without a hint of shame. "But we have caught two of the shits. The other two won't get far and I still have the jewel that you seek."

The ogre pointed at Thias and then towards the cage in which Irabo sat watching the drama that played out before him.

"Whoever these people are and given that they had the jewel in their possession, they must be brought before the Lady. We cannot afford to let them escape," ordered Rhaizen.

"I'll have my best men..." began the General.

"Don't bother you useless dolt," ordered Rhaizen. "I shall take care of this myself. Just keep the other two and the gem secure."

"My Lord Rhaizen, as always I follow your commands, but do you think it wise to go on alone with that injured arm of yours?" stuttered the General.

"My good one is more than enough!"

Thias now knew the name of the knight and noted the power of Commander Rhaizen's presence as the General began to tremble.

"Oedd," said Rhaizen as he looked around the encampment.

"Yes Sir," replied the second knight.

"You are in charge until I return with the other two. It won't take me long to find the bastards. We will then leave for Avolire and take the General and his thick skulled friends with us. We must get the Gem to the Silverwynn as soon as possible.

"I understand Sir," replied Oedd.

"Are you sure you really want to go alone? One of them is a Berserker," said the General.

"Just tell me which way they went," ordered Rhaizen.

"That way, towards the old ruins of Calistorn."

Thias could not think of anyone better than a Berserker to protect Llyat out in the wilderness. He felt that he had failed the youth and that now it was up Einar alone to guide and protect Llyat on his quest. Irabo was also restrained, unable to assist, and Thias felt a great sadness and sense of apprehension for himself and the young warrior. He could but hope that the Cutter would be quick to use her knife should they face torture at the hands of their captors. He closed his eyes and prayed that some of the gods were awake, still sober, and able to give Llyat the strength to carry on. A sudden gust of wind then bore down on the encampment and embers carried through the air spread flames to all the tents that made up the ogre's base. Soon the fire raged with the greatest of intensity while towards the horizon Thias saw Rhaizen riding at speed. As he then watched the complete destruction of the ogre's camp he at last allowed himself to smile.

22

Llyat's chest hurt to bursting point. He had never run so fast in all of his life and as he raced through the darkness he stumbled time and time again upon the rocky ground which crunched and crumbled under his feet. He gasped for air as he sped onwards and although he had never excelled in physical endeavour the thought that several large and blood thirsty ogres could be chasing after him focused all his efforts into self-preservation. He had to keep running despite the pain for there was no other option available. In the darkness of the barren land that surrounded him, Llyat saw the large form of the Berserker who bounded ahead. Running appeared effortless to Einar and the giant did not seem at all out of breath. Llyat prayed that he would not lose sight of his friend as they covered the ground amid the gloom that spread across the land, starved of Mona's light as the goddess hid amongst the clouds. The burning in Llyat's lungs eventually forced him to stop. He bent forward, placed both his hands upon his knees and exhaled to the very depths of his belly as his body attempted to catch each its breath. Without doing so he knew he would have passed out and then would have been at the mercy of the foul beasts that would surely follow once they had discovered that their prisoners had escaped. It was but by chance that Einar stopped at the same moment to scan the surrounding terrain. The Berserker turned and made his way towards Llyat where he then grabbed hold of the youth's leather tunic with considerable force and pushed him forwards.

"Come on," he ordered. "We cannot stop. They will by now know we are missing."

"Please! I need to rest," pleaded Llyat. "I need to breathe."

"Get a hold of yourself," yelled Einar. "I for one have no intention of being returned to that cage and carted off to Avolire."

"But..."

"Just move, you useless bugger."

Before he could argue the Berserker took off once again into the darkness and Llyat had little choice but to follow. Onwards he lumbered over the crackling ground. Every muscle in his body knotted in agony and yet he pushed himself harder than he had ever done before; the flight would either crush him or save him. He had no choice but to trust in the Berserker's decisions even though he had no understanding of where he was being led. Without breaking his stride Llyat glanced back to the origin of their flight. In the distance he saw the fire glow intensify in a most dramatic fashion. It illuminated the night sky and spewed black smoke high into the air. He could just about hear faint shouts from the ogre's camp that travelled on the wind. Although he could not make out the words that emanated from the creatures' foul mouths it was clear that something significant had just occurred. It had to be the work of Thias and Irabo.

"We can't just leave them," shouted Llyat.

"They made their choice," replied the Berserker. "Only the Moirai can serve them now. They ordered me to get you to safety and that is what I intend to do."

Llyat thought about his friends. It had been but a matter of minutes after the Bard had left to retrieve the sapphire that Irabo had followed him for the warrior of the Watch had decided that Thias would need help if he were to regain possession of the jewel. Llyat had pleaded with Irabo to reconsider his decision but he had been most insistent. His parting words had been directed to Einar. The giant was to take care of Llyat and after giving that order Irabo had limped off towards the ogre's camp. Llyat began to speculate on what could have caused the sudden conflagration.

Einar disappeared into the shadowy landscape as the distance between the two fleeing souls stretched further. Once again the crushing feeling in Llyat's chest became too intense to bare and it forced him to stop a second time and fight for air. Looking back towards the burning encampment, now a tiny speck of light in the distance. He thought of his friends and the dangers that they faced. When his lungs had been sufficiently aerated he shouted out into the darkness in the hope that Einar was still close enough to hear.

"We have to wait for them!"

Llyat stood in silence for what seemed like an eternity although in truth it was but a matter of seconds. Then Einar reappeared for a second time and began to drag Llyat away with him.

"We have to wait for them," repeated Llyat but Einar was not for changing his mind.

"You heard what the bard said. We wait for them in Calistorn and not before. We are too easy to locate out here in the open and we need to find somewhere to hide."

"But..."

"No Llyat! This is not the time and the place to argue. Now move!"

Once again Einar pushed Llyat forward across the porous ground. This time they set off side by side and every time that Llyat showed signs of slowing, Einar pushed again. Every bone in Llyat's body screamed out its discomfort and he prayed to any god listening to end his torture. In the light of Solaris on the previous day the ruins of Calistorn had seemed much closer. The crumbling structures that he had seen from the back of the cage were still nowhere to be seen. He stumbled and tripped but was caught by Einar who thrust him forward again like a houndsman driving his dog. The way that Einar bullied him exasperated Llyat and he felt his anger begin to grow. He understood too well that Einar was trying to save his life but just wished that the Berserker would fuck off. Once again Llyat began to falter and this time the Berserker raced on alone.

"Einar, please slow down! I cannot keep up with you."

No answer came and soon Llyat was left alone in the dark and stillness of the night. Amid his isolation not even the fleeting appearance of Mona through a break in the clouds gave Llyat any comfort. There was only one thing to do; he would continue on in a straight line in the hope that by some miracle or other he would catch up to his protector. As he restarted his run he began to notice the ground becoming firmer underfoot. He glanced down between his strides and saw that he was running along what appeared to be a paved road, similar in construction to those of the better streets of Parandor. Then in the next instant, emerging from the blackness, he saw the ruins of time ravaged buildings. So preoccupied was he with them that he failed to see the stationary Berserker until it was too late. Llyat's momentum carried him forward into the giant man off whom he then bounced and fell to the ground.

"For Fuck's sake Llyat, watch where you're going!"

The Berserker grabbed the youth by scruff of the neck and pulled him to his feet.

"I so sorry, I didn't see you! I was looking at the rubble."

"Just be careful," groaned Einar. "At least we have made it to Calistorn. We should be able to find some place to hide here and wait out the rest of the night. It's the best we can do although I don't like it. The gods alone know what foul creatures still dwell within this city."

Llyat then looked around but all he could make out were the dark shadows of the buildings. Llyat's night vision was hopeless in comparison to his companion. Without knowing where the thought came from, he remembered one of Cvyler Olin's comments. It was said that living so close to the dragons over many years had enhanced the Berserker's senses. The ability to see in the dark was one of them.

"Can you see any sign of them?" stuttered Llyat.

"It's too dark to tell, even for me," replied Einar. "My hawk eye is not great over long distances on the darkest of nights. I'm sure..."

Einar stopped speaking and focused back in the direction of their escape.

"What is it?" asked Llyat.

"There is something over there and it's moving towards us."

"Is it Thias?" said Llyat with a degree of excitement. "Is it Irabo?"

"It's not them, the shape is far bigger than any man and it's moving much quicker."

"An ogre?"

"Too fast for an ogre and it's moving at great speed. We must keep going. We have to..."

"Run?" said Llyat as he anticipated Einar's instructions.

"Yes do that. We have to find somewhere to hide right now."

Llyat did not wait to be told a second time. Off the pair ran deep into the ruins of Calistorn. A few minutes later Einar grabbed Llyat by the arm and pulled him towards some steps that led down into an old cellar. He pushed Llyat down them, followed, and then flung open the time battered oak door at the bottom. Llyat expected to find something similar to the cellars of Parandor but instead there was just a pile of rubble where the ceiling of the building had collapsed inwards and part blocked the doorway. There was just enough space for one person to squeeze past between the door and the rubble pile and before Llyat could argue Einar thrust him forward into that void.

"In there at once," ordered the giant.

"What about you?"

"Don't worry about me. I will be fine. I'll find my own hiding place nearby. Whatever you do, do not leave this place. Even if you hear the voices of

Thias or Irabo. I will come and get you when it is safe to do so. Do you understand me?"

Llyat did not answer. He did not know what to think for his emotions were shot. He began to fear that Einar was about to abandon him.

"Do you understand me Llyat?"

"Yes, I fucking understand."

Einar shut the door and left Llyat alone in the dark. Soon everything became still as Llyat allowed his eyes to adapt to his new place of confinement. A little light came from above as Mona peeked through the clouds and cast a beam upon the ruined street. Cracks around the doors allowed him to look out onto the street that he had left only seconds earlier. He allowed his breathing to slow and sought to recover from his exhaustion. Llyat was not alone in the confines of his small space for clinging to the door by their sticky feet were three small lizards. They did not move but watched Llyat with great intent. He remembered that Thamous had talked of creatures that acted as his watchers, his spies and ears as he referred to them, and he wondered if here were three of them.

"Are you watching me?" he whispered but the Gecko's did not answer.

Llyat felt like laughing but stopped as a new noise sounded in the street. It caused the Geckos to scuttle off into the dark shadows of the adjacent rubble. Llyat knew at once what the noise was for as it was a sound he recognised from journeys with his father on lazy summer evenings between Maplehill to Ashview. A horse approached. He tried to keep his fear in check and refused to let the madness of the night take control of his senses. Pushing his face up against the wood he stared out to the street above. Llyat half hoped to see Thias and Irabo riding upon one of the mighty mounts that had pulled the ogres cage. Trying to bring about what he thought about, he pictured Thias with the sapphire in his hand and the Dragon Whisper around his neck. However Llyat saw nothing and this just fuelled his anxiety.

The sounds of the horse upon the cobbled street grew ever louder, accompanied soon by the heavy snorting of its nose. Once again the youth stared out and this time he saw a black steed illuminated in Mona's weak light. As he focused upon the beast his anger started to build for sat upon it was the man in a skull adorned helmet. Then he noted with some surprise that the Commander had one arm in a sling but that didn't make the swine any less threatening. Fear forced Llyat to move away from the door until he came up against the rubble pile behind him and dislodged several stones. The small rocks clattered upon the floor and Llyat closed his eyes. His action had been foolish, the result of his mounting terror, and as such may well have led the Commander straight to his hiding place. Somewhere deep inside Llyat did not care if he was discovered for it would give him the opportunity to face the man who had murdered his parents.

A lust for revenge began to grip Llyat's heart. He moved back towards the door and looked out into the street above. The horse that carried his nemesis remained stationary at the top of the steps. The Commander, menacing in his helmet and ink black armour, looked in all directions as he sought out his prey. There was no doubt that the hunt was on and Llyat almost forced open the door with the intent of confronting the foul knight. Yet he did not for thoughts of the higher purpose of his quest battered through his consciousness and no matter how hard Llyat fought against them he found he could not bring himself to open the door. The intense urge to exact vengeance at last receded and Llyat stayed hidden. Once again he looked out to the street beyond the door and watched the knight dismount. The Commander stood still in the poor light and watched and listened as if sensing someone or something close at hand. The evil destroyer of innocents soon focused on the steps, then the door behind which Llyat hid. Slowly he moved forwards. It seemed to Llyat that he had no possible means of escape and yet something stirred inside the young man's heart and his courage began to grow again. He vowed that if caught he would not allow himself to be dragged away without a fight. The sound of the Commander's feet descending the steps caused Llyat to prey to the gods for a miracle. Then he became aware of a second sound, way beyond the walls of his hideaway. It was part screech, part howl and could mean but one thing.

"Nighthowler," he heard the Commander utter with contempt.

Llyat listened as the footfall receded back onto the cobbled street. He opened his eyes and looked through the wood just in time to see the Commander remount his horse. With a quick yank on the reigns the knight with skull helmet rode off and out of Llyat's field of vision.

"That was too fucking close," he whispered to himself as he leaned back upon the pile of rubble. In the darkness he felt something run over his hand and a Gecko scuttled between several of the larger stones.

"Some use you were," said Llyat to the emptiness that the creature left behind.

Time dragged amid the darkness of his hideaway and he lost all sense of it. With all that had happened since he had been cast into the river in Maplehill he realised how fortunate he was to be still alive. Once again he began to reflect on Irabo's belief that everything in life was predetermined but still the concept did not sit well with him. Tonousa had made it quite clear that everything a person does in life is the result of personal choice; unnatural entities were the stuff of simpletons and children. Without warning and while still lost in his thoughts the door to his hideaway was forced open. Llyat jumped to his feet in fear but his terror eased when he saw Einar's face appear from behind the wood.

"Did you see him?" exclaimed Llyat. "The man with the skull helmet that I told you about."

"Yes I did. I was in a building on the other side of the road watching every move that he made."

"That was the bastard who killed my parents," snarled Llyat.

"You did well not to act on impulse."

"What do you mean?"

"You showed control. If it had been me whose parents he had murdered then I could not have stopped myself from attacking the bastard. You showed great restraint and a good deal of sense."

Llyat was taken aback by Einar's words for this was the first time that the Berserker had treated him other than an unnecessary burden that he had been coerced into babysitting. He sensed a change in the giant's attitude towards him and wondered if their friendship had at last turned a corner.

"For a moment I thought he had discovered your hiding place. I could not face that bard again if anything was to happen to you. Be grateful that I know a few tricks. What did you think of my nighthowler call?"

"It was good, I thought it was the real thing," replied Llyat smiling.

"Well at least it worked and got you out of immediate danger."

Llyat climbed out of the door, stood at the base of the stairs, and looked up to the street above. He rather liked this new facet of the Berserker's personality.

"So what do we do now?" asked Llyat as he stared down the deserted road.

"I don't know about you, but I need food," replied Einar as he patted his belly.

Llyat nodded in agreement for he too felt his stomach churn with ripples of hunger. It then gurgled such that Einar could hear it and demanded to be filled. In their frantic escape from the ogres and the arrival of the Commander from Avolire, Llyat had forgotten how hungry he was.

"I'm famished."

"And where do you think you're going," demanded Einar as he stuck out an arm.

"I thought you said we were going to look for some food!"

"I said nothing of the sort," grumbled the giant. "I said we could do with some food. I didn't say you could leave your hiding place. The nighthowler ruse may have worked for now but I am not willing to risk you coming across him again. He may still be somewhere close."

Llyat accepted the logic of the Berserker's words and retreated back into the dark alcove behind the door. There he made himself comfortable on the floor with his back to the mound of rubble.

"It won't be for much longer, I promise you that," said Einar. "I'm going to scout out the area and make sure that he has gone. Then I am going to find us something to eat. I am certain from the stench in the air that there are wild Mathulath in these ruins."

Llyat sniffed but sensed nothing. Perhaps this was yet another Berserker skill, obtained from years of exposure to dragons. With his keen eyesight, acute sense of smell, fleetness of foot, and impressive fighting ability, it was obvious why Cvyler Olin had sent Einar to take him to Thamous. It was as if the old man had second guessed what dangers he would face and how he would soon come to depend on Einar's talents for his survival.

"Are you going to be safe all on your own out there?" asked Llyat. "I mean, if the Commander returns, I hate to think what he will do to you if he catches you. Do not forget he has the ability to wield magic."

"Aye lad, I remember. Let's pray that the Moirai have not yet decided to call time."

Einar then departed a second time and left Llyat alone in the dark.

The youth yawned and stretched out his arms. Ever since Einar's return he had felt more in need of sleep as each minute had passed. In the darkness and security of his hiding place he felt his eyes begin to close. He curled up against the fallen stones and sighed. When his eyes closed he was plunged into a deep and impenetrable sleep.

As Llyat began to dream he saw before him the Eastern Marsh in all of its foul and putrid glory. It stretched out towards the coastal waters of the west and to the south where it encroached upon the base of the Grey Mountains where they too swept towards the sea. He saw the fog that surrounded and settled over the muddy patches of water and the green reeds that grew where most other life had failed to gain a foothold. There amongst the harsh vegetation he noted that a white flower bloomed in abundance. It defied all the rules of nature in that fetid and inhospitable swamp that stank of rotten eggs. No matter how much he tried to switch his focus away from the dank waters of the marsh his vision always returned to the same place, a distant point on the horizon.

"Show him the city," cackled an ancient voice that echoed across his dream.

"Of course dear sister," replied a second which sounded just as old.

Llyat then found himself floating across the marsh at great speed. The surrounding land turned into a blur as he raced on towards to the distant point on the horizon that grew ever bigger as his dream moved forward. Soon all was clear and the object of his focus appeared before him.

"This is the city at the heart of the Eastern Marsh," said the first voice.

"The city of the Lizardmen," added the second.

Llyat looked down upon the vast sprawling metropolis. Fog covered the mud huts and woven reed shacks that made up the bulk of the structures, all erected on a mass of floating reeds. He could make out individual buildings and the wooden walkways between them but he could not move unaided amid their walls for he was being manipulated and controlled. He sensed he was being shown only that which he was allowed to see, not everything that he wanted to look at. Those in control spoke again.

"Show him the temple," said the first voice. "Show him Urthanock."

Llyat again felt himself move over the ground at great speed as the buildings and mist swirled. He was steered through the narrow gaps between the huts, always moving towards the centre of the city of reeds. Then as the mist lifted he saw Lizardmen, young and old, workers and warriors, but none acknowledged his presence. All were oblivious to his journey across their lands and lakes. Soon he came to a halt before a dry island in the centre of the marsh. On it stood a huge stone temple carved out of the rock and earth that had been thrust up out of the swamp in primordial times.

"Show him Urthanock," ordered the first.

"Who are you?" he cried out in an attempt to gain some control while the word 'Moirai' echoed around his head.

At last he was brought before the natural opening of the ancient cavern that served as the temple entrance and there he once again found himself dragged forward as if controlled like a puppet. Walls moved past at speed as he was sucked into the temple interior. In the next instant, amid an explosion of light, Llyat stood before a large statue of a reptilian warrior in the centre of a cavernous candle lit space. Several Lizardmen in brown robes attended to the statue yet all remained oblivious to his presence. Llyat had seen the statue before and he knew who it depicted.

"Llyat, seek the Gem of Thamous," said the first voice.

"Locate the Temple of Urthanock," said the second.

"Who are you? Why do you show me these things?" demanded Llyat.

"Moirai... Moirai...Moirai."

Llyat attempted to shake his head and clear his mind and yet his thoughts became focused on the stone alter at the feet of the statue of Urthanock. He could see offerings and gifts to the Lord of Fear set out upon its hard cold surface. Gold coins, rubies, and emeralds lay everywhere and upon a set of golden scales, weighed down on one side, he saw a multitude of amethyst crystals. Llyat looked closer at the balance but found he could not move any nearer to it for those who controlled him would still not permit him to move on his own. As he surveyed the pile of amethysts he sought to break the will of those who steered his experience.

"But which one is it?" he shouted.

"You will know it when you find it," said the first.

"But..." began Llyat.

"No, it is time for you to wake," said the second.

Llyat woke with a start, jumped to his feet, and brushed off three Geckos that had decided to explore his torso. In a state of high anxiety he then surveyed his immediate vicinity. The light of Solaris poured through the cracks in the wooden door, crept in silence over the heap of rubble, and illuminated his hiding space as if nothing better to do with their time. When Llyat moved he disturbed significant amounts of dust which then sparkled in the beams of light and reminded him of wood wasps warming themselves in the woods surrounding Maplehill. He wondered how long he had been asleep for he had no real idea. The main thought that troubled him was that the Commander may have returned. He stretched, yawned, and once again pressed his face against the wooden door as he looked up to the deserted street. He saw nothing of significance nor any sign of Einar, Thias, or Irabo. Of more immediate importance there was nothing to indicate the presence of a black knight from Avolire. Llyat then felt a dull ache in his lover legs and realised that cramp had set in for he had been cooped within the small space for too long. Pushing open the wooden door he allowed more of the light to flood in. He had expected to find some resistance to its movement but the portal opened with ease and allowed Llyat access onto the street. He mounted the steps and attempted to make sense of his surroundings which looked so much different than they had done in the midst of the dark night. The buildings that stretched before him were all dilapidated. The red stone had crumbled and most of the once magnificent edifices were unrecognisable as dwellings. Many of the buildings still carried a discernible coat of arms built into their lower stone work, two nighthowlers tearing a skyfawn apart while stood astride a shield of checked design. He tried to imagine what the city would have looked like at the height of its power and it struck him that it would have been much more beautiful than Parandor. A thought then came to him. If the city had been the home of the Lady of the Silverwynn before Calistorn's mutinous rebellion then how could it be possible that she was still alive? No one could be that old. He looked up into the sky and from the position of Solaris noted that it was mid-morning and still some time before Thias's deadline would pass. In his heart Llyat was certain that his friends would then appear. Another thought then popped into his head. Even if Thias and Irabo did arrive in Calistorn before the height of the disc's transit, how would they ever locate him in the vastness of the ruined city? In his cloud of frustration he shouted aloud in the hope that someone would hear him.

"Einar! Thias! Irabo!"

As the echoes of the three names fell away, Llyat was once again plunged into the deafening silence that filled the once magnificent city. He listened in all directions but still no answer came. Realising at last that he was all alone he swore he would not give into his fears. He had faith that his friends would soon return and that they could continue their journey together towards the Eastern Marsh. In his dream he had discovered the location of the amethyst, hidden at the feet of the statue of Urthanock, and he needed to share this knowledge with the others before the memory of his dream faded.

"Einar!" he shouted again.

Still there was no answer. He thought perhaps the Commander had found the Berserker and left him dead in some dark recess of the city. A noise from behind caused Llyat to turn and look towards a statue that lay fallen in the accumulated dirt. The sound had been generated by a simple sparrow which had taken flight. Llyat then focused with great interest on the fallen statue, left broken and crumbling amid the ancient dust. It was a figure of a young woman with a sheet draped around her body. With long flowing hair and despite being cracked it carried an attractive face. A wave of emotion then swept through Llyat as he was reminded of Heliana, the one person he wanted above all others to be with. Llyat smiled as his thoughts recalled the first time he had met the young woman on waking in Parandor. His mind created pictures of them both together, warm besides a fire in the servant's quarters of the Underkeep, naked and wrapped in a furs with their limbs entwined. Oh how he wished it could be so again. Then in solitary desolation he wept.

"Pull yourself together," he told himself. "What would Heliana think if she saw you like this? She would give you a right old roasting and dump you for some other spotty faced prick. Come on its time to stop wallowing in self-pity and take control of your life."

Llyat dried his eyes with his dirt encrusted sleeve but he was right, something inside him had to change. He had relied far too much on Thias and allowed the bard to make all the decisions. Yes, Thias had saved his life but what did he now have to show for it? He had been happy to play the role of an immature yokel but not anymore. He was the 'Marked' after all and needed to start acting like the hero that the Prophecy of Enderdetag demanded, not some billy-arsed bumpkin from nowhere. A fire of positivity, sparked from somewhere unknown, began to burn within his core. A few minutes passed and at last he felt better. Letting out a deep sigh he looked up and down the street in the hope of seeing his friends. Then he squinted up to Solaris. There was still some time before the deadline would pass but he began to face the possibility that his friends may never come. Should that be the case he knew where he had to go and what he needed to do; it had all been laid out in his dream. Once again a sound caused Llyat turn to look deep into one of the ruined and roofless buildings. As his limbs began to tremble he could find nothing to account for the sudden noise. Perhaps it was a ghost that haunted the ancient city, a spectre like something out of the stories that Denius Castor used to tell in the Red Mare. No, they just were stories, tales to frighten children. This was the here and now and he was no longer a child. He had to get a grip of himself, leave his world of fantasies, and believe only what he could see with his own eyes.

"Einar!" he shouted. "If that's you, then quit fucking about."

Having received no answer he looked about the ruins that surrounded him and wondered if he would ever see the Berserker again. Then he spotted what appeared to be a dome sticking out above the roof tops of some far off buildings. It was like nothing he had ever seen before and it sparked his curiosity.

"Interesting," he muttered to himself as he started to walk along the road in the direction of the spherical object. His stomach rumbled once again and he realised the seriousness of his situation. If he didn't find food soon, he would pass out and then starve to death. Even though Einar had told him to stay until he returned, Llyat could no longer depend upon the actions of others. It was time to stand on his own, to control his own destiny, and above all find something to eat.

"Einar!" he shouted one last time. "Fuck you then."

Off the youth strode with great urgency of step towards the distant sphere. As he passed through the ruins, with Solaris forever edging towards its zenith, he noted the absence of vegetation. This was in stark contrast to the ruins of Barad Elestor, deep within the snow covered wilds of Thengar. Llyat then remembered the solitary rose he had seen growing out of the snow and which had given him hope within that dark foreboding frozen forest. He wished for something similar as he tramped the streets and moved closer to the mysterious sphere. Einar had said there were wild Mathulath in the ruins but Llyat could not imagine what they could survive on. Then he remembered that the beasts preferred to eat meat but that still didn't resolve the enigma. He had no idea what he would do if he came across one and he did not linger on the thought. First he would find something to eat. Then he would somehow get back to Heliana for he feared something was about to happen to her.

After walking for half of an hour Llyat entered a large open space which he guessed must have been the central marketplace of the once prosperous city. Ruin lined streets radiated away as if lines on a sundial. In its centre, towering above the buildings that surrounded it, was the round object he had seen from afar. It was a perfect globe with various markings etched onto its stained marble surface. The enormous structure was held aloft by a pair of gargantuan naked statues, one a man and the other a woman. They stood back to back holding the sphere upon their shoulders. Around their feet were seven smaller figures in various poses which seemed to Llyat to be reaching up towards the two larger ones. He guessed at once what all this represented for he remembered the story he had heard tell on his travels. This was a depiction of the gods Egredor and Chalis with their seven children and they held aloft the world on which Llyat lived. It was the one thing in the city that did not appear to have been allowed to fall into ruin and Llyat thought it was beautiful.

As he walked towards the shadow that the mighty statue cast across the market place Llyat spotted two geckos that basked in the heat of the late morning light, warming their bodies with the life power that Solaris cast upon them. He paused for a moment and looked down to where they lay. For a second he felt the urge to pounce on one of them and consume it in a single swallow, but if these were indeed friends of Thamous then the last thing he needed was to bring down the wrath of the wyvern. It would be safer to leave them be. Feeling dizzy with his vision blurring he stumbled forward and fell upon one of the smaller statues. He knew at once what was happening. He was suffering from the effects of dehydration. If he did not find something to eat and drink soon then Heliana would have to walk the ground without him. Yet he was determined not to let that happen and so took a deep breath and steadied himself upon representation of Thinestar. He blinked several times and forced his vision to return. As he did so he focused onto one of the many cobbled streets that led away from the market place. There his eyes fell upon on a black spot in the distance and he tried make out what it could be. It seemed that the harder he tried to focus on the shape the more his vision played tricks with him. Squinting even more he thought perhaps it was Einar returning with food or even perhaps Thias and Irabo.

"I'm over here," he cried while waving his arms in the air.

Llyat continued to signal towards the black shape on the horizon when his vision cleared and he was able sharpen his focus. In that moment he realised the graveness of his mistake. The shape was that of the knight in black armour riding his horse.

"Fuck," cursed Llyat as he dropped his arms.

The terrified youth turned and began to run as fast as he could in the opposite direction. There seemed no logical explanation for his stupidity and as he ran he blamed the lack of sustenance for his actions. This was not the first time in his life he had not thought through the consequences of his actions. If he was to escape his pursuer and live to continue on his quest then he would have to put a stop to his recklessness. Thias was no longer there to protect him and he would have to find a way to survive what was coming. The sound of hooves clattered upon the cobbles while Llyat struggled through a stitch pain and air hunger. He was determined not to be caught and he had to get back to Heliana. He would not abandon her to a life without him and he still had to fulfil the Prophecy. The sound of the galloping horse grew ever closer. Llyat glanced back to check who it was that pursued him. It was the knight with the skull helmet. Llyat then caught his foot on one of the cobbles as he attempted to enter several ruined buildings in order to improve his chances of escape. He fell face first and landed with a thump onto the floor. His face exploded in pain as he burst his nose and spread much crimson over the adjacent ground. Then he heard the horse stop and its rider dismount. He attempted to regain his feet but as he rolled onto his back the armoured foot of the Commander crashed down onto his chest and prevented any hope of flight. Llyat looked up into the skull helmet and then the Commander spoke.

"Did you think I would give up boy?"

"Fuck you," snapped back Llyat.

"This that goes by the name of Calistorn has long been deserted," snarled the Commander. "Nothing lives in this hole save for a few feral Mathulath and the odd Kulkulkath. That being the case I know you must be one of the two shits that escaped from General Brosizrug and his inadequate ogres."

"Go jump on your sword," shouted Llyat after which he spat out a piece of tooth that had been dislodged on impact with the ground.

The Commander looked down and with a sudden swift swing of his good arm he removed the skull helmet from his head and cast it to the ground. Llyat stared at the grizzled, gaunt and pale features of the aging man before him.

"Brave words for one so young," sneered the Commander. "But it matters not. You'll be back with your friends before long. So tell me boy, before I cripple you to prevent you from escaping, who are you?"

"First tell me your name," replied Llyat. "Say who you are and then kill me for I am past caring for this life."

"Well if that's all it takes boy, I will indulge you," began the Commander as he drew his curved blade from its scabbard and pointed it at Llyat's neck. "My name is Rhaizen, Commander of the Knights of Avolire, and right hand to Sanura, Lady of the Silverwynn, last of her line. Now answer my question. Who are you? What did you want with the Sapphire of Barad Elestor? Who are your two accomplices who being now in chains will soon be on their way to Avolire? Where is other that you escaped with? Speak now and I will not harm you. The Lady wants you alive, but that doesn't mean I can't remove an eye or something else a boy of your age may value."

Llyat smiled. This Commander it seemed had no clue to who he was, that he was the true Marked mentioned in the Prophecy of Enderdetag. He realised in that briefest of moments that he still held the upper hand. Knowledge was power and he could use it to his advantage if only he could keep his mouth shut.

"You know only too well who I am?" said Llyat as the edges of his mouth turned up.

"I'll wipe that smile off your pretty face and leave it unrecognisable," responded Rhaizen. "Now let's play a guessing game. Perhaps you come from Avolire and for some reason of personal greed have decided to try and thwart our Lady's plans. By the way you are dressed you look more like one of the dragon fuckers of the Dragonas but you are far too puny to be one of their kind. I think it's more probable that your mother was just some pox ridden whore that I once had the unfortunate experience of fucking in some shit hole north of the Grey Mountains. "

Llyat's anger grew until his smile was replaced by a grimace of pure hatred.

"Don't you dare talk of my mother, not now, not ever, do you hear me?"

"Did I touch a raw nerve lad? Then perhaps I have stumbled on the truth after all. But that still doesn't tell me what you want with the Sapphire, one of the legendary Gems of Thamous. Tell me now before I render you unconscious and drag your worthless carcass back to my Lady. What is your name, you worthless piece of shit?"

Llyat gritted his teeth as he fought to remain rational. If Rhaizen knew the truth he would kill him there and then. Then for some bizarre reason he decided to tell him anyway.

"You murdered my father and my mother."

"No doubt they deserved it and I have killed so many over the years that it is of no consequence."

"My mother was Lyrusa Emgar," began Llyat as he clenched his fists in rage. "My father was Rukave Emgar. You killed my family, my friends and..."

Llyat did not have time to finish his sentence.

"You!" exclaimed Rhaizen as he raised his sword high up into the air with the intent to strike.

Llyat was about to close his eyes when from his left side a flashing blur collided with the Commander and threw him to the ground. In the next instant Llyat was free of the pressure from the armoured boot.

"Llyat!" shouted Einar over the sound of the startled horse. "Run, get away from here!"

Llyat wasted no time and was soon on his feet again. He looked down on what at first appeared to be a nighthowler wrestling with the Knight from Avolire. Then the pelt fell away and confirmed it was indeed Einar who had come to his recue. The aging knight with one good arm and the semi-naked Berserker wrestled together upon the dusty ground of Calistorn. Each punched and kicked as they tried to get the upper hand while Llyat looked around for somewhere to hide. He knew that to stay would be foolish but he also wondered how far he would get before being hunted down. Einar was fulfilling his role as promised and he owed it to the Berserker to flee to a place of safety. He raced towards the nearest wall and hoped that Rhaizen had not spotted the direction of his flight. There he hid and listened to the commotion in the street while trying to block out the sounds of the fight. Images of the attack on Maplehill flooded through his thoughts and it seemed that awful history was being re-enacted just paces away. Llyat had a chance to escape but his friend Einar did not. No, he could not leave the Berserker to die in Calistorn as he had once left Methladon Heyn to his fate.

Forcing himself to look from behind the wall he saw that both combatants were again on their feet. Einar held the Commanders curved blade and he swung it in front of him to keep the knight at a distance. Llyat then heard his friend cry out and as he looked again he saw Einar suspended in mid-air, his limbs pulled in different directions by some unseen force. The Berserker dropped the blade as the Commander stood motionless and dishevelled, his armour dented and scuffed, his sling long since ripped from his neck. Rhaizen extended his good arm and pointed a finger at the Berserker. Llyat sensed what was happening for it was the same magic that had been used on his father during the destruction of his home. He closed his eyes as painful images of his parent's death returned. Enough was enough and he had to do something. Llyat so wished he had Destiny's Song to hand but it either still remained in the ruins of Barad Elestor, embedded in the corpse of an ogre, or was being carried on to Avolire along with the sapphire. Llyat searched around for something he could use as a weapon and soon spotted a slither of rock, rough but dagger shaped, although bigger and heavier. He grabbed it with his right hand, jumped to his feet and then raced out from behind the wall. Without further thought for his own safety he jumped onto the back of the Commander and brought the shard of rock down onto the nape of the knight's neck. He thrust it into the unprotected skin with all the force of a terrified youth. Rhaizen howled in pain and threw Llyat from his back. Einar fell to the ground as the Commander's spell was broken. Rhaizen too dropped to his knees and clutched at his neck. Crimson spurted out from the edge of a deep wound and left spray patterns on his armour and the grey dusty ground. Llyat however wasn't finished. He jumped back onto his feet and with the shard of rock in his hand he charged back at Rhaizen. With another swing of his arm he lashed out with the jagged edge and severed the throat of the man who had killed his parents. Then Llyat took a slow step backwards and stared down at the fallen knight.

"Just fucking die!" he screamed.

The Commander of the Knights of Avolire clutched at his throat while torrents of red oozed through his fingers as they attempted to stem the flow. A gurgling noise then erupted from the knight's throat as horror and disbelief formed upon his dying face. Rhaizen did not take another breath and fell forward into the pool of red. Nor did he move again and yet Llyat was still not finished. He stepped up to the Commander's body and kicked it as hard as he could in the chest. Crimson bubbles flew from the gash in the severed beast's throat. Then Llyat kicked Rhaizen over onto his back and he dropped to his knees over the Commander's corpse. Without further pause he drove the splinter of rock into the dead man's face over and over again. He did not stop until it was beyond recognition.

"That's for my mother," he had cried as the stone's first blow struck its mark. "That's for my father. This is for the Heyns. This is for Catriana and Elita. This is for Denius and Mal. This is for...."

Before he got around to old man Chirth, Llyat felt a firm hand grip his shoulder and pull him up to his feet.

"You can stop now," said Einar. "He's well dead."

Llyat span around and held the shard of rock outwards and towards Einar to keep him at a distance. Excitement and adrenalin coursed through his body and he no longer felt scared.

"Where the fuck did you get too?" he cried.

"I was looking for food," replied Einar as he pointing to a dead Mathulath some paces away. "I thought I told you to stay put."

"And I bet you're so glad now that I didn't," snapped back Llyat.

"Yes, but you can drop the stone now."

Llyat continued to hyperventilate as Einar moved closer. The Berserker and then removed the shard of stone from the youth's hand and tossed it aside. Then he Llyat into his arms and hugged him.

"It's okay. Everything is going to be just fine."

Llyat pulled back, took several deep breaths, and stared at his friend. Then he looked to the crimson pulp that just minutes before had been the Commander's face. The feelings of hate dissipated to be replaced by a strong sense of purpose. There was no going back for the youth had crossed yet another threshold in his life. Never again would he be the same and once he had composed himself he began to smile. Somehow he felt Einar knew what he was thinking.

"So now what" asked the Berserker?

Llyat glanced up to Solaris and noted it had long passed the high point of its journey across the sky. Thias and Irabo had not appeared and that could only mean that Rhaizen had been telling the truth. His friends were being taken to Avolire. He and Einar would have to go on to the Eastern Marsh without them. Then after another sigh Llyat felt his stomach rumble. Turning to Einar with a degree of confidence he had never before experienced he gave his first order.

"First we eat. Then we finish this."

23

"What do you mean stolen?"

Tonousa Amberstone sat on one of the ornate wooden chairs that had been set out for guests in Lady Fullbane's solar. Amid the maze of her investigation a path had finally formed and it had brought her almost full circle. Once again she found herself in the company of the woman who had been saved from choking by the cordwainer of Valameer. This time however it was not the warm rays from Solaris that illuminated the great woman but the pale grey-blue beams of the goddess Mona. Mystic fingers silhouetted the enormous Lady against the window. This weak light was supplemented by several tapers that burnt atop of golden candlesticks, themselves scattered about the room. The radiance caused the Lady's silken gown to glow fiery silver before their flickering dance. While Tonousa sat and stared at Lady Fullbane her thoughts returned to the abattoir on Shaylotte Street and the events that had led her to visit this most peculiar chamber of the highborn. She recalled the coincidence of seeing a small pool of blood on the throat of Falaz Al Hizdor which she had linked with Danisun's comment about saving the life of the Lady. If Theoplous was correct she could not ignore such a coincidence and felt it her duty to explore the new concept. The shape of the crimson stain had reminded Tonousa of Thias's instruction that she should seek to locate Thamous's ruby. This memory, coupled with Danisun Dain's reference to Lady Fullbane while Darchus lay beneath an enormous pig had unlocked a sub consciousness thought process that linked all her ideas as one. They had told her exactly where she needed to look. In that brief moment within the slaughter house Tonousa had recalled where she had seen a ruby necklace once before. It was the first time she had visited the solar and it had hung down from around the neck of Thinata Fullbane between two enormous saucer sized nipples and made visible by the woman's then transparent morning attire.

Tonousa sighed. She could not believe what she had just heard. The one lead in the search for the ruby, the clue that seemed to make so much sense, had just slipped from her grasp as would a lamprey in a bucket. It added to the sense of hopelessness that festered inside her heart.

"It is just like I said Tonousa, I woke up one morning and the stone was gone from its chain," added Lady Fullbane as if the jewel had no real value. "Just the clasp and the golden rope remain."

Tonousa looked across the room to the one other present. If anything ever went missing from inside the Keep, it fell to the Lord Chamberlin to investigate and decide if any crime had been committed. Once Lady Fullbane had been made aware of the reason behind Tonousa's impromptu visit she had insisted that Gilebin Ystafell be present. Even though he was at first reluctant to join them deep into the night due to the quantity of fortified wine he had consumed with his supper, he was at last persuaded to make his way to the Lady's solar.

"I see Lady Fullbane," began the Chamberlin in his usual lisping manner. "However, forgive me for saying so but you don't seem at all put out by the fact that the ruby has gone."

"It was but a trinket Lord Ystafell," she replied as she tucked the golden chain back down into the depths of her voluminous cleavage. "Just a memento of times long past."

Tonousa glanced towards the Lord Chamberlin and could tell what he was thinking. He knew that Tonousa as a member of the City Watch was there to uphold the law but he was still unsure as to whether any crime had been committed.

"Why didn't you report this sooner? Why didn't you tell someone?" demanded Tonousa.

She had half expected Ystafell to back her up with some questions of his own but it was as if he had been struck dumb.

"It doesn't matter," replied Fullbane as she uttered a nervous giggle. "It was just one of many baubles my Enguerrand gave me before his unfortunate death. I have tried to put his memory behind me given the sadness it stirs in my heart. I try to focus my desires on younger meat these days, if you get my drift!"

Tonousa's ears picked up the comment in an instant. It seemed to her that there could be more to the story than Fullbane had so far divulged. It was strange that the ruby which she sought had been hidden in plain sight for so many years, so obvious to all who would have looked upon it and yet none had made the connection with Thamous's infamous jewel. It seemed that Fullbane was ignorant of the stone's true significance but perhaps the dismissive behaviour was just an act to throw Tonousa off the trail. Yet it was too much of a coincidence to ignore this particular ruby and she would follow the ways of the Cuvar and pursue the connection.

"I have lost count of all the jewellery that my husband procured for me over our years together," Lady Fullbane rambled. "Forget that piece of costume tat Tonousa Amberstone. Maybe there is something else I can tempt your interest in. A ring perhaps, a tiara, or even a golden locket."

"No thank you Lady Fullbane."

Tonousa raised her hand and stopped the Lady as she reached for a silver bell with which to summon her servants.

"It was the ruby I came to enquire about and nothing else."

"Pity," replied Fullbane as she leaned back into her chaise longue. "With such lovely eyes, something that sparkles around your neck would bring out their colour so well."

Tonousa sighed. Once again it seemed that her investigation had stalled. She felt the urge to shake the highborn lump but instead turned her attention to Ystafell who continued to listen with indifference to all that passed between the two women. If she were to have any hope of finding the ruby she would have to recruit the assistance of the Lord Chamberlin. Ystafell was not one of the four that her father had suspected and remained an innocent within the unfolding drama.

"Do you think there is any chance we could recover this missing jewel if stolen?" she asked.

"Knowing half of the servants down in the Underkeep as well as I do, then I would not hold out much hope of success in such a venture," lisped Lord Ystafell. "Most of the greedy little shites would seek to line their own their pockets with anything their paws could pilfer. They would sell such a valuable prize as quick their grimy little fingers could snap. The Thieves Guild would pay a high price for it.

"So you believe Lady Fullbane's jewel has most likely left the Citadel?"

"Not at all," replied Ystafell. "You see the doors to Lady Fullbane's chambers have not been forced open. The locks remain intact."

Tonousa glanced over towards the door at which Ystafell pointed. He was correct. There was no sign of forced entry and that left but two possibilities. The first was that one of Fullbane's own servants had stolen the ruby from off the chain. The second was far more interesting.

"Who else had access to the keys that would open Lady Fullbane's chambers?" she asked.

"Apart from her servants and myself, the one other with access, on the ground of security you understand, is Sir Byddin."

Tonousa sighed. One of her four suspects had resurfaced. She turned towards Lady Fullbane.

"Is it true that Sir Byddin has keys to your chambers? Did you know that?" she asked.

"Like the Lord Chamberlin says," she replied. "It was in the interest of security, that's all. I know you all think that I am desperate to bed anything with a heartbeat but the one eyed freak does nothing for my wanton appetite!"

"Lady F… F…Fullbane," stammered Lord Ystafell, shocked at what he had just heard. "Control yourself please. That is no way to talk about a member of Phauless Gylewu's Council."

Tonousa wondered what insult the monstrous woman would throw out next. She sensed some connection with Sir Byddin that the Lady was unwilling to divulge. There seemed an even deeper level to the mystery. Suspecting lust and blackmail was at play she returned to address the disappearance of the ruby.

"Lord Ystafell, if one of the servants has taken the jewel then there may yet be a chance that we could recover it. What more could you do to assist me?"

"I can ask around the servant's quarters and see what information I can gain from the grubby little buggers," replied Ystafell as he sought to remain awake. "I'll see what I can do, but I do have to ask, why all this sudden interest in the theft of a piece of Lady Fullbane's jewellery for which even she holds little value? I thought you had more important tasks to occupy your time Tonousa. Are you not supposed to be looking into all that Death Tubaria nonsense?"

Tonousa looked towards the Chamberlin and then back towards Lady Fullbane. She sighed for she could not divulge the importance of this part of her investigation. Neither could she talk to him of her father's message and the names of the four key suspects. She dare not mention the Gems of Thamous and their importance to the Realm's continued survival. It would be impossible to describe her bizarre dream or her new insight into the power of coincidental events. It was all too much to take in.

"To protect my sources, all I can say is that things are very complicated."

"Fair enough," replied Ystafell. "We all have our own business to attend to and I will take the importance of your questions on trust. I will not push you for answers nor indeed waste anymore of my time in trying to second guess your motives and intentions."

"I thank you for that Lord Chamberlin," replied Tonousa.

"I'll leave you now to talk with the servants and see what I can discover."

Tonousa thanked the Lord Chamberlin who bowed and exited the room.

Inhaling several times Tonousa searched her thoughts for anything she could have missed so far. She became obsessed with the idea of having overlooked something of great importance which would have led her to Fullbane sooner. The path to the Lady had formed in her dream but it had not come soon enough. Other than the slim chance of Ystafell turning something up in the Underkeep there seemed little hope of quickly locating the missing gem and time was of an essence. Then, in a moment of reflection, she tried to understand why out of all the people in the Realm, the ruby had fallen into the hands of Lady Fullbane, someone who appeared to be both ignorant of everything beyond her lips. Yet time and time again the Lady forced her way into Tonousa's thinking. Sensing she was on the right track she believed Fullbane was holding something back.

The Lady reached forwards to the table and picked up the small bell where it had sat in silence. She held it between her swollen fingers and began to generate a pleasant tinkle.

"Lady Fullbane, I hope you don't mind being..." began Tonousa, however Fullbane was quick to cut off the flow of her words.

"Please, first things first Tonousa Amberstone. You must join me in some midnight refreshment, some fruit perhaps, maybe some cheese and wine? I even have some smoked pizzle if you would prefer it! And of course wine, plenty of wine."

Tonousa tried her best not to lose her patience. Once again the mountainous woman was focused on filling her stomach and after the events of her last visit Tonousa did not relish the thought of staying to watch her eat. It had only been through Darchus's quick thinking that the whale had been saved yet it seemed the glutton had not learned anything from her recent near death experience.

"I thank you for your offer but this time I will give it a miss," she replied.

Tonousa then bit her tongue; it was not her place to warn Fullbane of the dangers of carrying so much weight. The Lady giggled and a hint of embarrassment formed upon her ball-like face.

"Fair point girl, maybe just for now I'll give my jaws a rest and stick to the drink."

"Yes, that would be a good start Lady Fullbane!"

Tonousa noticed a sudden change in the Lady's demeanour as she adjusted herself on her chaise longue. Her smile changed into a lecherous grin.

"I have to ask you; will your handsome friend be joining us again this evening?"

"I'm afraid Darchus is at present in the infirmary, if that is whom you refer to," replied Tonousa as she too smiled. "He took a nasty blow to the back of the head earlier today but you know young men, they soon get back on their feet."

"That is so true my dear. My Enguerrand was forever injuring himself while away serving our Sovereign Lord. But he always bounced back as quick as you like. Oh, he was such a resilient man, well at least until his unfortunate accident, if you know what I mean?"

"I do know for I have heard the detail of his death from the official record," replied Tonousa as the image her scrawny husband suffocating popped back into her thoughts.

"It's such a shame that the lad is not coming for I would like to reward him in my own special way for saving my life. He is such a good looker too. Remind me of his name again."

"Darchus," sighed Tonousa. "Darchus Arillius."

"And where did you say he was from again? "Valameer I think you..."

"Lady Fullbane please," snapped back Tonousa. "I have further questions that I need to ask you about your ruby necklace..."

"Oh, forget that worthless thing."

"No, I must insist that I am allowed to continue; the necklace I need to know of its origin."

"I have already told you Tonousa. My late husband gave me that trinket."

"And from where did your husband obtain it?" asked Tonousa.

"Oh, it was all so many years ago...."

"Lady Fullbane, please," demanded the irritated warrior.

Fullbane forced a sigh.

"My, my, Tonousa Amberstone," she began. "It would appear from your persistence and obvious frustration that there is more to my necklace than I ever envisaged."

"Look Lady Fullbane, please listen to me. I am just trying to do my job. If we are to make any headway in retrieving your stolen property, I need to know where the ruby came from. Only then may I ascertain its true value and in which market it will be sold. Do you now understand?"

Lady Fullbane rolled her eyes up into their sockets.

"Oh very well," she mumbled. "But let's make it a short conversation. This fixation on my costume jewellery bores me."

"Of course."

Tonousa sensed an opportunity to make progress but before she could open her mouth to speak the door to the room flew open and Heliana entered. She was dressed in her blue and white dress with her blonde hair tied up in a bun on the top of her head. Tonousa had jumped up at the unexpected opening of the door. Her hand had fallen at once to her sword but it dropped away on recognising the young servant.

"Do you want something my Lady?" snapped back Heliana. "You rang your bell I believe!"

Lady Fullbane attempted to turn her neck but its multiple rolls resisted the action.

"Yes I did ring, but do not get so angry about it. I know you have been feeling under the weather these past few days but there is still an expected way to behave in the presence of a highborn. I'll forgive your rudeness once child but do not embarrass me in front of my guests ever again."

"Thank you for your understanding your Ladyship," replied Heliana as she curtsied and blushed at the same time. "How may I be of service to you?"

"Bring me wine and an extra goblet for my guest."

"Yes, of course my Lady."

Tonousa watched Heliana leave the room. If the girl was indeed ill it would explain why she had not visited The Murdered Wolf during the past week.

"Is she under the weather?" asked Tonousa. "Do you know what is wrong with the poor girl?"

Lady Fullbane once again tried to make herself comfortable.

"I haven't the slightest idea. Young Ourri found her with her head in one of my gazunders, emptying her stomach contents for all to see. She denies having eaten anything tainted and has shown no sign of the pox or similar afflictions. If I was to hazard a guess, and given my knowledge of the ways of women, I would say that the young girl is with child. However when I questioned Ourri he said most thought Heliana preferred eating hairy fish, if you get my meaning. I would rather not spell it out to you."

"I think I follow your meaning," replied Tonousa.

It was obvious to Tonousa that if Heliana was indeed pregnant then the father of the child was without doubt Llyat for she had noted the strength of the attraction between the young couple. Knowledge of their feelings for each other it seemed had not percolated throughout the Underkeep prior to their travels to Valameer. Tonousa would need to talk with Heliana but right now she had unfinished business.

"My Lady, please may we get back to the issue that we were discussing before this latest interruption. Your ruby; from where did Lord Enguerrand obtain the necklace?"

Lady Fullbane once again rolled her eyes and sighed.

"First of all please understand that the necklace you speak of wasn't always a necklace. When Enguerrand was given the ruby he had it fashioned into one and then gave it to me in on my thirty fifth birthday."

"I see," added Tonousa, "but how did he come by it?"

"If I recall correctly, it was some fifteen summers ago that Enguerrand first came into possession of the stone that once sat upon my ample bosom. He said it was a present for all that we had done for him."

"Him? Who is this him?" asked Tonousa at once.

"He was a Historian that came from the lands beyond the Dirmark. Some say he'd been wandering the Realm looking into the demise of the civilizations of old and carried with him many of the trinkets that he had found on his travels. He even sold a few to a then rather young Llys Emeny I might add. The ruby belonged to the Historian. It was the most valuable of all his possessions and it surprised me when he handed it over to Enguerrand in gratitude for his assistance."

"This Historian," continued Tonousa as she racked her memory to remember where and in what context she had heard him mentioned before. "I think that I recall you talked of him during my interview with Lady Emeny, before your accidental..."

"Let's not discuss that mishap again," interrupted Fullbane as she raised her hand out in front of her body. "We've already been there once this evening and it pains me to think how that day I almost passed from this world. There is no reason to go over it all a second time."

"I apologise. Please do continue. The Historian..."

"Your memory is good; I did mention the man once before Tonousa. He became close friends with my husband and through conversations we were informed that the jewel came from an ancient dwarf crypt he had stumbled upon somewhere on the boarders of Dirmark. Do you know something, he made quite an impression on people, that man. He even managed to woo Enguerrand's sister during his time in Parandor."

Lady Fullbane paused for a moment as she tried to recall facts about the Historian.

"You speak of him like he had no name Lady Fullbane. By what was he called? You said he originated beyond the Dirmark, but where did he come from before he arrived in Parandor?"

"You know something my dear, in the five years that I knew him I was never completely sure that he was ever telling the truth. He was too shifty for my liking, always watching you and trying to work out your innermost secrets. It was like he was hiding something, a great secret of some sort."

"But what name did he give you? He must have answered to something."

Tonousa waited as the Lady paused and tried to remember. How she wondered did this mysterious Historian fit into her investigation. Once again the words of her dream skipped through her mind; 'A path will form.' It was perhaps another coincidence.

"If my memory serves me right, his name was Rukave, or something very similar. But like I said, I couldn't trust him. I was never too sure if that was his real name or not."

"And this man," continued Tonousa "This man called Rukave, what was his purpose here in the Capital. What did he want in Parandor?"

"As I recall, he turned up some fifteen years ago and entered Parandor with a young child in tow. The kid was no more than two or maybe three years old. He told everyone he was a wandering traveller from beyond Dirmark and that the child's mother had succumbed to the venom of one of those large scorpion like buggers that inhabit the Grey Mountains."

"Do you mean kulkulkath?"

"Yes, them," continued the Lady. "The Historian, Rukave, or whatever we will choose to call him, was first denied entry into Parandor by that shit Blackfayer. You know what that man was like with his rules and stipulations."

"Yes, I do. I remember only too well."

"Well, it was down to Fate that my Enguerrand happened upon the Historian and his child at the North Gate as he returned from one of his diplomatic excursions to Valameer. He took pity on them for some reason and even helped them gain access to the city. I still do not understand why the Historian didn't use his stash of valuables to bribe the City Watch."

"We're not all corrupt," grunted Tonousa.

"That's as maybe," continued Lady Fullbane. "My Enguerrand saw to it that the boy and his father were looked after by our servants and given everything that they needed. During the five years that they stayed in the city my husband helped find lodgings that suited the status of an important scholar. It was through his tales of the north that this Rukave informed us of all of the places he had visited, the Dirmark, Calistorn, and even Avolire. That was Enguerrand's weakness. He'd always had an interest in that awful place. Did you know that they once had the vilest ways to torture people that you could ever imagine? Well, I digress Tonousa. It was through these tales that my Enguerrand's friendship with Rukave grew and my dear husband became fascinated with the history of Avolire. He and Blackfayer also. Oh, and your father too Tonousa if I remember rightly. I'm surprised your farther never mentioned the Historian or introduced you to him."

"My father kept a lot of secrets," replied Tonousa as she reflected on the cards and letter she had found in the wall. "But Xix Blackfayer? Why would he have wanted to befriend the Historian?"

"That I cannot answer," continued Lady Fullbane. "But there were many who were interested in the stories and objects that friend Rukave brought with him from Avolire. As I have already told you, Lady Emeny for one, and Sir Byddin another. Even Jonas Tullage was taken in by all that the Historian had to say before he was arrested. Then of course Enguerrand's sister Lyrusa found him more than fascinating, so much so that after two years they were married."

"So this Rukave, what happened to him?" asked Tonousa. "Where did he go? Why did he leave the city? Is he still alive?"

Lady Fullbane laughed.

"Is everything alright?"

"I'm fine. I'm fine. I'm just so surprised at the questions my neckless has surfaced."

"I hope you won't mind answering a few more of them," replied Tonousa.

"If you insist then so be it, but let me continue while the story is still clear. It was about ten years ago, during the time that Heward Teulu first came to Parandor and just as the snake of Death Tubaria first started to raise its foul head. I recall that Enguerrand told me something most interesting. It seems that one day Rukave saw something in at Court and it was enough to twist his bowels. It frightened the life out of him. Anyway that's what he told Enguerrand in front of me. He said it was time to act; that it was time for him to go."

"Go?" queried Tonousa. "Go where?

"Of that I have no idea. All I know is that the Historian fled that night, aided by Blackfayer and your father. He took the boy and Lyrusa with him, and gave Enguerrand the ruby that you now seek."

Tonousa closed her eyes as a myriad of questions flowered in her mind. She tried to work out her father's role in the story and how Blackfayer could fit into the plot. She was determined to find out who the Historian was and what had happened to him. Perhaps he and the boy were still alive. Then she began to think why the scholar would give the ruby away and pondered on what he saw that could have spooked him so much. The answers alluded her.

"What was it that frightened Rukave so much that he fled the city?"

"That's where my memory fails me," continued Fullbane "All I know is that he left as soon as he could and took Lyrusa and the boy with him. From what Enguerrand later told me he went into hiding somewhere along the Tiaryer."

"Did you ever see him again?"

"No, he just vanished. Enguerrand never heard from his sister again, not a single letter or even a whisper from travellers of the Realm. It was as if one of those weird buggers from the Wizard's Guild had cast some form of enchantment and made them invisible. My husband did however tell me once after a skin full of wine that he believed he knew where they had headed for. He added that Blackfayer knew more but had refused to share any further information. Said I liked to talk too much and of course he was right. Even if he had known the location I doubt he would have told me. Enguerrand did say that one day he would go and check on them all and make sure they had settled into their new lives but then all that business with Tullage and Death Tubaria plunged us into anarchy. Did you know that Tullage had even murdered his own wife and kept her in a cupboard in the Underkeep with the intent of using the spells from that infernal book on the corpse? The mad bastard believed he could bring people back from whatever exists after death. He was convinced he could reanimate the stiff and the cold."

"Yes, I know something of that story," added Tonousa.

Tonousa did indeed know of the horrors that Tullage had subjected people to through the dark days of Death Tubaria. There were many tales of heinous crimes committed on innocent children as the mad doctor had experimented on the process of resurrecting the dead. She had lived through the rise of the cult and had apprehended several of its followers. A knock sounded on the door.

"Come in," shouted Lady Fullbane.

The door opened and Heliana strode in. She appeared to be less agitated and carried a silver tray upon which lay an ornate decanter and two goblets of similar design. While walking behind the chaise longue, she made eye contact with Tonousa. It was obvious that she had been crying. Heliana placed the tray upon the table and poured the wine.

"Your grape tonic my Lady," said the subdued servant.

"Thank you Heliana, now run along, there's a good girl."

Heliana turned and made her way out through the door, drying her eyes on her sleeve as she went. The action did not go unnoticed as Tonousa watched like an owl on a vole. She somehow sensed the truth but tried not to show it. Lady Fullbane finished her first cup of wine.

"I'm sorry to keep pushing you Lady Fullbane but if I could just confirm a few other things."

"Of course," replied the mountain as she refilled her goblet."

"So the Historian Rukave and your sister in law went into hiding somewhere along the river? You said Xix Blackfayer and my father assisted your husband in hiding them. Did they tell you anything else? I can't believe that even Blackfayer could hold someone's confidence for that long before using what he knew against them."

Tonousa paused once again. The hate for the man that had framed her father threatened to cloud her judgement. Fullbane finished her second goblet of wine, poured herself a third, and began again.

"I knew nothing about the meetings and discussions that the four men convened. I was never invited to share in their private discourse and at the time I never wanted to do so. However, now I come to think of it, Rukave the Historian grew ever more paranoid each year he lived in the Capital. He was suspicious of anyone he met and used to look at most like they weren't human. Only the gods know what he was looking for."

Tonousa wondered if Rukave had been aware of the presence of a shape changer within the Citadel. That however was over ten years ago and it seemed inconceivable that the swine she sought could have been spying on the Court for that length of time.

"Stranger things have happened in the history of the Realm," said Tonousa.

"Indeed," replied Fullbane

Tonousa then sat and pondered on what she had heard. It was clear that this Historian was linked to her investigation somehow, even if only at its periphery. What was more important was that that for the first time Tonousa believed she had direct proof that the jewel that she was looking for existed and that it was indeed one of the Gems of Thamous. She broke from her thoughts as Heliana returned with a second decanter of wine and began topping up the grotesque guzzler's goblet. Tonousa had not yet taken a sip of her own and did not dare to drink. She needed to make excuses before Fullbane began to embarrass herself and it was vital that she remembered all the information she had uncovered. Time was running short for she also had to call out the Watch and charge them with finding both the thief and the missing jewel.

"I won't take up any more of your time Lady Fullbane," said Tonousa as she stood from her seat. Lady Fullbane continued to slurp away at her wine allowing some to splash out and dribble down onto her clothes. "I have more than enough information to begin a search for your missing ruby!"

Tonousa bowed and turned towards the door but Fullbane called out.

"Yes that's it," she exclaimed. "I knew there was something I'd forgotten."

"And what would that be," asked Tonousa with more than a little excitement in her voice?

"It was just a word. It was a single word. Nonsense I think."

"And what was it?"

"The word was Cuvar. The four kept repeating it although I had no understanding as to what or who it referred."

Once again Tonousa smiled. This was further confirmation of the connection between the Historian Rukave and her attempt to unmask the murderer. Despite her excitement she was troubled by her father's link and by the possibility that Blackfayer could have been Cuvar, given the way he had turned on her father. She needed more time to think about this new evidence but she knew this was not the time and place. If she was to catch the thief she needed to call out the Watch.

"Thank you Lady Fullbane. You have been most helpful. I will endeavour to return your jewel as soon as possible."

"No, I must thank you Tonousa Amberstone. You are a credit to your dear departed father."

Tonousa turned and made her way through the door and into the corridor beyond. She spotted Heliana leaning against the wall and immediately feared for the young girl that she could read like a scroll. She stopped beside the young woman and then called back to Lady Fullbane.

"Please may I borrow Heliana for a brief time? I have an errand for her."

"By all means, but bring me more tonic when you return Heliana, there's a good girl," slurred the sot as she downed more wine.

"Once again I thank you my Lady. Come on Heliana, follow me," ordered Tonousa as she strode off down the corridor.

Heliana followed as ordered and the moment that the two women were well clear of the door, Tonousa scanned the corridor. There was not a soul in sight and all appeared secure in their beds.

"Are you well?" asked Tonousa.

"What is it you demand of me now?" snapped Heliana. "What else do you want me to do?"

Tonousa was taken aback by Helena's aggressive response.

"What's wrong? You do not seem your normal self."

"I'm fine," grunted back Heliana. "I've never felt better."

"Oh no you're not. You are far from it."

Tonousa pushed her face close to Heliana's and looked deep into her eyes. Amid the blue orbs Tonousa saw the sadness that engulfed the young woman. Then Heliana began to cry. Tonousa threw out a comforting arm and the pair moved down deeper into the shadows of the corridor.

"I'm so scared Tonousa," sobbed Heliana as she attempted to wipe away her tears.

"What is it? What's wrong?"

"I think..."stuttered Heliana through her tears, "that I'm with child."

"Are you certain?"

"I haven't gushed this month," replied Heliana.

"Oh, I see. But it's, good news, isn't it?"

Heliana sobbed and Tonousa detected her friend's sense of isolation.

"It's Llyat's child and I am at a loss as to what to do for the best."

"I see," replied Tonousa as Heliana sank into her embrace.

"I can't be fucked up, I just can't," howled Heliana. "Lord Ystafell will kick me out if I am carrying a bastard. It's not like I know a trustworthy inn keeper to look after the child once it's born. I will end up out on the streets with nowhere to go just as the city begins its war with Avolire...."

Tonousa looked deep into the young girl's eyes and saw great fear. She had to say something that would help.

"Heliana, you can trust me, I will look after you."

"But..."

"Listen to me girl, everything will be fine, that I promise. No one who works in the Underkeep will punish you. I sense that even Lady Fullbane has a wealth of compassion buried somewhere inside her mountainous chest. You are not going anywhere."

"Thank you so much for your support," sobbed Heliana. "What service do you require of me?"

"I have no task for you Heliana. I just wanted to get you on your own so we could talk."

"Well now you know it all," she sobbed.

Tonousa hugged the young woman and wondered what it must be like to be pregnant.

24

The steel sword, decorated with inlaid bronze, bounced off the black orichalcum armour of the Knight from Avolire. The man who swung the blade was a warrior of another kind for he was clad in gold. His intent was clear for he meant to strike down the evil one and destroy him for all time. The sword was not alone as it recoiled off the black metal for the tears of the gods sprayed down from above and bounced from the metal plates of the two who fought to the death. For hour after hour the rain continued in torrents as the golden warrior sought to destroy his opponent but the man in black was too powerful and would not yield. It seemed to eyes that watched that the golden one that he had no realistic chance of winning.

Around and around they circled, locked in an eternal combat, while behind them a great battle raged before a burning city. He who swung the blade could not recall the name of the place that grew from the edge of the mouth of a mighty river. In fact its name did not seem at all important. What mattered most was the defeat of his nemesis and those that followed him; the host of others he would need to dispose of if he was to win the day. All about him other knights battered away at each other as did a large number in leather armour that fought a swarm of reptiles. For the knights it was a battle not just of colour, gold against black, but also sigil against sigil. Those who wore the steel carried the golden cross over four coloured triangles while that of the men in black depicted beasts astride a checked shield. Each warrior fought the other with ferocious intent, thrusting steel against steel and smashing iron against iron. As men and beasts were cut down the mud sodden field became a lake of crimson soup. There was no rest for the warriors as no matter how many were slain, others took their place. It was an endless war, one destined to last until the end of time.

Once again the black knight defended a flurry of blows from his opponent. His shield parried most of them and the rest were blocked by his sword. As the golden one paused for breath the black knight thrust forward with his own curved blade and it penetrated his opponent's chest. The golden knight stumbled forwards and fell to his knees. In one swift movement the Knight from Avolire swung his weapon and decapitated his foe. The golden body slumped to the ground while its head fell some distance away. The black knight looked at the face within the helmet as it lay in the stinking mud of the field of slaughter. Eyes widened in disbelief as the gold knight's visor fell back and revealed the identity of his fearsome foe. The black knight could not understand what he saw. It was his own face that peered back at him from within the golden helmet. He struggled to understand how that could be while he threw down his shield and removed his own helm. Then he checked his face with his gauntlet covered hand. It was beyond all reason. There had been another, identical in features. He was at a loss to understand the meaning of it all.

"Methladon," shouted a voice that echoed across the battlefield. "Listen to me!"

The images of battle began to blur as he focused on the voice that called to him. The warrior found himself being dragged back into a different reality. The Seer's Stone would reveal nothing more this time. His eyes flickered as they attempted to adjust to light of the room, illuminated by seven candles. Amid the shadows of the Lady of the Silverwynn's chamber, the blacksmith's son sat before a wooden dresser. The sceptre of Urthanock rested with ease in his hands while the Dagger of Kha lay before him. The evil emerald in its hilt had lost its power over him and he was longer afraid.

Methladon then felt a hand fall upon his shoulder. Once again the voice that had dragged him out of the stone spoke.

"Methladon! Can you hear me?"

He knew the voice, brushed aside the hand from his shoulder, and then stared at the dwarf through the mirror before his eyes him. The diminutive man from the Dirmark was dressed in full armour and was both annoyed and concerned.

"What do you want Grovrouk," growled Methladon.

"You've been looking into that stone again. You're obsessed with it."

"And what if I am. What business is that of yours?"

Methladon looked through the reflection in the mirror and saw the little man's unease. He did not care what Grovrouk thought for the dwarf mattered little in the plans that he was formulating. Neither did he fear the dwarf's warnings of the consequences of looking into the stone, hour upon hour, day after day, for he was certain Urthanock's sceptre could not control his mind.

"I'm trying to help you, you pig headed piece of shit," continued Grovrouk as he replaced his hand upon Methladon's shoulder only for it to be brushed aside a second time. "I need you to find your humane side again. I need you to begin to care for the soul you lost down in the caverns of the Gathering. Something awful happened there and it has changed you for the worse. You have no time for your companions now and you speak to us as if we mean nothing more than the dirt on your boots. You are oblivious to fear and all that may happen to you. I'm trying to..."

Methladon readied his voice. It would be harsher than usual. Yet the mark on the back of his neck did not burn for he was in control of his anger.

"I know too well what I lost down in the darkness of that evil place. You left me to face the beast on my own. Yes, I have overcome my fears. I no longer worry about what future the gods may have mapped out for me. I say 'fuck the gods' for I cannot die and I will not be manipulated by them as they play their pathetic games. Why should I live in fear? Why should I worry what the Lady plans for me? If she wants me to open the doors to the Underworld then so be it. I am all powerful and I will not deny myself the chance to see into my future. Do not dare to try and counter my comments for I will not take heed of any tripe that spews from your mouth.

"I'm not saying that you shouldn't look into the stone or that the Lady should not take the throne of Parandor," replied Grovrouk. "Yet I have to warn you again of the power contained within the dagger and the sceptre. You are tapping into forces of which you have little understanding. You have seen what is happening to the Lady. She decays before our eyes and the gods alone know the reason for it. The powers that this room bestowed upon her essence have deserted her and now you..."

"What about me," demanded Methladon as he turned away from the mirror to look directly at the man from the Dirmark?

"I saw the way that you reacted when I first brought the Dagger of Kha into your presence. It almost destroyed you and yet now it sits there and you do not even flinch. What has happened to you Methladon? Where is the boy I first met in the cage, the one who cared about an innocent young girl and a woman with child..."

"And the point you are making short arse?"

"Forgive me when I say this my friend but you are no longer the blacksmith's son that was taken from Maplehill. You've changed Methladon and not for the better. The power that resides in you and feeds your immortality is corrupting your mind and body. The regenerative power of the Rift should have healed your scars and returned you to your old self, yet now you look more like..."

"Like what?" snapped Methladon as he rose to his feet.

He knew that he could kill the dwarf with little effort but he still had control of his anger. He sensed the dwarf's fear. In fact he could smell it.

"Tell me then hole-dweller. What do I look like when you gaze on me?"

"Like one of them."

"Like who?" he demanded Methladon as a deeper second voice dominated his own."

"Those fucking lizards," stammered Grovrouk. "You're even beginning to sound like them. You may not have noticed, but I have, and others have too. What has happened to you Methladon? What did Ssonsh and Ssleptaz do to you?"

As Grovrouk spoke, Methladon again looked at his reflection in the mirror and focused on the scars on his face. The dwarf was right. The burns had healed but left wounds like scales etched over one side of his face. As he listened to the dwarf's rant, he too wondered what had transpired.

"Don't listen to him," said the voice. "He knows nothing of your destiny."

"The Knights of Avolire are with...." continued Grovrouk, but Methladon turned and snarled.

"Fuck the Knights of Avolire!"

"Meth!" exclaimed Grovrouk.

"My name is Methladon Heyn."

"But..."

"Listen dwarf," he barked out. "If I could change anything then it is the curse of being able to understand your foul language. Do me a favour and piss off."

Methladon then sneered into the mirror. He knew that his words had hurt the diminutive stump. He did not care about such trivia now for he was focused on objects of far more importance, the Seer's Stone and the Dagger of Kha. Once again he picked up the sceptre, looked into the stone, and succumbed to its milky images.

Grovrouk snatched the sceptre from out of Methladon's hands. He then took several steps back towards the centre of the bedchamber. Methladon glared at the dwarf through the mirror and his hatred and anger boiled his soul, fuelled by the other voice that sought to control his thinking. Without warning the mirror fractured in several places and yet it did not fall to the floor.

"How dare you touch that object, you fucking imp of nonentity?" screamed his two voices.

"What has happened to you?" replied Grovrouk as he clutched the Sceptre and trembled.

"Didn't I tell you to piss off?" screamed Methladon as he stood large and loomed.

Grovrouk soiled himself.

"It doesn't have to be like this Methladon..."

"If you won't go then I will," replied the blacksmith's son.

The now Beast of Maplehill made his way towards the doors of the strange room. Once there he clicked his fingers and the two halves of wood swung open. On leaving he snarled one last time.

"If the sceptre and the dagger have been touched while I am gone then you are dead. Even the Lady will not save you. I will stuff you in the Lions myself. Do you understand?"

With that said he strode out of the room. The doors closed under their own volition and left the trembling dwarf to shed tears for the loss of the man he had once been proud to call friend.

Methladon wandered through the dark corridors of the ruined building. He was lost in his thoughts as he passed numerous Lizardman and several armoured knights moving through the shadows on business of their own. His thoughts returned to the dwarf's comments on his appearance and the scars that resembled the scales of the Lizardmen. He smiled for he liked that thought. His appearance had shaken Grovrouk and he wondered how many others had been disturbed by the nature of his new of his face as it had regenerated in a most unexpected way. He thought perhaps it was down to the power that resided within his essence rather than the magic of Lady's room. Perhaps it was also something to do with the Dagger of Kha but whatever the cause, it did not matter. His distinctive visage had a power of its own and he would not hide it from others. As Grovrouk had stated, he had changed and was no longer just plain Methladon Heyn, the youth who played at being a village warrior and who should have died so long ago. He was something else now and it felt all powerful.

Methladon touched the unaffected side of his face as he walked and the smoothness of its skin made him feel sick. He became filled with a revulsion for its texture and overcome with an intense desire to cover it. That was not the side he wanted others to see and he imagined making a helmet with a half visor to cover all but the scales. Then, as if out of nowhere, he spotted a discarded a helmet of orichalcum lying on the ground before him. He picked it up and with the magic contained in his fingertips removed half the visor as if slicing through soft cheese with an intense heat that emanated from their pulps He bent the metal with ease such that it then fitted his head and it somehow polished itself. His power and ability to manipulate the elements was growing ever stronger by the day. Now he would display only his reptilian side for that that would be more intimidating. Methladon suddenly felt in complete control of his rebirth.

After several minutes wandering amongst the ruins he stepped out into the long main street of Avolire. It was a place he had walked many times before and where he had witnessed the poverty of those who feared the war that was heading their way. The atmosphere was different than before. He was now surrounded by those who prepared for battle and the long march to Parandor. The many that formed the army of the Avolire busied themselves as they tried on armour while assisted by an equal number of shackled slaves. To Methladon they could not be considered true knights for they were impoverished and malnourished individuals who rattled around inside the metal plate that had been forced to wear. He knew they were a rabble and unfit for battle but he also knew that these innocents would form the first wave of the attack on Parandor and would give the true Knights of Avolire and the Lizardmen hoard a chance to detect and then attack the weak points of the Capital's defences. The Lady of the Silverwynn did not have a care for these sad unfortunates who had flocked to her side for protection and the hope of a better future. Such scum would hold no interest for her once they had served their purpose. As he continued to wander on down the street those who recognised him turned their heads away as they passed for they could sense the evil aura that his new persona projected.

"I know you can feel it," said the voice. "This is what you've always craved. You need never fear anything again."

Methladon smiled to himself for the voice spoke the truth. He passed several groups of wretches, dressed in grime encrusted rags and who stood around braziers in an attempt to keep out the cold of the night. Then he recognise the place that he had drifted into, the courtyard where he had first gazed up at the stars on the night following his release from the mines. It was the very same place that the dwarf had collected him from before the great change had begun. He moved towards a large piece of masonry that had fallen from the high crenulations of the outer ruined walls, a place had often sat and contemplated his future. There he noticed two rough looking men huddled around yet another makeshift fire. The two were not so in need of the fire as others he had passed for they wore black fur cloaks over their leather armour. In addition to the warmth provided the pelts part concealed the blades that hung at their sides but the beast knew they were there. Methladon guessed that they were mercenaries and he held such swine in contempt. He moved closer such that he could listen into their conversation for he was suspicious of their motives and sought to understand the true purpose for their presence in Avolire. As his ears tuned in he began to pick up the words spoken by the larger of the two.

"Do you remember what I spoke of in Fallguard, the story I told you L'Fare? The one about Nictis. All the stuff about him joining with the Knights of Avolire? Well, the rumour around here is that some whelp of a boy killed him down in that lion pit of theirs."

"Get out of here," sneered L'Fare as Methladon drew closer. "That's hard to believe but if true the bastard deserved it for the way he treated his brother."

"It's said that boy is now one of the Lady's toys," continued the first. "And you'll never guess what else?"

"Go on then," slurred the inebriated second. "What else have you found out?"

Methladon listened with great interest to this fated conversation.

"I've not yet worked out the Lady's motives, gathering us together with these slimy shits from the Marsh, but I have managed to gain employment in her service. You may find this difficult to believe but I have been appointed as her torturer and executioner. She has many prisoners on their way here and with Nictis dead she needed someone to continue his work. I put myself up for the job and she offered it to me once I had explained my expertise in such matters. I could not decline such an opportunity."

"So you've met her then Ventes?" asked the one called L'Fare "Is it true she is as beautiful as they say, that her tits are like perfect fruits and that her quim tastes of honey?"

"If you find crones attractive!" replied Ventes "Sorry, I forgot you fucked your granny's corpse."

"Fuck off!" snarled L'Fare "The Lady of the Silverwynn...Is she as all describe her? Was she...you know," he added while gesticulating.

"You haven't seen her yet! She's like a rotting corpse."

Methladon's anger grew as he was forced to listen to the insults cast against the Lady of the Silverwynn. The two sell-swords had agreed to fight for her cause and yet they dared to abuse the one who would soon be ruler of the Realm. He was about to walk away but the voice in his head thought otherwise.

"Do not let them talk of her like that despite her fading light."

"I advise you both to hold your tongue; the Lady has spies everywhere," ordered Methladon as he moved out of the shadows and startled the two men

"And who the fuck are you?" demanded Ventes.

Methladon looked back with menace but the two men were not intimidated.

"I am not your friend. Neither do I spy for the Lady.

"Then who are you?" demanded Ventes.

"Be careful, I don't like the look of this scale faced fucker," added L'Fare.

"What's your name snake face" demanded Ventes?

Methladon laughed in a strange manner which unnerved L'Fare. Ventes however held fast.

"That is for me to know," replied the beast. "I asked you your name."

"Let's just say that I am on the right side friend and that I am someone you can trust," added Ventes.

"I am not your friend and I suggest you both fuck off and leave this place," ordered Methladon as the two mercenaries dropped their hand to their swords.

"Hark at him L'Fare," said Ventes. "The mad bastard wants us to leave."

Ventes drew his blade from its sheath and pointed it at Methladon. L'Fare then mirrored his action. Methladon smiled for they could not hurt him. Again his inner voice issued its instructions.

"Kill them. Kill them both now. Use your power and be done with it."

Methladon's lips curled but the two mercenaries held their ground.

"I will ask you one last time. Leave now or you will not see Solaris rise."

"So, here you are! I have been looking for you everywhere," a hissed voice from behind.

Methladon turned to face the reptile Sslondash as the mercenaries sheathed their weapons.

"The Lady and Ssonsh wish to converse with you," added the Lizardman.

Methladon glanced to the mercenaries and replied. "Is it a request or a summons?"

"It will be to your advantage to hear what they have to say," replied Sslondash

"Where are they?" he asked.

"In the old church. I know you are familiar with that place for it was there that you first looked into the Seer's stone.

"So be it. I will not silence her messenger. Take me to her at once."

Sslondash began to move away from the brazier and Methladon turned to the mercenaries.

"I'll be back to sort you turds out later."

"And who the fuck do you think you are?" demanded Ventes.

"I'm the whelp that killed Nictis!"

The reborn turned to follow Sslondash and left the two mercenaries with jaws agape.

On his trek Methladon passed several more makeshift warriors preparing for war. Those that made eye contact with the former blacksmiths son had been drawn to the side of his face left uncovered by the half helm that he had created. They had stared at his scales and the cloudy eye which he had chosen to display. Sslondash did not once questioned his appearance and had somehow known where to find him. He then tried to guess the reason behind the summons. It had to be something so important that it would interrupt the Lady's preparations for war. Pools of water had formed on the uneven stone flags from recent rains. The wet, plus the debris from the collapsed ceiling slowed his passage across the once hallowed ground. At the far end of the temple, waiting for him on the raised stone platform, was a withered old crone. The once young and vibrant Lady of the Silverwynn was fading fast. Beside her stood the frog like creature known as Ssonsh and with whom she was engaged in whispered conversation. Methladon then noticed the shape-shifter called Ssleptaz who rested against the remains of an old pulpit while he sharpened his claws with a knife and listened to the Lady's conversation.

"I'm here! What do you want with me?" demanded Methladon

"I'm so pleased you could join us young Heyn," she answered. "I like your new look. You can now pass as a true servant of Avolire."

"Enough of such talk, what do you want of me?" repeated Methladon as climbed the platform.

"Will there be anything else my lady?" asked the Lizardman escort.

"Thank you, but no. That will be all Sslondash."

The Lizardman bowed in turn to the Lady of the Silverwynn and the frog priest Ssonsh. It then made its way back through the hall. Methladon turned to look at those who had summoned him.

"Well, what is that you want this time?"

"I assume you have witnessed the force of arms that I have ordered to mass in this city," replied the Lady. "This is the army that will march on Parandor and bring it to its knees. We will take their city in the name of Avolire and secure the throne for us both."

"I've seen the scum that flood the streets. They are but a rabble," he replied.

The Lady of the Silverwynn shot out her arm and gripped Methladon by the chin before he could move. She then forced his head to tilt from side to side and looked into his eyes with an intense curiosity. He wanted to push her away but decided to first listen to her words.

"I sense there is still a lot of anger inside you," she whispered as her eyes burned into his soul. "But don't let it control you Methladon. Be open to suggestions. Do not close your mind to..."

"Keep to the point old woman. What do you want from me?"

"That's it. Control the conversation," said his other voice.

The Lady of the Silverwynn glanced towards the two Lizardmen before releasing her gip on Methladon's face. Then she laughed in her most dismissive manner.

"I know you are aware of the Enderdetag Prophecy..." she continued.

"And what about it?" interrupted Methladon.

"Focus your eyes up there young Heyn," she continued while pointing to a gap in the roof with one of her withered hands. "Look to the stars and tell me what you see?"

Methladon focused into the dark night and there saw several dots of light in the centre of his field of vision. They looked like ordinary stars and he sensed nothing special about them.

"I don't..." he began.

"Look again Methladon Heyn," she continued. "Tell me all that you see."

The troubled youth glanced through the hole again and he looked at each individual star for several seconds before moving onto the next. He tried to fathom out what insight the Lady wanted him to gain from looking at them. In a flash it came to him. Their perfect alignment finally made sense.

"I see numerous stars. They are almost in a line. I have never noticed that constellation before. What does it signify? What does this all mean?" he asked

"It means that the Enderdetag alignment is at hand."

'Enderdetag'. It was that word again, the one he had first heard in the mines beneath the city. His fellow prisoners had talked of it and now the Lady was herself was fixated by the old prophecy.

"So what does this alignment..." he began before being interrupted by Ssonsh.

"These events were predicted in the writing of the Historian Rukave Emgar, translated from an inscribed tablet that he discovered in the Dirmark along with one of the Gems of Thamous. It had first been described by the Ancients and foretold the event we now witness."

"Do you know the words of that prophecy Methladon?" asked the Lady.

"I heard someone speak of it once, but I do not know the detail," he replied.

Everything was at last falling into place for the youth from Maplehill. Now he began to understand the significance of the mysterious conversations he had overheard, the cryptic clues left in his path by the Lady of the Silverwynn, her followers, and even the wyvern Thamous. If he was not the Marked he still found it hard to believe it could be Llyat Emgar whom he was certain had fallen during the destruction of Maplehill. The alignments appeared centred on him in some way. He was the all-powerful one and it was he would change the world forever.

"The words speak of the 'Marked' controlling the doors to the Underworld and destroying the Lord of Fear. I seek the power of that foul Lord," spat out Methladon. "That is what I desire most for then will I have the strength to bring down the House of Gylewu and all who support it."

"It is this same power that we have been harnessing through fractures in the Mighty Rift," added Ssonsh. "The power of the Underworld seeps into our reality through the cracks between the worlds. These powers, for some reason I am yet to understand, are now focused on you."

Methladon looked at the frog like creature who had confirmed what he had already begun to suspect.

"For some reason that even Ssonsh cannot fathom," continued the Lady, "the energy that manifests itself within my special room has deserted me. The power of Urthanock seeps through the Mighty Rift but it no longer bestows the gift of eternal youth upon my body. The Dark Lord has chosen you and you are the now the Vessel."

There again was that other word that tormented Methladon's thoughts. 'The Vessel', the object that the wyvern said needed to die. It all then made sense, why Thamous had wanted to kill him in the caverns beneath the Gathering. It was trying to prevent the return of Urthanock and his role in facilitating the evil Lord's return. Methladon smiled. He no longer worried about beasts such as Urthanock and there was nothing to fear from a spirit of the past. He would soon obtain his full power, one great enough to shape the Realm. Once again he looked to the wizen hag and pondered on the real reason that she had summoned him to her presence.

"When are you going to tell me what you want of me? I have already guessed that you need me to open the doors to the Underworld. Is that all you desire or is there something else you wish to discuss before I take my leave?"

"If these are the days of the Enderdetag..." began the Lady, but Ssonsh interrupted.

"It seems the time of the Prophecy has appeared before we have finalised out preparations. We will be forced to act before we are ready. We cannot allow the events described in the Prophecy to come to pass and for the Underworld to be sealed forever by the Gems of Thamous."

The doors to the church flew open and the Lizardman Sslashnash that Methladon had first encountered in Eastern Marsh raced down the central aisle. The Lady called out with what little strength she could muster.

"What is the meaning of this interruption?"

"I am sorry to burst in my Lady Silverwynn," replied Sslashnash as he gasped for air.

"You better have a good reason for coming here uninvited," croaked Ssonsh as he bellowed at his own kind. "Why do you dare to interrupt our meeting?"

Methladon looked on while the Lizardman gathered his breath. Ssleptaz remained silent but listened with great interest.

"General Brosizrug has returned!"

"So why the urgency?" croaked Ssonsh.

"I apologise for interrupting but the Ogre said you would want to have his news at once. It's to do with the sapphire and his prisoners."

"No doubt these are the ones from Barad Elestor, remember the message brought by the bird," said the Lady as a smile crept across her ancient face. "Tell Brosizrug to take the prisoners to the old prison and I will join him there. I have another task for him."

Methladon watched as Sslashnash remained still and started to tremble. Both Ssonsh and Ssleptaz recognised the signs of fear on their comrade's face.

"Well! What are you waiting for?" demanded the Lady.

"There is something else I must tell you," hissed Sslashnash.

"Then spit it out you pathetic reptile," she ordered.

"Not out loud my Lady. Someone may be listening."

Methladon sensed that Sslashnash had referred to him but he did not care what motive the Lizardman had, he would find out sooner or later for he was beginning to take control of the Lady's thoughts. She would tell him everything that he wanted. He then watched as the Lady moved to converse with Sslashnash, their voices lowered such that none could hear what passed between them. Methladon strained to listen but could not make out the words. He looked over towards Ssonsh and Ssleptaz who appeared in the process of devising some plot. They glanced back at him with their suspicious slit like eyes.

"What do you think they are talking about Frog?" snarled Methladon.

"Remember who you are talking to boy," hissed Ssleptaz as he pointed his dagger in Methladon's direction. "I could gut you here and now. No one would give an ogre's fuck."

"Piss off!" snarled back Methladon.

The youth stretched out his arm and clicked his fingers. In the next instant the knife in Ssleptaz's hand burned with an intense heat. It blistered the flesh that surrounded it and caused the changeling to drop his weapon and cry out in pain.

"Hurt him," cried the voice. "Make him suffer."

"You'll pay for that one day," hissed Ssleptaz as he took several steps back.

"Of course, I expected you to say nothing less," replied Methladon as he kicked the knife away.

The weapon clunked and clattered across the raised platform until it passed over its edge and fell into a pool of water. The noise of laughter that followed took Methladon by surprise. The croaking of the frog priest echoed through the hall.

"What's so funny?" demanded Methladon.

"The power of the Rift flows wildly through your essence," said Ssonsh "Just like me, you have a special relationship with its energy. I thought she was the special one when she came to us for help. She had a certain aura but she had nothing like your talents. Your skills will be much appreciated when she doesn't make it to the end."

Methladon noted the frog creature's lidless eyes flick towards the Lady of the Silverwynn.

"What do you mean? What do you know?" he asked. "Of course she will make it. She'll will sit on the throne of Parandor with me by her side. I have seen it come to pass."

Methladon then thought about the second time he had looked into the Seer's stone. He had sat on the throne without her. Now he realised what the stone had been trying to tell him, the Lady was dying!

"Explain all of this to me," he said.

"You've seen how frail she has become," answered the priest. "She will be lucky to survive a week at the rate she is aging. Urthanock has abandoned her and he has chosen you in her place."

"Yes, Yes," whispered the voice. "This is the power that you crave."

"I thought you didn't know the reason behind the power shift," said Methladon as he ignored the voice inside his head. "Yet you speak like you know what is happening to me. Do you believe that the Rift is responsible? Is it the power of Urthanock that feeds my curse mark and the reason why I cannot die?"

"Correct!" croaked Ssonsh. "But you haven't yet understood all that will soon be yours."

"If she dies before we take the city, the throne of Parandor will lie empty," said Methladon. "What then? Why should we then bother opening the doors of the Underworld? It will be pointless, unless..."

Methladon looked at the two Lizardmen who in turn glanced at each other.

"Think about it," said the voice. "If she is dying why wait. What has she got to lose?"

"She wants to bring forward her invasion, doesn't she?" said Methladon. "She wants to sit on the throne before she dies."

Once again Ssonsh croaked out a belly laugh. All the while the Lady of the Silverwynn remained focused on her conversation with Sslashnash.

"Again you are correct," replied Ssonsh.

"She is changing her plans isn't she? She doesn't want to open the underworld anymore. She wants me just as I am. I am her ultimate weapon?"

Ssonsh laughed but it was Ssleptaz that continued.

"You have become the key to our plan to open the Underworld. The Marked, the one spoken of in the Enderdetag prophecy, is either dead or has vanished into the mists. She is dying and she knows it. Even so she will do anything she can to gain revenge over the house of Gylewu. If it means using you the way you are now then that is what she will do."

Methladon tried to make sense of the Lady's intentions. If she was to bring her attack forward then there would be no need of the gems, except to keep them from any other who would seek to manipulate the portal. Yet there was still something missing and Methladon sensed that the Lizardmen had still to reveal its significance.

"What is it you are not telling me?" he asked.

"It had always been the Lady's intentions to open the doors to the Underworld, no matter what else happened," answered Ssonsh. "That is why we helped her in return for finding and eliminating the Marked. We desire that the portal is shattered and that it remains forever open," replied Ssleptaz.

"So are you telling me that her plans have nothing to do with what is happening up there in the heavens?" continued Methladon as he pointed towards the hole in the ceiling. "She's just fearful that she won't live long enough to take the throne of Parandor."

"There you have it," hissed Ssleptaz.

"She is weak but her armies will fight on," croaked Ssonsh.

Methladon looked at both the frog priest and the shape changer as he began to sense the next level of their plan.

"They want the Lady dead!" whispered the voice. "She threatens their plans."

"What are you bastards about to do?" demanded Methladon as he smelled the treachery.

"What do you think?" replied Ssleptaz. "It's just like a game on a board. We intend to sacrifice one piece and replace it by another much stronger."

"How can you speak such words?"

"And yet the dwarf told us what you saw in Ssterong's Sceptre," hissed Ssleptaz.

"He should learn to keep his fucking mouth shut," growled Methladon who could not believe that Grovrouk was party to the plot. Treachery it seemed was everywhere. First the two mercenaries, then the Lizardmen, and now Grovrouk.

"Why did you call it Ssterong's Sceptre?"

"Because that is who owned it before it became one of the Gems of Thamous," answered Ssleptaz in a whisper low enough such that no one else but the three of them could hear his words.

"I thought it was Urthanock..."

"They are one and the same," hissed Ssleptaz. "Urthanock is a term in our language that means 'Lord over Fear'."

"Are you saying that he was a Lizardman? I always thought he was..."

"Human?" croaked Ssonsh. "That shows your level of ignorance. Didn't your father pass on to you the great truth of this world, that the more you know, the more you realise you don't? "

Methladon felt confused and he tried to make sense of it all. The Lizardmen it seemed wanted the portal to the Underworld opened and the powers of the Lord of Fear released, one who it transpires wasn't human after all and just the spirit of yet another of the scale covered reptilians. The Lady intended to use him to bring down Parandor and was about to desert the Lizardmens' quest. He smiled as he realised the extent to which he was at the centre of all that was unfolding and how the power of the Underworld would be his alone to manipulate.

"That's it, you know understand what you desire most," whispered the voice.

Methladon touched the scale side of his face and focused on his realisation that Urthanock had been of lizard kind. The pads of his fingers moved across the skin left bare by his half helm and he thought perhaps this Ssterong had once been human just like himself. Maybe he too had become the Lord of Fear as the result of exposure to dragon fire.

"But what you talk of Ssonsh is still treason," whispered Methladon. "Even if the Lady is dying and there is nothing we can do to prevent it, it is still a foul act and you should be ashamed."

"Yet your emotions give you away," hissed back Ssonsh "As I told you, the dwarf talks. He told us what you saw in the jewel. You want the throne of Parandor for yourself once the 'Dragon Whisper' has finished his work in the Capital. Think about it!"

"The dragon what?"

"The Dragon Whisper," said Ssonsh.

"And what the fuck is that?"

"There is no word in the language of man to describe Ssleptaz's skill. Dragon Whisper is the nearest translation I can offer," explained Ssonsh." He has been key to our plans so far. I am sure you must have heard talk of the talent of the few special ones that hail from the Eastern Marsh."

"I know of such creatures," replied Methladon. "They can change their appearance from one being to that of another. From what I was told the copy is so perfect that even mothers cannot spot such a substitution. Yet I was also told that they can only ever imitate one other and that once chosen there is no going back."

"I understand that Ssleptaz has already revealed to you the form he takes in Parandor. However, he has been absent from the Capital for several days now and will soon be missed."

"Yes, he did reveal his secret," answered Methladon. "He's..."

"Infiltrated the centre of the House of Gylewu," interrupted Ssonsh. "His prime purpose over time has been to distract our enemy and Ssleptaz is our Dragon Whisper."

"There was only one in Parandor who ever discovered my identity and he was immediately eliminated, added Ssleptaz."

"And who was that?" asked Methladon.

"One who went by the name of Blackfayer, the Sovereign Adviser to the Court. He was most astute in deducing who I was and two weeks ago he caught me in the process of transformation. I eliminated him and made it look like he took his own life. I ought to have branded him just like I did with the others but I had already chosen my next target. The resurrection of the cult of Death Tubaria has followed a well-defined plan."

"What is that plan?"

"Well that would be..."

The sudden sound of footsteps caused Methladon to turn. The once beautiful Lady of the Silverwynn hobbled back onto the stone platform. Even in the few minutes since they had last conversed she looked much older. It was obvious that something serious weighed on her mind for her face displayed sadness mixed with much anger.

"My lady, what is the matter? What news did that foul creature bring?"

"Watch your mouth boy," hissed Ssleptaz as he rubbed his blistered hand.

Methladon ignored the comment and looked to the Lady for an answer. He gazed into her eyes and saw the sorrow that filled them. A lone tear fell down the side of her cheek.

"It's Rhaizen, he is dead" mumbled the Lady in a state of obvious shock.

"You're joking! How did that happen?" he exclaimed.

The Lady of the Silverwynn looked in turn to Methladon, Ssleptaz and the frog priest, Ssonsh.

"Brosizrug took four prisoners in Barad Elestor. Two escaped and fled into the ruins of Calistorn. Rhaizen gave chase but never came back. That Harbinger of his, Oedd, went looking for him the day after he failed to return and found him lying in the ruins of my former home, his head destroyed beyond recognition."

"And the prisoners?" asked Methladon. "Did this Brosizrug say who they were?"

A second tear welled in her eye before rolling down her cheek. Methladon sensed past history between the Lady and her Commander but it no longer mattered. This new a turn of events would not deflect him away from the power that he craved. Rhaizen's death would not be allowed to hinder the execution of his new plan.

"My Lady, what about the prisoners?" asked Methladon as he placed both hands on the Lady's shoulders and shook her out of her trance.

"What else do you know?" he said as the second voice overlaid his own.

The Lady of the Silverwynn looked to Methladon and within her furrowed face he saw her anger grow. It was suppressed primal rage and it sought a release.

"So you want to know about the fucking prisoners?" she bellowed as her voice grew ever louder. "I will find out who they are and what they were doing in Barad Elestor. Nothing shall be kept from me. They will suffer for what they did to my beloved Commander. It will not be long until they submit to pain and tell me about the other two. By the heat of Solaris I will have them grovel before me. They will suffer torture like they could never imagine possible and there will be a great reward for the one who can extract their motive for seeking out the sapphire in Barad Elestor. No method will be left untouched in breaking their silence. Time is running short and nothing must get in the way of my destiny. Fry their dicks if you have to but bring me answers."

The Lady of the Silverwynn stopped to catch her breath amid the passion that her frail body had somehow generated. Methladon placed his right arm across his chest and saluted.

"For Avolire."

"For Avolire," hissed Ssleptaz and Ssonsh.

"I will sit of the throne of Parandor and destroy all traces of the House of Gylewu. Ssleptaz!"

"My Lady," hissed the Lizardman.

"The time has come. Make your final strike."

"Of course. As you so demand," hissed the creature.

Methladon watched as Ssleptaz bowed. The changeling then twisted the small golden bracelet wrapped around his right wrist. A flash of blue energy filled the space where the Lizardman had stood and then just as it had appeared it was gone. So was Ssleptaz.

"Everything will still work out as I intended," she cackled. "Parandor will soon be..."

The Lady of the Silverwynn did not finish her sentence. Her eyes rolled back into her head exposing the white below the colour and before Methladon could react she collapsed to the floor. He rushed to her side, dropped to his knees, and cradled her head between his thighs. He felt her laboured breathing. She was too frail to exert herself and her anger had drained her of all energy.

Then as he knelt and held her head she opened her eyes.

"Take me to my chamber," she moaned. "Bring the sapphire to me. I must look into the diamond."

Methladon felt detached. He looked to the frog priest who mouthed three words.

"Think about it."

25

Tonousa moved with purpose through the narrow thoroughfares of the Capital. The cock had crowed but an hour ago and there were few people in the pungent alleyways that made up the city's rat runs. It was almost the time, when as one, the piss pots of Parandor would be emptied from on high. She was thankful to be minutes ahead of the slush hour.

Darchus and Danisun, both having recovered from the attack by Nedes Karoly and his one-handed accomplice, accompanied Tonousa on her current mission. It had been several days since the events at the slaughter house on Shaylotte Street and although they looked well the two men still suffered residual effects from the assaults upon their heads. Their reaction times were impaired and their memories somewhat muddled. Tonousa was grateful they were at least alive and on the mend. She was also content in the knowledge that Nedes Karoly was locked up in one of the foulest of the Underkeep's cells. There he would remain until such time as he could be brought to trial for horse rustling, the assault on members of the City Watch, and for abetting the murder of Falaz Al-Hizdor. That swarthy southerner had been a key element in her investigation; he had known the identity of the shapeshifter that she so needed to uncover. Sadly he was dead.

Her thoughts focused first on Al-Hizdor's murder and then how she had been led to Fullbane and the revelation that the Lady had once been the owner of the ruby, the very same gem that Thias had tasked her to find. She still reeled from the knowledge that it had been stolen but true to her word Tonousa had initiated an in-depth search after reporting the details of the crime to Commander Townsforth. A sweep of all the local thieves' dens had commenced and the Watch had already repossessed a hoard of stolen goods, far more than they had ever expected. But not the elusive ruby. She also knew that the Thieves Guild would not take these raids well and that she was at great risk of being found on the back of Cassius Underscroft's cart, ritually slit from clit to tit and with half her innards missing. At least the search for the missing jewel was underway and it provided the Watch with a welcome distraction from the ongoing preparations for war.

Darchus drew up alongside her and panted for breath.

"Remind me where we are going," he wheezed "If I'm not mistaken this is the route to the Southern Gate."

"The Temple of Fatumai," replied Tonousa.

"Why are we going there?" asked Danisun from her other side. "Are we looking for Heward Teulu?"

Tonousa nodded and then smiled. "I have just received news from Watcyn Dustfury. Heward Teulu has returned from Valameer. It is said that he arrived late last night and visited the Citadel Chapel where Dustfury saw him. Then he made a quick call on Phauless Gylewu before retiring to his rooms in the Temple of Fatumai."

"Who is this Dustfury?" asked Darchus.

"Sir Watcyn Dustfury started his warrior life in Watch, long before he was knighted and became one of the Royal Guard. He is also one of the few I believe to be unstained by the use of Lillywort."

"Do we yet know why Teulu buggered off to Valameer in first place?" asked Danisun.

"He left to go there soon after receiving news of the attack on the Bards Guild, just after I returned from that city myself. I am certain he was here on the day of my father's execution. The common talk is that he raced to Valameer to assist with the wounded in their hour of greatest need."

"Did you ever confirm this with his priests?" asked Danisun. "They would have known?"

"I think we've discussed this before," said Tonousa. "His priests will not speak to us without the implicit permission of their leader. They would hold their master's actions secret on fear of retribution in the afterlife."

"So that's why we are heading to the temple of Fatumai? To have him confirm his story."

"Correct. There is something about it that just does not add up. There are things I need to clarify. Everyone we have spoken with pointed to Lillywort being connected to the Death Tubaria murders. Remember, if you can, that Richemanus said the flower is used in the embalming processes that are practiced within the Temple of Fatumai. There is no better place to continue our investigation."

Danisun and Darchus did not respond yet Tonousa realised they had understood her message. Despite their concussion the two men put their faith in her leadership. It was a level of trust that was more than she felt justified for she was not convinced of her own ability to bring the investigation to a successful conclusion. How she wished for some comfort, someone to hold and someone to love. She had to keep focused.

Tonousa glanced at Darchus and reflected on how he had almost lost his life in the abattoir and how fortunate she had been to have had Theoplous with her. During the past two days Danisun and Darchus had been confined to their beds within the barracks of the Watch. She had been there on both occasions when Darchus's wife and child visited him and cursed him for bringing them to this most foul and wretched city. Yet the loyal woman had endless unconditional love and after each morning's rant her heart had always softened and precipitated a tender embrace. Tonousa then thought of Danisun slumped in a heap in Shaylotte Street and recoiled at the memory of how he appeared dead. He was her superior in every sense, a veteran of the City Watch who knew the ways of the low life and fostered connections with most. It would have been her fault had he died and so a small tear welled in her eye and trickled down her cheek. It left a track in the grime that had built up over the past week.

"Are you crying Tonousa?" asked Danisun.

"No, it's just a speck of dust," she lied as she wiped her eye.

The narrow alleyways opened up into a square surrounded by ramshackle buildings. In its centre stood the impressive Temple of Fatumai.

"Praise be the gods, we are here at last," mumbled Darchus.

The grey and white building had been constructed from the finest stone and marble. Each block had been carved to give it its almost perfect cylindrical shape. The roof of the building was a dome of sophisticated construction and it protected the interior from all the elements of nature. Leading up to the main central doorway was a small flight of steps, flanked on either side by two stone warriors. In normal times the temple would have looked magnificent in the centre of the otherwise empty square but now it was surrounded by a makeshift sprawl. Squalid structures acted as the shelter camp for the displaced refugees who had rushed into the city for protection and sought sanctuary amid the shadows of the holiest of temples.

Tonousa led her colleagues on through the miserable unfortunates who all appeared to be starving. It was clear that supplies of food were scarce. The already malnourished slum scum were at great risk of imminent death and the various religious orders were trying to feed as many as they could from their own meagre stores. Some of the poor had even joined the Watch on the hope of at least one good meal. There were too many to feed, too many to shelter, and the temple square had begun to fill with excrement. A human catastrophe looked imminent and inevitable.

"Spare a coin," said one of the unfortunates.

Tonousa declined the request and shook her head as she recalled stories of beggars who would cover their bodies with fake sores, bind their limbs, or use other devious tricks to dupe the unwary. Her reaction was not from spite or disregard for their suffering but if she gave a coin to one, word would spread like dragon fire, and she would be swamped by a multitude of others seeking the same.

"Bless you my daughter," said the disappointed wretch as Tonousa passed through the throng.

The words pulled on her strings. As much as she wanted to give away all the coins she had with her, she had to first look to her own safety. She guessed Irabo would have acted differently and that added to her shame.

"There are so many of them," whispered Darchus "They seem to be doubling in number by the day. Why do you think they chose this location rather than any other inside Parandor?"

"What do you see ahead of you?" asked Tonousa.

"The Temple of Fatumai. The home of the Fates," he replied.

"You sound uneasy Darchus. Is there a problem?"

"It's just that I don't... I mean... the people of Valameer don't believe in such nonsense," he added. "We believe that we make our own choices and create our own destiny. That is why you were dismissed by the Lady Flurdiana when you went to meet with her. She chose not to act because she could. She has free will and ignores the diktats of distant others."

"I think I understand what you are trying to say Darchus..." replied Tonousa.

"She sounds a bit like you," added Danisun.

"What do you mean?"

"When I first met you Tonousa, you held the same beliefs as Darchus. You didn't believe in the Fates and always insisted on making your own decisions. I remember you could never settle your differences with Irabo on such matters but now I see that the time spent in his company has rubbed off and altered your perceptions."

"As it would seem," smiled Darchus. "Even I have noticed the change..."

"Shut up you two. We have purpose in being here today," snarled Tonousa.

The three at last fought their way through the destitute and approached the base of the stone steps. There a group of four beggars sat cross legged and demanded alms. Close by and dressed in the robes of the priests of Fatumai stood a bald and wizen man who was tending to a wound on one of starving four. Tonousa stepped over a couple of bodies and made to the priest. Danisun and Darchus followed her without question.

"Excuse me sir," said Tonousa. "Where may I find Heward Teulu?"

The old priest turned his head away from the wound he was treating and brought his attention to the three members of the Watch. He eyed them with significant distrust before opening his mouth.

"The last time I saw him he was administering to a group of children within the inner sanctum. The poor souls require dressing of their festering wounds each day and his Holiness has the ability and strength to do that work."

"May the gods watch over you," Tonousa uttered in response, not wishing to waste time.

"And with you," muttered the priest while returning to his task.

The three warriors continued up the flight of stairs, pushed open the iron doors at the top, and entered into the temple proper. The space before them was vast with walls that rose high above the ground. Fixed amid them were doors at regular intervals which led off into numerous smaller anterooms and passages. There was no secondary roof, just the dome itself. Yet there was a stillness and peacefulness that calmed Tonousa as she walked across the threshold and into the depths of the building. It was as if all of her worries had been cast aside and she made her way towards the inner sanctum.

The sacred sanctum with its rounded stone walls had been constructed in the middle of the temple. From its base Tonousa looked up to the dome above and her attention was captured by the intricate paintings that adorned its surface. They depicted the primeval parent gods and their seven children who watched down on all below. Tonousa felt it strange that such frescos should have been dedicated solely to the worship of Fatumai. Then she remembered something she had once been told. The building was older than time and its original purpose had long been forgotten.

Surrounding the sanctum were circles of stone slabs, eroded over time by the bony arses of the many. They acted as seats for those who came to worship within the sacred space. The stones were bisected in the four points of the compass to allow the passage of feet from the outer walls to the centre. It had been down one of these aisles that the three members of the Watch had walked until they passed through the door and entered into the sanctum's inner confines. There before them stood the squat alter to Fatumai on which several street urchins sat and dangled their legs. The man that they had come to find stood before the children and cleaned a dirt encrusted wound on one of the urchins' legs.

"Holiness...a moment if you please," whispered Tonousa in reverence to both man and place.

"Tonousa Amberstone of all people," answered the aging man without lifting his head. "It is both a pleasure and I surprise to have you here. I don't think I've seen you in this sacred space before but you are most welcome. Let me say how sorry I am regarding your father's demise. I spoke up for him you know. But enough of that, what may I do for you on this fine day?"

"It's because of my father that I am here," replied Tonousa as she reached into her leather pouch and removed the four pieces of parchment found inside her father's wall. "What do you make of these?"

Within moments of handing over the cards Tonousa detected the hint of a smile on Heward Teulu's gentle face. It was one of recognition and it was clear he understood the symbols and their meaning.

"So you seek knowledge of the future," he replied. "Are you sure that you want to play the Grey Eye, or Fortunes Fate as it known in the more common tongue?"

Tonousa sensed the priest expected her to have an understanding of what his words meant. Despite Ligart Highroar's vow to obtain a full set of the cards he had not delivered on his promise. She so wished that Theoplous was with her to help her through her uncertainty but he was busy down in the docks, readying the Banshees Wail.

"Forgive me, Holiness, but I know nothing of these cards or their true meaning. This is what I know of them..."

Tonousa then told how she had found the four cards inside her father's room after detecting a message in his words upon the Richemanus Folly. She explained in some detail the previous conversations she had had with Sir Byddin, Lady Emeny, and Sir Richemanus and how the letter from her father, deciphered with a Cuvar code wheel, had assigned individuals to each of the four pieces of parchment. Teulu listened as if detached. All the while he continued to dress the child's wound.

"So what exactly do you want from me?" he replied once Tonousa had finished speaking and replaced the four the cards inside her pouch.

"Are you able to help me shed light as to their true meaning and why my father would have left them for me to find?"

In the brief silence that followed Tonousa wondered if the priest had worked out the true reason behind her visit to his temple

"There that should do it!" said Teulu as he finished his work. "Your leg will be back to normal in no time. Now go and play, the lot of you."

The child jumped down from the altar and along with his friends, ran up the nearest aisle, and then out through one of the doors in the wall of the temple. Once the children were out of sight, Teulu cast a cursory glance towards two other priests who knelt in prayer amongst the stone benches. Then he at last began to address Tonousa's question.

"To understand the Grey Eye you must first have a reading."

"If that is what it takes then that is what I will do" replied Tonousa.

"Then follow me Tonousa Amberstone, fearless daughter of Mathias."

Teulu rose to his feet. He made to move forward and his action was mirrored by the three members of the City Watch. The priest stopped and raised his right hand.

"Your friends must wait here. Nothing can interrupt the Fates once the game is underway and there can be no external influence."

Tonousa looked to her companions and shrugged her shoulders. There was nothing she could do or say for she needed time alone with the priest.

"Are you happy with this?" asked Danisun.

"Don't worry, I'll be fine," she replied as her tapped upon the hilt of her sheathed blade.

When Tonousa turned to follow Teulu she heard him call to the two priests at prayer.

"Fathers Lachesis, Father Atropos, I require your assistance. The Eye of the Fates calls to us. Come help me discover what the Moirai have in store for the daughter of Lord Amberstone."

Heward Teulu led Tonousa down a short flight of steps and into a small chamber beneath the inner sanctum. A large wooden table with three chairs on one side and a stool on the other almost filled the room. There was little space for movement but somehow Tonousa found herself sat upon the stool while the three priests occupied those opposite. Her gaze fell upon a stack of parchment cards in the centre of the table and two twelve sided dice. At last she was about to experience the mystical process known as Fortunes Fate.

"So how does it work?" she asked.

Teulu smiled as he fanned the cards out face down onto the table. Tonousa was transfixed by the pattern they displayed, a swirling mix of black and white.

"It is an exercise in divination that opens insight into the future. It requires the manipulation of forty seven cards and two twelve sided dice," replied Teulu. "If you look on the left hand corner, you will see the cards are numbered one through to forty seven."

"One through to forty seven, yes I see that now," mumbled Tonousa to herself.

"Cards one through to twenty two are white cards and these are known as the 'Attributes'. These are what govern your life. Examples would be 'Humour', 'Inclusion' or 'Redemption'. They are the kind your father left for you to find. Do you follow what I have said so far?"

"I think so," replied Tonousa.

"Cards twenty three to forty four are black cards and we refer to them as 'Characters'. Examples of such would be 'Hero', 'Condemned' and 'Keeper of Secrets'. These cards define who you are."

"And who am I?" whispered Tonousa.

"Patience child, we will come to that in due time. Now where was I... ah yes! The remaining three, the half black and half white ones, are the 'Assigners' and each depicts one of the three Fates. Have you heard of the daughters of Fatumai? They are the ones that we believe predetermine and control our actions. The three are known as Spinner, Allotter, and Cutter. Does that stir any memories for you?"

"A little of something," replied Tonousa, remembering a past conversation with Irabo.

"The rules of the game are simple," continued Teulu.

"If only they appeared so!" added Tonousa as she laughed out her nerves.

"We three priests will represent the Assigners. Father Atropos will assume the role of Cutter for he has taken a vow of silence. Father Lachesis will assume the role of Allotter?"

"As always," replied the priest.

"First of all," began Teulu. "We will define the period of time we are to envision, the duration of time that we ask the Fates to predict. For the purpose of this reading I shall choose days. Are you okay with that?"

"Of course," replied Tonousa as she shrugged her shoulders.

"Now the person who represents the Spinner draws a black card. This will confirm who 'the reading' is about. It is always placed face upwards upon the table."

Tonousa watched as Heward Teulu's left hand reached forward into the fan of cards. He selected a black one at random and turned it over onto the table. He then pushed it with a soft touch towards Tonousa. The picture on the card depicted a blond haired knight sat upon a mighty steed while carrying a hefty lance as if to fight in a tournament. Under the picture in black letters were the words that defined the card and the character.

"The Warrior?" gasped Tonousa and Heward Teulu smiled.

"A perfect choice, it seems that the Fate's know you well."

"Please continue. What happens next?"

"Now the one who represents Allotter draws three white cards and places them face down upon the table."

Without prompting the priest to the right of Heward Teulu selected three of the white cards and placed them in front of his superior.

"Thank you Lachesis. Now as Allotter turns each card over, the Cutter, Father Atropos in this case, roles the two dice. The number determined by the dice will define the time your Attributes will last for. In the case of this reading as stated earlier it will be days."

Without further prompting Father Lachesis moved towards the cards while Atropos shook and then rolled the dice. They fell upon the table where after spinning they at last came to rest. Father Lachesis turned the first card and Tonousa recognised the picture at once. It was one of the four cards she had recovered from her father's room and that at least proved they were not from the same pack.

"Card number fourteen which is Justice and the sum of the dice role is six," exclaimed Teulu.

"What does that mean?" asked Tonousa.

"It means that in six days from now, justice will prevail."

"And what does that mean?"

"You alone know the answer to that. We must now move on to the next?" ordered Teulu.

Tonousa tried to work out the meaning of the card's appearance. She prayed it meant that in six days hence she would apprehend the one who had framed her father and caused his execution. Without further ado Lachesis turned over the second of the parchment cards. He pushed it towards Tonousa. Atropos rolled the dice a second time.

"Card number sixteen. Success. And again, another role of a six. What are the chances of that happening I wonder?" said Teulu.

Tonousa looked at the new card. She saw the image of a man silhouetted against the sky on the highest mountain with an arm raised up high. Her thoughts jumped to the conclusion that it meant in six days she would indeed conclude her investigation. That was enough for her and she knew she did not need to know more.

"And now for the final card," said Teulu as Atropos picked up the dice once gain.

"I get the idea and I do not need to hear anymore," she said at the same time as Atropos threw yet another combination that summed to six. Tonousa's intervention caused Father Lachesis to pause and he did not turn the last card.

"Don't you want to know what the final card shows you?" asked Teulu, somewhat surprised. "You have thrown six three times. That is an act that carries great significance."

"I think we both know that we have been stalling for time," answered Tonousa. "I sense you have guessed my real purpose in coming here."

She searched for any change in the old priest's demeanour but Teulu's face did not move.

"You are very direct Tonousa, like your father. Lachesis, Atropos, please leave us."

Without hesitation, the two priests rose from the table, bowed in deference to their master, and then left the small chamber. They closed the door behind them. Being left alone with Teulu, Tonousa's heart rate quickened.

"So at last it comes to this," he began as his demeanour darkened. "I shall save you the trouble of asking the first question. I understand the investigative techniques of the City Watch for I had a personal teacher, Commander Townsforth."

"I assume you refer to your wife's demise and the reason that you turned holy?" she added.

"Ah! So you know about that little episode. My pardon is on the record. Fatumai saw I that was innocent and ordered Hamthor to destroy the gallows built for my execution. The House of Gylewu exonerated me and took me to their hearts. Blessed be Fatumai."

"And yet…" interjected Tonousa but the priest was quick to silence her.

"Let us have no 'and yet' on this matter. These are the last words that I will utter on the issue of my wife. I savoured her flesh in our time together but then I realised there was more to this life of ours than the emptying of the sack. We must focus on your investigation and I assume you would like to hear of any connection I may have had with the victims of the crimes you are charged to solve."

Tonousa was taken back. The priest was correct and he had anticipated her first question. She now prayed he would be truthful in his comments and offer information that could help her move forward. With renewed hope that the game of cards had given her, the fact that she could perhaps solve the mystery within six days, she sought to set her interrogation off in the right direction. Once again the voice of Lady Fullbane flitted through her thoughts as it whispered 'A path will form'.

"That would perhaps be the best place to start," said Tonousa.

"Yes it is, if you will pardon my rudeness," Teulu replied with a dismissive shake of his hand.

"Then please be as good as to enlighten me," she said, annoyed by the priest's tone of voice.

"They were all followers of my teaching, here in the Temple of Fatumai, apart from the stable boy Danbury and the two servants Flintwind and Underscroft. I did however know those three from my frequent visits to the Citadel. I don't just care for the souls of the highborn you understand"

"I see," replied Tonousa.

"Now let us get onto the next question that I am sure you wish to ask. You want to know where I was at the time that the murders were committed, including your father's if I am not mistaken."

"My father was..."

"Yes child! He was innocent of the crimes he was accused of yet he was still sent from this world by Sir Richemanus, one of the four that your father believed responsible. I too was at Stukeley Knoll when your father died but I was here in this temple when all the other bodies were discovered. My priests will vouch for that."

"I will need to ask them to confirm that fact. I hope you will instruct them to be truthful and to give me their full cooperation?"

"I may."

"That brings me back to the Stukeley Knoll," continued Tonousa. "I was there and saw what happened to my father but I cannot recall you being on the platform with the rest of the council."

"I was present Tonousa," replied the priest. "When the mark of Kha appeared on your father, Lady Emeny fainted. It was Blackfayer and I who helped her down from the platform. There is something else which I feel you ought to know. I'm not sure if you are aware of the lie that spread from the place of your father's death."

Tonousa tried to think what she could have overlooked.

"What do you mean?"

"The three circle brand, the Mark of Kha that was cast upon his head. That mark can form only in the presence of an unholy relic that takes the form of a dagger. It occurs when that hideous implement of Death Tubaria is placed against the skin of a victim as they breathe their last. Your father died first and then the mark appeared some seconds later. No one touched him with any dagger. You must agree that is the truth."

Tonousa was enlightened and in that moment she realised that the murders she was investigating had nothing at all to do with the resurrection of the cult of Death Tubaria.

"So I now understand," she exclaimed "The circles on all of the victims were fake."

"That is correct."

"Did you never think to reveal this vital piece of evidence to others, in particular those of us seeking to uncover the identity of the killer?"

"I did, but he ignored my comments."

"Who did?" exclaimed Tonousa as she grew ever more frustrated.

"The Sovereign Advisor, Xix Blackfayer. He was an unbeliever and not one for religious interference in the affairs of the Realm. You may or may not be surprised to learn that without the knowledge of the Sovereign or of the City Watch he was determined to solve these crimes using his own peculiar methods. He forbade me from burdening Phauless Gylewu with my insight. Let me tell you, I first suspected the truth after that kitchen boy Webb was murdered but it was after the events of your father's execution that I had the proof that I needed. But that worm Blackfayer would not listen. You may imagine my surprise to learn that after I left for Valameer he committed suicide. It is possible that the guilt of not listening to me had some part to play in his black thoughts."

"I assume his body was embalmed and lies in the crypts below this temple?" said Tonousa.

"Correct, and I know what you are thinking; was there a three circle mark?"

"Yes I am."

"The answer is no," continued the priest. "On my return to Parandor I even checked his body myself, shaved his head where he lay and found nothing. If Blackfayer had been another victim in the series of murders and had not committed suicide then I would have found the mark, but I did not."

"That leads me to my next path of my enquiry," said Tonousa. "I need to ask you about the embalming process and the specific use of Lillywort."

"Lillywort!" replied Teulu as if he had never heard of the flower before.

"Yes Lillywort," snapped back Tonousa. "A small white flower...."

"Yes, Yes, Yes. I know of Lillywort. We use it in the mummification of the highborn. It also makes for a decorative flower and Blackfayer had a wonderful wreath of such blooms placed around his head for his passage into the afterlife. Why do you want to know about Lillywort of all things?"

Tonousa then proceeded to explain the reasons behind this new line of enquiry. She told how Byddin, Emeny, and Richemanus had, in their own different ways, confirmed that the Royal Guard and many members of the House of Gylewu had developed a dependency upon the effects of powdered Lillywort. Teulu listened with care as this news sank in.

"So the whole of the Guard are taking that weed," he said sneering. "I cannot wait until I see Byddin again for we shall have a most interesting discourse on this matter."

Teulu's surprise appeared genuine and Tonousa sensed that the priest had no prior knowledge of the practice that now undermined the ability of the Citadel to function. Her thoughts raced in a multitude of directions. There was always the possibility he was just deceiving her but somehow she felt that wasn't the case. Yet since Teulu had been away in Valameer there had not been another murder that could be linked to the Death Tubaria. This fact alone seemed damming enough evidence to implicate the priest in some way. The suggestion that the marks of Kha had been faked troubled Tonousa for now her investigation seemed even more confused and complicated. The infiltrator had covered his trail well but she struggled to understand why he had bothered to create the copycat marks in the first place.

Tonousa then felt a cold sensation pass through her as if she were being watched by some evil presence. She felt her nemesis crushing the ability of Realm to respond to the threat from Avolire. The Royal Guard was rotting under the effects of Lillywort and it seemed that anyone who got too close to the infiltrator was dispatched without delay. Her one hope lay in unlocking the link between the flower and the spy in their midst.

"If you would permit your Holiness, it would be of great help to see where you store your Lillywort."

"I do not see why not. We keep it in the catacombs below the temple where it is cool."

"Thank you. That will help me get a much clearer picture of your embalming practice," she said as she rose from her seat.

Teulu led Tonousa on through a network of passages at the rear of the temple. After a brisk walk they came to a small room with a trap door fixed into the wooden floor. Next to it stood a small oak table and upon it an oil lamp and flint. Tonousa waited while the priest lit the lamp and then opened the trap door. Teulu then led the way down into the deep dark tunnels under the temple. Tonousa was reminded of those of the Underkeep and recalled the story of the hidden tunnel, the one said to connect the Temple of Fatumai to the Citadel. A musty smell hung in the air which Tonousa assumed was due to the damp although she could not be certain. They passed many niches built into the walls and inside which the remains of the highborn of Parandor rested for eternity. Soon Teulu stopped before a particular thick wooden door that that had been left part open.

"That's strange," said the priest. "This should be locked at all times. Someone has left it open. I do not understand..."

Then he moved towards the door but Tonousa stopped him and took hold of his arm.

"You must be careful Holiness. Whoever did this may still be in there. I would not wish to give them chance to escape or indeed do you harm."

The pair crept forward and peered into the darkness. It crossed Tonousa's mind that it could be a trap laid by Teulu himself and her hand gripped the hilt of her sword. The old priest went first with his lamp as they both stepped into the dark. Tonousa tried as best she could to take in her surroundings. In the room's centre stood an ancient stone slab. Around the walls its many shelves were stacked with rolls of embalming cloth and many clay urns which she surmised contained the Lillywort.

"Is anything missing?" asked Tonousa.

"No it doesn't appear..." began Teulu but then he gasped. "Oh dear. Look, over here!"

"What is it? What have you seen?"

The priest pointed towards one of the shelves and in the dust Tonousa saw the obvious mark where something round had once stood.

"One of the jars of Lillywort has been taken and it's not just any one of them."

"What do you mean?" demanded Tonousa.

"The Lillywort in the missing one is of the most potent kind. That is the reason we use it in the embalming procedure. The jars on this particular shelf contain the most refined concentrate of the flowers' seed heads. Should any of the Royal Guard partake of this variant they would not have to worry about their futures. The tiniest grain in their bodies would kill them within seconds. Its sole purpose is to prevent the decay of the dead."

Tonousa looked around the room and saw no sign of forced entry.

"You say that this door is always kept locked?"

"Yes, at all times and I have the only key. It is strange that there is no sign of the lock being broken," he replied.

"So now we have two connected thefts," muttered Tonousa to herself as she recalled the loss of the ruby. "Are you sure that no one else has a key to the door?"

"As I just told you, I have the only one," replied Teulu.

"Then show it to me now."

Teulu reached into his robe and pulled out the ancient metal key from inside one of his pockets. Having done so he drew back and winced as if in great pain. He uttered several curse words as the key dropped from his hand onto the stone floor with resounding clang. Tonousa looked up and saw the priest was in significant discomfort as he rubbed his injured hand with vigour. Tonousa reached down, picked up the key from where it had fallen, and then waited for the priest to compose himself.

"What happened to your hand?" she asked.

"I injured it when away in Valameer. I spilled hot oil into my palm. I was using it to stop an injured child's wound from festering. It has been slow to heal but it will get there in time.

"Are you sure this key has never left your possession, even for a brief moment? Could you have forgotten to lock it the last time you were here?" asked Tonousa.

"It has never once left my possession. I always have it with me. When I am away from the city I pass the responsibility to one of my priests"

"Who looked after the key during your trip to Valameer?"

"That would have been Father Atropos if my memory serves me well," replied Teulu.

"Is it possible that someone could have made a copy? Perhaps the key could have been taken without his knowledge, smuggled to the Thieves Guild, duplicated, and then returned in secret."

"That's a fanciful fiction, and most improbable," said Teulu as he dismissed the idea. "You know as well as I do that you don't find the Thieves Guild, they find you."

Tonousa sighed and retreated once again into her thoughts. She considered the possibility that the lock had been picked but why then had the door been left open. She found it difficult to imagine anyone reaching this isolated place and gaining access to the room without being seen or challenged by the temple priests. Then she recalled the supposed secret tunnel.

"It could be that our murderous infiltrator has mastered the art of picking locks and has been using the tunnel that links these catacombs with the Citadel."

"Preposterous! Using the tunnel would be out of the question."

"Please explain," replied Tonousa.

"I'll do better than that. I will show you so that you can see the truth with your own eyes."

Teulu lead Tonousa off into the labyrinth of tunnels and several minutes later they entered one whose passageway was blocked by several large boulders and much fallen brickwork. It was impossible to make further progress for the barrier was impenetrable to all but the rats.

"I see what you mean. If this is the link to the Citadel then it cannot be the route taken by the thief," said Tonousa as she vocalised her thoughts.

"Time has not been kind to the oldest of the tunnels. No man alive could move the rocks and stone that block this passage," added Teulu as he held his lamp aloft such that he could confirm his observation. "Do you see what I mean Tonousa, there is no way through. Now, is there anything else you would like to ask me?"

Tonousa sighed and delved deep into the depths of her thinking. Then she surfaced one final question that she needed to ask.

"Given your knowledge in the use of the Fortunes Fate cards, who would you select as murderer from the four that I showed you. Who is the evil one that I seek to uncover?"

"Well, as you would expect, I discard the one card that suggests my personal involvement," replied the priest. "If anything I would look to the least likely of the other three. Byddin searches for the power of Barad Elestor to strengthen his army. Richemanus is too addled by Lillywort, beer, and the pox. If I were a betting man, which of course is not permitted in our order, I would choose Emeny. She claims to be of a nervous disposition but I put it to you that is but a refined act to deflect any suspicion from her person. Look to Lady Emeny; that is my advice."

Tonousa searched for truth the priest's eyes. She had been surprised by his selection.

"What evidence can you offer to support your choice?"

"I'm afraid to say, none at all. You can choose to accept it as an inspired guess or just the ramblings of an old man but I wish you well in your quest," he replied with a softening smile.

"In that case I have no more questions just now. Please can lead me back to the surface so that I may re-join my companions. I am most grateful to you for giving up your time to speak with me Holiness."

Teulu bowed in affirmation to Tonousa's request and then led her back through the labyrinth, up to the trap door, and back into the temple above. As they walked Tonousa had reassured him that she would dedicate another of the Watch to investigate the theft of the Lillywort from the temple. Having returned to the inner sanctum Tonousa cast her gaze towards Danisun and Darchus who had awaited her return with some impatience. She could tell at once that both were relieved to see her still alive. Heward Teulu prepared to take his leave but as he turned away Tonousa took hold of his arm.

"One last thing Holiness, if you don't mind. The cards, the Grey Eye, or however you wish to name them..."

"You wish to know what the final card was?" replied the priest. "I'm afraid that time has passed. Atropos alone will have looked at it and he has committed his life to silence."

"No Holiness, my personal reading holds no interest for I have no faith in the cards. I see it as childish nonsense. However, the cards are important to my investigation. I would like to obtain a full set and examine them closely. Do you happen to have any spare that I can borrow?"

"Of course Tonousa. I will have Father Atropos bring some over to the City Watch."

"Not the Watch if you do not mind Holiness," whispered Tonousa. "Please have him deliver them to the room I have rented at The Murdered Wolf. The less people who know about this the better, if you know what I mean."

"As you so wish," replied Teulu, raising an eyebrow. "May Fatumai walk well with you?"

"And with you, Holiness."

Teulu then turned and made his exit. Tonousa watched his departure in silence with Danisun and Darchus still by her side. Danisun then spoke.

"Well what did you find out? Come on the suspense is making my head throb."

Tonousa turned to face the Man-at-Arms and replied: "In all honesty I don't think it's him."

"Why?"

"Not here, I'll explain later," she replied. "Someone may be listening."

It was clear to Tonousa that the Temple of Fatumai had been breached and not via the tunnel that had once connected it with the Citadel. Someone from inside the building had to be involved and she could not risk them lurking in the shadows and listening to her words. Danisun however looked agitated and he spoke back with authority.

"We do not have time for you to stall Tonousa. You'll need to tell all you know right now. While you were with the priest, Karkis Snouth came looking for us with a message from Townsforth."

"Steady yourself," replied Tonousa. "What was the context of his message?"

Danisun looked around to check they were alone before he continued.

"We three have been summoned to meet with Phauless Gylewu. The order was issued by Lady Emeny and we are to make our way to the Court without delay. Even our Lord Commander has been ordered to attend."

"Did Karkis say why we are we being summoned to meet with the Sovereign?"

"The scrap of information he was given said that the Grand Wizard has found something significant within the Lore of the Dead. Apparently it is related to a prophecy and could mean we are all in the greatest of danger."

26

Within the gloomy confines of a crumbling stone cell the cold gripped hold of Thias and sought to destroy the remnants of his resilience. He had been stripped of the clothes he had worn during his journey through the Dragonas, Thengar Forest, and the road to Avolire. The dank and musty cell provided the most miserable of environments that he could ever have imagined. A single hole in the roof, about the width of a man's shoulders, permitted the entry of a trace of light. Thias felt the icy night air bite into his bare skin for there was no warmth in that most pitiful of beams. He listened to the drips of water that leaked into his subterranean cell from the ruined city above and he realised that he had lost all sense of time. Unable to calculate how long he had been incarcerated his misery seemed unsurmountable. A meagre amount of food had been left once each day but it was insufficient to sustain his needs and that of his companion with whom he was forced to share his suffering. Thias's stomach constricted as the aroma of meat on the spit drifted down through the oculus in the roof. All he would get would be pitiful scraps, not fit for a pig, and left each day by a keeper of gross appearance who never spoke. Ever since he and Irabo had arrived in Avolire, Thias had seen no sign of ogres, Lizardmen, or the Knights of Avolire. No one seemed to want to question them and yet the voices that echoed down through the hole indicated the presence of many who were intent on war. Neither had there been any sign of their host, the Lady of the Silverwynn.

The bard sniffed the air. The pungent smell excrement and sweat felt all pervading as he sat against the wall, manacled and attached to it by a heavy rusting chain. He reckoned it would require great strength to loosen it from its fixing point, strength that had long seeped out of his starving muscles. He touched his face as he tried to think of any possible means of escape and his fingers passed through several weeks of hair that had sprouted from out of his chin. Thias's body itched and he sensed a serious infestation of lice. He so longed for a bucket of water with which to clean himself but such a luxury was not to be had in this Lady's guest house. He had been left to rot in his own filth and the lacerations sustained in his battle with the ogres had already started to fester. Thias looked towards Irabo who was chained by his wrists to the opposite wall and he shared his companion's pain. The warrior from the Watch had also been stripped and beaten following their attempted escape from the ogre's camp. Thias could not comprehend why his friend had been so foolish to have returned when he had been given strict instructions to take Llyat to a place of safety. Given the fury of his captors he had not yet had the chance to ask that question for they had both been gagged by the ogre whose brother Llyat had slain in Barad Elestor. Ever since the inception of their incarceration, Irabo had drifted in and out of consciousness and he now seldom made any attempt to talk. Brosizrug's ogres had been hard on Thias but for some unknown reason Irabo had faced most of their ire.

The warrior began to cough and Thias saw that his friend was at last awake.

"Hang on in there. Try and focus on staying alive. It will be over soon."

Thias paused for a moment. He sensed death would soon call and provide release.

"I'm glad you came along for the ride!" muttered Irabo amid his confusion.

Thias almost laughed but then Irabo spoke again.

"Perhaps this is what the Moirai had planned for us all along."

"What do you mean?"

"I think," continued Irabo between coughs, "that maybe it was always the Moirai plan for us to end up here. If only I hadn't been so stupid and followed you back to the ogres' camp."

"What are you trying to say my friend?"

"The question I am struggling with is this; did I make that choice or was it made for me? Did I choose to do it or did those three bitches decide I would end my life with you in this stinking hole?"

Thias hesitated for it appeared that Irabo was questioning his own beliefs. The young warrior had always made it clear that the Fates governed the lives of men.

"I don't know my friend," Thias replied in an attempt to avoid answering the questions.

"I made a deliberate choice to return to that camp," continued Irabo. "I cannot believe that the Moirai could be so cruel as to place me in this wretched hole."

"Who knows what Fatumai and her daughters have planned for us," said Thias. "Whatever happens, you must retain your beliefs. Do not let them falter for they are all that you have left. We don't know how long we are going to be held in this pit and the power of faith may yet see us through this nightmare. This is not the time nor place to deny all that you have grown up to believe. Within this cell, amid your darkest hour, you must find the strength to sustain your life-force. You must clear your mind of any doubt."

Thias heard the sound of a key turn in the iron lock and seconds later the door opened. Two Lizardmen, dressed in their strange mix of leather and iron armour, entered and stood either side of the door. They were followed some seconds later by a figure shrouded in a hooded cloak, draped over distinctive black leather armour. As this strange man moved to the centre of the cell he sharpened a knife upon a small block of stone that he held in his other hand. His presence and actions caused Thias to break into a fearful sweat. Then another entered, dressed in an ancient green gown with golden trim. The door closed and was locked from the inside. Thias had been expecting a visit from this Lady for some days but was surprised to see her look so old and prune-like.

"Sanura Silverwynn, I am pleased to meet you at last," exclaimed Thias.

"You will address her as Lady," hissed one of the Lizardmen.

"I do apologise my Lady. I meant no disrespect."

The Lady of the Silverwynn looked at both Thias and Irabo in turn and then answered;

"And the fuck who are you?"

Thias hesitated. He looked first to Irabo and then back towards the Lady. He contemplated telling lies but that strategy had not helped him so far.

"Thias," he replied. "My name is Thias Calavan."

"He lies," snarled the one under the hood "This man is known to me. I recognised him the moment I entered the room, despite the hair that has grown on his face. I came across him in the Three Sisters tavern back in Fallguard and where he announced himself as Vostag Heyn."

Thias stared at the man whose face was hidden in the shadow of his hood. He sought to remember his visit to Fallguard and those who had been present in the tavern that night. He recalled the landlord and his man-wife and then at last he recognised the distinctive voice. It belonged to one of the two mercenaries whose conversation he had overheard that night. Then he remembered the man's name.

"Ventes, is that who you are?" asked Thias, half in the hope that he was mistaken.

The man reached up, pulled back his hood and displayed a distinctive scar on his left cheek.

"I'm glad to see that I left a lasting impression on your memory," said the mercenary.

"How touching," exclaimed the Lady. "We are not here for a reunion."

"Enlighten me as to your needs," replied Thias with all the strength he could muster.

"I need to ask you some questions," continued the Lady. "I want to know who you are, that is all. There is no harm in that is there, and then perhaps we can all be friends?"

"Fuck you," spat back Thias as his anger suppurated.

"Then have it your own way," replied the Lady.

Thias watched as the lady of the Silverwynn clicked her fingers and signalled to the two Lizardmen on either side of the door. Both moved towards Thias and as he then struggled to free himself from their grasp they lifted him up from where he sat and held him up before the ancient hag.

"Is this the extent of your life now?" snarled Thias. "In bed with the treacherous Knights Avolire and these stinking creatures from the swamps. What could have driven you to stoop so low?"

The Lady did not answer but instead grabbed hold of Thias by his bearded chin. Even though old she still had strength in her body. She stared into Thias's eyes and then over to the mercenary beside Irabo who continued to sharpen the knife he had brought with him.

"For each answer you give me that I deem to be false I will order Ventes to take off one of your friend's finger tips."

"You cannot..."exclaimed Thias as the Lady removed her bony fingers from his face. "He is an innocent and..."

Before he could finish Irabo groaned.

"Don't tell them anything Thias."

"Shut your festering mouth," snapped Ventes as he thrust his stone into Irabo's face causing the young man to spit blood and a tooth upon the floor.

"Once his tips are gone, if you still refuse to tell me all you know, Ventes will start to remove what then remains of his fingers one by one," continued the Lady "He will then move on to limbs and other precious body parts. Let me be clear about this, he will do it in such a manner that your friend will be awake throughout it all."

Thias glanced over to Irabo who hung in his helplessness against the wall and he struggled to understand how anyone, least of all a woman, could be so cruel.

The aging highborn hag cast her gaze to where Irabo hung naked like a carcass in a butchers shop window. She signalled with her hand to Ventes. The mercenary then took hold of Irabo's right hand, gripped it at the wrist, and stretched out one finger. Thias watched on in horror as Ventes thrust his blade into Irabo's flesh and began to cut away the tip of the extended digit. The warrior's screams filled the room but the manner in which he was fixed to the wall prevented him from kicking out or moving his arms. He could offer no resistance to the blade and continued to wail in the most pitiful of ways. The sounds of woe hit Thias hard and he decided he had no choice but to talk if he was to save his friend from further suffering.

"Stop, I will do as you wish!" he exclaimed. "What do you want to know?"

"Good, I see we have arrived at an understanding," the Lady snarled. "Ventes said that he recognised you and that you go by the name Vostag Heyn? Yet my cellkeep says your friend calls you Thias. Can you explain the reason for that?"

Thias struggled to comprehend all that was happening. He suppressed intense desire to lash out despite knowing he would be better served being compliant. Despite his attempts to control his anger words spewed from his mouth.

"Go fuck yourself, you pox ridden whore!"

Once again the Lady of the Silverwynn turned to Ventes and clicked her fingers. The sniggering mercenary took hold of Irabo's hand and this time extending the second digit. It was already coated with blood from the wound inflicted on the first. Once again the blade sliced into the flesh and Irabo screamed out his woe.

"Stop! Stop!" screamed Thias above the noise of his friend's agony. "We ran into Ventes in Fallguard. I had two companions with me and we wanted to avoid any trouble. That is why we lied and gave false names. We wanted to keep well away from the war brewing between Avolire and Parandor. Vostag Heyn was a blacksmith I used to know long ago, far removed from here, and his was the first name that came to my mind."

Thias glared at the Lady of the Silverwynn as she noted his discomfort. He prayed that his answer had been sufficient and yet he felt unnerved at a slight change in her face, a simple moment of recognition in which he realised she had heard of the blacksmith before. The moment passed and the Lady spoke again.

"Then let me ask another question. Brosizrug, that dim shit of an ogre, found you in the ruins of Barad Elestor. On your capture they found two items in your possession which you later tried to retrieve during your pathetic escape attempt. One was a sapphire, an object that I also had been looking for. What purpose did you have for this gem?"

"We just came across it when exploring the ancient pyramid and it seemed of significant value. We thought it would bring our families many riches."

"And the other object?" demanded the Lady.

"That is a gift from one of my friends," replied Thias. "The one who escaped your ogres."

"Why does it glow so strong and in such a strange way?"

Thias thought of the stone and chain that Llyat had given him in Fallguard. He remembered that it had called out his name inside the General's tent but until this moment he had not considered whose voice it was. The Lady watched his expression change as he struggled to come up with an answer to her question. He then recalled that the stone had glowed in the presence of the sapphire inside the ogre's satchel. Perhaps the emission was activated by some deeper and more purposeful magic but he could not think of an explanation that the Lady of the Silverwynn would believe.

"I don't know."

Once again the Lady signalled to the mercenary who cut into Irabo's blooded hand for a third time. The warrior's screams were too much for Thias to bare.

"Please leave him alone," shouted Thias as he struggled against the grip of the two Lizardmen that held him. "I don't know why it glows. It is a mystery to me."

As Irabo continued to scream, the Lady of the Silverwynn looked at Thias and their eyes met. She smiled in a sinister way and then signalled to Ventes with her bony hand.

"Desist."

Thias looked to his friend who hung motionless from the wall, his screams having ceased. With no sign of movement not even a finger twitched. Irabo looked like a corpse.

"If you've killed him..." exclaimed Thias.

"He's just passed out my Lady," said Ventes who had moved his head close to Irabo in order to feel to his breath.

"Then wake the bastard up."

Thais squirmed as Ventes took the knife he had used to remove the finger tips and drove it through the flesh of the back of Irabo's hand. The force of the blade thrust pinned the flesh to the wall through a gap in between two stones. Irabo then woke, screamed, and squirmed against the wall as he tried in vain to free himself from his shackles. The agony of his friend's suffering brought tears to Thias's eyes. He felt destroyed, useless, and blamed himself for all the young warrior's suffering.

"Please, I beg you, leave him be."

"Then answer my questions and be honest!" replied the Lady.

"Yes, yes, I will tell you all," pleaded Thias. "He need not suffer more. What is it you want to know?"

The Lady looked at Thias before signalling for Ventes to stand down.

"Tell me about the two from your party who ran off into the ruins of my ancestral home. Who are they? What would a peasant boy and a Berserker want within the ruins of that tragic place? Why did they flee in that particular direction?"

Once again Thias hesitated and tried to figure out what he could say that would satisfy her and save his friend from further torture.

"They didn't want anything. I sent them in that direction as I thought it would be the safest and the easiest place to hide. I swear by the gods that both the boy and the Berserker are innocents."

The Lady's face seemed to soften as if she half believed for an instant what Thias had told her.

"Well, they won't get far," she continued. "To the east there is nothing but marsh and then the great sea. Those who dwell there will dispose of such trespassers, innocents or not.

Once again she made eye contact with Thais and her stare unnerved him. It was as if she was trying to see through his exterior and delve deep within his soul for the information that she wanted.

"What is it that you are not willing to tell me about these two? I sense you are hiding something. I will ask you just one more time; who are they?"

Thias took a breath and looked over to where Irabo hung. Again he hesitated as he tried to determine his best course of action. The Lady had however lost patience and she signalled to Ventes with her hand.

"No, no, please wait," pleaded Thias.

"Don't tell them anything," groaned Irabo.

"Do not worry my friend," shouted Thias. "You do not have to suffer. The Fates will watch over Llyat and Einar. We have served our purpose."

Ventes's hand lay upon the knife, still embedded in the wall but the Lady signalled that the blade should stay there.

"Wasn't that easy?" she added with a smile. "Thank you Thias for your cooperation. I am so pleased we do not have to continue with this nastiness."

The two Lizardmen that held Thias let out an expulsion of air which Thias interpreted as their way of demonstrating contempt.

"Forgive me Lady but I am revolted by the company that you keep," said Thias as he looked in turn at the two reptilians that held his arms. "However did you come by them? What could you or the Knights of Avolire hope to gain from mixing with such foul creatures?"

Thias felt the grip of the two tighten on his arms.

"They serve my purpose and I wouldn't be here without them. Now tell me Thias Calavan, who are the two who fled into Calistorn? I understand they call themselves Llyat and Einar?"

"Einar sounds like a name befitting a Berserker," added Ventes.

Before Thias could answer the mercenary then took hold of Irabo's chin and lifted it.

"Am I correct?"

Thias winced for he wasn't at all sure that Irabo would be able to answer.

"Correct," whimpered the shell of a man.

Ventes dropped Irabo's head and let it hang to the floor. The Lady of the Silverwynn then took hold of the hair on Thias's chin and forced him to look into her eyes.

"I will not let this rest. I ask you again who is this boy Llyat and what significance should I read into you having had a Berserker in your party? What is their mission and purpose?"

Thias stalled for time.

"Then first answer me this," he began. "As I am not going anywhere and as I have agreed to answer all your questions, please could you clarify something of great importance to me?"

"You speak like a member of the House of Gylewu," she answered as she released her grip on his face and moved to the centre of the room. "Well bard, what is it that you want to know. I will answer your question but then you will tell me all you know or so help me you will both died most horribly."

Thias hesitated. He had not expected the Lady to agree to his request.

"Why are you flirting with the power of the Rift," he asked. "I am aware that the Lizardmen use it to travel great distances and know it is how they gained entrance into the Bards Guild of Valameer which they then destroyed. I have also heard that the Lizardmen can use the portal unaided but others can only do so by means of a human sacrifice. Despite this knowledge I still fail to understand your reasons for harnessing its power."

"I am surprised you have even heard of the Rift," replied the Lady as she continued to indulge him. "As you seem to already know, the Rift is a fracture between the Underworld and our own middle plane of existence. The energy that the Lizardmen have tapped into is the very same that Kha bestowed upon Urthanock the Lord of Fear way back in history. Behind the door between the dimensions lies an unimaginable amount of power."

"Yes, so I understand," said Thias, "But for what end do you intend to use this power? Is it just to bring down the House of Gylewu?"

"You may well have worked out my ultimate goal but you must understand that several generations ago the Lizardmen of the Eastern Marsh witnessed the destruction of Calistorn by the bastards that hailed from Parandor. They began to realise the threat that those of Gylewu brought to their own marshlands. The Great Ssonsh, one who is now their leader, saw when he was but very young, how he could use me to further his own plans. He needed the support of the Knights of Avolire and I was the conduit he chose to make that happen. He encouraged me to harness the power of the Rift and it rejuvenated me. They reversed the passage of time and…"

"So what happened for I see it has stopped working?" said Thias forgetting his place.

The mercenary moved towards Irabo as if to inflict further torture.

"No Ventes, not yet. I am enjoying this conversation for it has been sometime since I've had the opportunity to converse with a man of intelligence. I will allow this question to be answered. You see bard, something has gone wrong with the rejuvenation process that even Ssonsh is at a loss to explain. The powers of the Underworld have turned their favour to another, a survivor just like myself."

Thias smiled for he believed he had highlighted a significant flaw in the Lady's plan. She may well have been able to amass an army of cut throats and others of foul intent but she would not it seemed live long enough to lead them in the final battle.

"What do you mean by another survivor?" probed Thias as the lady continued to indulge him.

"The doors to the underworld cannot be opened or indeed closed by any mere mortal. Sir Raulyn and that great worm Thamous saw to that. We foresaw a plan to use one known as the Marked and who was revealed to us in the Prophecy. We believed him capable of opening the door to the Underworld. Yet the Marked was stolen some years back and taken south by a Historian. He is probably now dead, yet this matters not."

"So if I understand what you are saying, the other survivor you talk of is also capable of carrying out this task."

"You guess well," continued the Lady. "He has been cursed by the god's and will be key to the destruction of the House of Gylewu in the war that I intend to prosecute. This other holds the greatest of all powers, that of immortality."

Thias was alarmed by the full extent of the Lady's plan for not only was she intent on exacting revenge against the Sovereign but she also intended to release the powers of the Underworld upon the world. It appeared the deluded old crone intended to release the Lord of Fear himself. The prophecy now made sense. In that moment he began to understand Llyat's purpose and why the Cuvar had sought to protect and hide him from the world. Thoughts raced through his mind but were broken when Irabo begin to whimper.

"No one is immortal," he moaned.

"So the corpse speaks," laughed the lady. "Project your voice louder wretch so we may all hear your wisdom."

"I said that no one is immortal," continued Irabo. "The Fates will not allow it."

"Yet after many attempts on this other's life, he still lives."

"It's just another of the three hag's sick games," added Thias.

"Then tell me bard," said the Lady. "Why has Cutter been unable to end his life? How can he still live when he should be dead? For what purpose could the Moirai keep him breathing?"

"So you also know the three sisters by that name," stated Thias.

"I know them by many names. The Fates, the Moirai, the Oracle. They are all one and the same."

"When the Oracle's crypt shall awaken...." began Thias and the lady looked back with surprise.

"So you know of the Enderdetag Prophecy?"

"Yes, I know something of it" he replied.

"It is the future that the Ancients foresaw when Sir Raulyn vanquished Urthanock from the Realm," she continued. "How do you know of such things? Why did you lie to me; I thought we had a mutual agreement?"

"I did not lie to you," replied Thias as he attempted to recall all he had heard in the past.

"If you know of the Enderdetag Prophecy then you know of the Gems of Thamous," she snapped back. "Ventes, take out your plaything's tongue."

Thias struggled against the grip of two Lizardmen who still restrained him. Ventes punched Irabo in the stomach and then wrenched his knife free from the wall. The pain induced by its forced extraction caused Irabo to cry out. The newly appointed torturer then took hold of Irabo's cheeks and exposed his tongue. Thias heard the pitiful mumblings of his friend and once again felt helpless.

"No, please, not my tongue. I beg you to leave it be," moaned Irabo.

"Bard, you have but three seconds to tell me why you took the Sapphire from Barad Elestor and how your actions fit into the Enderdetag Prophecy. Speak now or your friend will drown in his own blood," bellowed the Lady.

"I told you, we found it..."

"One!" said the lady as she signalled to the mercenary.

"You're making a great mistake,"

"Two!"

"Don't tell them anything Thias," moaned Irabo despite Ventes grip on his face.

"Three."

Thias cried out as the mercenary's blade entered into Irabo's mouth. Then he snapped.

"Stop now, I will tell you the truth. I will tell you everything," he cried out in despair.

The Lady raised her hand once again and Ventes retracted his blade.

"I'm so sorry Irabo," continued Thias. "I can't let them do this to you."

"Thias, no, you mustn't," groaned Irabo as he drifted out of consciousness.

"You choose well bard. Now talk!" snarled the Lady.

Thias sighed for he knew he had no choice in the matter. It was either speak or watch his companion slowly murdered before his eyes. It was all his fault and he would have to live with his choices for the rest of his days even though he did not expect to live longer than a few. He stared back at both the Lady and the mercenary in turn. Through his pent up anger he fired out the words of his story. He spat them out with great venom in the hope they would prevent Irabo from further suffering.

The bard told how he had been sent from Parandor by Phauless Gylewu to investigate the resurgence of the cult of Death Tubaria. In his investigations he was to seek out the dwarf known as Grovrouk the Despoiler at the Grey Keep and question him on the Lore of the Dead. He told of the Lizardmen attack and how he had then made his way to Valameer to seek the counsel of the bards. How once there he had met others from Parandor. He spoke of the Grand Physician who had come to investigate the murders linked to Death Tubaria. How there he had met a boy who had been fished out of the waters of the river Tiaryer and who, after the fall of the Bards Guild, accompanied him into the Dragonas in order to speak with Thamous. His mission had been to seek out and unite the Gems as had been written into the Prophecy. Thias then told of his escape from the Knights of Avolire at the Gathering and their subsequent adventures in Thengar Forest and the Temple of

Barad Elestor. Then at last explained how his small group had been captured by a platoon of ogres, how two of his friends had escaped, and were now somewhere out in the wilderness to the north of the Grey Mountains.

The Lady of the Silverwynn listened to all that Thias had to say. When he reached the end of his tale she began to ask more questions.

"If you were seeking to reunite the Gems of Thamous, then the boy that fled must be..."

"He is called Llyat Emgar," added Thias. "A youth from Maplehill."

"Then he must be the Marked, the child of the Prophecy. So you say he is still alive?"

"Yes, and well out of your reach it seems," added Thias smugly.

"And where is the Marked heading?" demanded the Lady. "What was your plan? Tell me all that the great snake tongue of Thamous revealed to you. Where are the remaining gems?"

The Lady asked her final question once again but this time she directed it at Irabo who had woken to a pain in his mouth and to Thias's treasonable disclosures. Irabo looked into her face, rolled blood stained spittle around in his mouth, and spat it out in her direction. As the drool hit her on the cheek she recoiled and threw out a look that would have withered Urthanock himself.

"Fuck you," snarled Irabo.

Ventes moved closer and punched Irabo in the face. Several teeth were expelled yet this did not stop Irabo from answering back.

"I'll die before I tell you anything you witch."

The Lady of the Silverwynn laughed once again.

"Perhaps," she said before turning her attention back to Thias.

"The question is with you now bard. Refuse to answer and your friend will die. One last time, where are the remaining gems?"

Thias sighed for he had no choice but to comply.

"Only Llyat was allowed to converse with Thamous. From what he told me, the wyvern could sense the approximate location of two jewels. The third he could not see at all for some strange substance surrounded it and resisted his attempts at remote sighting. The Sapphire as you now know was in the pyramid of Barad Elestor and the Amethyst..."

"I now have three of them. Where is the Amethyst?" demanded the Lady.

"It is in the Eastern Marsh somewhere," replied Thias as he dropped his head in shame. "The jewel has lain hidden under the nose of the Lizardmen for generations. I told you they are useless."

The Lady of the Silverwynn laughed and her voice echoed round the cell. Even in her dotage the news that Thias had delivered seemed to rejuvenate her essence.

"Well that's a large area of swamp to search," she said. "Please be more specific. Where in the Eastern Marsh did Thamous point to? Tell me now or I'll have Ventes remove your friend's eyes."

"When Llyat touched the Sapphire in Barad Elestor," continued Thias. "He experienced a vision in which he saw the Amethyst's location. He said there was a city on the eastern edge of the marsh, built upon a vast hidden lake and near to where the marsh meets the sea."

The Lady looked pleased. The Lizardman that restrained Thias's right arm then spoke.

"Xabkat," it hissed.

Silence fell while the lady processed this new information.

"How very interesting" she at last answered as she stroked her own chin. "So tell me, how does the Marked intend to infiltrate this great city of the lizards?"

"I do not know," replied Thias. "We never got to plan that far ahead. I don't think Llyat knew for he referred to it as 'looking for a dragons fart'."

After yet another pause the Lady turned to the two Lizardmen.

"You," she said while pointing to the one on Thias's left. "Go at once to Xabkat. Use the rift if you must but make sure that the city is placed on full alert. This time the Marked must be caught and eliminated."

The Lizardman hesitated and Thias sensed something amiss. He was sure that it exchanged a blink of its reptilian eyes with its colleague.

"What are you waiting for?" exclaimed the Lady. "Get to Xabkat, now!"

Thias looked on as the creature that restrained him grunted and then twisted a golden bracelet on its wrist. A second later a flash of blue energy surrounded the Lizardman and when it had gone, so had the reptile.

"So that is how they access the Rift?" said Thias in amazement "And that's how they infiltrated the Bards Guild."

The Lady did not respond and stood deep in thought. Thias took her silence as confirmation of his statement and would have liked to have examined one of the bracelets in more detail. He pondered over the mechanics of how the Lizardmen travelled the Rift until the Lady spoke again.

"Tell me more about this boy that you call Llyat, he who interferes with my plans. I must decide if he is the one that the Enderdetag Prophecy speaks of. What was his place of origin?"

"I know little about him," replied Thias. "Why does it matter anyway? You have your 'other' who can fulfil your needs. Why do you need to bother yourself with Llyat Emgar?"

"Do I have to remind you what will happen to your friend if you do not tell me all that you know? I want to know everything about this boy before he is killed. There must be no loose ends or my plan may yet fail. The door to the Underworld must be opened and stay open for I crave the ultimate power that my 'other' will release. We march to war in a matter of days but with the strength and power of Urthanock behind me then no one, not even all the dragons and the wyverns in the Dragonas can thwart my plan."

Thias tried to assess the threat from the crone's unbridled megalomania. He sensed that she risked everything on powers that were way beyond her understanding and ability control. If the Rift had indeed abandoned her for her 'other', how could she be certain it would continue to favour him once the door had been opened? Whatever was about to unfold, one thing was clear; the attack on Parandor was imminent. He prayed that Tonousa had identified the infiltrator and silenced him before he could bring the Capital down from within.

"You seem lost in thoughts," said the Lady. "I will ask you just one last time, what you know of the Marked."

"I am being honest with you," replied Thias. "I do not know much about him. He came from Maplehill and I met him there once, before I knew of his...."

Thias hesitated mid-sentence and looked towards the Lady of the Silverwynn. He could tell that something important had registered for her face began to show the signs of recognition. Even the mercenary noticed the change in the old woman's demeanour.

"Is there something wrong my Lady?" asked Ventes.

"Maplehill you say," she continued with suspicion in her voice. "That is very interesting and it ties up with the name you gave to Ventes as your own. Yes, it all makes perfect sense to me now."

"I'm sorry. I do not follow," said Thias.

"To you it will not matter," continued the Lady. "But to my plan it is most important. 'When a Marked is found amongst the Maples'. The words from the Prophecy confirm your boy to be the one I must eliminate. You may be surprised to learn that we both have connections to that insignificant little village along the banks of the Tiaryer, and I don't mean Rukave Emgar, the guardian of the Marked, the one who stole the boy from my care."

"But you cannot m...m...mean..." stammered Thias but the Lady cut him off.

"I speak of the Vessel, a boy like Llyat, one who cannot die. A young man that carries the three circle brand of Kha upon the back of his head. You see there is another 'Marked' and it will be the 'other' that sits by my side once Parandor has been destroyed."

Thias was stunned. Even though the Lady had not named the 'other' there was only one from Maplehill who carried the curse brand of Kha. Yet he was supposed to be dead. Thias searched the Lady's face for confirmation of his suspicion but all he saw was row upon row of wrinkles. The interrogation was draining her energy and her sand was racing to empty.

"This conversation has made me very weary. I must rest Ventes. Sslondash will escort me back to my chamber."

"As you so wish my Lady," replied the mercenary.

The old woman wilted and almost collapsed. Ventes and Sslondash moved forward to support her. The Lizardman took most of her weight while Ventes opened the door to the cell. As the three moved past Irabo the mercenary punched out one last time and shattered Irabo's nose. Crimson sprayed from his nostrils and down onto his body. Irabo coughed and spluttered while Ventes shook away the pain from his hand. The mercenary then gave his full attention to the Lady and helped to keep her upright. The iron door closed.

Thias felt a great weakness in his legs. He wanted to move across the room and support Irabo but could not for the manacle and chain around his leg prevented him doing so. All he could do was offer his young friend a few words of encouragement.

"Stay with me Irabo. Don't give up just yet."

A sudden cough and expulsion of blood demonstrated that Irabo was at least still alive and gave Thias a glimmer of hope.

"Are you okay?" he dared to ask.

"Never felt better!" groaned Irabo. "But who was she talking about? Who is the other 'Marked'? Do you believe there could be two of them?"

"At his moment in time, I just don't know," answered Thias but deep in his heart he now knew that Methladon Heyn was alive.

27

"They are all going to be here," said Tonousa as the large wooden doors of the white marble hall closed behind her. "All four of them."

Her searching eyes surveyed the gathering of the Lords and Ladies of the Royal Court who had all been summoned to the throne room. The collective multitude of perspiring bodies raised the temperature of the room to an unpleasant degree and hindered her intent to check the identity of all who were present. The sweating herd also proved a significant obstruction to her attempt to move to the centre of the chamber in order to get closer to the throne itself. Without warning a pair of large hands settled onto her back and propelled her through the first line of bodies. Danisun Dain continued to push Tonousa forward and he followed close behind so as not to create a gap for others to infill. Darchus Arillius, the third of their group, then did likewise.

"Keep moving Tonousa" ordered Danisun. "Remember our purpose in being here."

"Yes, of course, you are right as always," she replied as she sought to control her nerves.

Tonousa had every reason to feel apprehensive given all that she had been through in the past few weeks. Her mind raced and she tried to second guess the basis for Lady Emeny's summons. She was further intrigued to discover what those from the Wizard's Guild had found inside the Lore of the Dead, the book that haunted her investigation and which was never far from her thoughts. Through the crowd she pushed and to the annoyance of most present she elbowed her way to the front of the highborn wastrels. The lofty lot had all turned out in their finest attire and continued to pass their time in irrelevant and inane conversations. All waited in similar anticipation to hear the news which they expected was of great importance. Lady Emeny had somehow managed to mobilise the whole Court, shake them out of their apathy and collect them together in the same place at the same time. Tonousa reckoned this had to be a first in the long history of Parandor politics.

Having pushed through the crowd Tonousa at last came before the empty marble throne in the centre of the hall. There was no sign of Phauless Gylewu and Lady Emeny twitched from one foot to the other at the side of the regal seat. Tonousa then spotted Sir Byddin who stood a little way behind her. He was dressed in full armour and he signalled in turn to each pair of Royal Guards that had been posted at every entrance to the vast room. This was just as Tonousa would have expected given that the Sovereign was due to make an appearance and make an important pronouncement.

"It seems Sir Byddin has doubled the guard. Something is not right," whispered Danisun.

"And there's no sign of Phauless," replied Tonousa. "Do you think something could have happened to him?"

"No, I don't think so. We would have heard already."

"Yet something is up or Lady Emeny wouldn't have called everyone here like this. I suspect it is more than just a message from the wizards..." began Tonousa before Danisun interrupted.

"Promise me that you won't do anything rash. Remember what happened following your stupid actions at the Stukeley Knoll. We don't want to go through all that again. "

Tonousa did not answer. She had reflected with great discomfort on those events every day since being released from her incarceration in the Underkeep; how having turned up to witness her father's execution she had stolen a sword off another member of the Watch and had ran run through the crowd with the blade drawn. It stopped her from sleeping most nights and the images had grown ever more vivid as the weeks had passed.

Then through the crowd she made eye contact with Sir Richemanus. The executioner stood in formal garb and leaned against a closet built into the east wall of the room. There he sipped from a goblet having been the first to help himself to the free wine, an act that no one else had yet dared to replicate. Tonousa's investigations had unravelled the reality behind the fearful persona of Sir Richemanus of the Nightfall. She now knew him to be a nothing more than an over-powering bully and in debt to almost all who walked the streets of Parandor. Yet despite a trace of compassion, Tonousa still hated the man who delivered the blow that had severed her father's neck.

"Do not worry Danisun; how could I ever forget," she uttered under her breath.

The two comrades in arms looked once again at Sir Byddin as he waved out his orders to his guards. Tonousa watched him point to the crowd after which he gesticulated to Sir Horace Mandleworth in order to attract his attention. She pushed her way closer in order to see what Sir Byddin was pointing at and as the crowd parted her vision fell upon numerous wooden tables in the shape of the letter 'L' that had been placed before the raised plinth on which the throne rested. The trestle tables were filled with every conceivable type of rich and expensive food, resting on golden plates, and interspersed between flagons of wine. It was a feast beyond belief for the members of the Watch, unaccustomed as they were to the excesses of the Royal Court.

"I don't like this one bit. Something is not right," mumbled Tonousa. "The room is well guarded and yet it seems there is to be a celebration of some sorts. I wonder if Lady Emeny is going to reveal her news before or after the horn has blown for the race to the trough. Perhaps we need to say our piece before the tables are besieged by the highborn porkers."

Without pause Danisun took hold the nearest servant by shoulder and pulled him towards the three members of the Watch. Tonousa recognised the boy at once for he had been Xix Blackfayer's cupbearer. Now it seemed he was just one of the general pool of dog bodies.

"What is going on here lad? What's with all the food?" demanded Danisun.

"This great buffet has been ordered and provided by Lord Phauless on the recommendation of Lady Emeny," replied Arfon.

The lowly servant's voice trembled, confronted as he was by the two who had threatened his former master in his chambers.

"What purpose does all this food serve? What are we here to celebrate?" said Tonousa

"I have been told it is to lighten everyone's spirits given all the concerns and worry over the recent murders and the preparations for war," continued Arfon, trying not to trip over his words. "The message from the kitchens is that this food would go to waste if not eaten soon. It had been ordered to celebrate the wedding of our Sovereign's late brother, Lord Raorick."

Tonousa nodded in recognition of the plausible explanation. It seemed to make perfect sense and it surprised her how Raorick's demise had slipped from her consciousness. Now she recalled the importance of Thias's story of the slaughter at the Grey Keep.

"Thank you, your words are much appreciated," said Tonousa.

"Yes, well done lad, now fuck off," added Danisun.

Arfon made his way into the crowd while Tonousa's attention was drawn to the priest Heward Teulu whom she spotted amongst the gathered throng. He was immersed in deep conversation with two slender and beautiful blondes, Lady Calendrial Lorst and Lady Antviane Rirert. Tonousa tried to read his lips and was sure he spoke the word 'Lillywort' as he showed his injured hand to the two captivated women.

A loud crash sounded to Tonousa's right. The crowd then pressed forward to see what had caused the sudden commotion.

"It seems that fool is making mischief again," said Darchus who had been covering the backs of his two companions.

"Who do you mean?" asked Tonousa as she turned to face her friend from Valameer.

"The Court Fool, now what was his name? Ah yes, Lolly I seem to remember."

"What about the idiot" continued Tonousa?

"He's the one making all the racket," said Darchus as he pointed through the crowd. "He's got everyone's attention now, look even Sir Richemanus is laughing and that must be a first."

Tonousa searched through the multitude until her gaze fell upon the imposing figure of the executioner. She then followed his line of sight to a parting in the crowd. Lolly lay amongst a heap of fallen seats. He had been demonstrating his chair balancing trick but had as usual failed to bring it off. His arms and legs flailed amongst the weevilled wood and he cursed aloud to the gods for failing him in his moment of need. Even Tonousa raised a hint of a smile at the farce.

"Always the fucking imbecile that one," said a voice from behind. "He's just a knob-head like his father and his father before him."

"Well said Lord Commander," added Danisun Dain.

Tonousa looked to her side and with a nod of her head acknowledged her superior.

"Good, I 'm glad you're all here," he said.

"Do you know what this is all about?" asked Danisun.

Tonousa could only assume that the reason Danisun had forgotten they were answering the Sovereign Advisor's summons was the consequence of his recent head trauma.

"I understand that Emeny and the rest of the Council want to hear an account of your findings Danisun," replied Commander Townsforth. "Given that you let Tonousa off the leash in this investigation, I thought it best that she accompanied you. From what I have heard she seems to have upset a few important people with the manner of her questioning."

Tonousa looked to Sir Richemanus who was in the process of clearing the mess that Lolly had created. Then she switched her attention Lady Emeny who now waited with mounting frustration for the appearance of Phauless Gylewu. She sensed it had to be one or both of those who had made complaints against her.

"But what's all this about the Wizards Guild, Sir?" said Tonousa as she sought to deny the message from her Commander. "I was led to believe that Lady Emeny's summons was a consequence of the wizards finding something of significance within the Lore of the Dead. I don't see why their Guild would involve themselves in these matters for they have always refused to do so in the past."

"When that infamous book resurfaced, planted in your father's room by some unknown person who wished to frame him, Lady Emeny passed it on to the Wizard's Guild. They were instructed to hold it in their possession, for safe keeping, and in order to prevent any further mischief," continued the Lord Commander. "Archmage Iqotrix has apparently found something within the tome, something that refers to a prophecy and the possible resurgence of Urthanock. You may remember the threat to the wizards posed by Karoly and his vigilantes. As that menace has been removed the wizards feel it now safe to move outside of their Guild."

"I apologise Lord Commander," added Tonousa. "But how do you know all of this?"

"Sir Byddin let it slip by chance a few hours ago when we shared a glass or two of that firewater known as Hotch's Hooch and which I obtained from... Never mind where I got it! Did you know that Byddin had shown an interest in the infernal book? He told me that buried somewhere within its pages was a clue to the whereabouts of an object that could help us in our fight with Avolire."

"I don't trust that bastard," replied Tonousa while she tried to relocate Byddin within the room. Her eyes made contact with those of Heward Teulu, still engaged in conversation with Ladies Lorst and Rirert.

"Well, at least the book has been protected," added Danisun.

"You're right," continued the Lord Commander. "If I recall from the time that Death Tubaria first raised its ugly head, it is impossible to progress the aims of the cult without the content of that evil tome."

Tonousa recalled her meeting with Heward Teulu. If the priest's suspicions were true, that the resurfacing of the cult was just cloak and daggers, then the Commander had come to a false conclusion.

"There is something you need to know Lord..." began Tonousa.

As she sought to finish her sentence her voice was drowned out by the sudden call for silence from the centre of the room. The eyes of all present focused on Lady Emeny.

"Quiet; I must have everyone's attention."

The background noise subsided as the Lady who moved to the tables of food at the edge of the platform. Tonousa felt somewhat perplexed for the demeanour of the Lady was no longer that of a woman who lived on the edge of her nerves. No, it was that of a confident professional who appeared ready to take on any challenge that the world threw at her feet. Once again Tonousa's thoughts recalled words that Heward Teulu had spoken. *'Look to the most unlikely person'* he had told her and as Emeny spoke again Tonousa could not help but think perhaps this was not the real Lady but rather a servant of the Eastern Marsh, the very infiltrator that she sought to unmask.

"My Lords, Ladies, and others," began Lady Emeny. "I now ask that all who are not members of the Council remove themselves from the hall. The feast will begin soon and do not worry, you will all be invited back and will not miss out on the magnificent spread that our Sovereign has bestowed upon us. However, at this precise moment there are several things that I need to discuss with the Council and the four members of the City Watch that I see before me. What I have to say must be in private and therefore I thank you in advance for your understanding. I will conduct my business in haste so please do not wander too far or you may miss out on the best dishes."

None of those dismissed sought to show dissent despite their obvious disappointment. One by one the lower tier members of the Court and their servants funnelled out of the room. They passed through the various exits that would soon be closed, guarded from both inside and out. The elite waited upon the floor of the hall while Tonousa noted the positions of Sir Byddin, Heward Teulu, and Gilebin Ystafell in particular. Then without warning as the crowd thinned Lady Emeny raised her hand and called out.

"Not you Lolly. As much as it displeases me, you must stay. I have need of you this day."

Tonousa looked to where the Fool stood both surprised and still. A look of astonishment flashed across his face after which he bowed in a most comical fashion and then moved back towards the centre of the room.

"Thank you my dear, I feel most honoured, I think!" exclaimed Lolly as he stuck two fingers up at Gilebin Ystafell and took his place besides Lady Emeny at the edge of the feast.

"Why keep the Fool here?" whispered Tonousa to Commander Townsforth.

"I'm nonplussed," he replied.

"And where's Iqotrix?" she continued. "I thought he'd be..."

The last member of the Court at last left the room. Tonousa then noticed a tall slender man with spiked red hair and a youthful yet wizen face, marked with pox scars and thick black hairs that grew in a stubble from the end of his pointed chin. She had never seen this person before, one who stood at one end of nest of tables and poured himself a goblet of wine. Her eyes moved from the drinking vessel to the man's hands and there she noted several different coloured rings on long bony fingers. She knew at once who this strange looking man was.

"Don't worry, I've found him," she whispered to her Commander.

With the doors to the hall sealed tight by Sir Richemanus and Sir Horace Mandleworth, Lady Emeny turned towards Watcyn Dustfury who stood at attention by the portal that led to the Sovereign's chambers. The knight readied the horn that he held in his hands. With a nod from the Sovereign Advisor, Dustfury raised his trumpet and made ready to blow. A look of anger from Lady Emeny however made him think better of it and so he opened the door, pushed his head into the shadows, shouted something that no one else could hear, and then returned to attention at his post. All conversation ceased as Phauless Gylewu strode into the room, flanked by his personal body guard. On reaching his throne with his two protectors behind him, he turned to address his Council.

"I thank you all for coming at such short notice. Sir Richemanus, I am even pleased to see you here for it gives me comfort to know that I have your added protection against any who would seek to do me harm. Llys, I see that everyone is here that you asked for but also Lolly for some strange reason. Now without further delay please explain to us all why you have gathered us together."

The Sovereign took then took his place on the throne. Lady Emeny moved even closer to him and then began her address.

"First of all dear friends, Lord Phauless is most honoured that you have come to accept a share of the feast he has provided for us all today. Please show appreciation for his benevolence,"

The Council members began to clap their hands until Phauless raised his right hand.

"Your gratitude is noted," said the Sovereign.

"She's stalling," whispered Tonousa into her Commander's ear.

"Yes I think you are right," said Danisun.

Tonousa raised an eyebrow, surprised that her voice had carried to others. Then in the next moment, Phauless's demeanour changed and he snapped at Lady Emeny.

"Enough of this shit Llys. Just get on with it and tell us why you have dragged us all here today."

A flustered Lady Emeny tried to hide her surprise at the Sovereign's sudden change of mood. Tonousa was also perplexed, if not more so. Phauless Gylewu was known to be a fair and mild man who seldom raised his voice. However, these were troubled times and she thought perhaps that was the simple explanation for his change in demeanour. After all, numerous members of his household had been murdered and there had been an attempt on his own life by an unknown who had not as yet been apprehended. He had great reason to be on edge and suspicious of everyone and everything.

"You owe us all an explanation Lady," continued Phauless. "But first tell me why that cow's twat of a Fool remains in our company. You told me this was sensitive official business, not some mummer's farce."

"My lord, these are the most dangerous of hours," stuttered Lady Emeny. "Given the recent attempt to end your days and what we are all about to discuss I have a great fear that someone may attempt to poison you in the manner of the Death Tubaria murders. Therefore I propose to promote the Fool to the role of Royal Food Taster. From now on you will not eat or drink anything that Lolly hasn't first sampled, and of course survived. Should he die in the process, you will be spared and we will all be the better off for no longer having to listen to the idiot's words."

Phauless laughed.

"Llys, I cannot ask him to do that?" he replied shaking his head. "No one should put their life before mine in such a way..."

"Lolly would be most honoured to accept this role," replied the fool as he bobbed his head in his usual ridiculous manner. "Just think of all the wondrous concoctions that I will get to taste. I will endeavour to save some for you my Lord, unless of course I like them too much,"

"I cannot ask this of you..." continued Phauless but Lolly would not be rejected.

"I accept this honour. Indeed I insist that I have it my Lord."

Lolly then ran to nearest table and began to pick up samples from the dishes. These he shoved into his mouth until his cheeks began to bulge. Tonousa saw in that moment that Lady Fullbane would now have competition in the race to empty the larders of the Realm and that thought led her to realise that the big one was absent from the hall. She then remembered that the whale was not a full member of the Council. Without warning the Fool dropped to the floor and began to shake with uncontrolled violence. After several seconds in which all watched on in disbelief, Lolly spat the food out and jumped to his feet.

"Just joking!" he laughed.

Danisun whispered into Tonousa's ear such that the Commander could not hear.

"We can but hope that someone poisons the annoying little fucker."

Tonousa turned and glared at her colleague.

"It's just the concussion speaking!" he added with a cheeky smile on his face.

Tonousa looked back towards the Sovereign Advisor. She sensed that Lady Emeny was about to recommence her speech, however it was Sir Byddin's voice that she heard next.

"Well Llys, What have you to say for yourself? Dogs bollocks; what's going on?"

"Yes Emeny," lisped Gilebin Ystafell. "Explain yourself at once. We all have many other important tasks we need to complete this day."

Lady Emeny sighed and glanced towards Phauless Gylewu. The Sovereign then signalled with a wave of his hand for her to proceed and at last she began to explain her motives for calling the meeting.

"You all know Archmage Iqotrix I presume," she began, gesturing towards the strange looking man with the spiky red hair and with goblet in hand.

"Of course we know who he is," exclaimed Sir Byddin. "What the..."

"Let him speak and you will know," Lady Emeny shouted back. "Archmage, you may proceed at your convenience. As for the rest of you, please allow him the curtesy he deserves and as difficult as it may be, keep your ears open and your mouths shut while he speaks."

Tonousa looked on with much suspicion as the Archmage climbed onto the platform. There he bowed in respect to the Sovereign and then turned to address those present.

"He we go," said Tonousa under her breath.

"My Lords and Ladies of the Council and friends from the City Watch," the wizard began, his voice soft and direct. "I first sought out Lady Emeny on the matter that I bring before you as I was aware of her fascination and interest in the history of the ancient times. That plus her role as Sovereign Adviser made her the ideal member of the Council for me to approach with my findings."

"What fucking findings?" spat out Sir Byddin, unable to restrain himself.

"As you all know, ever since the arrest of Lord Amberstone and the recovery of the Lore of the Dead that was found in his chambers," continued the Arch Mage unmoved. "That dreadful tome has been in the possession of the Wizard's Guild following an order issued by Lady Emeny herself. We found no enchantment had been placed upon the book that would excuse a person to commit such atrocities as Lord Jonas Tullage did all those years ago. Whoever began to re-enact the secrets contained within its pages did so of their own free will. We therefore concluded that the book was not responsible for Lord Tullage's actions but nonetheless we are taken aback by its profound and wondrous content."

"Come on Llys," spluttered Sir Byddin. "What is the point of this? If we wanted more fucking riddles we could have just listened to the Fool."

Tonousa's smile disappeared when the Archmage moved at speed to the spot where Sir Byddin stood and squared up to the Head of the Royal Guard.

"I have heard Byddin that for some reason you sought access to certain pages of the tome."

Tonousa's ears pricked up. As far as she could recollect there were just two people who would have known about Sir Byddin's interest in the Lore of the Dead, her father and Xix Blackfayer. She then remembered two other possibilities, the Historian who hid as Rukave Emgar, and Lord Enguerrand Fullbane. The colour drained from Sir Byddin's face as the Archmage continued.

"You searched for a weapon didn't you? A most powerful one to use against the forces of Avolire, an axe that contains one of the lost Gems of Thamous. For those of you who do not know, these gems when brought together grant the power of access into the Underworld."

"That may be the case, but I don't see..." stuttered Sir Byddin.

The Archmage ignored the knight's response and continued his address.

"I do not know how many of you are acquainted with the Prophecy of Enderdetag. You need to understand the importance of this work for I have spent many days looking at its verses and have I have examined them in infinite detail. I must tell you this, the Prophecy is contained within the Lore and was written in blood; although whose it was even I cannot begin to guess."

Once again the room fell silent. After a few seconds a general murmur began to grow as members of the Council began to vocalise their fears. Tonousa knew what the Archmage had come to discuss. The summons was linked to the details of the old prophecy she had first heard in Valameer. She had doubted its relevance then but now its importance became clearer by the minute.

"From the look on a few of your faces, it is clear that some of you have heard of the Prophecy before today," said the wizard while making eye contact with Tonousa.

He could either read her mind or her facial expression had given up the truth of her concerns. Tonousa wasn't sure which as she waited to hear what was said next. Phauless Gylewu leaned forward for he too had much interest in this news.

"What is this Prophecy of Enderdetag and how is it linked to the armies of Avolire?" the Sovereign asked.

Tonousa would not have been surprised if the wizard had pulled the Lore of the Dead out from under his robes but he didn't. Instead he began to recite the Prophecy from memory.

When the Marked is found amongst the Maples,
And the armies of the east shall walk again,
With the Enderdetag alignment in the heavens,
Then shall be the end of good men.

When the Oracles crypt shall be opened,
And the choices we make must thrive,
The powers of evil shall be woken,
And no one alive shall survive.

From the innocent the savoir shall waken,
To the Bards he shall appear,
To reunite the Gems of Thamous,
And destroy the Lord of Fear.

The hall fell silent and the words reverberated around Tonousa's head. Her thoughts raced as she tried to envision who the infiltrator could be and the true nature of the great evil that was at work within the Capital. Desperate for some clue as to the identity of the murderer she sensed their evil presence. Scanning the faces of the council she sought see if the revelation of the prophecy had caused any significant change.

"Bollocks! Absolute bollocks!" exclaimed Sir Byddin whereupon Phauless raised his hand again and demanded silence.

"Lolly!" shouted the Sovereign. "Be of use and get me some wine."

"Yes at once your mightiness, ruler of the rich and randy; I am here to fulfil your needs."

Lolly bowed as low as only a fool can do and then moved to the table on which the wine stood waiting. He filled a goblet and took a gulp to show that he understood his new role. He winked and smiled when death did not follow and passed the goblet into his master's hands. Phauless took a couple of sips of wine and started to mull over the news of the Prophecy. Then he looked to Lady Emeny with a troubled frown.

"I am sorry if I appear somewhat dull but I still don't understand why you summoned us to be here today. What has this ancient piece of claptrap got to do with the murders that are happening in the here and now? Are you trying to say they are somehow connected?"

Once again a hubbub of background chatter rose inside the hall. Tonousa waited and wondered if the Sovereign had lost interest in the proceedings. It did not take long for Lady Emeny to sense that possibility and soon she shouted out from her position next to the marble throne.

"Please my Lord, I beg of you, let the Archmage explain."

"Very well, but make it quick. What does all of this mean wizard?"

"My Lord, in good time," began Iqotrix as he bowed and then turned to address his audience.

The weird man with the spikey hair and pox marked faced took the Council through the three verses of the Prophecy and then dissected each line with his own interpretation of its meaning. Tonousa had heard it all before and was pleased that at least the wizard had come to the same conclusion as the Bards of Valameer. Her thoughts began to wander until the Archmage began to bring his discourse to an end.

"The bulk of the Lore's text we have yet to dissect and decipher but you must all realise that the star alignment the Prophecy speaks of is already in the heavens. It has also been brought to my knowledge that a boy was found in the river by members of the City Watch. It is alleged that this youth came down the river from Maplehill and later left for Valameer. Is that not correct Lord Commander?"

The Court turned as one and all stared at the four members of the Watch. Without hesitation Commander Townsforth stepped forward and bowed low before his Ruler.

"That is correct. The wizard speaks the truth my Lord," he added with authority.

"I wonder who told the wizard that," whispered Tonousa as her thoughts raced.

"I understand that with your assistance the boy from the Prophecy was sent to meet with the bloated bards," continued the Archmage. "I do not understand why you did that Commander when all would have expected you make his presence known to this Council. You must see that the time of the Prophecy is now. The Armies of the East shall indeed march again and you have contrived to lose our potential saviour."

Townsforth grunted and took a step backwards.

"Bollocks and more fucking bollocks!" exclaimed Sir Byddin, deflecting attention away from the Commander of the Watch.

"Sir Byddin, remember whose presence you are in," ordered Phauless.

"Forgive me my Lord. I apologise for forgetting my place but as long as I breathe, I swear to you that no army of Avolire shall ever take this city."

With that said Byddin reached to the table, removed an apple, and sank his teeth into it. It was an apt move to prevent his mouth from causing more harm.

"But Lord, Avolire is in the north not the east," shouted a voice without warning; one which immediately gained the attention of all in the room.

Tonousa looked to her right in surprise as Darchus had stepped forward to address the hall.

"Forgive me, but who the fuck are you?" snapped out Phauless. "I do not think we have met. State your name."

"I am Darchus my Lord. Darchus Arillius of Valameer and now a proud servant of the City Watch of Parandor. I apologise for the interruption but Sir Byddin has failed to grasp the nature of the true enemy that we face. The words of the Prophecy do not relate to Avolire. It is those who dwell within the Eastern Marsh we should fear and their threat should not be underestimated."

"I beg to differ, this is all bollocks. I... I...," sneered Sir Byddin.

"Is there anything of relevance that you wish to share with us before I remove your tongue Sir?" added Phauless as he sneered at one eyed knight.

"I swear to you all that nothing can nor will breach this city's walls," Byddin exclaimed. "The gates are impenetrable. We have legions of troops encamped outside this city waiting for the inevitable attack from Avolire. We have constructed a vast number of machines of war and our defences are stronger than they have ever been."

"I also know your army has demolished the slums and that the poor remain homeless and helpless," shouted Phauless. "Have you failed to notice the tide of humanity that has swept to my protection and sought sanctuary around my temple?"

The Sovereign stepped forward to confront the one eyed knight.

"By the balls of Belanore," replied the Sir Byddin. "We could do without this religious shite."

Tension hung in the air as the Commander of the Royal Guard waited for Phauless to respond. Tonousa watched in anticipation. Sir Byddin coughed and muttered under his breath for it seemed his statement had been ignored. Then at last the Sovereign spoke and looked to Heward Teulu to answer his questions.

"What are we doing to help the unfortunates who have entered our city to seek my protection? What more we can do to help them?"

Then Phauless turned to Lolly "More wine, and fill my plate. Make sure you taste it all and try not to die on me. If you do not survive Fool, then today I shall go hungry."

Lolly responded at once to his Sovereign's order and made his way over to the feast. Phauless looked to Teulu for an answer to his questions.

"The unfortunates from outside the city walls are being cared for by my priests, despite the efforts of Sir Byddin's men and the armies of the Fifteen Keeps to drive them away into the wilds of countryside. The various faiths that practice within the walls of Parandor have come together to act as one. Those that follow Hamthor, Fatumai, Solaris and even Mona have put aside their differences for a greater and more pressing cause. We have united with the sole aim of feeding and protecting the masses. We are their shield against the horrors that are about to descend on this city."

"Our Sovereign Ruler is most appreciative of your efforts, Holiness," added Lady Emeny.

Phauless Gylewu hesitated as if not knowing how to respond. He turned to the Archmage and began a different conversation.

"Tell me in all truth, do we have the full support of the Wizard's if we go to war?"

"Of course my Lord, we would be honoured to support you. In the past we have steered clear of such conflicts, but given that your Royal Guards eliminated the vigilantes that had vowed to destroy all users of magic, we feel duty bound to assist you in your upcoming conflict; be it against the Knights of Avolire or those from the Eastern Marsh."

"Arrogant prick!" muttered Tonousa under her breath.

"Shush, be quiet," ordered Commander Townsforth.

"But we were the ones who stopped Nedes Karoly."

"Yes, but leave it be for now. There will be a time and a place to recognise your actions Tonousa. Right now we must listen to what more the Archmage has to say."

Tonousa could not but help wonder what the motive was behind the wizard's sudden willingness to join forces with the ruling house of Parandor. She began to contemplate that perhaps he too was Cuvar and party to the conspiracy that she had discovered between her father, Xix Blackfayer, Enguerrand Fullbane and the Historian. She vowed to explore that thought at a later date as she refocused on the Archmage's words.

"For too long wizards have hidden behind the enchanted walls of our Guild. Parandor will not fall to the Lady of the Silverwynn, her knights of Avolire, nor indeed the reptiles. We will not allow any such an evil to disturb the decades of peace that we have shared together."

"Hurrah!" bellowed Sir Richemanus.

The executioner's sudden exclamation caused Lolly to drop a small pie as he collected a selection of food for his master to sample. All present then focused on the monstrous man.

"Thank you Nightfall," replied Phauless. "I'm so pleased to hear that you have the wellbeing of the highborn ingrained in your heart. Your reaction has not gone unnoticed but I don't understand what you're doing here. You are not one of the Council and never will be."

"I apologise for my presence my Lord," replied Sir Richemanus as his cheeks flushed red.

"Just keep your mouth shut and do not interrupt again," ordered Phauless before turning his attention to the rest of those gathered. "I have to admit that I have not heard of the prophecy that the Archmage is so concerned about, well not until today. I find myself at a loss to understand why that may be. I am most surprised that our Librarian, or the previous Sovereign Advisor did not bring news of it to us earlier. Do any of you have any further knowledge or information that could be of use?"

Tonousa held her breath and remained silent. She wanted to reveal the conclusions of her investigations to date but the moment somehow did not seem right. She could not stand before her Sovereign and throw out sweeping accusations that she could not substantiate. While lost her thoughts Gilebin Ystafell spoke.

"I think I have something useful to add my Lord. If I recall correctly, Danisun Dain, the Man-at-Arms of the City Watch, may have found a weakness in the black armour that the Knights of Avolire are said to have developed."

"The metal they have fashioned from Orichalcum," interrupted the Archmage "It is the mystical ore of Calistorn that your ancestor Malistaire Gylewu went to war over but failed to obtain."

Phauless Gylewu leaned forward in his throne. He looked with great interest at the Lord Chamberlin.

"A weakness you say, why wasn't I told of this? What is wrong with you all? Why are you buggers keeping things from me?"

"Forgive me, my Lord," stammered Ystafell. "I apologise for not informing you of this earlier but after the attempt on your life which we first assumed was the work of Mathias Amberstone, Xix Blackfayer ordered me to remain silent. He said I was not to bother you with such details as you had more import issues to worry about!"

Phauless turned to his new and nervy Sovereign Advisor.

"Is this true Llys?"

"I'm afraid so," stammered Lady Emeny, her volume of voice withering as her words flowed. "Given what had happened to your brother, we felt it best to..."

Phauless thought for a moment and then turned to the Commander of the City Watch, his eyes demanding confirmation.

"Is it true that their armour has a significant weakness that we can exploit?" said Brynn Townsforth with pride.

"What the Lord Commander says is true my Lord," added Danisun as he stepped forward a pace. "It is where the breastplate fails to meet the helm, just above the shoulder. It leaves a significant gap. A blade aimed with accuracy could penetrate this space and deliver a fatal wound to the neck."

Phauless Gylewu deliberated over this revelation after which he turned his attention back to Sir Byddin.

"Are your men aware of this this weakness?"

"Yes, my Lord," affirmed the knight as he poured himself more wine.

"And what of the City Watch?" continued Phauless, "Are your men prepared for what is to come?"

"We are indeed my Lord," replied Commander Townsforth. "We have been training day and night for the past few weeks and have doubled all patrols. As you must be aware, Sir Byddin's forces will protect the outer walls, while we, the warriors of the Watch will look after all who remain inside the city. Anyone or anything that should manage to breach the outer wall will be slaughtered without mercy. However my Lord, as you wish to know all, there is one weakness in our combined defences that does cause me significant concern. You may not be aware but the mechanism that controls the work of the Narrow Gate is not as it should be. I have despatched some men to address this problem and they have been working hard to correct it. I must report however that progress has been rather slower than I had hoped."

"Sir Byddin, send ten of your strongest men to assist the Watch and ensure you guard it well until it is fully functional again," ordered Phauless.

"I will my Lord," the knight replied as he bowed low.

The Sovereign then turned his attention to the Fool who had just mounted the central platform while carrying a large plate of food. Lady Emeny had watched Lolly taste everything brought before the Sovereign.

"Thank you Lune," smiled Phauless as he took the plate from the Fool. "Oh most excellent! You have include the compote of wild mushrooms which is my favourite dish. I am being spoiled today. Now, have you tasted everything? If you are to continue in your new role then you must be thorough."

"Of course my Lord. I have doubled my weight already! I must say the mushrooms were the tastiest of all. Lady Llys has watched me savour everything."

Phauless took hold of the fork on his plate and after his first mouthful he spoke again.

"Llys, have we covered everything that you intended to raise before the Council today?"

Lady Emeny hesitated before offering an answer. In that brief moment Tonousa tried to connect the dots between the findings of her own investigation and the Prophecy of Enderdetag. She was now convinced they were linked just as Thias had long ago insisted, but she still struggled to make sense of it all. Lady Emeny at last replied.

"The Archmage has told his story and I have had my questions answered."

Phauless raised his hand and gestured to Commander Townsforth and the other three from the Watch.

"While you are with us," he began. "Please give the Council an update on your investigations into the resurgence of Death Tubaria, the sequence of the foul murders, and the attempt on my life. What progress have you made Lord Commander? Are you any closer to discovering who is responsible for these most appalling crimes?"

Tonousa looked from each of her four suspects to the next and made eye contact with all except Sir Richemanus who had his back turned to her. She wondered if he was hiding something and was then struck with a thought that made her legs weaken. Perhaps all four were in it together. Her interrogations had shown all were connected to the use and supply of Lillywort and they could be guilty of a more sinister and devious conspiracy. She began to tremble as she imagined the possibility of there being more than one shapeshifter in the room. After all, they were reputed masters of deceit and misinformation.

"As you know only too well Lord Phauless, we appointed Tonousa Amberstone to investigate the series of murders but the unfortunate events at Stukeley Knoll compromised her judgement," replied Commander Townsforth. "I therefore passed control of the investigation over to my Man-at-Arms, Danisun Dain."

"That is correct my Lord," interrupted Danisun. "However I must add that Tonousa has continued to assist me despite what happened to her father. Without her we would not have made the progress we have to date. I ask that my Lord Commander and the Council give her the floor and allow her to reveal her findings..."

"I don't think this is the time..." began Lady Emeny but Phauless raised his hand, silenced her, and then after another mouthful of food displayed his full authority.

"Be quiet Llys, let Tonousa Amberstone speak. I would very much like to hear what she has to say. Whatever she has done has inhibited the perpetrator of the crimes for there hasn't been another murder since the mark appeared on her father's severed head. I do of course exclude Blackfayer's suicide. I also note that no murders occurred while Teulu was away in Valameer!"

Tonousa witnessed a knowing look pass between Phauless and Teulu. It seemed there was more to the priest's visit to Valameer than he had told her? She would need to question the priest over the statement when her thoughts became clearer. Then she remembered what the cards had told her. She would solve the mystery inside six days.

"I don't know how to respond to that..." muttered Teulu.

"Then say nothing," ordered Phauless. "I wish to hear what Tonousa and the Watch have found out and if they are any closer to discovering the identity of the one responsible for the crimes that haunt my waking hours."

"Allow me then to start my Lord," began Tonousa.

Without further hesitation Tonousa poured out the details of her investigation. She started from the moment Danisun Dain had released her from the Underkeep following Blackfayer's suicide. She then went on to describe how Danisun had given her full control of the investigation as she was without doubt the best person to finish the task. Soon she moved on to explain how she had found four cards hidden in her father's room along with a message that hinted at four possible key suspects. She did not mention the fact that the message was in code for she felt that Theoplous had helped her enough without being dragged before the Ruler. Nor did she surface the link with the Cuvar for she had not as yet realised its full significance. She then proceeded to tell how each one of the four cards symbolised one of those now present in the hall. As Tonousa named each of the four she looked to them in turn. All were quiet and listened, as indeed did the rest of those present.

"I still don't see..." interrupted Lady Emeny but Tonousa talked her down.

She recounted how she had met and spoken with each of the four suspects in turn. Without hesitation or fear of the consequences she revealed how Sir Byddin and Lady Emeny had both been interested in the Lore of the Dead for personal and different reasons and that both had confirmed that a mind disturbing compound called Lillywort that was harvested from the Eastern Marsh was being used to subdue the members of the Royal Court, the Royal Guard, and the Armies of Parandor. This revelation resulted in a torrent of disbelief. The outcry continued when she revealed that Richemanus had been blackmailing several of the Death Tubaria victims because he too was peddling the substance.

"So this Lillywort?" said Phauless. "Where do you think our infiltrator gets his supply from and how does he get it into the Capital? Do you have any idea at all?"

"There is a collapsed tunnel that links the Citadel with the Temple of Fatumai," answered Tonousa. "The priests keep a significant amount of the flower extract in a store close to that tunnel because they use it in the embalming process of the departed highborn. I have seen this tunnel for myself earlier today and at first inspection it seems impassable. It cannot be the conduit for the flow of the compound. I'm sorry, I forgot to say that a jar of concentrated Lillywort has been stolen from Heward Teulu's subterranean store and that may be of some relevance. But I ask you all to cast your minds back to the murder of Mikus Danbury, the stable boy who was killed by a giant boulder. It is my belief that our murderer is a shapeshifter from the Eastern Marsh and that he has the ability to use magic to manipulate stone and earth. This I believe is how he uses the tunnel for his own ends. He or indeed she, moves the boulders at will to clear a passage and then seals it again once used."

"Bollocks! Not one of us here are capable of such magic," spat out Sir Byddin. "This is a preposterous proposal."

"That's a lie and you know it Sir," shouted out Richemanus of the Nightfall. "I know how you lost that eye of yours."

"Please gentlemen, stop this turd mouthing and let the woman finish," ordered Phauless with authority. "Amberstone, please continue."

Tonousa took a deep breath. She looked to her colleague's faces and realised that having started her story she would have to finish it alone. Without fear she gathered her thoughts and recommenced the summary of her investigation. She continued with the revelation that Heward Teulu had informed Xix Blackfayer that those banded with the curse mark of Kha had been murdered in the absence of the artefact known as the Dagger of Kha. The whereabouts of this foul weapon was unknown. If the branding had not been caused by the dagger them some other magic was afoot. Her belief was that the murderer was using the fear of a resurgence of Death Tubaria to mask a more sinister plot. Then Tonousa threw in the fact Lady Emeny was known to have a deep interest in ancient artefacts and in particular those from Avolire. This caused a further commotion but Phauless did not respond other than to cough and try to clear his throat.

Tonousa paused for she realised how precarious her position was given that the shapeshifter could be within several paces of where when now stood. She sensed it would be most foolish to let slip that she was also searching for the Ruby. It was fortuitous that Lady Fullbane was absent for she would no doubt have let that fact tumble out from her ever moving jaws. Tonousa then recalled that Gilebin Ystafell was also aware of the hunt for the Ruby. He too remained silent and Tonousa put that down to his inability to make the appropriate connection between the missing stone and the Gems of Thamous. When she had at last finished, the members of the Council all looked at each other as their eyes betrayed their depth of fear and suspicion. None of them knew who they could trust and the tension within the room grew ever more palpable. Even Lolly and the Archmage looked at all others with accusing eyes but all that Tonousa could do was smirk. She had thrown a large rock into the Council's pond of complacency.

"Well-spoken Tonousa," whispered Danisun into her right ear.

"Thank you for your support!" she replied as her cheeks flushed.

"So Tonousa, you believe that one from the Eastern Marsh has infiltrated the Council," said the Archmage as he stroked his chin.

"This is ridiculous," interjected Lady Emeny. "How could one of the Sovereign Council be a shape changer? We would know at once."

"Don't be stupid Llys," snapped back Sir Byddin. "That's the whole point of a shapeshifter, or Dragon Whisper as they call them north of the Grey Mountains. You're not meant to be able to spot one of the fuckers."

"You seem to know rather a lot about the Eastern Marsh, Sir," replied the flustered Lady. "I call you out as the spy. You are the shapeshifter that we seek. Richemanus will confirm you have long practiced certain aspects of magic. I accuse you of being a 'sleeper' in our midst. You must have been plotting our downfall for many years, up to this point in time when the stars are magically aligned. Come on, confess man. All the evidence adds up and our fingers point to you."

"You cow's arsehole Llys. You've lost the plot. Never in my life have I heard such bollocks!"

"Please Sir Byddin, Lady Emeny, calm yourselves..." shouted Gilebin Ystafell with an exaggerated lisp.

The Lord Chamberlain's plea fell on closed ears and Sir Byddin and Lady Emeny continued to assault each other with every profanity they could muster. Tonousa smirked again as she waited for the outcome of the spat.

"It's my job to know of such things," continued Sir Byddin as he regained his composure. "As head of the Royal Guard it is my role to know the enemy. That's why I know of terms such as Dragon Whisper. Yes of course I wanted to access the Lore of the Dead but only for the purpose of obtaining the fabled axe and jewel that I could turn against the power of a resurgent Avolire. If you must know, I even sent some of my men out into Thengar Forest in an attempt to find it but they never returned. You saw what happened those who followed Sir Britta Rainmark ten years ago. They all went mad. I will not let it happen again, not to my men."

"Sir Byddin, please. Remember where you are," lisped Gilebin Ystafell but the knight continued his rant.

"If you feel the need to point the finger at someone then just look to your hand Llys. There will be three pointing back. You have always worried me with your fascination for the history of Avolire. It's you isn't it you gushless crone. Why else would you hold such a connection for that infernal place?"

"It's just a hobby, that's all," she screamed. "Everyone is entitled to have one. It's not a crime to collect objects from the past. But I say this Sir, if you are nor the swine we seek then who in the name of the god's should we look to accuse next?"

Sir Byddin turned towards Sir Richemanus and glared. Tonousa sensed something but could not put her finger on what it was. Richemanus made a grab for Byddin and threw him to the floor. The monstrous man then placed his foot upon the knight's chest.

"To who else do you owe money?" screamed Sir Byddin from the floor. "Do we have to wait for them to die too before we know the answer?"

"There is no one else, I swear," answered the executioner as he removed his foot from Sir Byddin's chest. "Everyone that I owed money to is now dead."

"I beg to disagree," shouted Sir Byddin

The Commander of the Royal Guard leapt to his feet and punched Richemanus in his face with his gauntlet. Crimson flew in all directions and splattered across the pristine marble floor.

"Lord Commander, Do something please!" cried Gilebin Ystafell.

Townsforth acted at once. He strode to where Sir Byddin continued his assault on Richemanus and forced the two men apart. Tonousa was surprised that the few guards that remained on the inside of the doors made no effort to intervene. It was at moments like this that Tonousa understood how Brynn Townsforth had risen to the top of the City Watch.

"Stop this nonsense you pair of arseholes," demanded Townsforth.

"Oh, what great entertainment," shouted Lolly from his seat on the floor by the throne.

"And you can shut your fucking mouth before I fill it with my fist," shouted Townsforth.

Tonousa watched as Commander Townsforth pushed Sir Byddin to one side. Gilebin Ystafell helped the executioner onto an empty chair at the side of the room and then sought to arrest the bleeding from the injured knight's nose with a cloth he had snatched from one of the feasting tables. The Archmage looked bemused, still intrigued by the story that Tonousa had recounted. Tonousa was disturbed by the wizard's demeanour and his continued presence in the hall.

"I can't believe this is happening," whispered Danisun into her ear.

"Me neither" she replied. "The pair of them are total wazzocks and have no respect for our Sovereign. He should quarter their privates for such behaviour!"

"I don't think he's even noticed it," replied Danisun.

Tonousa gasped. Her stomach sank deep into her belly at the implication of those few words.

"What did you say?"

"I don't think he saw the confrontation" added Darchus. "He's been asleep for some minutes. Look at him."

Tonousa ignored all that was going on around her and looked to where Phauless Gylewu sat slumped on his throne. A sickening feeling washed over her and she screamed out in panic.

"Everybody be quiet, all is not well!"

"What more have you to say you evil bitch?" said Lady Emeny.

Tonousa rushed across the floor of the hall. Danisun and Darchus followed as all eyes gazed upon the lifeless figure on the throne with a plate of mushrooms still on his lap. The enormity of the situation grew ever larger with every step that Tonousa took and it seemed an eternity before she at last reached her Sovereign. She took hold of Phauless's right hand and it felt colder than she had hoped.

"My Lord." she shouted.

"The old bugger's fallen asleep," sneered Sir Byddin.

Ignoring the comment Tonousa placed her hand in front of the Ruler's mouth. She felt no breath and the Sovereign's lips had turned blue. There was no sign of life.

"No. No. NO!" screamed out Tonousa as she began to shake the Sovereign's body.

Lady Emeny appeared by Tonousa's side and tried to stop her assault upon the Ruler.

"What do you think you are doing," she exclaimed. "Unhand Lord Phauless at once you..."

Screams echoed throughout the room as even the Sovereign Advisor realised the truth of the moment. Tonousa then grabbed Darchus by the sleeve and pulled him towards the lifeless body. If this was murder it had happened before their eyes and they were all guilty of incompetence.

"You know what to do. Do what you did for Lady Fullbane and save him for all our sakes."

Darchus nodded to indicate that he understood the command. He pulled Phauless Gylewu down from the throne and caused the regal head to crack against the hard marble floor. Darchus then checked for signs of breathing and found none. He ripped open the Sovereign's tunic to expose his chest and then looked to Tonousa. She too had noticed the mark on Phauless's neck, the three circle mark of Death Tubaria.

The man with special skills lowered his mouth towards that of the Sovereign in order to breathe air into his lifeless body but their lips never met. A strong arm pulled him back and ordered him to stop.

"Do not touch his mouth young man, he has likely been poisoned," ordered Heward Teulu. "I suspect it was the mushrooms and you will follow him into the Underworld if you continue."

Darchus did not have to be told twice and he pulled his head away from that of Phauless Gylewu. A cold silence spread across the hall.

"Is there anything else you can do?" pleaded Tonousa.

Darchus proceeded to pound up and down on the chest of the once vibrant Ruler but there was no response. After several minutes of hard toil while everyone else looked on in shock he abandoned his heroic efforts. Tonousa then looked to the Archmage and called to him to use his great magic but the wizard just shrugged his shoulders, and dropped his head.

Phauless Gylewu IV was as dead as a man could be and in that moment Tonousa Amberstone realised the enormity of her failure. In the silence that followed the Royal Guards sealed the room.

28

On leaving the ruins of Calistorn, low clouds gathered and threatened to engulf the two travellers in the same unseasonal weather that they had first encountered in Fallguard and then on their journey through Thengar Forest. To Llyat it seemed that the cold air was determined to chase him and prevent the fulfilment of his quest. The snow caught up to them on the second day out of the city. Llyat was most grateful for the Mathulath furs that Einar had skinned amongst the derelict buildings. He was also pleased with the length of the hair on his head which had grown long and wild. It added further insulation as did a fine down of bum fluff that had sprouted unchecked upon his face. Einar had refused any fur and still braved the elements with chest laid bare. The Berserker no longer wore the nighthowler pelt over his head for it had been abandoned in the flight from the ogres. This allowed Llyat to look with awe upon the grizzled features of the giant from Falahorn.

Their journey from Calistorn was otherwise uneventful. The hard yet porous ground had given way to grassland on that second day and was of a type similar in appearance to that which flourished between the Valmuhsh and the Tiaryer. It was amid this tall verdant grass on the middle of the third day that they came across a stream which they sensed fed into the distant marshes to the east. There Einar had managed to fashion a water bladder out of the rabbit pelt, a beast he had caught and cleaned. Even in amongst land of abundant liquid Einar was keen to ensure he had an emergency supply with which to sustain them should the marsh water become unpotable. They would not travel far without water but food was not an issue. Einar had cut enough Mathulath meat to keep them free of hunger for many days, enough they hoped to get them to the temple and statue of Urthanock deep within depths of the Eastern Marsh. The homeward journey, assuming they were successful, would be different story.

Later that third day they came across a reed boat, abandoned on the edge of one of the waterways that fed into the interlaced lakes of the marsh. Llyat joined in with Einar as they thanked the Fates for the provision of transport across the stinking waters of the festering swamps. Once they had pushed away from solid ground Llyat ruminated for some time over the Berserker's last message. 'There are things in the marshes better left unmentioned'. No more was spoken about them for Einar had also said that to do so would cause Llyat to turn back. Legend had it that there were beasts in the swamp that liked the taste of men.

Llyat knelt in the front of the boat and worked his paddle on the left hand side of the vessel. Einar sat behind him on a plank and paddled to the right. Their joint effort propelled the small boat through the still waters of the marsh with ease. Cutting light ripples on the water the vessel glided through the frost filled fog that came at it from all directions. Llyat somehow knew the precise direction to take yet had to convince Einar that he was correct. On the second day on the water the Berserker challenged Llyat about the accuracy of his navigation. The youth reassured his friend and never once showed any hint of uncertainty for he had obtained a new sense of confidence and courage. It had begun the moment that he had killed the

Commander of the Knights of Avolire. All Llyat's thoughts of revenge had left him and had been replaced by intense feeling of purpose. He was on a divine mission and he would not fail, not if he had any choice in the matter. If the Fates had already decided his end, and he didn't like it, then he would tell them to fuck off and work out a more favourable ending to his life story.

"So tell me again," asked Einar. "How is it you know where to go?"

"You wouldn't believe me even if I told you," sneered Llyat.

"I'm willing to give it a try lad. Go on, test me."

The Berserker's once harsh persona had evaporated in the mist and the two friends now interacted as equals. Llyat's growing self-belief enabled his response.

"I first saw the city and the statue when I looked into the sapphire back in Barad Elestor. Then when you hid me in Calistorn I fell asleep and in a dream saw more detail where we needed to go. The visions come to me all the time now. The voices that return each night are always a little different. They tell me where to go next and I have been following their instructions."

"I see; that's rather interesting," said Einar after much deep thought.

"I knew you wouldn't believe me."

"I never said that I didn't," replied the Berserker as a light snowfall settled on the surrounding reeds "There are many strange things in this Realm and the hearing of voices is far from being the weirdest. How many did you hear?"

"There were two, both old yet so very different."

"Interesting." Einar replied.

"What do you mean?"

"Back in Falahorn, most folk believe in the voices they hear in their dreams and follow what they say with confidence. They understand such insight comes from the Moirai themselves. I have no doubt that it was their words that infiltrated your sleep and that they are guiding you on your quest."

"So you believe me?"

"Believe you!" answered Einar. "I think your fucking blessed. So what did the voices tell you last night?"

"They said we should carry on for a few days more until we reach the edge of the great lake.'"

That was how the brief conversation ended but the voices in Llyat's head continued to visit him each time that he slept. The marsh land stretched as far as the eye could see, mile upon mile of interconnected waterways with reed strewn islands and muddy banks, all covered in a dense thick fog that blocked out all reference points within the flat landscape. Llyat knew from old tales that the waters of the Eastern Marsh were fed by the north flowing river Awyth that swept down from the Grey Mountains and while the boat drifted on he began to think of other unexplored sources, perhaps long lost or dried up like the mighty river Wistulla that had once flowed out into the Dirmark. He also knew that somewhere to the South lay the passage through the mountains where the Grey Keep stood. At last his thoughts drifted down the road that led to his former home in the once proud village of Maplehill, now destroyed by the Avolire swine.

Some hours later as the two companions propelled their boat across the stagnant waters Llyat refocused on the present. He stared into the freezing fog and watched the steam form on his breath.

"Where does it end?" he asked. "Do you know how far east the bog stretches?"

"That I could not tell you," replied Einar. "In fact I don't think any without scale has ever dared to make the crossing. Those who sail the coast hint that the domain of the Lizardmen stretches all the way out to the sea. Although some consider this area still part of the Realm, the reptiles who dwell here will never pay homage to the rule of Phauless Gylewu."

"Do you think we will find the city amongst this fog and maze of waterways?" asked Llyat.

"With you leading the way, of course we will. Do not start to doubt yourself again. The Moirai have led you this far and I doubt that Cutter is sharpening her blade just yet. You seem to be the one they are most interested in and your relevance to their plans grows ever more certain to me. Have faith for we are not yet beaten."

Llyat smiled. It felt good that the Berserker showed him respect, after all they had travelled this far with his guidance. On the pair paddled with Llyat acting as lookout while they cut through the thick and impenetrable haze. The islands of green became covered in snow and frost and as he stared at them Llyat could not help but think that the Moirai were determined to make his life as difficult as they could. They were turning the marsh into a cold unending nightmare.

A moment later, away off in the fog, Llyat noticed a strange faint glow. It formed into a shape like an inverted flame and it bobbed up and down just above the level of the water. The light then vanished only to reappear a few seconds later a short distance away.

"Einar," whispered Llyat. "There's something out there in the mist."

"Where?"

"It's over there," he replied at once, but as soon as he pointed to the light it disappeared. "It doesn't matter, forget it. I must be seeing things. Perhaps my imagination is playing tricks with my eyes."

"What did you see? Tell me, it could be important."

"It was like a light that moved up and down as if beckoning us to follow"

"Wisp!" added Einar after a moment's thought. "Do you remember what I told you when we found the boat on that mud flat and you asked why it had been abandoned. I told you there were things in this place that would give you terrors. Wisps are one of them and I would rather not have had to think about them. Whoever owned this boat could have been taken by those same foul creatures."

"What the fuck is a wisp?" demanded Llyat while searching his memory for anything Denius Castor may have told him.

"You may know them by their full name."

"And what is that?" asked Llyat.

"In the common language, will-o'-the-wisp."

Llyat was somewhat embarrassed that he had not made the connection. Einar went on to explain that the will-o'-the-wisp was a water dwelling creature that fed off living flesh. Legends had it that these demons of the wetlands would lure travellers to their death with a tentacle like appendage that had its own natural luminosity. They were also rumoured to be present in large numbers in the Eastern Marsh. Those who had seen them and lived to tell the tale spoke of a flickering light or ghost like spectre. No one had ever lived to describe what the full creature looked like or how many of them there were. It was clear to Llyat that they should be avoided at all costs.

"It's not the wisps we need to worry about," continued Einar "There are said to be far worse things in the water than those buggers. I once heard a story of a gigantic reptile, not dissimilar to a dragon or wyvern that inhabits the deeper waters; a creature with jaws so fierce that it can swallow a Berserker whole and still have room for a farm boy. Those are the kind of serpents that worry me. We can see wisps coming but not the others."

"Thanks for sharing that!" said Llyat.

The pair paddled through the marsh for a further two days. They stopped just to relieve themselves of over the side of the boat and to take on water. Yet even then they did not dally long just in case some swamp monster should be lurking nearby. Whenever Llyat's eyes tired from the strain of staring through the fog, Einar took over at the front of the boat. All the while Llyat continued to follow the directions revealed in his dreams. He went off instinct for there were still no landmarks or stars in the sky that could confirm the path that he steered through the swamp. He became ever more attuned to his surroundings and heard many noises made by creatures that lurked within the mist. He picked up the sounds of fish as they hunted for insects and broke through the surface of the water. Most of all he was grateful that the waterways had not iced over for that would have meant abandoning their boat. The plant life that grew amongst the reeds and mosses soon began to attract Llyat's attention. There he spotted strange white flowers, tinted in parts with pale yellow. They grew on what resembled small bushes that populated the edge of many of the islands. Llyat was reminded of the solitary rose he had seen poking through the snow during the journey through Thengar Forest and it warmed him to see this new white flower as it clung to life in an otherwise hostile environment. Floating alongside one particular bush Llyat reached out to pick one of the wild blossoms when Einar shouted from behind.

"I wouldn't touch them if I were you lad."

"Why is that?" he asked as he pulled his hand away. "Are they poisonous?"

"They are called Lillywort," replied Einar. "Parts of that plant have powerful properties and I don't want to witness what would happen if you touched it."

"Thanks for the warning," said Llyat as he gulped in air.

"I've heard that a man can go mad after contact with that flower and that a concentrate made from its pollen can kill in an instant," continued Einar. "It just stops you breathing."

"And there I was about to pick one."

"Like I said Llyat, I'm glad you didn't. It is also whispered that there are some who have a natural immunity to the flower's poison and that includes the Lizardmen. The scale-shites use the plant's properties for both recreation and for war. They sometimes coat the tips of their arrows and swords in the stuff. Either they send you mad or they kill you outright depending on the strength of the coating they use."

Llyat did not share Einar's enthusiasm for talking about the flower, in fact the thought of it made him shudder. He struggled to understand how something so beautiful could be so lethal. In those seconds of contemplation he wanted to flee from the unique bloom but then as he looked around he realised they were everywhere.

"Thank you so much for coming with me."

"If you remember, I swore an oath," said the Berserker. "Thias made me do it; to protect the 'Marked' come what may. I pray that Fatumai still favours him and that he and Irabo are still alive."

Llyat sighed and reflected on the potential fates of his friends. At best he presumed they had been taken by the ogres to Avolire. If that was the case he feared for the torture they would no doubt endure. Yet this was a more preferable outcome than imagining they were already stiff and their bones picked at by the beasts that roamed free across the lands north of the Grey Mountains.

"I'm sure they alive," said Llyat without much conviction.

The journey through the marsh continued to slip by in silence. It gave Llyat time to think back to all that had happened to him since the attack on Maplehill had fractured his life. He also began to dwell on thoughts of Heliana and prayed she had made it back to Parandor. Yet wherever she was, he hoped she had not forgotten him. The thought of her in the arms of another was too painful to contemplate. He longed to feel her touch and have her both comfort and excite him. Through the long frozen days within the swamplands this was the one thought that sustained his positivity. Then from time to time his troubles surfaced. He tried to imagine how he could gain access to the Lizardmens' city without being seen or noticed. If, as he was led to believe, it lay in the centre of a lake surrounding a rocky island, the temple of Urthanock would not be easy to approach without being seen. His dreams had not so far revealed any weakness in the reptiles' defences. The one decision he had made however was that he and Einar would need to travel to the island under the cover of a misty night if they were to retain any element of surprise. He still had no idea how he would make it through to the temple once landed and so decided to leave that to a later time when he hoped an answer would reveal itself. Then as if from nowhere he had an idea. If they managed to reach the island they could create a significant distraction. That tactic always seemed to work in the stories that Denius Castor used to tell over the froth of his beer. With that idea implanted Llyat turned to Einar

"What do you know about the city of the Lizardmen?"

"Until you mentioned it in Barad Elestor I did not know it existed," replied the Berserker. "I have never heard even a sniff of a rumour about the place. Why do you presume I would know of it?"

"My visions indicate that the city floats on something, but on what I wonder?"

"Well, I could make a guess and say that the island is made of the same material as their houses," continued Einar. "I remember Geir and Gulbrand returning once from a reconnaissance on the edge of the marsh. They had been sent there many years ago by Cvyler Olin with the instruction to observe one of the Lizardmen villages. They reported that the buildings were made from mud and Tetorak, the reed that grows in great abundance amid the marshland. Perhaps that is what the island floats upon, a raft of Tetorak. Anyway, why do you ask?"

"No reason," answered Llyat. "I was just trying to devise a plan to get us onto the city. We are going to need a good one if we are to get to the temple unnoticed."

"You do surprise me lad. What ever happened to the scared pup I met in Falahorn?"

"He is long gone," said Llyat. "He's just a distant memory."

"So what have you got in mind?"

"Fire!" replied Llyat as he made a right fist and exclaimed, "Promethelumous."

Llyat did not know if the spell would work. The last time he had attempted to cast it was in the back of the ogres cart near Calistorn but with heightened confidence he hadn't thought twice about trying again. His hand ignited into a ball of flame and yet he felt no pain nor sniffed any burning of flesh. All he sensed was the warmth of the magic as it flowed down his arm from the centre of his body. His confidence grew by the second following the success of his experiment.

Throughout the next day Llyat continued to formulate his plan to infiltrate the floating city and despite the fact they hadn't yet reached it he knew what their next course of action would be. They would approach the city from the south under the cover of darkness. There they would ignite the reeds that formed the base of the island and while the Lizardmen attended to the fire, he and Einar would take the boat to the northern most point of the city and disembark during the chaos. He had, however, still not worked out how to reach the temple unobserved. It wasn't long before Llyat got the chance to confirm that his plan would work. The next morning after yet another iteration of his dream the small boat entered into a great lake which stretched out to the horizon in all directions. The freezing fog that had so hampered their journey dispersed within minutes and allowed the two travellers to see the lake in its full majesty. That was when then both saw it, the floating metropolis that lay in the centre of the swamp.

In order to take stock of their situation they moored their boat for a time on a small island that lay in the mouth of the waterway that fed into the lake. Llyat stepped onto dry land for the first time in days and stared across the vastness of the water towards the island in the distance. The city was just as his dreams had revealed. There upon an enormous floating raft of Tetorak, was a sprawling mass of squat reed and mud buildings. The city stretched for several leagues and at its northern end a long rickety bridge constructed from similar materials connected the island to the marshland at the side of the lake. Llyat could just about make out a collection of moored boats, similar to the one they had themselves found abandoned. He squinted as he tried to spot the signs of movement either from within the city or on the bridge but the distance defeated him. Then his gaze was captured by that which he had come to find. In the centre of the city, rising above everything else, was a large outcrop of rock that had the appearance of a small mountain. It was certainly big enough to house a Temple. Llyat's thoughts returned to the vision he had experienced when he had touched the sapphire in Barad Elestor. It had shown him this very place where Lizardman warriors hid within a sprawl of wood, reed, and mud. The words of the Prophecy resonated through his mind as he scanned the island's shore line and looked for signs of activity.

'And the Armies of the East shall march again.'

He next tried to estimate how many Lizardmen he would need to avoid in order to reach his goal. The city went on as far as the eye could see. All of its surface was covered in huts, each he reckoned large enough to house two or three lizards. A quick estimate suggested he would have to avoid several thousand in order to complete his mission. He remained puzzled by the absence of significant activity on the island and hoped that meant that the army of the Eastern Marsh had already embarked on its long journey to Parandor. Then he remembered the Rift and that they had perhaps used it to leave the city. He turned to Einar who guarded their precious boat.

"Back in the Dragonas, at the Gathering, I understand your friends Geir and Gulbrand saw the Knights of Avolire approach from a great distance. Do you also have that gift of far sight?"

"All Berserkers do," added Einar as he left the boat and made his way over to Llyat.

"Excellent, that was the answer I was hoping for. What can you see on the island? I have spotted some limited movement but cannot see enough detail on which to help plan our next move. Can you see any signs of their army or indeed anything else that we need to avoid?"

Einar looked out towards the floating city. He lifted his right hand above his eyes to block out the glare from Solaris and scanned the length of the visible shoreline.

"I see just a few females of their kind and some of their offspring down by the water's edge," he began. "There are old ones which appear to be fishermen and a couple of metal workers. The place does not look fortified or even guarded."

"That's very fortunate for us."

"I guess that you still intend us to cause a fiery distraction?" added Einar.

Llyat paused for a moment and thought long and hard. If the army had moved on and the city had been left depleted of swamp scum then perhaps a fire would be unnecessary and indeed only cause the Lizardmen to return. Stealth and the cover of darkness could perhaps be the best plan.

"I'm not so sure now,"

The youth continued to scan the distant shoreline and soon he spotted a small area of flattened reed which was devoid of houses.

"There," said Llyat as he pointed with his finger. "That's where we shall head for. We will sneak in under cover of darkness. Once on land we shall move behind the nearest buildings and regroup in their shadows. With a bit of luck we may get in without being seen. We can then decide whether to set the island alight."

Einar thought on Llyat's plan as he too fixed his attention onto the same area.

"Llyat, I think your plan may work. I vote to burn the place down."

When at last night fell Llyat's plan was actioned. Cloud had returned and it covered the sky with a dark curtain that hid any light from Mona. Having filled their bellies with the last of the Mathulath meat they took to the boat again. As before Llyat sat in the front and at speed they navigated their vessel across the open waters of the lake. Throughout their journey they broke the surface of the water with their paddles with great care so as to reduce both the sound and the ripples from the craft's bow. The journey took a little longer than Llyat had expected but eventually they reached the southern end of the island. Save for the occasional light from an inquisitive wisp the journey was uneventful. The boat reached the line of reeds at the planned location and there Llyat reached out and took hold of the nearest tuft of Tetorak.

"Are you ready?" he asked with urgency of voice. "Once I ignite this stuff we will need to move fast. I hope the cloud cover persists. Do you understand what we need to do?"

Einar indicated that he both understood and was ready for the off. Llyat closed his eyes and concentrated on his hand. He ripped out a bundle of Tetorak and held it aloft.

"Promethelumous," he whispered, but nothing happened.

"Promethelumous," he whispered again and this time the reed bundle in his hand ignited.

Llyat waded through the shallows to firm land, ran to the nearest structure and placed the burning foliage against the buildings dry reed and timber supports. The flame took hold at once and the base of the building began to burn with zest. Wasting no time Llyat made his way back the boat and jumped back in at the front.

"It's now or never," he exclaimed and having gripped his paddle he pushed back against the edge of the island. As quick as they could the two friends backed away from the burning island and into the darkness of the waters of the great lake.

Llyat watched as the fire took hold; its red and yellow flames jumping from one building to another in the small isolated harbour of the city. Its intensity grew exponentially and having raged for less than a minute it created a terrifying and ever expanding conflagration. Dense and acrid smoke began to rise and drift over the waters of the lake. Soon the flames spread further amongst and reed houses and the city seemed destined for complete destruction.

"Come on, let's get out of here," ordered Llyat.

He moved his paddle in the water so as to turn the boat to the left. A few minutes later Llyat heard a multitude of screams uttered in a strange language. He felt the heat that drifted over the water as the fire jumped from building to building. Loud crackling noises filled his ears while his nostrils stung from the smoke. Several groups of Lizardmen attempted to contain the spread of the fire by using containers of water and by pulling down sections of houses to act as firebreaks. Lizardmen were then everywhere, all sizes, some fatter than others with a more frog-like appearance. But there was no evidence of an army. The vision he had seen when he had touched the sapphire in Barad Elestor had shown one and its absence both perplexed and troubled him.

"I think that got their attention?" whispered Llyat, loud enough such that Einar could hear.

"Time alone will tell if it's all of them," replied the Berserker. "We will know for certain when we get to the other side of their city."

It took a good twenty minutes of furious paddling to reach the dark northern tip of the island. As they had moved along the coast Llyat noticed the land come awake and a wave of lamps rolled from building to building. So as the fire spread so did the commotion it caused in the populace. Flames engulfed the entire southern aspect of the metropolis while ash began to fall from the sky like snow.

"Do you think I've over cooked it?" asked Llyat, feeling a hint of remorse.

"Not at all," added Einar. "Just think what they would have done, or indeed will do if they ever catch you. Focus on that if you have to think of anything."

"Yes, you're right," replied Llyat. "What's the loss of a few hundred huts in the saving of the Realm? I will not grieve their loss given what the bastards did to Maplehill and the Bards Guild."

The bare rocky outcrop towards the northern tip of the island was devoid of activity. Soon they moored their boat and looked towards the nearest building that stood some two hundred or so paces away. No activity or light came from within its confines. In the dark Llyat and Einar moved to the base of the building and there crouched down with their backs to the wall while deciding on their next course of action.

"Now what," whispered Einar?

"We make for that large rock in the centre."

Llyat peeped out from behind the house of reeds. He looked towards the looming mass of stone, illuminated by the glow from the burning city. Seeing no evidence of reptilian activity he sensed the time was right to move on.

"Come," he ordered. "Follow me, this may be our one chance."

The two friends moved with great stealth, always keeping low to the ground. All remained quiet as Llyat led Einar from building to building. Their progress seemed a little too easy and that caused Llyat concern. Given that his plan was working, he soon dismissed his doubts and focused on finding the temple and the statue of Urthanock. For the first time in his life, Llyat felt in control. He no longer needed his dreams to point the way forward nor a bard to lead him by the hand. He was in charge and his confidence continued to grow. On he inched towards the rocky mound where he somehow knew the temple was located. By morning he expected to have long departed the island.

The noise of movement from around the side of the next building reached his ears. With great care he poked his head around its corner in an attempt to assess the danger ahead. An armoured Lizardman stood guard with a spear in hand. This was the first sign of the army that Llyat had seen in his vison. The jewel it seemed had told the truth.

"Fuck!" Llyat whispered "We've got company."

"Where" asked Einar, lowering his voice?

"See for yourself."

In silence Einar and Llyat swapped places. The Berserker peered round the building where he also assessed the situation. Llyat was then startled as he felt something run across his hand. Somehow he managed to control his fear as a small marsh gecko leapt off and disappeared into the darkness.

"Any ideas what we should do next?" asked Llyat.

"I could break its neck and take it out."

"But we would risk it calling out and alerting many more to our presence."

Einar paused and thought on the issue. While seconds passed like days Llyat tried to devise another plan.

"There is the obvious Berserker trick," Einar added. "In the same way that I distracted that bastard in Calistorn with the sound of a nighthowler. I will move away from here and make a similar noise. That I hope will allow you run on to the Temple. I will follow on as and when I can."

"That sounds a better plan than a direct assault," said Llyat.

"Then let's do it."

Einar did not hesitate nor give Llyat time to argue. The Berserker made his way back round the side of the building and left Llyat alone in the darkness. The wait seemed endless and Llyat's thoughts turned to the marsh gecko that reappeared in front of him. The creature, now out in the open, was bathed in the orange light from the encroaching inferno. Just like in is hide away in Calistorn he wondered if this was yet another of Thamous's many spies. With nothing better to do in that moment Llyat began to whisper to the creature.

"Thamous, I'm in the Eastern Marsh. Things are going better than they did in Barad Elestor."

The marsh gecko twitched its head, flicked out its tongue and then disappeared at the sound of a nighthowler call that rose from some distance away. Once again Llyat looked around the corner of the building. The guard began to head off in the direction of the bestial howl and Llyat took his chance to move towards the rock. He darted towards the remaining buildings, always keeping within the protective apron of their shadows. Having passed the spot where the Lizardman guard had stood he ran on without caution. Einar could look after himself and Llyat was convinced that the giant would soon catch up with him. The thought of his ease of progress once again worried him as did the absence of any more guards.

Soon Llyat found himself at the foot of the imposing rock wall that reached high up into the smoke filled sky. This was the place of his visions, the site of the temple, the statue of Urthanock, and the amethyst that he had come to collect. The rocky outcrop of once molten stone was made up of minerals that Llyat had never seen before, strange, irregular, and yet with a smooth external surface. A wide smile formed on his face for in his dreams the Moirai had guided him to the entrance of the cavern. A black hole opened before him. Even more remarkable was the fact that the entrance had been left unguarded. He thought for a brief moment that it could be all a trap but there was no alternative but to press on. Stopping at the threshold of the cavern he whispered as loud as he dared.

"Einar, Einar!" but all was silent save from the cries of those who still fought the fire.

"Einar." he whispered one last time.

Llyat then realised he would have to finish the quest alone and so he began his descent into the dark. He was soon reminded of the cave in which he had met Thamous but this one was narrower and longer. The internal rocks were of the same type as those outside and it was at once obvious that the tunnels had been created by the hands and tools of the Lizardmen and not from dragon fire. The journey through the long passage was made easier by the presence of light from burning metal braziers that were fixed to the walls every twenty paces or so. Still he saw no one nor heard any noise, not even Einar's footfall from behind.

For some reason Llyat then became distracted. His anxiety dropped away and his thoughts returned to Heliana. He began to wonder how different events would have been had she accompanied him north from Valameer. It was unlikely that she would have survived the Ivory pass and she would without doubt have succumbed to the cold during the long days spent in the Thengar Forest. Frightful visions of what the ogres would have done to her body tormented his progress. One thought alone heartened him. If he ever met her again he would protect her until the end of their days.

The sound of a rolling pebble caused Llyat to turn around but despite the dim light cast by the burning braziers he saw nothing. He did not hear the sound again and assumed that his imagination was playing tricks. On he moved while picking up his pace. For the first time in days he felt feelings of self-doubt seek to force their way back in. Slamming his mind door shut he refused to let them grow. The senselessness of his past was gone and he answered his voice of doubt; 'Don't be stupid. Look how well you are doing.'

Llyat smiled for his inner voice was right. He had devised the plan that had got him deep into the centre of the city and he would keep reminding himself of that fact to sustain his new found confidence. Llyat knew that Heliana would do the same for she never give a toss what anyone thought about her. She valued herself and he admired her natural ability to live that way. How he longed to be with her once again, to hold her tight, saviour her breasts, and fuck without risk of interruption.

The tunnel through the rocks eventually opened out into a larger cavern that reached up into the small mountain; so high that Llyat could not see the roof because the light did not penetrate that far. Soon he stopped for directly ahead of him in the centre of the natural space stood the largest stone statue that he had ever seen. The figure of the most hideous Lizardman imaginable had been fashioned from the mountain, dressed in its battle armour and with a sword in its hand.

Around its base had been placed a black streaked marble alter upon which a myriad of offerings had been left. They formed a treasure fit for dynasty of Sovereigns.

"I never realised that that it would be so fucking huge," he whispered.

Once over his immediate surprise Llyat looked around to ensure that he was still alone. In addition to the statue of Urthanock the space contained numerous carved stone pillars around its circumference which Llyat guessed were there to support the roof although they were well decorated and could just as well been placed there for effect. They were made from the same strange material as the rest of the rocky mound and they created a separate space between them and the rock wall from where eyes could watch unseen. At regular intervals he noted black openings into several additional passages that led further in to the depths of the small mountain. The entrance of each was highlighted by the light from a candle that sat in a small alcove at each of the opening's edge. The longer he looked the more Llyat was filled with awe and it took him some time to regain his focus. With still no sign of Lizardmen he began his search.

Having moved to the base of the deity he focused his attention on the treasure trove that dazzled his eyes. Hands sifted through the piles of golden coins, rubies, emeralds, and gemstones of every conceivable colour. He lifted up tiaras, golden ornaments, and those made from other precious metals. Their collective wealth was too great for Llyat to contemplate and he calculated that just a single pocketful would have made him the richest man he had ever known. With regard to the amethyst, he knew he had found it the moment that he saw it for the Moirai had revealed its location in his dreams. In the middle of the treasure sat a set of golden scales, covered with intricate markings and weighed down on one side by a collection of amethyst crystals of differing shapes and sizes. One of them had to be the jewel he had come to find.

There Llyat paused as he wondered how to identify the precise one that was Thamous's infamous stone. He knew that he could not take them all with him. One would go unnoticed but to take them all would reveal evidence of his crime. He then thought back to events at Barad Elestor and what had happened when he had removed the sapphire from the hilt of Sir Raulyn's battle axe. The blue gem had taken over his being, forced a vision to appear, and shown him the location of the Temple of Urthanock. Thias had told him how the Kundalish Aura had erupted and caused him to thrash and scream until the stone had fallen from his hand. Llyat knew what he had to do and despite the pain that was inevitable he did not feel afraid. Without hesitation he thrust his hand into the pile of amethysts and one by one took hold of them between his fingers. After several tries in which nothing untoward happened he thought that there might be something else that he needed to do in order to find the 'One'. However, when he then took hold of the largest of them, an amethyst about the size of his own fist, an intense pain shot through his body. The Kundalish Aura poured out from his pores and Llyat's mind went blank.

He woke lying on the floor with his right hand outstretched, pointing to the large amethyst that was just inches away. He sat upright and looked up to the shadow that loomed over him. The giant figure of Einar stood smiling down with his hands on hips.

"Welcome back to the world of the living," said the Berserker as Llyat tried to refocus his thoughts. "I thought you were dead until I checked your breathing."

"How long have I been unconscious?" asked Llyat as he then looked around the temple?

"Ten, maybe fifteen minutes at the most," said Einar as he offered Llyat his hand and then pulled him up onto his feet. "So what happened? I leave you for a just a few minutes and I find this!"

"I found the amethyst, touched it, and then passed out," jabbered Llyat in his excitement while pointing to the stone.

He made to reach for the gemstone but Einar's long and powerful arm pulled his own back.

"Are you mad?" said the Berserker.

"Not at all. The stone won't affect me a second time, not now that it has shown me the location of the last of the Gems of Thamous."

"So where is it?"

"Well that's the strange thing. All I saw was a spongy kind of blackness and then for a brief moment I saw Heliana..."

"Who is Heliana?" interrupted Einar which confused Llyat for he had talked of her many times.

"She is the servant girl that travelled with me to Valameer. Like I said, there was blackness and then I saw Heliana holding a heart shaped ruby. I'm fucked if I know why she would have it."

"This realm is full of many strange things..." said Einar before stopping abruptly.

At first Llyat assumed that his friend had lost his line of thought but then he saw the depth of anxiety etched on the giant's face.

"What is it? What's wrong?"

"We have company."

"Where?"

"It sounds like they approach from the main entrance."

Llyat turned and looked into the tunnel he had earlier passed through and saw the silhouette of three approaching Lizardmen.

"Quick, take the amethyst and let's get out of here," ordered Einar.

"But which way should we go?"

"One the other tunnels must also lead to the surface, if not all of them. We must not let these creatures have the satisfaction of taking us to the Lady of the Silverwynn. Come on, move your sorry arse."

Llyat did not argue as Einar moved towards the nearest tunnel. Without hesitation and with complete faith in his friend, he picked up the amethyst from where it had fallen. Much to his relief it had no further effect on him.

"Einar wait, please wait for me."

On entering the tunnel he was immediately engulfed by darkness. Without further thought he reached back and snatched hold of the candle that burned in the alcove. On he ran down this new narrow corridor, shielding the flame with his left hand to stop it from blowing out. He could not see Einar but could hear his footfall in the passage ahead and realised that their roles had reversed. He was again chasing the decision of another's and it left him feeling most uncomfortable. In his heightened state of anxiety he tried to think if the giant had done the right thing but it had all happened so quickly and there was nothing he could do other than face the consequences of the Berserker's decision.

The tunnel started to slope down and then it turned back on itself. Llyat sensed he was dropping ever lower into the small mountain and he did not like it. The reptilian footfall behind offered him no choice but to keep on running. Llyat then calculated that he must have travelled below the water level of the Eastern Marsh and that the tunnel was a most improbable means of escape. Without warning the tunnel opened up into yet another enormous cavern similar to that where he had encountered Thamous. He found himself upon a wooden walkway that had been constructed and fixed upon a small ledge half way up the cavern's wall. Ahead of him this walkway turned to steps that led to the bottom of the vast natural space, eroded and formed over centuries by the stream that crossed its floor. There Llyat saw a multitude of lights which flickered yellow and red and indicated the presence of a thousand fires. Once again he was awestruck and tried to make sense of what he saw. Then he noticed that Einar had ceased his mad dash for freedom and now stood at the edge of the walkway while looking down into the depths of the cavern. The Berserker turned and made his way back to Llyat.

"Where the fuck have you brought us, you lolloping turd?" exclaimed the youth as he tried to reassert his authority.

Einar placed his finger to his lips. "Hush!"

"Don't you fucking hush me," snapped back Llyat.

Einar's hand gripped Llyat's head and forced the youth to peer down into the cavern's abyss.

"What is it then?" demanded Llyat. "What is it you've...."

Llyat did not finish his sentence for he then saw the focus of Einar's attention. Amid the glow of the many braziers and furnaces swarmed a mass of lizard men. There were thousands of them, all hidden deep beneath the marshland and away from the prying eyes of the Realm. This was the true city of the Lizardmen and it was a most formidable subterranean fortress. It was the most perfect place to hide an army.

Llyat turned to Einar: "We need to get out..."

The massive form of Einar began to change into something that Llyat already feared. The youth's jaw dropped as the Berserker's skin began to ripple with a life of its own. Then it fell away to an amorphous shape before in the next instant it began its rebirth into the distinctive shape of a Lizardman.

"How!" stuttered Llyat, "When?"

"The deception was easy once we recognised that your friend's nighthowler call was a crude imitation of the real thing. You never suspected did you?" answered the beast.

The beast swung its fist into Llyat's face. For the second time in minutes, all went black.

29

The Great Hall was shrouded in a dense cloak of silence as the members of the Sovereign Council, the City Watch, and knights of the Royal Guards gathered around the pale corpse of their once proud and vibrant ruler, Phauless Gylewu IV. The Guard had acted with both speed and clarity of decision making and sealed the room as soon the death of the Sovereign had been become apparent. Whoever was responsible for the heinous crime was now trapped within the confines of the Great Hall. The faces of those gathered around the body were etched with deep furrows of concern, sorrow, and complete confusion. All sought to comprehend how the murderous event could have occurred before so many eyes, all of which had missed the crime being committed. The unerring silence continued for several minutes until at last Tonousa found the courage to speak.

"Which one of you bastards dared commit this foul deed?" she demanded as she looked to each of her father's suspects in turn. "All four of you had at one point or other approached the feasting table so any of you could have slipped poison onto the food. Which one of you shits was it?"

Then as one, Sir Byddin, Lady Emeny, Sir Richemanus, and the priest Heward Teulu began their protests. They screamed out their outrage at being so accused by a low level servant of the Watch. One shrill voice fought to be heard over the shouts of the other three.

"It was that Fool!" exclaimed Lady Emeny as she pointing at Lolly. "He did it. He poisoned Phauless. Sir Byddin arrest the idiot and slit the little bastard's throat before he can spew forth a denial."

Lolly the Lune looked as dumbfounded as the rest of those present. Sir Byddin turned in a flash and made to restrain the jester by taking hold of his clothes. Lolly jumped backwards and avoided the knight's grasp after which he began to proclaim his innocence.

"It wasn't me, I swear it. If he was poisoned then I would have died first."

"I'll kill you myself when I get hold of you," bellowed Sir Byddin as he lunged forward once again, his hands still stained from his earlier assault on Sir Richemanus. "You've played your last piece of tomfoolery in this Court. Come here while I rip off your cock and stuff it down your throat. I'll make you juggle with your own balls, so help me I will!"

Danisun moved forward between the two and thwarted the impending violence after which he then spoke up in Lolly's defence.

"He also ate the food. Lady Emeny took pains to make him the taster."

The focus of those present fell upon Emeny who looked more flustered.

"Well...I...." stuttered the Lady, her nerves getting the better of her.

"It cannot have been poison," said Sir Byddin, trying to reassert authority.

"So how else did he die," lisped Gilebin Ystafell?

"It must have been magic," bellowed back Byddin. "Someone here must have whispered a spell to stop his breathing."

Tonousa contemplated that possibility. It had been Heward Teulu who had stopped Darchus from attempting to breathe life into the Sovereign and who had suggested that poison could be present on the dead man's lips. The miraculous appearance of the Mark of Kha made Sir Byddin's suggestion more than plausible.

"Is this possible?" she asked the Archmage who stood and stroked his chin.

"It is..." he began before Sir Byddin interrupted.

"There you have it," he shouted. "Someone used magic to kill him."

"Sir Byddin, please," ordered Commander Townsforth as he stepped forward. "This investigation is now the responsibility of the Watch. I ask you with the utmost of humility to be quiet, but if you don't understand that, then try this...Just shut your fucking prattle! Let us all hear what the Archmage has to say."

Byddin shrivelled back as all in the hall focused on the wizard. Tonousa knew that the knight would back down for he was no longer in a position to challenge the authority of the Commander and the collective wishes of the Sovereign Council. She began to focus on Iqotrix's words.

"As I was saying before I was interrupted, it is possible that magic may have been used but I am almost certain that it wasn't. There is an ethereal glow given off when magic is invoked and it is called the Kundalish Aura. I assume that none of you have so far encountered this phenomenon."

Tonousa recalled what she had witnessed in Valameer.

"This aura," continued the Archmage, "no matter how strong it is, can be detected by other magic users and I can tell you all now, there is not even the slightest hint of that aura present in this room. It therefore does not seem that magic was used, at least not the kind I have experience of."

"Then what did kill him?" asked Ystafell as he scanned the faces of all present.

"I don't honestly know," replied the confused Archmage

"Bollocks!" bellowed Sir Byddin. "You wizards are all the same. You're just like the Physicians and the alchemists. You seem to know what a person is going to do before they do it. That's too fucking convenient for my liking. I say to all here present that you're involved somehow in this foul murder. I have not decided if you did it or are just covering the back the one who did. I say, fuck you and all your kind!"

"I note your feelings Sir!" hissed the Archmage as evil intent oozed from his eyes.

"Sir Byddin! Will you please control your outbursts? This is not the time nor the place for such wild accusations," exclaimed Commander Townsforth.

"Then someone explain what is going on," shouted the knight.

As if on cue the room then filled with a cacophony of screaming accusations. Those of the Watch were the only ones to remain calm as venomous insults flew through the air. It turned into a most disgraceful spectacle of disrespect towards the ex-Ruler of the Realm as he lay dead upon the cold hard floor. Tonousa became more and more frustrated until at last she could no longer hold her tongue.

"Will you all just shut up and be quiet. I'm trying to think!" she exclaimed and on her command the room fell silent. "I am as shocked as all of you at what has happened here today, but please show our Lord some decency and respect."

Ashamed faces stared back as Lady Emeny turned to address Gylewu's bodyguards.

"Sir Lightmain, Sir Cragtalon, please find something to cover him with."

The two knights nodded in affirmation, moved down from either side of the throne, and made their way through the door from which the Sovereign had made his final entrance.

"And don't speak a word of this to anyone!" bellowed Sir Byddin who then turned to the remaining members of the Royal Guard and barked out his orders.

"No one else is to enter here. Not without permission of the Council. Do you understand?"

Each member of the Guard looked to each other, unable to read the situation and who to now take orders from.

"I have given an order you worthless turds. Do you understand?"

"Yes Sir!" they replied as one.

"Good then make sure you carry out my order to the letter!"

"So what are you going to do now; how do you propose we figure out who killed him?" asked Lady Emeny.

"Well..." said Townsforth, his uncertainty obvious to all. "If Tonousa's story about her father's suspicions are to be believed then there are four prime suspects."

Townsforth pointed them out in rapid succession.

"Bollocks!" spat back Sir Byddin.

"No! No! No!" snorted Lady Emeny.

"Why must it be one of us four?" said Richemanus, his face still reddened from Sir Byddin's assault. "Why not the Lord Chamberlin? Why not you Commander? Why not her, the Amberstone bitch?"

"I err..." hesitated Townsforth as he struggled to find an appropriate response.

"Sir Byddin makes a good point. Why should we believe what Amberstone said? Why should we entertain such ludicrous insinuations?" added Lady Emeny.

"Because they are the cards of the gods," said Heward Teulu. "They are the Fortunes Fate, the true messages from the daughters of Fatumai."

"And I say bollocks!" snapped back Sir Byddin. "The evidence is as slack as a beggar's bag. We must keep this investigation free from any religious clap-trap for it will not help us here today."

"Ignore the Faith of Fatumai if you so wish but you should trust my father's message for it relates to the Enderdetag Prophecy. That is why you should listen to it and because he was a devotee of the Moirai and a Cuvar," said Tonousa with authority.

"A what? What are you talking about now?" said Byddin. "My mother's arse talked more sense than your mouth does now."

"The Cuvar is a secret society, not a religion. If you will..." began Tonousa but her answer was squashed as Archmage Iqotrix continued the explanation.

"It is a secret order that seeks to ensure that the Enderdetag Prophecy will come to pass. Their members move amongst us and in plain sight and yet we do not know who they are. The prophecy was created by Anyle Belanore and it states that the Marked of Maplehill must fulfil his destiny. He must be there when the Oracles crypt is opened and reunite the Gems of Thamous to destroy the Lord of Fear."

Tonousa smiled. The Archmage in that brief description had explained all that the Sovereign Council, Sir Richemanus, the Lord Commander of the City Watch needed to know. Yet still they looked bewildered.

"Are you saying that your father was one of these Cuvar?" lisped Ystafell.

"That is indeed what I am saying," replied Tonousa. "He was investigating the murders in his own way and by himself. I guess he suspected they were somehow connected to the Prophecy and he feared for the life of the Marked. It seems he and perhaps other Cuvar gathered enough evidence to ensure that you four were the chief suspects. I don't however have access to that evidence but given what I have seen over the last few weeks I am more than willing to follow his lead and try and finish what he started."

"You hint that others were involved. Who are they?" asked Lady Emeny.

"Xix Blackfayer for one, Enguerrand Fullbane, and a traveller who came to this city with his son," replied Tonousa.

The Council seemed stunned and even Lolly raised an eyebrow.

"And why have you never mentioned this conspiracy before?" asked Sir Byddin.

"I explained my father's role in this investigation when I first met with you Sir, although I did not mention the name of his secret society."

Tonousa tried to recall the conversations she had had with the four suspects and if she had ever mentioned the Cuvar by name. She remembered showing each one of them the cards and asking their opinion of them. She also remembered telling them how she found the cards hidden in her father's wall. Yet as hard as she tried she could not swear whether she had used the term 'Cuvar'. Her thoughts drifted to the Historian and she recalled that he had apparently seen something in this very hall that had caused him to flee from the Capital. He must have discovered the identity of the infiltrator who had been active for so many years. One question after another popped into her head and yet she still felt certain that he father must have been on the right track. The shapeshifter had to be one of the four.

"I guess the question is, what now?" said Ystafell.

"If this fairy tale is to be believed and the combined forces of Avolire and the Eastern Marsh intend to march upon us then we must redouble our preparations for the defence of this city," responded Sir Byddin. "We have already sent requests for assistance to Lady Flurdiana, Cvyler Olin, and even as far away as the Dirmark; but none of our carrier birds have as yet returned. We must arm everyone, from the feeblest old man to any child that can lift a weapon. We must also arm the womenfolk for we will need every available hand to defeat what is coming."

"And I suppose that you think that you should continue to lead them?" said Lady Emeny.

"And what do you mean by that?"

"The last thing any of us want is a shape changer from the Eastern Marsh leading the armies of Parandor. We need to be confident in the actions and motives of such a leader. I for one do not want to have to worry what mischief is being planned!"

"How dare you suggest I step down, you old crone," shouted Sir Byddin.

"And yet she is right," added Townsforth. "We can't have four influential yet flawed people such as yourselves in charge of anything to do with the city's defence until we discover which of you were spawned in the swamps. We cannot risk further plots against us."

Tonousa saw the faces of Byddin, Emeny, and Teulu change with the realisation that none of them would hold power as the crisis deepened. Only Richemanus remained expressionless.

"You can't do this!" exclaimed Byddin. "You cannot remove us from the Council."

"It would be ridiculous; without us there would be no Council," added Lady Emeny.

"What in the name of Fatumai has got into you Commander?" asked Teulu.

"Ystafell, please back me up," exclaimed Sir Byddin as he turned to face the Lord Chamberlin. "Talk some sense into this fucking Watch wanker before I do something I may later regret."

"I'm afraid he is right Rayner," lisped Gilebin Ystafell. "If the Cuvar are to be believed and one of you is a traitor or even worse, then we cannot have any of you involved in our planning. That would be both foolish and..."

"Who then would organise the defence of this city..." snorted Sir Byddin.

"Commander, do you think that you are up to the task? I for one would be happy to put my future welfare in your hands," said Ystafell.

Tonousa looked to her superior and witnessed a smugness roll through his aging wrinkles.

"I will be honoured do my duty as requested by the Council. I will lead to the very best of my ability," replied Townsforth after which he bowed to the Lord Chamberlain.

"You can't do this Ystafell," spluttered Sir Byddin. "You have no authority. Just stick to looking after the piss pots!"

"I'm afraid he does Byddin," said Lady Emeny "Phauless made a decree, witnessed by both myself and the Archmage. In essence it states that should any of the Council become a threat to the Realm and the Sovereign be in anyway incapacitated then power would pass to the next highest ranking official who is without suspicion. Isn't that right Iqotrix?"

"That is correct Llys."

"Phauless Gylewu is dead," continued Lady Emeny. "Xix Blackfayer is dead. You and I Byddin are disqualified for we are both now implicated in this murder of our Sovereign and therefore cannot hold authority. Control then falls to the next inline which happens to be Ystafell, our Lord Chamberlin, and examiner of the Royal Pot."

Sir Lightmain and Sir Cragtalon returned carrying a large blackened tapestry. The two knights made the way at speed towards their fallen Lord whereupon the small gathering parted and allowed them to drape the material over their once proud master.

"And so begins the final journey of Phauless," began Ystafell as all present lowered their heads in a mark of respect. "The last member of the House of Gylewu has gone to join his ancestors."

"It was you! You fucking did this didn't you? You are manipulating this situation to better your own ends," bellowed Byddin.

"Sir! Please show some constraint," ordered Commander Townsforth but the one eyed knight continued his rant undeterred.

"You have access to all of our chambers. You could have planted the evidence that Tonousa found knowing well that Amberstone's daughter would one day search her father's rooms. It could have even been you who stole the Lore of the Dead and framed the Lord Librarian. You also had the means to attack Phauless from the shadows in his room. You are the keeper of the keys."

"Sir Byddin, this is you're final warning," ordered Townsforth

"This is just a fucking grab for power," snarled the one eyed knight. "You have eliminated us all now. There is but you left. Who are you going to appoint onto your council then? Go on, tell us you suppurating furuncle. The Archmage? The Lord Commander of the Watch? Do share your insight and intentions."

"Sir Byddin!" exclaimed the Lord Commander but the Knight was beyond relentless.

"I hope this fucking infiltrator takes the whole fucking lot of you down."

"I've had enough of this nonsense," exclaimed the Townsforth. "Sir Lightmain and Sir Cragtalon, take Sir Byddin to his chambers and restrain him there until we decide how best we can contain his temper. He must not to leave his rooms until you hear again from me."

Without warning the now redundant bodyguards of Phauless Gylewu moved forward and each took hold of one of Byddin's arms.

"Let go of me or you will live to regret your actions."

Lightmain and Cragtalon held their captive fast and as they sought to evict the Head of the Royal Guard from the hall, they collided with Lolly and knocked the Fool to the floor.

"And if that idiot tries to speak of this to anyone, you are ordered to take out his tongue," added Townsforth.

"I'll get you bastards for this affront on my honour," screamed Sir Byddin but it was to no avail for he was at once removed from the hall. The doors were sealed.

"Thank the gods we have peace at last." muttered the Lord Commander. "That man is intolerable. He makes more noise than a banging door in a storm."

Tonousa stared at the horrified faces of Emeny, Teulu and Richemanus as each struggled to find an appropriate answer in response to the Commander's message. Silence hung in pendulous clouds over the room.

"And what of the rest of us?" asked Lady Emeny at last. "What do you propose we do next?"

"You can't keep us all confined to our rooms," added Heward Teulu. "Those poor innocents out in the streets need me. You cannot deny them food and shelter on a vague suspicion that we four are involved in the murder of our dear departed Phauless; may Fatumai watch over his soul."

"He does make an important and reasonable point Lord Commander," added Danisun Dain.

Townsforth then began to think. He was joined in deep reflexion by both Gilebin Ystafell and Archmage Iqotrix whose faces told of the troubled thoughts that passed through their minds. Tonousa began to consider that Sir Byddin could have been on to something when he had accused the Lord Chamberlin of being the shapeshifter. Then she let that thought pass for it would complicate her investigation to a level she was unprepared to tolerate.

After several minutes the Lord Commander spoke once again, this time with the authority that Ystafell had bestowed on him.

"After much consideration I feel it will be important to avoid panic amongst the rest of those who dwell within the Citadel, the greater population of Parandor, and the armies amassed outside our walls. Therefore you three suspects will be allowed free access and movement throughout the Capital in order to conduct your basic business. You will however not be permitted to join the meetings of the Council, nor move outside of the city walls. Any attempt to flee from Parandor will be taken as an admission of your guilt and result in your confinement until you can be brought to trial and execution. Does that sound a fair and sensible course of action Lord Chamberlin?"

"I concur with all you have said Lord Commander," replied Ystafell.

Tonousa once again tried to read the expressions on the faces of the three remaining suspects.

"One further constraint on your freedom of movement is that you must not speak of what has happened here today," ordered the Lord Commander. "That order applies to everyone else here present. No one outside of these four walls must know that Lord Phauless is dead. Anyone caught discussing it will be punished beyond pain, on that I give you my word! Should anyone ask, then tell them that Phauless is both angry and indisposed? In a fit of temper he cancelled the banquet for the food turned out to be rotten. That will buy us sometime to decide on what to do in the long term. I hope you have you all got that!"

The executioner then raised his hand into the air.

"Yes Sir Richemanus?"

"There's one fact that still troubles me," said the brute. "Do we still believe that it was poison that killed our Lord and not magic..."

"Oh for fuck sake Richemanus, keep up will you!" sneered Lady Emeny. "We've gone through that already."

"No, hear me out please," he continued. "If the Archmage says he cannot detect any presence of magic then how did the three circle brand appear. No one had the opportunity to create it physically while we were watching."

Tonousa could only agree with the executioner's observation. She had been so preoccupied with the petty arguments of the Council that she had failed to register the importance of that fact. Perhaps the Archmage could solve the conundrum.

"Is Sir Richemanus is right?" she asked. "If no magic was used then how did the mark get there?"

Iqotrix hesitated as he looked down the body beneath the tapestry.

"Even I cannot explain many of the powers of the Underworld," he replied. "This is a deeper magic than even I can make sense of. There are some things better left alone."

"Well at least that answers one question," replied Tonousa.

"Just one!" sneered Heward Teulu.

"What I meant to say Holiness is that the Archmage has confirmed what you suspected right from the start, that the cult of Death Tubaria was not, and is not, responsible for these atrocities," continued Tonousa. "I would wager my reputation that everything we have been investigating was designed to distract us from a much greater threat to the Realm. Remember, there is every indication that two armies are about to appear before the gates of Parandor. If we fail to complete our defensives they will walk right in and it will be end of all we hold dear."

"It all sounds so unbelievable..." began Lady Emeny.

"Believe it Llys, it's happening," lisped Gilebin Ystafell.

"I see the relevance of the evidence presented by Tonousa. Her fears are well justified."

"Thank you for your support Lady Emeny," said Tonousa.

"I will also say this," continued the Lady. "As per the decree of our late Lord Phauless, and to comply with the will of the Lord Chamberlin, I will agree to step away from my duties on the Council and allow the City Watch to complete their investigation. I wish you a speedy success Townsforth in bringing the guilty one to justice."

"Thank you for your cooperation," added Ystafell, "but there is still the issue of what we are going to do with Phauless's body given we cannot yet tell the citizens of Parandor of his demise?

"If I could be excused," began Heward Teulu. "I could return to the Temple of Fatumai and send back priests to escort his body in secret to his family crypt. We can't leave him to fester here for the stench of decay would soon permeate the corridors of the Citadel. The sooner we begin the embalming process the better for us all."

"Agreed," muttered the many in support.

"We all need some fresh air. I for one am feeling a little faint," added Lady Emeny.

"So be it, you are all dismissed," lisped the Lord Chamberlin. "But remember, should any of you try to flee the city you will die as traitors. Speak of this to anyone and I'll remove your tongues myself."

The trio of suspects bowed their heads in deference to this new authority.

"You have my word on it," grunted Richemanus as if speaking for all.

Tonousa watched as the three subjugated figures made their way past the feasting tables to the main entrance and then departed. The doors closed behind them and were bolted once again from the inside. Watching all, Tonousa cast her mind back to her card reading with Heward Teulu and his priests. He had given her a time limit of six days in which to solve the most complicated investigation imaginable. She had so little information to go on and the erratic nature of her four suspects made it all the more difficult to bring her investigation to a logical conclusion. She was however resolved to succeed, if not for herself, then for her father and Phauless Gylewu.

"So now what," asked Danisun Dain?

"I suggest we retire to the Council Chamber," replied Ystafell. "We can't stay sealed up in the Great Hall while the four suspects are free to walk the corridors of the Citadel. We will have to impose identical restrictions on Byddin and have him understand the implications of any transgression. Commander, will you send a messenger to that effect?"

"Do you think they will keep to their bond?" asked Tonousa.

"I do hope so," replied the Lord Chamberlin. "Otherwise there will be anarchy."

"I'll make sure they are watched at all times and from a discrete distance," added the Lord Commander.

"Thank you Townsforth. I'm going to need all your help to steer us through these most difficult of times."

After a last bow to the covered body of their deceased Sovereign Lord, the members of the Watch, the Archmage, the Lord Chamberlin, and the Court Fool turned and made their way towards the exit. Two members of the Royal Guard dipped their heads and then opened the double doors. Tonousa heard them close behind her back as Ystafell then gave his final order to the Guards who manned the outside of the door.

"No one is to enter on my orders. Do you both understand? "

"Understood," muttered the first of the two knights.

"The exception is the priests that will soon arrive from the Temple of Fatumai."

"Fatumai... Got it," replied the second knight. "But what about that lot over there, the members of the Court who are still waiting to join the feast."

"Tell them the banquet is cancelled, the food has been spoiled, and Phauless is not in the mood for it to continue. Just tell them that and send them on their way.

The flustered Lord then scuttled off while avoiding all eye contact with the expectant crowd.

Ystafell appeared overwhelmed by the pressure that now rested on his shoulders. Tonousa reckoned he had been party to the creation of Phauless's decree and therefore felt little sympathy for the man who was clearly out of his depth and just about coping with his new responsibilities.

The Lord Chamberlin signalled for the group to follow him down the corridor. Most also kept their heads down as they progressed forward. Tonousa did not. She noted how many of the courtiers and servants that she passed looked on in confused bewilderment. They had all heard the raised voices of Sir Byddin and the Lord Commander, the shouts and screams of Lady Enemy, and the general hubbub of noise when Phauless Gylewu had breathed his last. Tonousa saw the concern in all the piercing eyes that watched her pass, those who had yet to grasp the enormity of what had just occurred behind the vast metal doors to the throne room. She then began to try and second guess how Teulu's priests would remove Phauless Gylewu's body without giving away news of the Sovereign's death. Then from out of the crowd she heard a familiar voice shout her name and when she turned she saw Heliana pushing her way through the highborn mob.

"Hi Tonousa! What the fuck is going on? I've just seen Sir Byddin being escorted by..."

"Not now Heliana, please,"

"I heard Lady Emeny scream? Is she okay?"

"I will tell you later Heliana; not here and not now. I'll explain everything as soon as I am allowed," whispered Tonousa so low that others did not hear.

"I also have something important to tell you. Don't be too long for you will surely want to hear my news," replied Heliana with pride thumping out from her bosom.

Tonousa had other things on her mind; the murder she had failed to prevent.

"Yes, yes, later... I'll come and find you when I can but I'm rather busy just now," she added while moving away.

It took a several of minutes to negotiate the corridors and the main stairs up to the Council Chamber on the first floor of the Citadel. With great purpose Ystafell pulled from his pocket the master set of keys for the entire edifice. He searched for the correct one while those gathered around waited in silence. Then one by one they entered the room until at the rear Commander Townsforth stuck out his arm in order to prevent the last of the group moving inside.

"That's as far as you go Fool," he said. "Food taster or not, your presence is not required. So just piss off! Do you understand?"

"I do, Sir!" replied Lolly.

The Court Fool then skipped off along the corridor and the bells on his coat tinkled as he jigged.

Once the Lord Commander had closed the door he, Danisun, Darchus, Tonousa, and the Archmage each sat down around the large wooden war table. When the Lord Chamberlin at last took his place he let out a deep sigh and sank into Phauless Gylewu's regal seat.

"So what do we do now?" Ystafell mumbled, his face showing signs of distress. "I cannot rule this realm alone, not in the long term."

"What about a bloodline," asked Darchus? "Didn't our Lord have brothers and sisters, children, or maybe even bastards?"

"He did have one brother but Raorick Gylewu was murdered by the marsh scum."

"And offspring?"

"None that anyone has ever been aware of," added Ystafell. "He always seemed to be too preoccupied with his wealth or young boys than to lay with quim. I'm afraid the House of Gylewu died with Phauless."

"In cases like this, who then takes control of the Realm?"

Once again silence fell as those present sought to think of the answer.

"The Lady Flurdiana of Valameer," said Ystafell a few seconds later.

"Why her?" replied Darchus?

"In event of anything happening to Phauless Gylewu, the leadership of this realm would have fallen to his brother," continued Ystafell. "Raorick Gylewu was committed to a marriage that Phauless had brokered with Lady Flurdiana. The plan, as I can work it out, was for her to be the future bearer of Gylewu Princes. As Phauless was either unwilling or unable to dip into her pot, he planned for his younger brother to do the job for him. Her children would have been rightful heirs to the throne and provided for the succession. She is the obvious choice and is highborn after all."

"Do you think she will come to our aid given everything that has happened and the threats that we now face," asked the Lord Commander.

As the question sank in, Tonousa thought back to the attack on the Bards Guild, how when she had approached Lady Flurdiana and asked for the assistance of her Trident Guard she had been dismissed out of hand. The Lady had appeared both fearless and stoic in the face of adversity but it still galled Tonousa that she had been more concerned about her breaking her fast than assisting those who had escaped death from the inferno at the end of the Bridge of Athuna. It was hard to imagine that same Lady being willing to come to the aid of Parandor and take up the mantle of Sovereign Ruler. The faces of others present indicated they too were troubled.

"Unless you are able to think of another option Lord Commander then we have no choice but to approach her," continued Gilebin Ystafell, his words changing pitch in response to the stress. "Once news gets out of Phauless Gylewu's murder it will be but an ugly anarchy that reigns across this Realm. Our forces may fall apart with Sir Byddin indisposed. We need someone to rule who would be assured to hold the respect of the military. Who better than the Lady Flurdiana and the Trident Guard."

"It is my understanding that the Council sent birds to Valameer and Falahorn some time ago requesting their aid. Did you ever receive a reply," asked Tonousa?

"Not as yet," replied Ystafell.

"Then we'd better send more," suggested Iqotrix.

"And risk them being intercepted by the Knights of Avolire and spies of the Eastern Marsh? I don't think that would be very wise," added Danisun Dain.

"Then what do you suggest, wise one of the Watch?" replied the Archmage as he glared back across the table.

"You arrogant bugger," shouted Danisun

The Man-at-Arms slammed his palms down upon the table, much to the surprise of all present. The action was so out of character that Tonousa assumed that her colleague still suffered from the effects of Nedes Karoly's assault.

"Calm yourself Danisun," she ordered as she pulled him back down on his chair.

"I'm just saying that birds can be intercepted," grumbled Danisun. "We cannot risk the enemy gaining sight of our plans. Byddin, Richemanus, Emeny, and Teulu will be under close observation and as such will be unware of this plan to put Flurdiana on the throne. The guilty one must not be able to alert the Lady of the Silverwynn and the Knights of Avolire. Just for once we may have the upper hand. The Silverwynn will be waiting for confirmation from her changeling of Phauless's death and we must seek to prevent such a message reaching her for as long as we can."

"So what do you propose we do then," asked the Archmage.

"Send someone we know and trust; someone who knows her, how she thinks and operates," continued Danisun. "Dispatch that person with a personal request for help."

"You mean Darchus don't you?" said Tonousa.

"Of course I do."

Darchus rose to his feet.

"I would be honoured to take the message and I will do everything in my power to bring the Lady Flurdiana and her legion of Trident Guard back to Parandor."

Archmage looked at Darchus with suspicion.

"And why you?" he asked.

"Because he hails from Valameer," said Commander Townsforth.

"How long do you think it would take you to get there?" Ystafell asked.

"If I set off today I could make Valameer in five days, perhaps four at a push. It would depend on the quality of the horse I was given."

Tonousa feared for Darchus's safety upon the open road and she too jumped to her feet. She felt a great responsibility towards the man from Valameer. The honourable cordwainer had come to Parandor with his family to seek her out. She had travelled that same road herself and was aware of its dangers. The packs of skyfawn and nighthowlers and now perhaps the Knights of Avolire could be lying in wait for such an easy picking.

"Danisun, are there any horses readied for such a journey?" asked the Commander.

"Several my lord. They could be saddled and ready to go within the hour."

"Are you up for this lad?"

"Of course I am and I pledge you my life to this goal."

"You cannot send him on that dangerous road alone," exclaimed Tonousa "He could easily be taken. If Darchus is going, then so am I. He still has a wife and child here in the city for whom I feel responsible. I would find it difficult to live with myself should anything happen to Darchus while he performs our dirty work. He will need as much protection as we can afford to give him."

Tonousa sensed that Darchus felt embarrassed at her sudden outpouring of concern. All eyes looked to her but no words could describe her confusion.

"I agree with your sentiments Tonousa," said Commander Townsforth.

"Thank you, my Lord..." sighed the weary warrior.

"However, it will not be you that accompanies him Tonousa. You are needed here in Parandor,"

"But..." she began but the Commander spoke over her words.

"You must understand that we need you here. You are the one that has the insight to uncover the infiltrator. You surfaced the Royal Guard's use of Lillywort and the enormity of Richemanus's debts. I sense you are near to solving the mystery that haunts us and therefore I cannot allow you to leave the city. Someone else must protect our messenger."

Tonousa knew that her superior was correct in his assessment even though it frustrated her. She sighed and sat back down at the table. Having checked her emotions she looked across to Darchus who smiled and winked.

"I'll be fine Tonousa," he said.

"Of course he will," snorted the Lord Commander. "He's a man of the City Watch now."

"If I do not accompany him, who will you send in may stead? It has to be someone with great skill and ability," said Tonousa.

"Danisun will accompany Darchus to Valameer with four others from the Watch. That should be sufficient to ward off any threat," replied the Commander.

"Yes sir, as you so wish," acknowledged Danisun.

"Well, man?" Townsforth bellowed. "What are you waiting for?"

Tonousa watched as Danisun's face then flushed. The Man-at-Arms rose from his seat and made towards the door while Darchus followed in his wake. Tonousa jumped up to intercept them before they could leave the room.

"Please be careful," she whispered as her hand reached out and touched Danisun's shoulder.

"Don't worry about us, just catch the killer for me when I've gone."

"I'll try my very best; take care."

"Relax Tonousa," smiled Darchus. "We are going to be fine. Please check on Ailora and Finian while I am gone and ensure their needs are met."

"Of course I will."

Danisun and Darchus then left the room. As the oak doors closed Tonousa returned to her seat amongst the ever dwindling Council of Parandor.

"I hope that Lady Flurdiana will respond well to our invitation," lisped Ystafell. "We can leave that task to our messengers and turn our attention elsewhere. There is much that I need to hear from you Tonousa Amberstone. I need to know all that you have concluded so far. Which of the four do you believe to be the killer? Have we missed something important like; do we understand the truths behind the crimes? Why would any of the four we suspect want to kill Phauless Gylewu or indeed the others? Please share your thoughts for I need to understand what is going on."

Tonousa sighed for it seemed the Lord Chamberlin had not registered any of what she had already reported.

"Focus on the fact that one of them is not human. This will help you pull it all into some sort of meaning," began Tonousa amid her despondency. "Whoever our murderer is, he or she is in reality a shapeshifter from the Eastern Marsh. I have applied all my skills to this investigation and interviewed all four. It seems to me that each one of them had a motive for killing Phauless Gylewu but I do not sense any of them to be of the lizard kind. Sir Byddin and Lady Emeny have always lusted for power. Richemanus was in debt to the Crown and Heward Teulu, despite his holy order is a manipulative toad with a history of murder on his hands."

"From which the gods saw fit to pardon him," added the Lord Commander.

"Yes, that is true," continued Tonousa. "But the point that I am trying to make is that at every turn of my investigation the four were linked to the abuse of Lillywort. Despite that fact, and no matter how hard I looked, I could not find sufficient evidence to prove that any one of them was guilty of murder. After my visit earlier today to Teulu's temple for a reading of Fortunes Fate, and later when on route to the Citadel, I realised that I was looking at it all wrong. The murderer didn't have a motive to kill anyone in particular, no his purpose is much simpler. The beast is simply intent on creating terror and the randomness of its actions support that aim. It wants to eliminate the opposition, yes, but in no particular order. I believe the crimes are opportunistic and that any anyone will fit its purpose."

"So are you are telling us that there is no way of deducing who will be next to die. It seems to me that the only way to prevent further misery is to apprehend the bastard in the act of committing a crime," asked Ystafell.

"That is my belief also," continued Tonousa with a nod of her head. "During my interrogations of the four I asked many questions that would reveal their true nature. I discovered many interesting facts about them all but nothing to suggest one is a changeling. I've thought through every possible scenario and when those ideas didn't work for me, I even tried to think the impossible. There is but one constant, the connection between the Lillywort plant and the Eastern Marsh."

"Are you saying that your investigation has faltered, if not altogether failed?" asked Ystafell.

Tonousa felt the eyes of the Lord Chamberlin, the Archmage, and the Commander of the Watch burn into her soul as she sought to think of something to say that could disprove that conclusion. A sudden thought came to her rescue; it was something she had missed in the chaos of the past few days and it brought a smile to her face.

"There's one possible lead that could be relevant," she said, stumbling over her words.

"And that is?" asked the Lord Chamberlin.

"The detail of the Lillywort supply chain," continued Tonousa. "Cassius Underscroft of the Thieves Guild once told me that his son Webb, prior to his murder, had been involved in distributing and selling the substance in the Citadel using his cover as a kitchen boy. Richemanus later confirmed this to me along with the name of his personal supplier. However there were others who assisted in the peddling of the compound and I almost had one in my grasp some days ago. He was in my opinion, the lead contact with our murderer who I am convinced was also the mastermind behind the distribution of Lillywort. This go-between called Falaz Al Hizdor had his throat slit just as I was about to ask him the name of his supplier. The one who silenced Falaz now rots in one of the cells of the Underkeep, unless of course Tharik Mastisan has destroyed him already with his perverted practices."

"I fail to see where this is going..." interrupted Ystafell.

"Please my Lord," uttered the Lord Commander. "Let her finish."

"Nedes Karoly, according to Sir Richemanus, was the member of the Thieves Guild responsible for the spate of horse rustling across the city, including the theft from Stable Master Treveyn's establishment. He was also an acquaintance of Falaz Al Hizdor and that link is of great importance. A path has opened in my thoughts you could say. From what I witnessed in the slaughter house in Shaylotte Street, I conclude that Nedes Karoly and his accomplice Fieggis had figured out that I had discovered Falaz's connection to the shapeshifter and that they feared he could crack under interrogation. I'm sad to say they found him first and killed him in my presence before he could divulge the name of the one that we seek."

"I understand that bastard Karoly was also the head of the vigilantes who have been threatening and abusing us wizards," added the Archmage.

"It was staring me right in the face and I just realised..."

"So are you are saying that this Nedes Karoly knows who the murder is?" asked Ystafell.

"Both Nedes Karoly and Fieggis were without doubt members of the Thieves Guild." continued Tonousa without hesitation. "There must be a direct link between the man we hold in the Underkeep and the infiltrator from the Eastern Marsh, just as there was with Falaz."

"So what do you suggest the Lord Chamberlin does next?" asked the Archmage.

"Thank you Iqotrix," lisped Ystafell. "I can speak for myself. So Tonousa, what do you suggest we do with this information? We must act in haste for I don't know how long we can keep Phauless's death a secret."

"I have a plan of sorts but I'll need your full support Lord Chamberlin; you also Commander."

"Let's hear it first, but of course I will support you if I can," replied Townsforth.

"I'll support anything that leads to the capture of the swine," added the Lord Chamberlin.

"I propose we set up a sting," continued Tonousa, her mind improvising as she talked. "We will use Nedes Karoly to facilitate a meeting with the perpetrator through his contacts with the Thieves Guild. We should use a real name as bait, someone of importance who will assume the role of purchaser of the potion. We will position them as desperate to get their hands on the mind rotting powder. Then we will set up an exchange, money for powder, and define the place, date, and time to our choosing. We will then wait and pounce on the bastard when he shows up for the trade."

"And do you think that would work?" pondered Ystafell.

"Depends which name we give. It has to be believable," added the Lord Commander.

"Then who do you suggest we use?" asked Ystafell.

"It cannot be anyone who was present when Phauless was murdered," said Tonousa with confidence. "I suggest Lady Fullbane. What she doesn't know will not hurt her. You've seen the decadent life she leads. I guess it wouldn't be too much of a surprise to the murderer if she was to start asking about Lillywort to satiate her ever growing gamut of desires."

"I couldn't have thought of anyone better," responded Ystafell as he laughed out loud. "But do you think this Nedes Karoly character will go along with the plot? I for one think that most unlikely."

Tonousa hesitated. Karoly was the only one who could make it succeed.

"Perhaps we could dangle an offer he couldn't refuse," she continued.

"Such as what," asked the Archmage?

"His freedom and a full pardon for all the crimes he has ever committed."

The expressions on the faces of the others showed that the idea did not sit well with them.

"You cannot be serious girl. We just cannot let him out to roam at will amongst us," said the Archmage. "His home spun justice will result in the death of many from my Guild. We can't..."

"If this is the only way, then I will support it," interrupted Ystafell. "I can have a warrant for his release written at once. How long do you think it would take to set up the sting Tonousa?"

Tonousa smiled for there was but one answer that she could give.

"Six days."

"Six days!" gasped Ystafell as he had expected a much shorter time frame. "I suppose that in the greater scheme of things that is not too long to wait if it results in an end to this nonsense. However, I don't know how I'm going to keep Phauless's murder quiet for six long days. You lot will have to help me with that."

"The Watch can be called upon to assist," said the Lord Commander.

"And those from the Wizards Guild," added the Archmage.

"I thank you all," continued Ystafell. "We all now have roles to play so let us agree to put Tonousa's plan into action. Lord Commander, please return to your barracks and ensure your men have all they need for their journey to Valameer. Tonousa, make your way to the dungeons of the Underkeep and if Tharik gives you any trouble send him to me. Archmage you are to remain by my side. As the Royal Council is as good as destroyed then I will need all the help you can give me until Lady Flurdiana gets here."

As the small group stood and prepared to leave the table Tonousa had yet another thought.

"Before we go Lord Chamberlin there is one last thing I need of you."

"Anything with in my power, daughter of Amberstone."

"The guards confining Sir Byddin to his rooms; we need to remember to make sure he has the same freedom of movement as the other three suspects. If he is the one we seek, we need to allow him the confidence to attend what he thinks is a meeting with Fullbane."

"Of course, I will ensure that point is made to those watching over him."

"I will also speak to the Royal Guard," added the Lord Commander. "I'll make something up, and I'll ensure that the four to roam the Citadel but their movements will be observed and monitored by the best men that I have available."

Tonousa was delighted that her investigation was at last moving forward and she prayed that her entrapment would work. Lady Fullbane's words returned: 'A Path Will Form.'

At the top of the main stairs Tonousa and her Commander stopped and gazed down upon the stained glass window before them; Sir Raulyn and his mighty battle axe illuminated by a shaft of evening light. Both warriors of the Watch took it as an omen of success but they did not linger.

"Take care of yourself, Tonousa. This is dangerous work that you do."

"And you too," she replied with respect.

"No, I mean it. I know the history between you and Karoly. Promise me that you'll behave yourself. I don't want a repeat of what happened at Stukeley Knoll."

"I will be a good girl," she replied.

Tonousa felt the pain of the comment as the two went their separate ways.

She traversed the corridors of the Citadel in rapid time and soon came upon the stone stairs that led down into the Underkeep. Her thoughts focused her imminent challenge, the turning of Karoly. She fought against the memory of witnessing Phauless Gylewu's murder and not knowing how it had been achieved. The vision of his body, still cold in the Great Hall, awaiting collection by the priests, prodded at her consciousness. Anger festered at her failings and self-doubt hammered away inside her head. Had she missed some vital clue along the way, something that could have prevented the Sovereign's murder? Still uncertain as to the cause of death, whether it was poison or some unknown magic, it was beyond her wit to figure out how the Mark of Kha had appeared. Fighting against idea that perhaps the Archmage wasn't telling the truth she questioned his apparent inability to detect an aura of magic. Then it hit her like a sword to the helm; perhaps it wasn't one of the four after all and her father had got it all wrong. She began to perspire as that idea grew and she fought against the image of the Archmage as the killer. Worse was to come for she then imagined it being the Lord Chamberlin and then, most painful of all, her own Lord Commander. The only two she was certain she could exclude were Danisun and Darchus. She refused outright to contemplate the possibility of it being either of them, besides Darchus was an outsider and was absent when the vast majority of the crimes had been committed.

Tonousa had six days to solve the case. Her thoughts retreated to the Fortune's Fate reading and the three cards that she had chosen. It had taken place that same morning but so much had happened since that it seemed a week ago. She remembered the first two cards, "Justice" and "Success" and that the message from the dice that said that she would identify the killer in six days. But then there was the third card, the one she had declined to view for some reason that now seemed most strange. Perhaps the last one would have revealed a vital clue and she kicked herself for not turning it over. Maybe Teulu had looked at it and could send her a clue to its identity. She was clutching at straws and her thoughts moved on to the

Historian who appeared to have a key role and was somehow linked to the Enderdetag Prophecy. Then at last she sought to make the connection between Rukave and the boy spoken of in the verse, the very same lad that Irabo had pulled from the Tiaryer, Llyat Emgar. Tonousa had become so lost in her thoughts that without conscious effort she had found her way to the cell in the Underkeep where a few feet ahead she knew that Nedes Karoly was being held prisoner. She hammered upon the door and within seconds it was opened by the grotesque form of Tharik Mastisan.

"What the fuck do you want," he snarled?

"I'm here to see the prisoner Nedes Karoly," she replied.

Mastisan looked Tonousa up and down before he turned and beckoned her inside.

"This way, if you must."

Tonousa followed the steps down into the stone chamber and into a cell very much like the one that she had herself had recently occupied. Within the confines of his cage, caked in his own dirt sat Karoly. The unkempt man rested against the wall, his hands bound in shackles which in turn were suspended from metal hooks high upon the wall. Rats scurried past his exposed feet which stank so foul that even then rodents wouldn't bite them. Had it been anyone else Tonousa may have shown pity but this was Nedes Karoly and she had a score to settle.

"And what brings the ravishing Tonousa Amberstone of the Watch to my bed chamber," said Karoly with a lecherous grin on his face. "I'm sure that Tharik here will find you a stool to sit on. I apologise for having nothing finer to offer but I seem to have fallen on rather hard times of late. It's such a shame what you did to Fieggis. I'm sure he would have liked to share your quim with me down here in the Underkeep."

"Shut your foul mouth," barked Tonousa though the bars. "I'm here to make you an offer which once you hear it, I'm sure you will not refuse."

Despite the dirt and grime that covered the blacksmith's face Tonousa could not help but recognise the evil that burned in his eyes. At least she had his undivided attention.

30

The cage that hung high above the cavern floor reminded Llyat of the one that Brosizrug and his ogres had used to transport their prisoners from Barad Elestor to the wastelands around Calistorn. The most significant difference was that this one was built from wood rather than metal. The cube was suspended by a large thick rope which itself was attached to a pulley system that his captors used to lower and to raise it. When Llyat first woke inside its confines he felt like vomiting for his head spun due to the swinging motion of the cage. He was not alone. Not counting a rotting corpse of a forgotten beast that hung through the bars, he was surprised to note that Einar shared his place of confinement. The size of the cage was too small to accommodate the giant with any degree of comfort and it forced the Berserker to either have to stoop or sit. Llyat's emotions fluctuated between relief and fear for the last time he had cast his eyes upon the giant he had morphed into a Lizardman. On seeing that Llyat was awake Einar sought to regain the young man's trust by describing in detail events that only he and Llyat could know. The youth was soon persuaded that this Einar was not a changeling when the Berserker repeated what he had been told relating to Heliana's seduction back in Parandor; an intimate tale shared on their journey together. Einar had spared none of the details and described activities that a Lizardman would have neither understood nor been interested in.

Once he had established that his fellow prisoner was indeed a friend Llyat then looked for the amethyst he had taken from the statue. He checked to see if he had concealed the stone amongst his furs but then he recognised the truth of the matter. There was no way the Lizardmen would allow him to keep it.

"You won't find it," mumbled Einar. "They took it off you before they threw you in here."

The thought that the Lady of the Silverwynn had acquired yet another of the Gems of Thamous was hard for Llyat to reconcile. He felt a wave of despair and it threatened to crush him with self-pity. And yet he had accomplished so much in such a short time that his confidence had doubled. He would not allow it to be snatched away by a moment of regret.

"So how did it happen?"

"They were waiting," began the Berserker. "Somehow they knew that we would be coming. All I can guess is that when you lit that fire in their village, they knew that you had arrived and that triggered a number pre-planned actions. It was a trap and we walked straight into it. That sentry was not alone and the rest took me by surprise. Once I was incapacitated they sent another of their own in my place."

"You weren't to know..." added Llyat but Einar just kept talking.

"I should never been caught like this. My guard dropped and now we're fucked. I am sorry."

Surprised that the once stoic giant now exhibited raw emotions Llyat feared that the Berserker had given up all hope. That was something that Llyat had no intention of doing.

"Stop wallowing," he ordered. "There is always a way forward. If a single rose can penetrate the frozen snows of the north then we too can triumph against all odds. We just need to find the right answer for the right moment."

"What nonsense are you spewing out now?" grumbled Einar.

"Back in Thengar Forest there was a solitary flower. A single rose that had broken through the snow covered ground and created a point of beauty amongst the old gnarled trees. It is an image that has stayed with me, the knowledge that no matter what hardships we may encounter there is always a chance that life lives on. We can yet still succeed if we hold on to the beliefs that we can influence the outcome."

Llyat did not know where his new strength came from as he was always the first to give up when faced with a problem. Now he would not be beaten, not now, not ever. He had come so far that it was impossible to contemplate an end, even if his plight was so desperate. All he could do was keep strong and ride each moment. Some chance event would appear that would help him escape."

Time dragged and Llyat estimated he had been confined beneath the Lizardman temple for some six days and nights, although it was difficult to be sure given the perpetual dark. As the days passed he began to sense the seriousness of his predicament. Throughout this time in limbo he had often thought about using the fire fists spell on the wood and rope but always decided against it. Such action would cause the cage to plummet amongst the enormous stalagmites that covered the cavern's floor. For many long hours he ruminated on other ways to freedom. Much of his time he spent observing the activities of the Lizardmen and what they had constructed underground. He noted buildings of similar construction to those he had seen upon the floating island although there were others that had been carved out of the rock. The varied nature of the structures intrigued him for they did not all appear to be houses. Most were multi-levelled and connected to each other by walkways and ramps that gave height and grandeur to the reptilian metropolis. This city of the Lizardmen was unique to anything he had ever seen before. The cavern itself was lit by an eerie glow, a deep red generated by various furnaces that were scattered amongst the more substantial stone buildings. Llyat at one point tried to estimate the numbers of the Lizardmen and worked out there had to be at several thousand. They came in various sizes, many having differing roles but most were warriors.

Food and water had been provided at regular intervals and always to a predictable timetable. This was one of the observations that Llyat had factored into his calculations of the passage of time. At feeding times the wooden cage would first be lowered, stopping just short of the jagged rocks and where the cage door abutted against one of the many wooden walkways that weaved throughout the city. Once the cage had descended, the prisoners would be greeted by at least six Lizardmen warriors, one of whom would provide the strange meat-like nourishment and muddy water in order they would not to starve. Neither Llyat nor Einar knew what the substance was but being so hungry they ate. It was perhaps best not to know.

"They are determined to keep us alive for some reason," said Einar on one occasion.

"Do you think they know who we are?" replied Llyat.

"I'm not sure and can only speculate as to their motives."

Once Einar and Llyat had eaten, the cage was always hoisted back to the full height where they were left to wait until fed once more. Even though they were trapped without hope, Llyat found it amusing when Einar at last snapped out of his depression and decided to void his bowels, aiming at one of the creatures below. When Llyat had asked why he would do such a thing the Berserker had responded with a thunderous laugh.

"If they are going to keep two men in a cage without a pot then they have but themselves to blame. There is just one way and that is down. Anyway, you stink so much from all we have been through that I do not want to add to it."

"And you my friend have reeked from the moment I first met you. A little more would make no difference!" said Llyat in response.

The sixth day of captivity was like all the previous ones except for the fact that Llyat had decided that it would be the day that he would somehow escape from his place of confinement. He wasn't sure how he would achieve this end but there was nothing that would stop him from trying. It was also the day that he first noticed other creatures being corralled below. Strange beasts were enclosed in robust wooden enclosures adjacent to some of the more distant stone buildings. Llyat recognised what they were despite only having encountered one of their kind.

"Kulkulkath!" he said as he pointed Einar in the direction of his line of sight. "They have Kulkulkath down there."

"I'm not surprised," replied Einar, his movement causing the cage to swing. "I've given up trying to understand these reptiles. What is it they want from us?"

Llyat was about to answer when the cage began to descend.

"I guess we may soon find out," he said as their captors broke their own routine.

The cage descended slowly and took several minutes to reach the loading platform. In that time Llyat ruminated on possible answers to Einar's questions. It was clear that the Lizardmen had been waiting for their arrival in the Marsh. He guessed that the Lady of the Silverwynn must have sent word of his intended movements, no doubt aware he would lead the Lizardmen to the amethyst. By know she would have Thias and Irabo within her clutches.

Once the cage had reached its docking platform they were met by four burly Lizardmen, each armed with a shield and spear. Amid this escort stood yet another variant of the reptile kind. This one was different from all others that Llyat had ever seen. Its skin was brown instead of green and it wore purple robes over its metal and leather armour.

"What is it that you want with us?" shouted Einar.

Llyat made eye contact with the robed creature which stared back without blinking. Then the beast began to examine Llyat and Einar with its slit like eyes before issuing an order to the other four.

"Restrain and bring them, with us, Ssobekk wishes to talk."

"Who is Ssobekk?" barked out Einar but none replied.

The door to the cage opened and scale covered hands reached inside. They grabbed hold of the weakened and emaciated prisoners and removed them from the cage. It took Llyat and Einar several minutes to regain their land legs. Once steady and unlikely to fall they were then pushed forward into the maze of the subterranean city.

"Fuck you all," shouted Einar as he was prodded in the back.

The closest reptile struck out with the shaft of his spear and connected with the Berserker's head. Einar dropped to floor.

"Did I say you could speak," hissed his assailant. "Now get up and move on!"

Einar, with a little assistance from Llyat, did as ordered. Once back on his feet he and Llyat were pushed forward once again. Llyat so no point in causing further trouble for he wanted to follow the one in purple and understand who or what Ssobekk was.

"Don't antagonise them," he whispered to Einar. "We will soon know what they want."

The purple reptile led the way along the walkways. As Llyat had already suspected from observations on high, the buildings were made of the same reed like tetorak that grew in the marshes. Those that were more solid were older and gave further proof that the city had been there a very long time. A multitude of eyes watched him as he passed. They belonged to reptiles of various ages and came in numerous shapes and sizes. Some were old and a few were young, some had green skin and others brown which tended to resemble frogs rather than lizards. The Lizardmen children delighted in throwing whatever came to hand at the two prisoners. The adults spat and hissed in a manner that Llyat assumed were curse words. It was clear the prisoners were neither loved nor welcomed. Llyat then felt several small stones strike him across the back of the head and he tried not to flinch. He would not give the reptiles the satisfaction of seeing his fear. He focused his thoughts on escape. Some of the streets where they met the cavern walls passed on into tunnels which appeared similar to the one that he had followed the changeling down from the statue. They appeared to be exit points and Llyat tried to work out if they could lead to the surface.

"Who do you think this Ssobekk is?" Einar whispered.

"I don't have a clue," replied Llyat. "Something with slit eyes and a forked tongue no doubt. Have you noticed how varied the buggers are?"

Llyat glanced at their escort but the Lizardmen did not seem concerned by their talk.

"We know that the Lady of the Silverwynn controls the Knights of Avolire and all those who have aligned themselves to her cause; yet we know nothing about the leadership of the Eastern Marsh except that hundreds of years ago they followed the fearsome Urthanock. Perhaps this Ssobekk is their current ruler."

"Well, we are going to find out soon enough," replied Einar.

"What makes you say that?" asked Llyat.

"Because of that!"

Llyat looked beyond the Berserker's finger. There ahead was a building much larger than any other within the cavern. Its foundations had been built from rock while its roof was supported by timber and tetorak columns and gave the impression of being some kind of fortress. Soon they came before two large studded iron doors which the purple reptile soon thrust aside. The two prisoners were pushed through the portal where Llyat was taken aback by the sheer size of a vast chamber that opened up before his eyes. Forced into the very heart of the structure he tried to work out the purpose behind its construction. The most striking feature was the large pit in its centre and towards the edge of which he and Einar were then taken. This hollow was at least a hundred paces across with a depth some five times that of a Berserker's height. Its floor was covered in fine white sand and upon its surface Llyat noted a scattering of human remains in various states of decomposition. A solitary passageway led out from the pit and was guarded by a strong wooden gate. The ground seemed to ripple from time to time as if something large burrowed beneath the sand. Set back a few paces from the pit edge stood stone terraces. In a natural break in the rock, directly opposite to where he stood, Llyat noted a canopy. It too was constructed from stone and under it sat a fine carved throne created from the bleached bones of strange creatures. Llyat thoughts returned to the arena back in Barad Elestor where having drunk Berserker juice he had fought the ogre. He realised he was looking at yet another arena but this one had not been abandoned. A gathering of Lizardmen warriors stood on the terraces, were positioned at all levels, some dressed in hoods with their faces obscured, and others with helms upon their heads. Each one appeared to be in heightened anticipation of some event and Llyat feared what it could be. Then as he and Einar were pushed forward to the very edge of the pit the Lizardman in purple shouted out:

"Ssobekk, I bring the prisoners before you."

From the far side of the arena the largest of the warriors began to move towards the prisoners.

"I have a bad feeling about this," muttered Einar.

Llyat ignored the comment for he was too preoccupied with the features of creature that walked in his direction. As the beast approached he began to appreciate its true size. It dwarfed even the Berserker. A long tail swished as it plodded forward and soon Llyat began to make out the detail of its rough skin. The most hideous deformities poked through gaps in armour way too small. One suspicious eye looked over a pointed snout. Where a second eye should have been was a dried out socket, no doubt the result of some long past altercation. It even waddled in a disconcerting fashion as it shifted its bulky body between two very different hind limbs. One, its right, was its natural leg while the other was a grotesque wood carved replacement. A memory stirred as Llyat remembered stories of the fabled crocodile warriors of the Badlands. This beast was more than lizard.

"Are you sure these are the two that Avolire warned us about?" snarled the creature.

"Yes Ssobekk," replied purple robes.

Ssobekk the beast stared at his captives with its one searching eye; its face encroaching such that Llyat reeled from the putrid stench of its breath.

"Is this the one that desecrated our sacred alter?"

"Yes Ssobekk, it is," replied the purple one.

Ssobekk's eye continued to examine Llyat with great interest until without warning the creature raised its hand and signalling for the prisoners and their escort to follow him. Once again Llyat felt the shaft of a spear push into deep into his back and it forced him around the side of the pit. Purple called out to Ssobekk, bowed, and then left the group. Llyat and Einar were now under the control of the one who commanded authority over all others. The creature moved on to the chair of bones when it then it stopped.

"So you are the Marked, the boy of the Prophecy,"

Llyat remained quiet. If he about to die he had no intention of giving answers that would aid the reptiles or the Lady of the Silverwynn.

"What if he is?" spat out Einar. "What is it too you?"

The nearest Lizardman swung the shaft of his spear and connected with Einar's head. The Berserker fell to his knees and moaned.

"You will speak only when asked a question," ordered the Lizardman.

"Fuck off!" snapped back the Berserker.

Einar jumped to his feet and turned on the Lizardman but was soon pushed back by the points of numerous spears. Llyat watched as his giant friend submitted. Ssobekk sat relaxed upon the bone chair and snorted in a way that Llyat assumed was laughter.

"Berserker, you might like to know that the spears that my warriors carry are tipped with a poison so lethal that one grain of its purest form can kill even the largest of creatures. I'm sure it would have the same effect on a dragon fucker."

Llyat saw the anger grow on Einar's face and feared his friend was about to start a war. He reckoned that their chances of escape were slim and he hoped Einar would desist.

"Let it go Einar, it's not worth dying for," shouted Llyat as Ssobekk laughed again.

"Listen to the Marked my friend. He seems by far the wisest, despite his desecration of the shine of Urthanock. Tell me young man, what is so special about this object."

Ssobekk reached into the r pouch that hung at his side and pulled out the amethyst. He held it aloft for the lizardmen to see. Llyat was once again transfixed by its presence.

"From the look in your eye, I see this stone means a great deal to you," snorted Ssobekk. "Could it be that you, the Marked has surfaced one of the legendary Gems of Thamous, one that has been hidden for a very long time? The changeling that found you unconscious told me of your vision in which you saw a young girl with yet another jewel in her hands. That interests me lad for I suspect it is the other that we seek"

Llyat did not answer and so Ssobekk continued.

"I'll take your silence as confirmation. It appears we now have four in our possession. Tell me of your vision and where the fifth can be found."

"The Lady of the Silverwynn will never unite the Gems of Thamous; the bitch will never control the Underworld."

"The Silverwynn, don't make me laugh," snorted Ssobekk. "That fool has desires that exceed her usefulness. You needn't bother yourself about her."

"What do mean by that?"

"Long ago, when we agreed to support the Lady's desire for revenge, Ssonsh the Priest Lord believed her to be an ideal vessel with which to contain the powers of the Rift. The energy that Kha himself had once bestowed upon Urthanock has begun to leak out from the Underworld through a fractured portal. Ssonsh saw in the Lady a great potential as did the powers of the Rift. Together they fuelled her desire for power and vengeance. A special room was created over the fracture where the Lady could absorb the energy as it leached out. It has nurtured and sustained her for many years."

Llyat struggled to follow the story and remain focused.

"Then something most unexpected happened," continued Ssobekk. "Another of your kind was found in the mines below Avolire. This new someone has a natural and unexplainable link to the magic of the Rift which has shifted its allegiance from the Lady and refocussed on him. The Lady of the Silverwynn is dying. Her value has been lost and her service to our cause is no longer required. Avolire and Parandor are alike in so many ways and both will fall to the might of the Lizardmen. The time of men, the race descended from the Ancients, is almost over. The Eastern Marsh is about to conquer all and complete what Urthanock failed to achieve during his first time amongst us."

Llyat's mind exploded in a burst of thought. He had been taken aback by the realisation the Lady of the Silverwynn had been but a mere counter in a Lizardman game. It seemed the scale swine had seduced her to their will with the temptation of harnessing the energy of the Underworld. Now that they had found someone younger she had been dismissed. He questioned if he was being told the truth yet throughout his ruminations he kept his gaze fixed on the amethyst, still secure within Ssobekk's leathery hands.

"So who is the real Marked? I wonder..." continued the crocodile beast as it tossed the amethyst high into the air and caught it with the same hand. "Is it you or this other in Avolire? Rest assured, the Lady of the Silverwynn will not live to reunite the Gems of Thamous. The armies of the Eastern Marsh are ready to march on Parandor. We await the command of our new leader and the return of Urthanock."

"So now I get what this is all this is all about," said Llyat. "The powers of the Underworld are being channelled through this new other. You aim to create a host for the spirit of Urthanock."

"Quite so," said the beast. "Once the portal has been opened the Underworld's power will fill the Vessel and he will become omnipotent."

"And that's why you want the Gems of Thamous,"

"Correct," continued Ssobekk. "The jewels are the key to the door. However, if the Enderdetag Prophecy is to be believed then another Marked will open the door and defeat the Lord of Fear. This is my dilemma; which is the true Marked and which is the one chosen to be the vessel for Urthanock. I think I know which you are and if I am correct we have a common purpose you and I. It would seem that we both want to control the door but for different reasons. You, I sense, are a great risk to our cause but you may yet be needed to unlock the portal."

To Llyat everything then made sense. He now understood his purpose and why he had to collect and own all five of the gems. It was he alone who could open and close the portal. His destiny was to seal the essence of Urthanock in the Underworld and destroy this 'other'. The thought threatened to overwhelm him but then Einar intervened.

"So why drag us all the way here to tell us this shite? You could have just left us to rot in that cage and the Prophecy would have died with us. Instead we have had to endure all that spews from the end your putrid snout."

"Einar, stop it, please!" exclaimed Llyat. "This will not help."

"You will respect Ssobekk," hissed one of the four guards as it prepared once again to hit the back of the Berserker's head.

This time Einar was ready for the assault. He snatched at the shaft of the spear and the speed of movement caught the Lizardman unaware. It recoiled backwards.

"Try that again and I'll rip out your guts," exclaimed Einar.

Llyat expected the other three guards to retaliate but they remained still. The beast upon the throne of bones began to laugh.

"I love the Berserker's lack of fear," snorted Ssobekk. "I'm so pleased we chose him to entertain us today in the great pit..."

"So what would you have me do for you down there?" snarled Einar as he pushed on the spear shaft of the nearest guard.

"The pit," continued Ssobekk, "is the palace of sport for those who dwell in this city. But before we go any further, what do they call you Berserker for I cannot remember your name?"

Ssobekk replaced the amethyst inside his pouch as Einar spoke his name. The beast then rose.

"Einar the Berserker, a name we will remember long after your death. I needed to be sure who you are and if Avolire was correct when then warned us that the Marked would seek to infiltrate our great city. Now that your identities are confirmed to my satisfaction I can give my most trusted followers some well-deserved entertainment."

"And what is it you have planned?" asked Einar.

Llyat looked at the warrior crowd and a bad feeling grew in his gut.

"This!" exclaimed Ssobekk.

In one swift and unexpected movement Ssobekk kicked out with his good leg and connected with the Berserker's stomach. The force of the clawed foot pushed Einar back over the edge of the pit. Llyat then heard the sound of his friend hit the sand covered floor. He stepped forward to the edge and peered down and then dropped to his belly.

"Einar, are you okay?"

The Berserker managed to stand and dust off the fine white sand that clung to his trousers.

"When I get back up there, you're going to wish you had never been hatched, you three legged lump of swamp shite."

"Are you okay?" bellowed Llyat.

"I've never felt fucking better," growled Einar.

Llyat did not have time to respond before he felt hands grab hold his leather clothes. They yanked him back to his feet and prevented any chance of him aiding his friend.

"Let go of me!" cried Llyat. "Who the fuck do you think you are?"

"I am Ssobekk," laughed the creature. "Head of the Army of the Eastern Marsh, Lord of this city, and the second in command to Ssonsh."

Llyat heard the words but they failed to register. As if possessed by a mighty warrior's essence he sought to break free from the creature's grasp. Einar's threats and curses were drowned by Ssobekk's laughter and the hissing of guards that now filled the arena.

"Let me go..." shouted the youth.

Then Llyat froze for he noticed the sands at the far end of the pit begin to ripple like waves on the shore. There was something in the ground and it wouldn't be anything good.

"Einar!" he shouted. "You've got to get out of there now."

"If he tries to climb the walls use your spears," shouted Ssobekk to the circle of warriors.

"What is it?" screamed Llyat. "What is it that you want from me? What is in there?"

"You are about to watch the mother of all battles lad," hissed Ssobekk. "When we heard that a Berserker dared to enter our territory I could not deny those that captured him the opportunity to witness a fight to the death. I want to see how he defends himself."

"But what is down there with him? Defend himself against what?"

"A kulkulkath from the Howling Hills," answered his captor. "This one is a queen, the most lethal of their species."

Llyat felt his stomach churn. He recalled images of the juvenile he had encountered in the Ivory Pass and how Thias and Irabo had both been terrified by its destructive potential. He knew that Einar was in great peril but there seemed nothing he could do about it.

"If the Berserker defeats the Kulkulkath then I promise you that I will allow him to live," snarled Ssobekk. "But I have other plans for you!"

"Go drown yourself in the marsh," spat back Llyat. "You and all you're fucking kin."

Llyat did not have chance to curse again before a sudden explosion of sand rose up from the centre of the pit. It was followed by a second and third. Each time the movements of the ground came ever closer to where Einar stood with eyes wide open and fists clenched.

"You've got to be joking!" bellowed the Berserker.

A further explosion was followed by the appearance of an enormous hairy creature that broke through the surface of the sand. Its claws snapped in the air while the venomous tail stinger zipped from side to side. This kulkulkath, at least three times the size of the juvenile, was primed to kill.

"Get out now!" screamed Llyat while he lost sight of Einar in a cloud of sand dust.

"Let the sport begin," snorted the crocodile Lord.

As he struggled to free himself from Ssobekk's grasp, Llyat focused on all that he could see through the haze. Einar raced towards the centre of the pit with the giant creature in hot pursuit. Jeers and shouts of Lizardmen warriors filled the space as they hissed as one in anticipation of the kulkulkath's kill. Llyat shouted as loud as he could and prayed that that Einar would both hear him and follow his advice.

"Find something to defend yourself with," he bellowed as his eyes noted the many carcasses that lay on the arena's floor.

"Many have fought the Queen and yet none can speak of victory," whispered Ssobekk. "The creatures hide is so thick that it cannot be penetrated by mortal weapons. Her claws are as sharp as razors and her stinger contains enough venom to kill a whole city. I cannot wait to see what my pet makes of a Berserker from the Dragonas."

"He'll find away a way to escape from your bitch," cried Llyat.

Einar continued to avoid each swing of the beast's claws and tail.

"Then he will only be the second to have done so," snorted Ssobekk.

"Who was the first?" asked Llyat.

Ssobekk did not answer but instead tapped his wooden leg with his free hand. Llyat understood the message. In the vastness of the arena the kulkulkath continued its efforts to cut Einar in half. It lunged forward and the Berserker used all of his skills to jump one way and then the other. Llyat realised that for Einar this was a lost cause. The Kulkulkath show no signs of slowing and Llyat wondered how long his friend's stamina could last. If only Einar had the access to the Berserkers fighting fluid.

An almighty cheer then echoed around the arena as Einar fell onto the sand. He had lost his footing as he had weaved in and out of the creatures killing zone. The Kulkulkath sensed its moment, scuttled forward, and brought its stinger flashing down over its head. Einar was too quick for the beast and as he rolled away the point missed.

"Your friend is a good mover, I'll give him that," laughed Ssobekk as he jeered at the one sided fight. "It thought he was gone that time."

"I'll not let you get away with this, you evil bastard," growled Llyat.

"But I already have!"

"Is that all you've got you black hairy turd," screamed Einar.

Llyat saw his friend square up to the creature which for a moment stood motionless and stared out from under its mass of fur. Llyat failed to understand what the creature could be doing or why it was waiting. His concern grew but then the creature pounced. As Einar dived for cover the creature buried itself deep into the sand. Einar rose again to his feet. With stealth he moved to the nearest corpse and picked up the sword that lay in the fallen warrior's bony hand. The sounds of jeering and shouting fell away and an eerie quiet passed along the terraces. Llyat feared for his friend. At least before the creature had gone to ground the Berserker knew where the kulkulkath was. Now it could be anywhere!

"Is that all you've got; have you had enough?" bellowed Einar as he readied the blade in his hand. "Are you scared to face me you oversized fucking ant?"

Without warning the kulkulkath's tail shot out from the sand. Einar attempted to swerve to one side and deflect it with his sword but he was too slow. The stinger connected with the skin on his bare torso and left a deep laceration.

"No" screamed Llyat.

Once again he tried to free himself from Ssobekk's grip but this time the world seemed to move at a much slower pace. His ears heard the cries and shouts for the kulkulkath victory but all were muffled. It was as if his essence had become suspended in time. His eyes stared in disbelief as Einar fell to his knees, dropped his blade and slumped forward. The beast stung again, and then again and Einar fell dead with shock etched upon his noble face. The beast's tail then wrapped itself around the Berserker's body and dragged it beneath the sandy surface. Tears filled Llyat's eyes. He turned on Ssobekk and began to beat the creature's chest with his fists.

"You bastard," he screamed. "You fucking, hateful bastard!"

Then as if from nowhere, Llyat clenched his fists and focused deep within his body. With all the strength he could muster he cried out;

"Promethelumous."

The youth's fists ignited and he punched upwards into the gaping jaws of Ssobekk. He felt the burn of the fire upon the scale flesh and in an instant the beast pulled its face away. Yet it still held onto Llyat's wrist.

"You little shit," hissed Ssobekk.

The monstrous lizard lost its balance and as its wooden leg gave way it tumbled over the edge of the pit. Ssobekk still would not let go of his prize and Llyat felt himself falling towards the sandy surface. He bounced off the sloping side of the arena and came to rest in the sand beside Croc Lord's gigantic frame.

Llyat was the first to his feet. A group of Lizardmen who stood above on the edge of the pit began to whisper and then shout out as they shared their uncertainty for the outcome of this sudden change in events. Llyat fought his fear for it seemed that he too would end his days as another meal for the black sand beast. Somehow he had to escape from the pit of death.

"Don't move a muscle if you value your life," whispered Ssobekk.

Llyat then knew that Ssobekk wanted to keep him alive. He scanned the sloping walls of the pit and realised there was no way that he could climb the slippery wooden sides. The one viable exit was through the wooden gate which was closed and very solid. He was trapped and at a loss as to what to do next. Suddenly a glint of light caught his peripheral vision. He focused onto the sand before his feet and his heart lightened. By some miraculous turn of fate, when both he and Ssobekk had fallen from the platform, the pouch that had contained the amethyst had opened. The Gem of Thamous now lay free upon the sand. An opportunity repossess the gemstone now presented itself to Llyat.

"I see what you're thinking," shouted Ssobekk. "Leave the stone where it lies or you will die."

It unnerved Llyat to think that Ssobekk could be looking out for him.

"Why should I trust you," he screamed with raw emotion.

"You have no choice lad. The stone will be retrieved later when the beast sleeps."

Llyat glanced at the amethyst as it sat in the centre of a well of sand and then back to the giant reptile beside him. The ground was quiet and there was no sign of the Kulkulkath. Llyat realised that he had but one chance to escape.

"No, don't move!" hissed Ssobekk as Llyat ran forward.

Once he had reached the amethyst Llyat picked it up and locked it into the palm of his right hand. The sand remained still and he and let out a deep sign.

"Maybe it wasn't hungry..." began Llyat but he did not have time to finish his words.

The claws of the kulkulkath burst from out of the sand and missed cutting his neck by mere inches. Then the remainder of the beast rose from out of the ground; its stinger poised to strike and jaws that still dripped with crimson ready to bite.

"Run lad!" shouted Ssobekk. "Run as fast as you can."

Llyat did not have to be told twice. As the creature prepared to launch itself towards him Llyat raced towards the centre of the arena. A roar screeched from the mouths of a thousand reptiles and echoed around the bowl of death. The amethyst remained secure in Llyat's hand, its flame having been extinguished during the fall into the pit. The one sound Llyat did hear was the scuttling of the creature behind as it rustled over the surface of the sand. The urge to look behind was too great and in an instant he turned his head. Seeing it approach at speed and with the reflexes of youth, Llyat somehow managed to duck as the stinger passed over his head.

The crescendo of noise from the sides of the arena then captured the attention of the kulkulkath. For several seconds it circled in confusion. Llyat looked over to the platform and the throne of bones where several Lizardmen were trying to raise the Ssobekk's great bulk from out from the pit. In this brief moment of respite Llyat took stock of his surroundings. He searched at once for an alternative means of escape but eventually refocused on the wooden gate. A sudden inspiration told him to burn the gate down.

With that idea implanted in his mind Llyat raced across the open sand. The kulkulkath was distracted by those still trying to drag Ssobekk to safety. A little of Llyat wanted to stay and see if Ssobekk survived the attentions of his pet but most thought better of it. Within seconds he was before the gate where he realised it was not made of wood after all but compressed reed bundles. He then gripped two its struts and closed his eyes as he sought to summon up the fire. Nothing happened except that the sand begin to move.

"Promethelumous," he shouted once again as his grip tightened on the gate.

Again nothing happened. He counted for ten seconds and shouted out the spell a third time. This time he felt the fires surge through his body and they exploded through his hands with a force that took him by surprise. The energy he had released was far more intense that anything he had seen from Thias. The door burst into flame and burned with a great heat. Llyat felt powerful and for a brief moment, in control.

"What the fuck do you think you are doing?" screamed Ssobekk from across the arena. "Don't let it out?"

The kulkulkath bounded over the ground. It jumped towards Llyat, its claws thunderclapping as in the wildest of storms. Without time to think what he was doing Llyat leapt to one side and then having landed rolled away across the sandy floor. He lifted his head he saw the kulkulkath collide with the gate whereupon the beast's mass of black hair ignited into a ball of fire. The creature howled, crashed through the already disintegrating gate, and raced on into the streets of the subterranean city. Llyat covered his ears as the kulkulkath's screams battered against his eardrums. The flames spread rapidly to the wood and reed supports that held up the stone terraces of the arena while Llyat turned one last time to see Ssobekk watching in disbelief from beneath his throne of bones. For a split second the two adversaries stared at each other before Llyat fled through the burning hole left by the incensed kulkulkath. Ssobekk's words chased him as he ran.

"Get after the little shit; The Marked must not be allowed to escape."

Having exited the gate Llyat gazed upon the carnage the beast had initiated. Many buildings were already alight as the monster snapped and clawed at the Lizardmen who attempted to subdue it. Several attempted to slay the creature but were cut down by the snapping claws and the whirling stinger. Llyat felt no sadness towards those who fell, just a desire for vengeance as he grieved for his friend. More Lizardmen appeared from the side of the arena and Llyat guessed they had been despatched to catch him and recapture the amethyst. Llyat was determined that he would not be taken and with the gem clutched in his fist he set off on his run.

On he raced and never once paused to catch his breath despite the tightness in his chest. He zipped between the wood and stone buildings and dodged gathering crowds of reptiles who did not seem to notice him pass. Llyat had no idea where he was heading and he felt that his life hung by the thinnest of strings. He had to trust in his own abilities for he was the Marked of the Prophecy. There was no alternative, he had to survive and he had to destroy the Lord of Fear. He alone could crush the Vessel that now lay hidden within the ruins of Avolire.

Then somehow Llyat knew where he needed to go. He remembered the many tunnels that led off into the cavern's walls, those he had seen on his journey from the cage to the arena. Although he could not be certain, his instinct told him they would all lead out of the city and into the swamps. A terrifying crash from behind caused him to stop and as he turned he saw to his horror that the kulkulkath was once again on his trail; now just a bald and smoking lump on legs. The guards that Ssobekk had sent after him had long since retreated and so he turned and ran. The nearest opening was still a hundred or so yards away but Llyat was not yet beaten. He knew that one wrong move, one moment of indecision, and all that he and his colleagues had sacrificed would not have be for nought. He hated kulkulkath like he had never hating anything before.

A few seconds later he made it to the passage that cut deep into the rock. Relieved that its entrance was too narrow to permit the passage of the beast he charged deep into tunnel. He heard it collide with the rock behind him and finally he sensed that he was safe. He stopped, looked back, and saw the frustrated creature retreat from the tunnel entrance intent on bringing death to more of those who had held it captive for so long. Llyat was content to be alive, at least for now.

He looked at the amethyst, still clutched in the palm of his right hand, and began to question if it had been worth the sacrifice to own it.

"Einar, you will not have died for nothing," he moaned as tears welled in his eyes.

Llyat wiped his face with his free hand and stared into the gloom. He saw that the tunnel inclined upwards and he felt a stream of cold air, sucked down to fan the flames that still spread within the cavern behind him. Escape now felt certain and his mind span. All he had to do was return to Parandor and find a way to put an end to the madness once and for all time.

On he ran until the night sky appeared overhead; only then stopping to rest. Soon he became aware of voices from behind. He turned and looked back. In the distance he saw torches moving towards him and knew he had to keep moving despite having little energy left in his legs. Llyat managed to keep going but half an hour later he could go no further. He was lost deep within the frozen marsh lands, alone and without hope. The tunnel and those that sought to hunt him down had been consumed by both distance and the dense mist. Then as he gathered in his breath and looked around for a landmark, something wrapped around his foot. It pulled him off balance and dragged him to the ground where his head collided with a small rock. Llyat could have perhaps have saved his skull from damage had his hand still not clutched the amethyst. With his head spinning he looked down to his right leg and saw a grey serpentine appendage that had snaked its way out of a nearby pool and coiled around his foot. A second bizarre tentacle then rose out of the water. It emitted an eerie glow from its tip and crept towards his face. Llyat could not believe that he had come so far to be dealt this final twist of fate; an end in the depths of the Eastern Marsh and devoured by a wisp.

The snake like tendril dragged Llyat over the frosty ground towards the pool where the bulk of the creature lay hidden. It pulled Llyat through the squelching swamp mud and on to his watery grave. Hauled helpless into the pool on his back he looked up to the sky one last time. A vast darkness then blocked out the little light that Mona had managed to push through the swirling mist. Llyat knew it was the end. He closed his eyes and slipped into unconsciousness while clutching the amethyst to his chest. In those final moments as he embraced his fate he contented himself with the knowledge that at least the Lizardmen of the Eastern Marsh would never gain possession of the precious stone.

31

The midmorning light from Solaris seeped through the shuttered window of the rented room at the rear of The Murdered Wolf. There Tonousa Amberstone sat alone at the table and examined the set of Fortunes Fate cards that lay face up before her. A priest from the temple of Fatumai had delivered the parchment cards to the tavern on the very same afternoon that Phauless Gylewu IV had been murdered. With Teulu's promise fulfilled Tonousa now sought to try and understand their meaning in the hope they would unravel the mystery that consumed her every waking thought. Her father had after all used similar ones in his bid to identify the infiltrator. Tonousa strived hard to follow his lead.

While studying them for the umpteenth time that morning, she removed the four that she knew held significance to her investigation; Strength, Justice, Judgement, and Temperance. She then set the others to one side, still face up as she examined the special ones. Her mind focused onto the key suspects who over the last six days had all been kept under detailed surveillance by the Watch.

Strength and Sir Byddin. She reflected on how the once proud yet pompous Knight, Head of the Royal Guard and the Armies of Parandor, had been released from confinement late on the afternoon following the Sovereign's murder. Sir Byddin had not been impressed by the whole affair and blamed Richemanus for the Ruler's death. In his view, the executioner had much to hide and a great deal to benefit from Phauless's demise. The Commander of the City Watch had decided to monitor Sir Byddin's activities himself under the belief that the knight was the most volatile and likely suspect.

Justice and Sir Richemanus. The brute of a man had taken to drink and for six days had sought to drown his sorrows with whatever alcohol he could lay his monstrous hands on. The knight that was once the most feared in Parandor had been reduced to the most wretched of souls. On several occasions had been found unconscious in the street only to be dragged home to bed by members of the Watch.

Judgement and Lady Emeny. Once removed from her role as the Sovereign Advisor, the Lady's composure had deserted her. She had succumbed to her nervous debilities and confined herself to her room. There she had refused to see any visitors save for Lady Calendrial Lorst who had tried to entice her out of her seclusion. Lorst however had her own motives for snooping. She had always been one of the great gossips of the Citadel and was desperate to understand what it was that troubled Lady Emeny, why the doors to the Court had been sealed, and why Phauless Gylewu was not conducting business.

Temperance and the High Priest Heward Teulu. According to Karkis Snouth, the holy servant of Fatumai had remained in prayer in his temple and had never once left it. The body of Phauless Gylewu had been collected by Teulu's priests as per his instructions and somehow they had managed to get it to the temple without being seen. This seemed to Tonousa to be a minor miracle and yet it pleased her for had the body been spotted she was sure the population of Parandor would have gone into meltdown. She could imagine with great clarity the effects of such mass panic and hysteria.

Tonousa placed the four back upon the table and began to think to back to her own reading. She remembered the two cards she had revealed 'Justice' and 'Success' and how it had been predicted that it would take six days for that success to manifest itself. This was the sixth day. Picking up the two she examined them for several minutes. If Heward Teulu's reading was true, then this day would be the one that she would solve the mystery of the murders. She would at last gain revenge for the injustice inflicted on her late father by the evil swine amongst their midst. At the back of her thoughts dwelt the ignorance of the third card that she had declined to view. How much she now regretted that decision. Of the white Attributes there were twenty other possibilities as to what that third might have been. It would have made her task much easier had she seen it. Perhaps it would have unlocked the mystery and she cursed her own stubbornness and lack of faith. Whatever that card had been it was too late now; and yet, if the game was to be believed, by the end of this day she would have all the answers that she needed.

Tonousa closed her eyes and thought about the gods that the unenlightened said resided in the heavens. If they had answered her once in her father's room then perhaps they would help her again.

"When you're ready up there!" she said, but her plea went unanswered.

"A little of your help would go a long way to aid my cause," she uttered.

A firm knock from the door brought Tonousa to her senses and forced her to open her eyes. She did not have to question who was there for it had been the distinctive secret rap of her Lord Commander. Tonousa waited and then as the door opened she was proved correct. Townsforth forced his presence upon the room. He was accompanied by another from the Watch, Lolye Throissler, who once inside closed the door behind him. Both new arrivals joined Tonousa at the table as she continued to look down at the cards.

"Any luck?" the Commander asked but Tonousa shook her head.

"I can't make any sense of them. I thought there would be something to help me move forward, but I am at a loss to find anything of use".

"Just keep at it Tonousa," said Townsforth as he placed a reassuring hand upon her shoulder. "I'm sure you will solve this riddle somehow. You just need to have faith in what you already know. You'll figure it out soon; you just need that moment of inspiration to push you forward and as you have kept telling me, a path will form."

"And what if it doesn't?" sighed Tonousa. "And then what do I do? It all seems impossible. Anyone of the four could have done it and I'm getting nowhere in trying to identify which of the buggers it is. My one hope lies in the assistance of Nedes Karoly, to help flush out the infiltrator, but I haven't seen hide nor hair of him for the last three days. I have nothing to report Sir and I feel that I am letting you down."

"Well Tonousa, remember the old saying; 'When you have eliminated the shit, then what remains, however improbable, must be the pot'."

The Commander's words sought to encourage his warrior colleague and boost her confidence. Tonousa knew that his concern was heart-felt but she so much did not want to let him down. She would not be able to live with herself if she failed.

"Am I right in guessing that you're not here to give me advice," said Tonousa. "I thought you were supposed to be keeping an eye on Sir Byddin?"

"Byddin is being watched over by Lightmain and Cragtalon," began the Lord Commander. "Even though they are from the Royal Guard and may have been dabbling in Lillywort, I do still trust them to follow my orders and keep a close watch on their leader. However, you are correct in your assumption. I'm not here to give you advice but to let you know that even though you haven't seen him for several days, Karoly has resurfaced and has passed on a message for you through the first member of the Watch that he encountered."

"And who was that?" demanded Tonousa.

"Young Throissler here, isn't that right lad?"

Tonousa glanced towards the young officer of the Watch who had become transfixed by the cards on the table.

"Isn't that right Throissler?" barked the Lord Commander again, causing the young warrior to jump to attention.

"Well!" added Tonousa. "Spit it out man?"

"Nedes found me about half an hour ago," began Throissler. "I was down by the Narrow Gate. He said he was looking for you and would speak to no one else. I informed him that we hadn't seen you in several days and that I would be happy to pass on any message. I apologise in advance for did not know that he was so vital to the outcome of your investigation. Had that been the case I would have brought him straight to the barracks myself."

"That's okay Throissler," said Tonousa as she smiled. "There was no way we could have informed everyone of Karoly's significance."

"Well lad, tell her what he had to say?" barked the Lord Commander.

"He said that his time was short and his cover would be blown if he was to be caught talking with a member of the Watch. He said he had to see you on a matter most urgent concerning the details of a rendezvous that you had asked him to arrange. I said again that I didn't know where you were but would get the message to you as soon as possible."

"So what was the message?" demanded Tonousa with growing impatience.

"I was coming to that," and with those words Throissler reached into his tunic and pulled out a small piece of parchment which he then handed over to Tonousa. "He said you would understand what this means. I hope I did right by you Tonousa."

"You did fine," she replied as she took hold of the parchment.

Tonousa was disappointed not to have received Karoly's message first hand. There was much she would have liked to have discussed regarding the setting up of the sting. She wondered if Karoly had relayed the right message, a transaction under the guise of obtaining a significant supply of Lillywort intended for Lady Fullbane. Deep down she sensed he would do the right thing, after all he had a lot at stake, a short life of incarceration versus a complete pardon and new identity. There had to be a trace of goodness left in Karoly somewhere. Tonousa glanced at the cards again.

"Did he have anything else to say?" she asked, more in hope than expectation.

"Nothing of any significance except to thank you for the bath and the fresh set of clothes," continued Throissler. "He said that you should not go looking for him and he apologised for all the trouble he has caused you, in particular the death of Falaz Al Hizdor."

"So the man repents!" exclaimed the Lord Commander.

"Did he give a name?" asked Tonousa. "Did he say who I was to meet at the rendezvous?"

"No name was offered. He just asked me to pass that parchment on to you. That's when I sought out the Commander Townsforth in order to find your whereabouts."

"Thank you Throissler," said Tonousa. "You have done very well indeed."

Even though she was disappointed with the lack of a name it seemed that Karoly had kept his word and used his influence with the Thieves Guild to organise a meeting with the infiltrator. Unable to wait any longer, Tonousa opened the small folded piece of parchment and looked at the words it contained. There were not many of them, but at least they had some meaning. '*Meet here at the setting of Solaris.*' Underneath the words had been scribbled a crude map and Tonousa recognised a familiar floorplan. A small 'x' indicated the precise location of the meeting point.

"Well," asked Townsforth impatiently. "What does it mean?"

"It's a map." replied Tonousa as she studied the parchment.

"A map of what?" he asked. "Don't leave us guessing."

Tonousa looked from her Commander and then to Throissler who had once again focused his attention on the forty seven cards laid out on the wooden table. She then passed the parchment over to her superior.

"It depicts the Underkeep beneath the Citadel," she said. "I'd know that layout anywhere. As my father had been a long serving member of the Court he often used to take me down there as a child. I have also been there on a few other occasions when taken against my will."

Tonousa emphasised the last few words of her sentence as if to reiterate the fact that following her father's death she had spent several days in one of its cells at the hands of the Watch.

"It says to meet at the setting of Solaris." continued Tonousa as Townsforth studied the parchment. "It appears that Karoly has kept his part of the bargain."

"And are you going to trust him; the one who maimed you and left those vicious scars upon your back?"

"What choice do I have? The trail died with Falaz Al Hizdor. Our four suspects are not giving anything away. It's the one option we have left."

Tonousa felt the tension in the room grow. It was evident that the weeks of toil were at last getting to her and yet somehow she managed to hold herself together. She sighed again, sat down at the table, and stared at the cards.

"I'm sorry," continued Townsforth as once again he placed a reassuring hand upon her shoulder. "This whole affair is getting to us all but if your intuition and these cards are correct then all will be brought to a head tonight in the Underkeep. By the gods of thunder we will unmask our villain soon."

"I just hope you are right," she replied.

Tonousa felt the tears well in her eyes and she so much wanted to cry. The great burden that she carried threatened to consume her soul; but no matter what, she would not give in. She would see it through to the end and would not be beaten.

"How is Lord Ystafell coping in his new position of power?" she asked, changing the subject in order to remove the focus from her own emotions.

"What is there to say?" replied Townsforth. "Like the rest of us he is struggling to keep it together. I don't know how he did it but he has somehow concealed the death of our Sovereign Lord from the rest of the populous. I offer my helm to him for that."

"Well that's at least one thing we can be thankful for."

"It seems Iqotrix has been a great help," continued Townsforth. "The weird wizard has been locked in the Council Chamber for the past six days and nights. It makes me wonder if his kind have an ulterior motive in this affair but perhaps that's a thought for another time. I'm just pleased they've got that bloody book under lock and key."

"The Lore of the Dead and Jonas Tullage have lot to answer for," said Tonousa. "It is now clear that Death Tubaria has not risen again and that we have been deceived. I just hope that Darchus and Danisun have managed to persuade Lady Flurdiana to come to our aid."

"Indeed," replied the Commander. "We received a bird this morning which confirmed they had arrived in Valameer."

A sudden gust of wind came from under the door and swirled through the room like a sand devil from the Badlands. It twisted is way across the table and threw the cards into the air. Most fell back upon the wood but some dropped to the floor. In a state of disorganised fluster Tonousa tried to prevent the rest from blowing away. Then as she bent down to pick up those that had fallen on the floor, she misjudged her movements and hit her head on the edge of the table. The force of the impact caused her to drop to her knees.

"Bastards!" she screamed though her gritted teeth. "Fucking bastards, bastards, bastards..."

Tonousa stilled. She continued to stare at the floor and the seven black backed cards that lay before her gaze. As she focused on the pictographs she shook her head. She could not believe what she saw or how she had missed the connection until now.

"Are you okay?" asked Townsforth with concern. "You need to be more careful girl."

"Fuck being careful," snapped back Tonousa. "I can't believe I didn't figure this out earlier. I've worked it out, and I've got a bloody good idea who it is as well."

"From a bang on the head?" questioned Throissler.

"Yes, exactly!"

Tonousa jumped to her feet and laid out the seven cards that had fallen on the floor. One by one she called out the name of each card in turn as she returned it to the table.

"The Hanged man; The Warrior; The Lovers; The Scholar; The Farrier; The Condemned; The Emperor."

"What about them?" exclaimed her Commander?

"It's them!" spluttered Tonousa.

"Who?"

"The ones that have been murdered," she shouted before pointing to each one of the cards. "The Hanged Man is Sir Tobius Faros. The Warrior, Sir Britta Rainmark. The Lover, well that covers both Golda Flintwind and Webb Underscroft. The Farrier is the stable boy, Mikus Danbury. The Condemned is my father and The Emperor is Phauless Gylewu. The murderer is choosing his victims using a deck of Fortunes Fate cards."

The Commander manoeuvred around the table to where Tonousa stood. He too then stared at the cards. From the change of expression on his face Tonousa realised that he too could now see the connection.

"You've got to be joking?" he exclaimed.

"I wish that I was," continued Tonousa. "It's too much of a coincidence to ignore."

The words of the Cuvar echoed through her mind. They had led her to Lady Fullbane and the last known location of Thamous's ruby. Now they had sent her another sign, the very one she had been hoping for.

"It seems a bit of a long shot though and you can't call the Royal Treasurer much of a scholar," said the Commander.

"But it fits so well," continued Tonousa as she struggled to contain her excitement. "These aren't random killings. Neither are they connected to Death Tubaria, or to the peddling of Lillywort. We have to believe this coincidence."

Once again Tonousa found herself using the words of the Cuvar. She reckoned Theoplous would have been surprised how much her beliefs had changed since they had first met on the Banshees Wail all those weeks ago. She hoped that he would be proud of how she had accepted her father's mantle and got so close to flushing out the enemy. Yet there was no way she could tell him of her success for he was otherwise engaged. Tonousa then realised how much she was on her own.

"Coincidence or not," began Townsforth as he tried work out the implications of Tonousa's discovery. "So the crimes have nothing to do with the resurgence of Death Tubaria but a hit list based on these cards. Why? Explain this to me."

"I don't know myself," replied Tonousa. "All I know is that these cards are used by the priests of Fatumai to predict the future. As you know, I myself had a reading six days ago. The victims were chosen from the pack, maybe at random, maybe not."

"So given this new insight who do you think the killer is? You hinted that you may have an idea. Tell me now and stop forcing me to drag it out in pieces."

"There can be but one possibility," replied Tonousa as her thoughts jumped around her head. "The killer would need access to a set and know in detail how they worked to be able to allocate them to different members of the Sovereign Household. I doubt Sir Byddin would have the patience and neither would Sir Richemanus. I could imagine Lady Emeny having cards somewhere, but only for show given her fascination for ancient artefacts."

"That means that there is just one it could be then."

"Yes it does!" exclaimed Tonousa, her mind racing. "It has to be him. There is no other possibility. At first I thought it couldn't be the priest due to the theft of the Lillywort from his personal store. But there is no way that anyone could have got into his storeroom without having access to the key. I'm telling you, Heward Teulu is our man."

"Then what are we waiting for," barked out the Lord Commander? "Forget this bloody nonsense with Karoly. Let's go and get the murderous monk right now."

Tonousa understood his eagerness to rush out and arrest the holiest man in Parandor. Then she remembered that Townsforth had been the chief investigator into the death of Teulu's wife and had been convinced of his guilt. Had it not been for the intervention of Hamthor, Heward Teulu would have swung from his neck years ago. Tonousa guessed that her superior was out for revenge.

"Remember sir," she began. "The real Heward Teulu would be long dead and his corpse festering somewhere in a darkened tunnel beneath the Citadel. The one who I go to meet is a changeling, a shapeshifter from the Eastern Marsh. A public challenge and arrest will cause the creature to remain in human form. We need to catch him in the act. He needs to be alone when I strike. I need to induce the change."

Commander Townsforth reflected on Tonousa's words while she looked again at the forty seven cards upon the table and pondered on their meaning. For some reason that she couldn't explain, her thoughts became fixed on the card she had failed to turn during her personal reading. If only she knew which one it had been.

"Who do we send to make the arrest?" asked the Commander.

The two warriors connected eyes and she saw that he had guessed her intentions.

"No." he exclaimed. "Not for all the power in the Underworld. I will not let you go alone."

"But it has to be that way," argued Tonousa. "No one else knows the case like I do. I think you owe me this one. I must have the satisfaction of bringing our killer down after what he did to my..."

"To your father," interrupted Townsforth. "It is because of your father I don't want you to do this. Your emotions are too are too caught up in this investigation. It has become personal vendetta, a mission driven by vengeance. I can't let your anger allow Teulu to escape."

"That's not going to happen."

"You're right, it's not going to happen," ordered the Lord Commander. "I'm just trying to protect you from yourself."

Once again a heavy silence filled the room and as it passed Tonousa made eye contact with Throissler who had been waiting with both patience and confusion. The puzzled look on his face demonstrated how uncomfortable he had become with the discussion. Tonousa signalled towards the door.

"Throissler, leave us for a moment will you," she ordered.

Throissler nodded and made his way out of the room. Tonousa turned to her Commander.

"It has to be me Brynn. I don't know why but I have to be the one who finishes this."

"Then at least take someone with you. Allow me to come. Two blades are better than one."

"No," she replied with a shake of her head. "I have to do this alone. The moment Teulu sees the Watch waiting for him he will flee and we will see no more of him. Remember, he is expecting a trade on behalf of Lady Fullbane. The trap must not be obvious. It must be sprung at the very last moment."

"But what if he changes?" asked Townsforth. "What if he assumes lizard form?"

"I can handle a Lizardman. They couldn't stop me at the Bards Guild and one on its own will be no match for my skills; after all it was you who trained me!"

"Please be on your guard and trust no one," continued the Commander. "And don't get arrogant like you sometimes do. Keep your wits about you and the day will soon be ours. And I don't need bloody cards to confirm that fact."

Tonousa looked down to the table and smiled. There would be no going back; the plan had been set in motion. Everything she had experienced in life so far had led her to this point in time, the climax of her destiny. The words of her strange dream floated through her subconscious, 'A path will form'. One had at last done so. This would be the day that Tonousa, daughter of the long line of Amberstones, ended the threat to the Realm. This time tomorrow she would have the infiltrator in chains, and through torture, would understand the Lady of the Silverwynn's evil plans. She looked to Townsforth and winked.

"Let's go and get that bastard priest."

Solaris was setting when Tonousa arrived at the courtyard entrance to the Underkeep, the closest door to the meeting point suggested on the map that Nedes Karoly had procured from the Thieves Guild. She moved into the dark corridors, lit by intermittent torches that cast dancing shadows upon the grey stone walls of the ancient edifice. The passageways were filled with the screams of the incarcerated that rose up from even deeper dungeons. Tonousa was focused and alert as she approached her intended destination. She knew exactly where she was going for the location of the main pantry was common knowledge to all who had spent any time in the Underkeep.

A few feet from the iron door that guarded the food stores entrance Tonousa heard movement behind her. She turned and peered into the dark, sure that someone was following her. A shadow seemed to pass in an instant and she thought perhaps her mind was playing tricks. Then as she turned back towards the pantry she collided with the colossal bulk of a very large man.

"Get out of my fucking way!" he bellowed.

Tonousa recognised the unmistakable form of Sir Richemanus of the Nightfall as he swept past and disappeared into the gloom. It troubled her that he was in this vicinity and she wondered why he would be there if he was not the one that she sought. No other was present in what was normally a very busy thoroughfare and that fact worried her.

Placing her hand on the iron door she moved its handle down, pushed it open, and entered. The pantry was much smaller than she had remembered from her childhood. The store of food and drink had been laid out in a most methodical manner. Barrels of grain, wheat, and rye flour were segregated and placed to one side. Cured meats hung from a rack in one corner, barrels of ale in another, and in the centre stood a large stone slab with its surface covered with baskets of fresh fruit and vegetables. Apart from the food and Tonousa the room was empty. Her stomach rumbled from the smell of the cured meats for she had not eaten anything all day having been too preoccupied with the cards and their meaning. She then began to close the door but left it ajar in order to hear the footfall of anyone who should approach.

Amid the pungent smell of the meats she then began to detect another, a hint of something rotten that from experience meant decomposed flesh. Her eyes failed to reveal anything to account for the source of this new and distinct odour. This also worried Tonousa and she then began to explore the pantry with increased care until at last the source was revealed. Beneath a set of tall shelves lay several rat traps, clever contraptions that had worked as intended for all three held rodent carcasses. Her nostrils tingled and she recalled the information that Lady Emeny had given during her first interview, the time when Darchus had saved Fullbane's life. Emeny had said that her Lillywort contact had met her somewhere that had smelled of death. This had to be the same place. The mixture of the cured meat and rotting rat must be the same that Lady Emeny had experienced and later attempted to describe.

Tonousa began to think how she could use this odd location to her advantage should her adversary become violent but the sound of approaching footsteps broke her concentration. In an instant she pushed herself against the wall behind where the door would open. There she waited and held her breath so as not to give away her presence. After what seemed like an eternity the door pushed open and someone entered. It was the last person she had expected to see.

"Heliana!" she exclaimed. "What in the name of the gods are you doing here?"

Heliana jumped with fright, squealed, and span around.

"Bloody hell, you scared me shitless. I could ask you the same thing," shouted the serving girl. "Why are you sneaking around here in the dark, what the fuck are you up to…?"

Before Heliana could finish, Tonousa gripped her arm and began push her out of the pantry.

"You cannot stay here."

"And why ever not. I have duties I must complete. Lady Fullbane requires an evening meal. As her servant I have every right to be here. You should tell me what you're doing here for that is more relevant. Then you can tell me what's been going on in the Court. Where is Phauless? What's happened to the Council? Why are the wizards...?"

"Heliana, listen to me," ordered Tonousa as she continued to push the girl through the door. "It is vital that you leave now. Your life is in great danger."

"Why?" snapped back Heliana, freeing herself from Tonousa's grip. "Why would I be in danger? Why should I go? Why are you here?"

"I do not have no time to..." replied Tonousa

"Argue! Is that what you were going to say? Go on, explain then. I've been trying to talk to you ever since that day we passed outside the Great Hall. That was six days ago but every time I have tried to approached you, you've either not noticed me, pushed me away, or told me not to bother you. I'm part of your investigation, no matter how much that displeases you."

"Now you listen to me Heliana," pleaded Tonousa. "You need to leave at once. I'm on the verge of solving the mystery. I am about to catch whoever is responsible for the murder of Phauless Gylewu..."

Tonousa ceased mid-sentence but the damage had been done and the secret was out of its box. She looked into Heliana's eyes and saw them cloud with the shock of the revelation of the Sovereign's murder. Heliana's hands dropped to clutch the swelling of her belly as if to protect her unborn from hearing such dreadful news.

"Phauless is dead?" she gasped. "How?"

"He was killed either by magic or poison although we are not sure which. It happened in the Great Hall, the very same day you say that you first tried to gain my attention. Now perhaps you will understand why I have been so distracted. Did you never wonder why silence descended and the Council began to act in such strange ways?"

"I must confess, I did," replied Heliana in a state of disbelief. "I guess that explains why Gilebin Ystafell has been in constant meetings with the wizards and why most of the Council have kept themselves isolated."

Tonousa placed her finger to her lips to hush Heliana. The last thing she needed was to alert others in the Citadel of Phauless's demise or the infiltrator to her presence. Without more ado Tonousa shut the door and slipped its bolt from the inside.

"You must not repeat any of what I have told you, not to anyone, do you hear me?" ordered Tonousa while Heliana nodded back in agreement. "We have to keep this information secret and go about our business as usual. There will be a time for the Realm to grieve but it is not now. Just for once we have a slight advantage over the murderer and I have set up a meeting here..."

"Given all I've done so far, maybe I can help you," said Heliana.

"I cannot ask you to put yourself in danger. Neither you nor your baby."

"Don't bring my unborn into this," barked back Heliana. "Considering what I've been carrying these last six days, that which I have been trying to talk to you about. I've been in more fucking danger than all the rest of you together."

"What are you blabbering on about? We don't..."

"The ruby!" exclaimed Heliana. "That Gem of Thamous. The ruby necklace that belonged to Lady Fullbane. I found the jewel six days ago and I've been trying to tell you ever since. So let's have no more of your verbal shite. I can look after myself, okay!"

The fact that Heliana had found the ruby stunned Tonousa. She convinced herself she must have misheard the servant's words and had to ask her to repeat them. How foolish she had been not to have allowed Heliana to speak earlier. She had indeed kept the young girl in great danger without ever realising it.

"Let me see it?" demanded Tonousa despite expecting Teulu to arrive at any moment.

Without further delay, Heliana reached into the top of her blue and white gown and pulled forward the heart shaped ruby that she had attached to a tight thick chain that fitted snug around her neck. Tonousa could not believe her sudden change of fortune. She was finally getting somewhere.

"Give it to me at once," demanded Tonousa as she held out an open hand. "Whoever the killer is he cannot see you with this around your neck. Nor can anyone else for that matter as they would conclude you had stolen it for yourself and turn you over to Ystafell.

"Not a fucking chance." replied Heliana. "Not if it means you getting rid of me. Remember, I was at the Bards Guild and I know the significance of this stone. I have helped you every step of the way and I haven't come this far to be shut out now. Either you let me help you, or the ruby stays with me."

Tonousa sighed into her boots and saw that she had no choice but to pander to the whim of the stubborn wench who stood before her. As Heliana slipped the jewel back beneath her dress collar Tonousa quickly explained the plan, how Nedes Karoly had arranged the meeting through his links with the Thieves Guild and that she, Tonousa, had come under false pretences to procure Lillywort for Lady Fullbane.

"Then wouldn't it be better coming from me?" replied Heliana.

"What do you mean?"

"Well, I'm one of Fullbane's servants. She could have sent me so as not to incriminate herself. You could hide behind the door and surprise whoever comes in."

Tonousa smiled. Even though she felt protective of Heliana and did not wish to subject her to any further danger, the young woman's suggestion seemed to make perfect sense.

"That's quite a good idea," she replied.

"Then I can stay?"

"Yes, we will go with your plan."

Tonousa sensed she didn't have any other option but to trust Heliana. The day was drawing to a close and she would soon unmask the killer that she had sought for so long. Everything was falling into place. She relaxed a little and leaned back against the central stone slab which she used to support her weight.

"Are you going to tell me where you found the ruby?" she asked.

Heliana smiled and then smirked. After that she began to laugh.

"What is it?" asked Tonousa. "What's so funny?"

"You're not going to believe this but Fullbane had it the whole time."

"Are you serious? And yet she reported it missing," replied Tonousa.

"Fullbane never knew she had it. You'll never believe where I found it."

"Heliana, please," pleaded Tonousa. "Stop teasing me."

"Six days ago," continued Heliana through a spate of giggles. "The very same day that Phauless had organised that feast using all the food he had originally intended to donate to his brother's wedding. Well, that day coincided with my Lady's monthly bath of indulgence, the time when she would wallow and be washed by her unfortunates. Just imagine what it's like to have to go cleaning out all those cracks and sweaty crevices. I was up to my elbows in one of the great folds that hang around her neck and shoulders. Having lifted out an old chicken bone the ruby then kind of popped out!"

"Popped out!" exclaimed Tonousa. "From where?"

"Don't ask me how it got there for I don't wish to know or imagine," continued Heliana. "All I know is that the infamous gem that we thought was stolen had been wedged in amongst the lard. It must have fallen off her neck chain one night while she slept and got trapped in a deep crevasse."

"And does she know you have it?" asked Tonousa as her voice hurried at full speed.

"Not yet. I managed to hide it from the other servant's with the full intention of passing it over to...."

Heliana did not have time to finish her sentence before the pair were disturbed by the lifting of the latch on the outside of the pantry door. As fast as she could Tonousa slipped back the bolt and then threw herself against the wall where the door as it opened would hide her. She watched as Heliana adjusted herself and made it look like she was waiting for whoever approached. The door sprang open and obscured Tonousa's view. Someone had entered the room. To Tonousa's surprise the voice that spoke was again female. It was not Heward Teulu after all.

"What are you doing in her girl?" exclaimed then woman.

"Nothing," answered Heliana with a hint of anxiety.

"Then stand aside. There is a bottle of good red wine in here that has my name on it. I hope you're not hanging around for shifty shag young lady, although I see from your swollen belly you've already passed that point of no return."

Tonousa listened to the sound of movement in the room as the other searched for her prize. It didn't take long and just as quick as she had entered Lady Emeny left and closed the door.

"Well it seems it isn't her," whispered Heliana.

"That was too close for comfort," replied Tonousa in a low whisper. "The last thing we wanted was for Lady Emeny to cause a scene and frighten off Teulu."

"Is that who you think it is?" asked Heliana.

Just as she finished her sentence the door opened again. This time Tonousa did not have time to hide and as she faced the new occupant she gazed upon yet another she had not expected to see.

"Hello, what have we here then, a pair of kitchen thieves in the dead of night?" said the Fool as he stood in the doorway and laughed.

"Fuck off Lolly!" exclaimed Heliana. "Can't you see that we are busy?"

"Oooo, upon my word," squeaked the joyous idiot as he stepped into the room with a beaming smile. "Girl on girl, how exciting, may I stay and watch? In all my fifteen years as a servant and Fool to Gylewu the Grand, I've longed to see the likes of this."

"It's not like that at all, you dirty old bugger," protested Heliana as Lolly then began to search for something amongst the baskets of food. "Now do us both a favour and fuck off. You're going to ruin everything..."

"What she means is we have a meeting planned regarding recent events in the Great Hall," said Tonousa and she placed her hand over Heliana's mouth to prevent the young woman from saying more. "The Lord Chamberlin has asked us to meet him here, to discuss what needs to be done. You do know what I am talking about, don't you Lolly?"

The jovial jester looked up from his search. He still wore a smile that stretched from ear to ear but showed no intention of leaving.

"Lolly is very hungry," he said in a dismissive tone. "Lolly will just get his supper and then leave you to your private doings."

And so he continued, searching the pantry for tasty morsels as Tonousa became ever more impatient at the Fool's lack of a sense of urgency. He gathered together pieces of bread, meat and vegetables and piled them high upon a metal plate that he had brought with him. At last he noticed the two women's agitation and smiled once again. His face changed as his eyes caught a glimpse of a red object that had popped out from the top of Heliana's dress.

"That's a wonderful pendent you have girl," said Lolly as he took a bite out of an apple and pointing to the jewel. "It looks to me like the one that used to sit around piggy Fullbane's neck. You can tell me your secret, where did you find it? Does she know that you have it?"

The two women exchanged glances. It seemed somewhat odd that the Fool would have noticed such a thing or indeed have been aware that the ruby was missing. Tonousa assumed that Ystafell had been asking the Court if anyone had seen it.

"That's none of your business," snapped back Heliana.

Lolly remained beside the one of the wooden shelves that contained various cooking utensils and recipe books. He continued to giggle in his usual irritating manner.

"Temper! Temper!" he retorted before sinking his teeth back into his apple and spraying out juice and spittle.

Lolly then returned to the task of filling up his plate with whatever food he deemed was unwanted. Tonousa feared that her plan was at risk of failing before it had even started. The fool was enough to deter anyone seeking to exchange drugs for coin.

"Lolly, I must ask that you to leave right now. It is important that only Heliana and I are present when our meeting takes place. It's so secret..."

"A secret meeting! Lolly loves secret meetings. I won't get in the way. I promise. I'll just hide over there between the meats and the ale."

"Lolly, I insist."

Tonousa stepped forward and grasped the lune by the arm that carried the plate. She then sought to direct him towards the pantry door.

"Get off of me you temptress," shouted Lolly. "I'll shout for the guards if you do not unhand me at once. I am not going to engage in a threesome no matter how rampant your quims; so just back off."

"Then I'll have you arrested for interfering in crucial matters of the Realm. You will rot in the cells of this Underkeep with just the rats to listen to your inane prattle," snarled Tonousa.

With a grimace forming across her face she lost her patience and pulled hard on Lolly's sleeve. The result was that the plate of food dropped and crashed upon the stone. Its contents scattered across the pantry floor.

"Now look what you've done you split ended siren," squealed Lolly in response to the shock of Tonousa's sudden assault. "That was Lolly's supper."

Tonousa didn't care what the idiot had said and once again latched onto his arm. This time however Lolly was not caught unawares and he reached out and snatched at a bracket that held up one particular section of the wooden shelves. In his attempt to resist being ejected from the room he anchored his feet on the ground and pulled with his arm. The bracket did not hold and as Lolly pulled, it moved and issued a loud click. Somehow the shelf did not fall and Tonousa assumed it had to be nailed to the wall.

"Now see what you've done," exclaimed Lolly. "The cook will have something to say about this damage. She'll fry your tits and stuff them into one of her game pies."

Tonousa then let go of Lolly's arm but not because of his protests. Her ears had picked up a most unnatural sound. It seemed as if some great whirling mechanism had been set in motion and the sound continued to spread behind the wall that held the damaged bracket. She listened as best she could despite Lolly's protestations.

"I will never forget this is attack upon my person," he wailed as he sought to hold back his tears. "Lolly did nothing wrong. All he wanted was his supper."

"Will you please just shut up and listen you good-for-nothing turd," shouted Tonousa as she turned on the Fool and forced his voice into submission.

With Lolly now quiet Tonousa returned her focus the sounds of the moving mechanism. Heliana then made her way from the door and stood beside her companion, unsure as to what to do next.

"What is it?" asked the servant. "What is it that you hear?"

"Listen," replied Tonousa pointing to her ear. "Something is unlocking. I think there is a door behind here and it seems Lolly opened it when he grabbed hold of that bracket."

"You see, I am good for something..." began Lolly but Tonousa glared and he knew to be quiet.

After another loud click the wooden shelves began to shake and as the three looked on it moved to one side and revealed a dark hole within the stone wall.

"Holy Solaris!" exclaimed Heliana as the shelves stopped moving. "I thought I knew all of the tunnels of the Underkeep but I've never heard of this one. I wonder where it could lead."

Tonousa paused and looked into the gloom. For the first few paces it was very dark but beyond lay a much larger chamber that was lit by dim candle light. She could just make out evidence of some basic furniture that indicated someone had no doubt used the space as their hiding place. A new and different musty smell lingered in her nostrils as the air from the tunnel mixed with that of the pantry. This must have been where Lady Emeny had been brought. It had to be another secret conduit that joined the Citadel to the Temple of Fatumai. Tonousa sensed she had found the infiltrator's lair and half expected Teulu appear at any moment. Failing to answer Heliana's question Tonousa stepped into the darkness. Her hand gripped the hilt of her sword and she readied it for war. Sensing Heliana and Lolly following her she turned to give her orders to her friend.

"Heliana, wait in the pantry and keep that idiot quiet."

The young woman understood and nodded. Tonousa then began her decent into the darkened recess hoping that the Fool also understood the seriousness of their predicament. In haste and with purpose Tonousa marched the short distance to the candle lit room in the expectation that she was about to snare the killer. Once inside, and as her eyes became accustomed to the dim light, she was disappointed to find the room empty apart from the furniture and a general mess. She noted a bed, a chest of drawers, a wooden cupboard and weapons rack, and the entrance to yet another small tunnel that led off into black. The clutter of discarded clothes, scraps of food, and other detritus that lay around pointed to it being the killer's lair. Tonousa then proceeded to examine the contents of the room in more detail, to try and spot something that would prove Teulu to be the one that she sought. She searched the desk and through piles of papers left upon it, all with writing in a language that she could not understand. There was nothing to implicate the priest. Turning her attention to the weapon rack, her eyes scanned the swords and daggers that were typical of those from the Eastern Marsh. In addition there were pieces of the leather and iron armour of the type that she had seen on those who had attacked the Bards Guild.

Something much more significant then caught her eye and she took it as evidence that Heward Teulu was the man she sought. Nailed to the wall between the cupboard and the new tunnel entrance was a selection of cards. They had been placed into two rows of equal numbers and they depicted twenty characters from the Fortunes Fate pack. A blood soaked 'X' had been scrawled over seven of them. They were the same seven that had been blown to the floor of The Murdered Wolf. Her theory was now confirmed.

A nasal tremor caused Tonousa to refocus on the musty smell which seemed to become more pungent the closer she got to the cupboard. An uneasy feeling began to trouble her as she took hold of its handle in order to see what was stored inside. Wasting no time she pulled the cupboard door open whereupon an old mummified body fell out. Tonousa jumped backwards to avoid being hit by the bones which then fell to the floor in a haze of dust. While the powder settled she moved closer to investigate. Before she could make progress Tonousa was then distracted by sounds from Heliana back in the pantry. It appeared she was trying to prevent Lolly from leaving. A second later Tonousa turned to examine the human remains on the floor and amid the powder she detected a hint of coloured woven material.

A loud scream which could only have come from Heliana forced Tonousa to retrace her steps back to the pantry. From the passage way there was no sign of either Heliana or Lolly. It seemed the killer had entered through the door to the Underkeep. Tonousa sped down the short passageway until her feet hit the stone of the larder floor. She felt a sharp blow to her side. Something penetrated her leather armour and thrust its way up into the organs at the base of her chest. The shock of the blow had taken her by surprise and she remained unaware of the seriousness of the damage inflicted. Tonousa fell to her knees as first pain and then a great numbness consumed her body. With some effort she looked up to see where the blow had come from and her eyes made contact with the last person she had ever expected to brandish a weapon.

"You!" she exclaimed. "It can't..."

"Oh yes it can," hissed her assailant in his lizard tongue.

"But you're not one of the four," she exclaimed. "This cannot be."

The one before her started to laugh as Tonousa sank down further to the floor. Even though her assailant had removed the blade from her side she still felt intense agony from where it had pierced her flesh. Blood poured out of her side and she struggled to arrest its flow while pressing down on the hole with both of her hands. Vast quantities of crimson seeped through her fingers and down over her legs where it then began to pool on the floor.

"Did you think I would let a Cuvar ruin the mechanics of my plan," laughed her assailant in a distinctive mocking tone. "You need to realise that your father, and those other cunts who tried to work their magic behind my back, never got close to knowing the truth. Old Amberstone made many mistakes and came to the wrong conclusions. Do you know something Tonousa, when I heard you speak in front of the Sovereign Council about Fortunes Fate cards, I so wanted to laugh. I had to keep quiet but I did enjoy seeing you floundering and squirming before the highborn. "

While the warrior from the Watch lay slumped on the ground everything starting to rotate around her like some mad uncontrollable spinning top. She looked ahead and spotted Heliana who also lay motionless some distance away. Tonousa prayed the girl was not dead for she could not bear the guilt of having let the killer take her life.

"What have you done to Heliana?" moaned Tonousa despite her agony and dizziness.

"Nothing too serious as yet," replied her assailant. "She's alive for now but if she ever wakes she will have the mother of all headaches."

"Are you going to kill both of us," asked Tonousa? "We both know who you are now!"

"You don't have any idea who I am," laughed the figure before her eyes.

The human form began to ripple in a bizarre and unnatural way. Her assailant melted away and left behind a skinless amorphous shape. Then just as it shed its skin, a new one replaced it from beneath the covering of the green and red. A reptilian tail protruded backwards as a well-built Lizardman replaced the Fool of Parandor.

"See," sneered the Lizardman. "You don't know who I am at all."

"You won't get away with this," she moaned as the room grew dark.

"I already have."

Tonousa felt disorientated and found it hard to focus her thoughts. Then as she coughed up a large bolus of blood the truth came to her. She was beyond saving and her life was coming to its end. If help did not come soon the Lizardman would be unstoppable.

"As I am going to die, then tell me something. Why Death Tubaria? How did you kill Phauless Gylewu? Did you use magic or something else? How did you move that boulder that killed the stable boy?"

The Lizardman laughed.

"You know the answer to those questions already," it said, hissing and taunting her with the truth. "Death Tubaria was the perfect ploy to distract Parandor from the preparations of the Army of the Eastern Marsh. Gylewu was killed with poison..."

"But you ate the food," replied Tonousa as she spat out more blood and slumped to the floor. "I saw you. You ate all that Phauless ate."

"I have a natural immunity and I would have thought those in the City Watch knew that the flower has no effect on those hatched within the Marsh."

The Lizardman moved over to the wall and pushed up the bracket that had revealed the hidden room. The sound of the mechanism clicking into reverse and the sliding back of the shelves against the wall forced its way into Tonousa's consciousness. She could not believe how foolish she had been. She had indeed known of Lizardmen immunity and yet she had failed to make the connection. The answer had been there all the time and she struggled to make meaning of it all. Sensing her end approaching she issued the one threat that she could muster.

"You and your kind will be thwarted. My friends will find the other Gems of Thamous."

"Ah, the Gems of Thamous!" hissed the creature. "The way you said 'other' tells me you already have one in your possession."

Tonousa at once recognised the enormity of her blunder. Her eyes betrayed the secret and the creature smiled in its lizard-like way.

"So the ruby around your friend's neck is the last of the Gems."

Tonousa did not answer for there was no point in such a waste of effort. She rolled onto her back to try and ease the pain in her side and keep control her thoughts. Then she looked at her hands which were stained deep crimson with her own blood. Her lips sought to utter a few words but failed. Her thoughts were darkening and she was getting very cold.

"Heliana," groaned Tonousa, her breath both shallow and rapid.

Despite her weakness she forced herself to once again look to the young servant girl lying on the floor. She watched the Lizardman trying to release the lock on the chain that had become ensnared in Heliana's dress.

"Damn the bloody thing," it hissed when the lock would not open "It looks like I will have to take her with me. No matter, I'm sure someone in Avolire will be able to remove it."

The reptile kicked out at Tonousa and hit her in the centre of the chest. It caused spasms of intense agony to radiate through her body. Then as the creature turned it took hold of Heliana's hand. A blue flash of energy flooded the pantry and when it had dispersed both Heliana and the Lizardman had gone. Tonousa knew she had failed.

Lying on the hard floor of the pantry with her breath ebbing away Tonousa looked up to the ceiling and allowed the sensation of falling to envelope her whole being. Her thoughts of failure tormented her final moments and at last she closed her eyes. Somehow her brain kept working and she thought back to her Fortunes Fate reading with the innocent Heward Teulu. She focused on the one card she hadn't turned over. There was only one that it could have been and its prediction had come to pass. Perhaps it was just as well she hadn't known earlier which one it was.

"Oh father, what have I done?" she forced herself to whisper.

Tonousa's eyes flickered open at the sound of three people walking close to her head. The footsteps were soft, unlike the hardened boots of those who dwelt in the Citadel. She opened her eyes and was surrounded by tiny strings. They reminded her of the cords of puppets but seemed formed from vibrant shafts of coloured light that were attached to her body. Each rose up and disappeared through the stone ceiling above her head. Trying to take in the strange vision she fought to take her last breath. Three figures came into view and they bent over her body. They were haggard old crones, their faces shrouded by black hoods. One carried a scythe.

"I wasn't expecting that sister," said the first.

"Nor I," said the second. "Far from it; not part of our plan. Someone is changing the rules."

"And she was such a good game player," continued the first. "Well sister, it's time."

"Who are you?" whispered Tonousa in a voice that was barely audible.

"We are the Moirai," said the first and with a nod of the head she signified the end.

The third figure, one who had not spoken, swung her scythe and sliced through the strings of coloured light. Then all was still in the pantry. What had been done, had been done, and there was nothing that could change it now.

32

The air cracked and popped. The sounds were then followed by an explosion of blue light. Methladon found himself standing in the dark shadows of the ruined church, the place where he had first been forced to gaze into the milky depths of the Seer's Stone. His body felt alive as his blood pounded and all his hairs stood on end. Of each of the times he had attempted to manipulate the Rift, guided as always by Ssonsh, this had been his most successful effort. An overwhelming feeling of power filled his every bone, organ, and the skin that coved them. Even the burnt half of his face, scarred lizard like, tingled as if with a life of its own.

"I did it!" he exclaimed. "I can't believe I managed it at last."

"You did well," croaked Ssonsh.

The frog-like creature was the only other present inside the ruined hall. The priest moved forward to join Methladon on the raised platform at the front of the ruined church. There it bathed in Mona's midnight light as the goddess broke amongst the clouds and shone through a large gap in the derelict building's roof.

"Short distances are always best when first learning to use the Rift and yet I sense somehow that it likes you. It will not be long before you can travel as far as I can."

"I feel so alive," gasped Methladon as he gripped the gold band around his wrist. "I can sense its power flowing through my body."

"Excellent," croaked Ssonsh, clapping reptilian hands. "The power of the Underworld grows strong in you. I witness the change and what you are becoming."

"So the toad sees the truth," whispered the voice at the back of the youth's mind.

Methladon had heard the voice more often as the week had passed and it manifested more after each traverse of the Rift. Despite his awareness of his growing powers, that he could do weird things such as manipulate matter within his immediate vicinity, the voice still bothered him. Every day it entered into his head and pushed him further. It offered ever more power like a great serpent tempting him with the glory that its poison could deliver. Yet he always liked what the voice had to say. It complimented him and made him feel worthy of the energy that the Rift bestowed. The voice also knew the truth, that the youth could not die within the Middle Realm and that a great force was building. Methladon could feel it and he liked it a lot. He no longer cared about his disfigured face, burned by Thamous's fiery kiss. Neither did he waste his time thinking about the Lady of the Silverwynn and her need of his assistance. Fuck the House of Gylewu. All that was just a game for he knew that something of even greater magnificence awaited him behind the doors of the Underworld. Once he had taken what he needed from Kha he would rule the Middle Realm for all time.

"I'm going to go again," exclaimed Methladon as the urge to sample the ecstasy of the Rift returned. "This time I am going to go much further."

"Good," said the voice. "Show him that you are worthy."

Ssonsh parted his arms palms upward and encouraged Methladon to try again. The blacksmith's son recalled everything that he had been taught. It was essential that he focused on his intended destination for a lapse in concentration could result in an endless drift through the void between the realities. He focused on the door to the church, way down beyond the aisles of abandoned seats. Placing his hand on the gold bracelet he manipulated it as shown by the frog.

A second thunderous noise then filled the church and it was followed by yet another flash of blue light. Methladon felt as if he was being stretched in all directions but within an instant he found himself by the church door, panting for breath yet full of the energy of life.

"Fuck yes!" he exclaimed while the blue sparks coursed through every cell of his body and lifted his senses to a plane they had never before experienced.

"Once again, you impress me," croaked Ssonsh from the opposite end of the Church. "You have mastered in mere days what can take for some of my kind years to achieve."

Methladon was not surprised by the comment and the energy gleaned from the Rift fired his ego. He now knew that nothing could stand in his way. He had even learned to control the mark on the back on his head. Channelling its burning power made him feel invincible. A thought then entered his mind and the voice brought it to the forefront of his consciousness.

"It felt different this time," said the voice. "Something else just happened."

"I also need you to explain something," shouted Methladon as he made his way back up the central aisle. "I have often observed Lizardmen using the Rift, heard the noise and seen the blue light which comes from the crack in the dimensions. Yet I am confused. When I first met you that night in the Eastern Marsh, when you murdered my friend Mal Castor, you told Rhaizen and the other Knights of Avolire that a sacrifice was needed for men to pass through the Rift. Yet, I have just demonstrated that to be untrue. We have made no sacrifice and yet I moved through it with ease."

As he re-joined Ssonsh the creature laughed and croaked back its answer.

"Cloak and daggers, a mummer's farce. The Knights of Avolire, even though descended from an ancient race of thieves and magic users remain most gullible. They are as naive as the rest of you men. They have never dared to use the Rift alone and believe the stories that we tell them. The fools never once questioned the myths that I propagated."

"But they must know that you use these bracelets?" exclaimed Methladon.

"There are some that know the truth," continued Ssonsh. "Others may have guessed our secret. The bracelet you wear is the only way known to manipulate the Rift. Forget human sacrifice. We do that for sport."

"But the clouds, the rain, the lightening that you summoned up in the Marsh. What was all that about?" continued Methladon.

"Like I said my young friend, it was all cloak and daggers. We know a few tricks and it was easy to impress the likes of Rhaizen and Nictis. Changing the weather, no matter to what degree, has always been a speciality of my magic."

"So you are telling me the events in the Marsh were all for show, just a lie, and that Mal died for nothing," growled Methladon as his curse mark burned.

"A lie that served its purpose," sneered Ssonsh. "It got you to Avolire."

"Forget that bastard's wife. Put her behind you for the event has no significance," snapped the voice in his head.

"Are you just going to stand there like a frightened pup?" croaked Ssonsh, "or are you going to try again."

Methladon glared at the creature before him. Even though it had been tutoring him in the ways of the Rift, he still felt a great hatred for it. He knew that he could kill it in an instant. He could do whatever he wanted. Methladon reached for the golden bracelet on his arm but before he could use it again a distinctive crack and pop coupled with another blue flash of energy signified the arrival of another. Someone else had accessed the Rift and as the figure materialised out of the ether both Methladon and Ssonsh turned to face the new arrival.

"Why are you here?" croaked Ssonsh with surprise.

"I was discovered and had to act in haste," exclaimed the muscular Lizardman who had appeared between them. "The City Watch of Parandor set a trap and I was forced to act on impulse."

Methladon recognised the Lizardman at once. It was the shape changer called Ssleptaz who had infiltrated Parandor disguised as the Court Fool; he that was referred to as the Dragon Whisper. From the look on Ssonsh's face it was obvious that the leader of the Lizardmen was not pleased about this new turn of events.

"What do you mean they set a trap?" croaked Ssonsh. "You were always careful to cover your tracks."

"And I did," hissed Ssleptaz. "But a bitch from the Watch was waiting. I overheard her plotting with this serving girl..."

Methladon and Ssonsh looked down to the feet of the Dragon Whisper. Their eyes fell upon a young woman dressed in a blue and white dress. The swelling of her lower belly indicated she was with child.

"Why did you bring her here?" stuttered Ssonsh. "Why did you not just kill her?"

"I would have done, if it hadn't been for the bitch from the Watch," replied Ssleptaz. "The girl screamed and Townsforth's agent became suspicious. I managed to silence that warrior but I couldn't risk being caught in the place where I killed her."

"But why bring this girl with you?" demanded Ssonsh as his green skin turned a deep purple.

"Because of an object around her neck," hissed Ssleptaz, disturbed by his Masters ire.

"What thing," demanded Methladon?

"Take a look for yourself."

Methladon bent down to where the young girl lay. He turned her over and for an instant admired her beauty. Then he saw the reason for Ssleptaz's comment, a heart shaped ruby on a chain fixed tight around the young girl's neck.

"It's just a ruby, nothing more," sneered Methladon.

"Not just any old ruby," hissed Ssleptaz. "It is one of the five Gems of Thamous. Don't ask me how the City Watch managed to find it when I have sought it for so long. From what I heard it had hung round the neck of the fat Lady they call Fullbane. See, the cheap and solid chain is trapped in the girls dress. All that time it was missed by my eyes, hidden in the great canyon on Fullbane's chest. It is the one we have been searching for."

"But you still haven't explained why you brought the girl with it,"

"There wasn't time to extricate the jewel before being discovered. The chain is tightly bound and locked. Her screams could have alerted others and I couldn't get the clasp undone," continued the changeling.

"Ssleptaz, you fat fingered fuck," croaked Ssonsh. "Why didn't you just remove the bitch's head and rip the dress off with the jewel; you didn't have to bring her here."

In the silence that followed the two Lizardmen and Methladon stood and stared at the young girl while a growing tension filled the void of the ancient church. Ssleptaz uttered a subservient hiss.

"I acted on impulse. I didn't have time to think."

"You're right," croaked Ssonsh. "You didn't think it through."

Methladon contemplated the potential outcome of the reptiles spat.

"Just leave them to it," said the voice.

The youth then knelt down beside the unconscious young girl and in an instant used his abilities to manipulate metal and free the chain. Standing with the chain in his right hand he allowed the ruby to swing before the two reptiles. Three pairs of eyes watched its gentle sway with great reverence.

"So that's four of the five in our possession," whispered the voice. "We will soon open the door to the Underworld. Already I feel it calling to us. Unlimited power will soon be ours."

Methladon shook his head to disperse the voice that taunted him and focused back on the reptiles' conversation.

"They going to miss you? Will they not suspect?" croaked Ssonsh.

"They will this time if I am absent for any length of time," replied Ssleptaz. "I managed to disappear for a few weeks once before but now they have the whole of the Citadel locked down. Should you not hear from me again you must assume that the enemy has discovered my disguise. I will return to Parandor at once and destroy any clue that the Watch could use to their advantage. I must cover my tracks."

Methladon did not know what Ssleptaz meant by tracks. He assumed it possible that someone had already worked out the reptile's deception. Yet as he stood and listened to the conversation he found himself focusing on the ruby in his hand. He became transfixed by its presence and his attention drifted away from the Lizardmen. It was as if the ruby was beckoning him into its crystalline structure and seeking to hold him there.

"Hey!" croaked Ssonsh. "Wake up!"

"Yes sir," exclaimed Methladon as he was forced out from his musings.

"Pay attention before Ssleptaz knocks some respect into your thick skull."

"I'm sorry, I don't know what happened."

"Oh yes you do," said the voice. "You we mesmerised by the ruby."

"I apologise; it won't happen again," said Methladon as he forced the voice to quieten.

"It had better not," croaked Ssonsh. "You might be immortal, the Rift may have chosen you as the 'Vessel', but I can still inflict pain on you."

Methladon felt the back of his neck burn as the power began to flow again. This was not the time to confront the reptiles and he knew that the passage of time would serve him better. Once he had subsumed all that the Underworld had to offer he would then exact his revenge on those who had murdered his friends. For now he would humour their pathetic game but when the time was right he would strike them all down. Forcing several deep breaths into his lungs he caused the burn to evaporate. It left him less energized than when he had traversed the Rift but at least his anger was controlled and thoughts clear.

"I think its best that I put it with the other three," he answered while starring at the jewel.

"Yes, that might be best," added Ssonsh before turning to Ssleptaz. "Take the girl down to the cells and put her with the other two. Then get your scale arse back to Parandor and wait for further instructions. Phauless Gylewu will fall..."

"He is already dead," interrupted Ssleptaz. "An opportunity arose and it was too good to miss. Right now the throne of Parandor is vacant and his once most trusted, now disgraced, followers are all under suspicion. It is time to march on Parandor. The fruit of war is ripe."

As Methladon listened he witnessed a slight smile on the frog priest's face.

"So the throne is empty and nothing now stands in our way."

"Just the Knights of...." began Ssleptaz.

The main doors to the ruined church then opened with a crash as Oedd, last of the Harbingers, entered in full armour.

"What do you want? This is a private meeting," demanded Ssonsh.

"The Lady of the Silverwynn sent me to collect Methladon Heyn," replied the knight without fear. "She has things to discuss with the boy."

Methladon looked to both Lizardmen and they nodded in recognition of his disguised intent. Following Oedd from the church more words from the reptiles' leader reached his ears.

"Take the red prize to the old crone, I'm sure she will be more than pleased to see it."

Methladon clutched the Ruby in his hand before magically manipulating the chain and slipping it around his own neck. The gem fell beneath his tunic and rested against the skin of his chest. Oedd had already exited the ruin and Methladon ran to catch up with the brute of a man. His eardrums picked up Ssonsh's repeated order. Ssleptaz was to take the pregnant girl to the dungeons then return to Parandor.

Oedd led on through the ruined streets of Avolire. Methladon did not actually need an escort for he knew the way to the Lady of the Silverwynn's enchanted room. This was where she now spent all her time as her life ebbed away with each passing hour. Soon she would be no more. It was obvious to all who saw her that she continued to decay. Lizardmen even placed bets on whether she would die before turning to dust and whether her spectral spirit would be let loose to haunt the ruins. The two wandered for many minutes through the derelict streets.

They passed amongst the Army of Avolire that continued to gather. Men and reptilians all tended to their animals and readied their armour and blades. Mighty siege weapons had been loaded in parts onto the back of a multitude of carts and all were ready to go. Yet as Methladon looked on, he knew that the majority were not well-honed warriors. Most were simple sods who held a deep grudge against Parandor. They would not fare well in the heat of battle and most would be cut down and slaughtered by a well-trained army.

Methladon drew alongside Oedd while the voice directed his thoughts.

"I wonder what the ancient hag wants and what do you want from her?"

"Nothing!" exclaimed Methladon. "I have no clue so get out of my head."

"Are you okay lad?" demanded Oedd as he turned towards the youth.

"I'm fucking fine, except for a voice in my head that won't leave me alone."

"I see," replied the Harbinger. "Grovrouk was correct. I didn't believe what the hole-dweller said until now. You're losing it Methladon. You're talking to yourself all the time."

"The dwarf should learn to keep his fucking mouth shut," spat back Methladon. "And what business is it of yours anyway?"

"I'm just saying that I now witness it for myself."

Methladon did not see the point in responding further. Ever since he had been rescued by Rhaizen on the slopes of the Gathering the dwarf had been sticking his bearded face into his affairs. Far too many times had the short arse told him what he should and shouldn't do; he was sick of the dwarf's interference and vowed to put an end to it. No longer would he tolerate being dictated to, not now that the energy of the Rift coursed through his body. He was becoming stronger by the day and Grovrouk was just another hindrance to achieving his full potential.

"The dwarf must to go, as must this Harbinger," whispered the voice.

Methladon thought about responding but chose not to give Oedd cause to comment further. He focused his attention onto a group of men in leather armour who stood talking besides a wall. He watched them with suspicion and they caused him to ask Oedd a question.

"Am I correct in assuming we are about to leave Avolire, head through the Grey Mountains, and attack the Parandor at the earliest opportunity?"

"You've got it in one," replied Oedd.

"That seems a waste of time when the Lady could use the Rift to transport her entire army before the walls of Parandor."

Oedd smiled and laughed.

"What's so funny?"

"Oh how little you know," said Oedd.

"Then tell me what I have missed."

Again the Harbinger smiled.

"The Army of Avolire will march on Parandor and fight whatever their Royal Guard sends out to face us. What you don't know lad is that there is a hidden army, a secret one that hides within the caverns under the Eastern Marsh. It is led by one called Ssobekk. This General will use the Rift to enter the Capital while the Army of the Realm fights with the Knights of Avolire before the walls of Parandor.

The city will fall from the inside out. As soon as our spy has killed Phauless Gylewu..."

"He already has," said Methladon.

"Then our work will be easier than we could have hoped. It gets even better, for there is rumour that the Marked has been captured and being held in the caverns under the Marsh. Everything seems to be falling into place."

Methladon thought back to all he had heard about Parandor. It was obvious that anyone caught inside or outside the walls would be massacred. The old, the poor, the worthless and the infirmed; all would struggle to survive once the fighting began. Parandor's army would be rapidly stretched to breaking point following such a duel attack. Given the skills of the select few knights worthy to be called that name and the ruthlessness of the Lizardmen, Methladon was sure the Capital would soon fall. Approaching the doors to the Lady's chamber he focused his thoughts onto his most recent Seer's Stone visions in which he had sat alone on the throne of Parandor. It was clear that the Lady of the Silverwynn was no longer part of the diamond's plans. Outside the doors he and Oedd stopped and listened. Two Lizardmen guards stood either side of the door through which loud voices boomed.

"Who is with her now?" asked Oedd of the Lizardman to the left of the door.

Methladon tuned in to the raised voices that emanated from within the room. Before the reptile could answer it was obvious to all who the verbal combatants were. The Lady of the Silverwynn screeched at Grovrouk the Despoiler and he replied with great angst in his diminutive voice. By some strange magic the room translated the language of the Dirmark into manspeak such that all could understand the dwarf's utterings. It seemed to Methladon that the Lady must have regained some of her powers and he was at a loss to explain how that could have happened.

"Do you think we should knock?" said Methladon while turning to Oedd.

The Harbinger did not have time to answer before the doors to the room were forced open and Grovrouk exited like a stone fired from a pult.

"And you can shift out of the fucking way!" bellowed the dwarf as he stormed off.

In the wake of Grovrouk's departure, Methladon followed Oedd into the chamber where the Lady of the Silverwynn stood by her bed. She was a most sorry sight to behold and a shock to Methladon's eyes. The old crone was even more ancient and dishevelled than the last time he had met with her. Clutching a warped wooden staff in her hands she sought to keep herself upright.

"I've have delivered Methladon Heyn as requested," said Oedd.

"I thank you," she replied, her voice weak and frail. "My dear Knight of Avolire, I must however ask you to leave. I have some things I need to discuss in private with this young man."

"Just as you wish my Lady," replied Oedd who then bowed and exited the room.

Left alone with the once great woman Methladon sensed some barrier had fallen between them. She looked back at him with an intense suspicion as she gripped onto her staff of life. It was clear that the old woman was no longer fit for purpose. Her journey into the next world was clearly imminent.

"The bitch is almost dead," said the voice but Methladon ignored it.

He began again to ponder on why he had been summoned and the purpose of this meeting. Even though without fear, the uncertainty of the moment caused his pulse to quicken. Then in the spur of the moment he held aloft the chain with its attached ruby. He let it dangle before her cloudy eyes and said the first thing that came into his head.

"I've brought you a gift."

The Lady of the Silverwynn glared across the open space between them.

"And what would I want with a trinket like that," she snapped.

It was obvious that whatever had passed between her and Grovrouk still troubled her thoughts. His words flowed without prior thought.

"Ssonsh said you may like to know that we have the ruby. We now have four of the five."

The Lady of the Silverwynn raised an eyebrow and in so doing showed the deep wrinkles carved into her forehead. Her face spoke the truth. She did not trust the frog anymore.

"Did he now?" she answered as she pointed to the dresser where the other Gems lay. "So the one that was stolen by Emgar and the Cuvar has returned at last. Put it with the others boy."

"What's got into the old cunt now?" whispered the voice.

The Lady watched his every step as he moved towards the dresser and the objects that sat upon it; the jewel encrusted Dagger of Kha and the diamond headed Sceptre of Urthanock. It was not difficult for him to deduce that the blue Sapphire that lay next to the dagger was the one that the Ogres had taken from their prisoners in the Forest of Thengar. There were however two other objects on the table that he did not recognise as he placed the ruby between them. One was a sword and the other a pendent of crafted metal with a small white oval stone set into its middle.

"The blade and the white stone, what are..." he asked?

"Spoils taken from the prisoners," snapped back the Lady. "The ancient sword was used to slay one of Brosizrug's platoon. The stone was found on the bard that we have incarcerated down in Avolire's prison."

Methladon was sure that the white stone had suddenly glowed. His good eye blinked and then refocused but then the luminescence had gone.

"So where did that fat frog find the Gem that we thought was lost for ever?" she asked.

"It wasn't Ssonsh," replied Methladon. "It was Ssleptaz."

"And how did the Dragon Whisper come by it?"

"It was around the neck of a servant girl," continued Methladon. "Ssleptaz was on the verge of being discovered and had to act with great haste. He brought the girl with him and Ssonsh has dispatched her to the dungeons. The ruby was round her neck but even the so called Dragon Whisper doesn't know how the wench came by it."

"And how is he so sure it is one of Thamous's Gems?"

"Ssleptaz overheard one from the City Watch talking about the stone. He was forced to take the warrior out before the alarm was raised."

"So the City Watch of Parandor know about the Gems of Thamous," mumbled the Lady. "How very interesting. This day gets ever better."

Methladon hesitated. There was something amiss. The Lady's manner displayed more than a hint of disbelief and he was still intrigued by what had transpired between her and the dwarf. Perhaps Grovrouk been interfering in her business just as with his. That could perhaps explain her mood.

"Something is wrong," said the voice.

"Are you well my Lady?" asked Methladon and he reached out touch her shoulder only to have his hand knocked back by her staff.

"Do not touch me!"

"I'm sorry, I meant no disrespect. I only... " replied Methladon in surprise.

"When I want your views or advice I will ask!"

Again Methladon was stunned at the open hostility that his leader showed. He had followed all of her instructions, all of her rules, and had been at her beck and call ever since the events before the Lions of Avolire. His mind struggled to work out the reason behind her sudden change of attitude. There could only be one answer, Grovrouk had said something to poison her opinion of him.

"May I ask why you sent for me?"

The Lady of the Silverwynn glared back through ancient eyes.

"Rumour has it that you are being taught how to travel via the rift."

"Yes, that is correct my Lady," he replied. "Ssonsh insisted that I learn to use the power that now flows through my being. He said that there was no better way to do that than manipulating the Rift."

"And how did it make you feel?"

"Wonderful," smirked Methladon. "Every time that I travel through it I feel that I can accomplish anything. It leaves me feeling omnipotent as if something has unlocked my internal constraints and released my true potential. I no longer know what drives me, the curse mark or the power sucked out of the fracture. Both seem to flow with an equal intensity. It's like my blood becomes pure energy. I already feel all powerful but some weird darkness wants to push me further."

"How dare you refer to me as that, you ignorant trail of slug snot," whispered the voice. "You and I have another name, one more ancient than you would ever believe."

"Not now, just fuck off," thought Methladon as he tried to drown out his tormentor.

"Oh, so it is a darkness that flows through you?" said the Lady as she cast a sly smile.

"I think so."

"Then just remember this young man, relishing the darkness of the Underworld could cost you your... well you know what I mean."

The strange cryptic message from the aging hag confused Methladon.

"I've no idea what are you are fucking talking about."

The Lady of the Silverwynn turned her back and made her way towards the dresser.

"Tell me what it is that you hint of!" demanded Methladon and he felt his anger surface again.

"Using the Rift will not just cost you your sanity, it will cost you your life. For many generations I have sought the power of the Underworld to use as a weapon against the House of Gylewu. I craved revenge for the destruction they brought upon my family and home in Calistorn. I dedicated my whole life to ensuring that Parandor is brought to its knees. I gave myself over to those bastards from the Eastern Marsh and just look where it has got me. My prolonged life has been one of ever increasing suffering and I wouldn't wish it on my worst enemy. Despite all I have sacrificed, they and their fucking Rift have abandoned me as if on a whim. They do everything just to suit their own selfish ends."

"You're so wrong," growled Methladon. "I can control it."

"Good, that's every so good," whispered the voice. "You have great potential."

"No one can control the darkness Methladon Heyn," the Lady cursed. "Not me, not the Eastern Marsh, and certainly not a runt like you."

Methladon could not understand what point the Lady strove to make. It was as if she was repenting in front of him for all the atrocities she had committed. He felt sure she was trying to lay the blame elsewhere and was puzzled by her sudden dislike for the power that she had so long craved.

"The dark essence of Kha has much to answer for?" she ranted. "Do you not see what you have become? You are no longer the slave from the mines in whom I saw so much potential. You are something else, a Vessel for the darkness."

"It wasn't the darkness that did this to me," said Methladon as his deformed face contorted. "It was Death Tubaria that gave me my curse mark. It was the Knights of Avolire that murdered my friends and family. It was that sadistic fuck called Nictis that awakened my body and soul to the power of Kha. It was that fucking bastard Thamous that burned me beyond recognition. As for you, you evil crone, you've mislead me each and every day since you released me from being a slave in your mines. You should have left me to rot down there."

"Good, very good. Let your anger flow," whispered the voice

"How dare you suggest that the power I am blessed with is to blame for what I have become," he continued. "The energy of the Rift and the Mark of Kha are the only positives in the nightmare that my life has become, one full of torture that you helped to create. Their energy has given me something you could never have done, meaning and purpose to my shit awful life. I am now all powerful and everlasting. I am the Almighty."

"Such delusions of grandeur will not make you content," said the Lady as she trembled and held onto her staff. "Methladon Heyn at last reveals the true extent of his evil."

"Fuck you! Is this why you wanted to see me today, just to put me down and hurl abuse? You were never worthy of the power from the Rift. It should have been mine from the beginning. The Lizardmen should never have allowed you to experience what the forces of the Underworld are capable of bestowing."

"And is power all that is important to you now?" she asked weakly.

"What is she getting at?" asked the voice.

"Is it more important than the friends you have made since coming to Avolire?" she asked.

"What shite are you uttering hag?" growled Methladon.

"Grovrouk was right. You're not the boy that we once knew and tried to shape to our will. You have become something else, something that must be eliminated."

Methladon laughed.

"Ah, so that's what you and the hole-dweller were talking about. That dwarf has a dangerous habit of interfering."

"And I chose in the past not to believe what he had to say," continued the Lady. "Now I see the truth of his allegations and the conspiracy which he is committed to uphold."

"And what conspiracy would that be? Do tell for I am intrigued."

Methladon was angered by Grovrouk's treachery and was surprised that even a dwarf could stoop so low. It was now obvious that all who were not of the reptile race had turned against him and were intent of taking away his power. Grovrouk was a major threat and would need to be eliminated at the earliest opportunity. But first he had to deal with the Lady of the Silverwynn.

"The dwarf tells me many things," continued the Lady. "He's observed you looking into the Seer's Stone and how it has corrupted you. He has witnessed your behaviour in the company of those of the Eastern Marsh. Your attitude has darkened to towards everyone else. Then there is the way you talk to yourself. It is as if something evil has control of your senses. A darkness is forcing its way out..."

"And what is it to you if these things that you speak of are true?" he shouted.

"As you have already said, I should have left you to rot in the mines..."

"I would have found a way out without your help. It may have taken me longer to realise my full potential, but I would have got there somehow. I would still have killed you BITCH."

Methladon waited for the Lady's response. Grovrouk had turned her against him, poisoned her mind, and she had abandoned her prodigy. The Lady of the Silverwynn had vented her fury and he had not taken it well. His fulminating fury peaked as she dared to bring a smile to her face.

"There it is, the dark essence has emerged at last."

"And that essence now belongs to me alone," he growled.

"It will consume you and destroy you Methladon Heyn, just as it has destroyed me."

"It has no power over me. I don't fear what I have become. I control the darkness, not it me. I am more than worthy of its power."

The Lady of the Silverwynn laughed. "You do have an abundance of confidence, poor deluded child, and yet you have no conception of the evil you have awakened."

"I've done nothing!" exclaimed Methladon. "You're just fucking jealous."

"As I said, you are deluded."

Methladon snapped and a deeper voice took over his mouth.

"I dare you to say that again, BITCH!"

"And so it begins. Don't you think I already knew this moment would come? I have also looked into the Seer's Stone and seen a different outcome. The power you seek was mine once, and will be so again."

"And you call me deluded," sneered Methladon. "You will never hold the power."

"That's it, you tell her," shouted the voice. "Finish it now!"

Before Methladon could react, the Lady of the Silverwynn stood tall and let her staff rest by her side. It was as if she had found a last reserve of energy with which to confront him. This surprised Methladon and caught him off guard. He hesitated and the she sensed his surprise. Fuelled by this minor advantage the old woman laughed and spoke again.

"Did you believe that all my power came from the rift?"

"I had not thought about it," he replied.

"How naïve of you then. I knew much magic before the marsh dwellers gave me access to this room. It is with that knowledge that I will destroy you. Let us now see if it is true that you cannot die?"

In the blink of an eye the Lady of the Silverwynn gripped her staff and pointed it at Methladon. A Brilliant green flash erupted from its tip and threw him across the room. His back hit the dresser with considerable force and dislodged the sword and artefacts that had lain on its surface. They flew through the air and clattered to the ground. Despite this sudden assault Methladon was without fear but the green energy caused every fibre of his body to pulse with a pain far greater than he had ever felt before.

The Lady of the Silverwynn moved forward with a satisfaction radiating from her face. With her reserves of magic saved for this one moment in time she took the fight to the corrupted youth.

"Grovrouk told me of your plan," she screamed as she moved in for the kill. "He was right when he advised me not to trust you. I know that you have been plotting to take me down but don't think for a moment that you and Ssonsh could take Parandor without the armies of Avolire. We will not bend to your will, at least not without a fight."

Something majestic awoke inside Methladon. He felt the energy of the rift surge though his body and the power of Kha flood in through the back of his neck. Sensations of omnipotence coursed through his veins and once again all of his hairs stood on end. The intensity of his enrichment escalated as each second passed.

"I will not let the lizards use me for their own ends," screamed the Lady.

"You mean like you used them?"

"They gave me a means to succeed but then deprived me of it," she ranted. "Why did they chose you over me when I had been so instrumental in the creation of their strategy? I should have been allowed to keep the power that I have worked so hard to secure. Believe me when I say this, I am going to turn my armies of Avolire on those scale skinned shits and force them to follow me again. No one will stop me from taking the throne of Parandor."

Methladon took the opportunity of her moment of insanity to regain his feet. On his way up he reached forward and picked up the ancient sword from where it had fallen a minute earlier. He took a firm grip and readied himself for the Lady's next move.

"There are other ways to take Parandor without the help of those from the Marsh or what lies behind the doors to the Underworld," continued the Lady "At this very moment Brosizrug and his ogres are laying waste to Griginor and opening the route my army will take through the Grey Mountains. The armies of Avolire are stronger than they ever have been and we will take Parandor with ease. You see young Heyn, or whatever you have become, my strength comes from those who have followed me for a very long time and not some slime spawn from the swamps. Once Parandor has fallen I will take my revenge on anything found slithering in the Eastern Marsh. Their floating city will sink forever beneath its foul waters."

"But you will not to see that day you demented old crone. You are dying."

"Oh, but I am determined to survive," she screeched in a strange manner.

In an instant the truth was obvious. It was the woman who was mad not him. Then the voice in Methladon's head spoke again and this time he took notice.

"Kill her. Kill her now and the armies of Avolire will be ours to command."

"Come on then bitch," screamed Methladon. "Do your worst."

Lifting her staff again the Lady of the Silverwynn pointed it at Methladon but this time he had anticipated her attack. In an instant he threw his sword like a javelin and before she could react the blade embedded itself deep into her shoulder. An explosion of pain caused her to drop her staff and she collapsed to the floor. Methladon felt yet another great surge of energy and his mind became clouded. He felt uncertain as to what was happening and the voice took command of his mind.

The old woman writhed in agony while her crimson life fluid seeped out of the wound in her shoulder. Methladon moved forward and began to gloat. A few seconds later he clicked his fingers and suspended the Lady in the air, just as he had seen Rhaizen do to others in the past. He stared into her ancient eyes and sensed her fear. She tried to move her lips.

"I'm so sorry, I cannot hear you," he sneered. "You'll need to speak a little louder."

"I will have my revenge in this life or the next," she groaned.

"I'm quivering with terror, can you not tell!"

"The Eastern Marsh will never triumph. The Marked will stop you. He will close the portal and destroy the source of your power," cursed the Lady.

"The Marked will fail for he has no chance of ever defeating me," boomed out the deeper voice.

"No you are so wrong, he does have the means to stop you," she cried.

A strange insanity filled Methladon's head and all rationality left him.

"Fuck the Marked, I have the power to end your suffering right now."

Reaching up he took hold of the Lady's cheeks. He felt her life essence drain from her and enter into his being. There it mixed with the darkness that already coursed through his centre. With the sickest of smiles he watched as she withered away before his eyes. The lady's walnut flesh and crumbling bones turned to dust and fell to the floor. A gust of air appeared out of nowhere and scattered her remains to the four corners of the room. The sword remained hanging in the air until he looked at it with curious eyes. Once the connection had been made it fell to the floor with a clatter. The blacksmith's son from Maplehill screamed and dropped to his knees. He felt confused yet within his pit of despondency and remorse he realised that he had never felt so alive.

"Excellent," whispered the voice. "Now you are the Vessel."

"What do want of me," demanded Methladon.

"Give yourself up to me and the power you desire will be yours for an eternity."

Methladon did not answer. He closed his eyes and sensed a swirling cloud of evil envelop his mind. His thoughts flickered like a failing candle and soon all reference to the innocent of Maplehill were locked in to the furthermost reaches of his subconscious. He stared at the residual traces of the once great Lady of the Silverwynn and he felt his body twitch and convulse. Even this did not trouble him for there was nothing that could scare him now. Fear held no sway for he saw it like a mere insect waiting to be crushed. For an indeterminable time he remained on his knees inside the gloom of the strange chamber while the darkness behind his eyes swirled. And yet he delighted in its presence. No complex thoughts of the past or the future came to trouble his thinking for his mind was captivated by the present as wave upon wave of power swept through him. He had been reborn and he was unstoppable. All his fingers tingled with something he could neither comprehend nor describe. When at last he managed to open his eyes he looked to his hands and smiled at the blue energy that passed between his fingertips. A manic smile stretched across his face and he soon began to laugh. It started small and then built to a crescendo. When he thought it could get no louder or more bizarre he surrendered into its presence. Madness had taken control. The Vessel reached up to its face and it screeched as a hand hit the cold metal of the half helm. Casting it to the floor he set about stroking the damaged half of his face. The roughness amused him and fed his mania.

The doors to the chamber then burst open and the Vessel looked quickly to the entrance as two Lizardmen stepped inside. They were followed by Ssonsh who approached in a hurry.

"News from the Marsh. The Marked has escaped with..."

The Vessel turned his head and glared. All three reptiles froze on the spot, stunned by two eyes that emitted diamond light.

"What has happened?" croaked Ssonsh. "Where is the Lady of the Silverwynn?"

The Vessel smirked and then laughed. "She tried to kill me but I struck first."

"Where is she?" demanded Ssonsh as he scanned the room.

The Lizardmen guards readied their spears and pointed them at the youth before them. The Vessel did not speak but scooped up a trace of dust from the floor and flicked it high into the air. It caught the light and sparkled as it floated and defied the pull of the ground. The Lady hung in the air, suspended and free from her earth held traumas. Ssonsh understood the meaning of what had happened and signalled the two guards to stand down.

"She had planned for Avolire to turn against you. Have them all killed and spare none of their knights," he said calmly.

"On whose authority," replied the Ssonsh?

"Mine!" he ordered.

"And who the fuck are you to give orders?" croaked Ssonsh.

"I am Urthanock, Lord over Fear," he replied.

The voice that had answered was not that of a young man. Ssonsh and the two Lizardmen paused, then bowed low, and after a brief hesitation fled the room.

Several hours later Urthanock stood within the last high tower of Avolire and watched the carnage unfold before him. He revelled as those from the Eastern Marsh fought and sought to destroy what was left of the best of the Knights of Avolire. He laughed as the ruined city began to burn and the scum that had rallied to the Lady's banner were forced to fight for their lives. The Lord over Fear, the foul one spoken of in ancient prophecies had been reborn. He now had full control of a Vessel and had embarked on the destruction of the Realm. The beast realised that the Marked had to be found and eliminated.

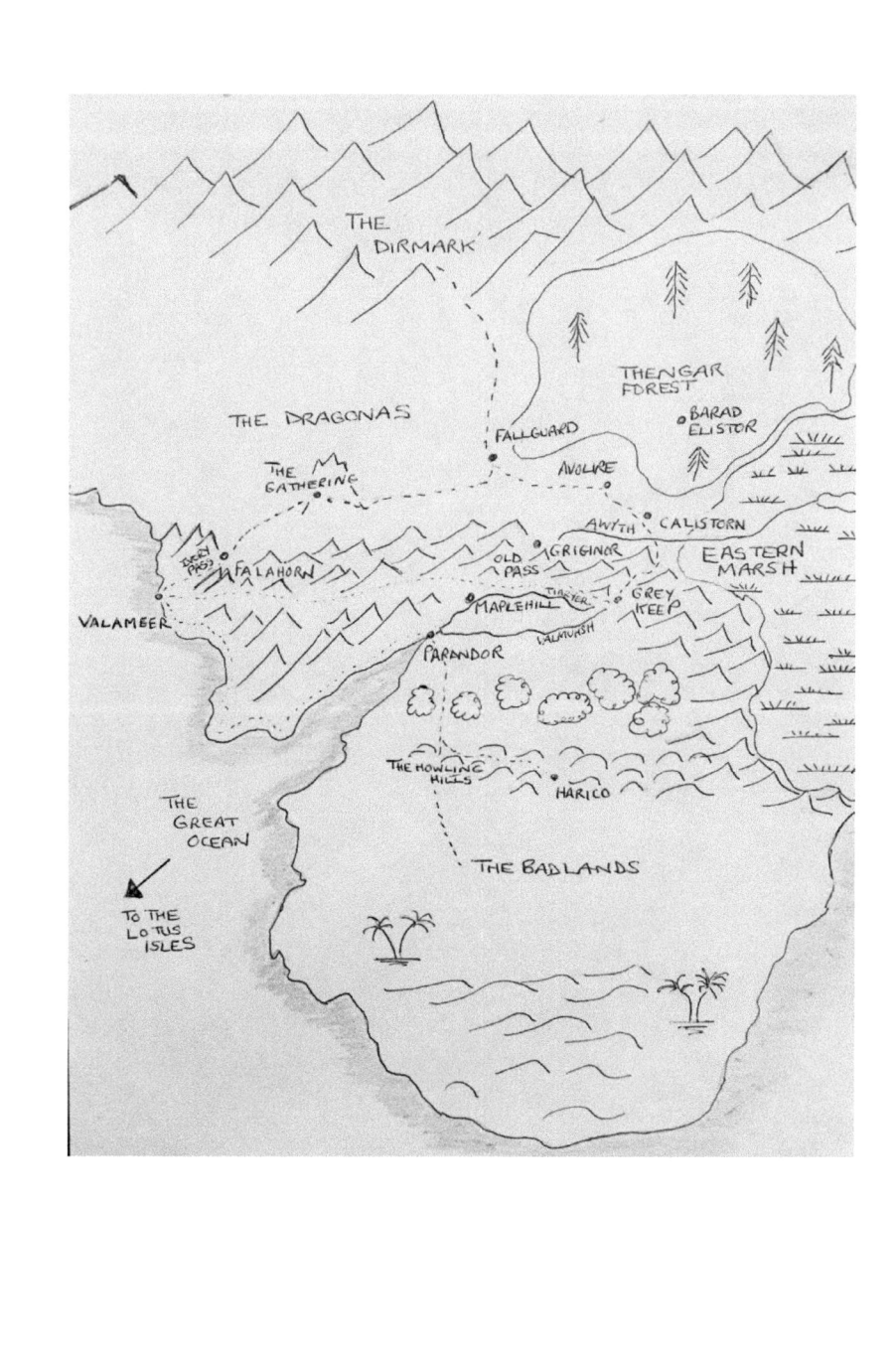